SPACE DUMPLINS

CRAIG THOMPSON
WITH COLOR BY DAVE STEWART

graphix

AN IMPRINT OF

SCHOLASTIC

"They had dumplings, too; small, but substantial, symmetrically globular, and INDESTRUCTIBLE DUMPLINGS."

MOBY-DICK
BY HERMAN MELVILLE

Library of Congress Control Number Available

ISBN 978-0-545-56541-7 (hardcover)
ISBN 978-0-545-56543-1 (paperback)

10 9 8 7 6 5 4 3 2 1   15 16 17 18 19

Printed in China   38
First edition, September 2015
Edited by David Saylor & Adam Rau
Color by Dave Stewart
Book design by Craig Thompson & Phil Falco
Creative Director: David Saylor

STAR MAP

GYROMETER

NAVIGATION

SW

MAGNITUDES · ★ ✦ ✴ ❋

01

GIMME SHELL-TARR

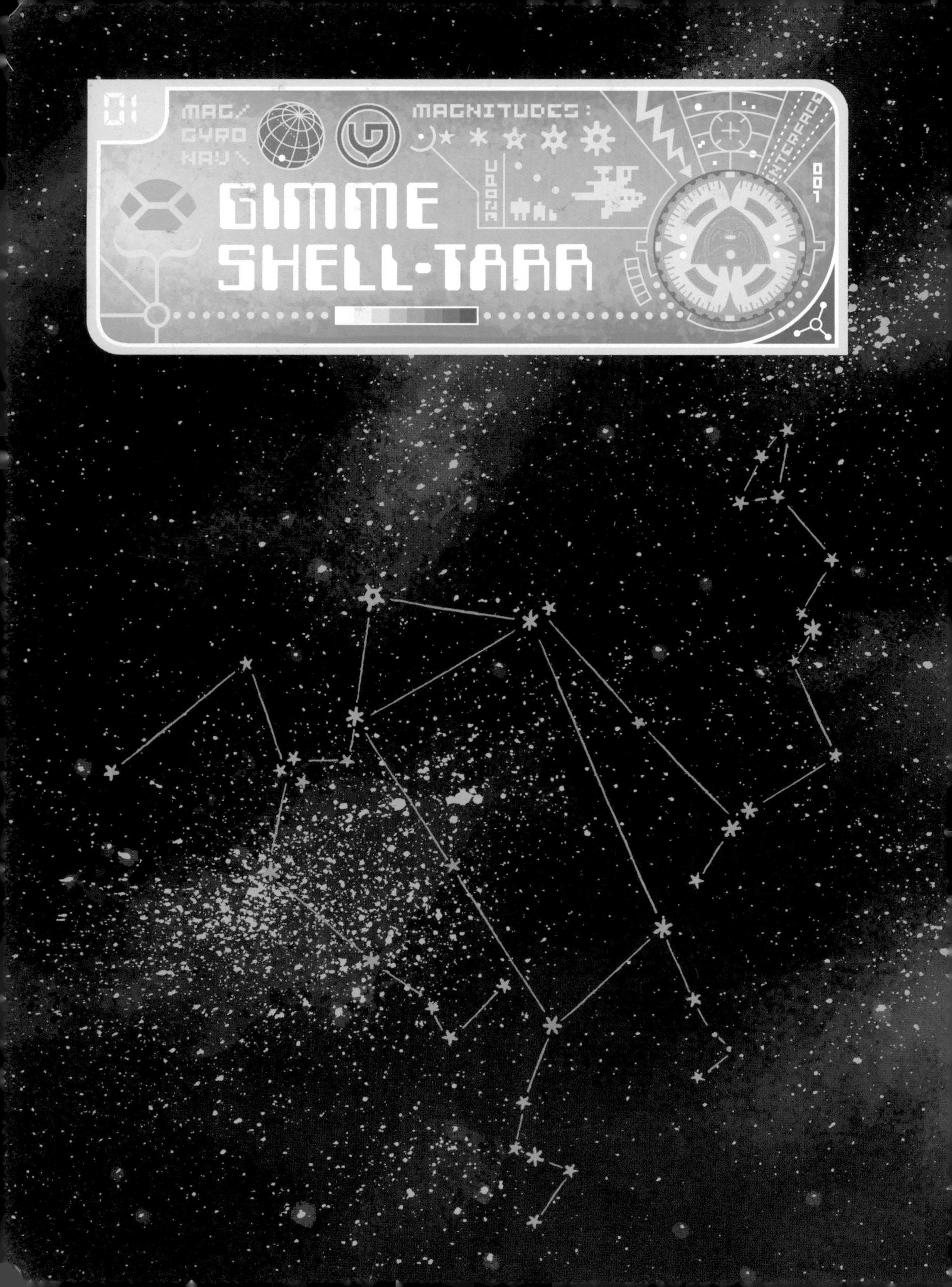

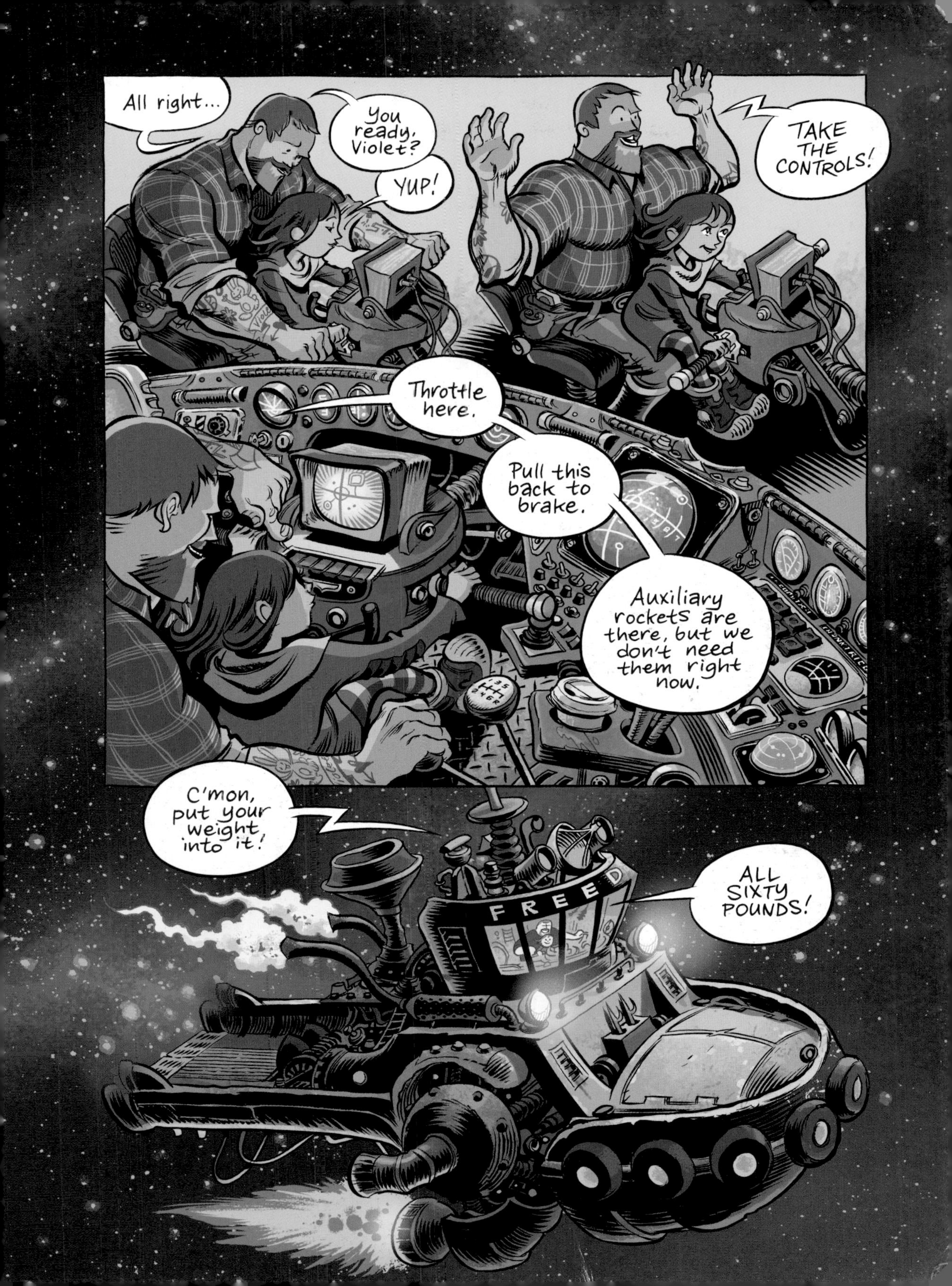
All right...
You ready, Violet?
YUP!
TAKE THE CONTROLS!
Throttle here.
Pull this back to brake.
Auxiliary rockets are there, but we don't need them right now.
C'mon, put your weight into it!
FREED
ALL SIXTY POUNDS!

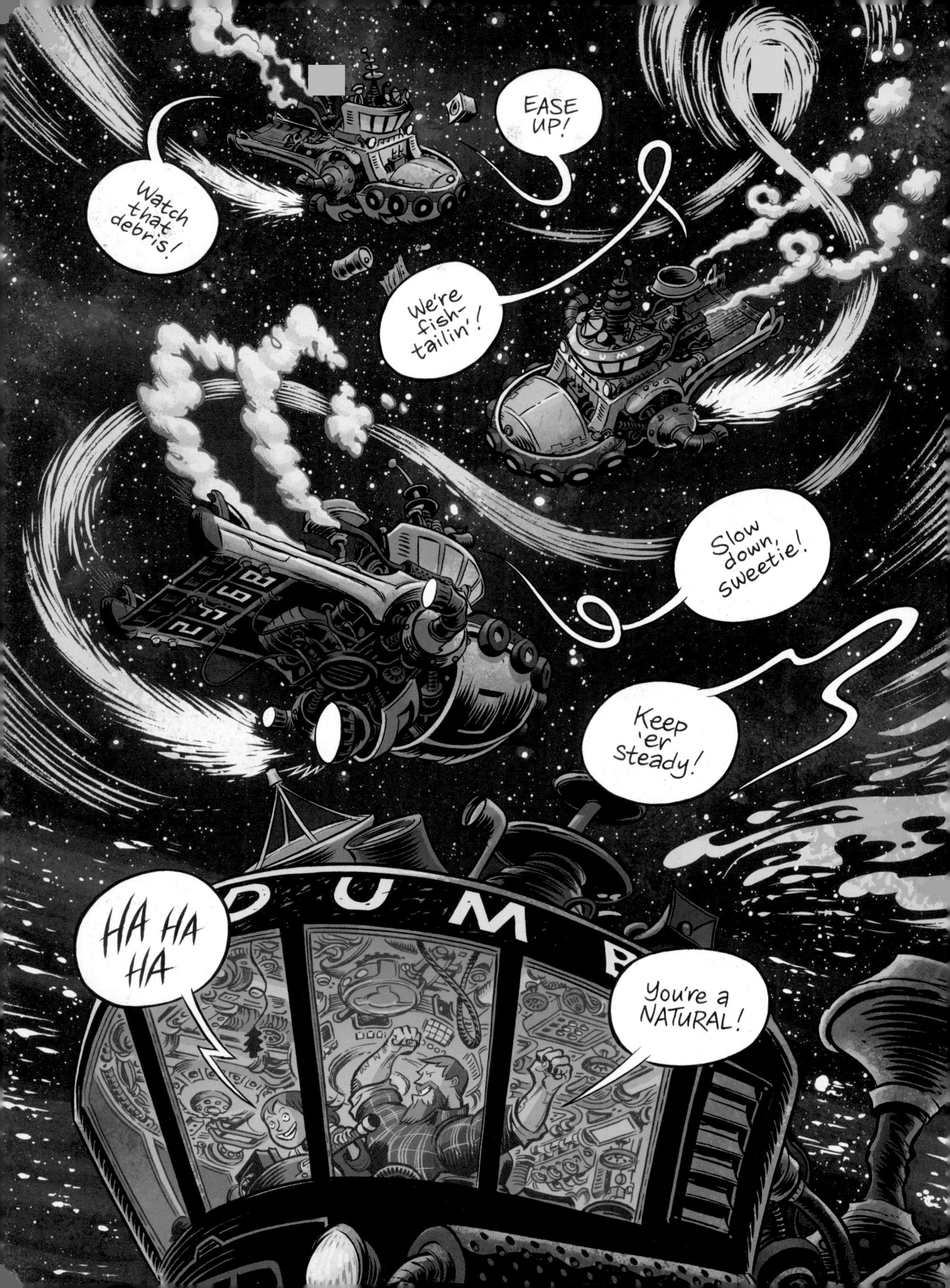
Watch that debris!
EASE UP!
We're fish-tailin'!
Slow down, sweetie!
Keep 'er steady!
HA HA HA
You're a NATURAL!

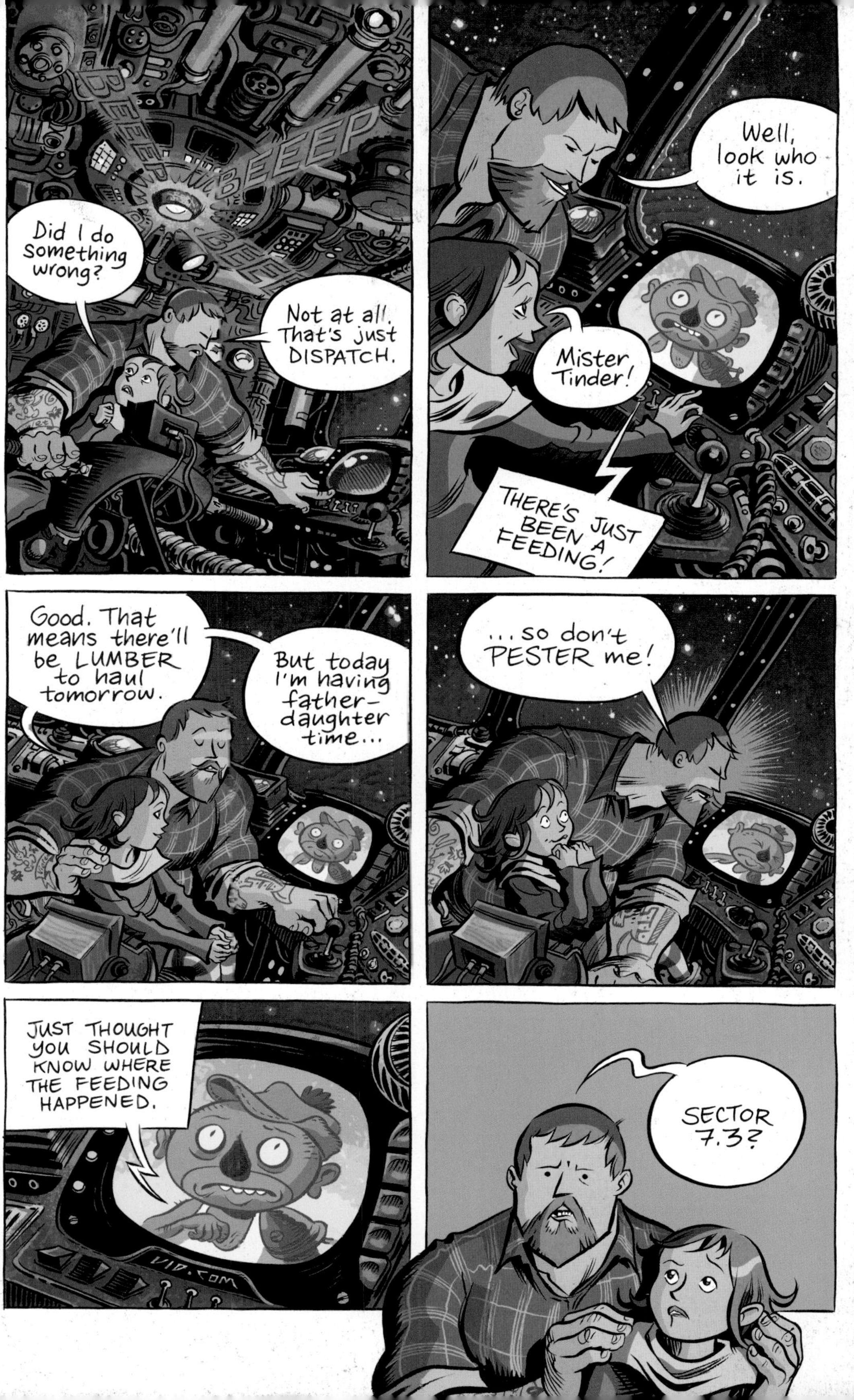
BEEEP BEEEP BEEEP
Did I do something wrong?
Not at all. That's just DISPATCH.
Well, look who it is.
Mister Tinder!
THERE'S JUST BEEN A FEEDING!
Good. That means there'll be LUMBER to haul tomorrow.
But today I'm having father-daughter time...
...so don't PESTER me!
JUST THOUGHT YOU SHOULD KNOW WHERE THE FEEDING HAPPENED.
VID.COM
SECTOR 7.3?

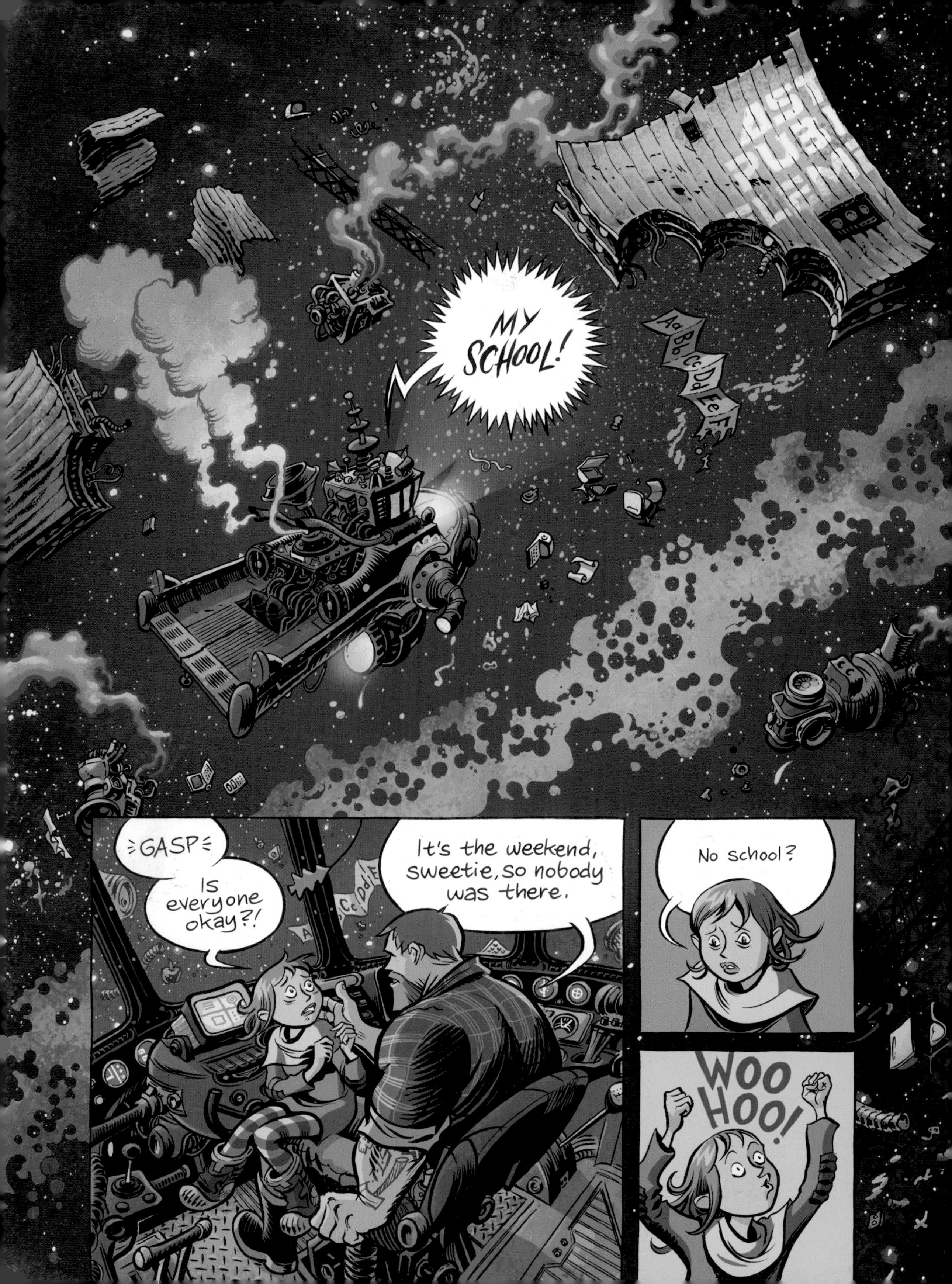
MY SCHOOL!
Aa Bb Cc Dd Ee F
GASP
Is everyone okay?!
It's the weekend, sweetie, so nobody was there.
No school?
WOO HOO!

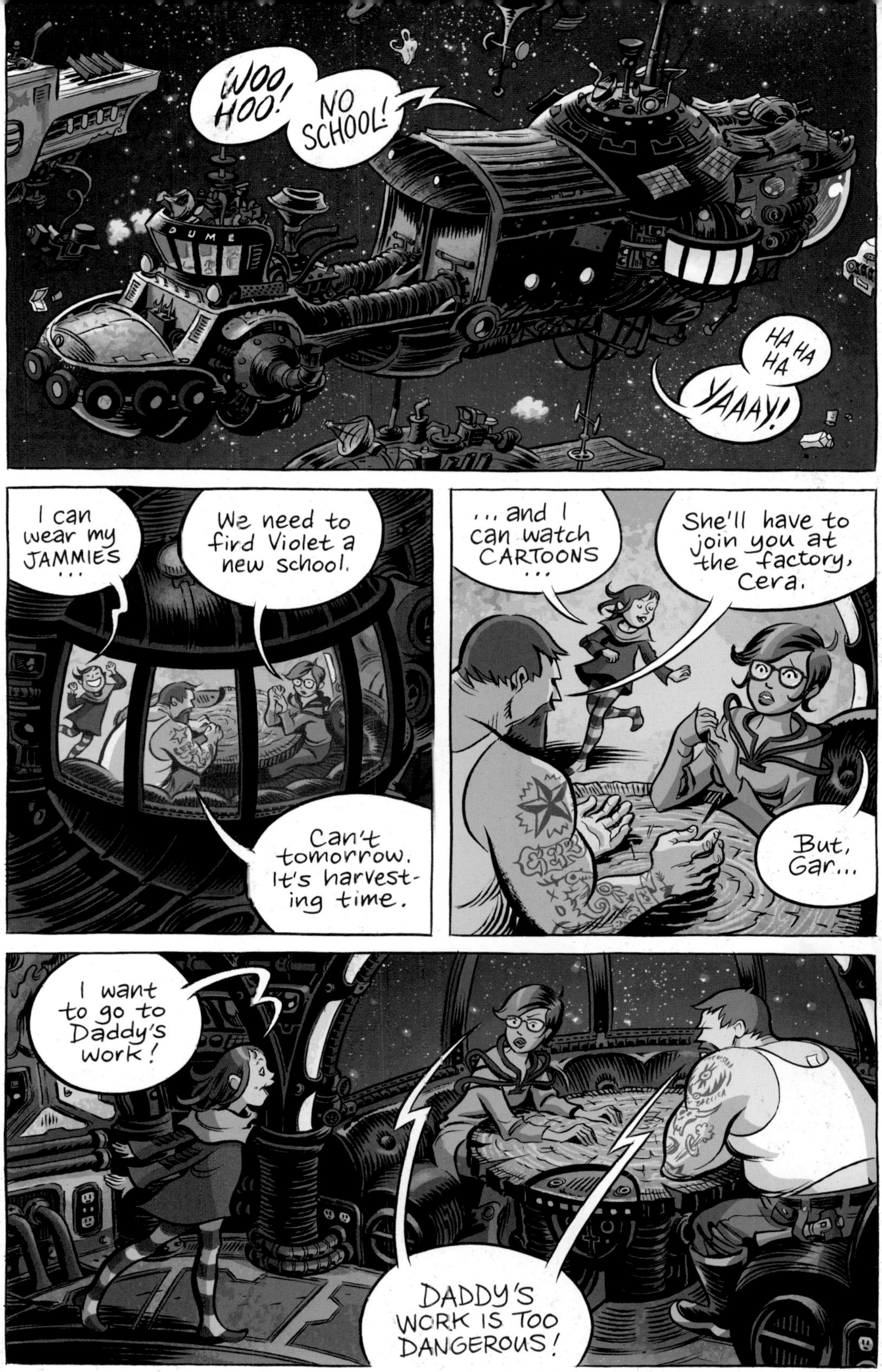
WOO HOO!
NO SCHOOL!
HA HA HA
YAAAY!
I can wear my JAMMIES ...
We need to find Violet a new school.
Can't tomorrow. It's harvesting time.
... and I can watch CARTOONS ...
She'll have to join you at the factory, Cera.
But, Gar...
I want to go to Daddy's work!
DADDY'S WORK IS TOO DANGEROUS!

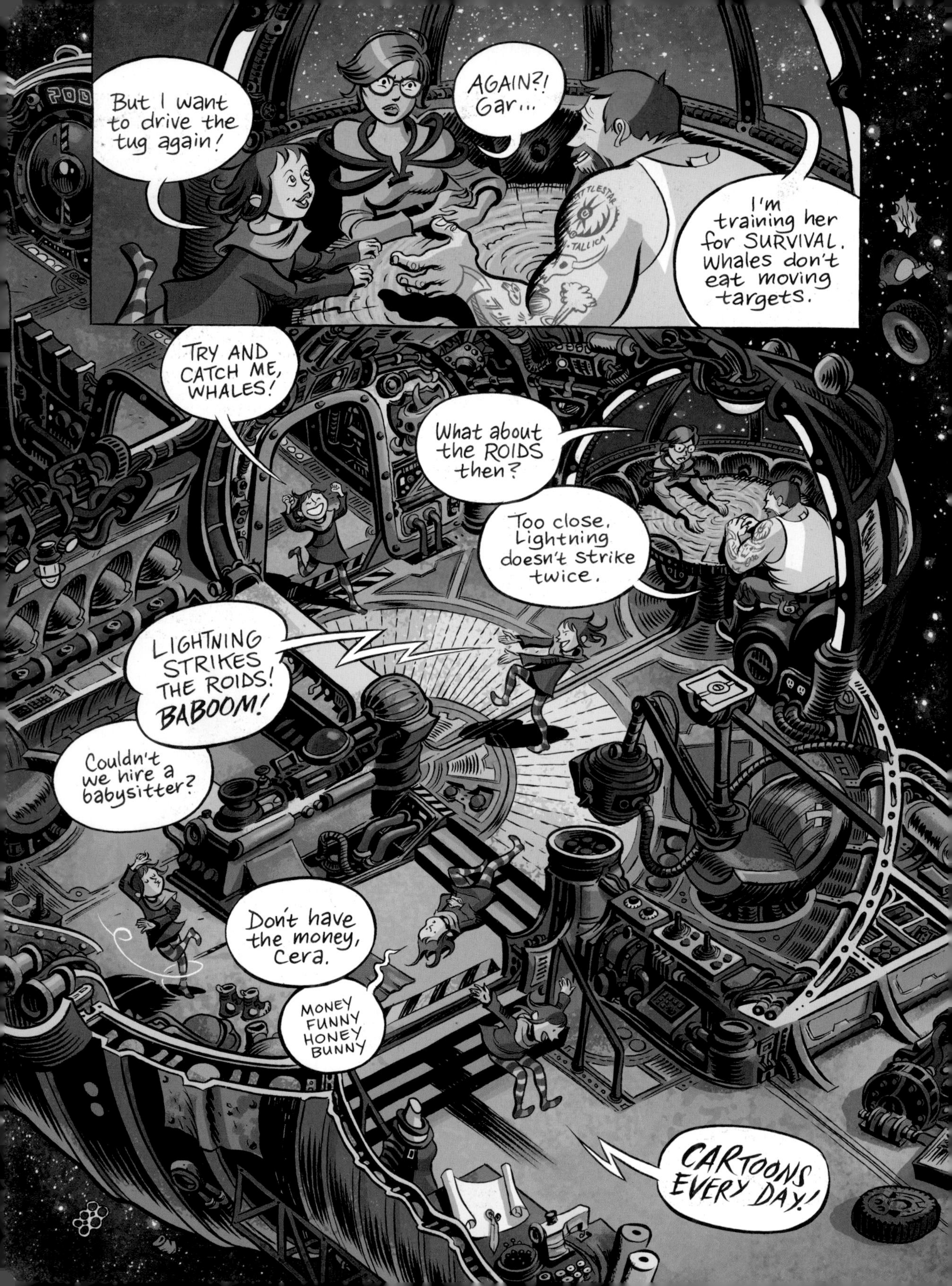
But I want to drive the tug again!
AGAIN?! Gar...
I'm training her for SURVIVAL. Whales don't eat moving targets.
TRY AND CATCH ME, WHALES!
What about the ROIDS then?
Too close. Lightning doesn't strike twice.
LIGHTNING STRIKES THE ROIDS! BABOOM!
Couldn't we hire a babysitter?
Don't have the money, Cera.
MONEY FUNNY HONEY BUNNY
CARTOONS EVERY DAY!

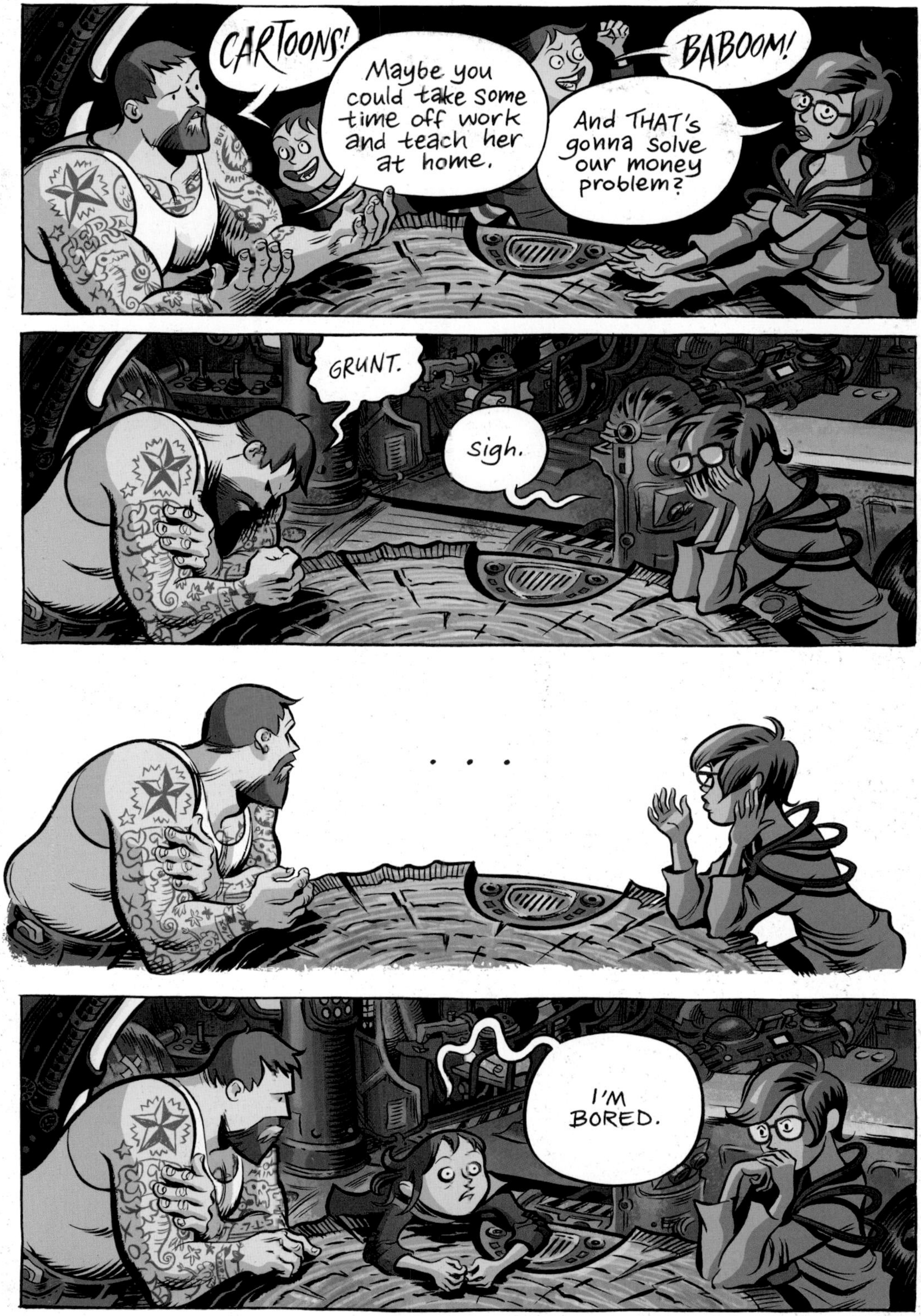
CARTOONS!
Maybe you could take some time off work and teach her at home.
BABOOM!
And THAT's gonna solve our money problem?
GRUNT.
sigh.
. . .
I'M BORED.

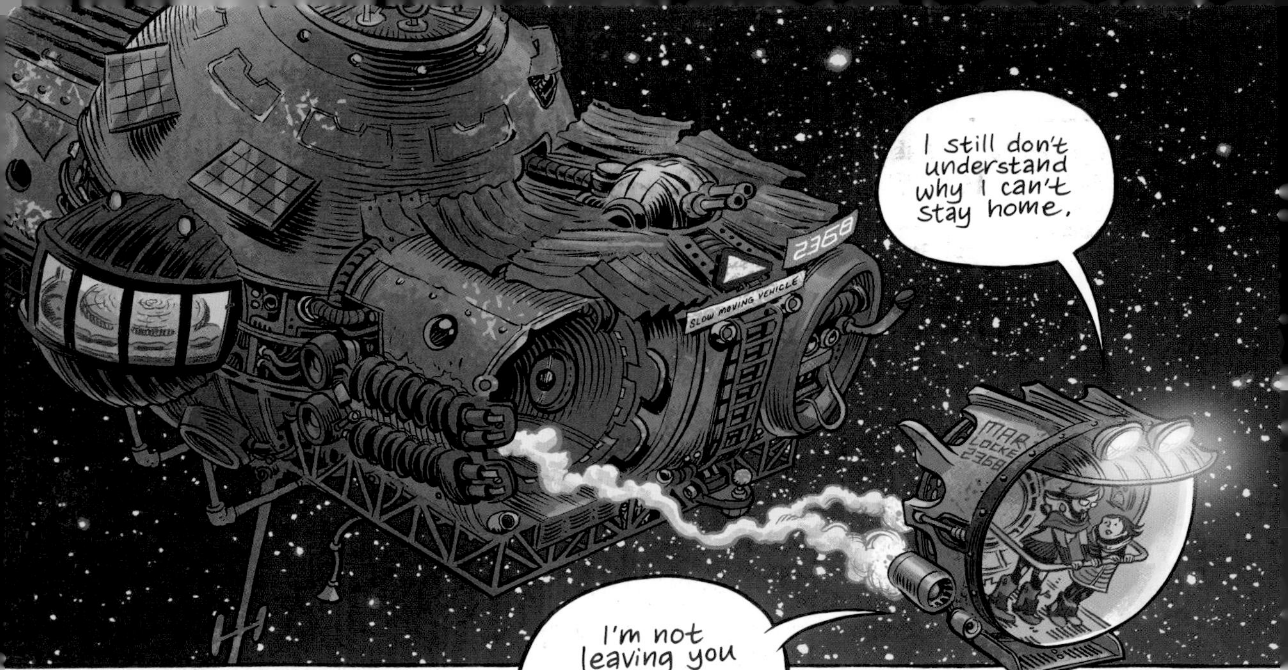
I still don't understand why I can't stay home.
2368
SLOW MOVING VEHICLE

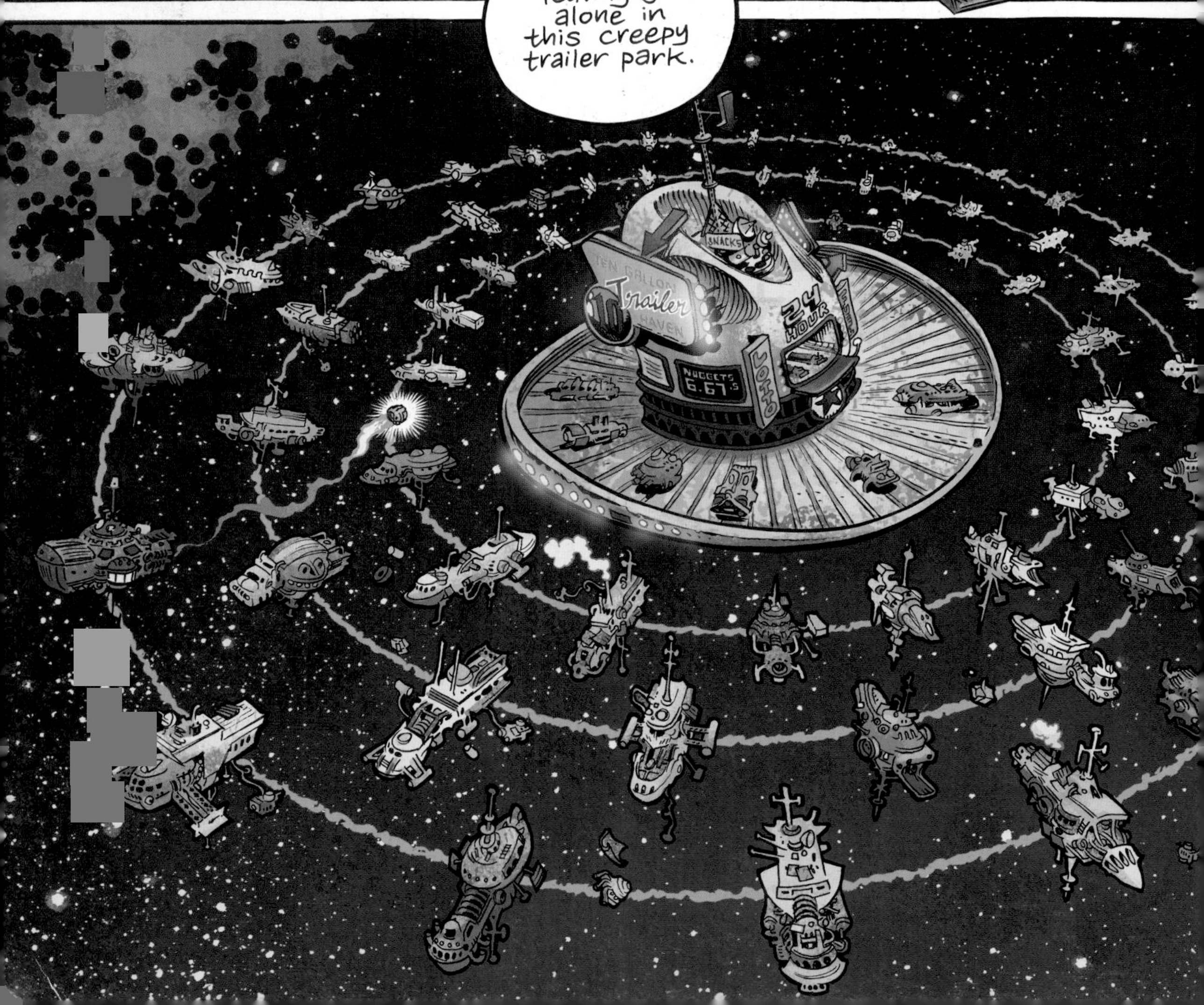
I'm not leaving you alone in this creepy trailer park.
SNACKS
TEN GALLON Trailer HAVEN
24 HOUR
NUGGETS 6.67
LOTTO

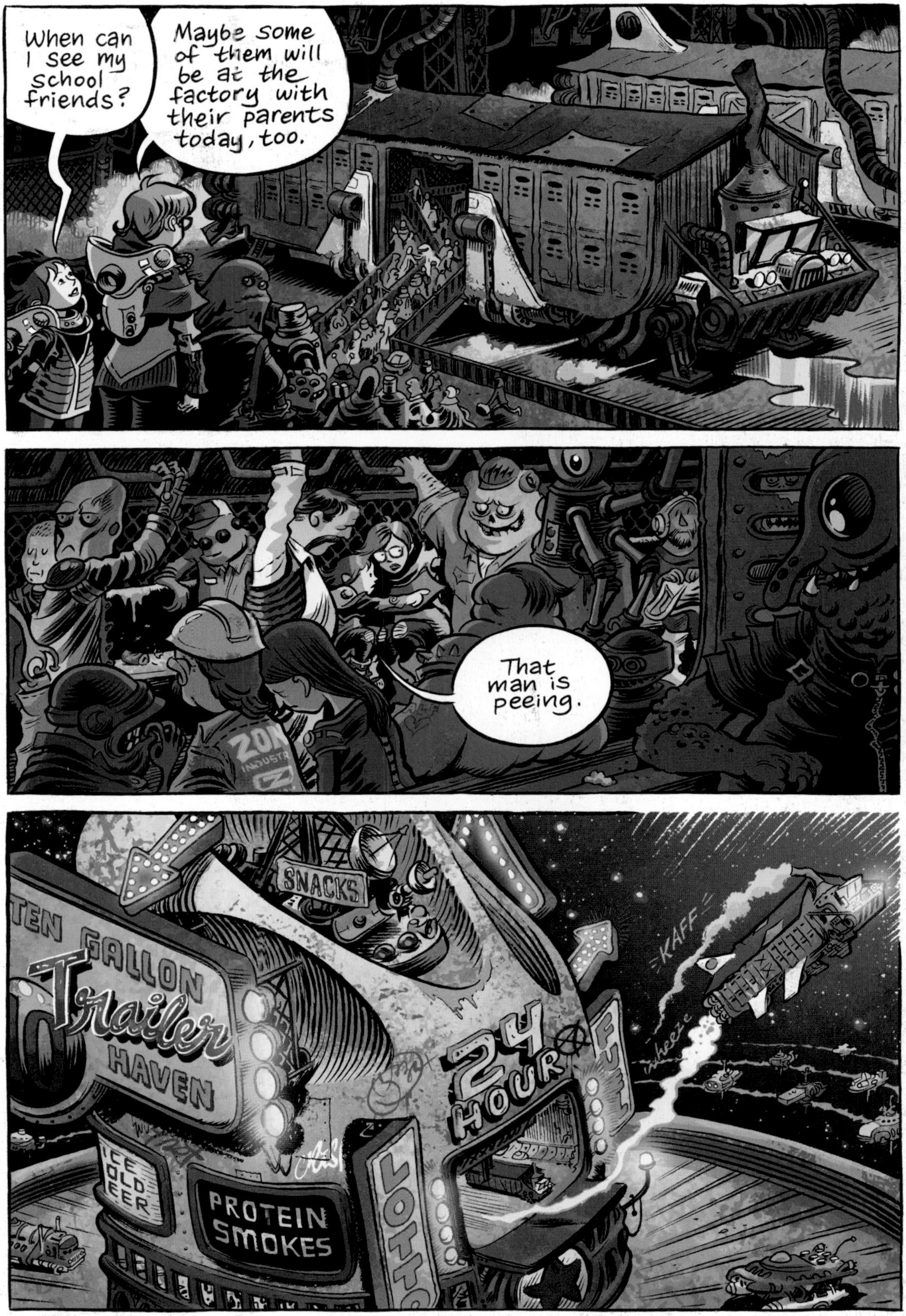
When can I see my school friends?
Maybe some of them will be at the factory with their parents today, too.
That man is peeing.
SNACKS
TEN GALLON
Trailer
HAVEN
24 HOUR
PROTEIN SMOKES
KAFF
wheeze

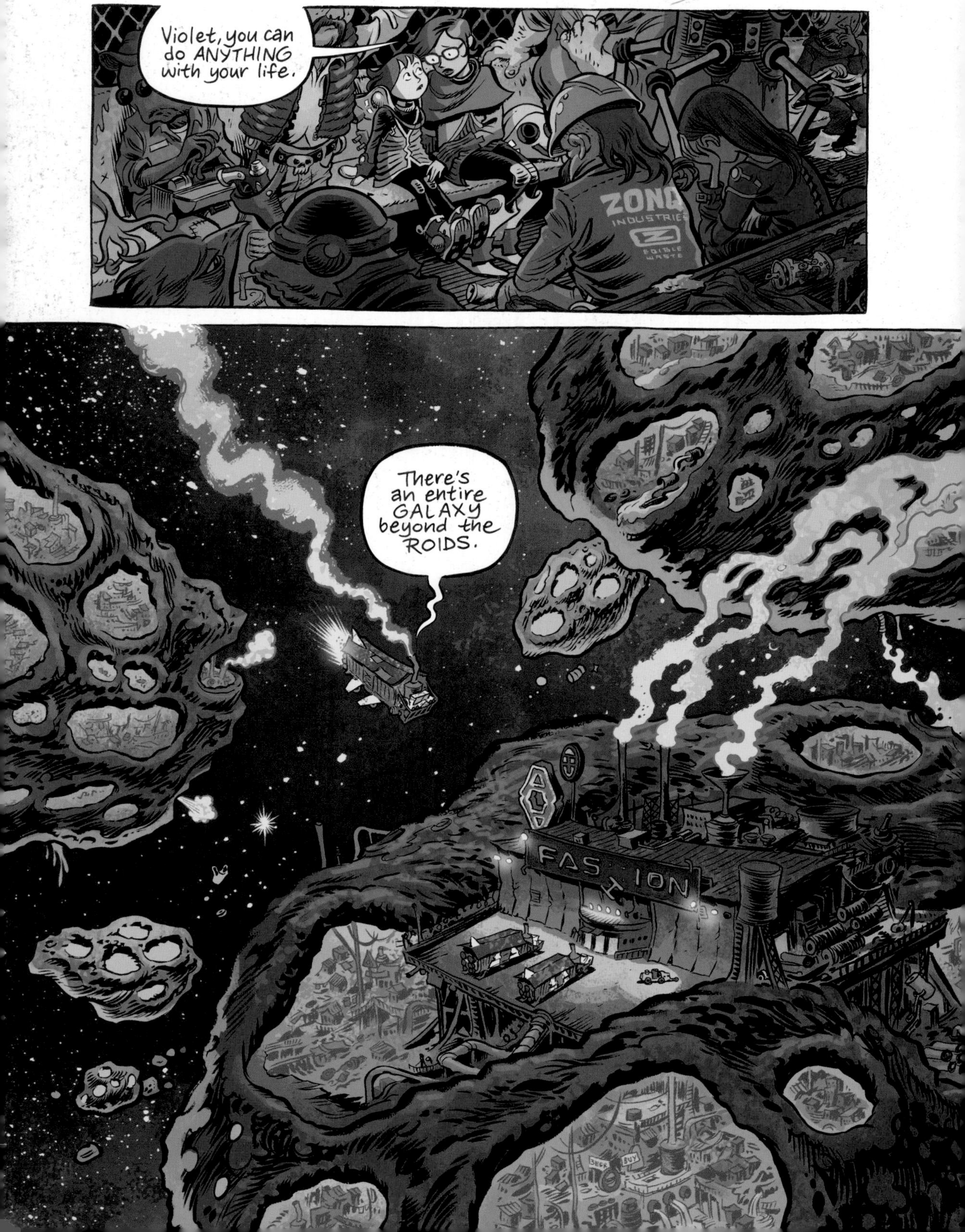

Violet, you can do ANYTHING with your life.
ZONQ INDUSTRIES
EDIBLE WASTE
There's an entire GALAXY beyond the ROIDS.

Mrs. Nurget, where's Livonia?

Playing at home and watching cartoons.

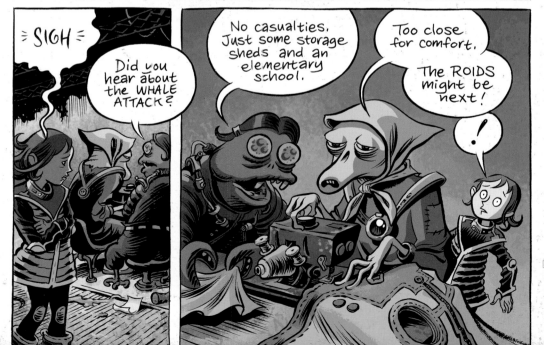

= SIGH =

Did you hear about the WHALE ATTACK?

No casualties. Just some storage sheds and an elementary school.

Too close for comfort.

The ROIDS might be next!

!

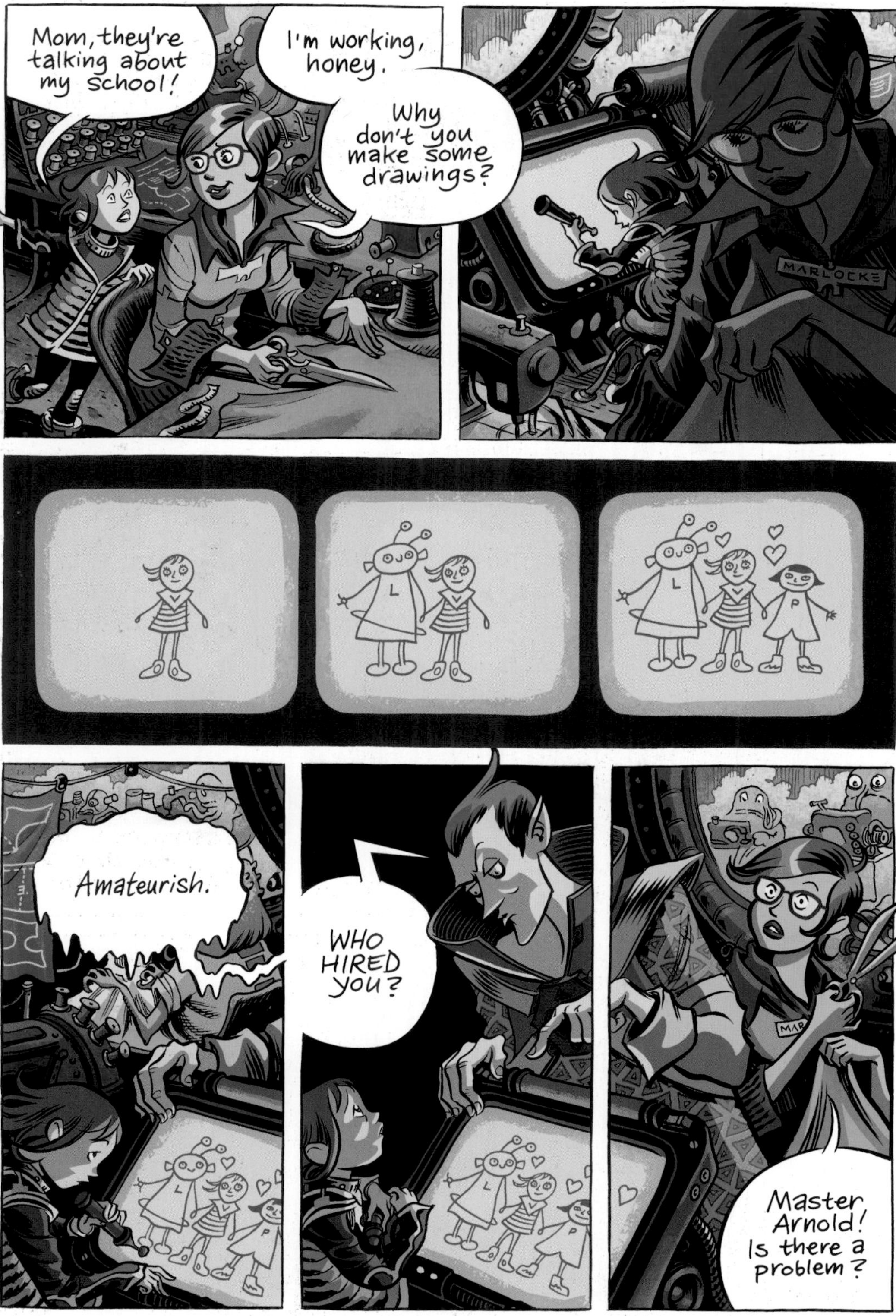
Mom, they're talking about my school!
I'm working, honey.
Why don't you make some drawings?
MARLOCKE
L
L
P
Amateurish.
WHO HIRED YOU?
MAR
Master Arnold! Is there a problem?

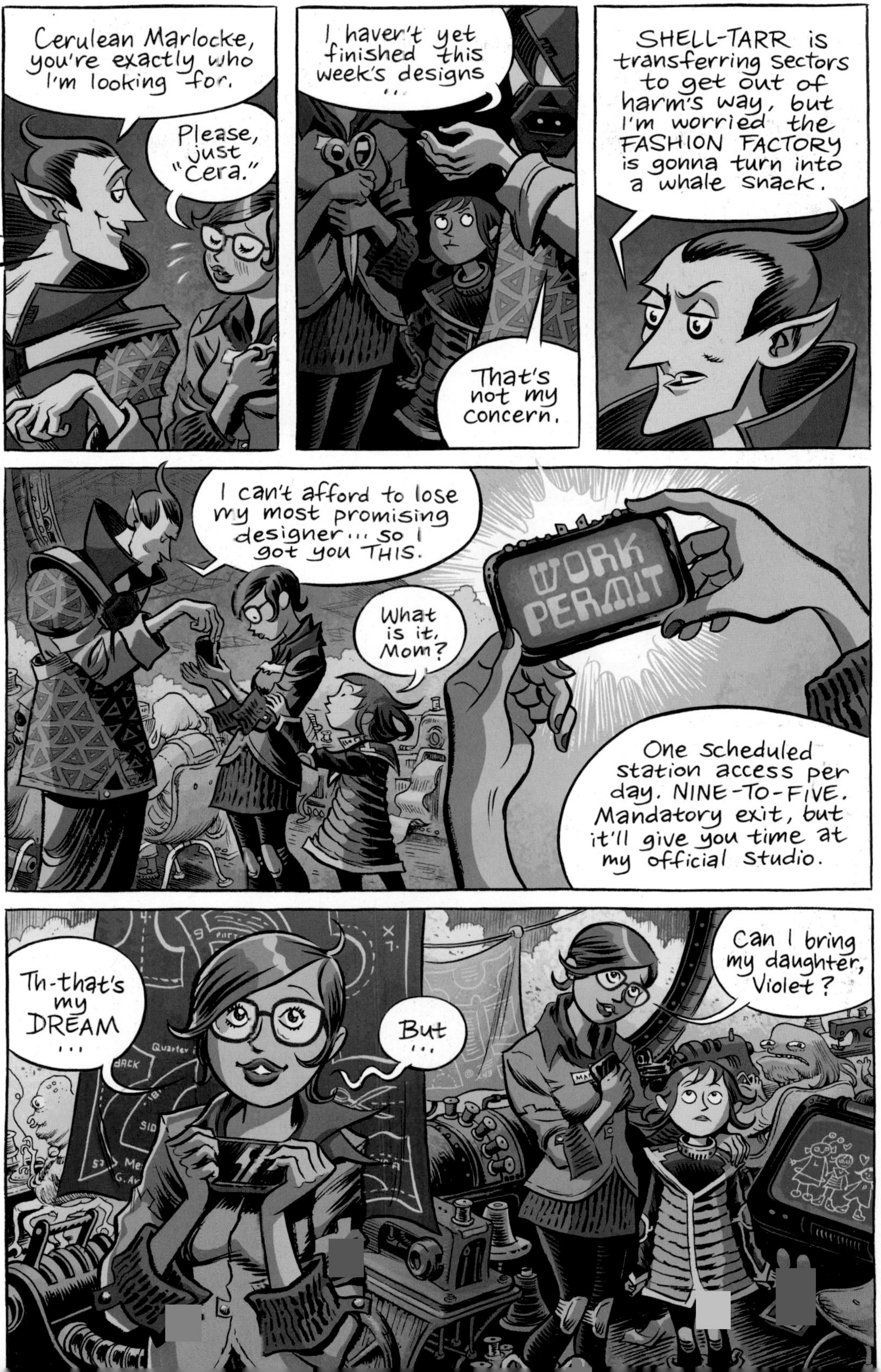
Cerulean Marlocke, you're exactly who I'm looking for.
Please, just "Cera."
I haven't yet finished this week's designs . . .
That's not my concern.
SHELL-TARR is transferring sectors to get out of harm's way, but I'm worried the FASHION FACTORY is gonna turn into a whale snack.
I can't afford to lose my most promising designer... so I got you THIS.
What is it, Mom?
WORK PERMIT
One scheduled station access per day. NINE-TO-FIVE. Mandatory exit, but it'll give you time at my official studio.
Th-that's my DREAM . . .
But . . .
Can I bring my daughter, Violet?

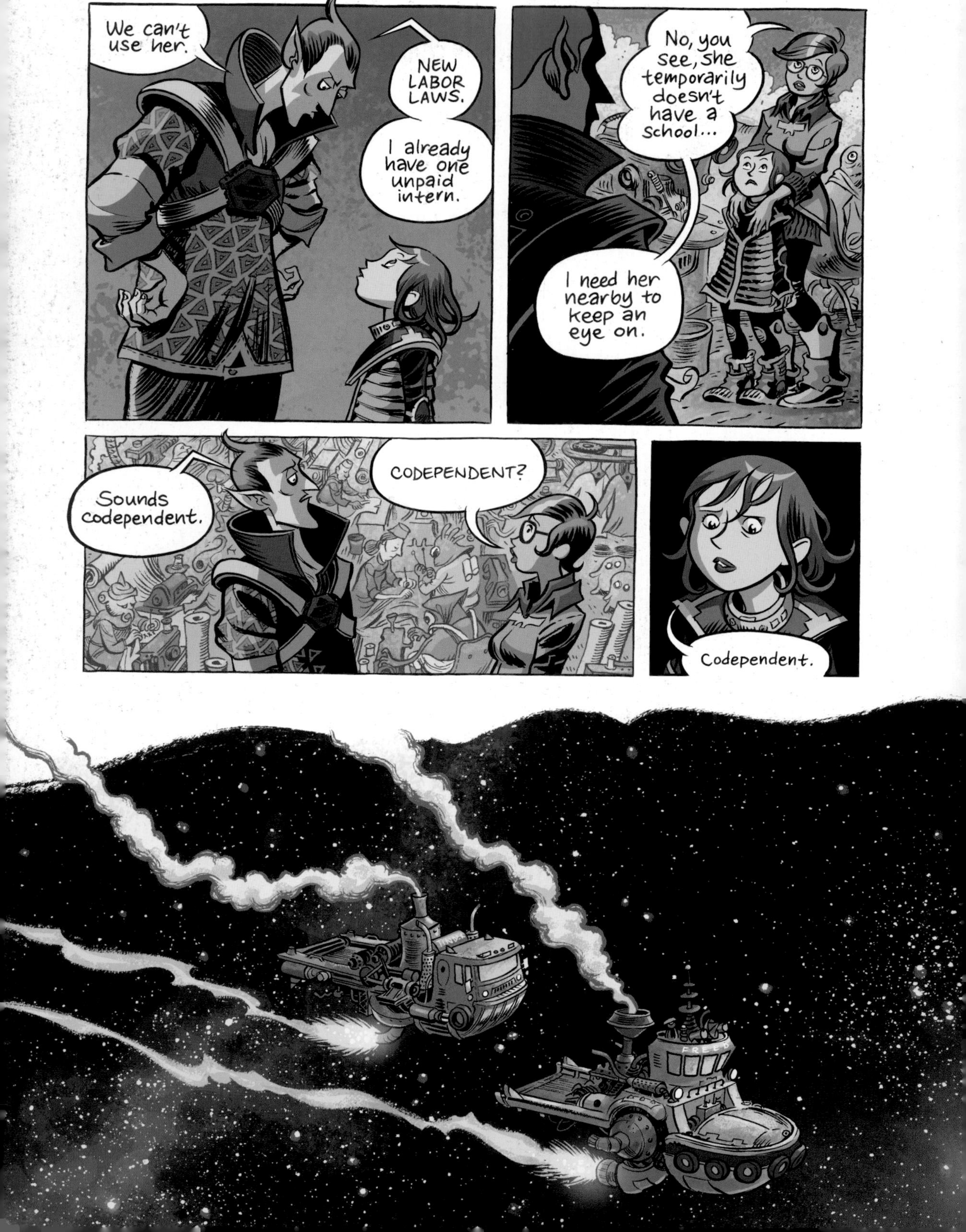
We can't use her.
NEW LABOR LAWS.
I already have one unpaid intern.
No, you see, she temporarily doesn't have a school...
I need her nearby to keep an eye on.
Sounds codependent.
CODEPENDENT?
Codependent.

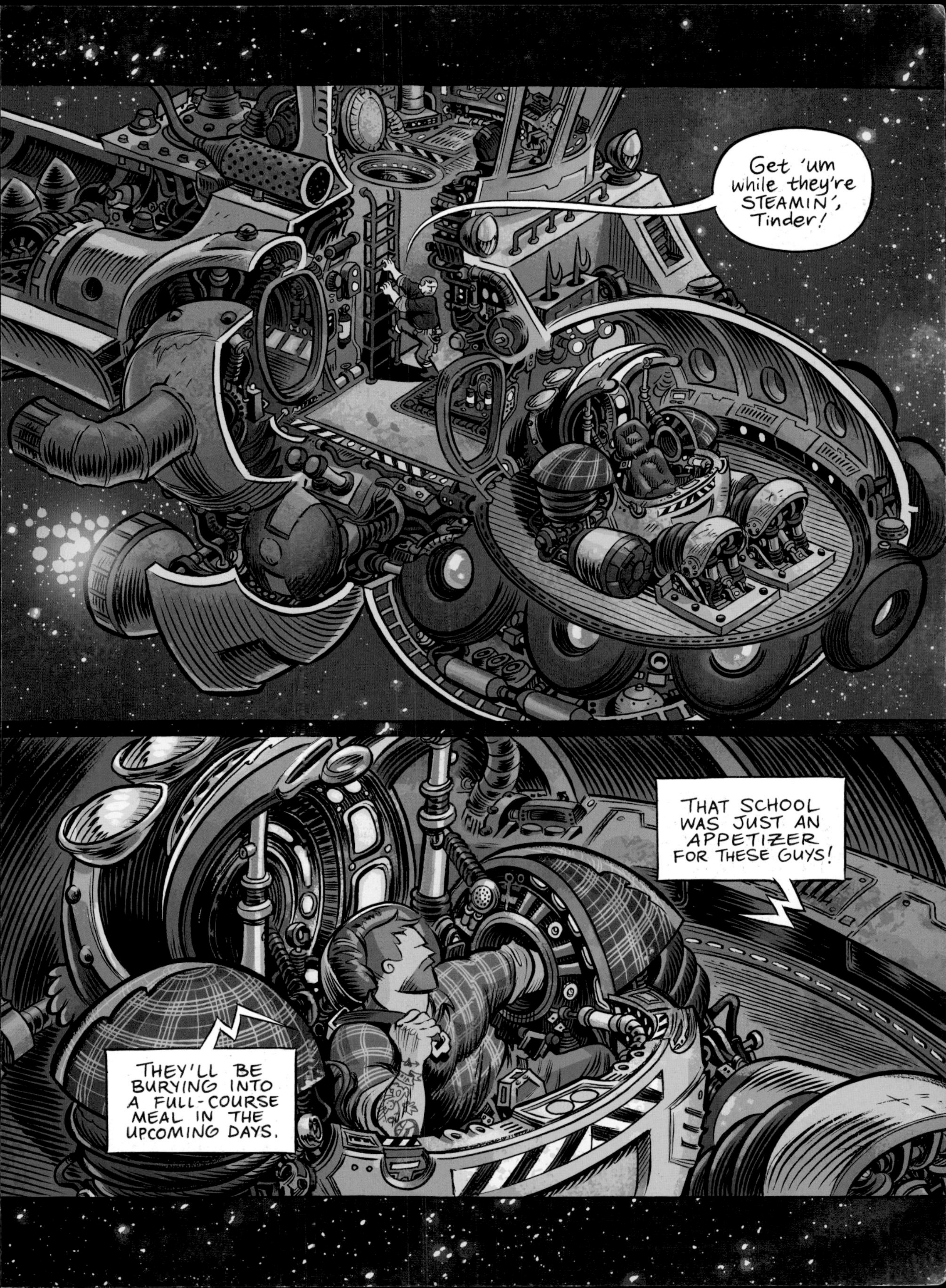

Get 'um while they're STEAMIN', Tinder!
THAT SCHOOL WAS JUST AN APPETIZER FOR THESE GUYS!
THEY'LL BE BURYING INTO A FULL-COURSE MEAL IN THE UPCOMING DAYS.

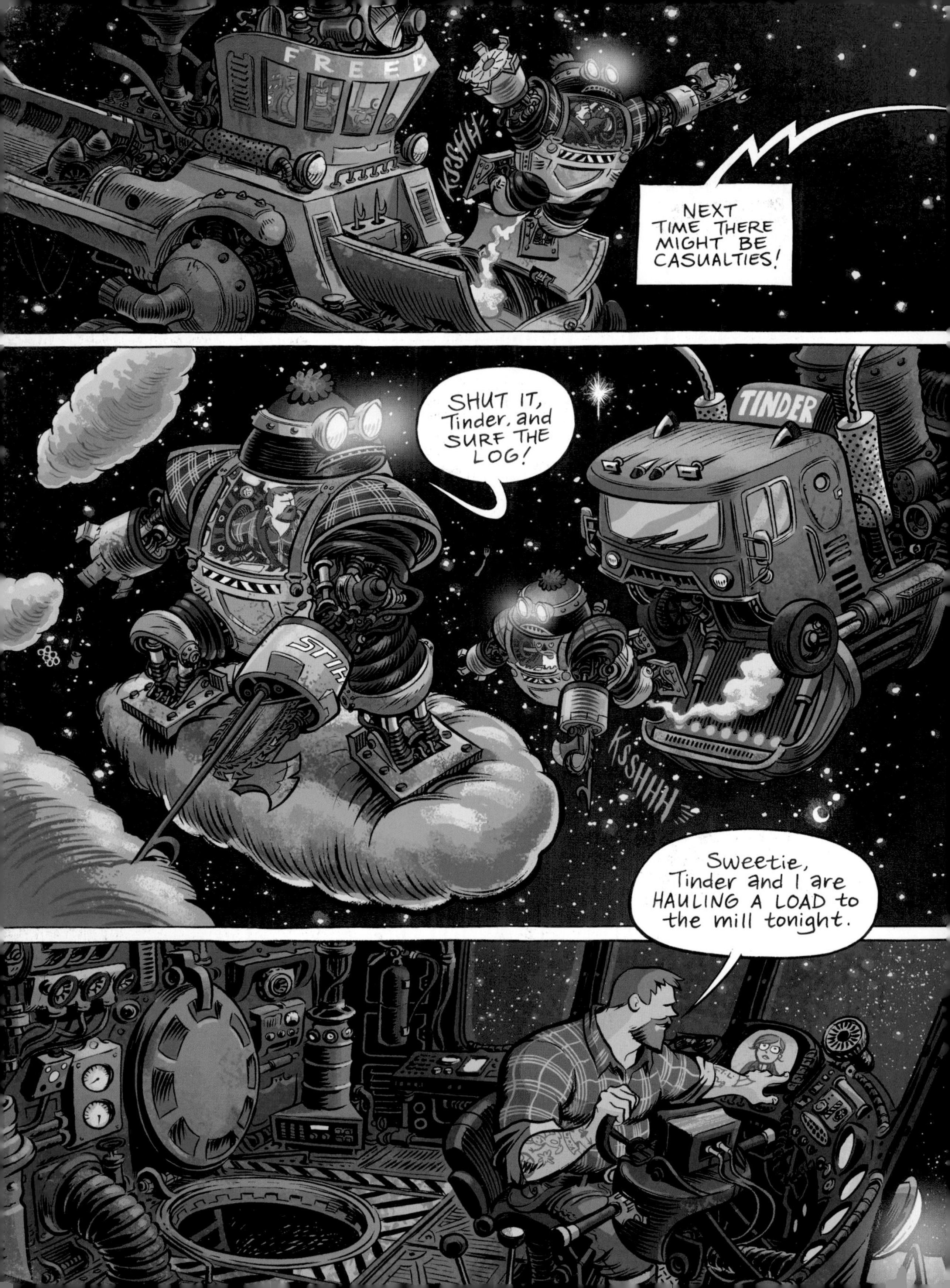
FREED
KSSHH
NEXT TIME THERE MIGHT BE CASUALTIES!
SHUT IT, Tinder, and SURF THE LOG!
TINDER
KSSHHH
Sweetie, Tinder and I are HAULING A LOAD to the mill tonight.

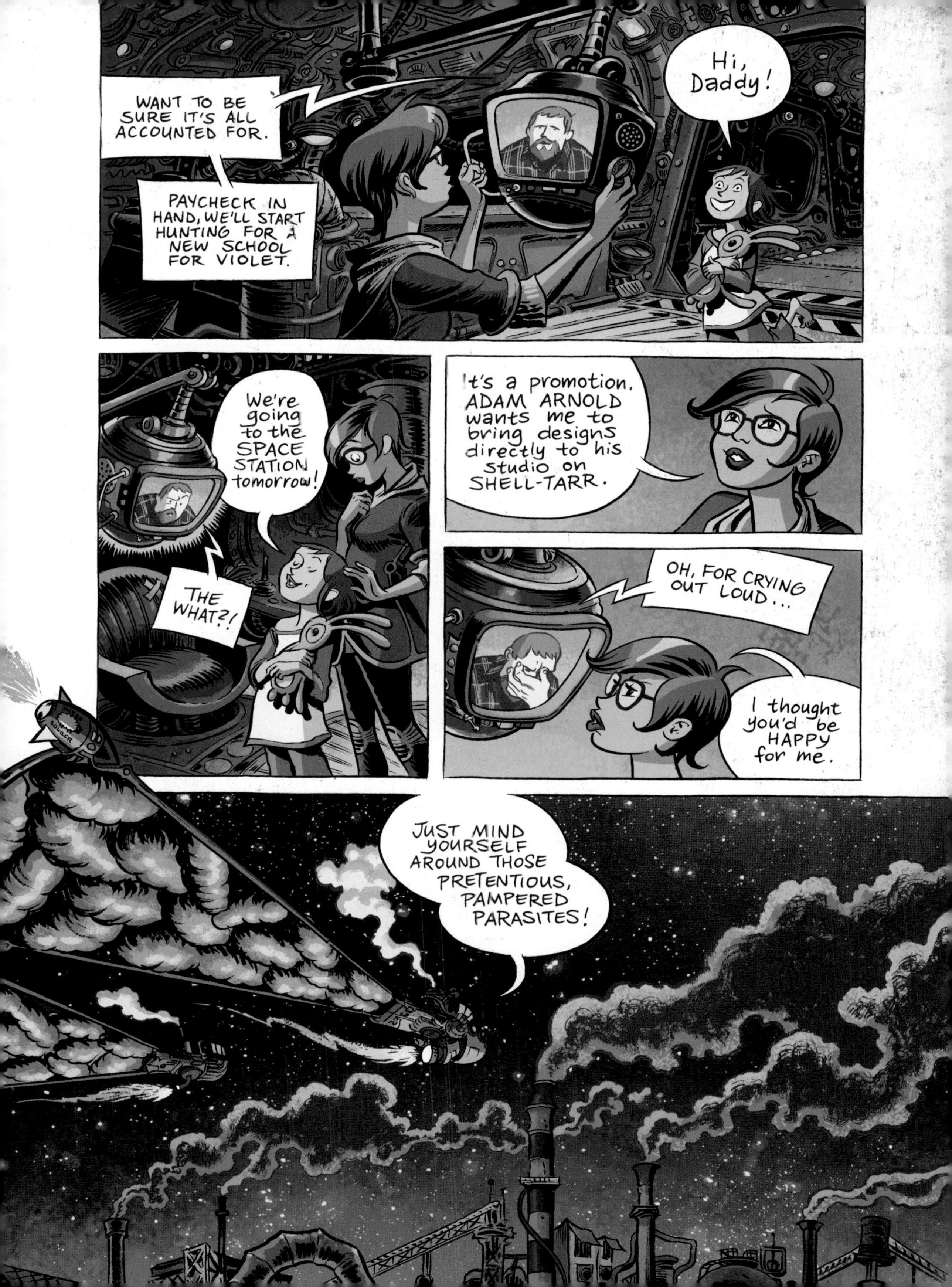
WANT TO BE SURE IT'S ALL ACCOUNTED FOR.
PAYCHECK IN HAND, WE'LL START HUNTING FOR A NEW SCHOOL FOR VIOLET.
Hi, Daddy!
We're going to the SPACE STATION tomorrow!
THE WHAT?!
It's a promotion. ADAM ARNOLD wants me to bring designs directly to his studio on SHELL-TARR.
OH, FOR CRYING OUT LOUD...
I thought you'd be HAPPY for me.
JUST MIND YOURSELF AROUND THOSE PRETENTIOUS, PAMPERED PARASITES!

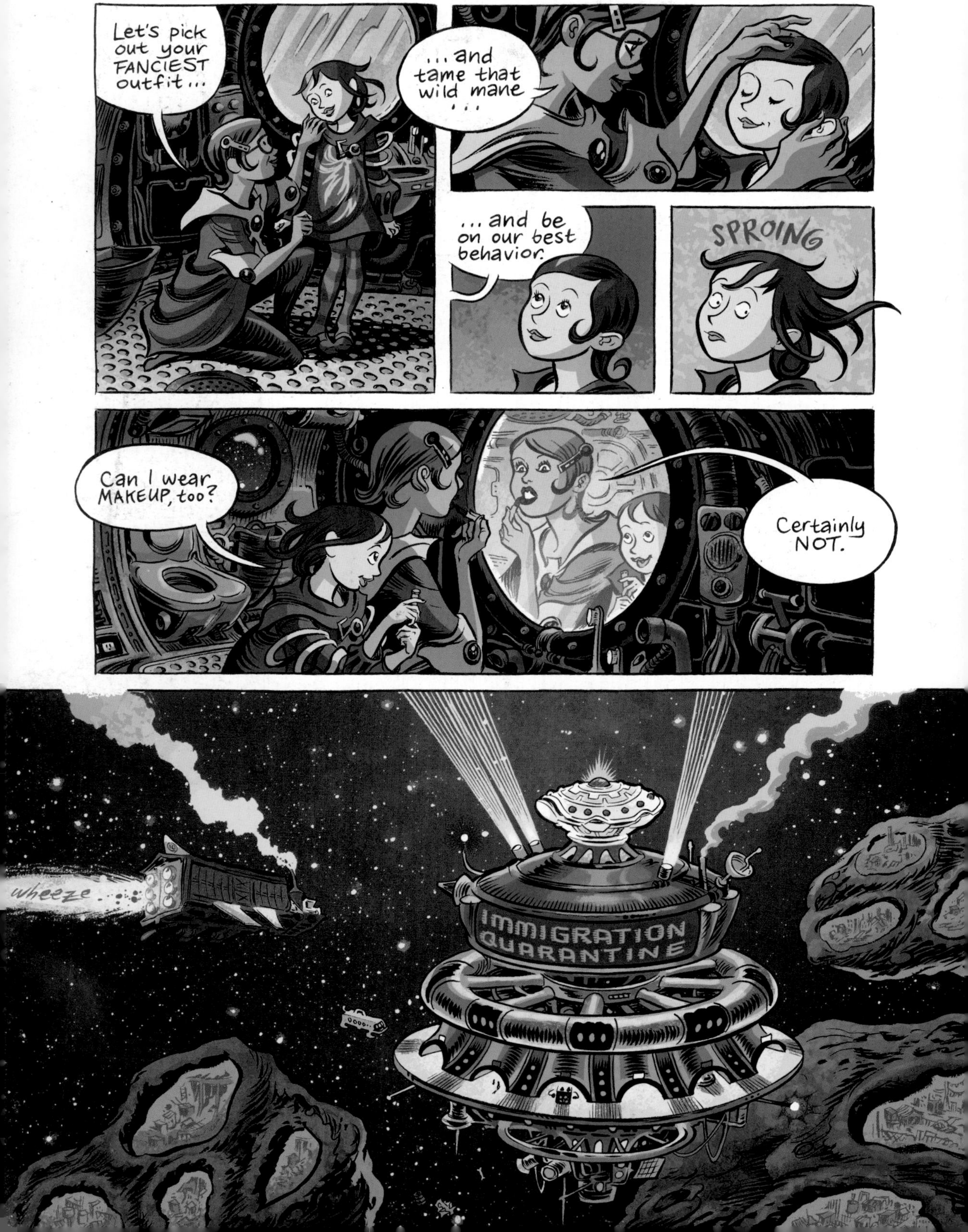
Let's pick out your FANCIEST outfit...
...and tame that wild mane...
...and be on our best behavior.
SPROING
Can I wear MAKEUP, too?
Certainly NOT.
wheeze
IMMIGRATION QUARANTINE

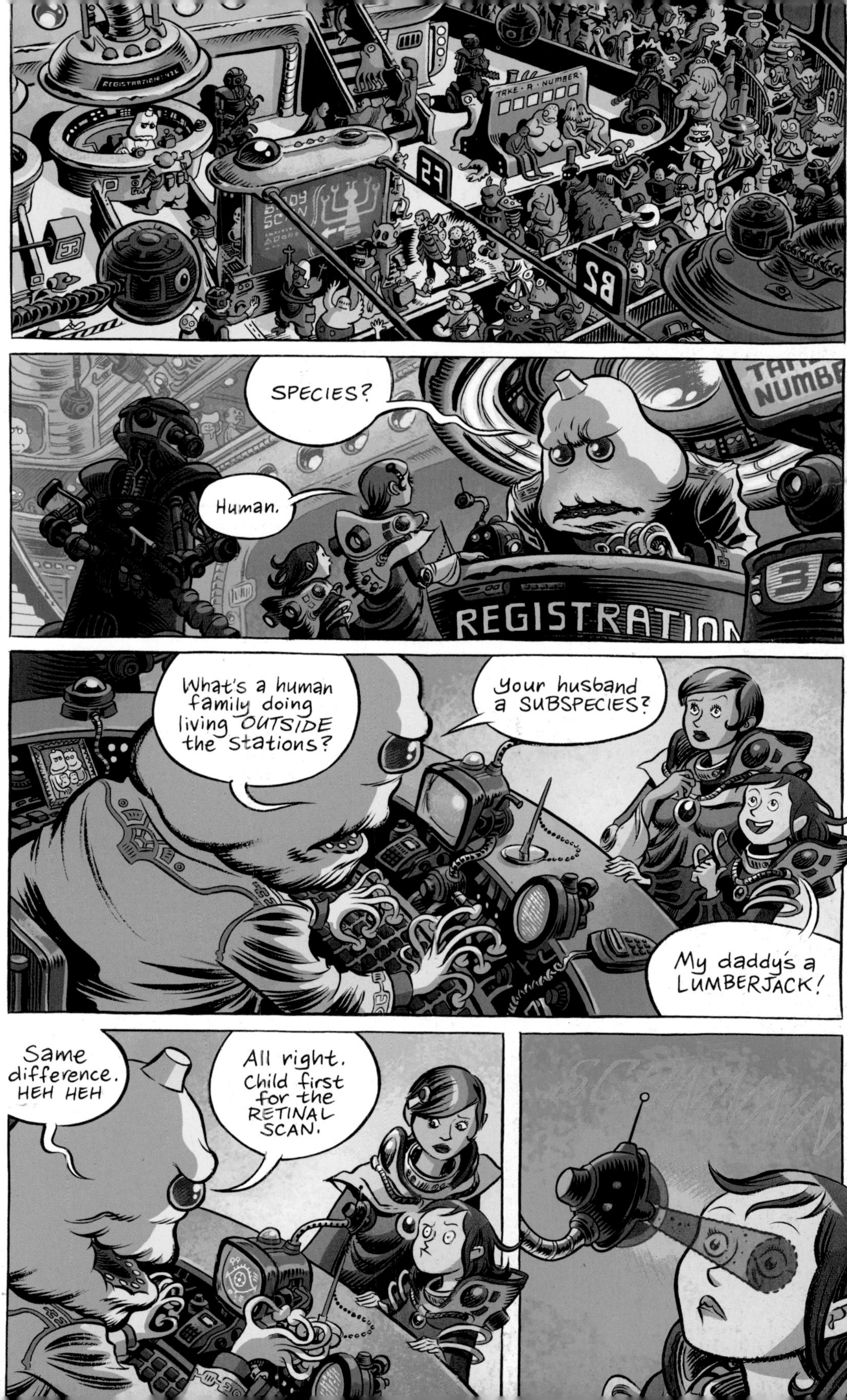
REGISTRATION
TAKE A NUMBER
BODY SCAN
23
B2
SPECIES?
Human.
What's a human family doing living OUTSIDE the stations?
Your husband a SUBSPECIES?
My daddy's a LUMBERJACK!
Same difference. HEH HEH
All right. Child first for the RETINAL SCAN.

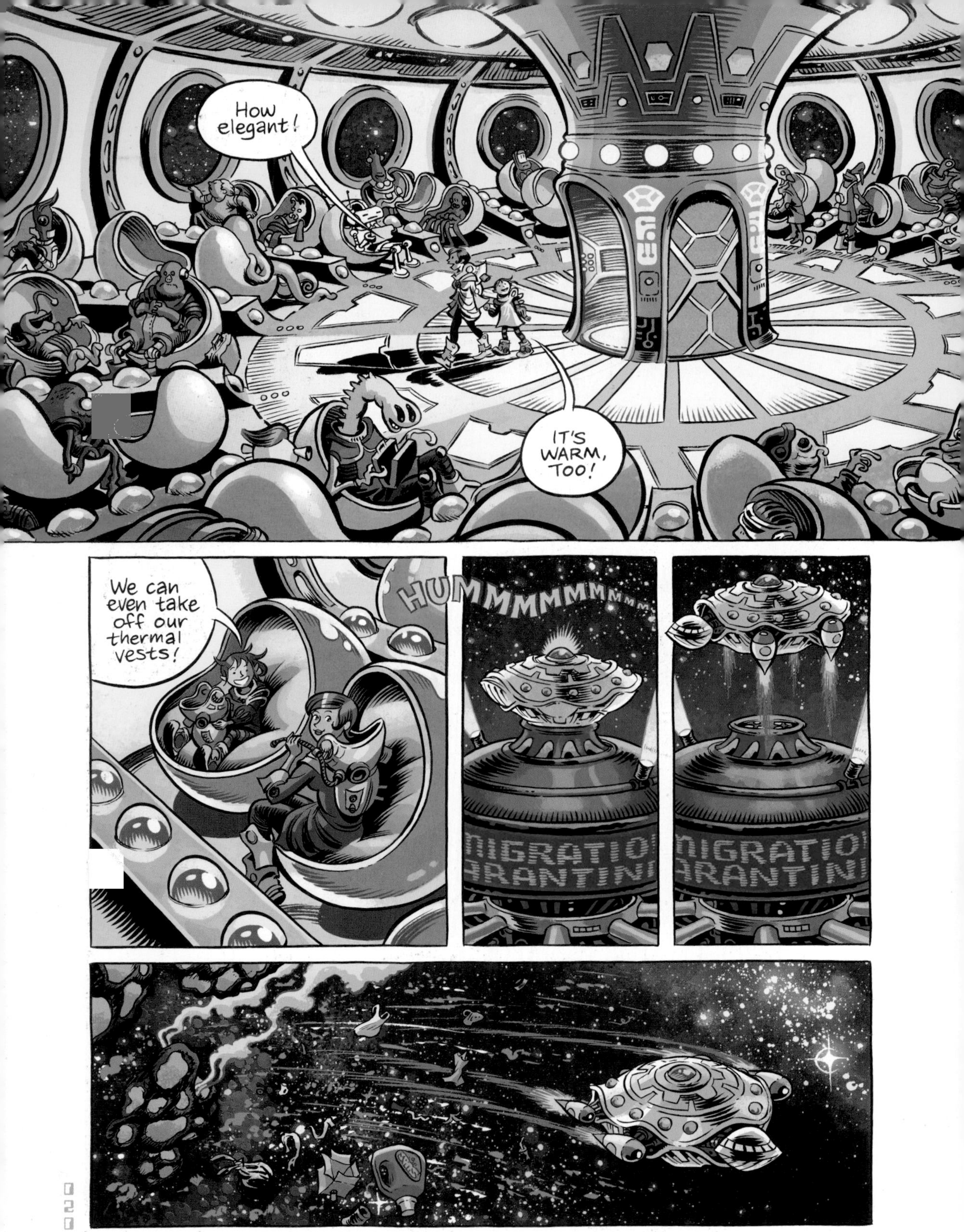
How elegant!
IT'S WARM, TOO!
We can even take off our thermal vests!
HUMMMMMMMMMM

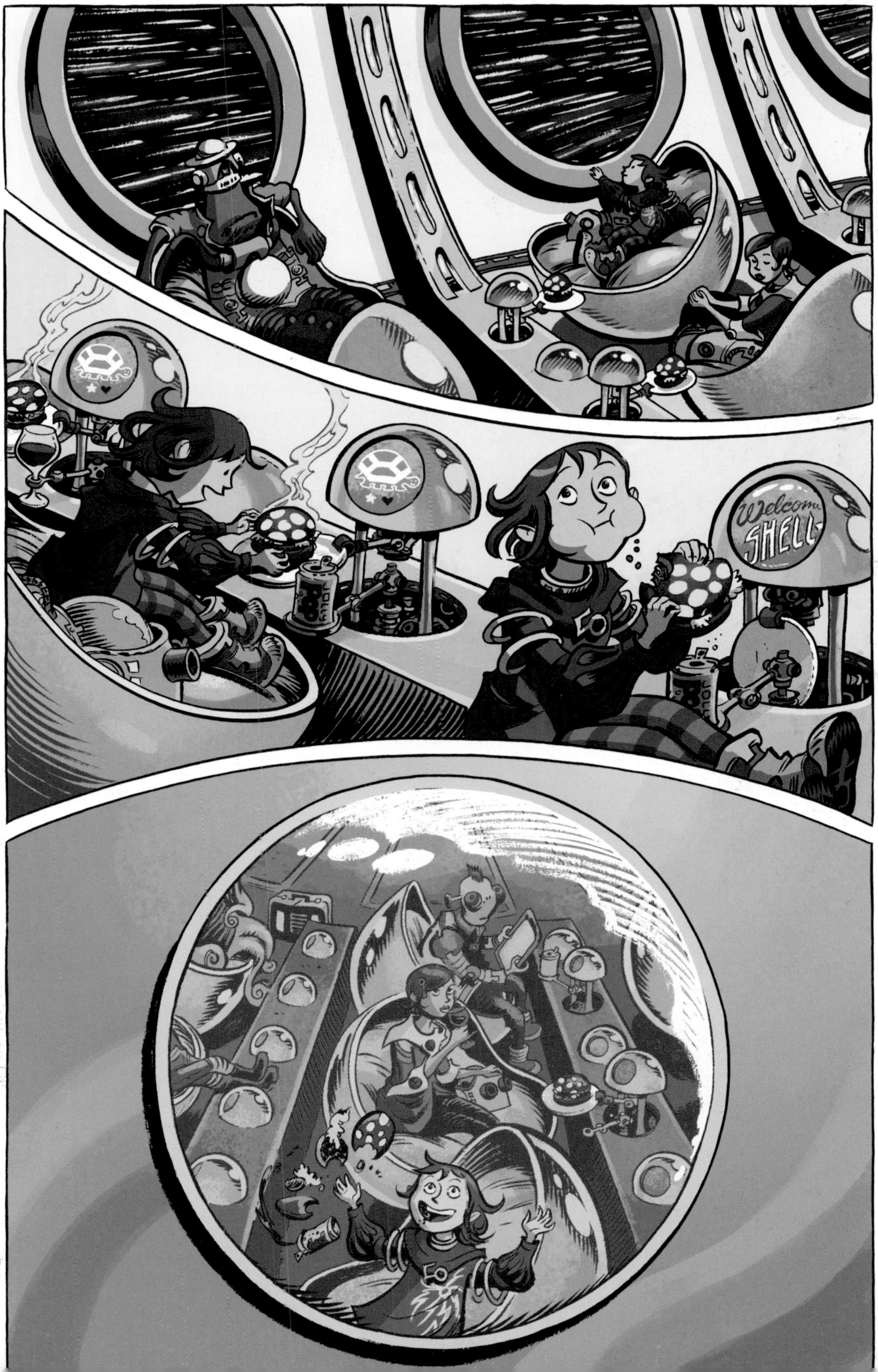
Welcom
SHELL

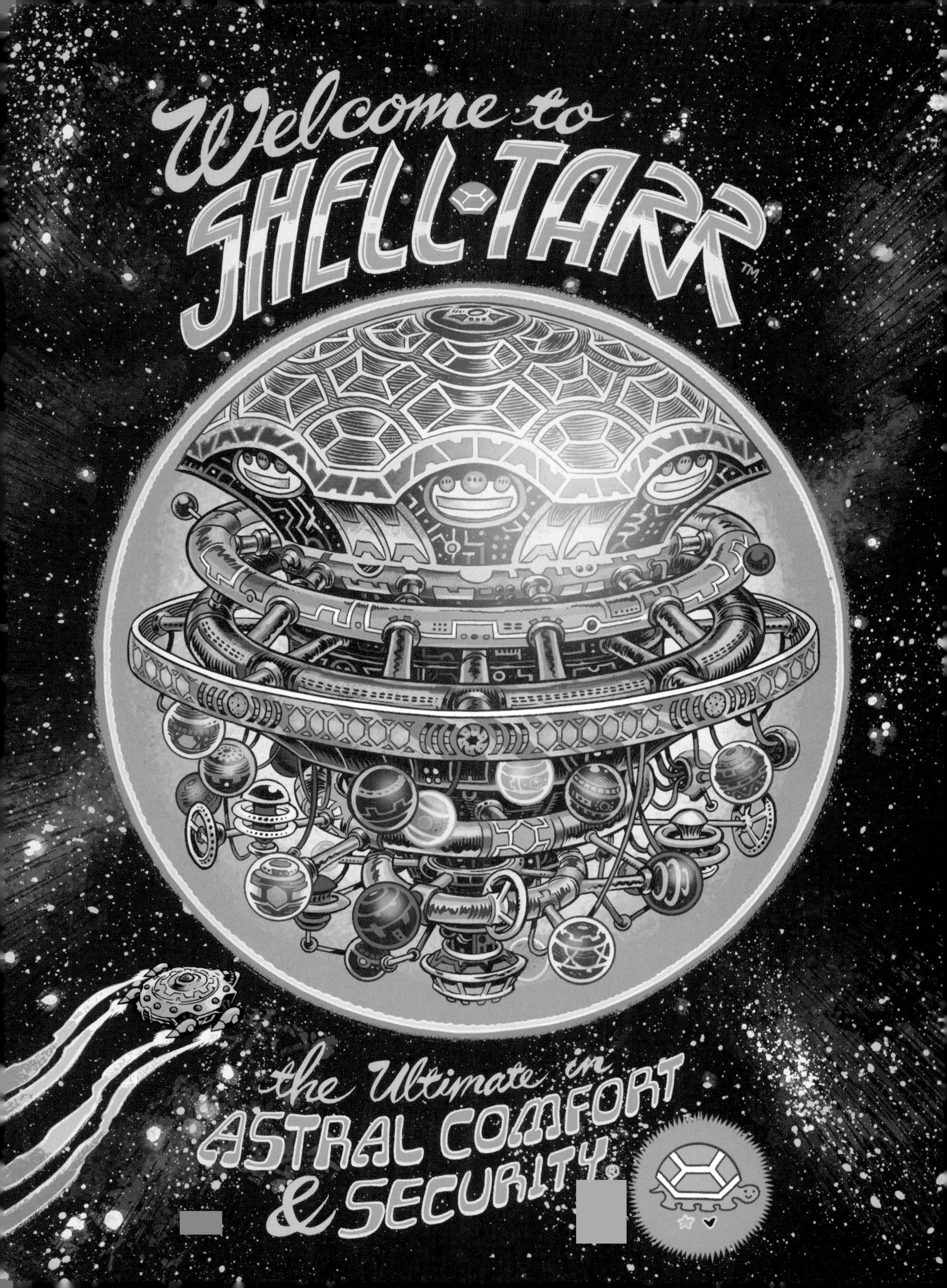
Welcome to
SHELL-TARR™
the Ultimate in
ASTRAL COMFORT
& SECURITY®

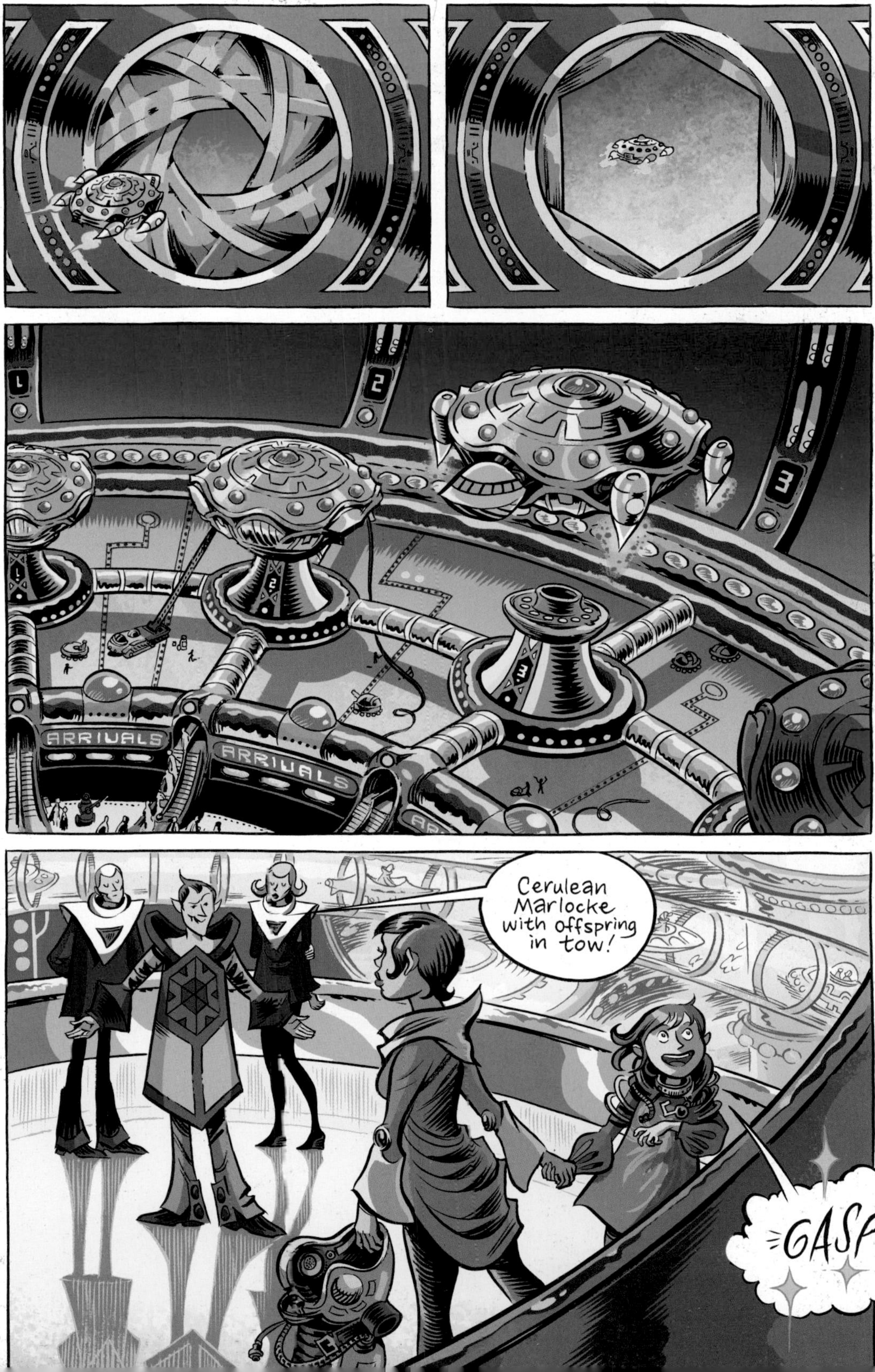
ARRIVALS
ARRIVALS
Cerulean Marlocke with offspring in tow!
GASP

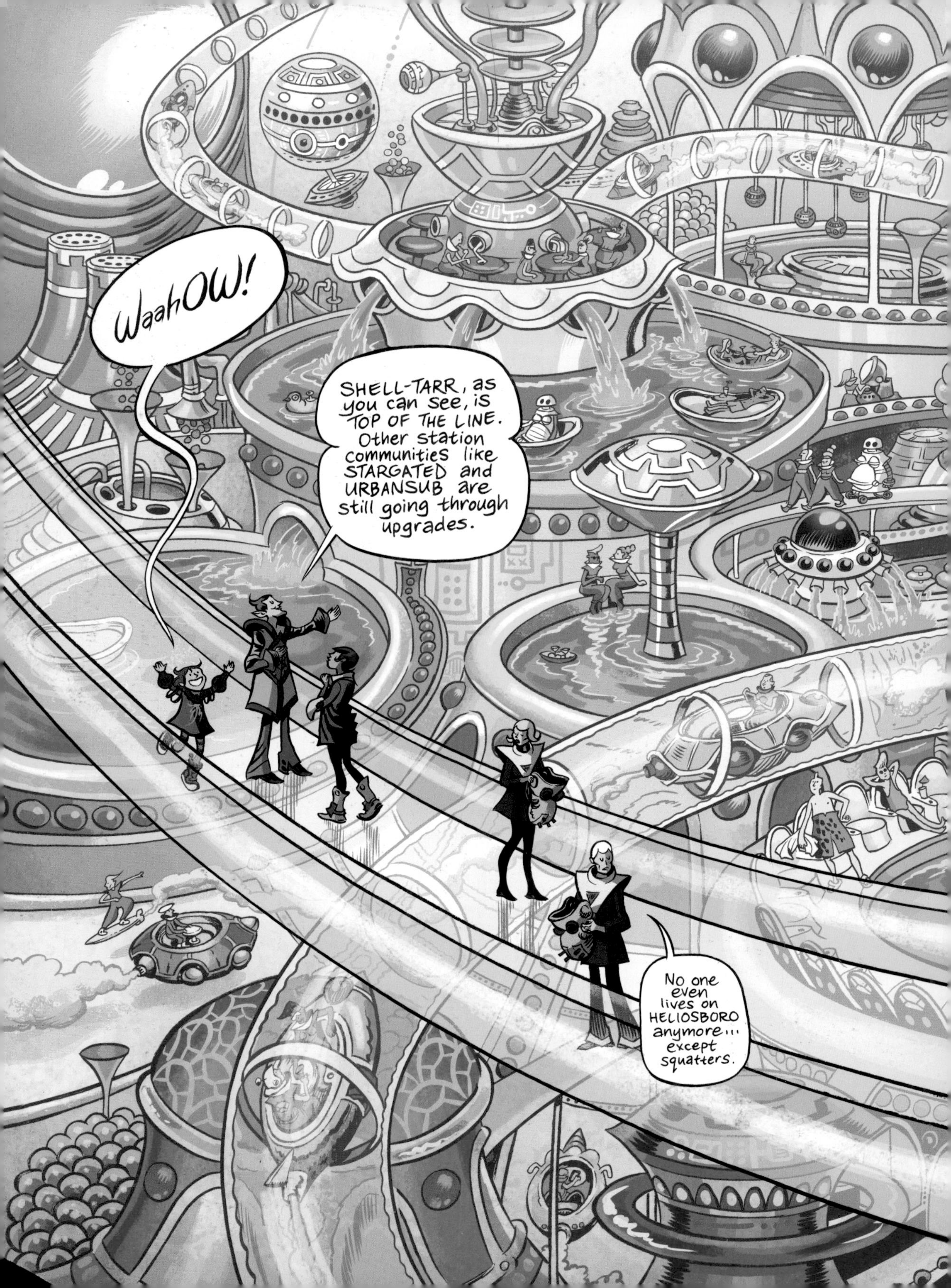
WaahOW!
SHELL-TARR, as you can see, is TOP OF THE LINE. Other station communities like STARGATED and URBANSUB are still going through upgrades.
No one even lives on HELIOSBORO anymore... except squatters.

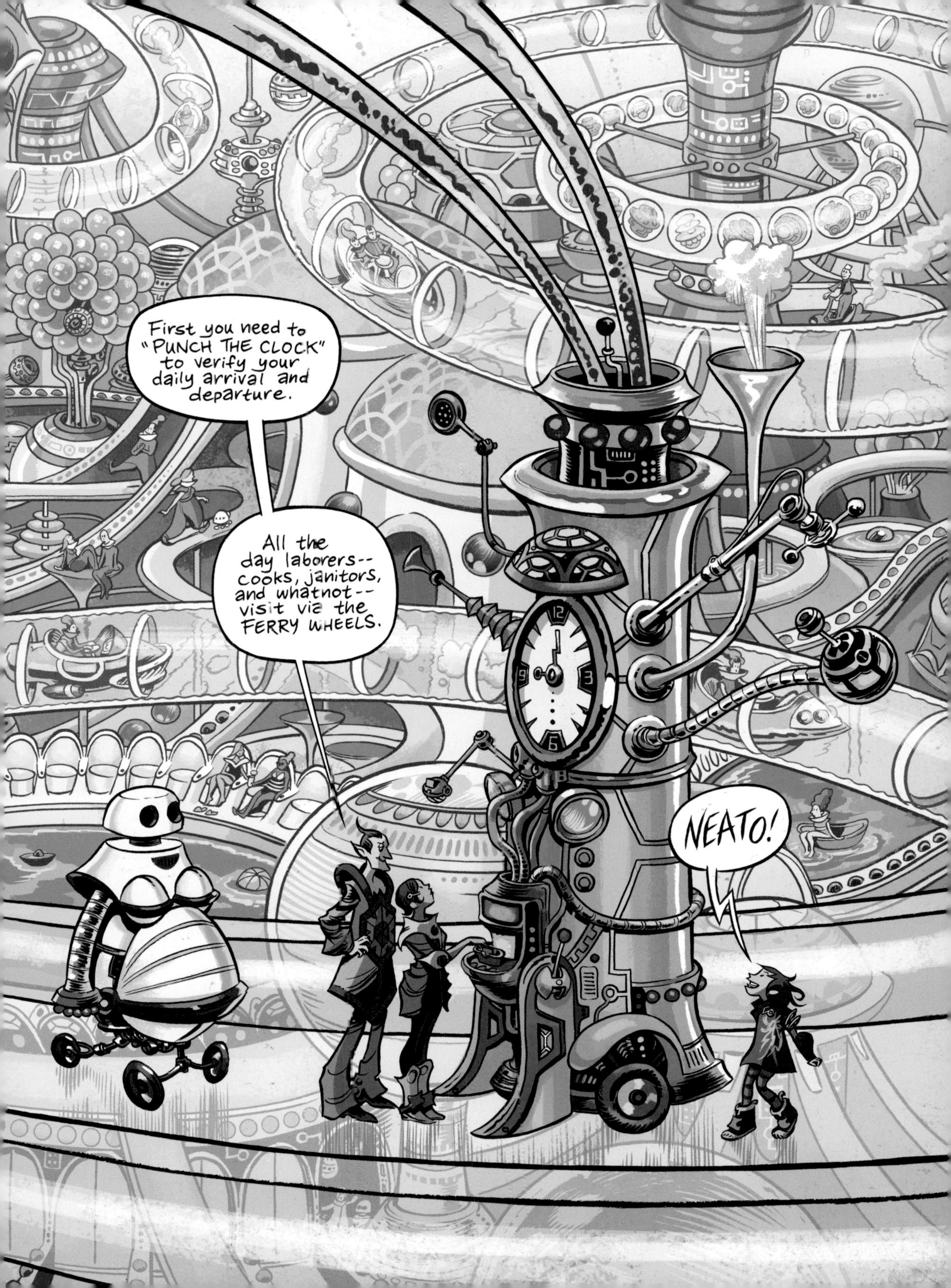
First you need to "PUNCH THE CLOCK" to verify your daily arrival and departure.
All the day laborers--cooks, janitors, and whatnot--visit via the FERRY WHEELS.
NEATO!

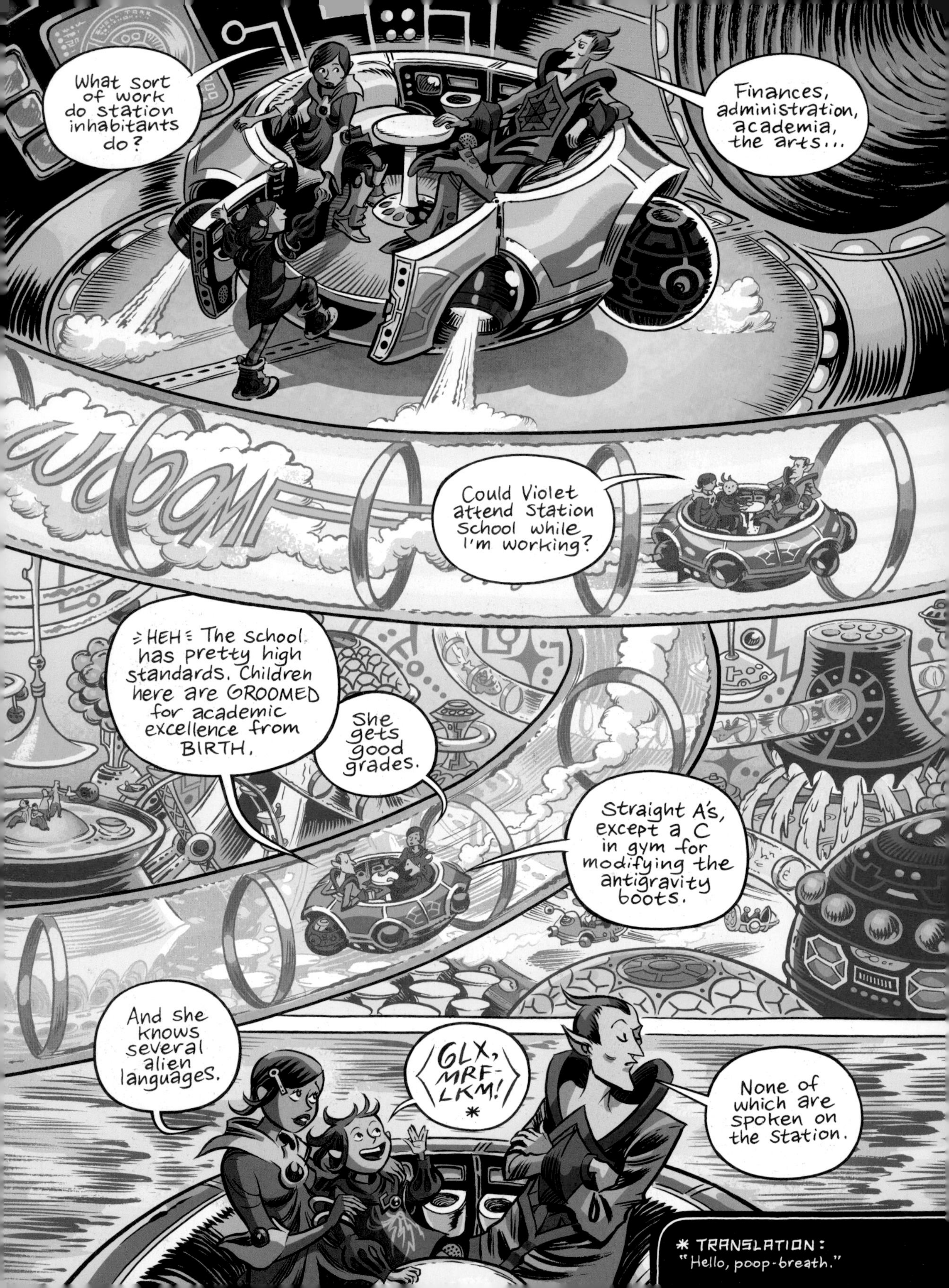
What sort of work do station inhabitants do?
Finances, administration, academia, the arts...
WOOOM!
Could Violet attend Station School while I'm working?
HEH The school has pretty high standards. Children here are GROOMED for academic excellence from BIRTH.
She gets good grades.
Straight A's, except a C in gym for modifying the antigravity boots.
And she knows several alien languages.
GLX, MRF-LKM! *
None of which are spoken on the station.
* TRANSLATION: "Hello, poop-breath."

SHELL
If it's really so important, you can tour the school TOMORROW.
Today, let's focus on getting started at the studio.
What fashion NEEDS, Cerulean . . .
Please, just "CERA."
. . . is some of that EDGE your people have.
My PEOPLE?
Outer-space dwellers.
Real RUSTIC folk!

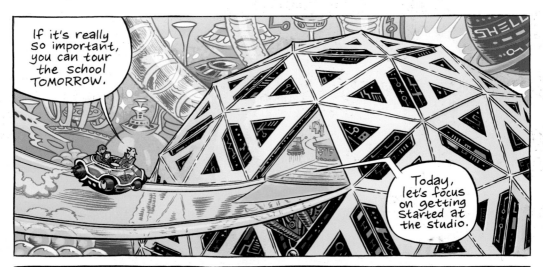

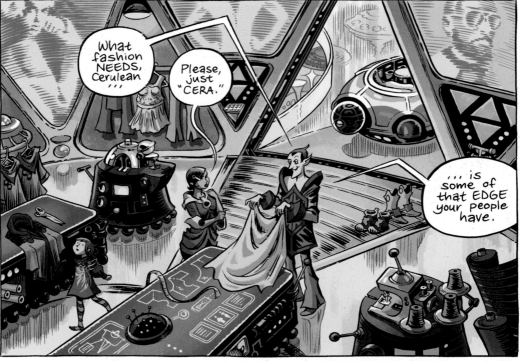

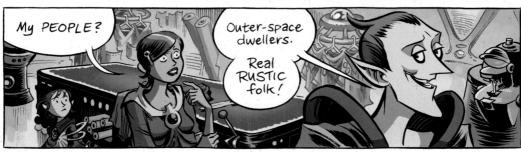

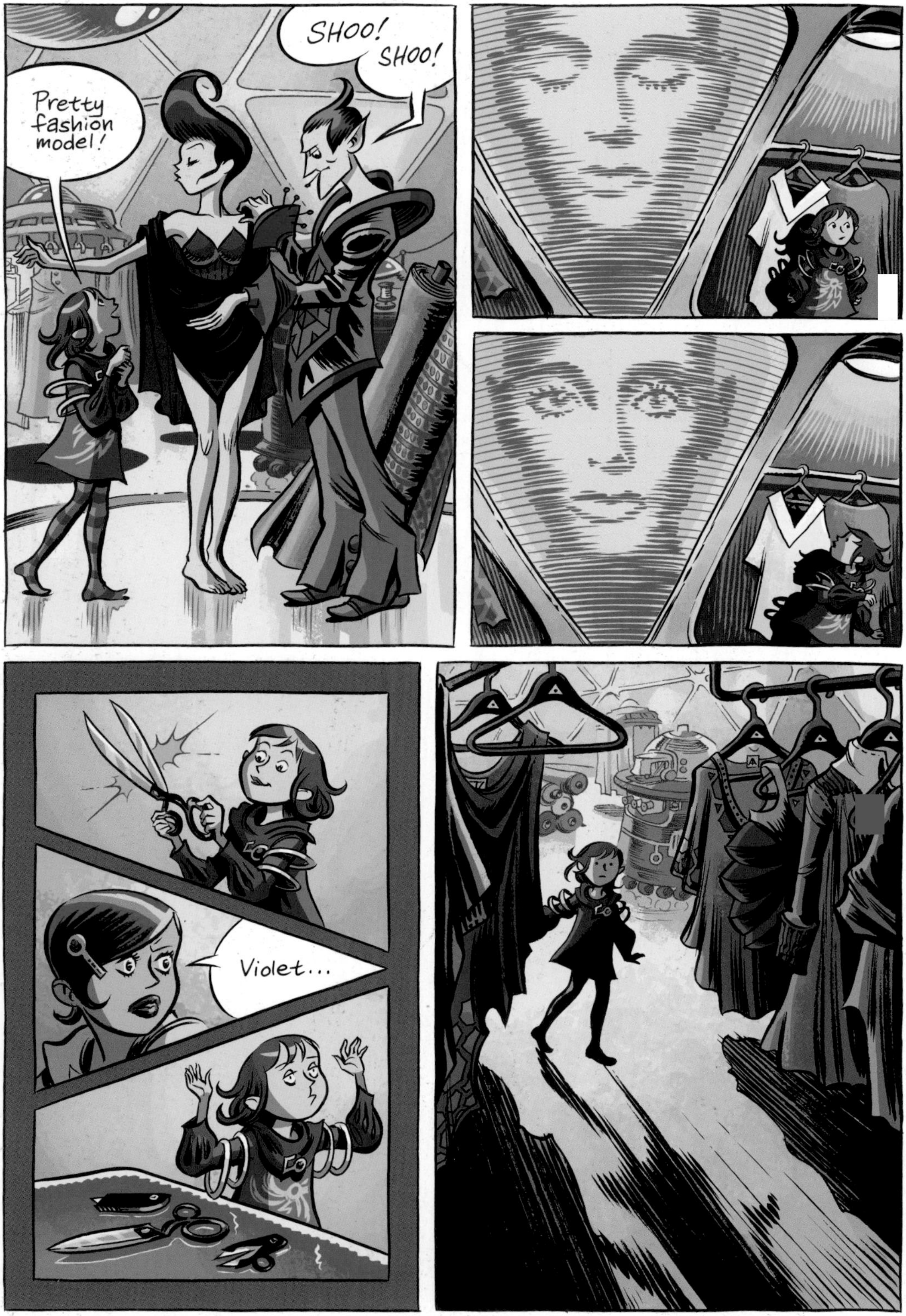
Pretty fashion model!
SHOO! SHOO!
Violet...

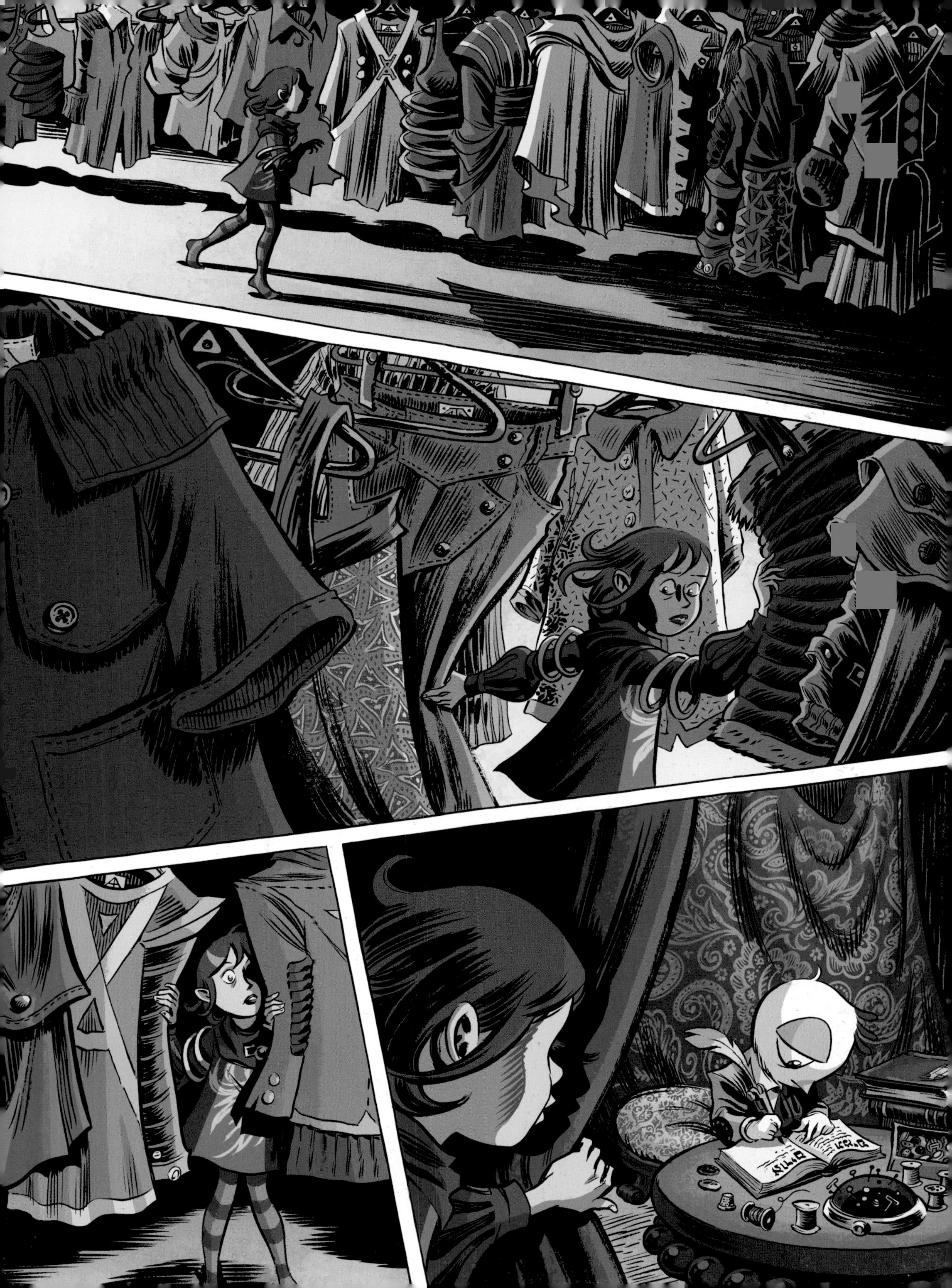

What are you doing?

...?

Do I... ...KNOW you?

My name's VIOLET. What's yours?

ELLIOT MARCEL OPGENORTH.

Now let me be.

What is THAT?

It's a book.

Don't you read?

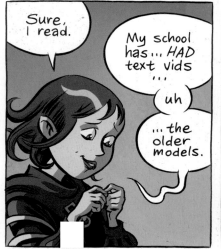

Sure, I read.

My school has... HAD text vids... uh ...the older models.

What kind of fabric is this?

It's PAPER. It's made from an extinct species of plant life.

DON'T CRINKLE IT!

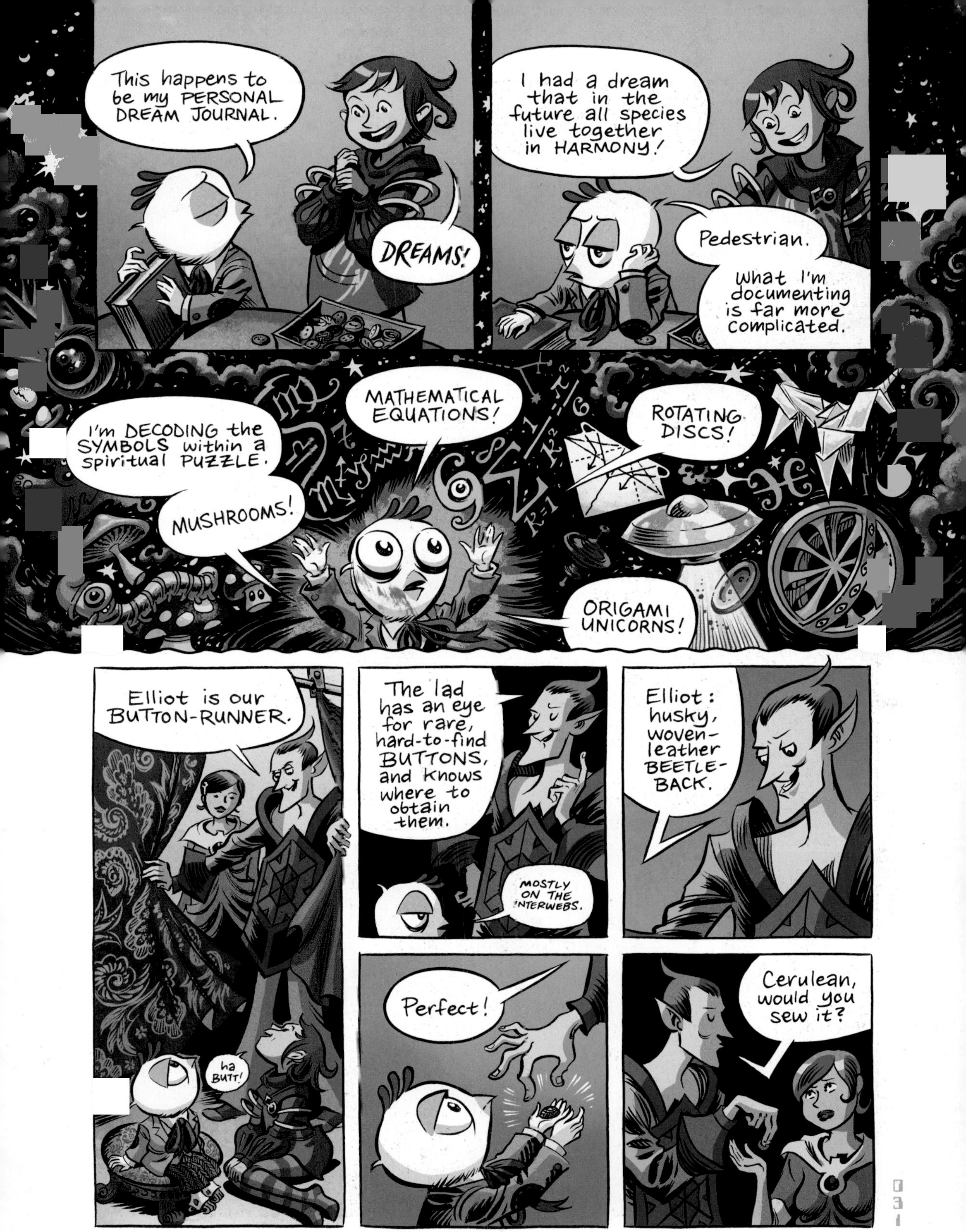
This happens to be my PERSONAL DREAM JOURNAL.
DREAMS!
I had a dream that in the future all species live together in HARMONY!
Pedestrian.
What I'm documenting is far more complicated.
I'm DECODING the SYMBOLS within a spiritual PUZZLE.
MATHEMATICAL EQUATIONS!
MUSHROOMS!
ROTATING DISCS!
ORIGAMI UNICORNS!
Elliot is our BUTTON-RUNNER.
ha BUTT!
The lad has an eye for rare, hard-to-find BUTTONS, and knows where to obtain them.
MOSTLY ON THE INTERWEBS.
Elliot: husky, woven-leather BEETLE-BACK.
Perfect!
Cerulean, would you sew it?

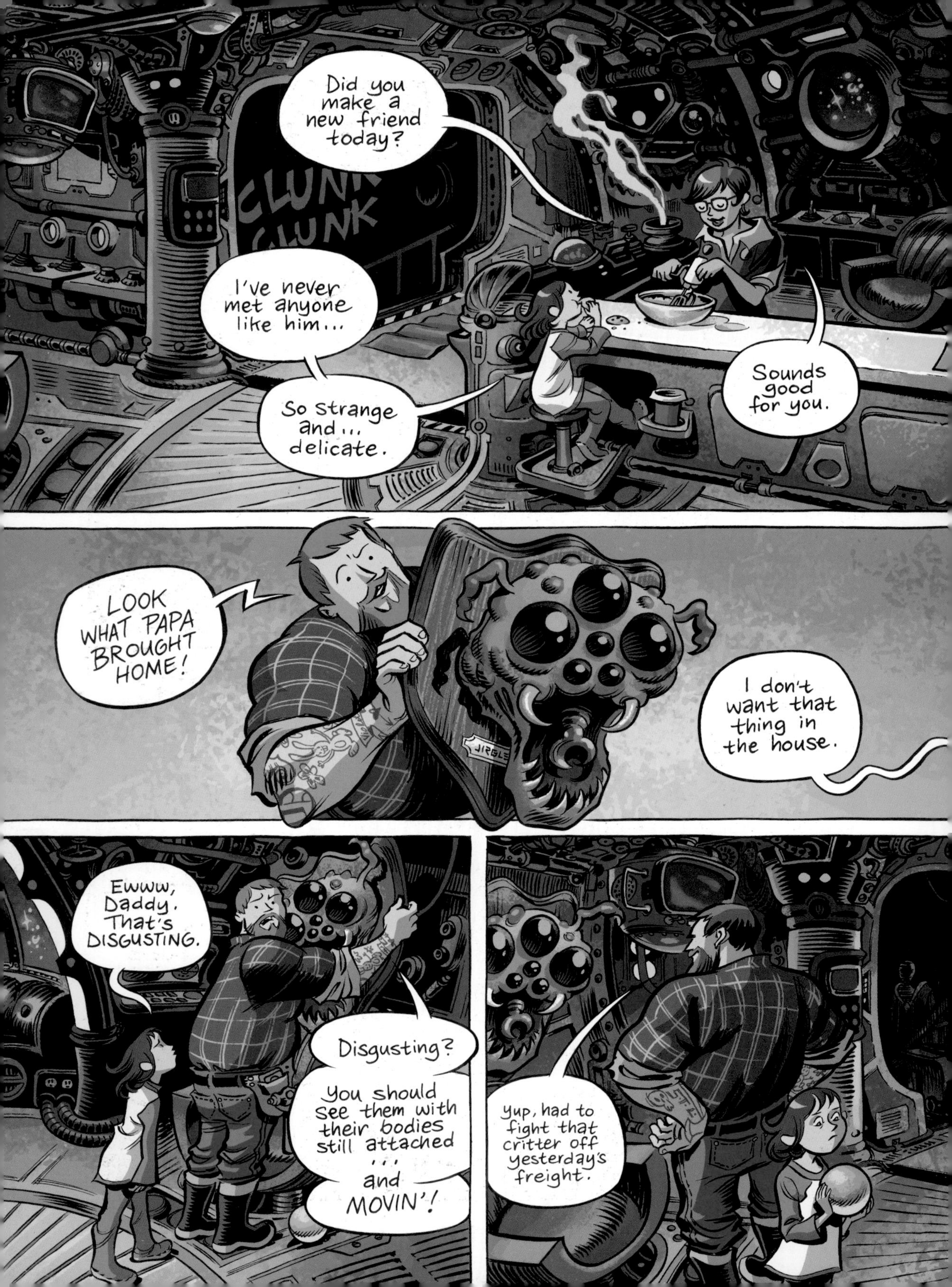
Did you make a new friend today?
CLUNK CLUNK
I've never met anyone like him...
So strange and... delicate.
Sounds good for you.
LOOK WHAT PAPA BROUGHT HOME!
I don't want that thing in the house.
Ewww, Daddy. That's DISGUSTING.
Disgusting?
You should see them with their bodies still attached ... and MOVIN'!
Yup, had to fight that critter off yesterday's freight.

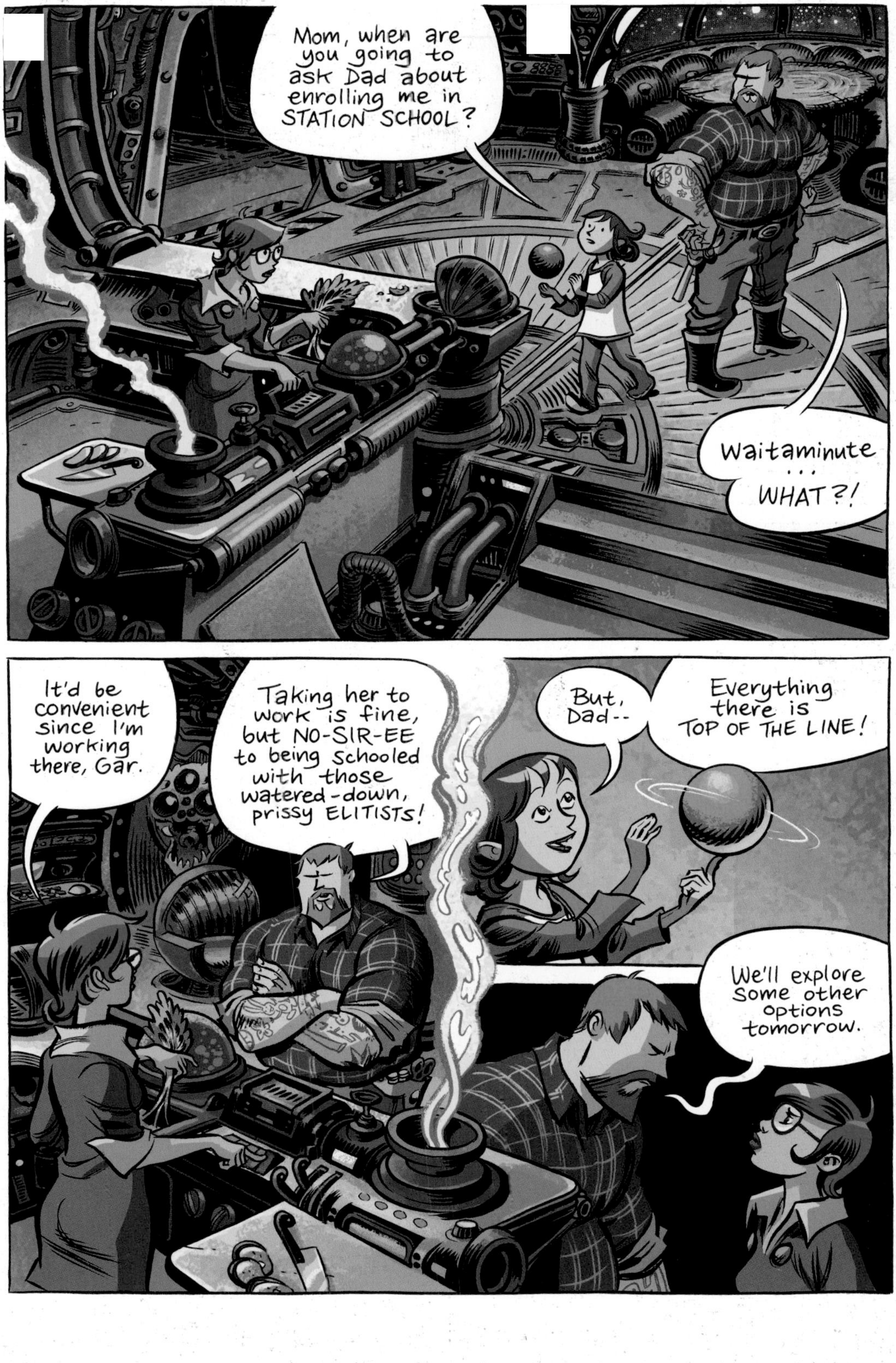
Mom, when are you going to ask Dad about enrolling me in STATION SCHOOL?
Waitaminute . . . WHAT?!
It'd be convenient since I'm working there, Gar.
Taking her to work is fine, but NO-SIR-EE to being schooled with those watered-down, prissy ELITISTS!
But, Dad--
Everything there is TOP OF THE LINE!
We'll explore some other options tomorrow.

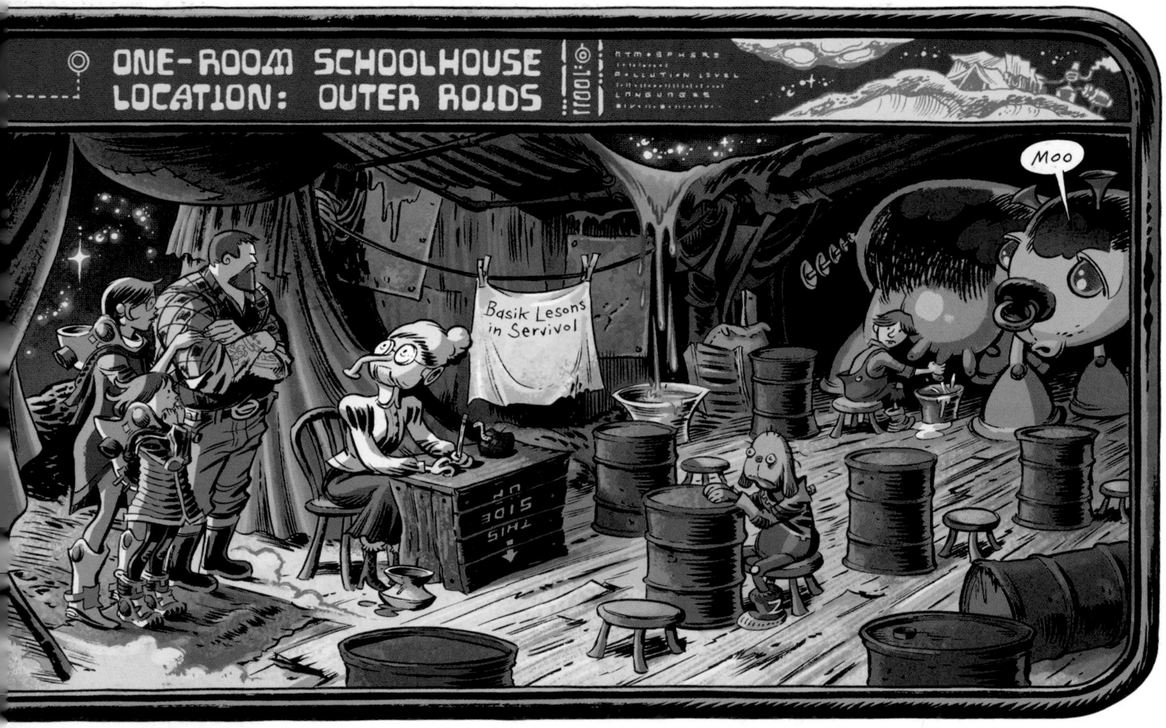
ONE-ROOM SCHOOLHOUSE
LOCATION: OUTER ROIDS
Basik Lesons in Servivol
THIS SIDE UP
Moo

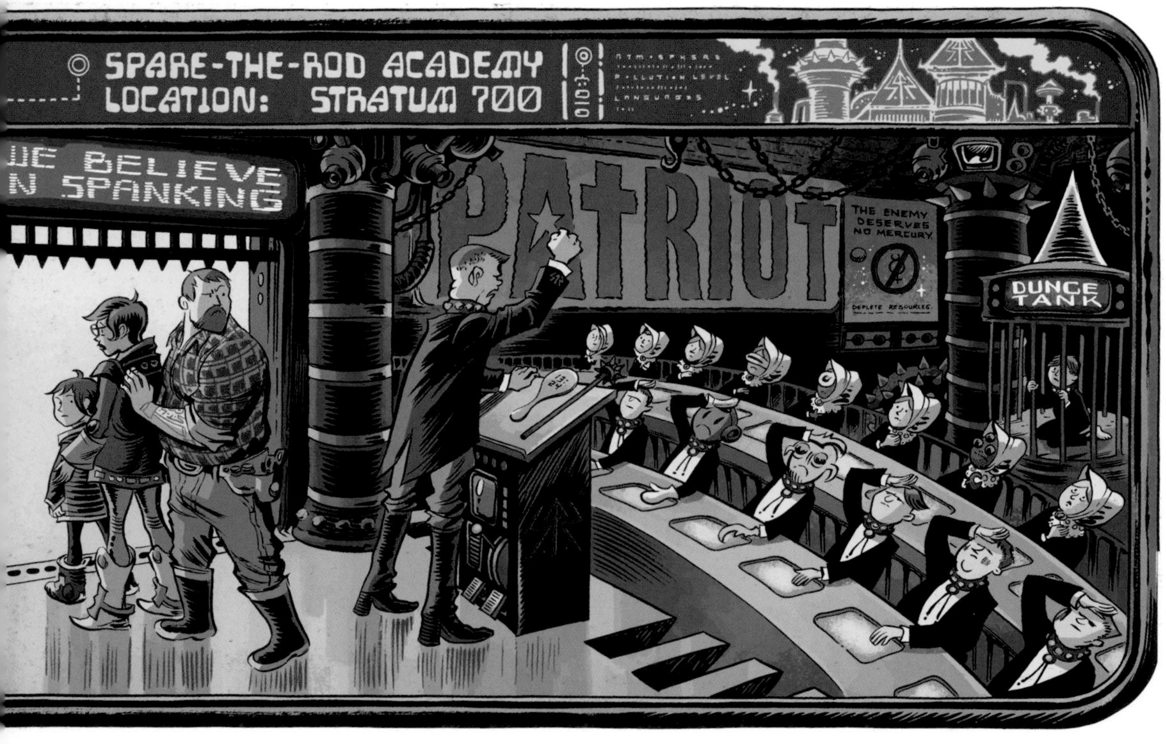
SPARE-THE-ROD ACADEMY
LOCATION: STRATUM 700
E BELIEVE
N SPANKING
PATRIOT
THE ENEMY DESERVES NO MERCURY.
DEPLETE RESOURCES.
DUNGE TANK

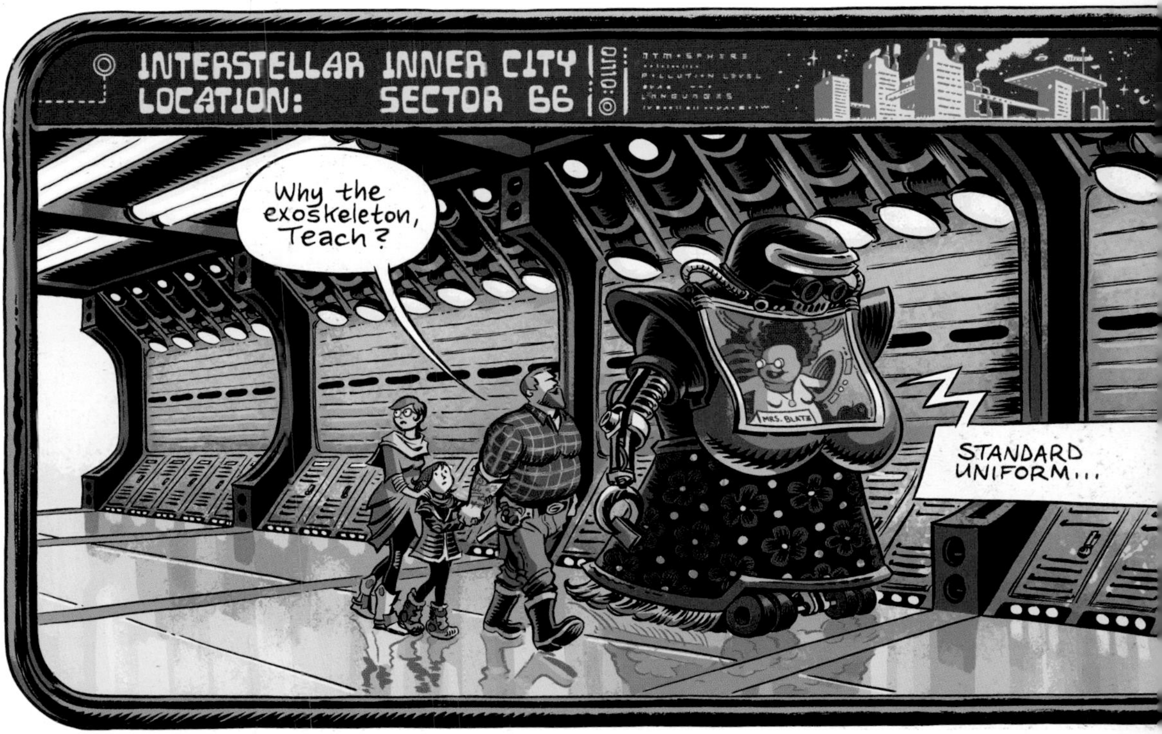
INTERSTELLAR INNER CITY
LOCATION: SECTOR 66
Why the exoskeleton, Teach?
MRS. BLATZ
STANDARD UNIFORM...

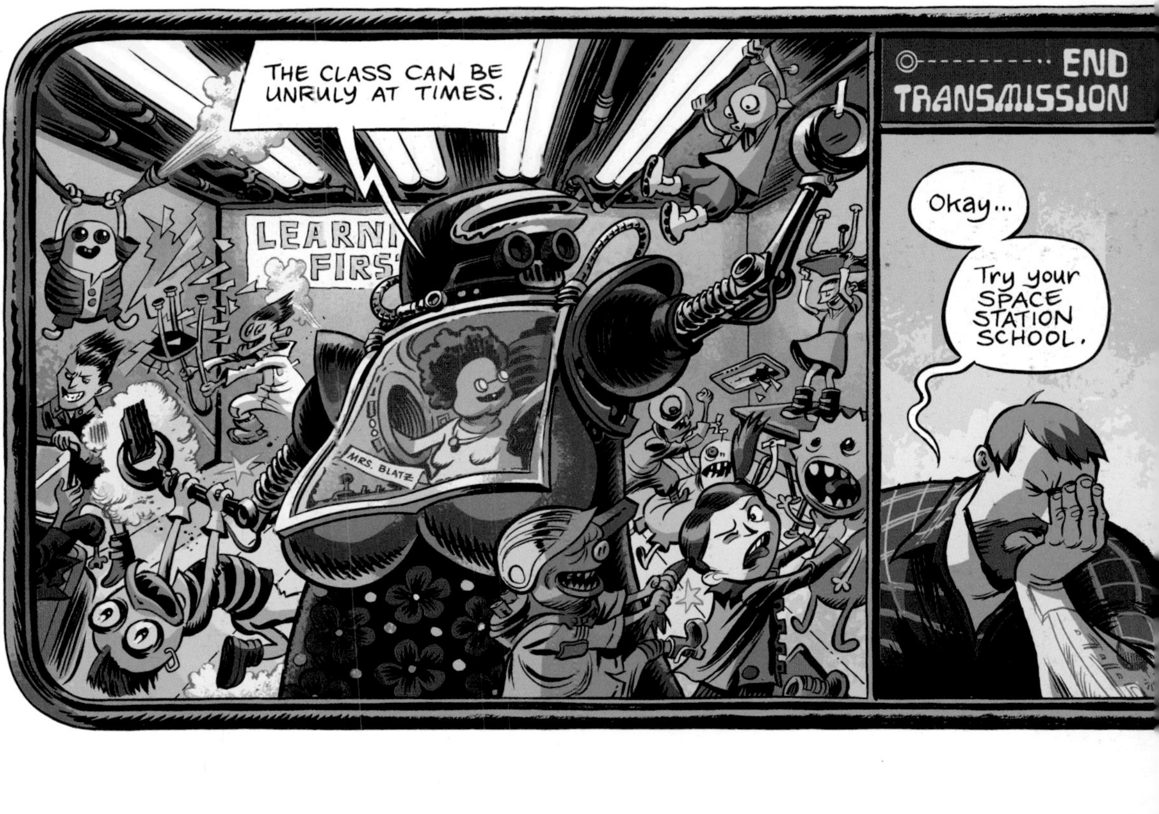
THE CLASS CAN BE UNRULY AT TIMES.
MRS. BLATZ
END TRANSMISSION
Okay...
Try your SPACE STATION SCHOOL.

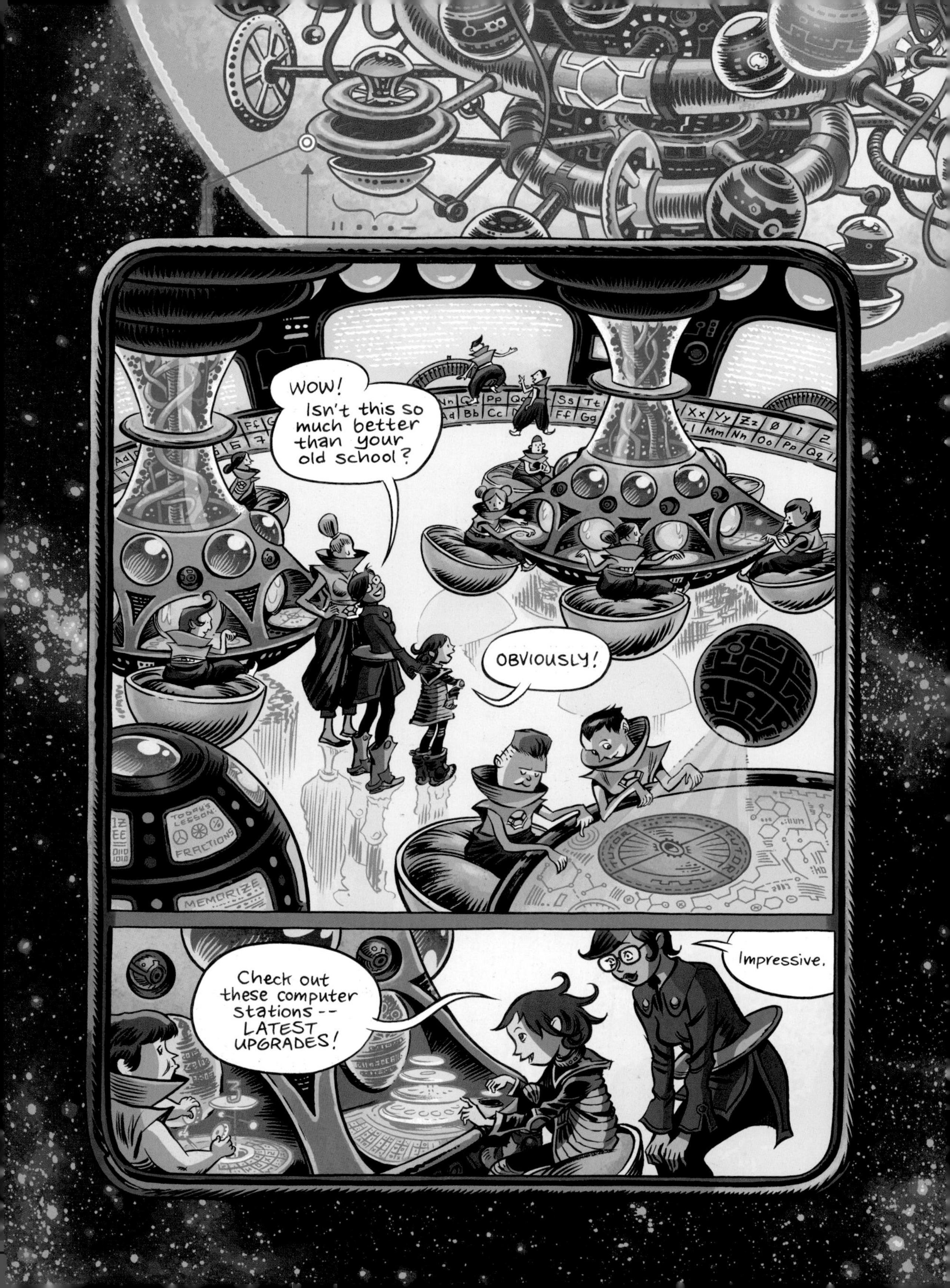
WOW!
Isn't this so much better than your old school?
OBVIOUSLY!
TODAY'S LESSON:
FRACTIONS
MEMORIZE
TUTOR
Check out these computer stations -- LATEST UPGRADES!
Impressive.

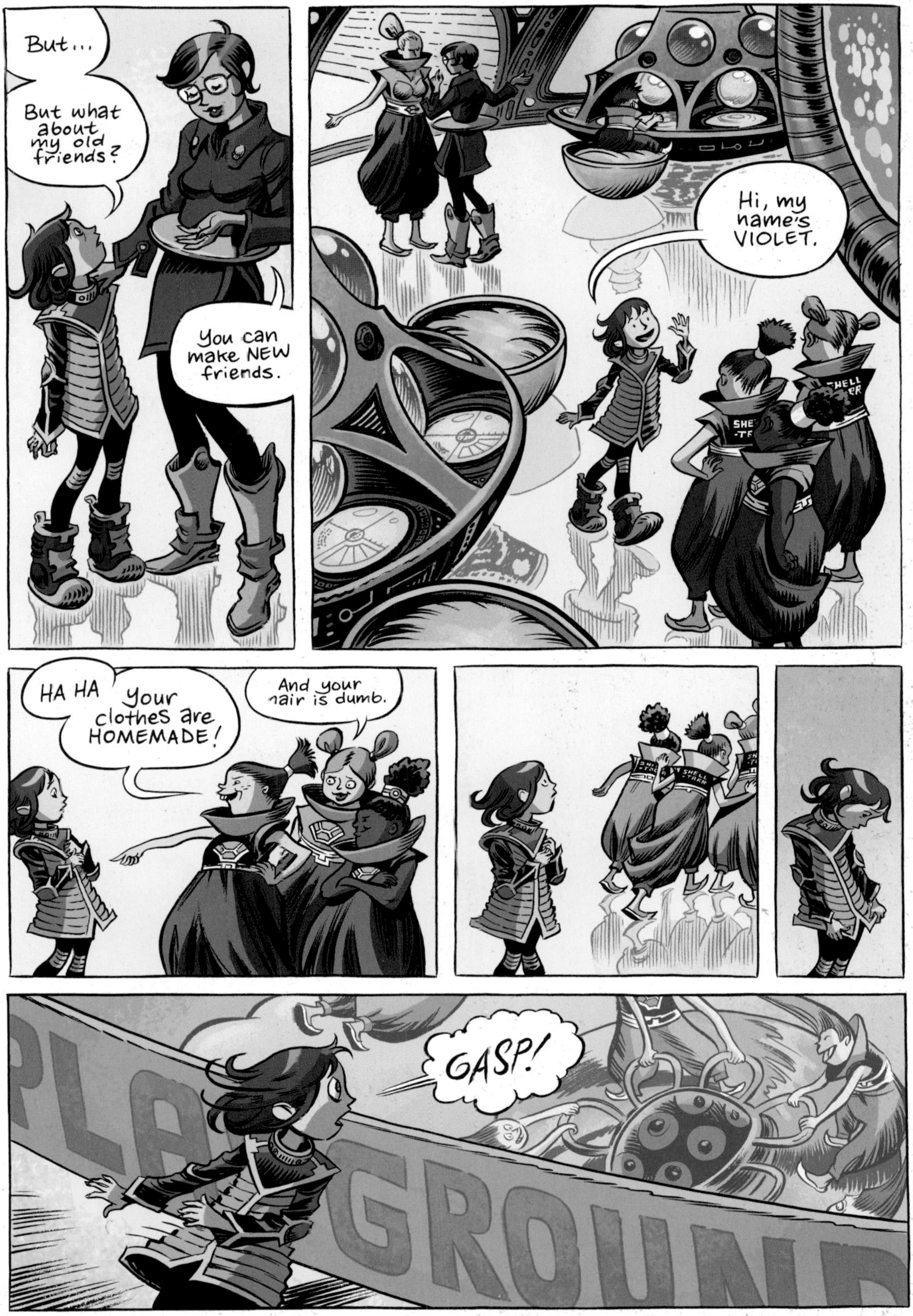

But...
But what about my old friends?
You can make NEW friends.
Hi, my name's VIOLET.
SHELL -TER
SHELL -TER
HA HA Your clothes are HOMEMADE!
And your hair is dumb.
SHELL -TER
SHELL -TER
GASP!
PLA GROUND

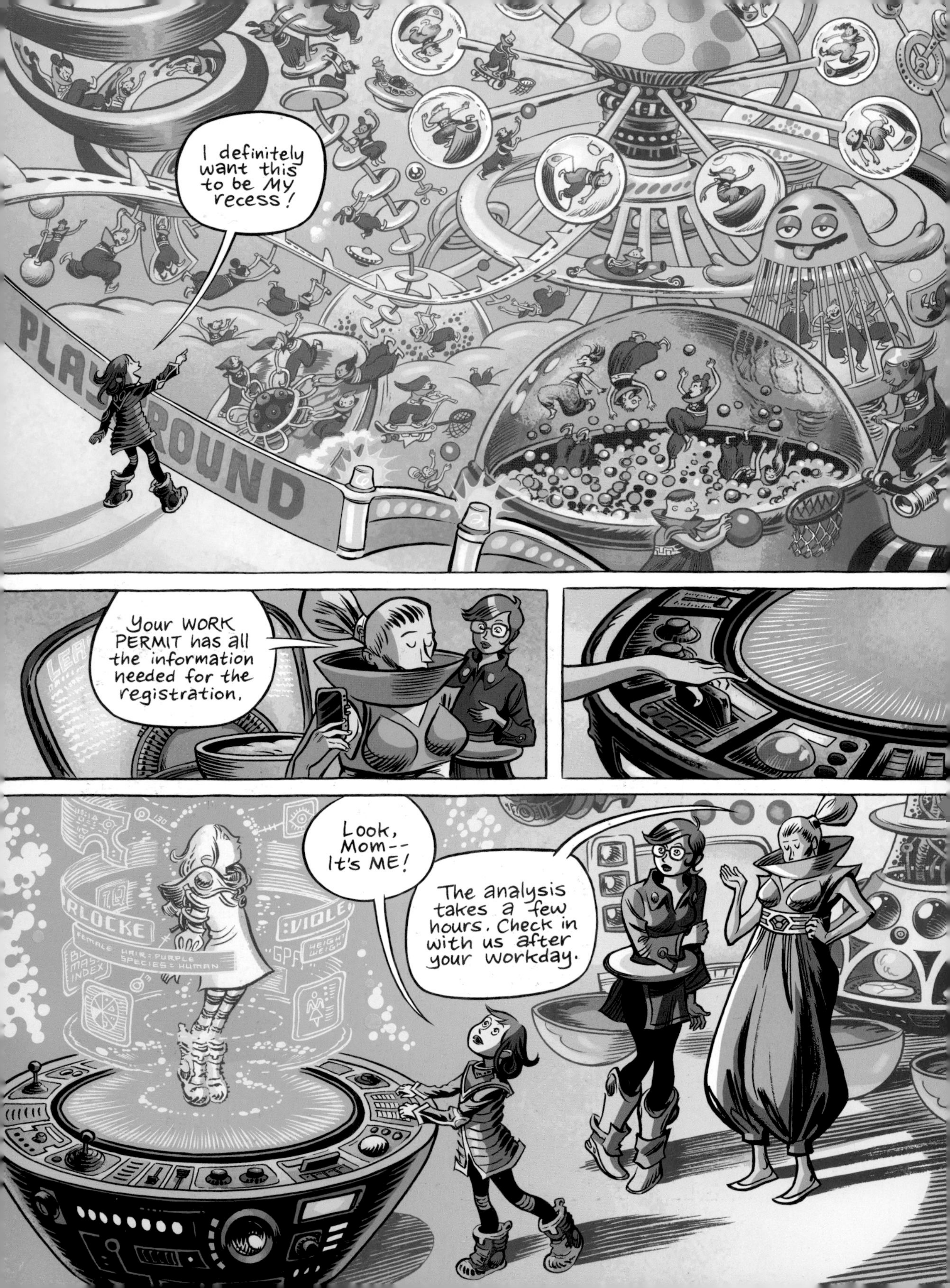
I definitely want this to be MY recess!
Your WORK PERMIT has all the information needed for the registration.
FEMALE HAIR: PURPLE
SPECIES: HUMAN
Look, Mom-- It's ME!
The analysis takes a few hours. Check in with us after your workday.

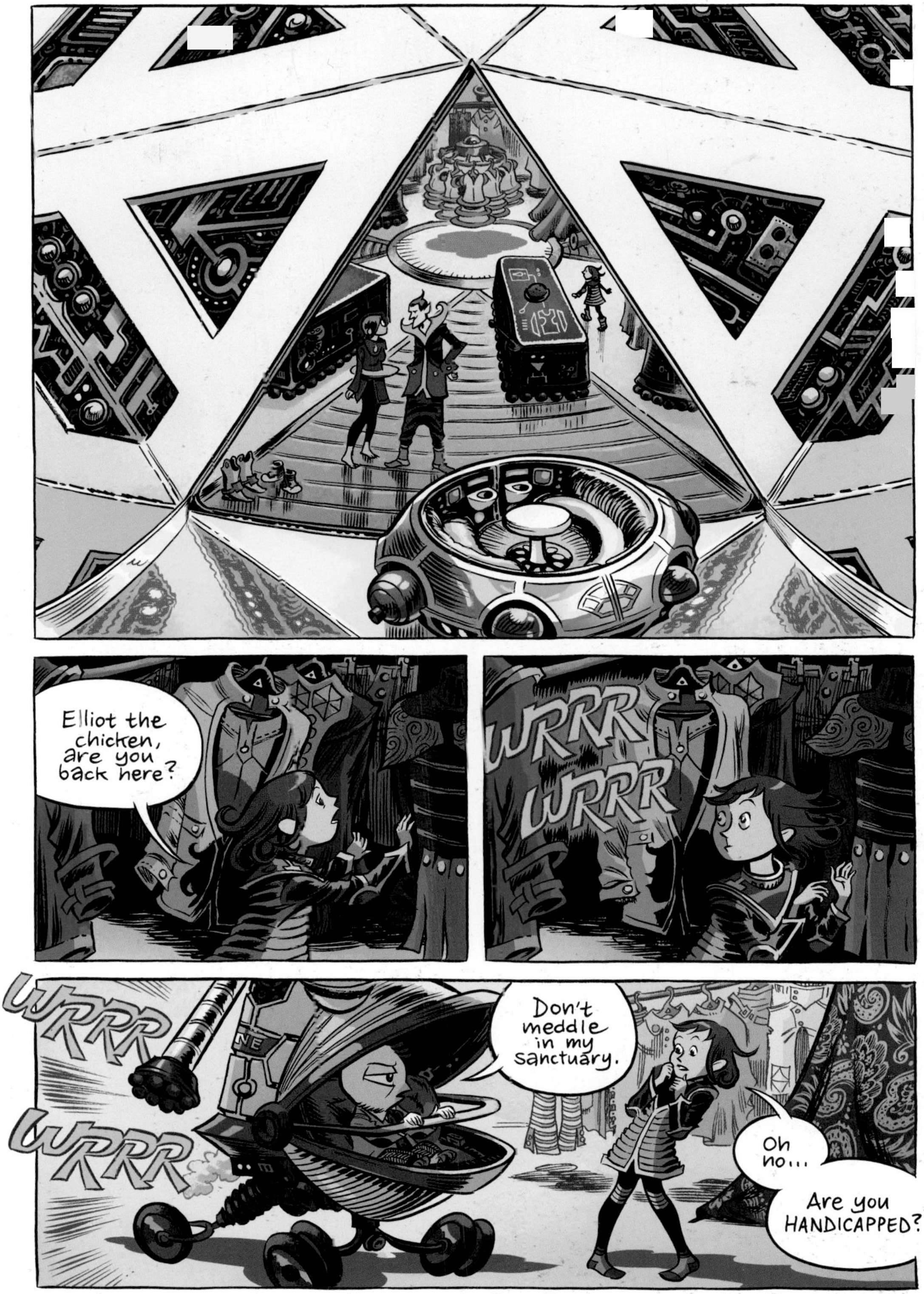
Elliot the chicken, are you back here?
WRRR
WRRR
WRRR
WRRR
Don't meddle in my sanctuary.
Oh no...
Are you HANDICAPPED?

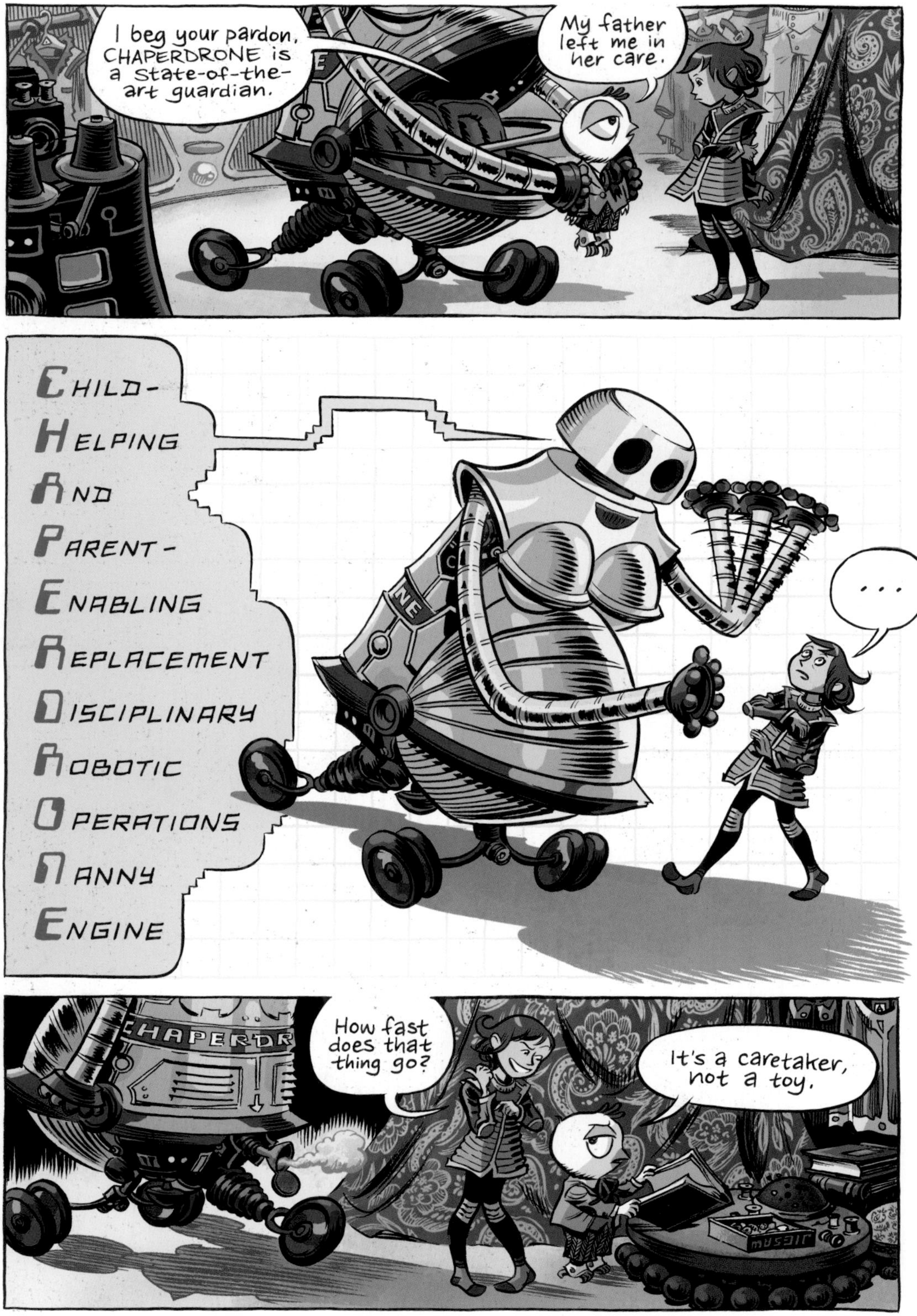
I beg your pardon, CHAPERDRONE is a state-of-the-art guardian.
My father left me in her care.
CHILD-
HELPING
AND
PARENT-
ENABLING
REPLACEMENT
DISCIPLINARY
ROBOTIC
OPERATIONS
NANNY
ENGINE
...
CHAPERDR
How fast does that thing go?
It's a caretaker, not a toy.
JIGSAW

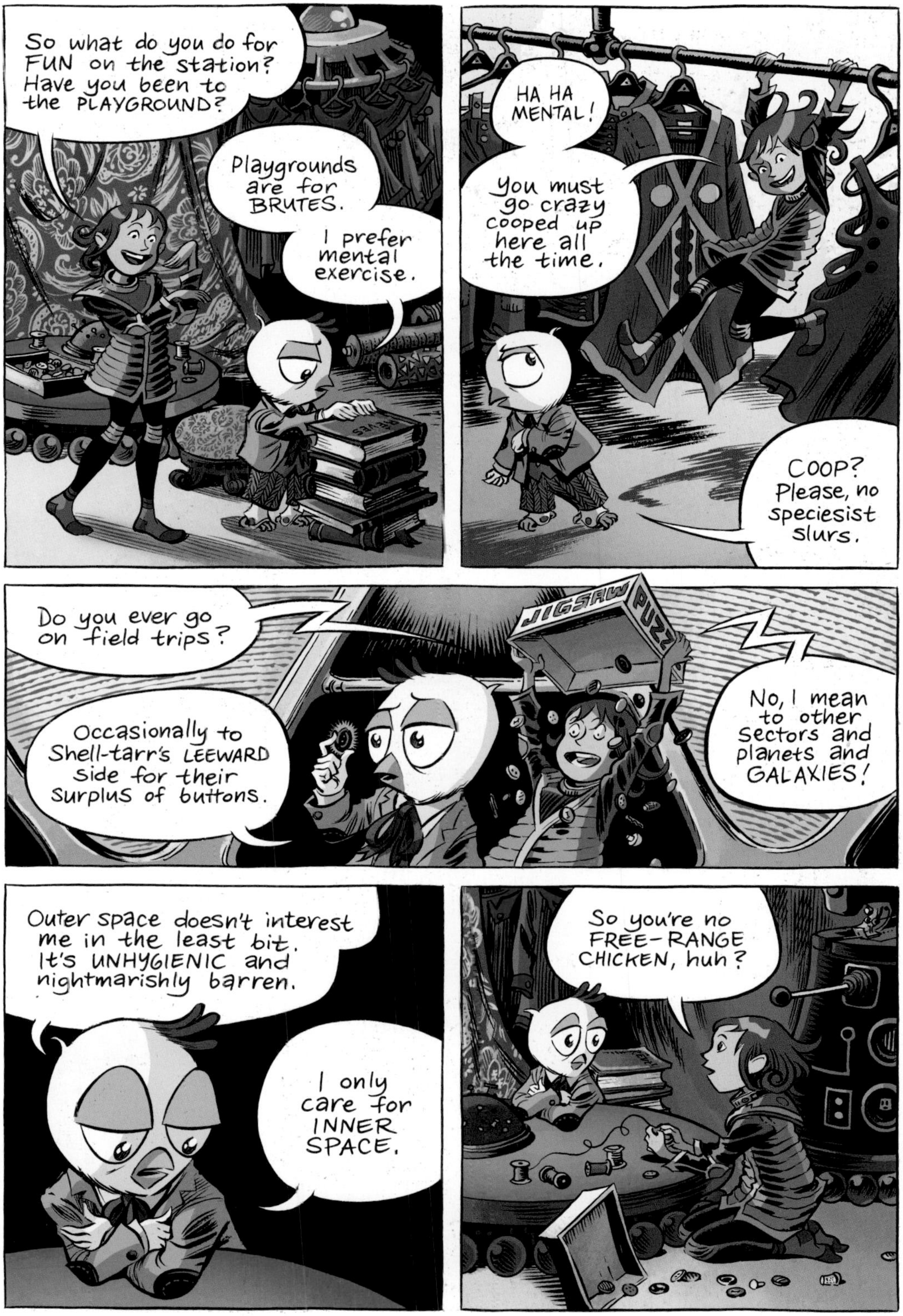
So what do you do for FUN on the station? Have you been to the PLAYGROUND?
Playgrounds are for BRUTES.
I prefer mental exercise.
HA HA MENTAL!
You must go crazy cooped up here all the time.
COOP? Please, no speciesist slurs.
Do you ever go on field trips?
JIGSAW PUZZ
Occasionally to Shell-tarr's LEEWARD side for their surplus of buttons.
No, I mean to other sectors and planets and GALAXIES!
Outer space doesn't interest me in the least bit. It's UNHYGIENIC and nightmarishly barren.
I only care for INNER SPACE.
So you're no FREE-RANGE CHICKEN, huh?

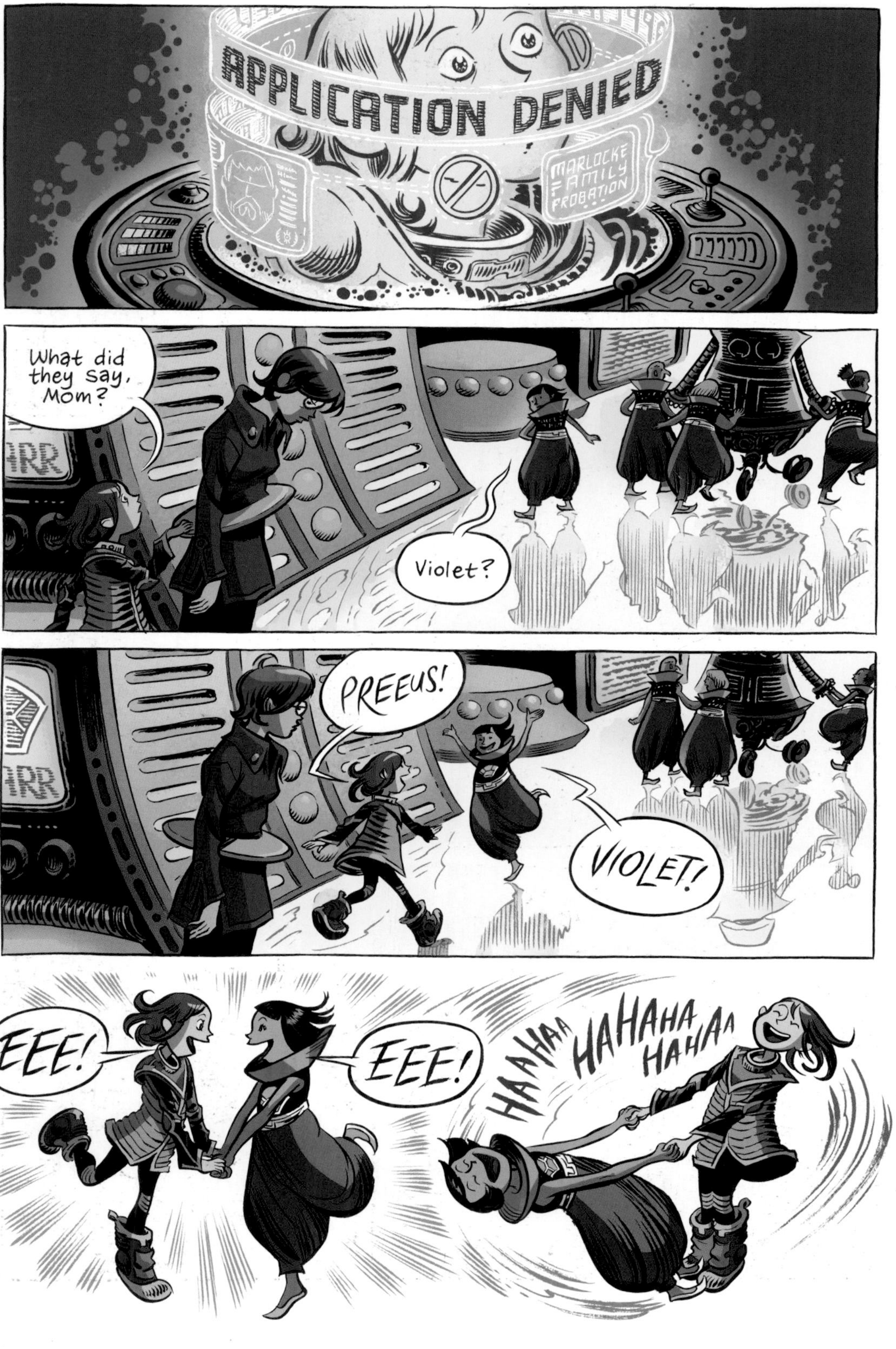
APPLICATION DENIED
MARLOCKE FAMILY PROBATION
What did they say, Mom?
Violet?
PREEUS!
VIOLET!
EEE!
EEE!
HAHAHAA HAHAHA HAHAA

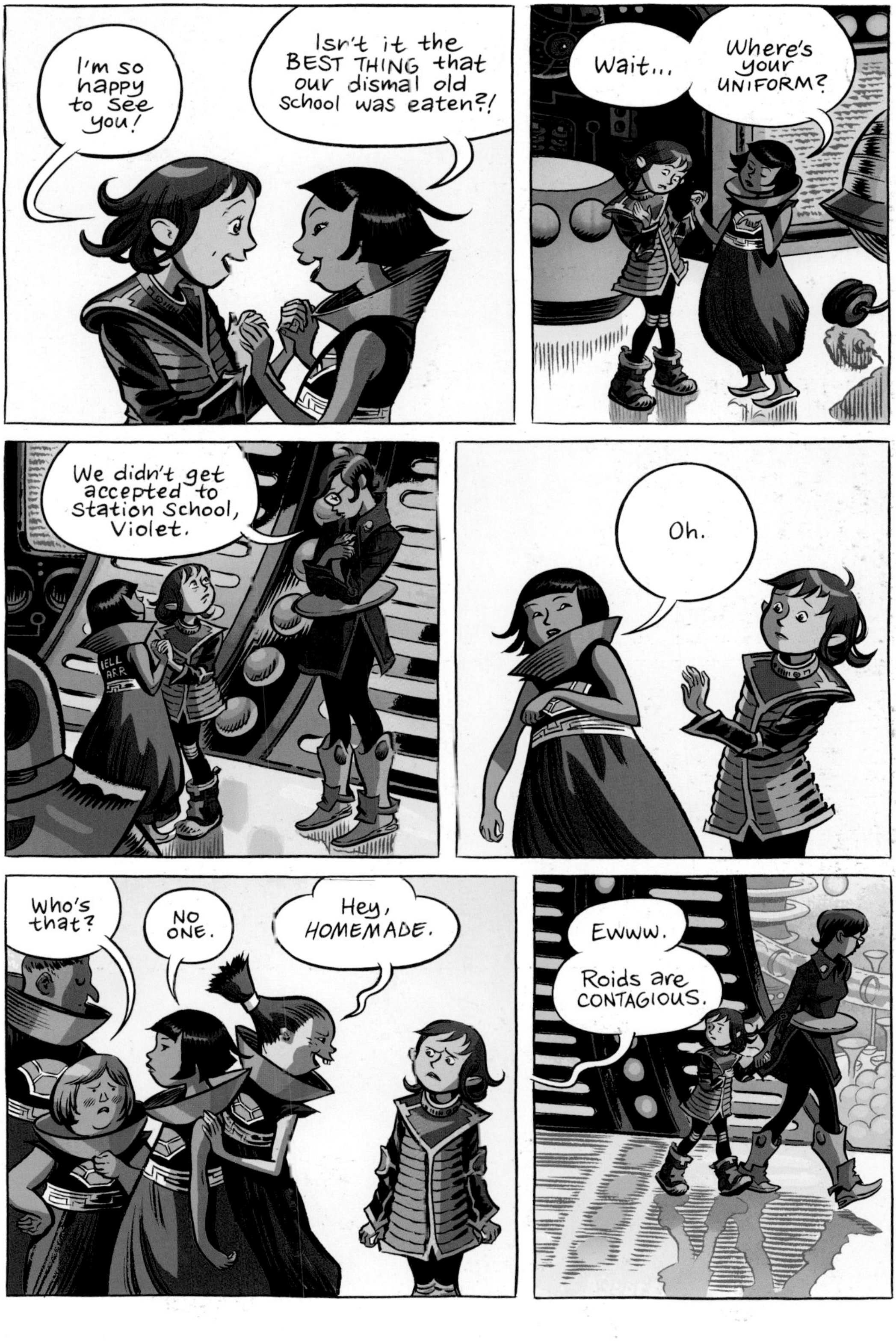
I'm so happy to see you!
Isn't it the BEST THING that our dismal old school was eaten?!
Wait...
Where's your UNIFORM?
We didn't get accepted to Station School, Violet.
Oh.
Who's that?
NO ONE.
Hey, HOMEMADE.
Ewww.
Roids are CONTAGIOUS.

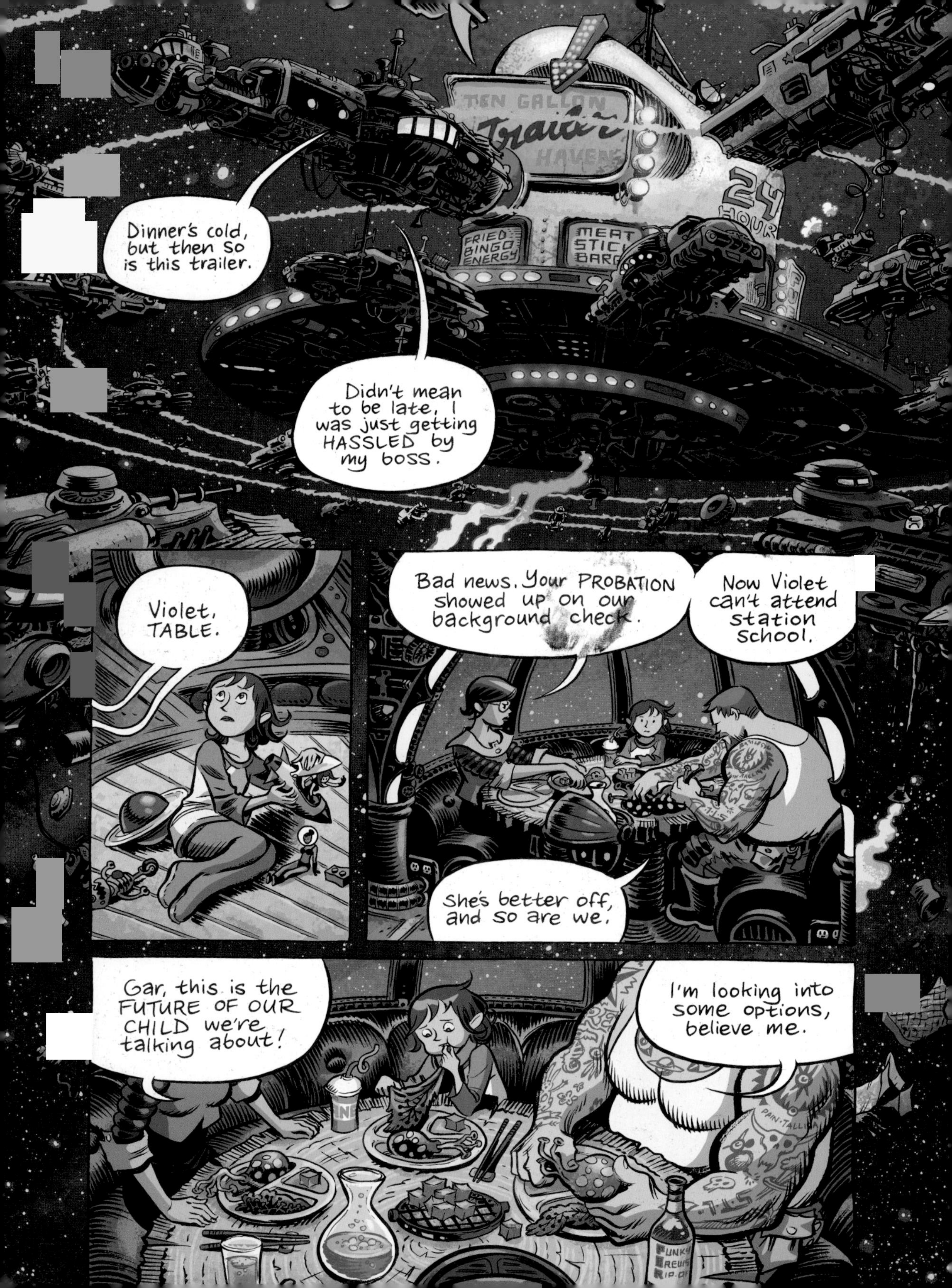
Dinner's cold, but then so is this trailer.
Didn't mean to be late, I was just getting HASSLED by my boss.
Violet, TABLE.
Bad news. Your PROBATION showed up on our background check.
Now Violet can't attend station school.
She's better off, and so are we.
Gar, this is the FUTURE OF OUR CHILD we're talking about!
I'm looking into some options, believe me.

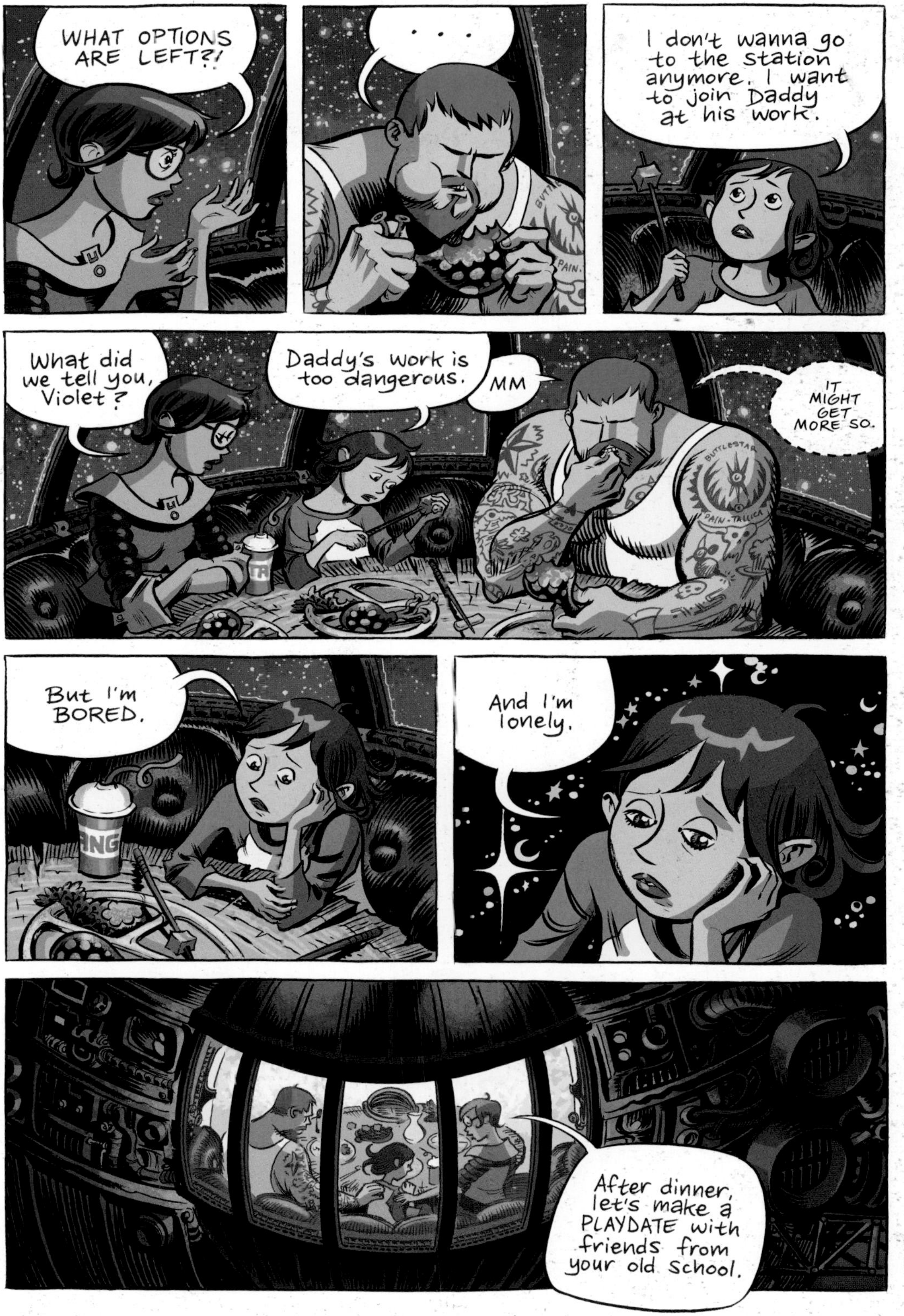
WHAT OPTIONS ARE LEFT?!
. . .
I don't wanna go to the station anymore. I want to join Daddy at his work.
What did we tell you, Violet?
Daddy's work is too dangerous.
MM
IT MIGHT GET MORE SO.
But I'm BORED.
And I'm lonely.
After dinner, let's make a PLAYDATE with friends from your old school.

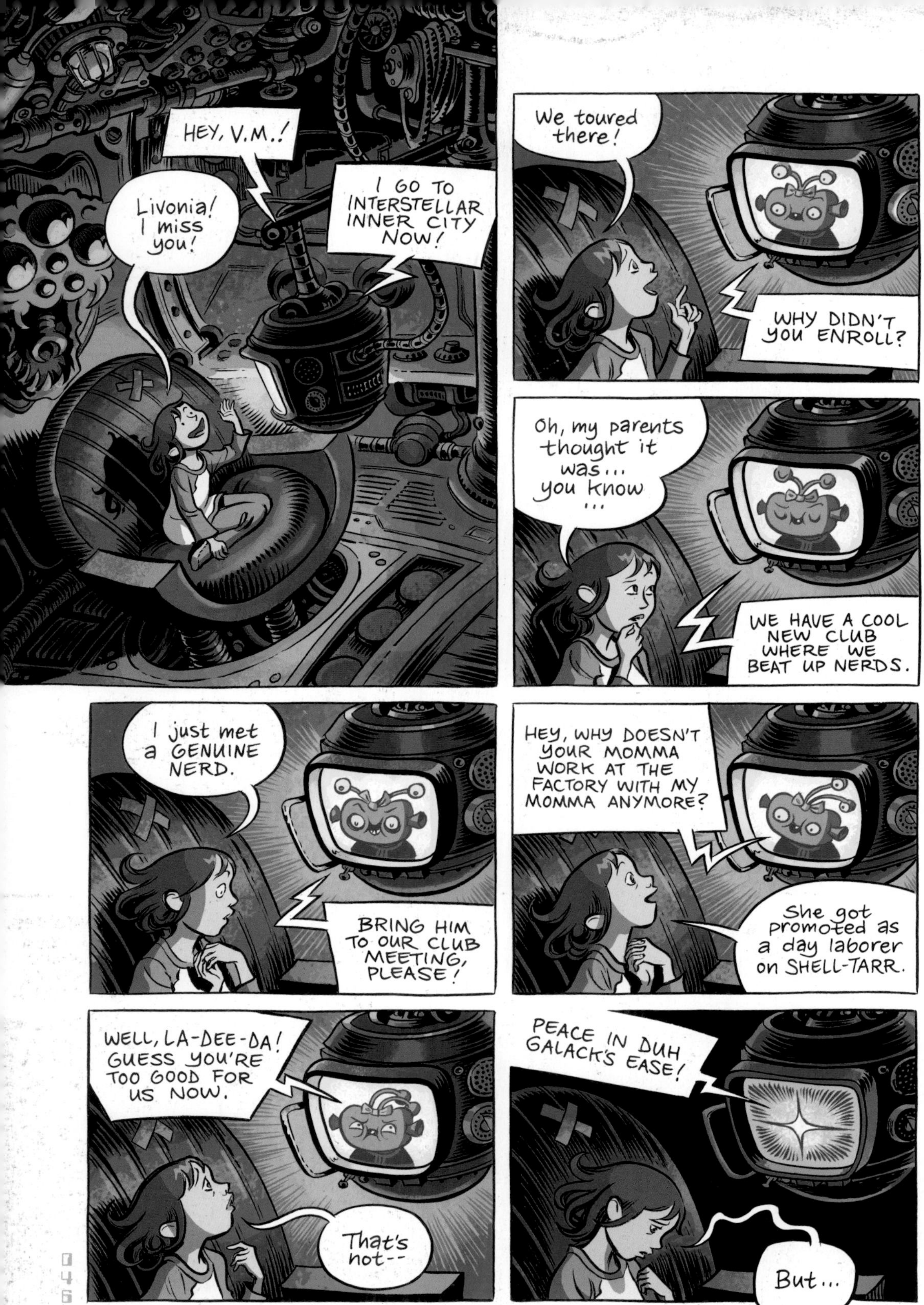
HEY, V.M.!
Livonia! I miss you!
I GO TO INTERSTELLAR INNER CITY NOW!
We toured there!
WHY DIDN'T YOU ENROLL?
Oh, my parents thought it was... you know ...
WE HAVE A COOL NEW CLUB WHERE WE BEAT UP NERDS.
I just met a GENUINE NERD.
BRING HIM TO OUR CLUB MEETING, PLEASE!
HEY, WHY DOESN'T YOUR MOMMA WORK AT THE FACTORY WITH MY MOMMA ANYMORE?
She got promoted as a day laborer on SHELL-TARR.
WELL, LA-DEE-DA! GUESS YOU'RE TOO GOOD FOR US NOW.
That's not--
PEACE IN DUH GALACK'S EASE!
But...

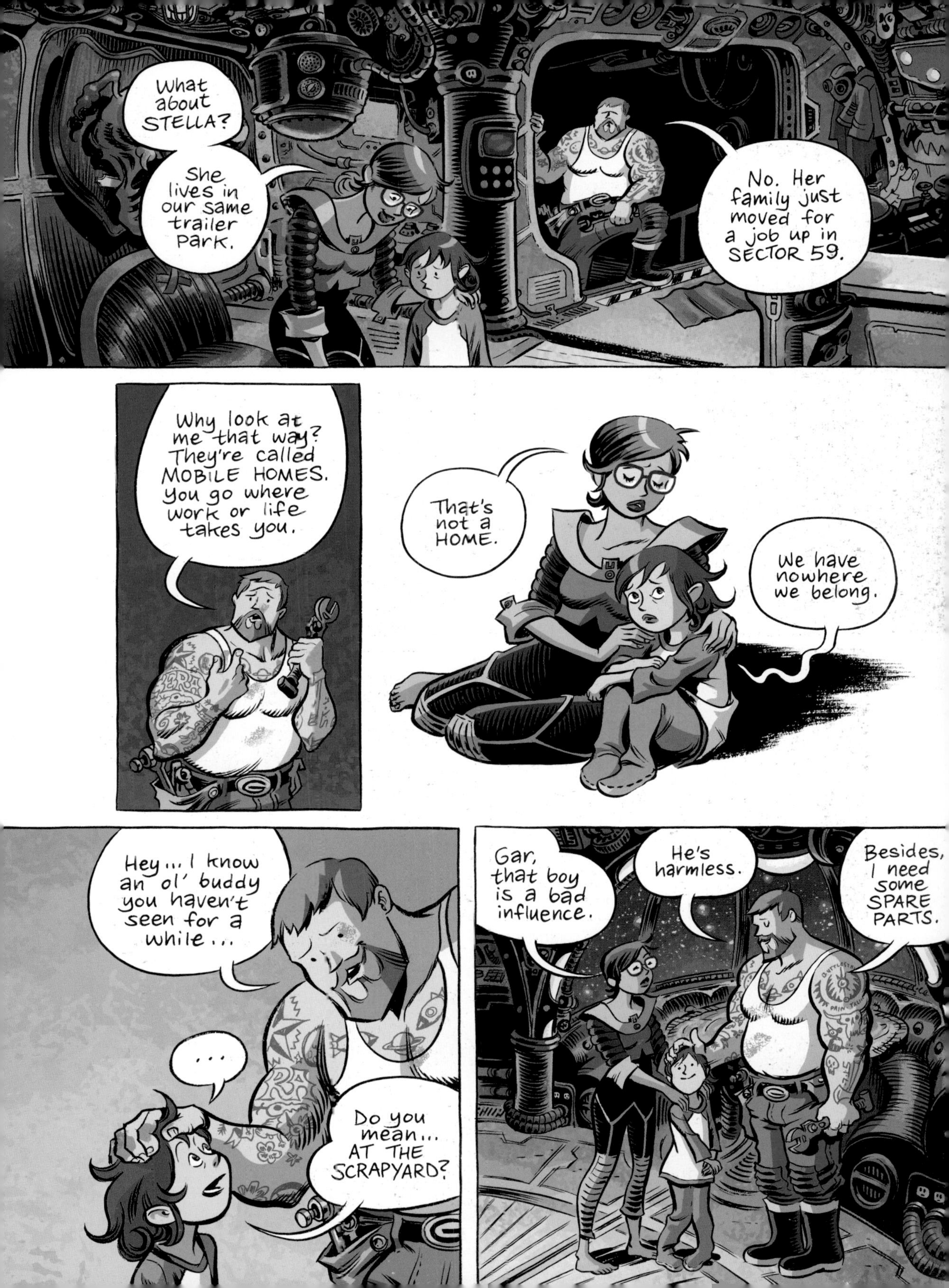
What about STELLA?
She lives in our same trailer park.
No. Her family just moved for a job up in SECTOR 59.
Why look at me that way? They're called MOBILE HOMES. You go where work or life takes you.
That's not a HOME.
We have nowhere we belong.
Hey... I know an ol' buddy you haven't seen for a while...
...
Do you mean... AT THE SCRAPYARD?
Gar, that boy is a bad influence.
He's harmless.
Besides, I need some SPARE PARTS.

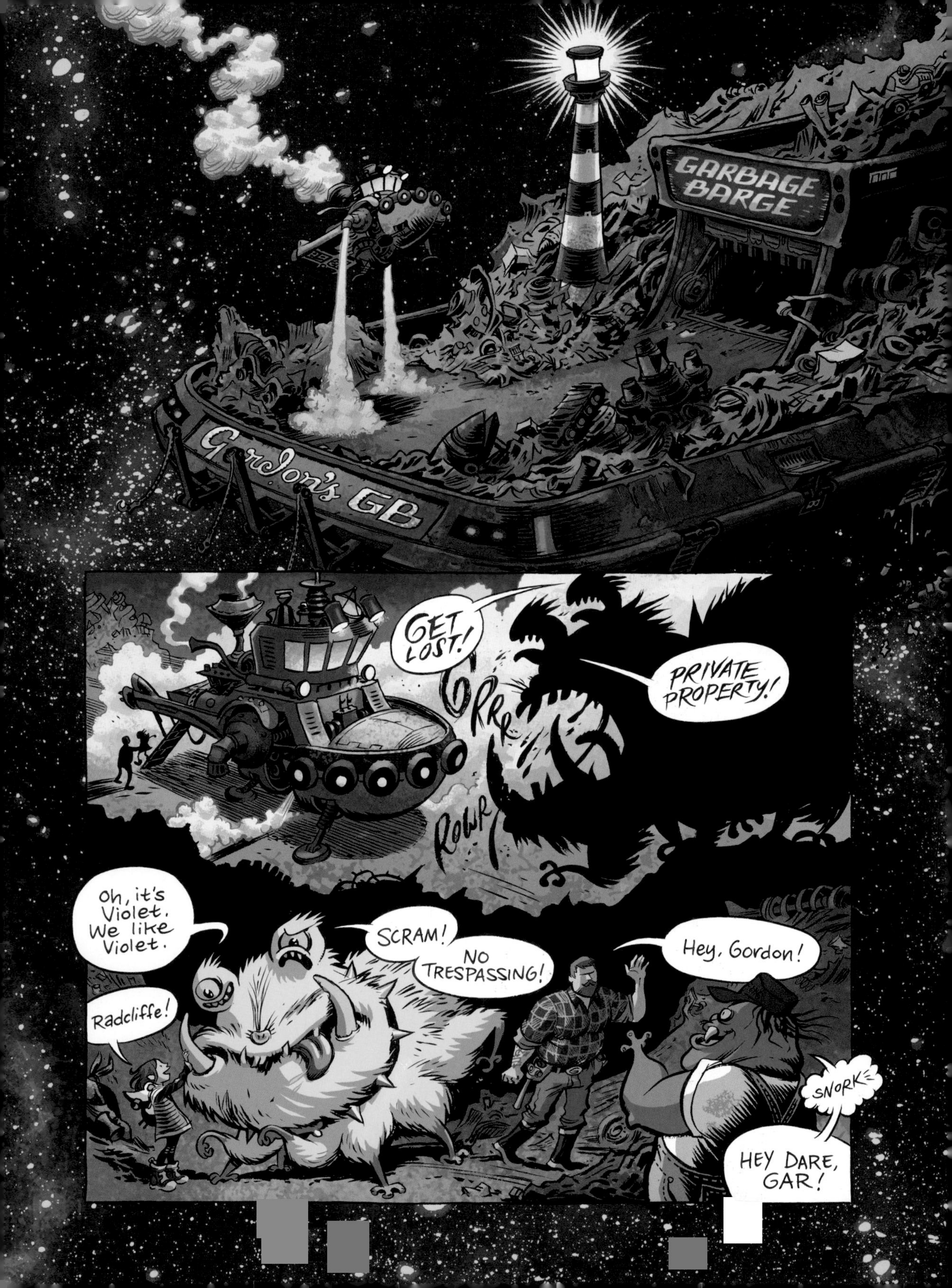
GARBAGE BARGE
Gordon's GB
GET LOST!
PRIVATE PROPERTY!
GRRR
ROWR
Oh, it's Violet. We like Violet.
SCRAM!
NO TRESPASSING!
Radcliffe!
Hey, Gordon!
SNORK
HEY DARE, GAR!

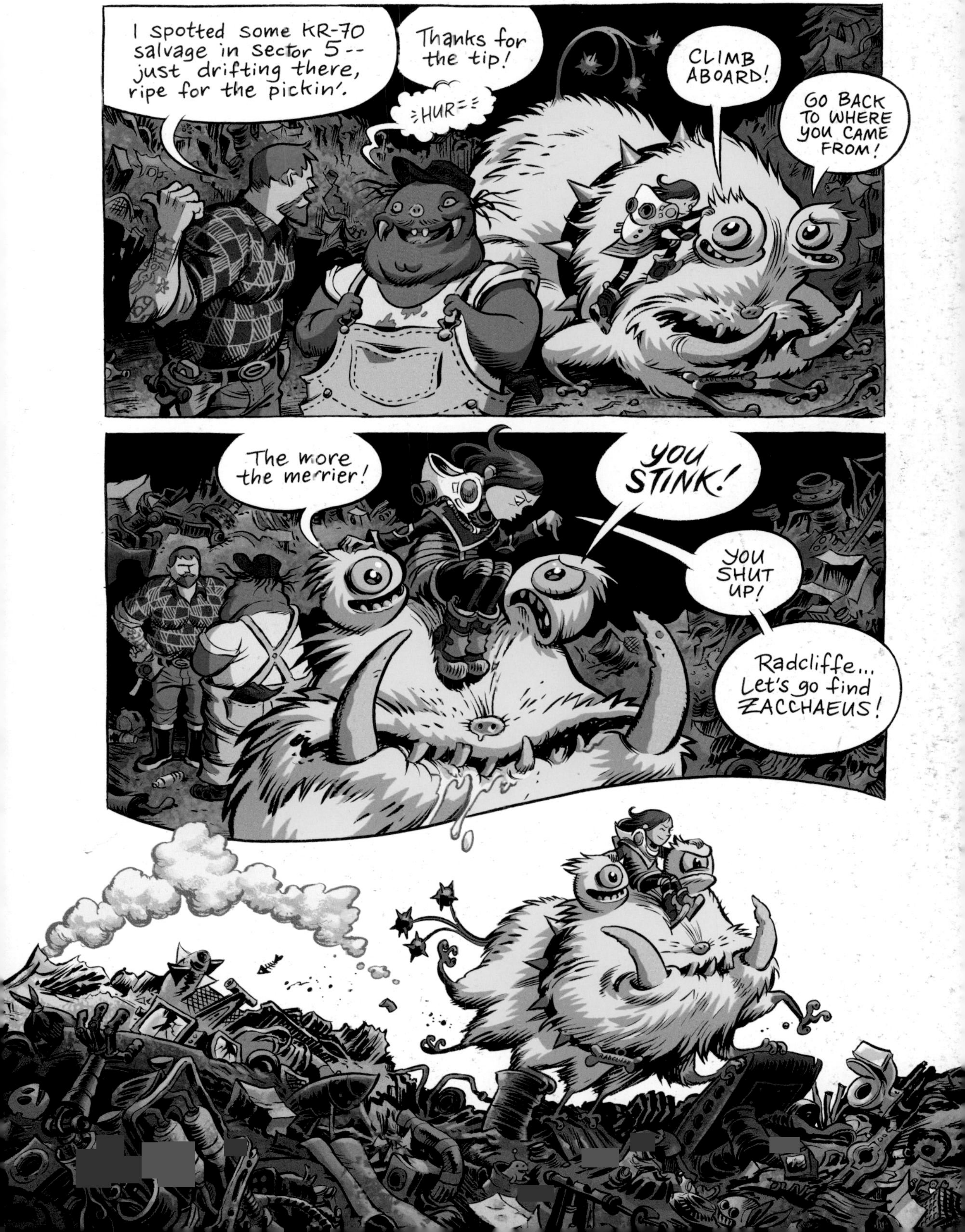
I spotted some KR-70 salvage in sector 5-- just drifting there, ripe for the pickin'.
Thanks for the tip!
HUR
CLIMB ABOARD!
GO BACK TO WHERE YOU CAME FROM!
The more the merrier!
YOU STINK!
YOU SHUT UP!
Radcliffe... Let's go find ZACCHAEUS!

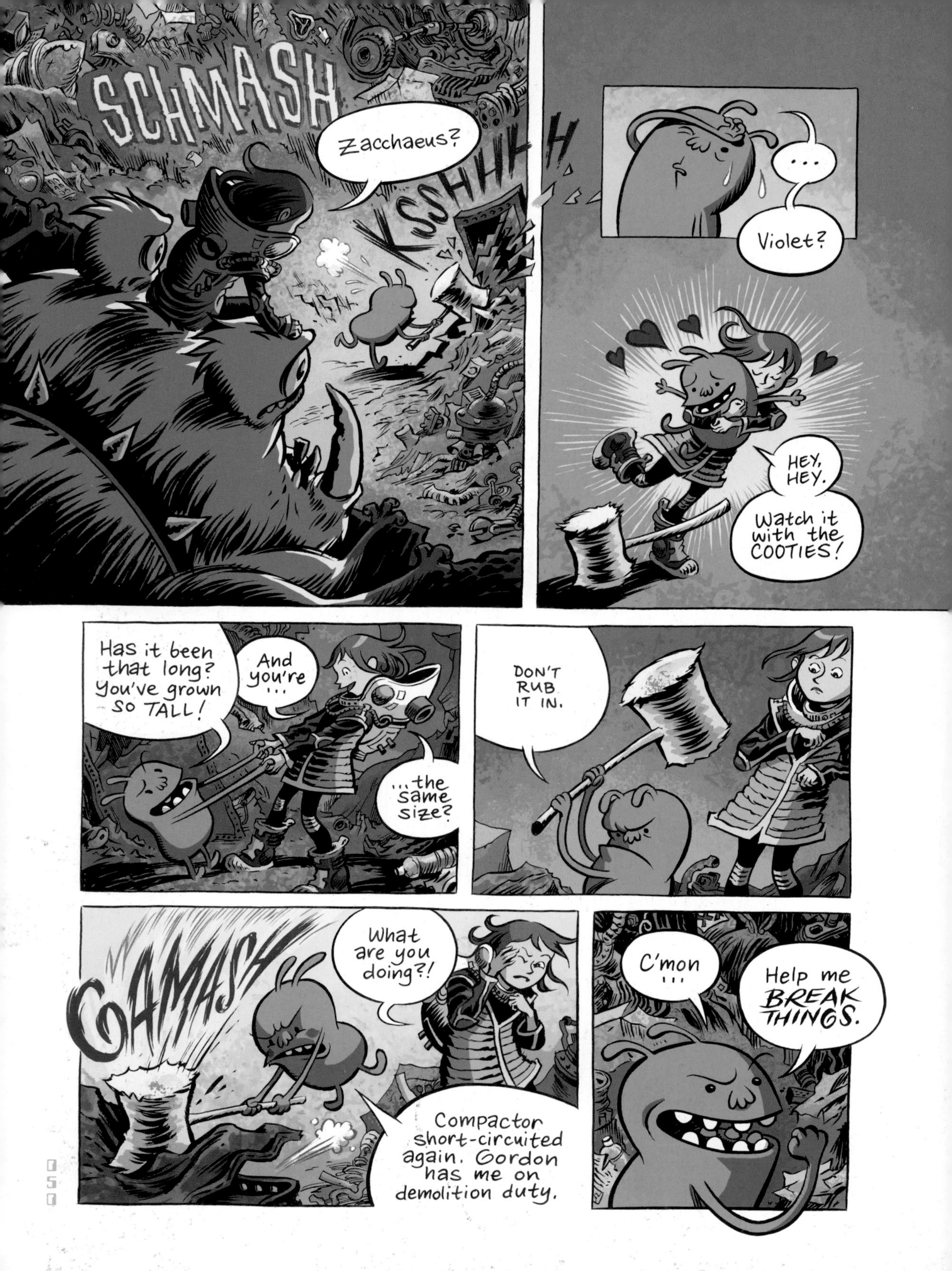

SCHMASH
Zacchaeus?
KSSHHHHH
...
Violet?
HEY, HEY.
Watch it with the COOTIES!
Has it been that long? You've grown SO TALL!
And you're ...
...the same size?
DON'T RUB IT IN.
What are you doing?!
Compactor short-circuited again. Gordon has me on demolition duty.
C'mon ...
Help me BREAK THINGS.

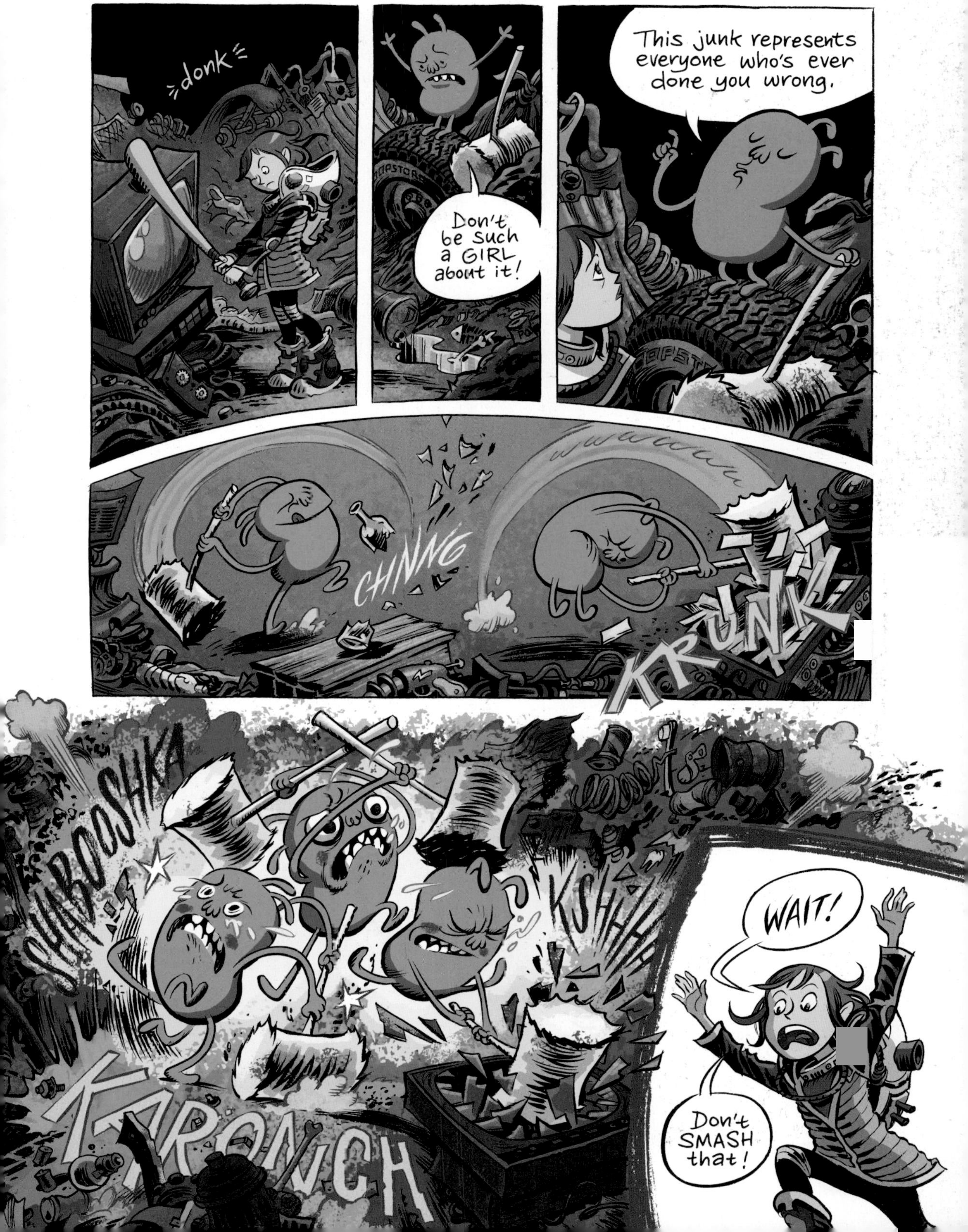
donk
Don't be such a GIRL about it!
This junk represents everyone who's ever done you wrong.
CHINNG
KRUNK
SHABOOSHKA
KSHHH
KARONCH
WAIT!
Don't SMASH that!

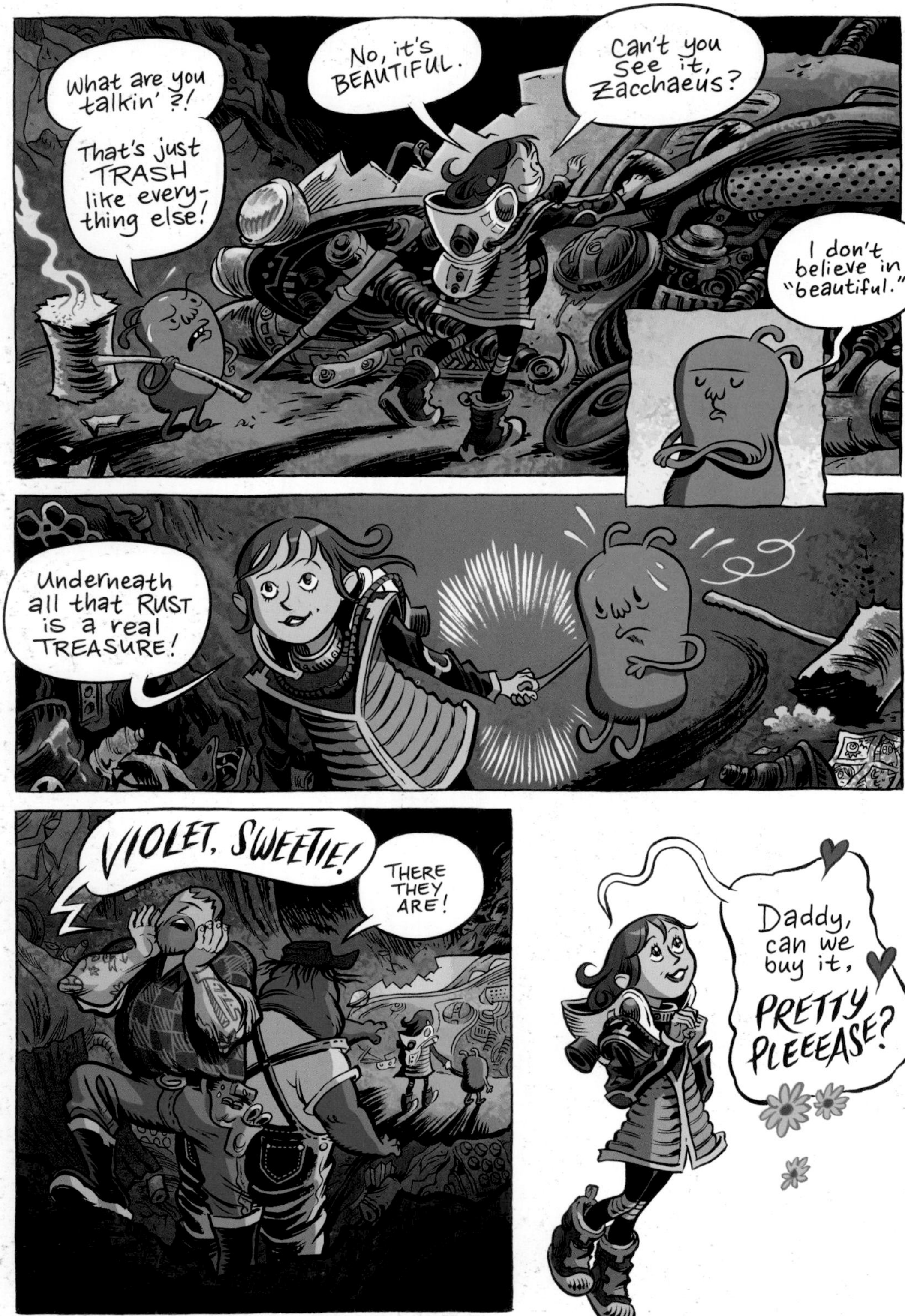
What are you talkin' ?!
That's just TRASH like every-thing else!
No, it's BEAUTIFUL.
Can't you see it, Zacchaeus?
I don't believe in "beautiful."
Underneath all that RUST is a real TREASURE!
VIOLET, SWEETIE!
THERE THEY ARE!
Daddy, can we buy it, PRETTY PLEEEASE?

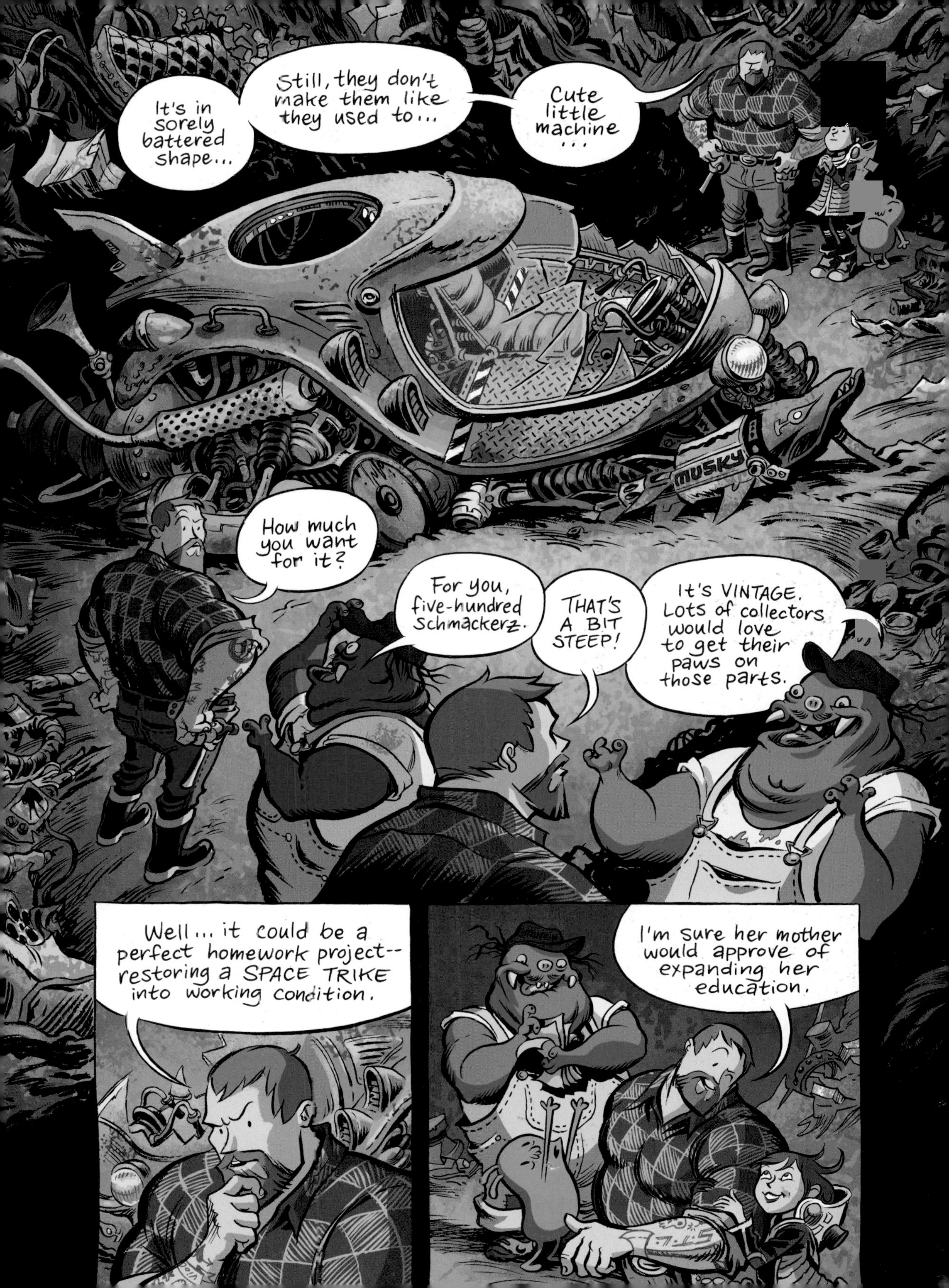
It's in sorely battered shape...
Still, they don't make them like they used to...
Cute little machine ...
MUSKY
How much you want for it?
For you, five-hundred Schmackerz.
THAT'S A BIT STEEP!
It's VINTAGE. Lots of collectors would love to get their paws on those parts.
Well... it could be a perfect homework project-- restoring a SPACE TRIKE into working condition.
I'm sure her mother would approve of expanding her education.

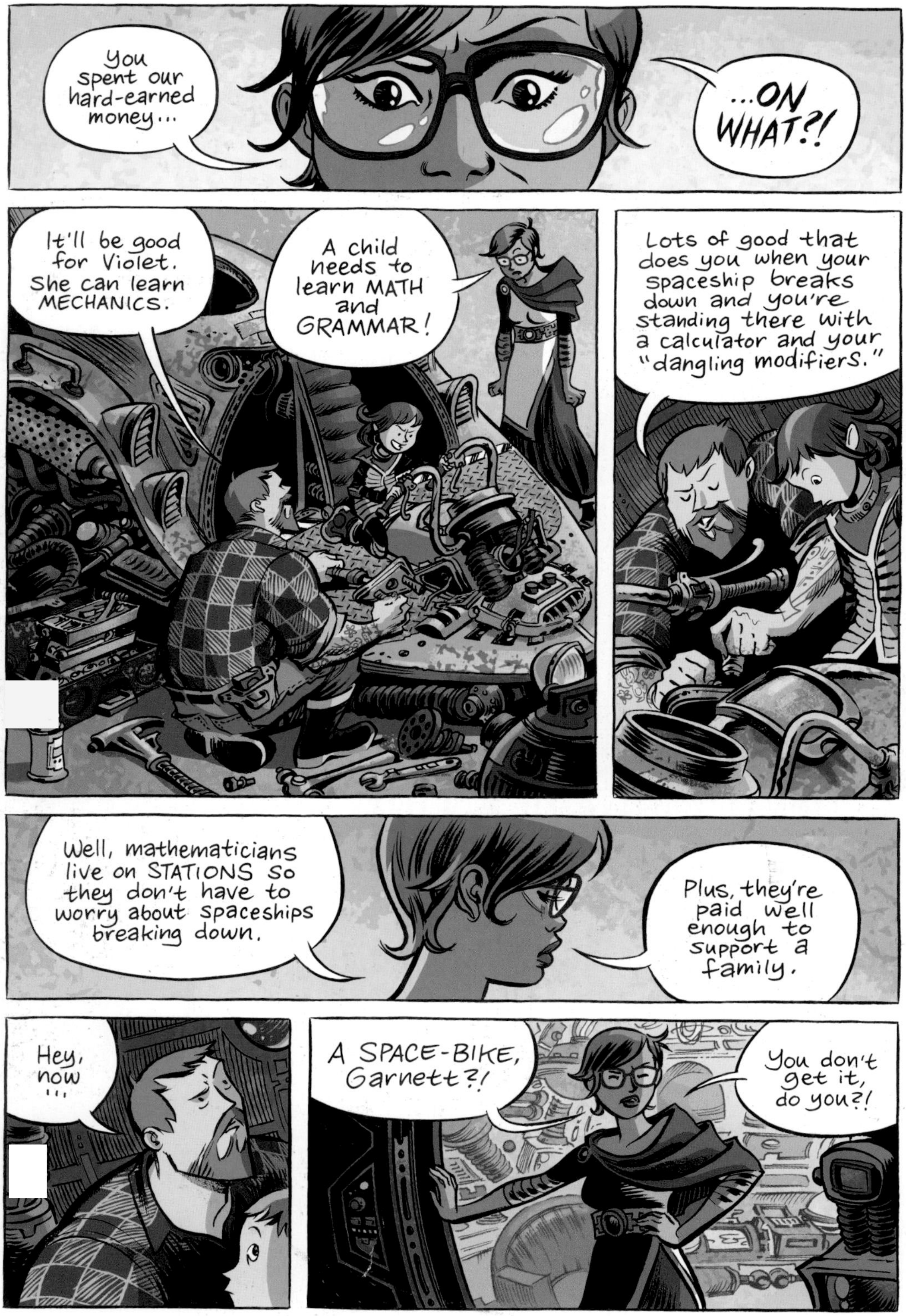
You spent our hard-earned money...
...ON WHAT?!
It'll be good for Violet. She can learn MECHANICS.
A child needs to learn MATH and GRAMMAR!
Lots of good that does you when your spaceship breaks down and you're standing there with a calculator and your "dangling modifiers."
Well, mathematicians live on STATIONS so they don't have to worry about spaceships breaking down.
Plus, they're paid well enough to support a family.
Hey, now ...
A SPACE-BIKE, Garnett?!
You don't get it, do you?!

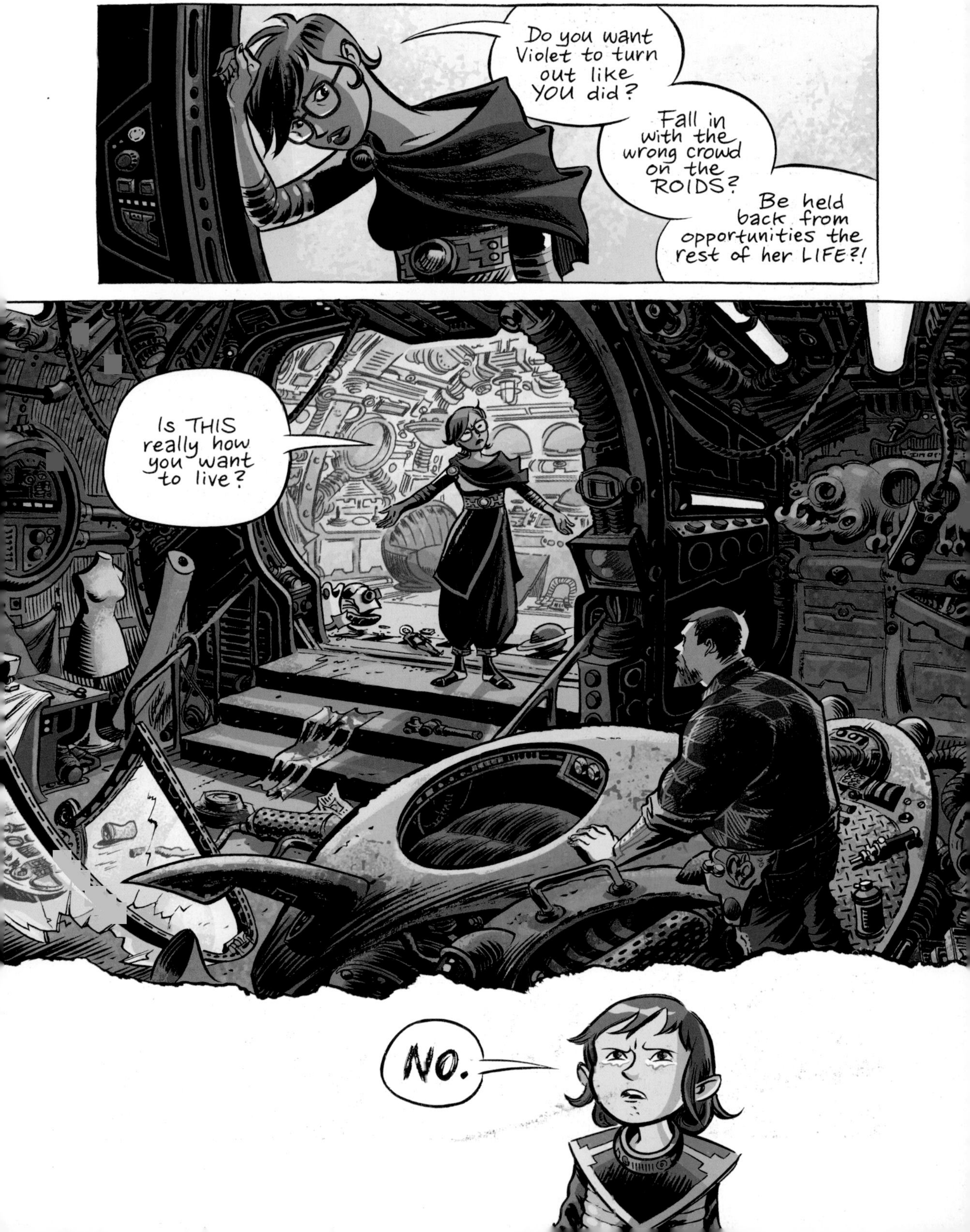
Do you want Violet to turn out like YOU did?
Fall in with the wrong crowd on the ROIDS?
Be held back from opportunities the rest of her LIFE?!
Is THIS really how you want to live?
NO.

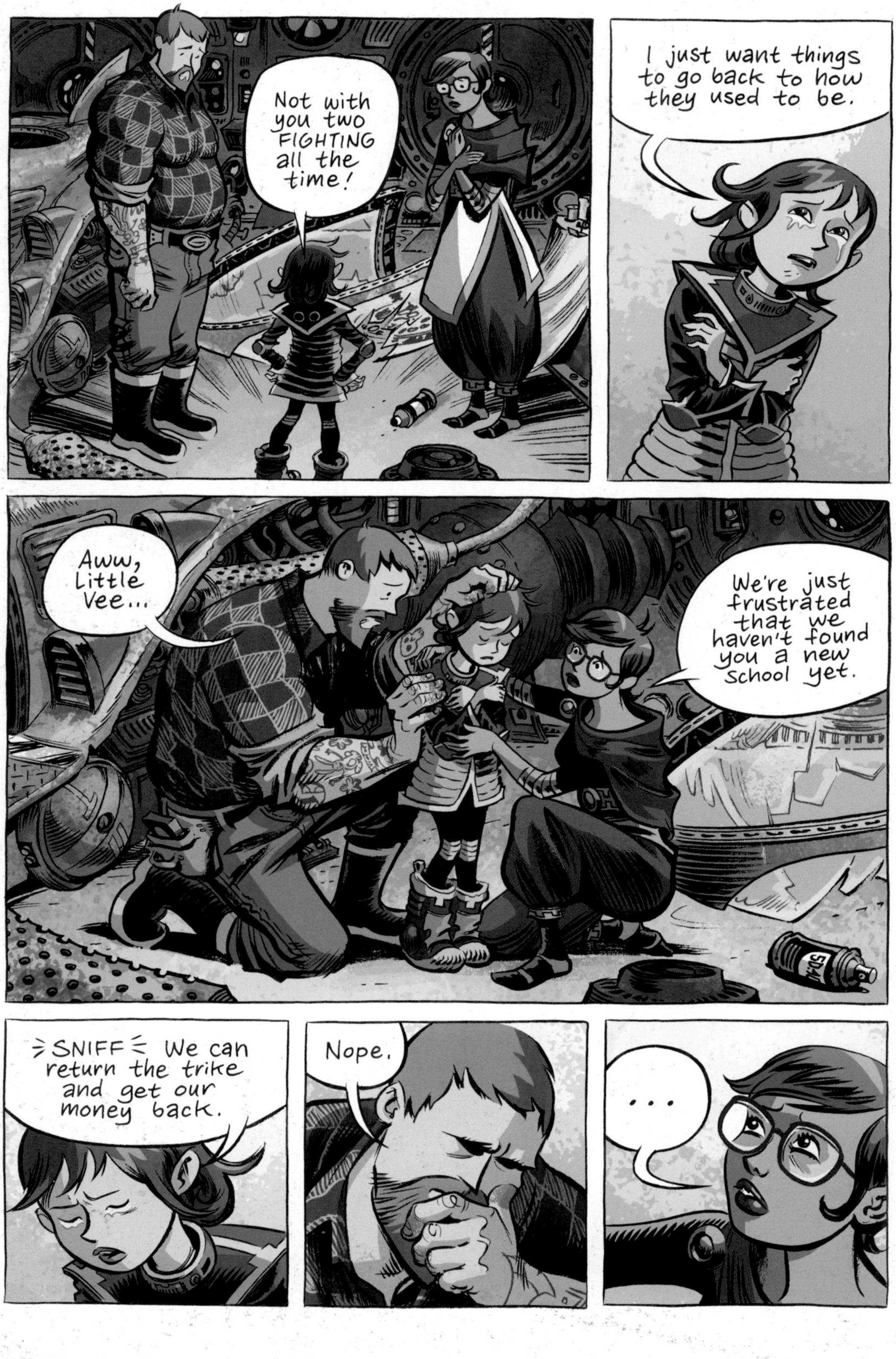
Not with you two FIGHTING all the time!
I just want things to go back to how they used to be.
Aww, Little Vee...
We're just frustrated that we haven't found you a new school yet.
SNIFF We can return the trike and get our money back.
Nope.
...

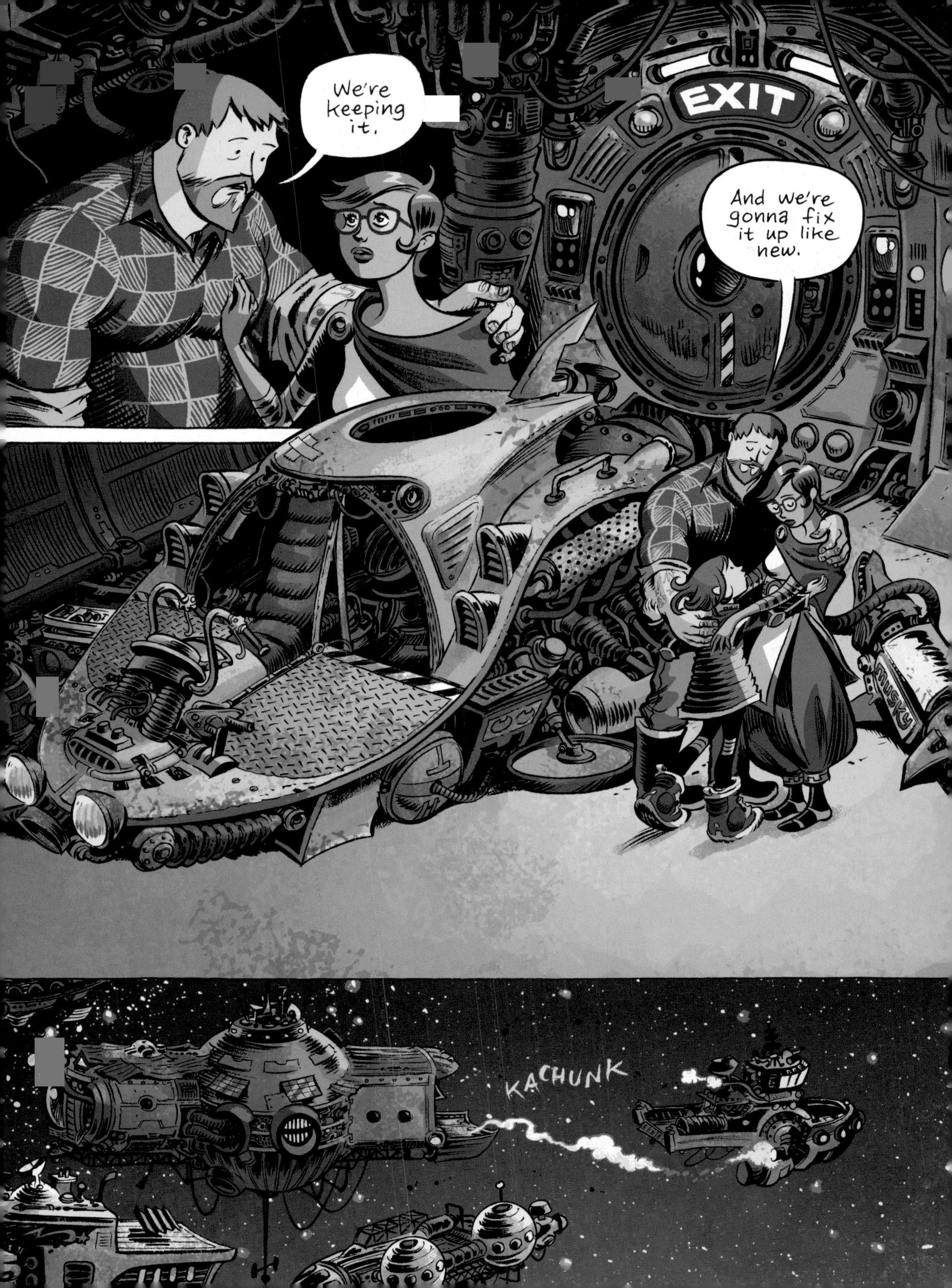
We're keeping it.
EXIT
And we're gonna fix it up like new.
musky
KACHUNK

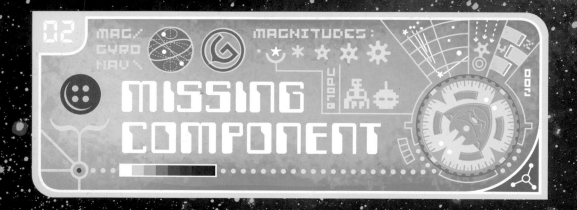

02 MISSING COMPONENT

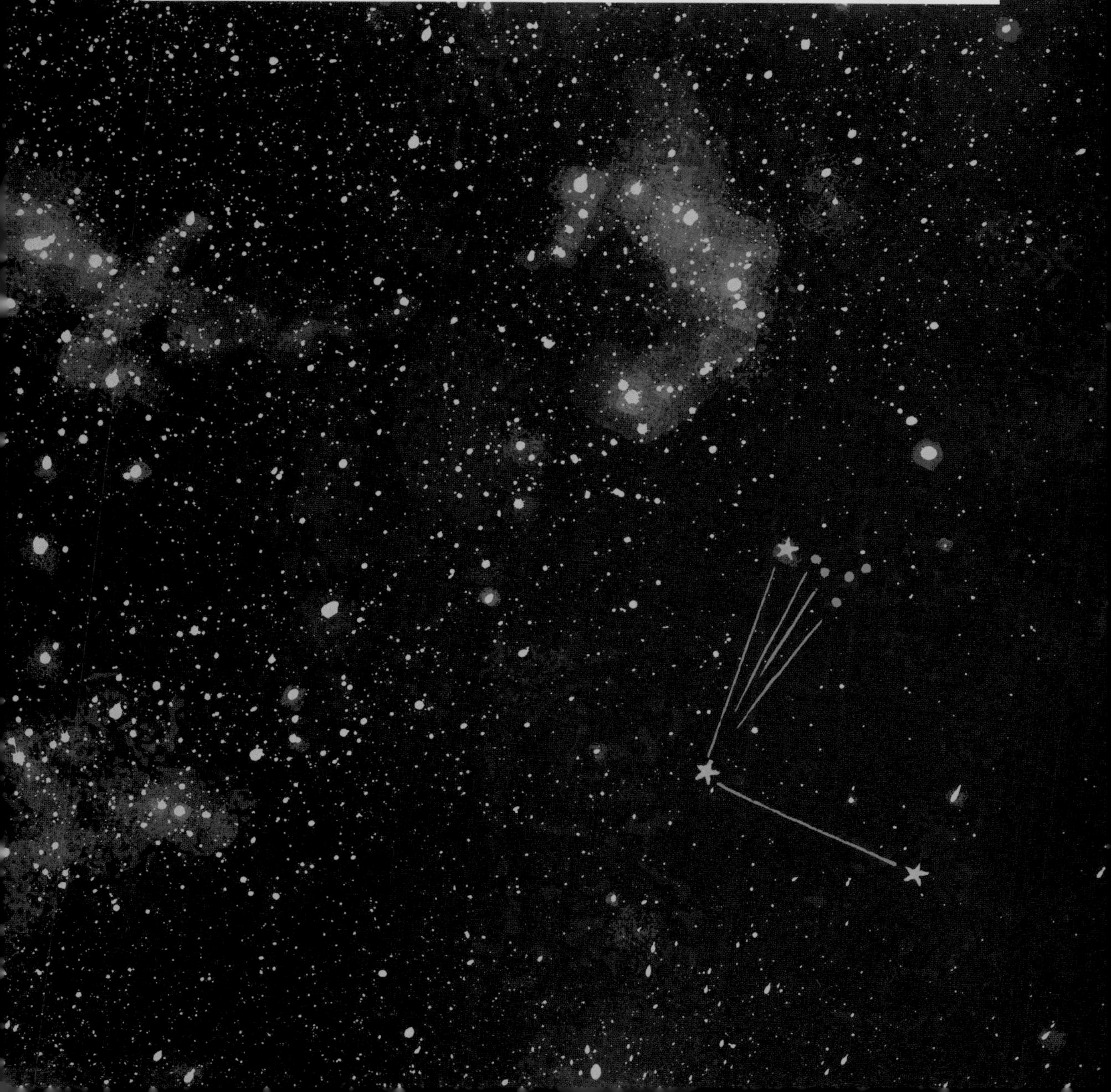

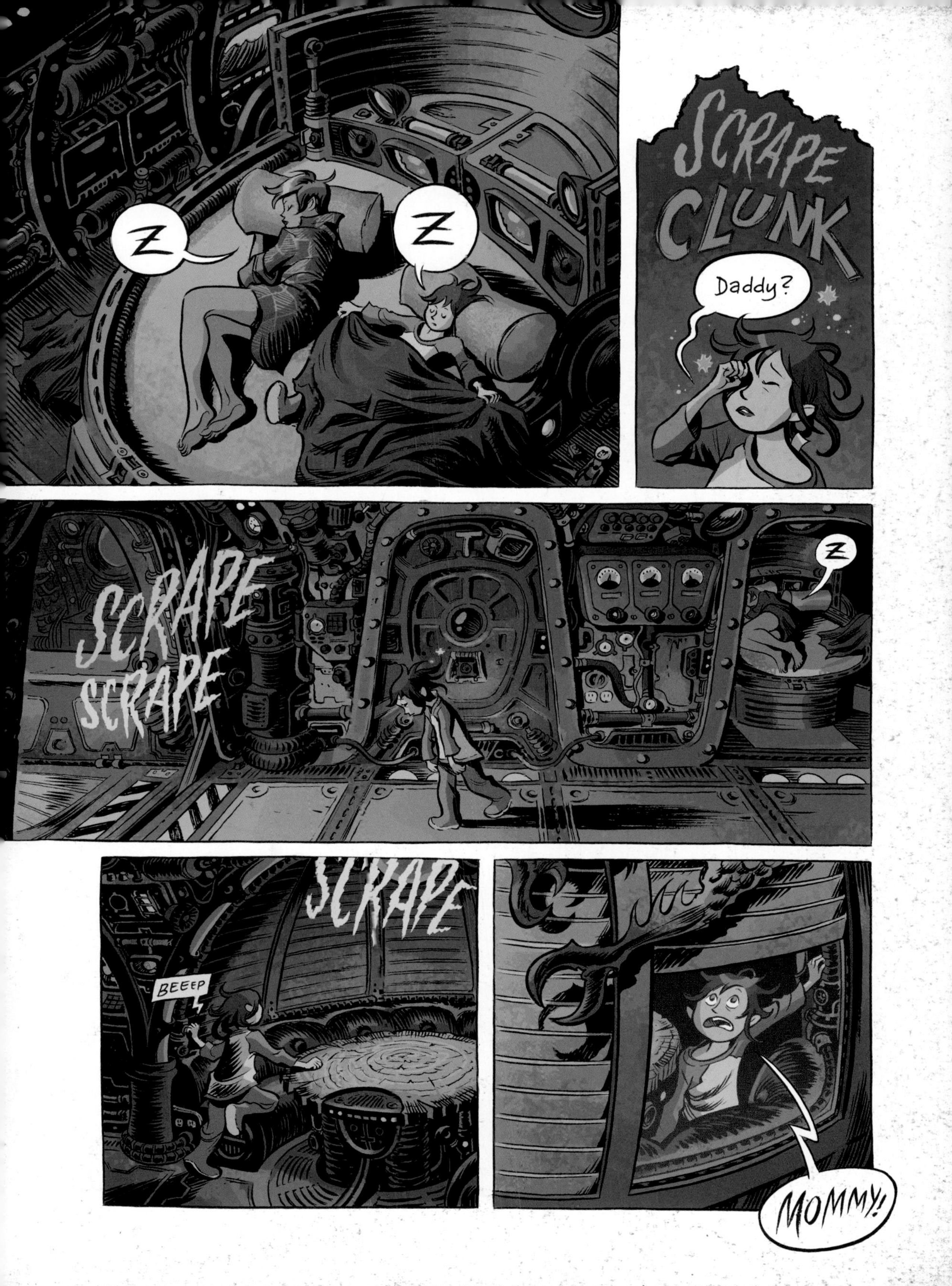
Z
Z
SCRAPE
CLUNK
Daddy?
SCRAPE
SCRAPE
Z
SCRAPE
BEEEP
MOMMY!

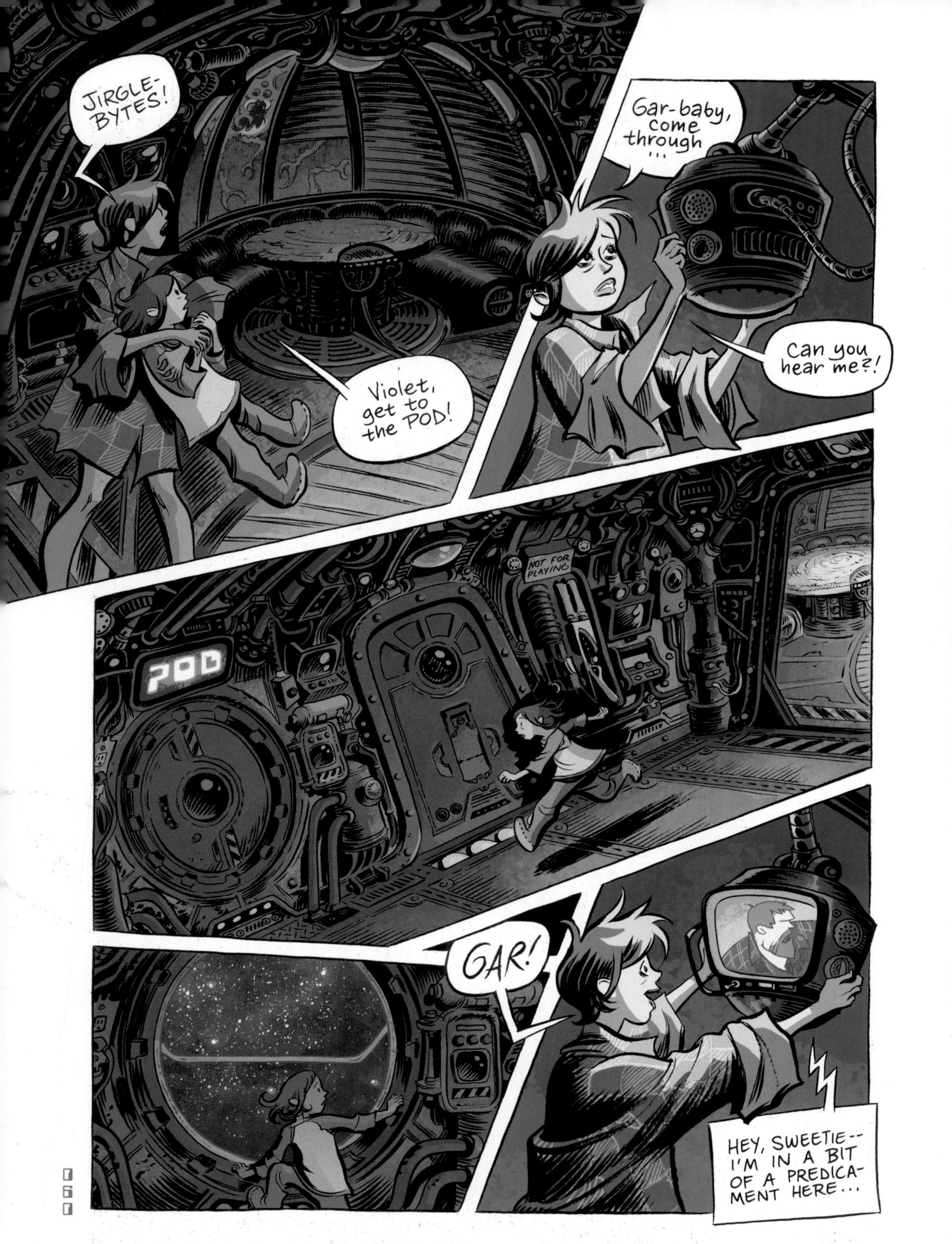
JIRGLE-BYTES!
Violet, get to the POD!
Gar-baby, come through...
Can you hear me?!
NOT FOR PLAYING
POD
GAR!
HEY, SWEETIE-- I'M IN A BIT OF A PREDICAMENT HERE...

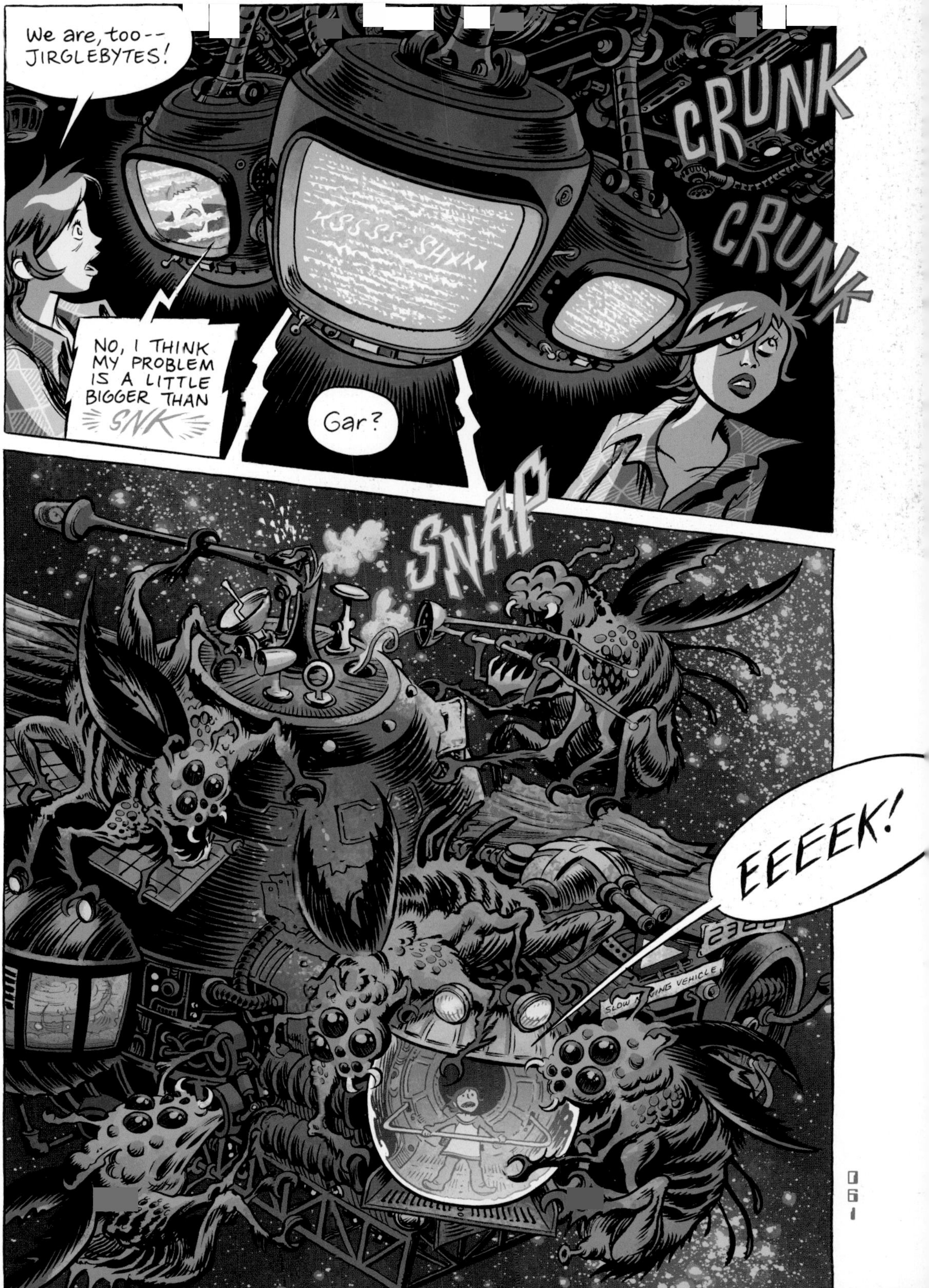

We are, too-- JIRGLEBYTES!
KSSSsSHxxx
CRUNK
CRUNK
NO, I THINK MY PROBLEM IS A LITTLE BIGGER THAN SNK
Gar?
SNAP
EEEEK!

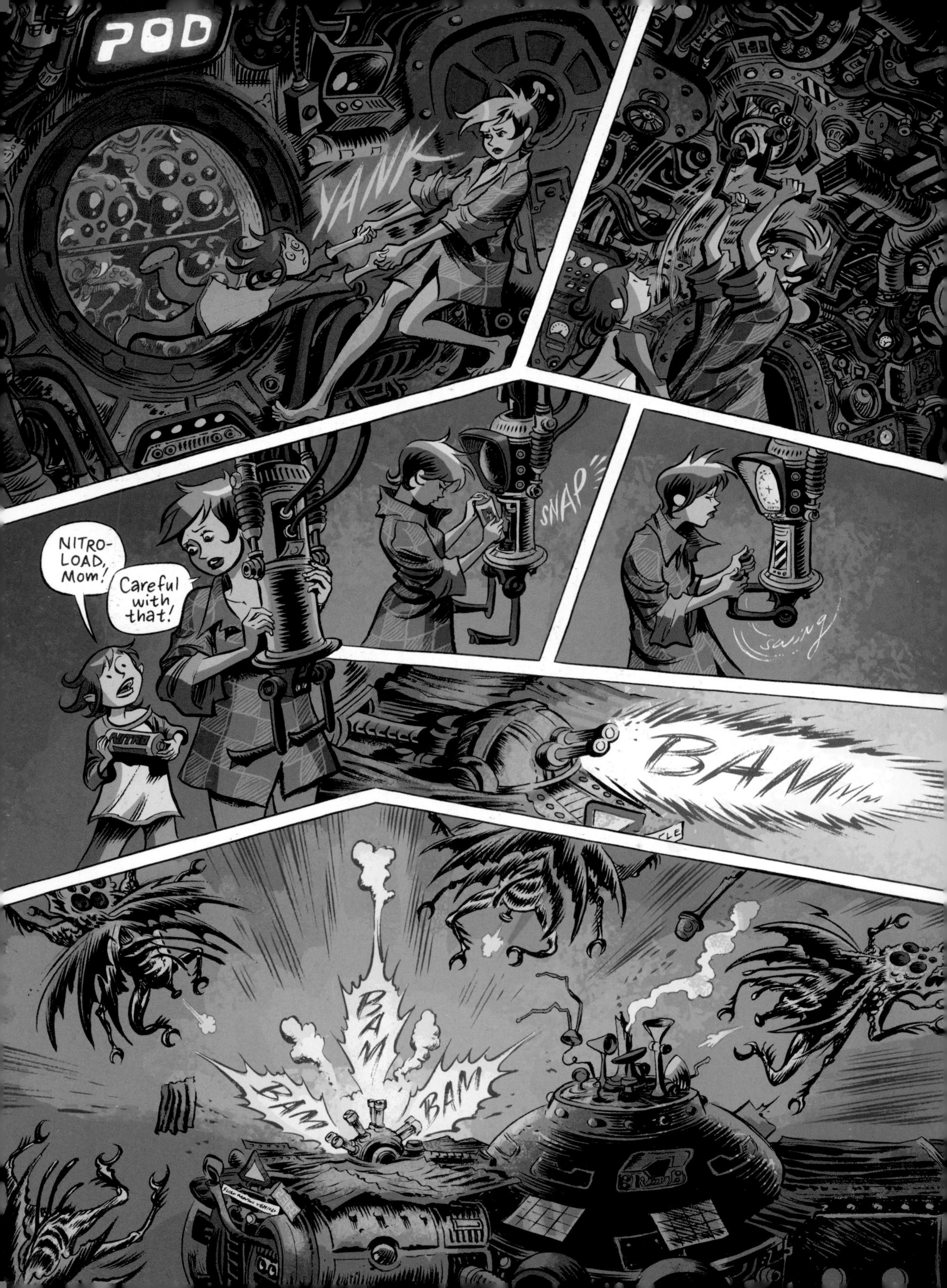

POD
YANK
NITRO-LOAD, Mom!
Careful with that!
SNAP
swing
BAM
BAM
BAM
BAM
BAM

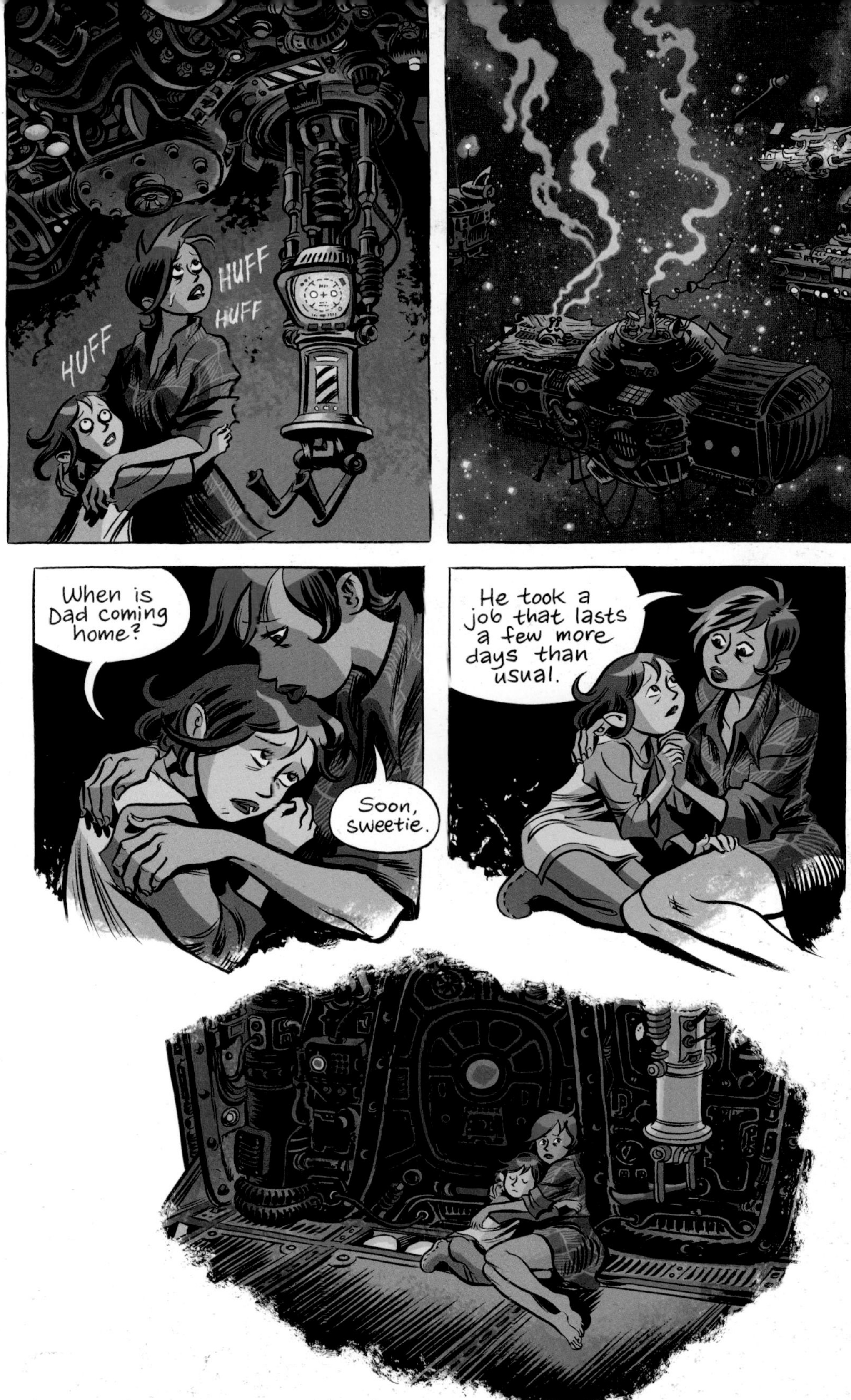
HUFF
HUFF
HUFF
When is Dad coming home?
Soon, sweetie.
He took a job that lasts a few more days than usual.

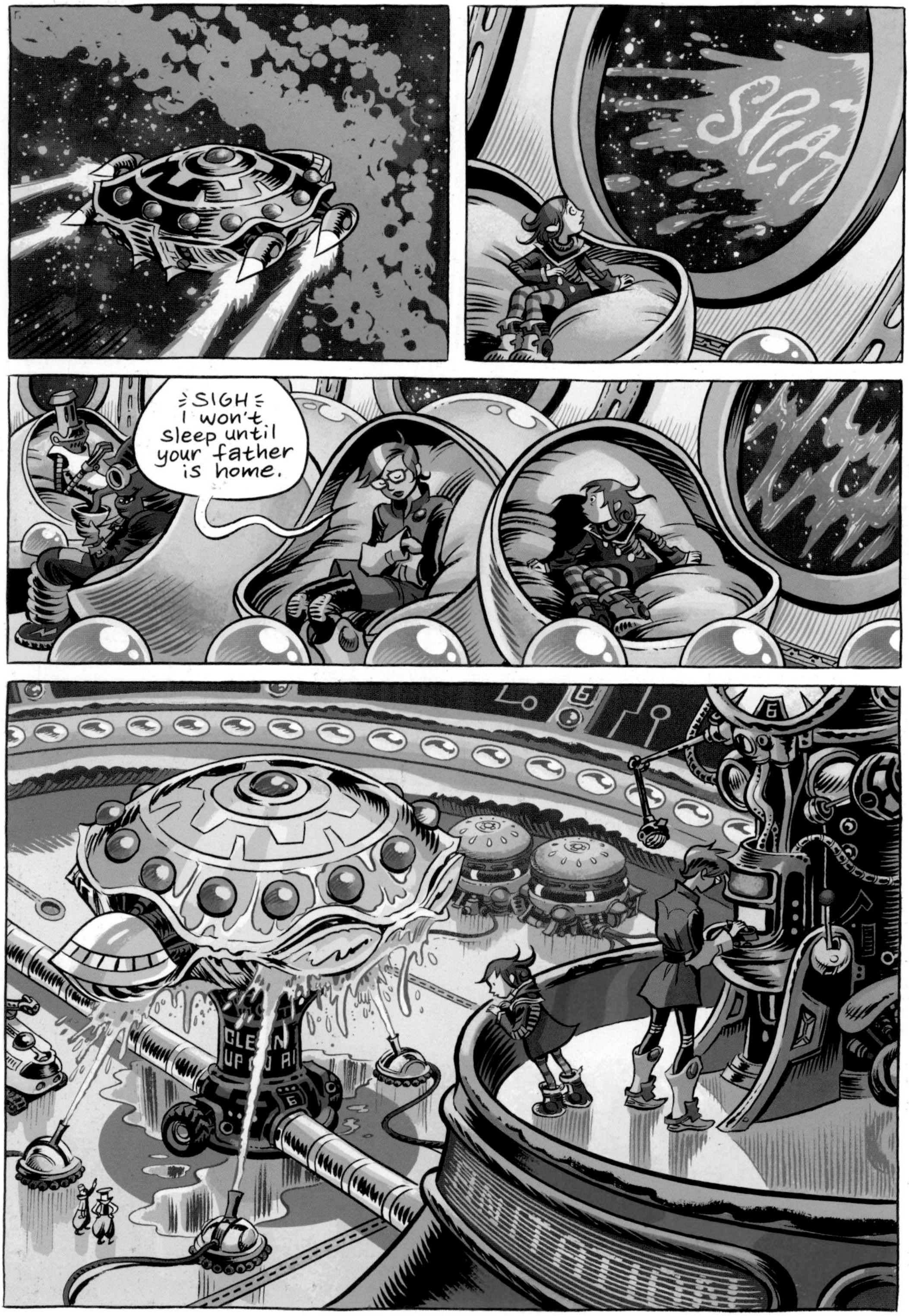
SPLAT
SIGH I won't sleep until your father is home.

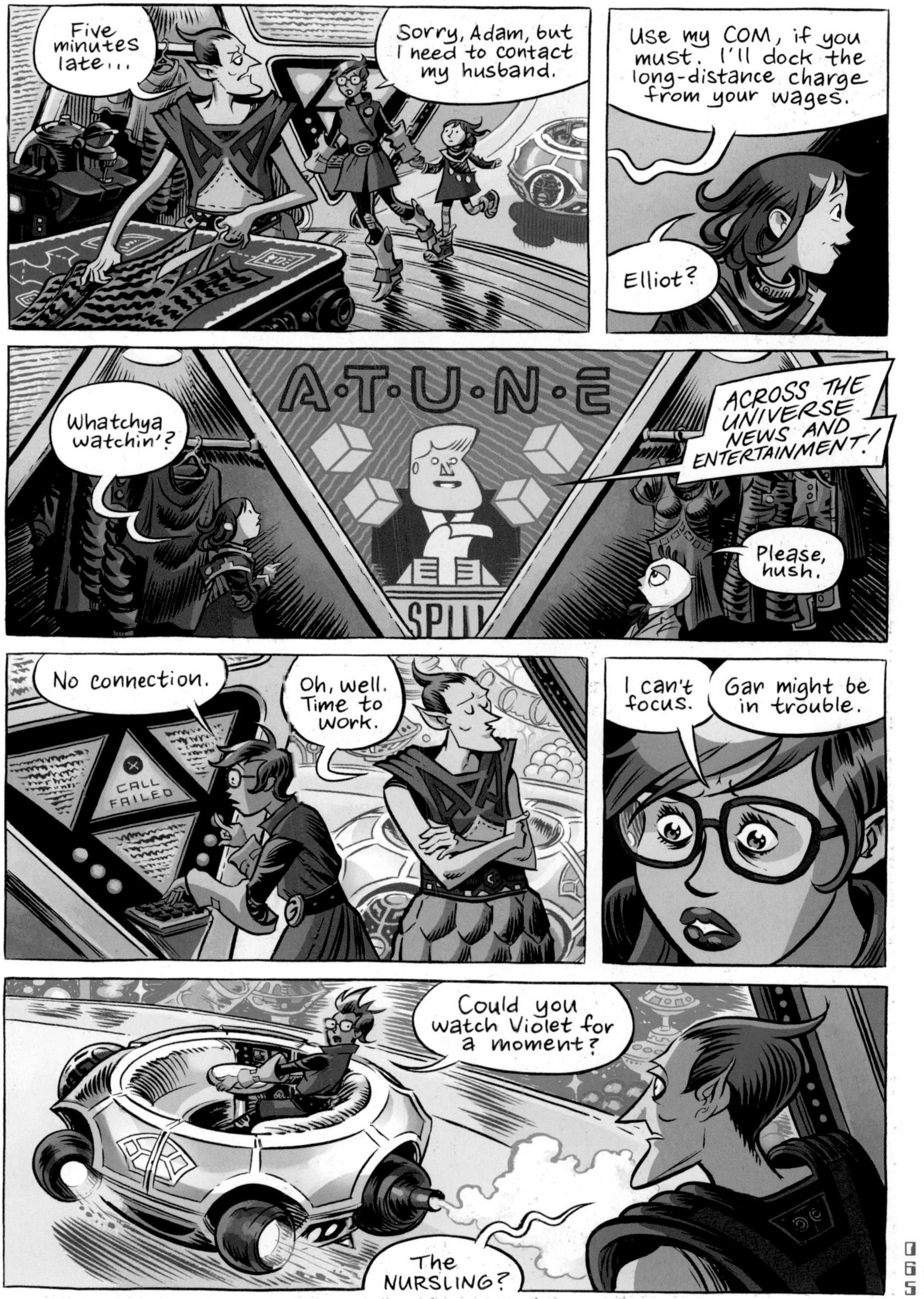

Five minutes late...
Sorry, Adam, but I need to contact my husband.
Use my COM, if you must. I'll dock the long-distance charge from your wages.
Elliot?
A·T·U·N·E
Whatchya watchin'?
ACROSS THE UNIVERSE NEWS AND ENTERTAINMENT!
Please, hush.
No connection.
CALL FAILED
Oh, well. Time to work.
I can't focus.
Gar might be in trouble.
Could you watch Violet for a moment?
The NURSLING?

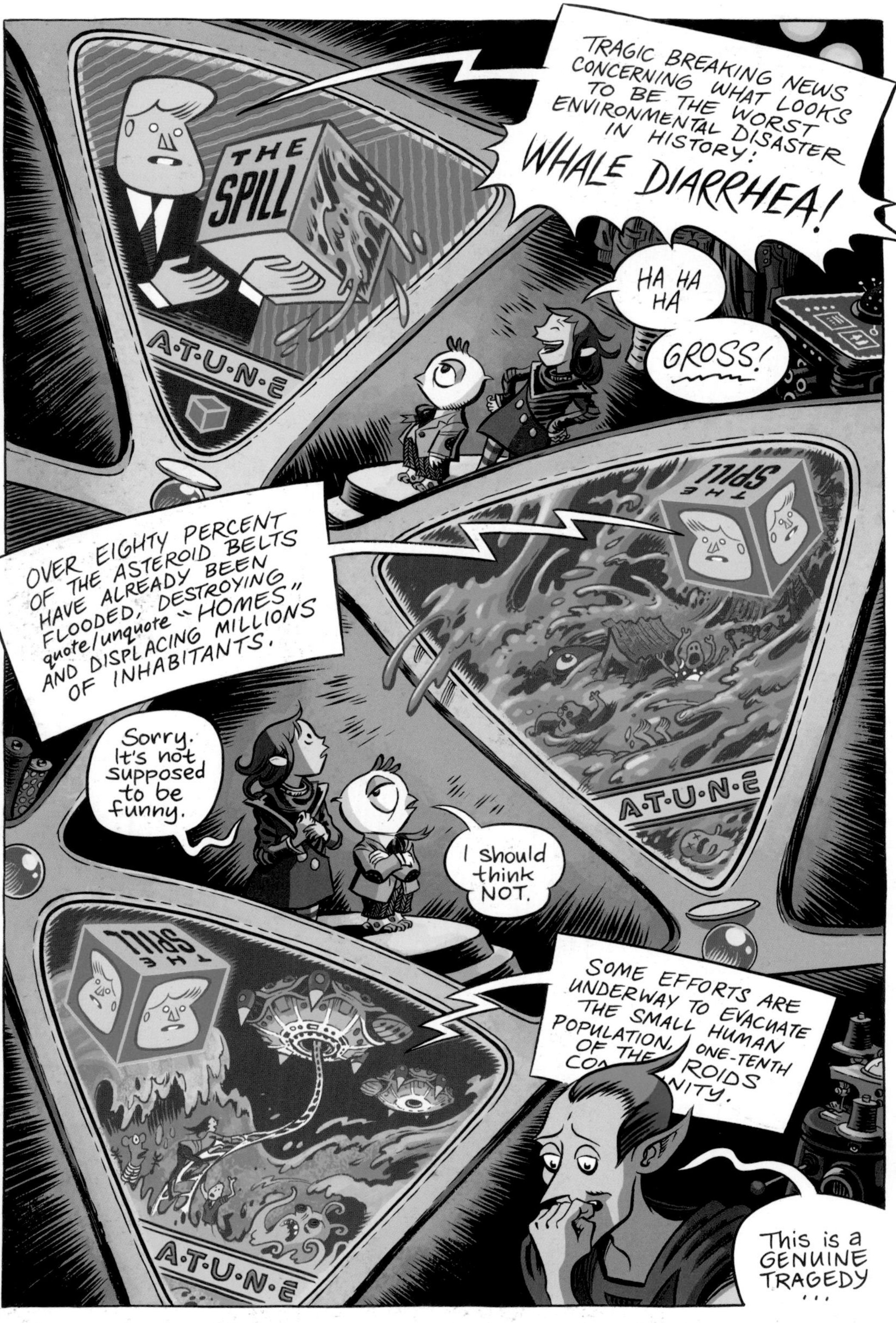
THE SPILL
A·T·U·N·E
TRAGIC BREAKING NEWS CONCERNING WHAT LOOKS TO BE THE WORST ENVIRONMENTAL DISASTER IN HISTORY: WHALE DIARRHEA!
HA HA HA
GROSS!
OVER EIGHTY PERCENT OF THE ASTEROID BELTS HAVE ALREADY BEEN FLOODED, DESTROYING quote/unquote "HOMES" AND DISPLACING MILLIONS OF INHABITANTS.
Sorry. It's not supposed to be funny.
I should think NOT.
SOME EFFORTS ARE UNDERWAY TO EVACUATE THE SMALL HUMAN POPULATION, ONE-TENTH OF THE
This is a GENUINE TRAGEDY . . .

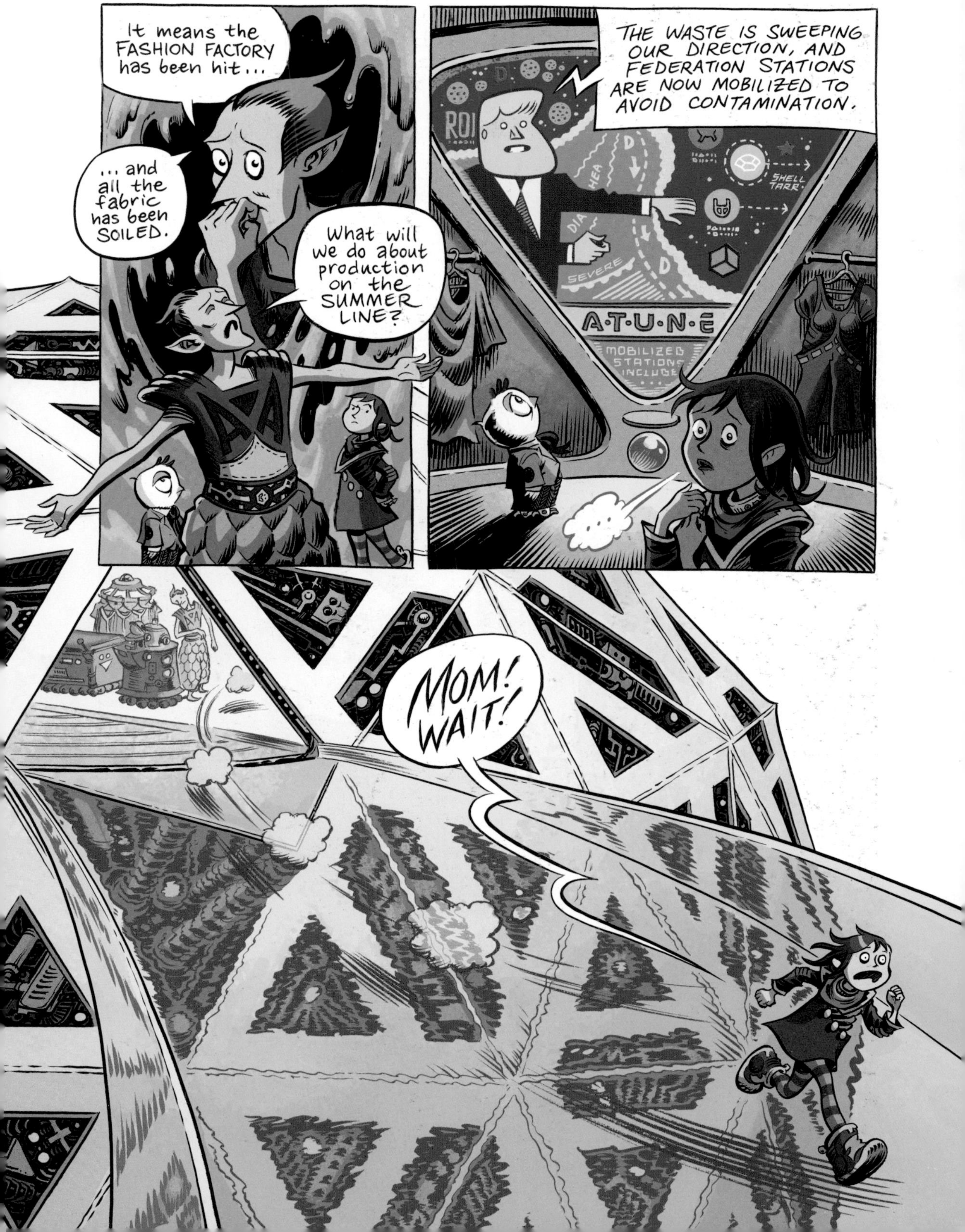
It means the FASHION FACTORY has been hit...
...and all the fabric has been SOILED.
What will we do about production on the SUMMER LINE?
THE WASTE IS SWEEPING OUR DIRECTION, AND FEDERATION STATIONS ARE NOW MOBILIZED TO AVOID CONTAMINATION.
SHELL TARR
SEVERE
A·T·U·N·E
MOBILIZED STATIONS INCLUDE
MOM! WAIT!

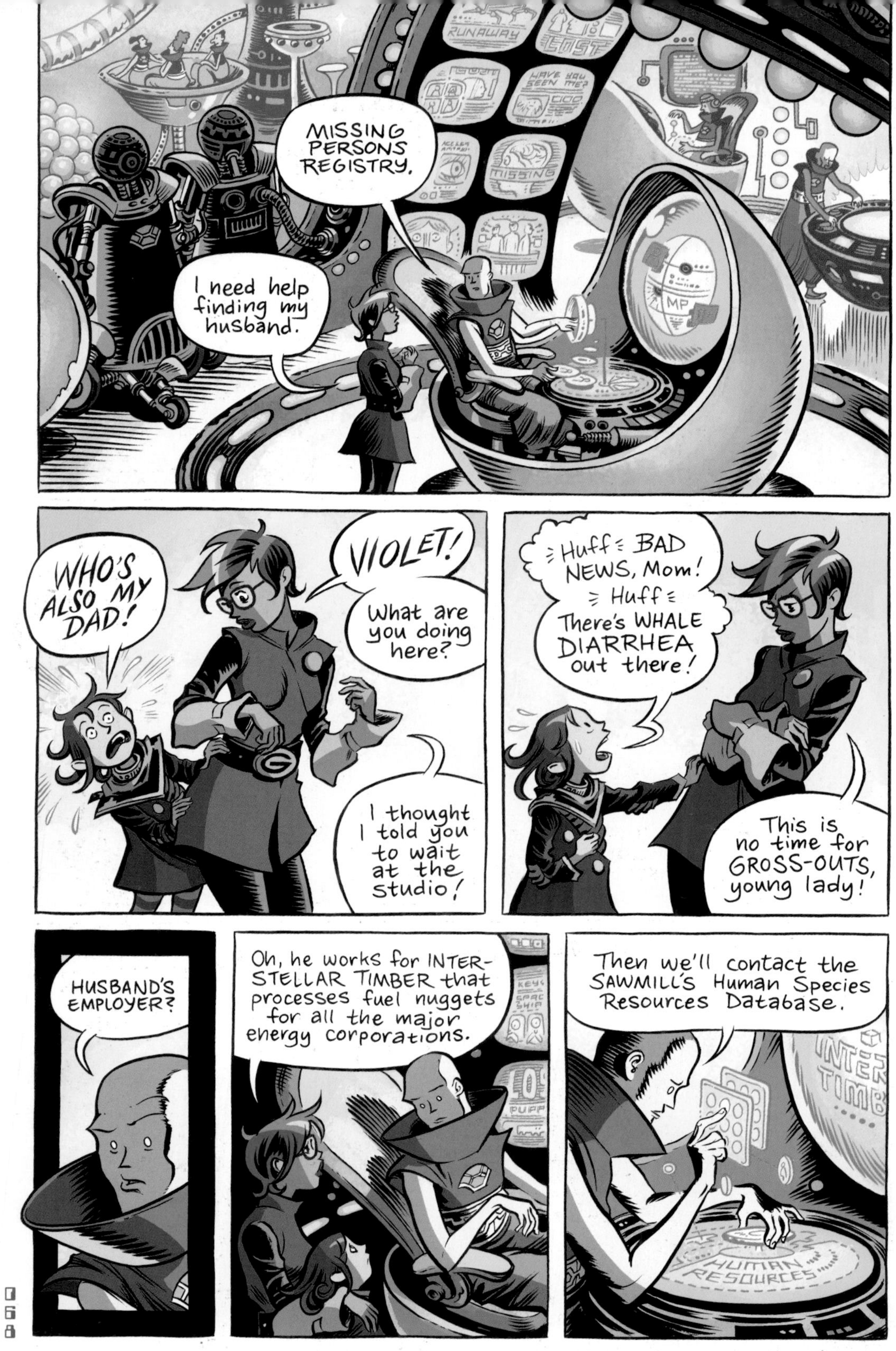
RUNAWAY
LOST
HAVE YOU SEEN ME?
MISSING
MISSING PERSONS REGISTRY.
MP
I need help finding my husband.
VIOLET!
What are you doing here?
WHO'S ALSO MY DAD!
I thought I told you to wait at the studio!
Huff BAD NEWS, Mom! Huff There's WHALE DIARRHEA out there!
This is no time for GROSS-OUTS, young lady!
HUSBAND'S EMPLOYER?
Oh, he works for INTERSTELLAR TIMBER that processes fuel nuggets for all the major energy corporations.
Then we'll contact the SAWMILL'S Human Species Resources Database.
HUMAN RESOURCES

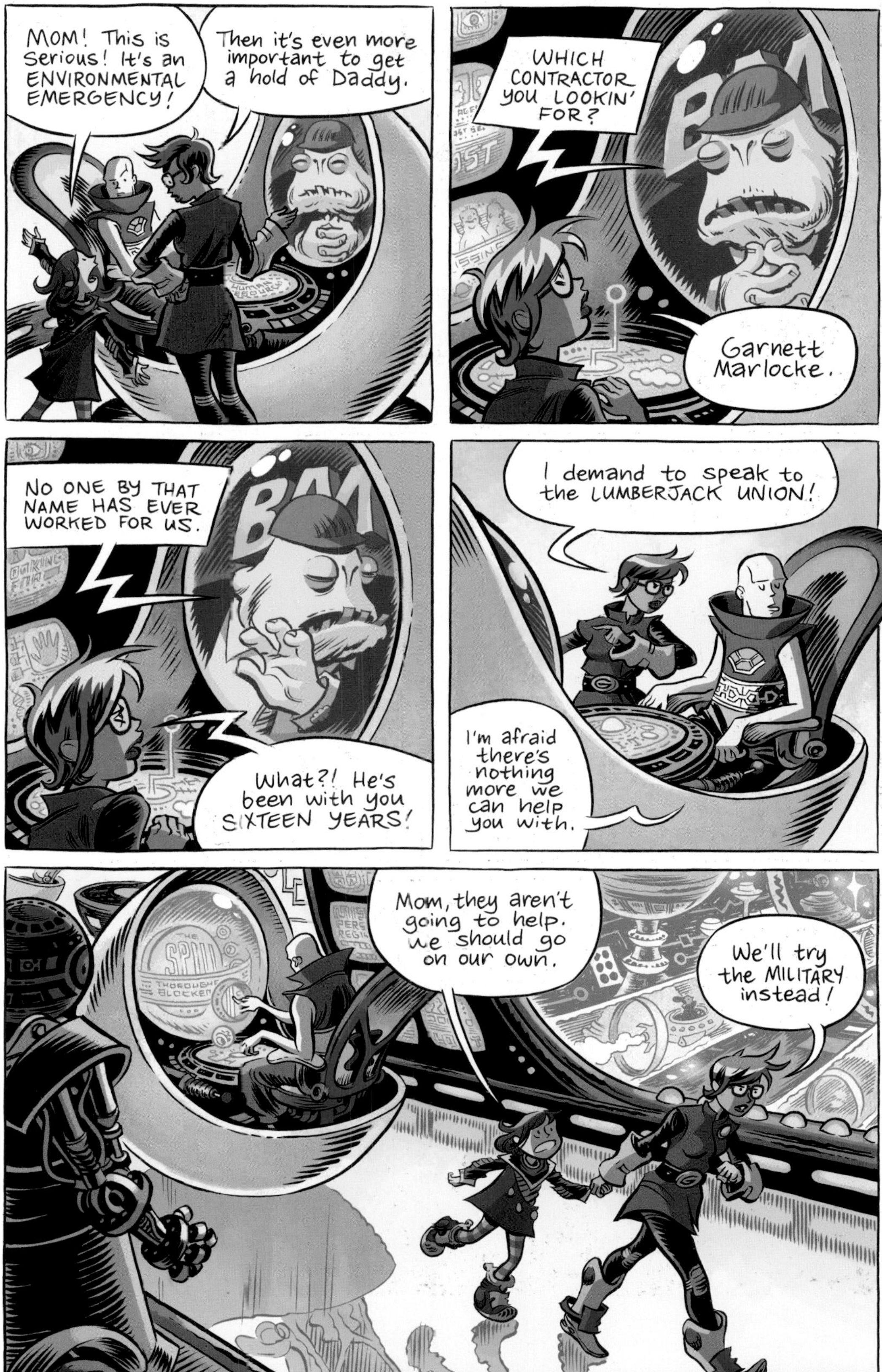
MOM! This is Serious! It's an ENVIRONMENTAL EMERGENCY!
Then it's even more important to get a hold of Daddy.
WHICH CONTRACTOR YOU LOOKIN' FOR?
Garnett Marlocke.
NO ONE BY THAT NAME HAS EVER WORKED FOR US.
What?! He's been with you SIXTEEN YEARS!
I demand to speak to the LUMBERJACK UNION!
I'm afraid there's nothing more we can help you with.
Mom, they aren't going to help. We should go on our own.
We'll try the MILITARY instead!

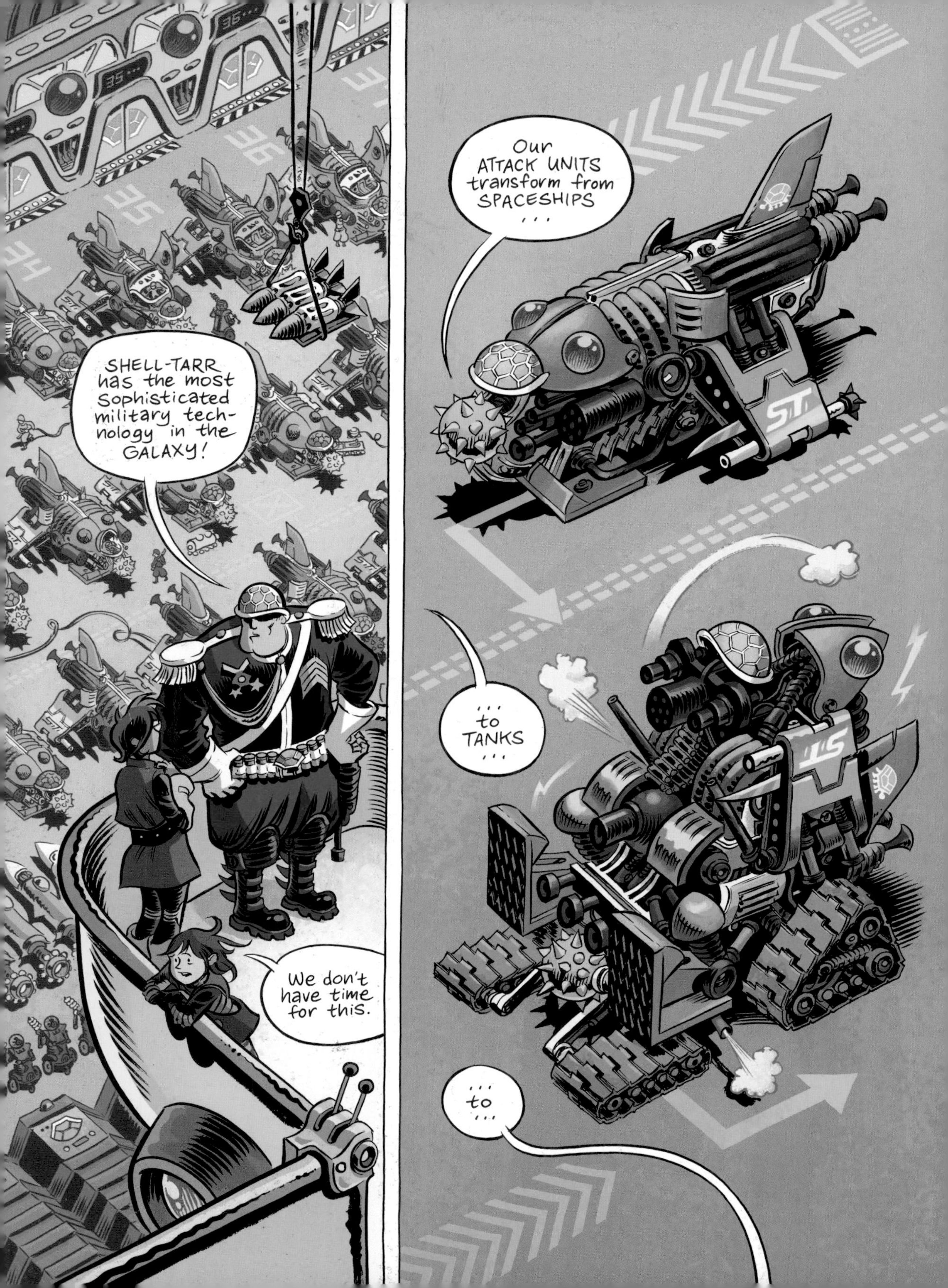
SHELL-TARR has the most sophisticated military tech-nology in the GALAXY!
We don't have time for this.
Our ATTACK UNITS transform from SPACESHIPS ...
... to TANKS ...
... to ...

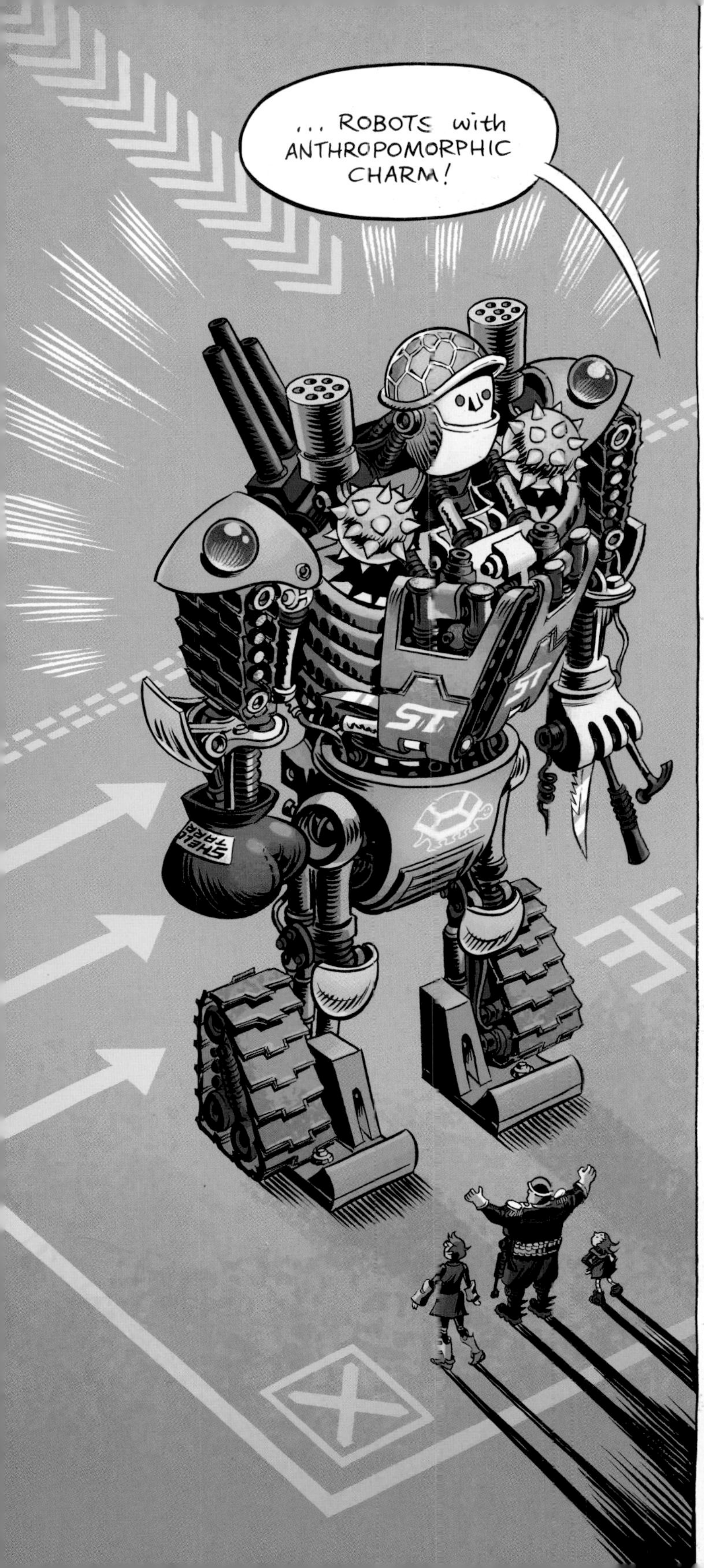
... ROBOTS with ANTHROPOMORPHIC CHARM!

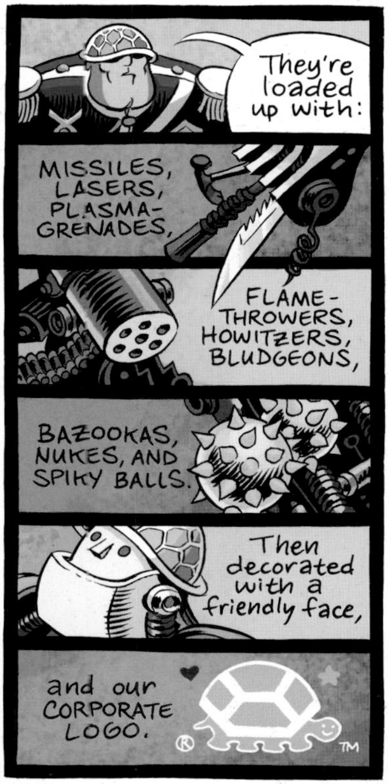
They're loaded up with:
MISSILES, LASERS, PLASMA-GRENADES,
FLAME-THROWERS, HOWITZERS, BLUDGEONS,
BAZOOKAS, NUKES, AND SPIKY BALLS.
Then decorated with a friendly face,
and our CORPORATE LOGO.

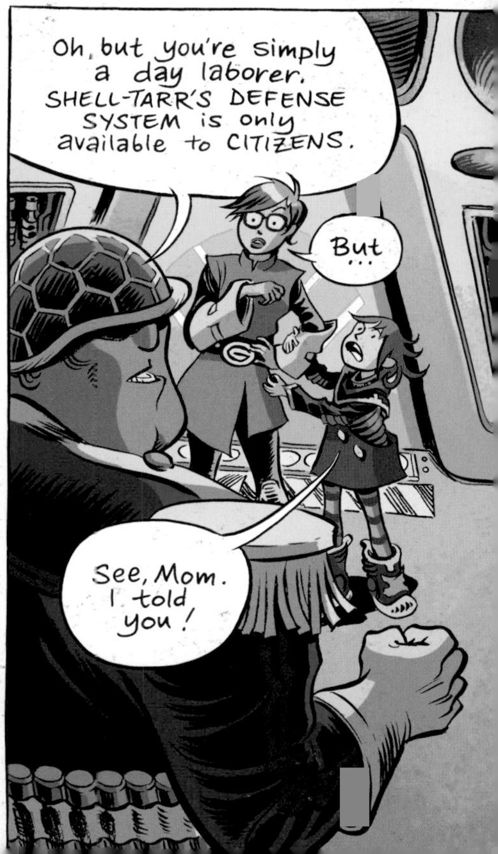
Oh, but you're simply a day laborer. SHELL-TARR'S DEFENSE SYSTEM is only available to CITIZENS.
But ...
See, Mom. I told you!

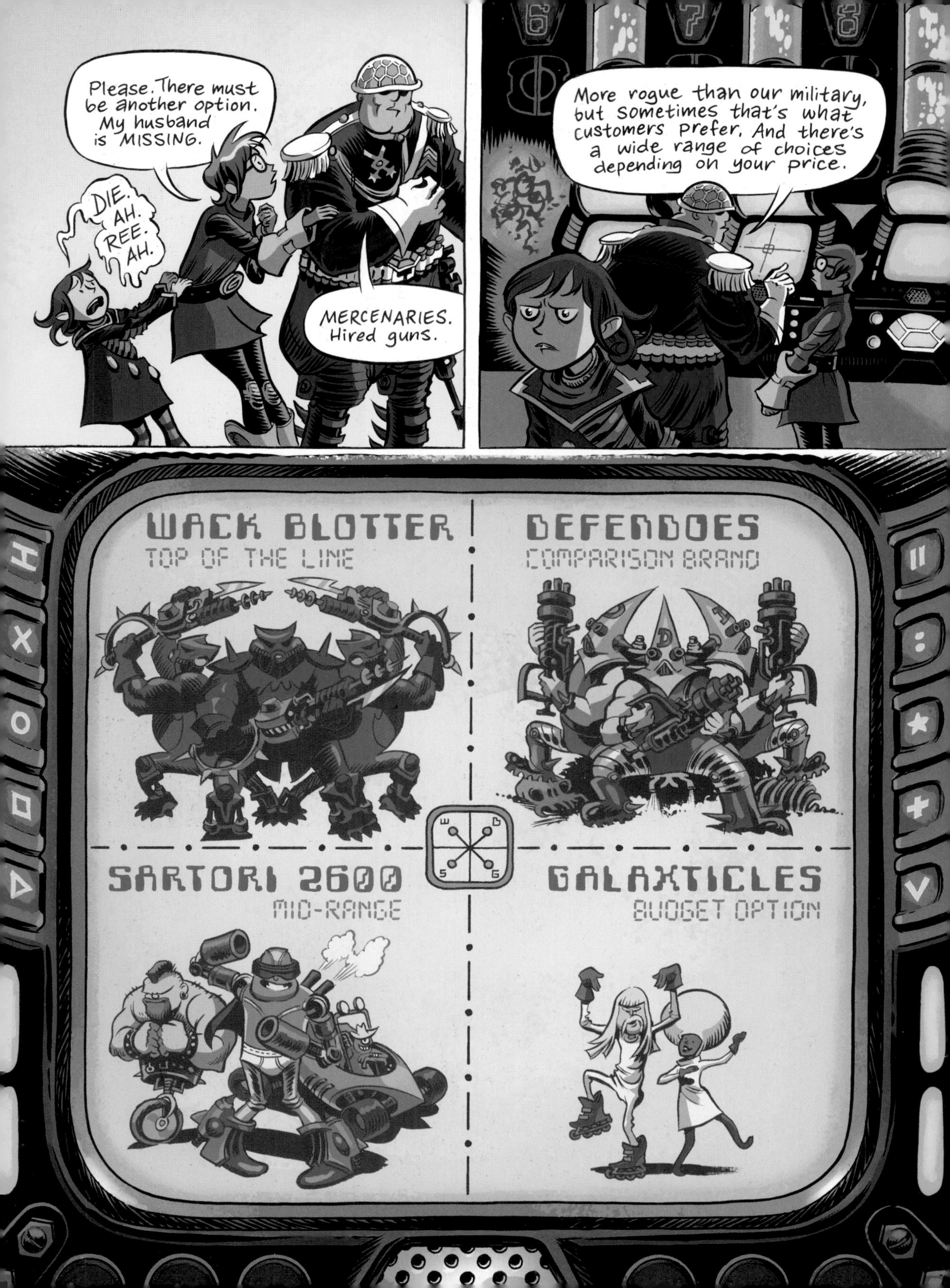
Please. There must be another option. My husband is MISSING.
DIE. AH. REE. AH.
MERCENARIES. Hired guns.
More rogue than our military, but sometimes that's what customers prefer. And there's a wide range of choices depending on your price.
WACK BLOTTER
TOP OF THE LINE
DEFENDOES
COMPARISON BRAND
SARTORI 2600
MID-RANGE
GALAXTICLES
BUDGET OPTION

...rd
...e.
...s.
Even the ones
you included for
comedic relief.

Mrs. Marlocke?

I'm here
on behalf of
MISSING PERSONS
REGISTRY.

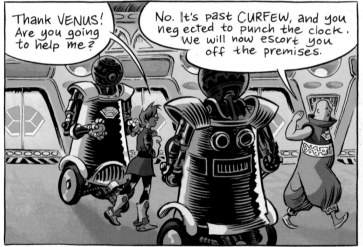

Thank VENUS!
Are you going
to help me?

No. It's past CURFEW, and you
neglected to punch the clock.
We will now escort you
off the premises.

Violet?

VIOLET!!

WHERE'S
MY
DAUGHTER?!

All noncitizens
will be aboard
the FERRY WHEEL.

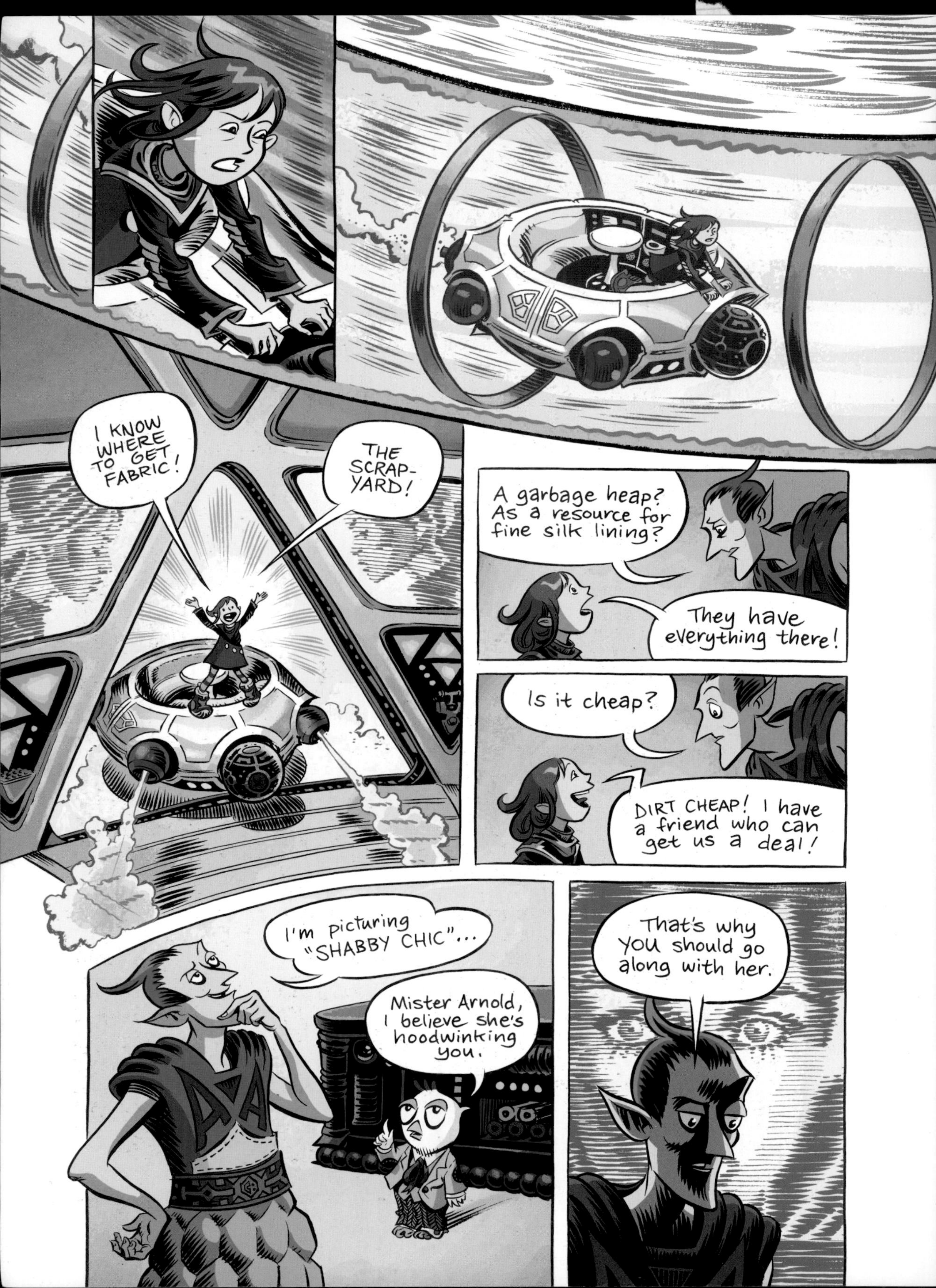
I KNOW WHERE TO GET FABRIC!
THE SCRAP-YARD!
A garbage heap? As a resource for fine silk lining?
They have everything there!
Is it cheap?
DIRT CHEAP! I have a friend who can get us a deal!
I'm picturing "SHABBY CHIC"...
Mister Arnold, I believe she's hoodwinking you.
That's why YOU should go along with her.

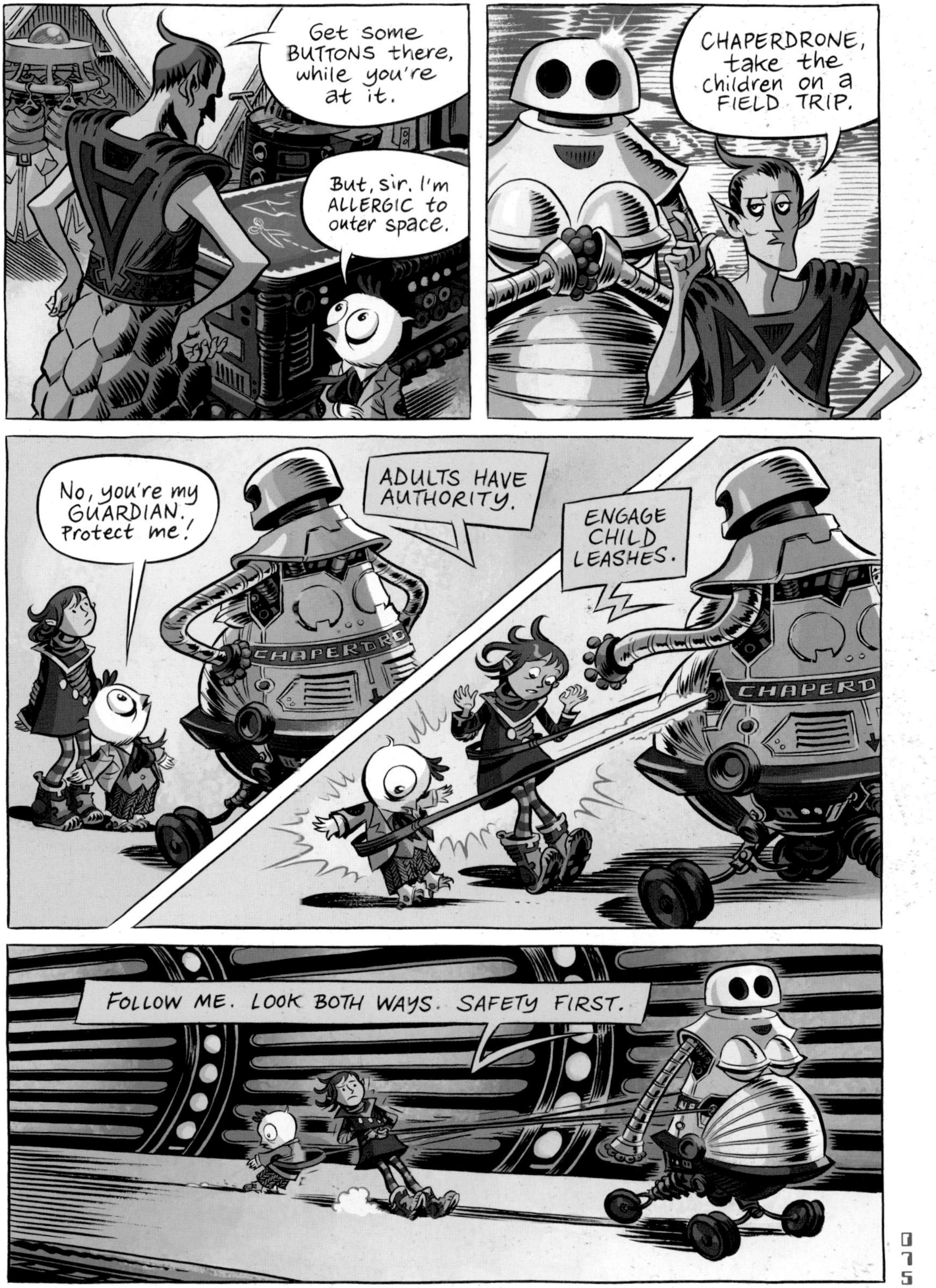
Get some BUTTONS there, while you're at it.
But, sir. I'm ALLERGIC to outer space.
CHAPERDRONE, take the children on a FIELD TRIP.
No, you're my GUARDIAN. Protect me!
ADULTS HAVE AUTHORITY.
CHAPERDRO
ENGAGE CHILD LEASHES.
CHAPERD
FOLLOW ME. LOOK BOTH WAYS. SAFETY FIRST.

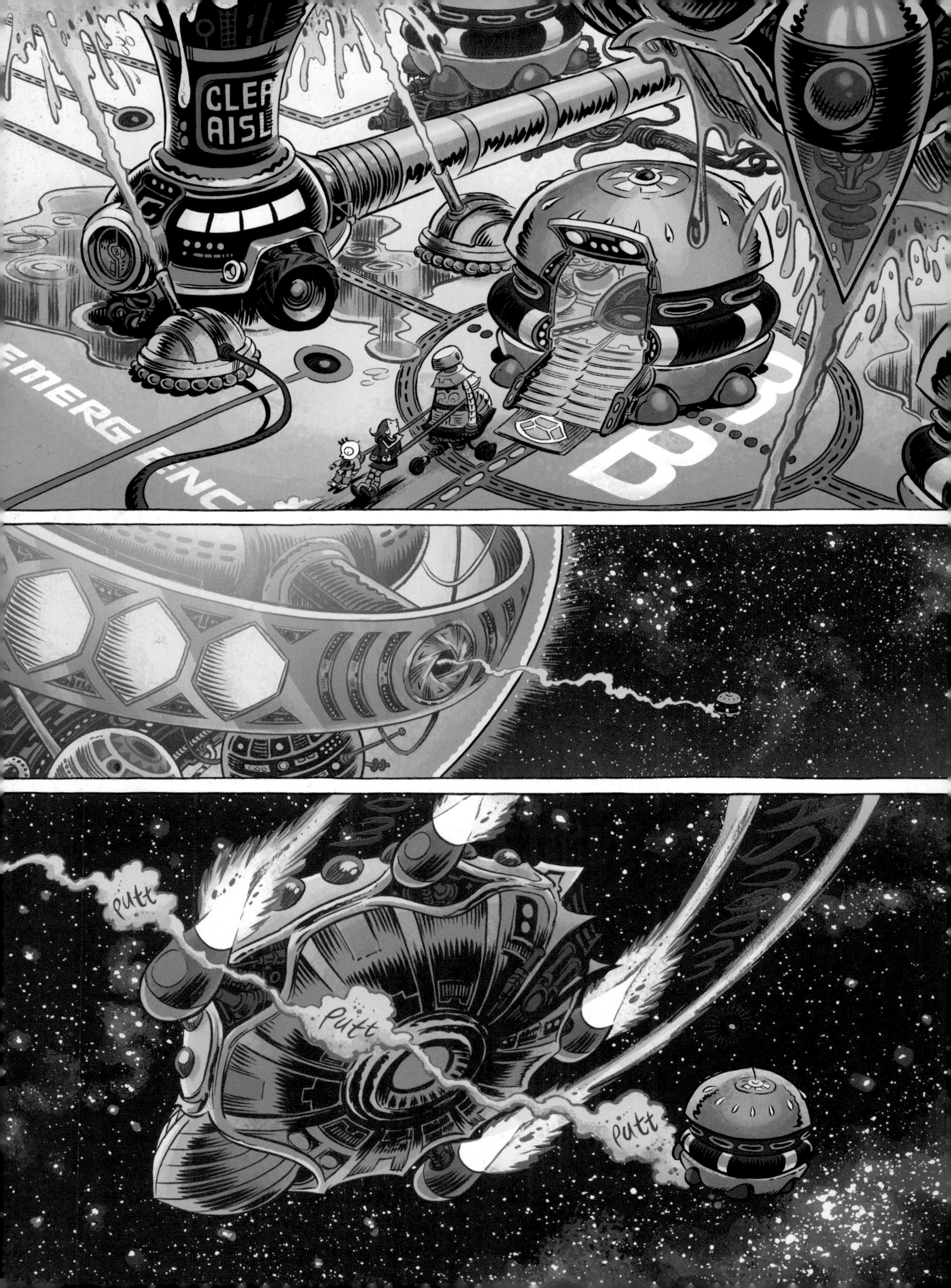
CLEA
AISL
EMERG ENC
B
putt
putt
putt

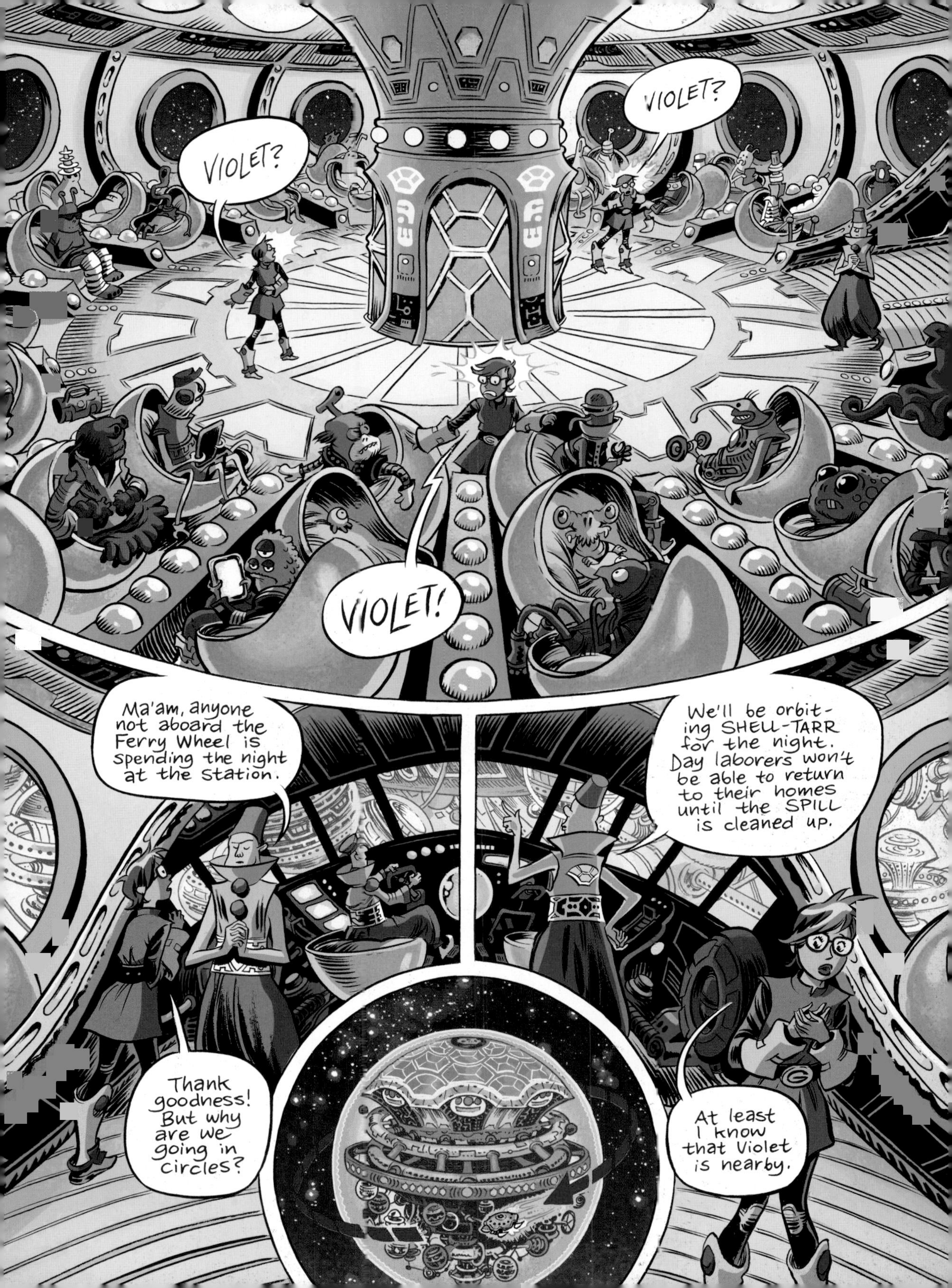
VIOLET?
VIOLET?
VIOLET!
Ma'am, anyone not aboard the Ferry Wheel is spending the night at the station.
We'll be orbit-ing SHELL-TARR for the night. Day laborers won't be able to return to their homes until the SPILL is cleaned up.
Thank goodness! But why are we going in circles?
At least I know that Violet is nearby.

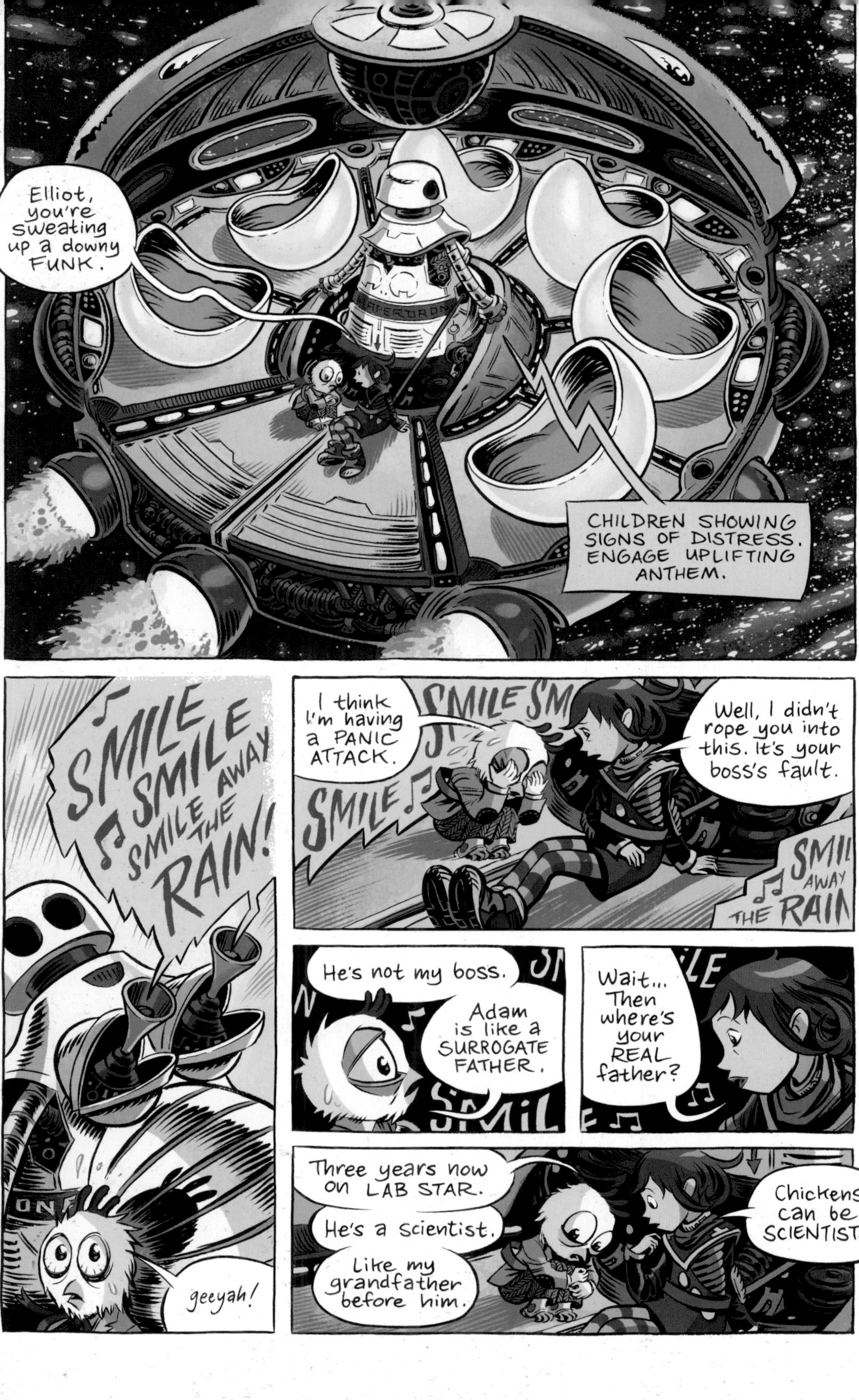

Elliot, you're sweating up a downy FUNK.
CHILDREN SHOWING SIGNS OF DISTRESS. ENGAGE UPLIFTING ANTHEM.
SMILE SMILE SMILE AWAY THE RAIN!
geeyah!
I think I'm having a PANIC ATTACK.
Well, I didn't rope you into this. It's your boss's fault.
SMILE
SMILE
SMIL AWAY THE RAIN
He's not my boss.
Adam is like a SURROGATE FATHER.
Wait... Then where's your REAL father?
Three years now on LAB STAR.
He's a scientist.
Like my grandfather before him.
Chickens can be SCIENTISTS?

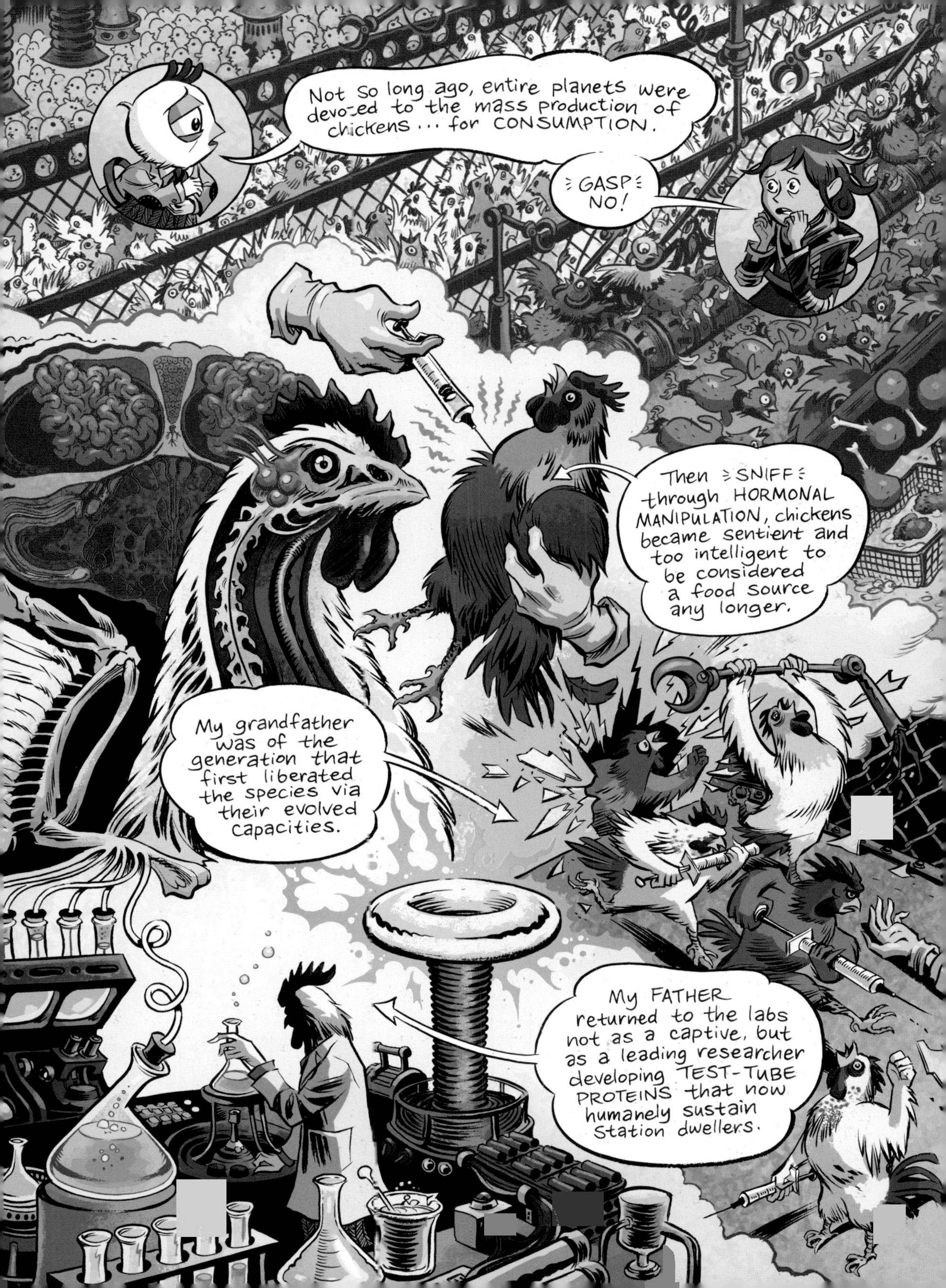

Not so long ago, entire planets were devoted to the mass production of chickens . . . for CONSUMPTION.
≡GASP≡ NO!
Then ≡SNIFF≡ through HORMONAL MANIPULATION, chickens became sentient and too intelligent to be considered a food source any longer.
My grandfather was of the generation that first liberated the species via their evolved capacities.
My FATHER returned to the labs not as a captive, but as a leading researcher developing TEST-TUBE PROTEINS that now humanely sustain Station dwellers.

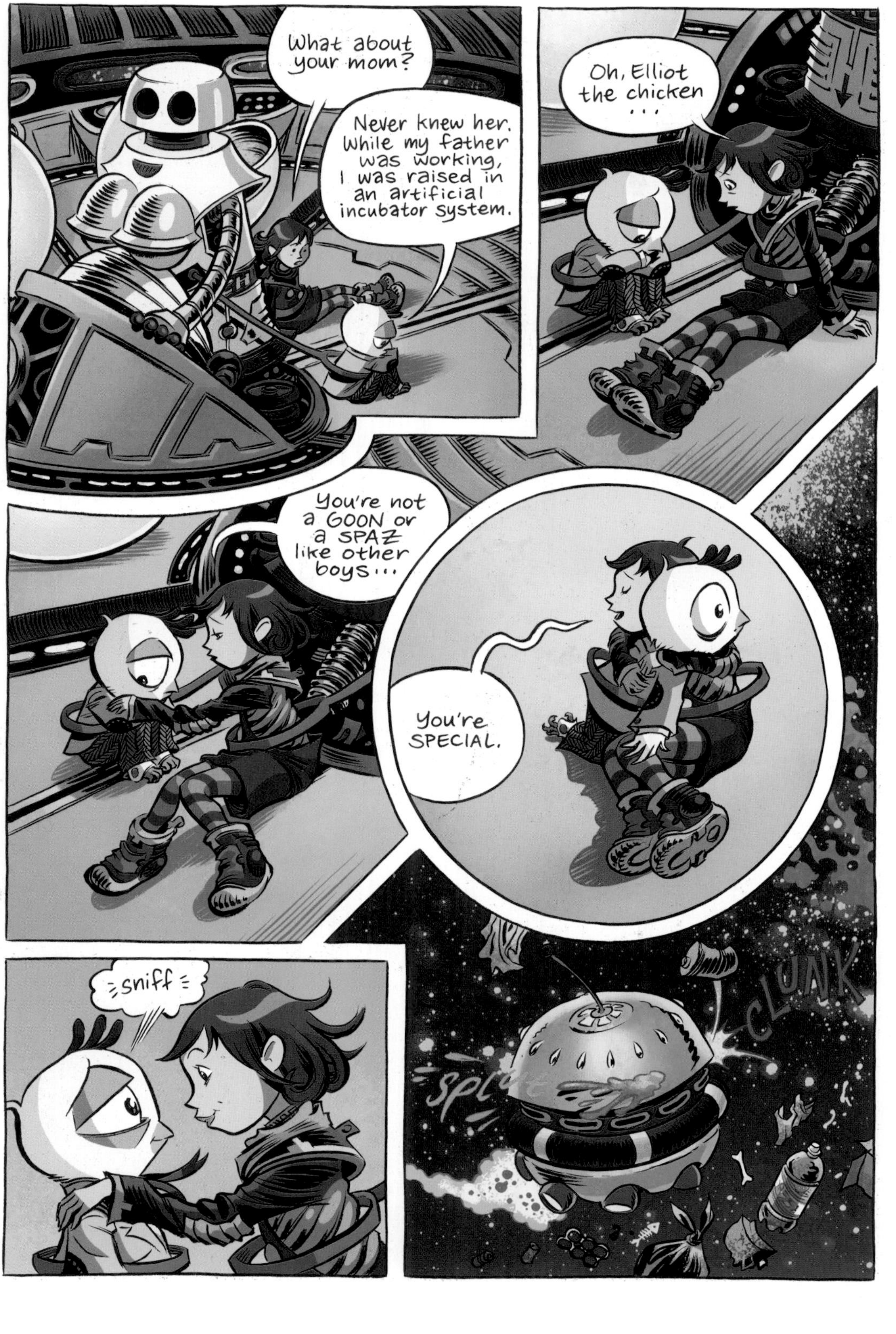
What about your mom?
Never knew her. While my father was working, I was raised in an artificial incubator system.
Oh, Elliot the chicken . . .
You're not a GOON or a SPAZ like other boys . . .
You're SPECIAL.
sniff
SPLAT
CLUNK

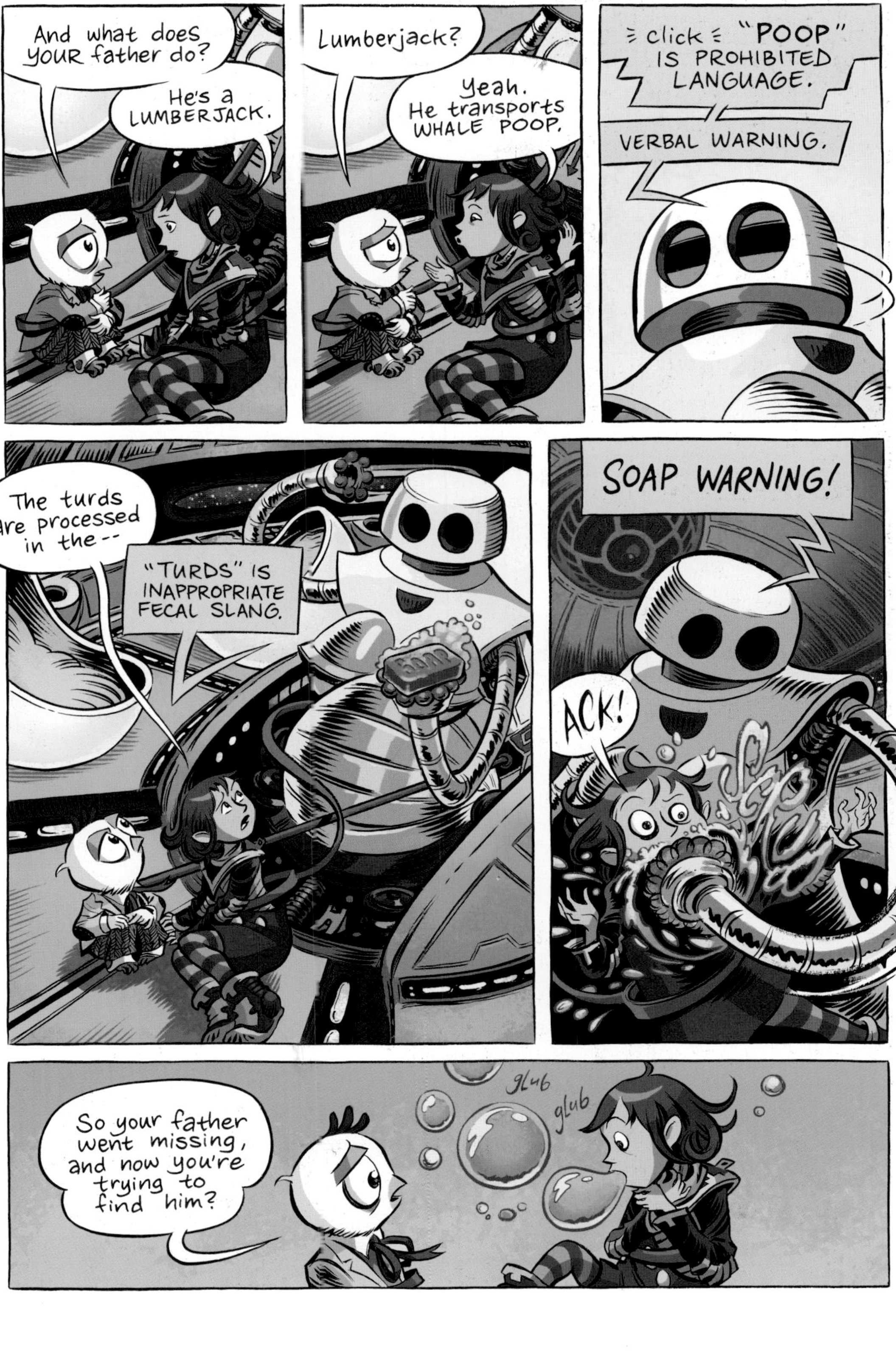
And what does YOUR father do?
He's a LUMBERJACK.
Lumberjack?
Yeah. He transports WHALE POOP.
click "POOP" IS PROHIBITED LANGUAGE.
VERBAL WARNING.
The turds are processed in the--
"TURDS" IS INAPPROPRIATE FECAL SLANG.
SOAP
SOAP WARNING!
ACK!
So your father went missing, and now you're trying to find him?
glub
glub

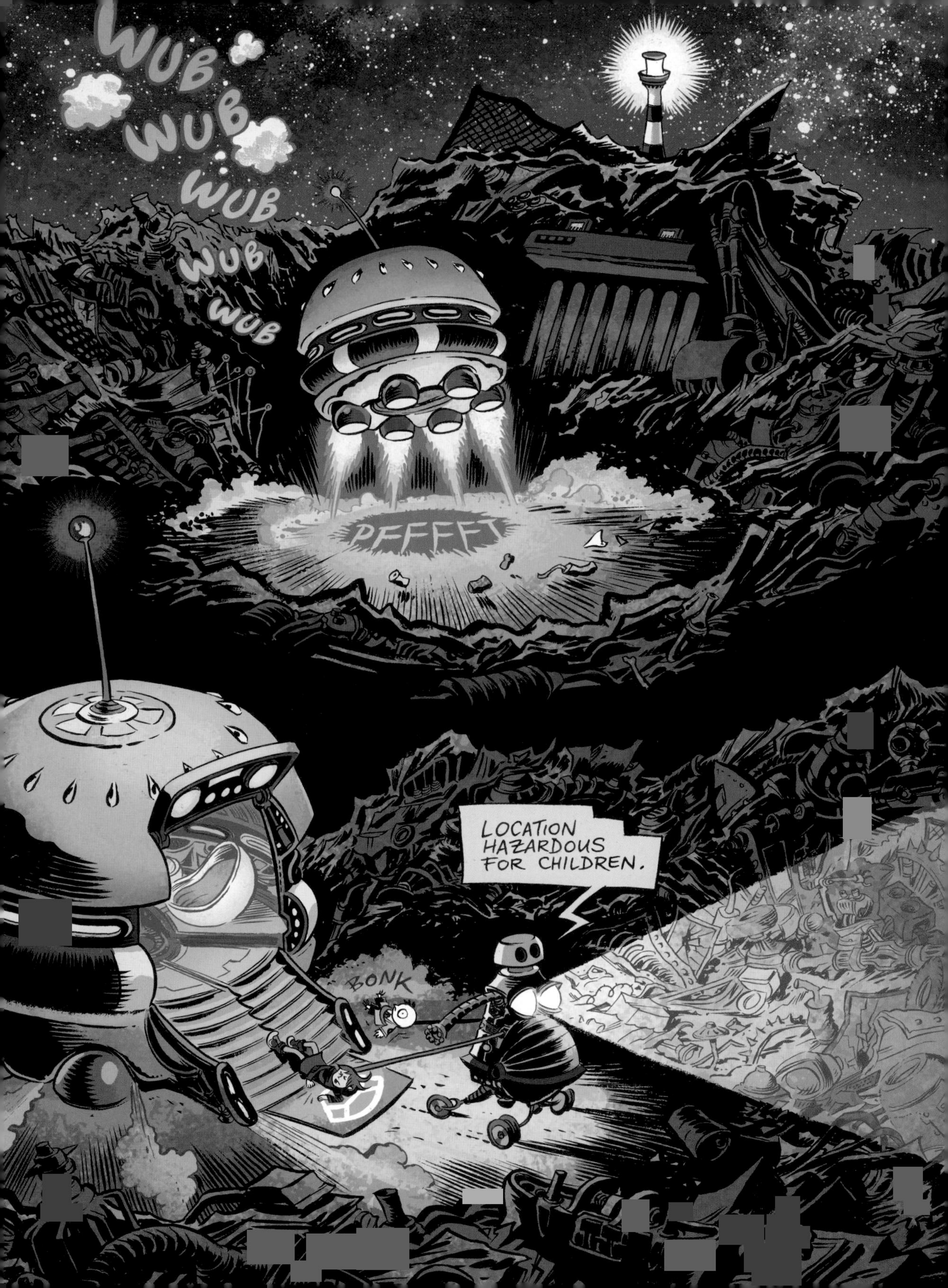
WUB
WUB
WUB
WUB
WUB
PFFFFT
LOCATION HAZARDOUS FOR CHILDREN.
BONK

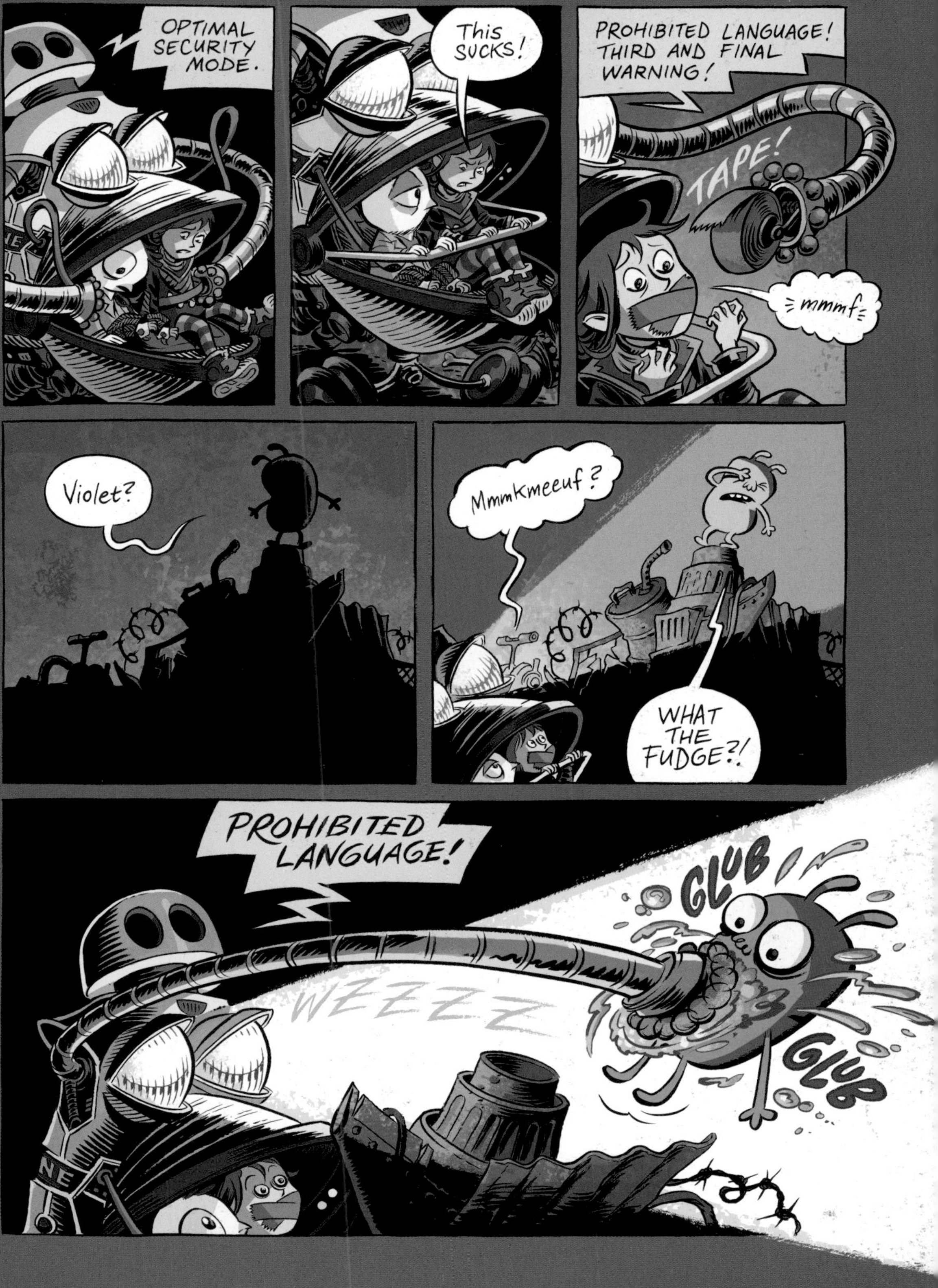
OPTIMAL SECURITY MODE.
This SUCKS!
PROHIBITED LANGUAGE! THIRD AND FINAL WARNING!
TAPE!
mmmf
Violet?
Mmmkmeeuf?
WHAT THE FUDGE?!
PROHIBITED LANGUAGE!
WZZZZZ
GLUB
GLUB

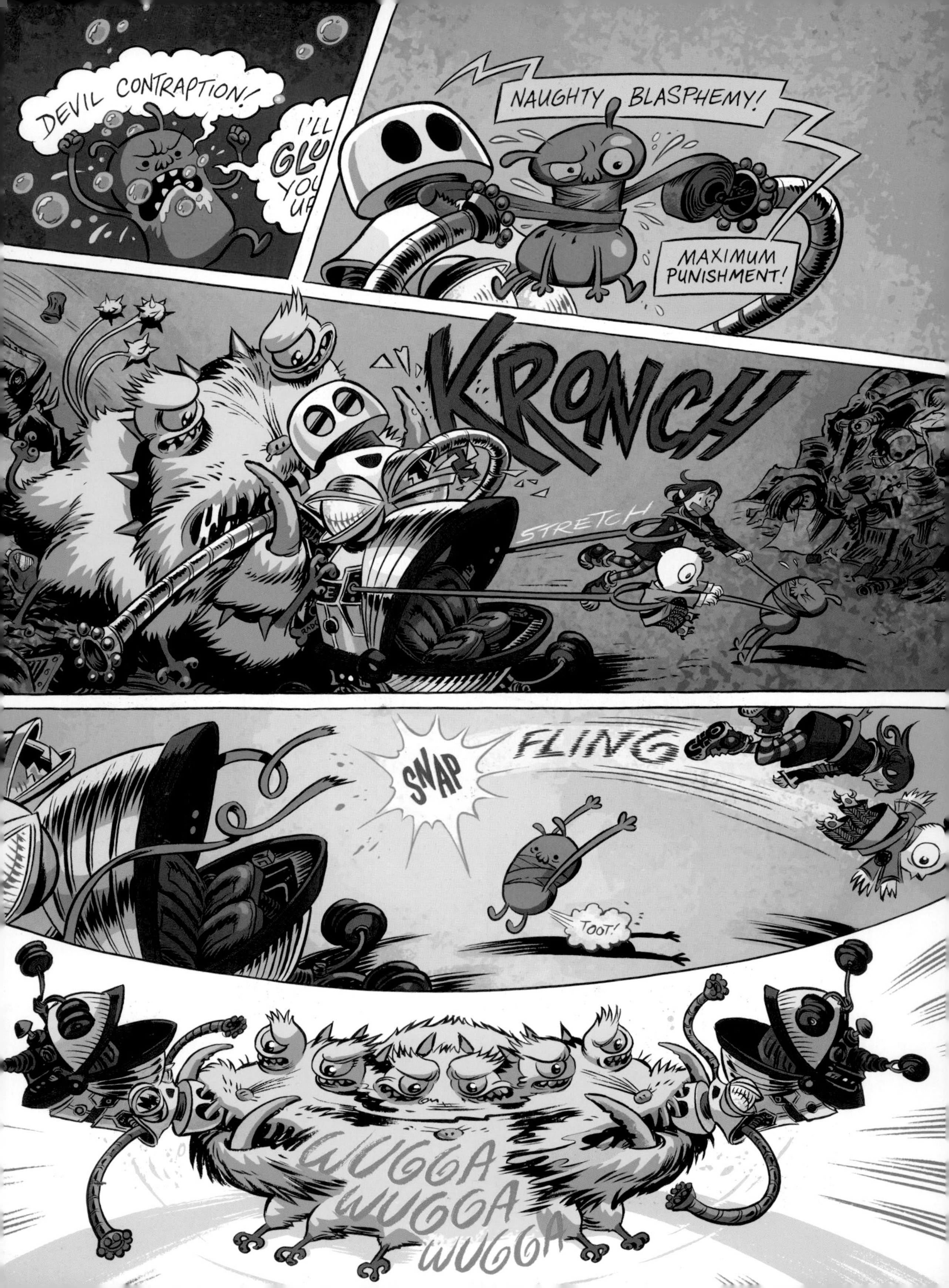
DEVIL CONTRAPTION!
I'LL GLU YOU UP
NAUGHTY BLASPHEMY!
MAXIMUM PUNISHMENT!
KRONCH
STRETCH
SNAP
FLING
TOOT!
WUGGA
WUGGA
WUGGA

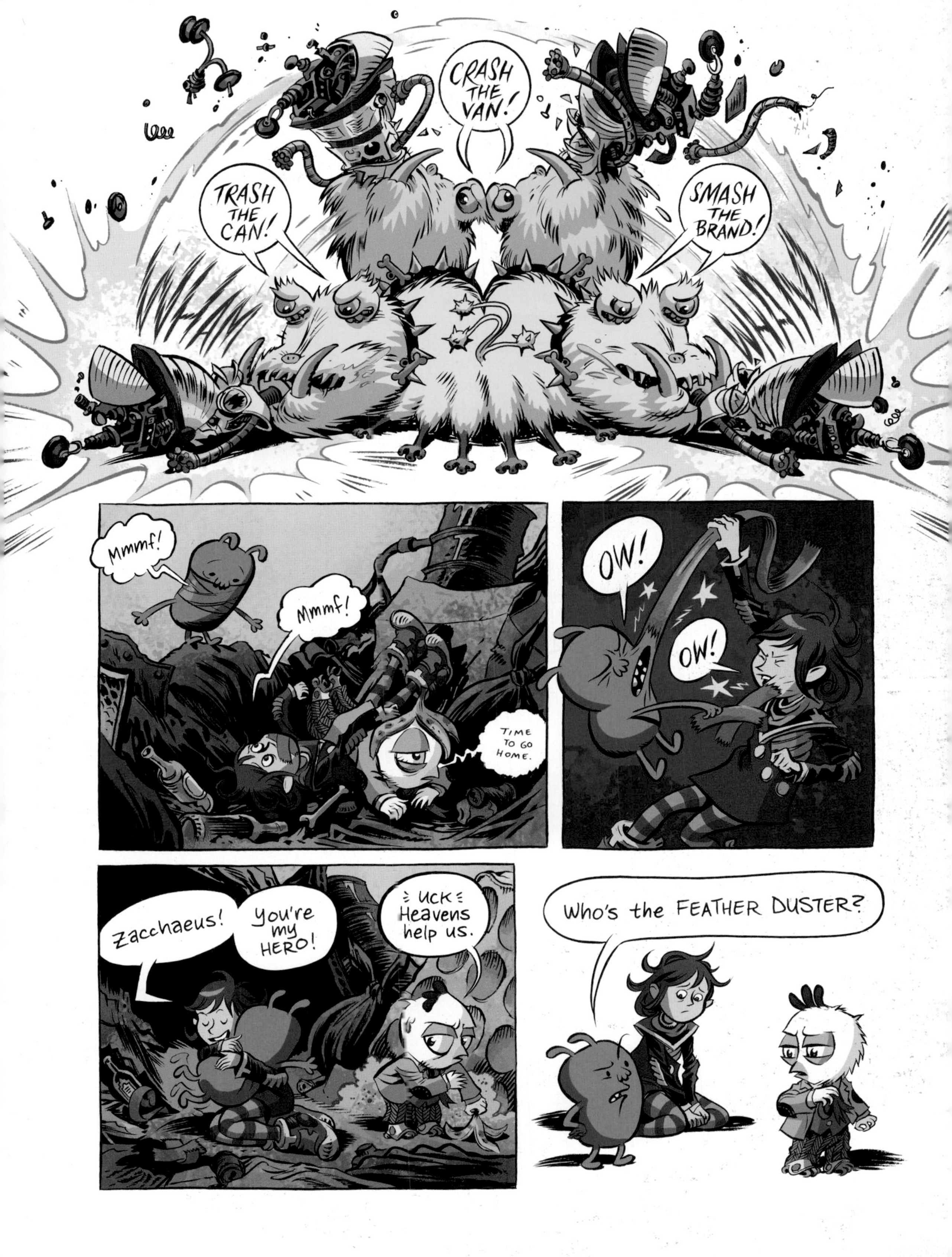
TRASH THE CAN!
CRASH THE VAN!
SMASH THE BRAND!
Mmmf!
Mmmf!
TIME TO GO HOME.
OW!
OW!
Zacchaeus!
You're my HERO!
UCK Heavens help us.
Who's the FEATHER DUSTER?

Elliot, I need your BUTTON-HUNTING skills to find that MUSKY part...

...then we can go search for my dad!

"WE"?

I'll HOT-WIRE the burger bus for MANUAL control!

That guy is a CRIMINAL!

No... He's my friend Zacchaeus!

Is he named after the wee, little man who climbed the sycamore tree?

Are you MOCKING me?!

TOSS

It's a biblical reference.

Well, I'm not religious. And I'm no "wee man."

I'm the LAST LIVING LUMPKIN!

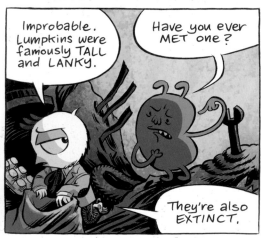

Improbable. Lumpkins were famously TALL and LANKY.

Have you ever MET one?

They're also EXTINCT.

Not while I'm still kicking.

That's right.

I'm the ORPHAN OF MY SPECIES!

Hmmm... Hand-carved ivory swirlback.

Rare specimen.

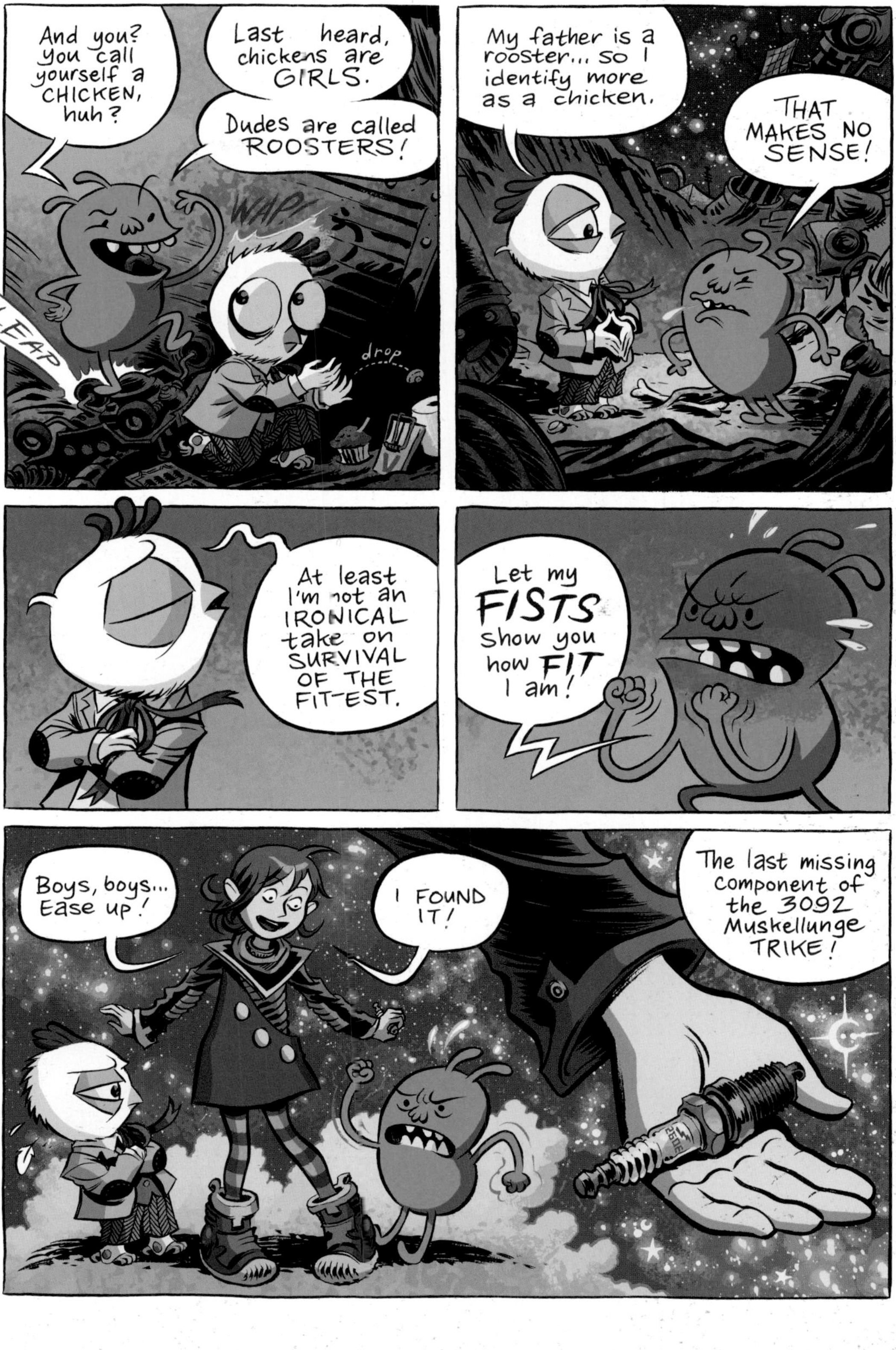
And you? You call yourself a CHICKEN, huh?
Last heard, chickens are GIRLS.
Dudes are called ROOSTERS!
WAP!
LEAP
drop
My father is a rooster... so I identify more as a chicken.
THAT MAKES NO SENSE!
At least I'm not an IRONICAL take on SURVIVAL OF THE FIT-EST.
Let my FISTS show you how FIT I am!
Boys, boys... Ease up!
I FOUND IT!
The last missing component of the 3092 Muskellunge TRIKE!

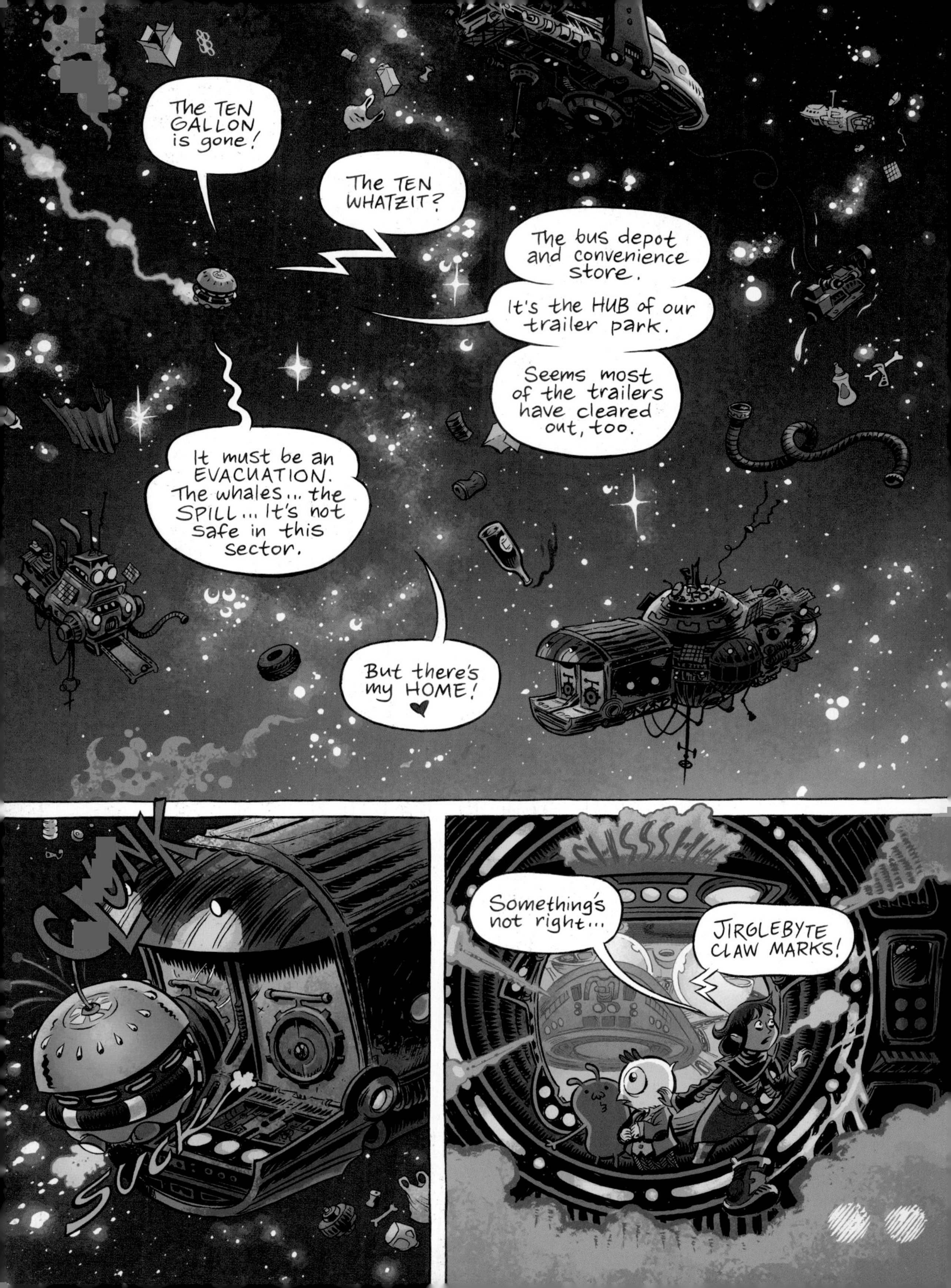
The TEN GALLON is gone!
The TEN WHATZIT?
The bus depot and convenience store.
It's the HUB of our trailer park.
Seems most of the trailers have cleared out, too.
It must be an EVACUATION. The whales... the SPILL... It's not safe in this sector.
But there's my HOME!
SUCK
Something's not right...
JIRGLEBYTE CLAW MARKS!

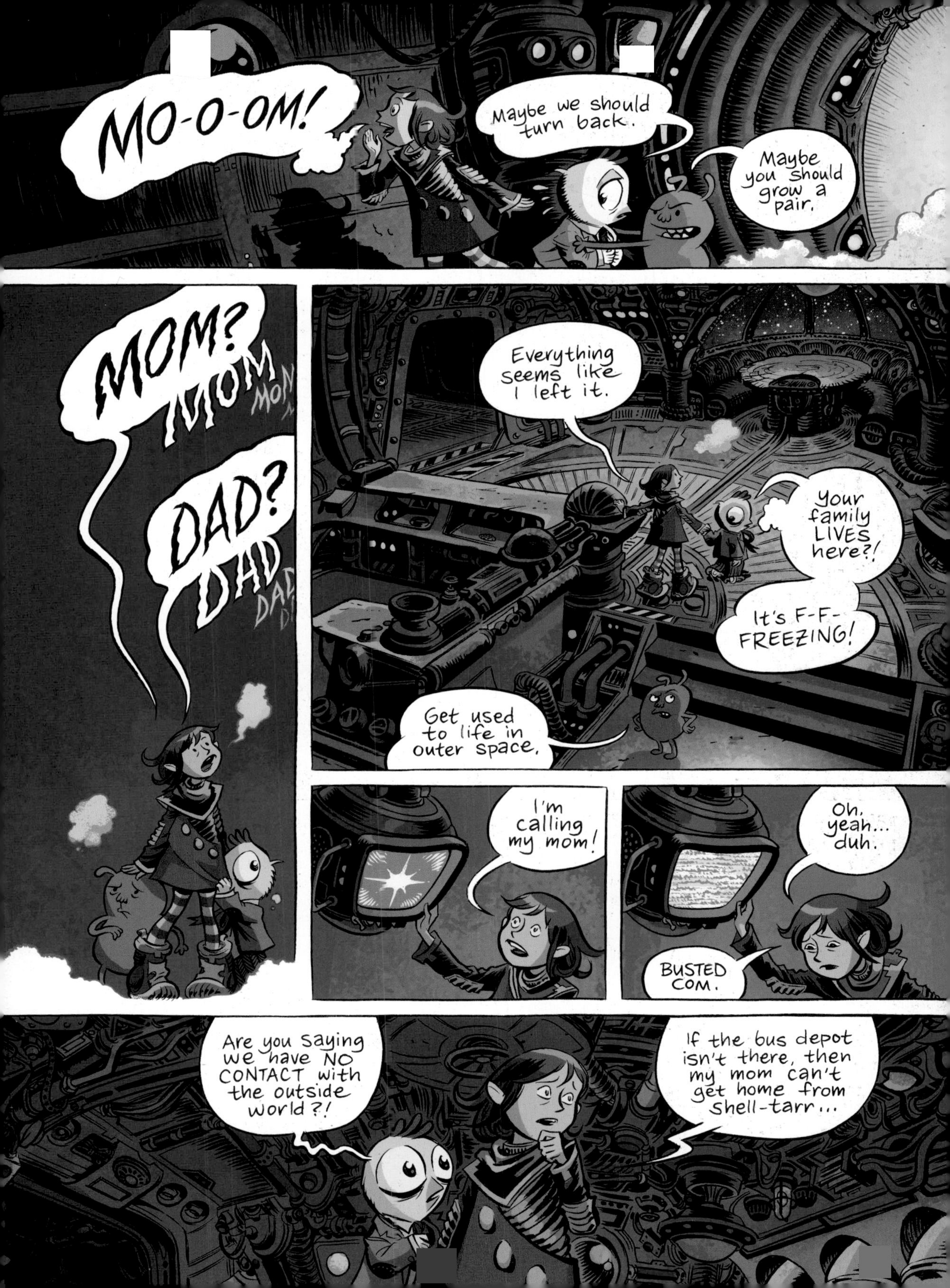
MO-O-OM!
Maybe we should turn back.
Maybe you should grow a pair.
MOM? MOM MOM
DAD? DAD DAD
Everything seems like I left it.
Your family LIVES here?!
It's F-F-FREEZING!
Get used to life in outer space.
I'm calling my mom!
Oh. yeah... duh.
BUSTED COM.
Are you saying we have NO CONTACT with the outside world?!
If the bus depot isn't there, then my mom can't get home from Shell-tarr...

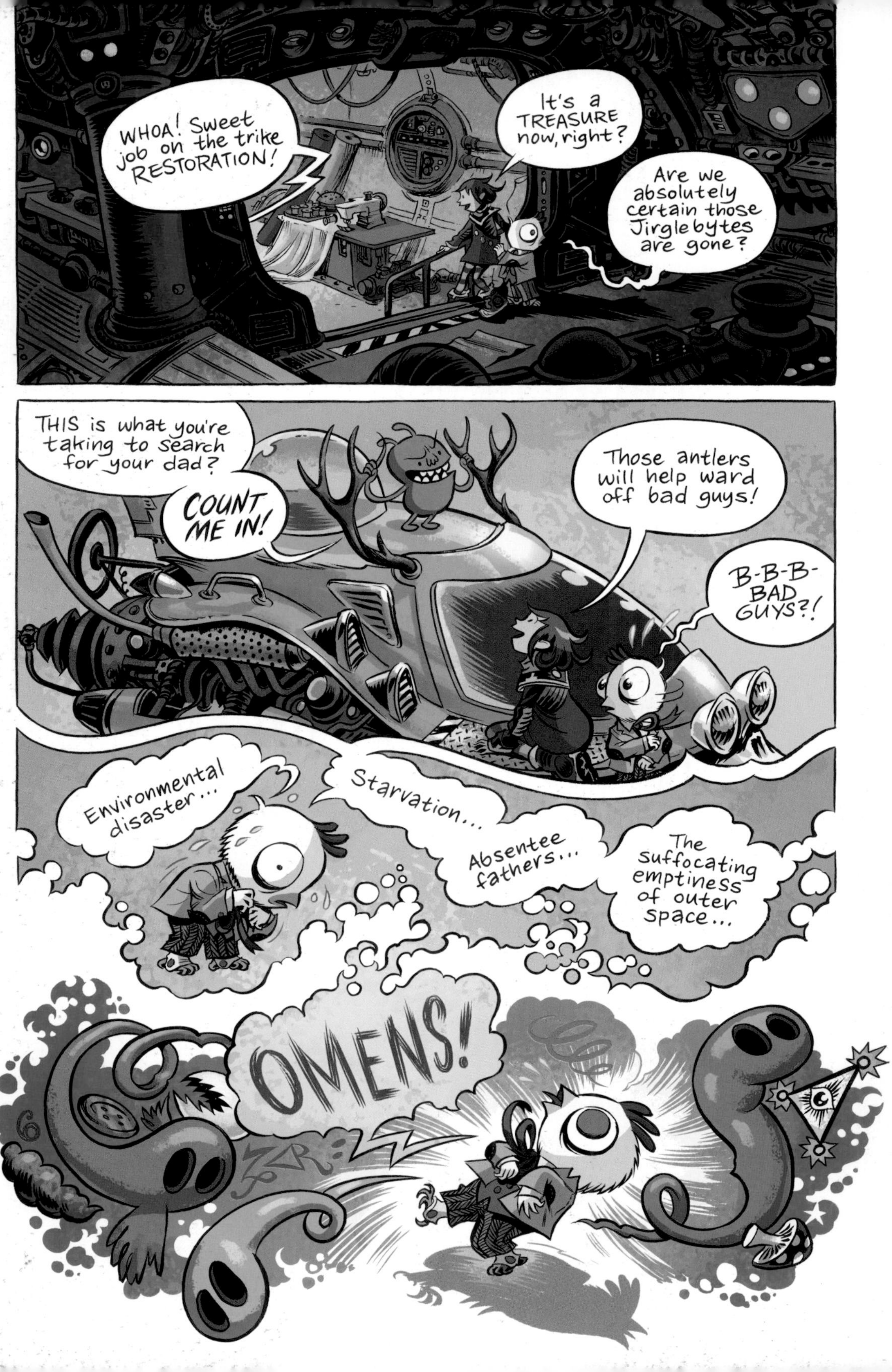
WHOA! Sweet job on the trike RESTORATION!
It's a TREASURE now, right?
Are we absolutely certain those Jirglebytes are gone?
THIS is what you're taking to search for your dad?
COUNT ME IN!
Those antlers will help ward off bad guys!
B-B-B-BAD GUYS?!
Environmental disaster...
Starvation...
Absentee fathers...
The suffocating emptiness of outer space...
OMENS!

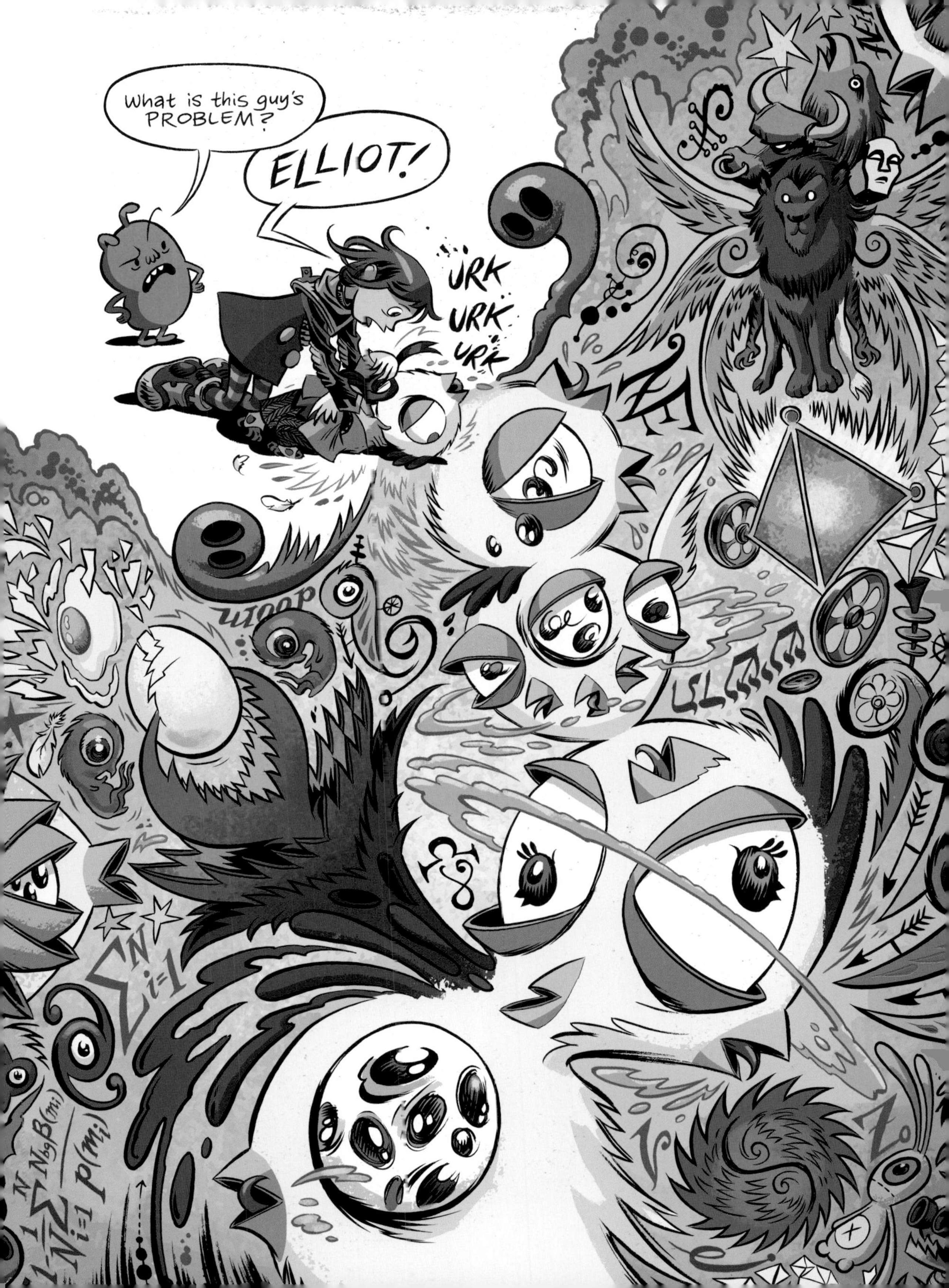

What is this guy's PROBLEM?
ELLIOT!
URK URK URK

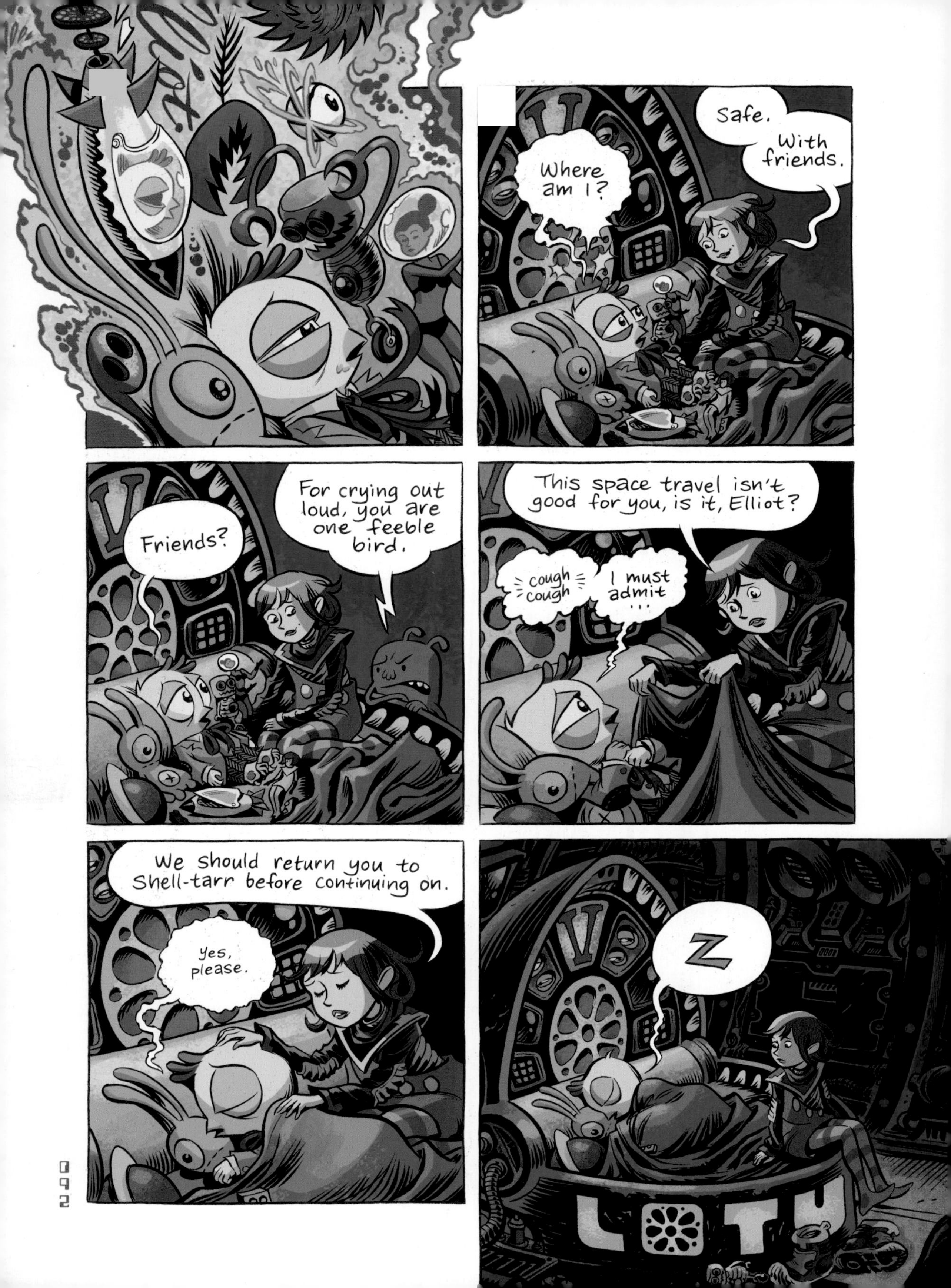
Where am I?
Safe.
With friends.
Friends?
For crying out loud, you are one feeble bird.
This space travel isn't good for you, is it, Elliot?
cough cough
I must admit . . .
We should return you to Shell-tarr before continuing on.
yes, please.
Z

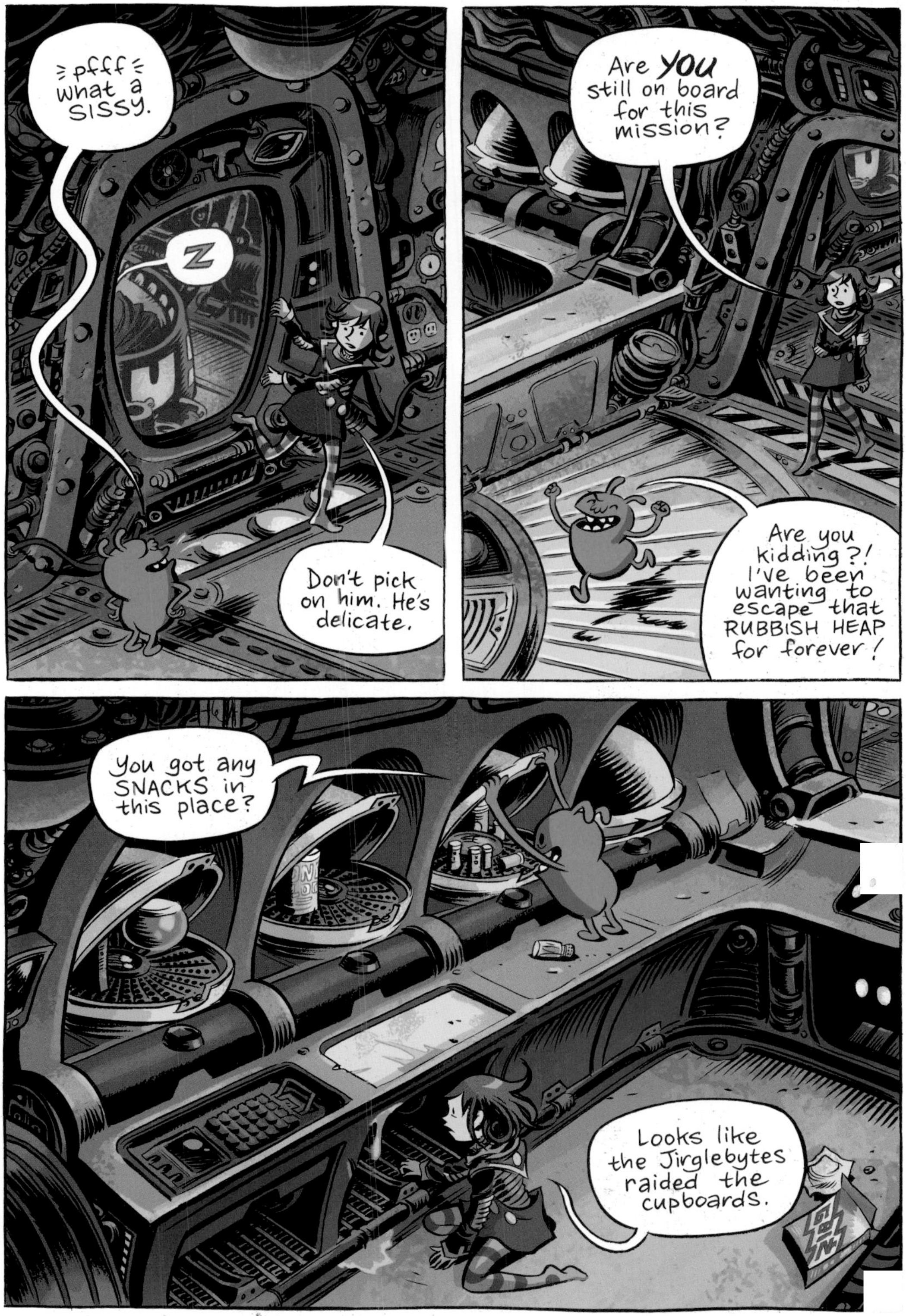
pfff what a SISSY.
Z
Don't pick on him. He's delicate.
Are YOU still on board for this mission?
Are you kidding?! I've been wanting to escape that RUBBISH HEAP for forever!
You got any SNACKS in this place?
Looks like the Jirglebytes raided the cupboards.

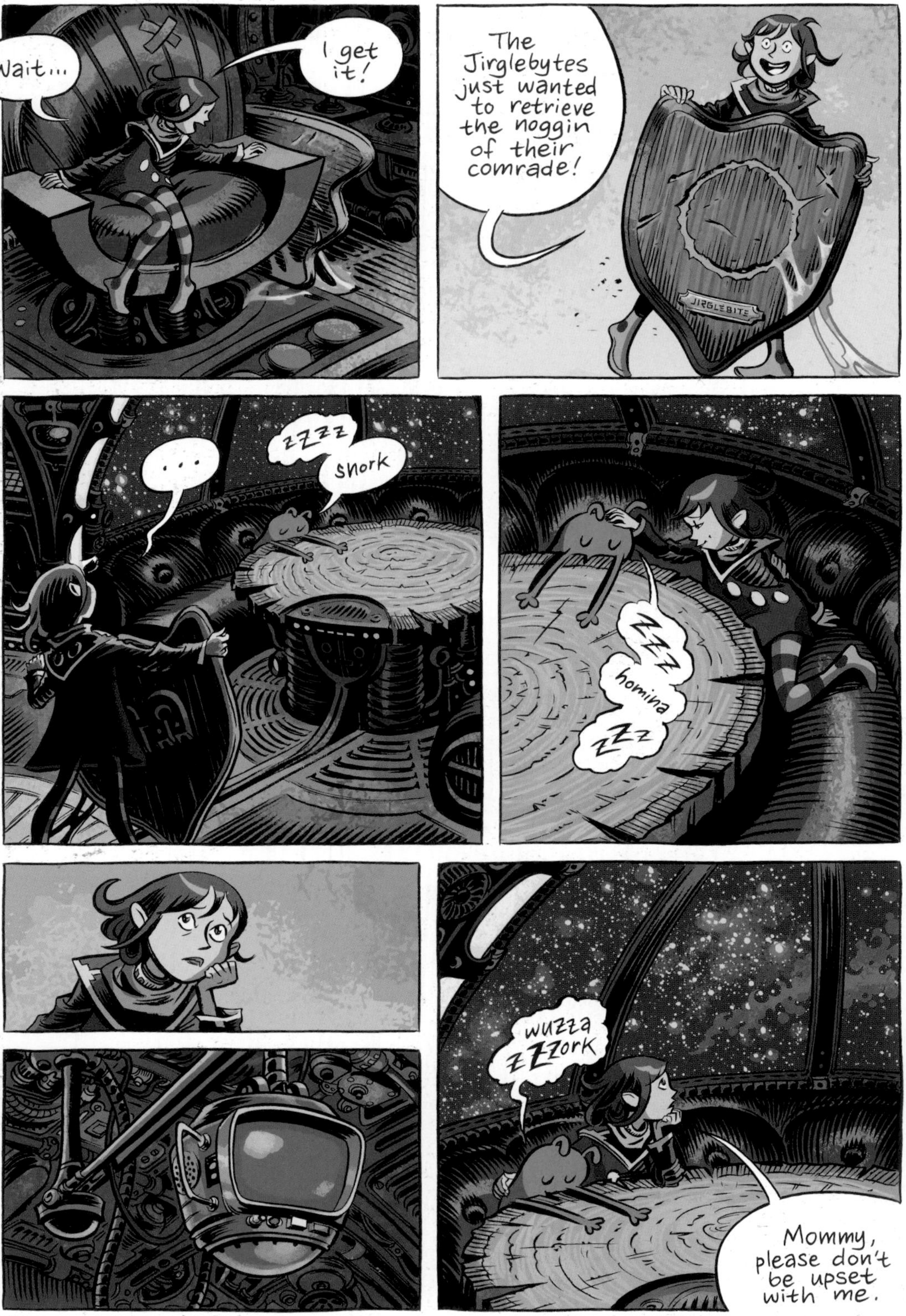
Wait...
I get it!
The Jirglebytes just wanted to retrieve the noggin of their comrade!
JIRGLEBITE
...
ZZZZ
snork
ZZZ
homina
ZZZ
wuzza ZZZork
Mommy, please don't be upset with me.

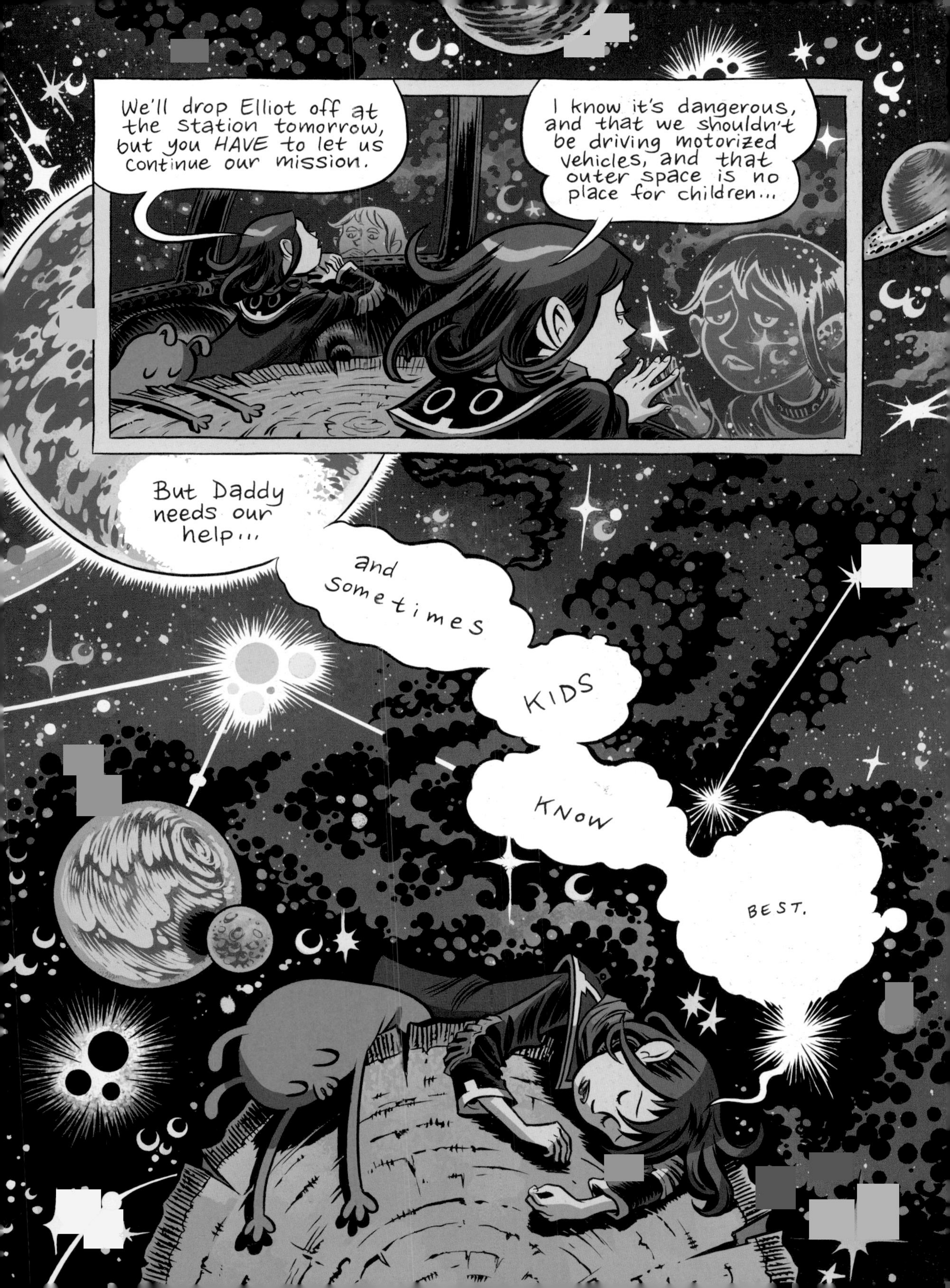
We'll drop Elliot off at the station tomorrow, but you HAVE to let us continue our mission.
I know it's dangerous, and that we shouldn't be driving motorized vehicles, and that outer space is no place for children...
But Daddy needs our help...
and sometimes KIDS KNOW BEST.

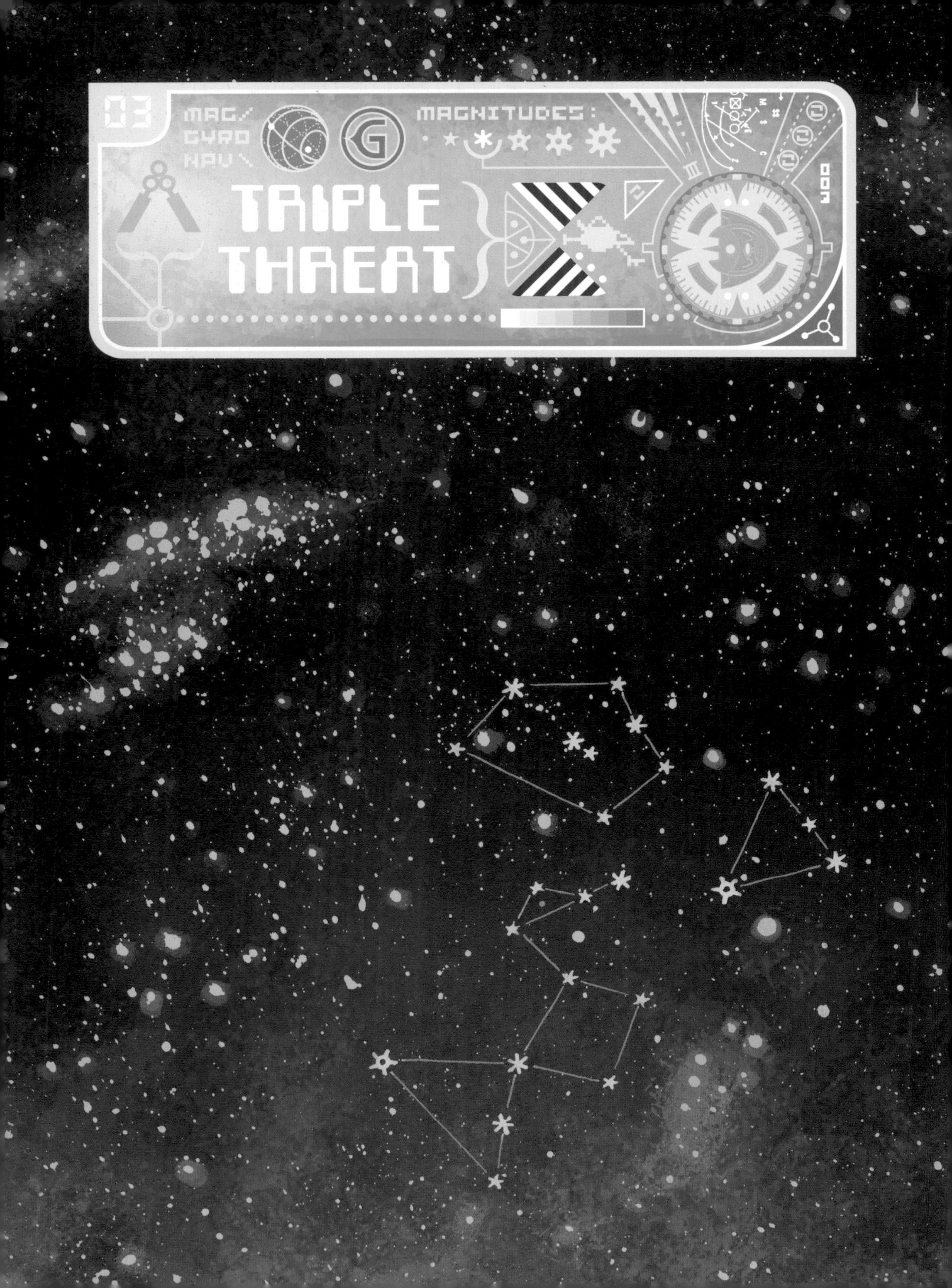
03
MAG/
GYRO
NAV
MAGNITUDES:
TRIPLE
THREAT

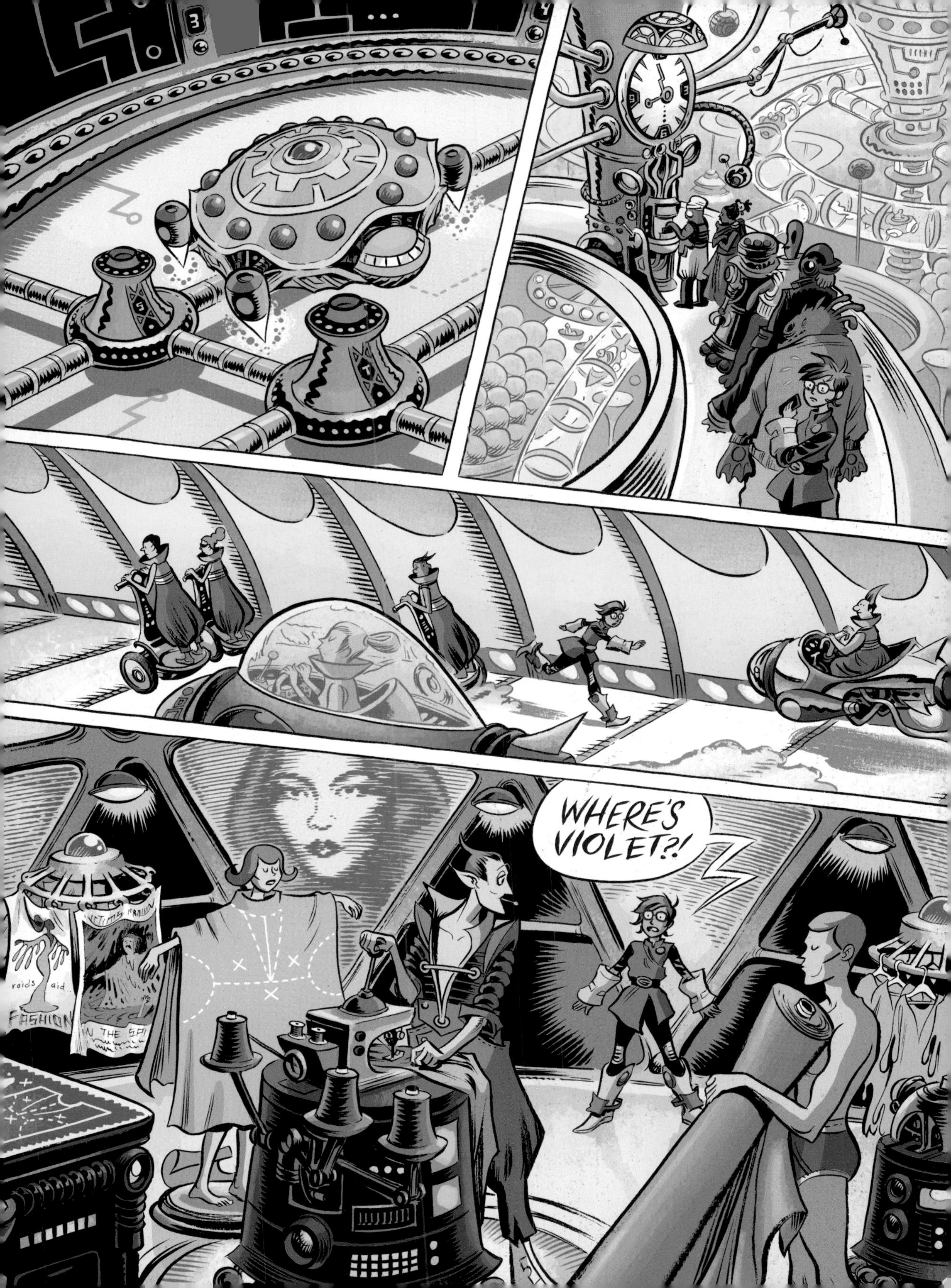
WHERE'S VIOLET?!
FASHION

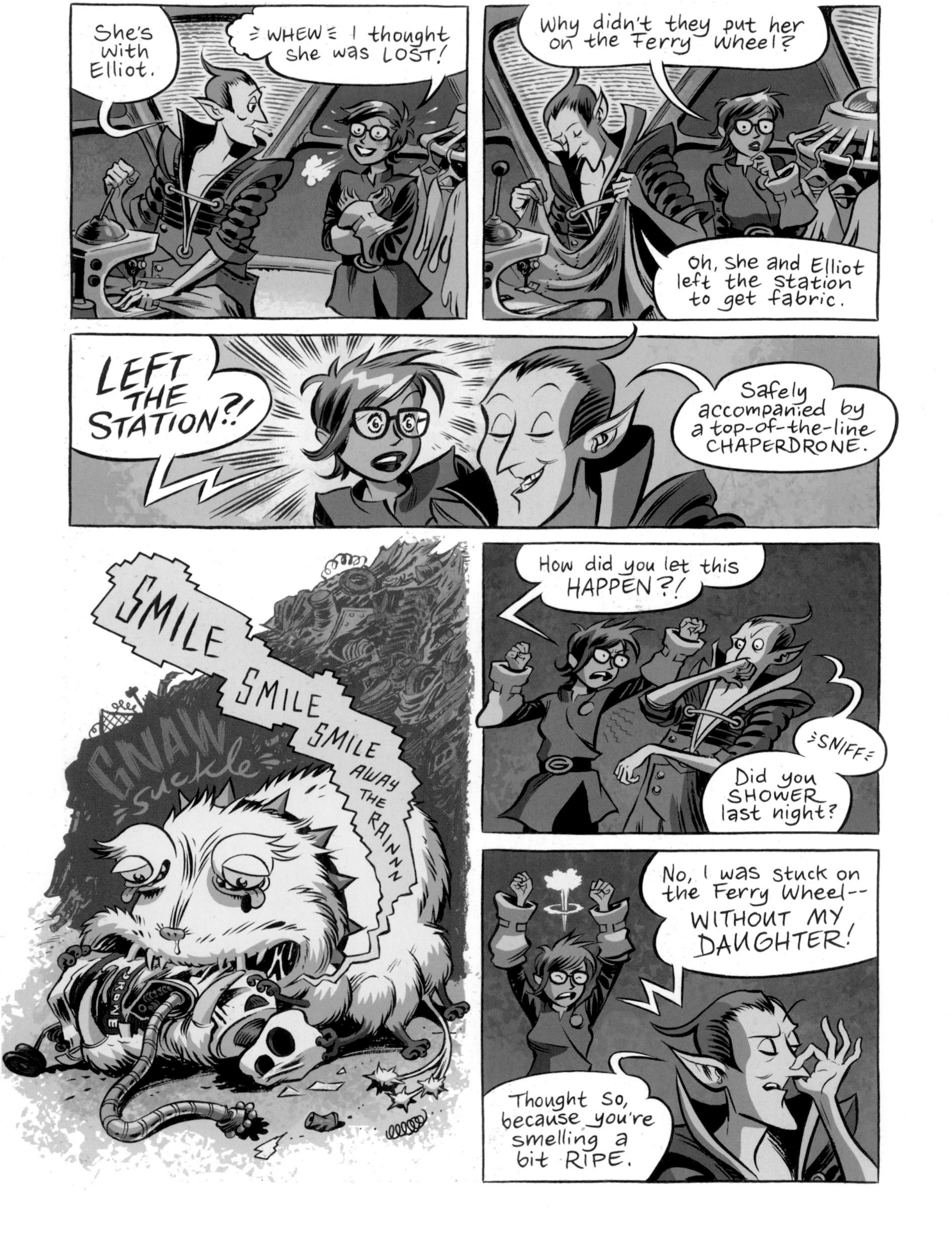

She's with Elliot.
WHEW I thought she was LOST!
Why didn't they put her on the Ferry Wheel?
Oh, she and Elliot left the station to get fabric.
LEFT THE STATION?!
Safely accompanied by a top-of-the-line CHAPERDRONE.
SMILE
SMILE
SMILE
AWAY THE RAINNN
GNAW
suckle
How did you let this HAPPEN?!
SNIFF
Did you SHOWER last night?
No, I was stuck on the Ferry Wheel-- WITHOUT MY DAUGHTER!
Thought so, because you're smelling a bit RIPE.

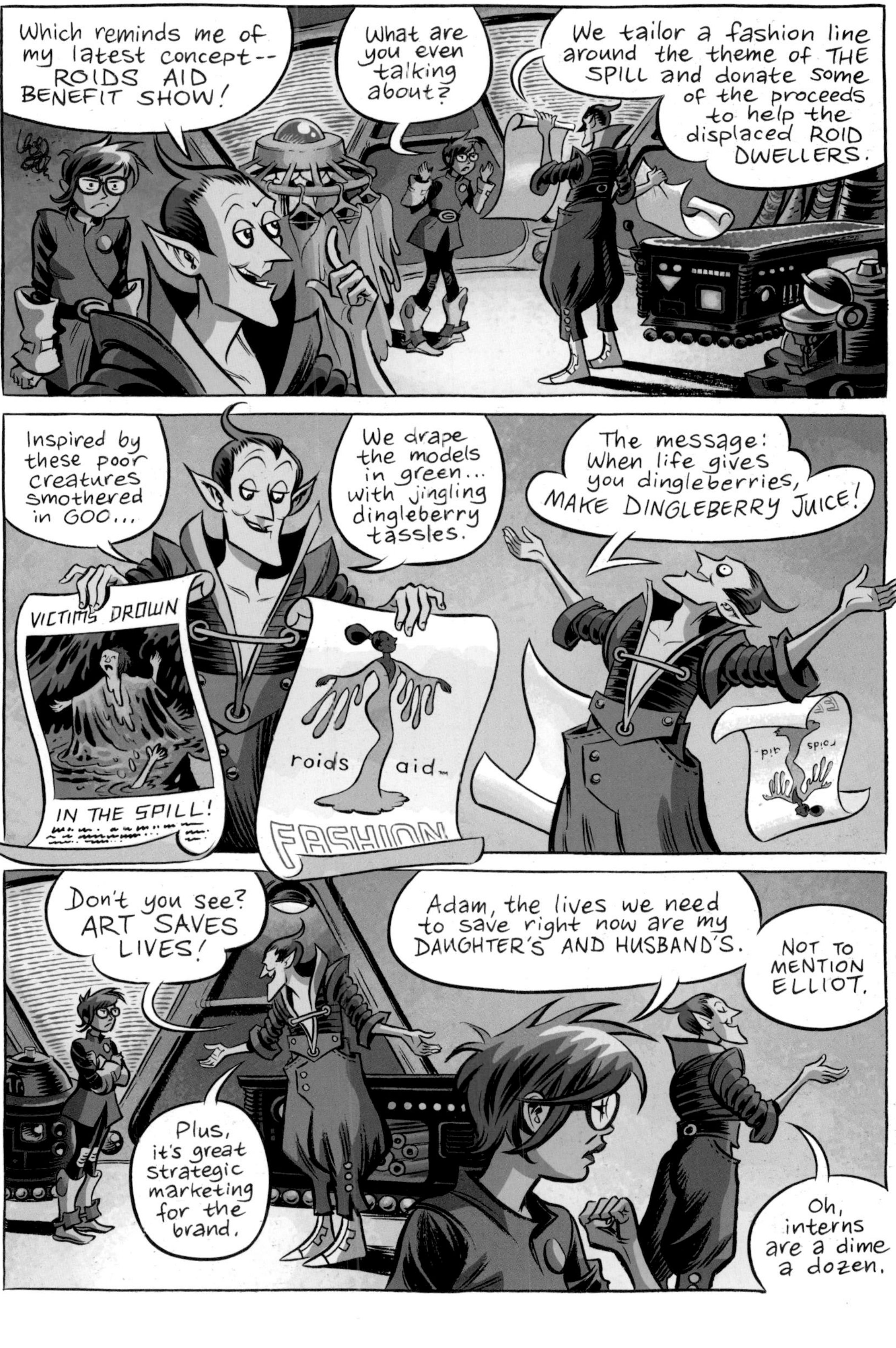
Which reminds me of my latest concept-- ROIDS AID BENEFIT SHOW!
What are you even talking about?
We tailor a fashion line around the theme of THE SPILL and donate some of the proceeds to help the displaced ROID DWELLERS.
Inspired by these poor creatures smothered in GOO...
VICTIMS DROWN
IN THE SPILL!
We drape the models in green... with jingling dingleberry tassles.
roids aid™
FASHION
The message: When life gives you dingleberries, MAKE DINGLEBERRY JUICE!
Don't you see? ART SAVES LIVES!
Plus, it's great strategic marketing for the brand.
Adam, the lives we need to save right now are my DAUGHTER'S AND HUSBAND'S.
NOT TO MENTION ELLIOT.
Oh, interns are a dime a dozen.

GEEYAH!

Elliot! Were you having a NIGHTMARE?!

AN ESCHATOLOGICAL VISION.

Scatological?

NO!

Well... kind of.

ESCHATOLOGY is the serious study of the END OF THE WORLD.

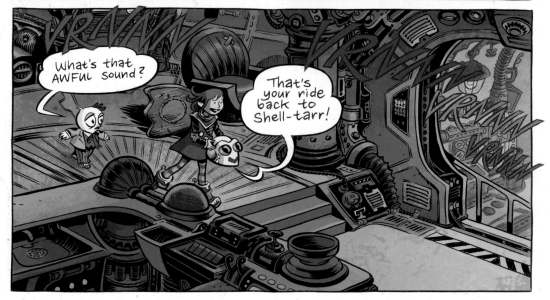

What's that AWFUL sound?

That's your ride back to Shell-tarr!

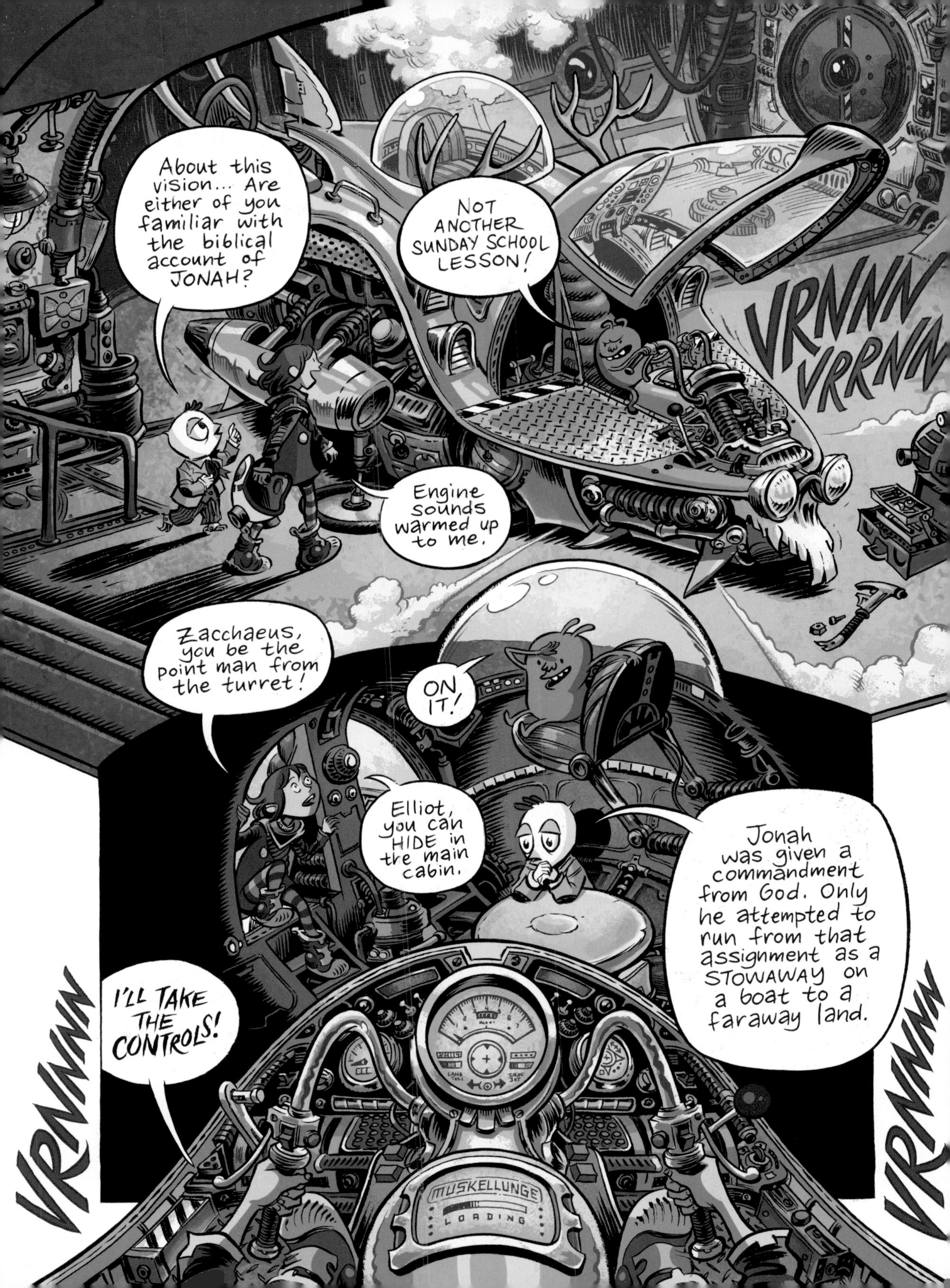
About this vision... Are either of you familiar with the biblical account of JONAH?
NOT ANOTHER SUNDAY SCHOOL LESSON!
VRNNN VRRNN
Engine sounds warmed up to me.
Zacchaeus, you be the point man from the turret!
ON IT!
Elliot, you can HIDE in the main cabin.
Jonah was given a commandment from God. Only he attempted to run from that assignment as a STOWAWAY on a boat to a faraway land.
I'LL TAKE THE CONTROLS!
VRNNNN
VRNNNN
MUSKELLUNGE
LOADING

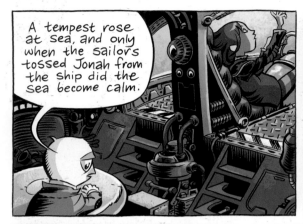

A tempest rose at sea, and only when the sailors tossed Jonah from the ship did the sea become calm.

Here goes...

Perhaps I'm this mission's JONAH...

KSSSH

...and after you UNLOAD THE BALLAST, it'll be smooth sailing for you from here on out.

Sounds about right to me.

On the other hand, maybe there's some COSMIC REASON for me being here. Maybe if I walk away, I'm simply fleeing my destiny.

Neither of us understand a WORD you're saying.

What I'm saying...

...is that despite common sense...

...I want to join you two.

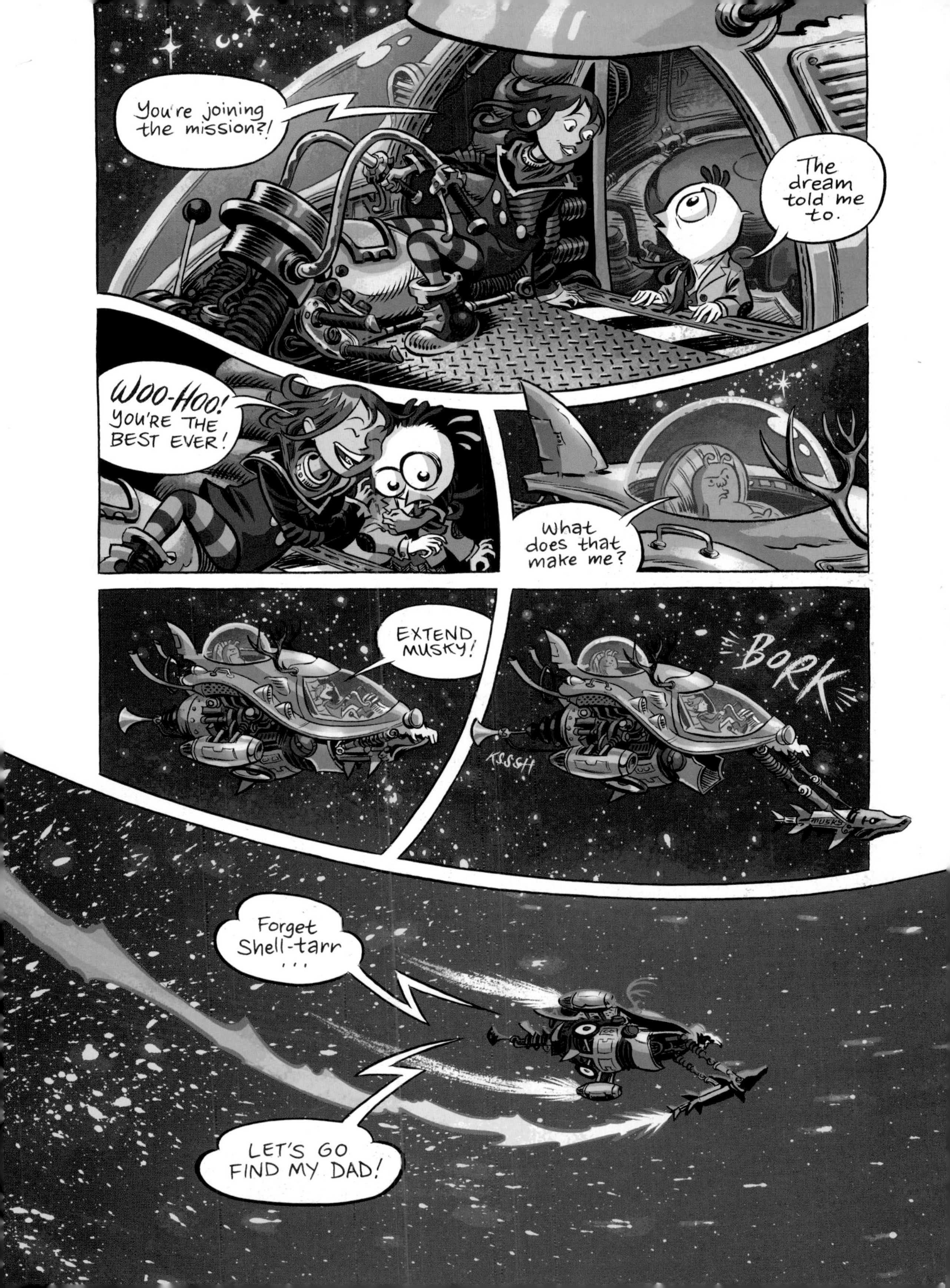
You're joining the mission?!
The dream told me to.
WOO-HOO! YOU'RE THE BEST EVER!
What does that make me?
EXTEND MUSKY!
KSSSH
BORK
MUSKS
Forget Shell-tarr . . .
LET'S GO FIND MY DAD!

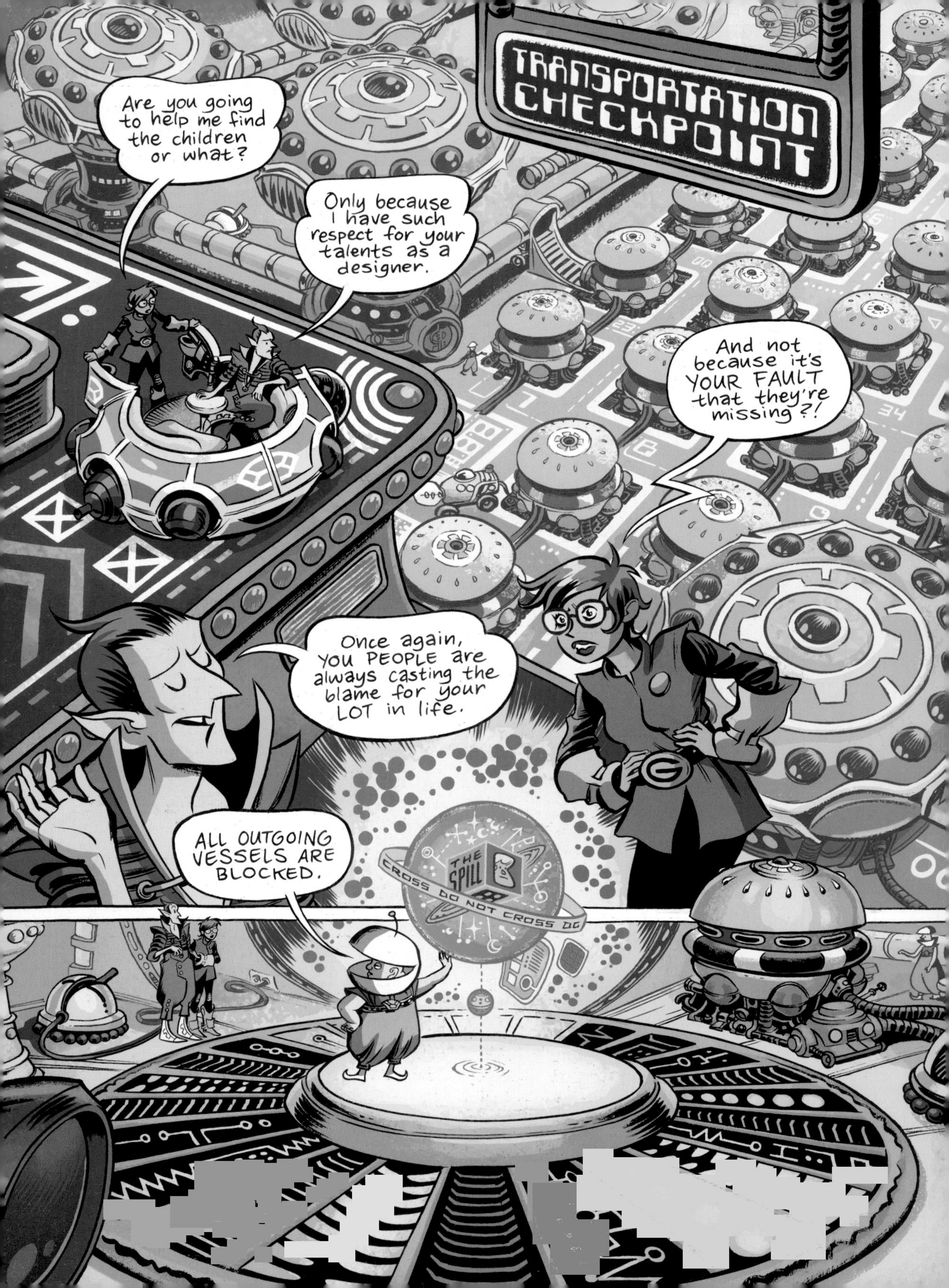
TRANSPORTATION CHECKPOINT
Are you going to help me find the children or what?
Only because I have such respect for your talents as a designer.
And not because it's YOUR FAULT that they're missing?!
Once again, YOU PEOPLE are always casting the blame for your LOT in life.
ALL OUTGOING VESSELS ARE BLOCKED.
THE SPILL
CROSS DO NOT CROSS DO

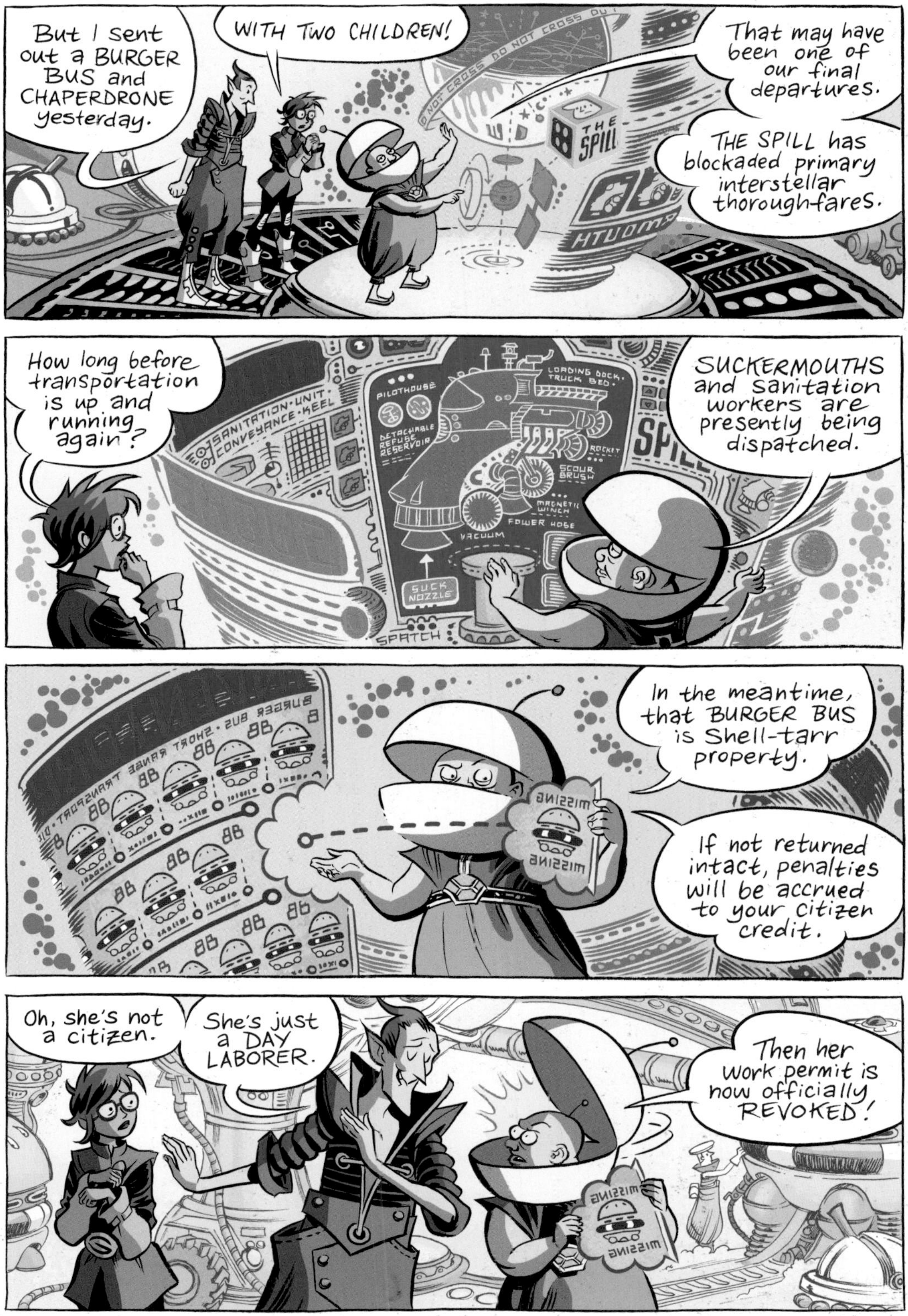
But I sent out a BURGER BUS and CHAPERDRONE yesterday.
WITH TWO CHILDREN!
That may have been one of our final departures.
THE SPILL has blockaded primary interstellar thoroughfares.
THE SPILL
How long before transportation is up and running again?
SUCKERMOUTHS and sanitation workers are presently being dispatched.
SANITATION · UNIT · CONVEYANCE · KEEL
PILOTHOUSE
LOADING DOCK, TRUCK BED
DETACHABLE REFUSE RESERVOIR
ROCKET
SCOUR BRUSH
MAGNETIC WINCH
POWER HOSE
VACUUM
SUCK NOZZLE
SPATCH
In the meantime, that BURGER BUS is Shell-tarr property.
If not returned intact, penalties will be accrued to your citizen credit.
Oh, she's not a citizen.
She's just a DAY LABORER.
Then her work permit is now officially REVOKED!

Ma'am, without your permit, you're prohibited from station grounds.

Let me make one last COM CALL, please!

I could call Tinder . . .

No. I'm not THAT desperate.

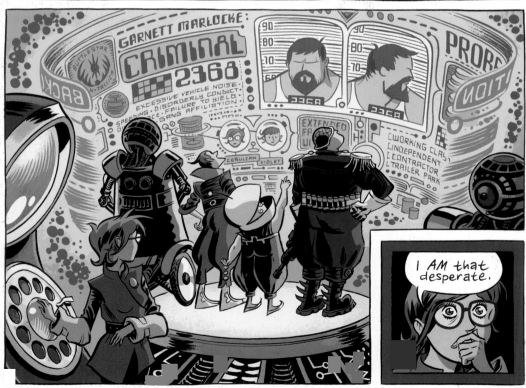

GARNETT MARLOCKE: CRIMINAL 2368

EXCESSIVE VEHICLE NOISE · SPEEDING · DISORDERLY CONDUCT · FAILURE TO YIELD · GANG AFFILIATION

CWORKING CLAS LINDEPENDENT LCONTRACTOR LTRAILER PARK

I AM that desperate.

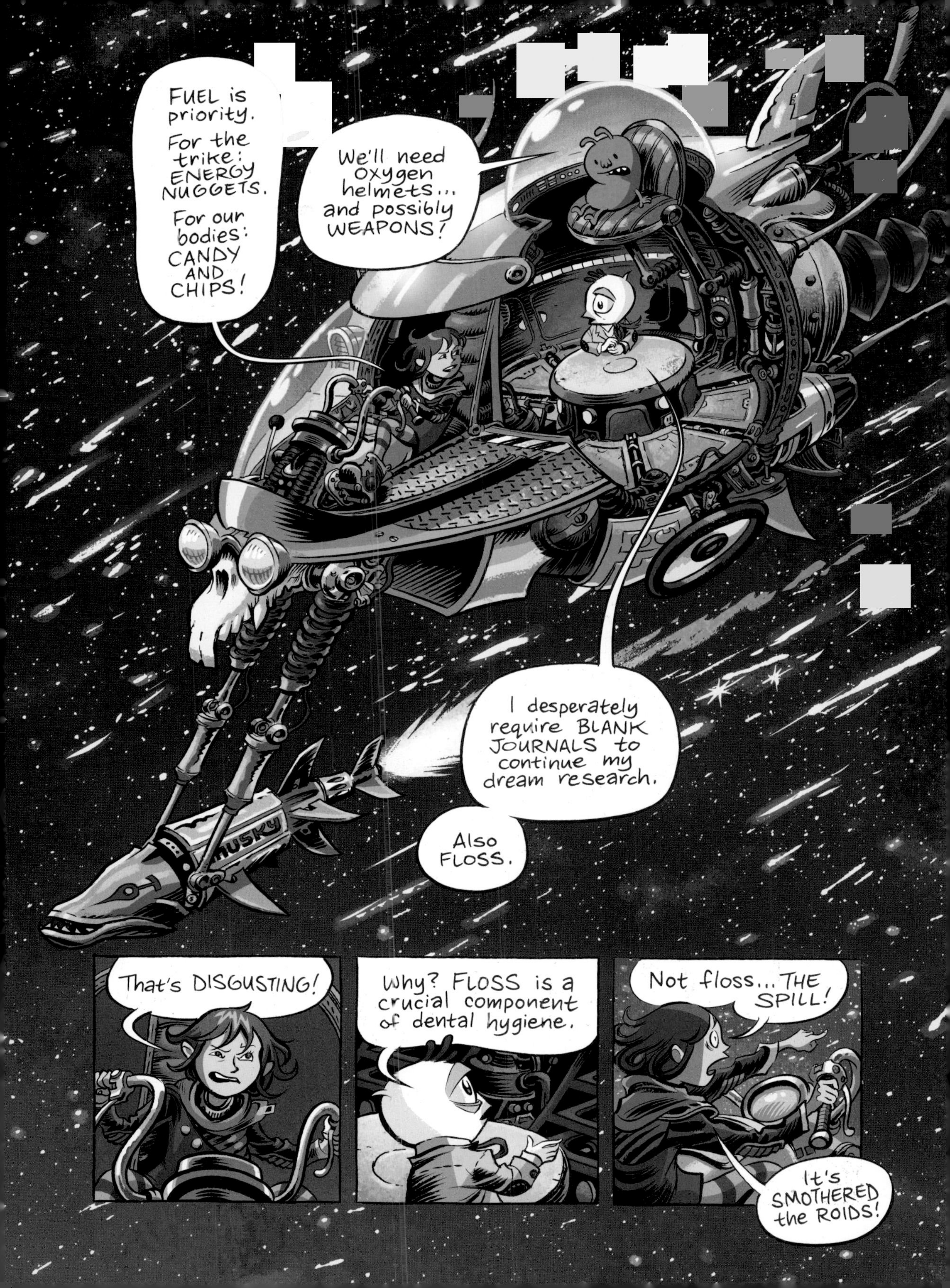
FUEL is priority. For the trike: ENERGY NUGGETS. For our bodies: CANDY AND CHIPS!
We'll need oxygen helmets... and possibly WEAPONS!
I desperately require BLANK JOURNALS to continue my dream research.
Also FLOSS.
MUSKY
That's DISGUSTING!
Why? FLOSS is a crucial component of dental hygiene.
Not floss... THE SPILL!
It's SMOTHERED the ROIDS!

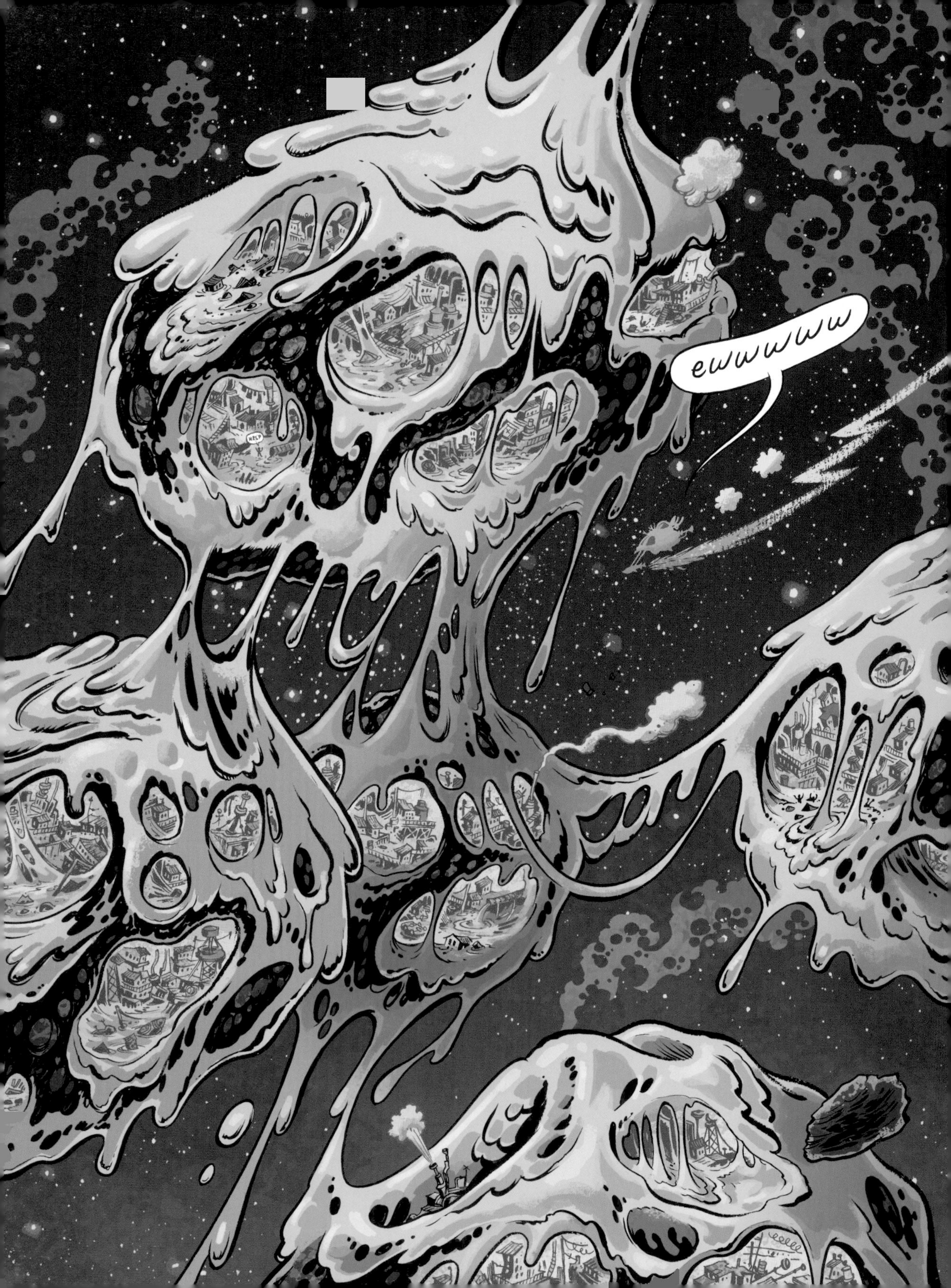
HELP
ewwwww

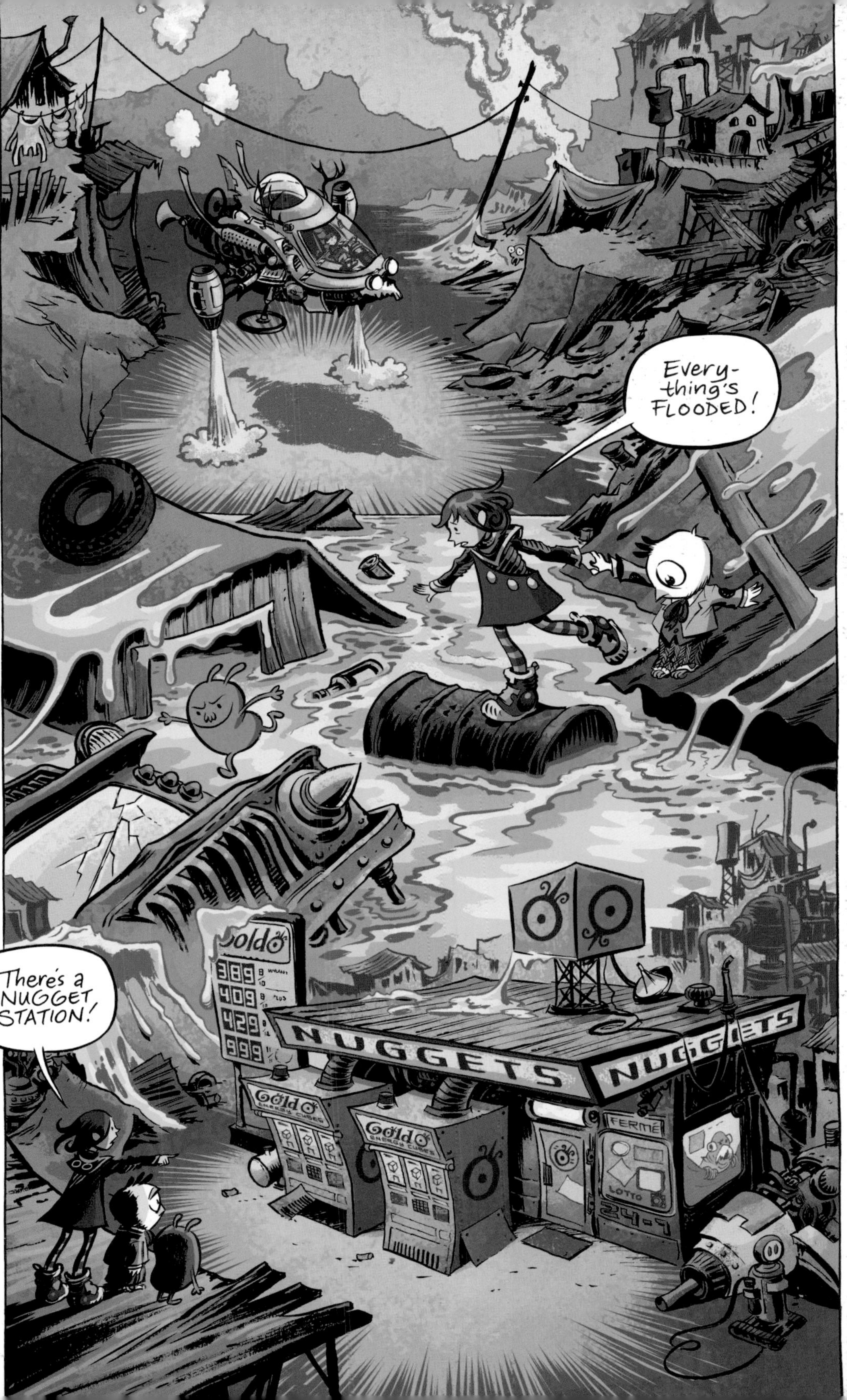
Every-thing's FLOODED!
There's a NUGGET STATION!
NUGGETS
NUGGETS
Goldo
Goldo ENERGY CUBES
Goldo ENERGY CUBES
FERMÉ
LOTTO
24-7

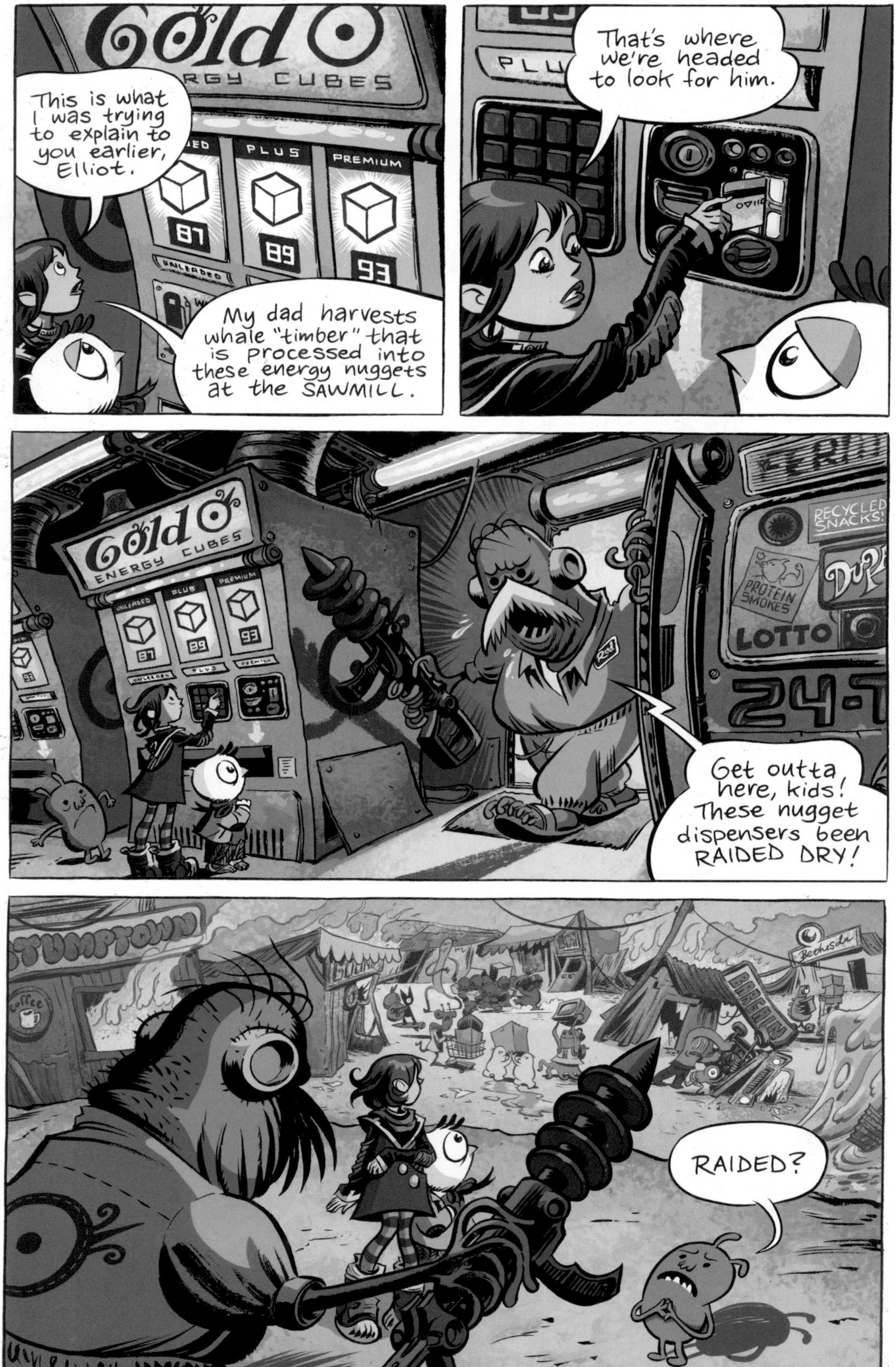
Gold
ENERGY CUBES
This is what I was trying to explain to you earlier, Elliot.
UNLEADED
PLUS
PREMIUM
87
89
93
My dad harvests whale "timber" that is processed into these energy nuggets at the SAWMILL.
That's where we're headed to look for him.
RECYCLED SNACKS!
PROTEIN SMOKES
LOTTO
Get outta here, kids! These nugget dispensers been RAIDED DRY!
STUMPTOWN
Coffee
BARGAIN
RAIDED?

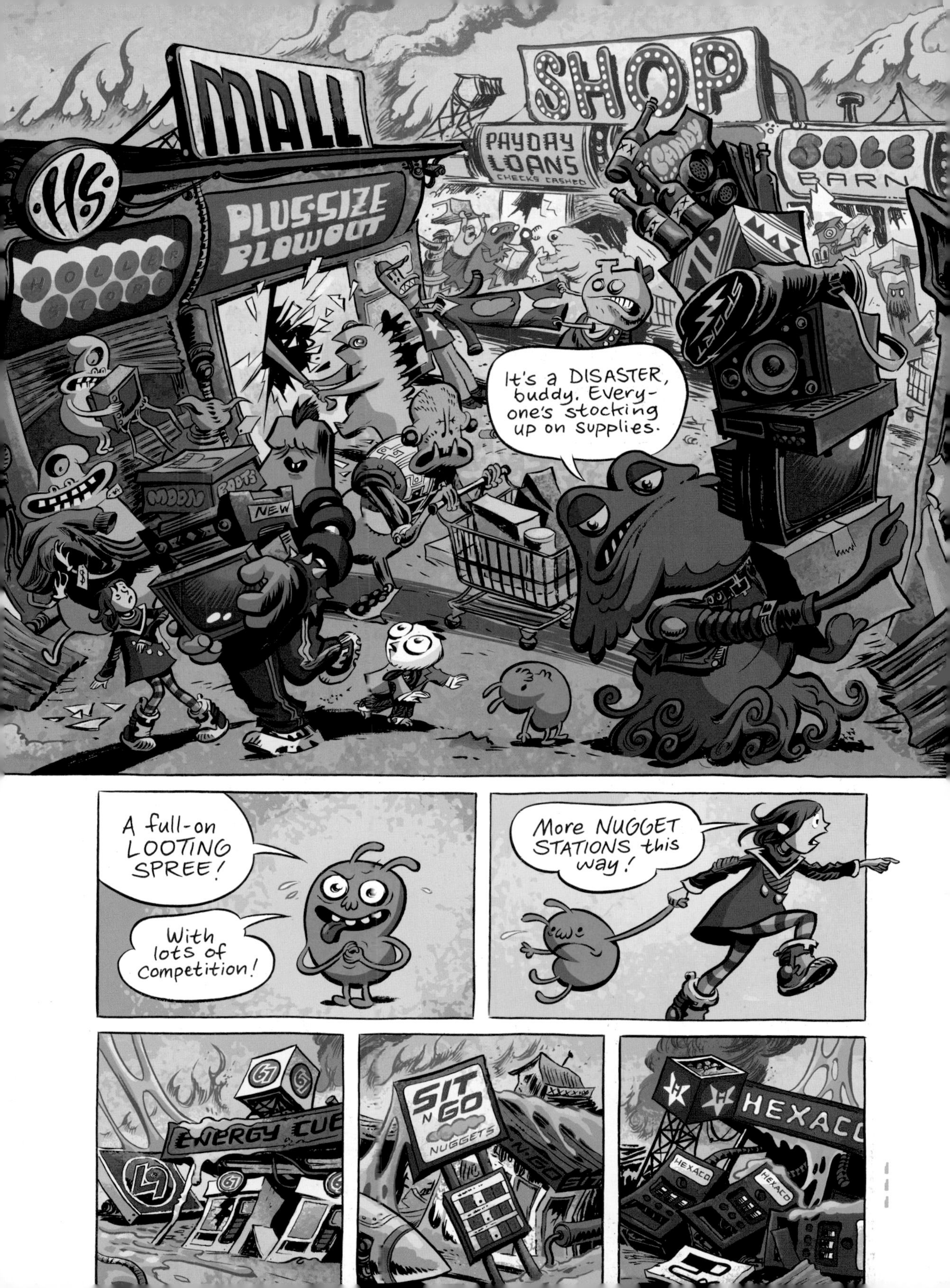
MALL
SHOP
PAYDAY LOANS
CHECKS CASHED
SALE BARN
PLUS-SIZE BLOWOUT
MOON BOOTS
NEW
SPORT
It's a DISASTER, buddy. Every-one's stocking up on supplies.
A full-on LOOTING SPREE!
With lots of Competition!
More NUGGET STATIONS this way!
ENERGY CUB
SIT N GO
NUGGETS
HEXACO

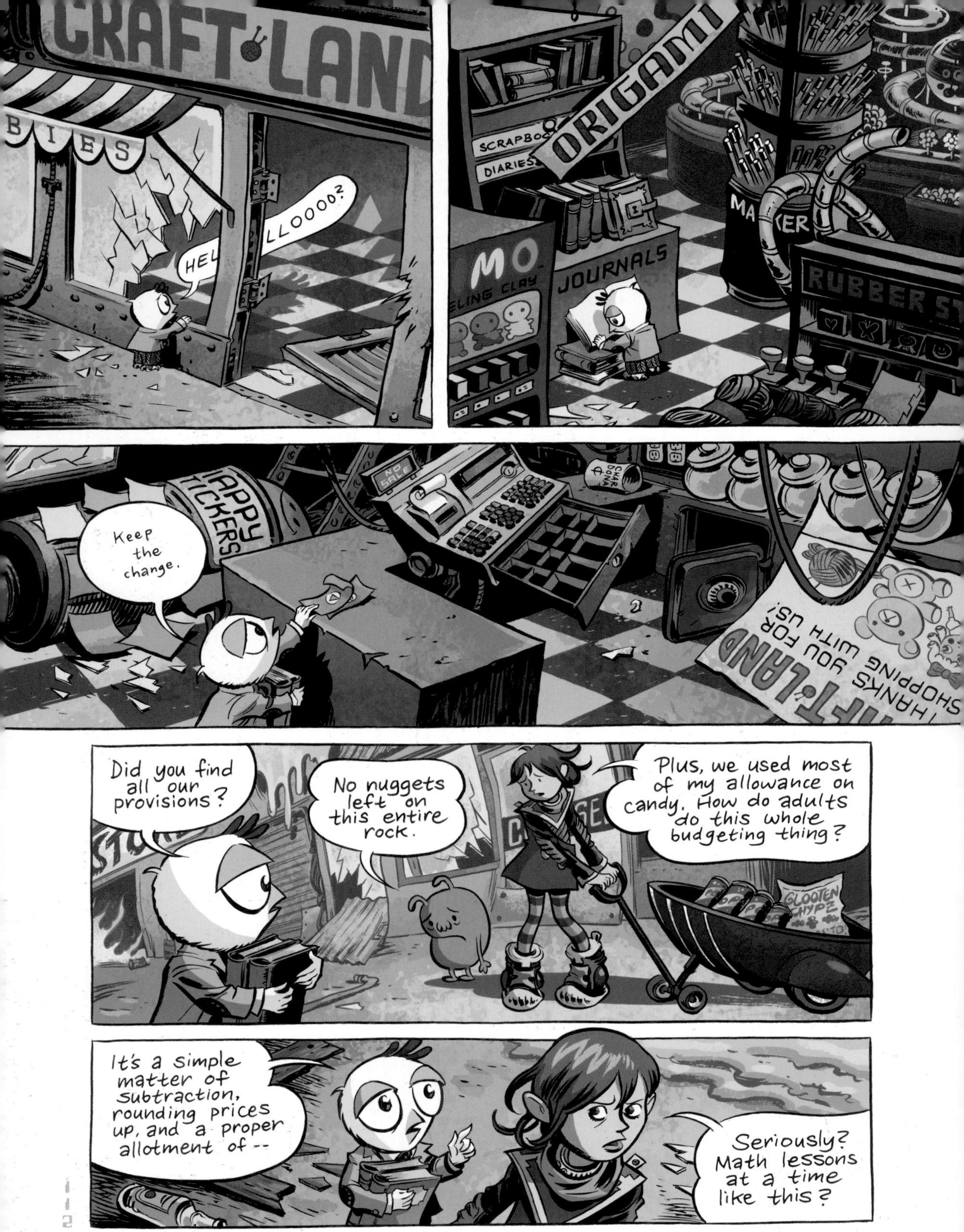

CRAFT LAND
HELLOOOO?
ORIGAMI
SCRAPBO
DIARIES
JOURNALS
MO
ELING CLAY
RUBBER ST
NO SALE
APPY TICKERS
Keep the change.
Did you find all our provisions?
No nuggets left on this entire rock.
Plus, we used most of my allowance on candy. How do adults do this whole budgeting thing?
GLOOTEN CHYPZ
It's a simple matter of subtraction, rounding prices up, and a proper allotment of --
Seriously? Math lessons at a time like this?

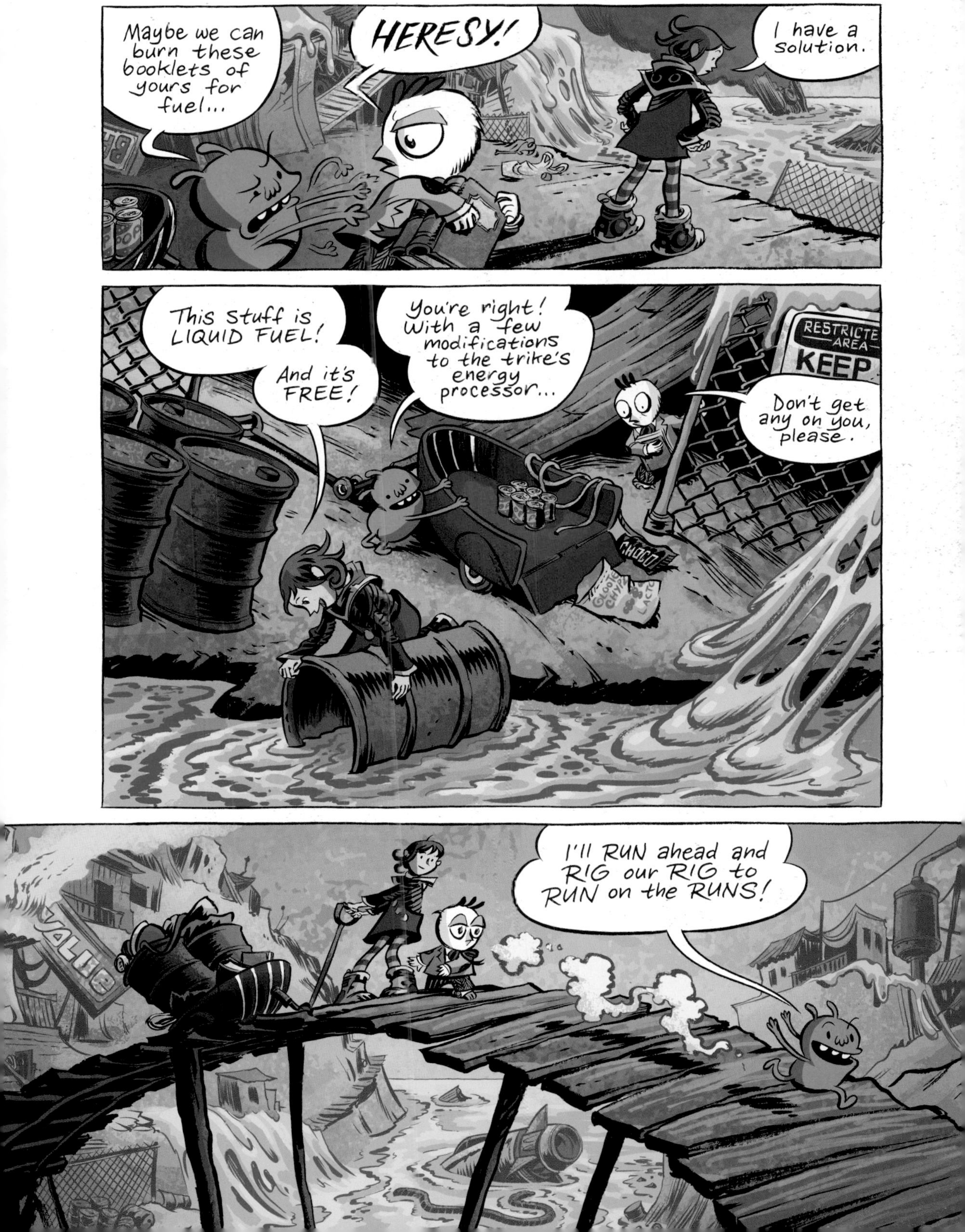
Maybe we can burn these booklets of yours for fuel...
HERESY!
I have a solution.
This stuff is LIQUID FUEL!
And it's FREE!
You're right! With a few modifications to the trike's energy processor...
Don't get any on you, please.
RESTRICTED AREA
KEEP
I'll RUN ahead and RIG our RIG to RUN on the RUNS!

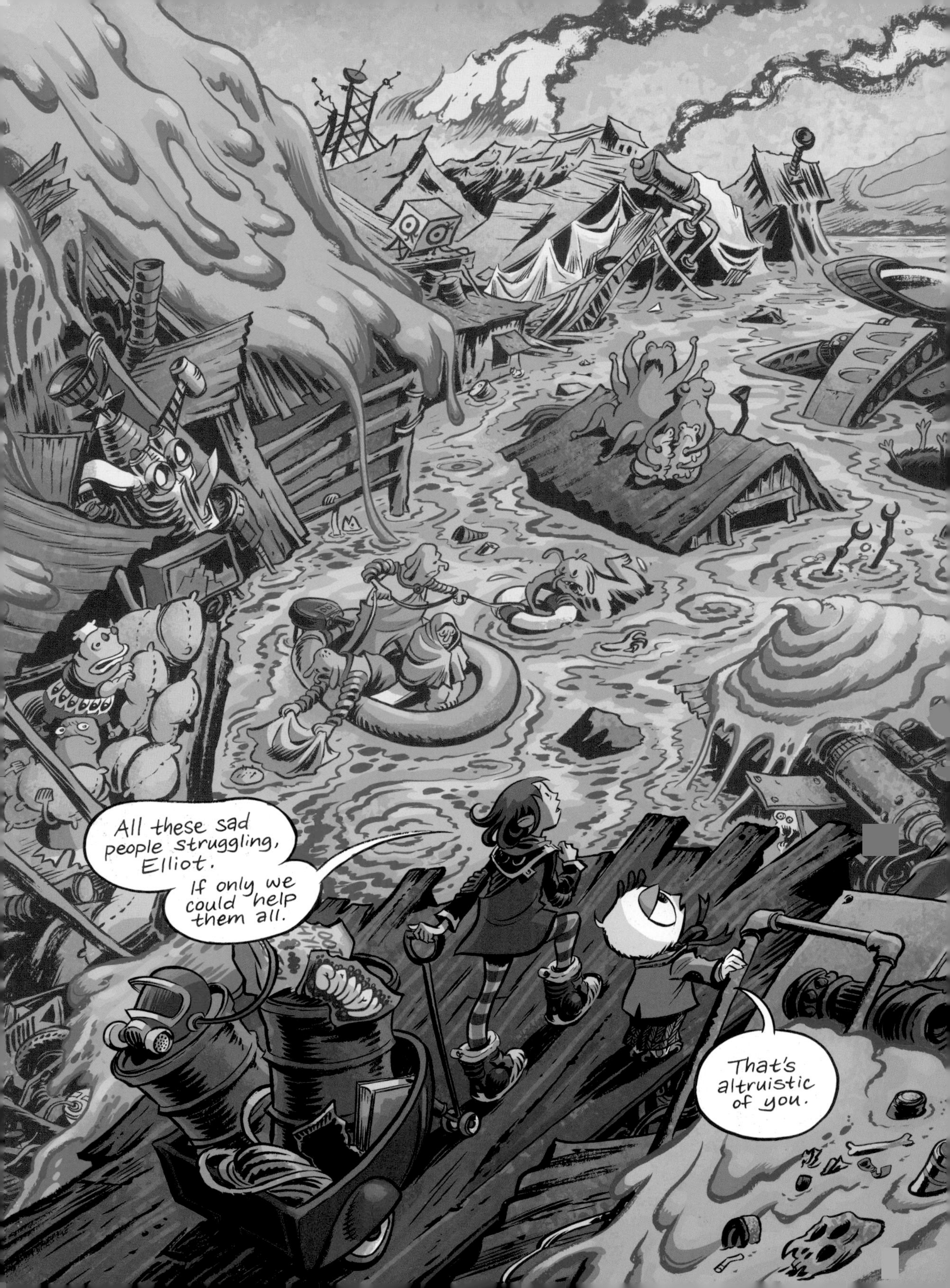
All these sad people struggling, Elliot.
If only we could help them all.
That's altruistic of you.

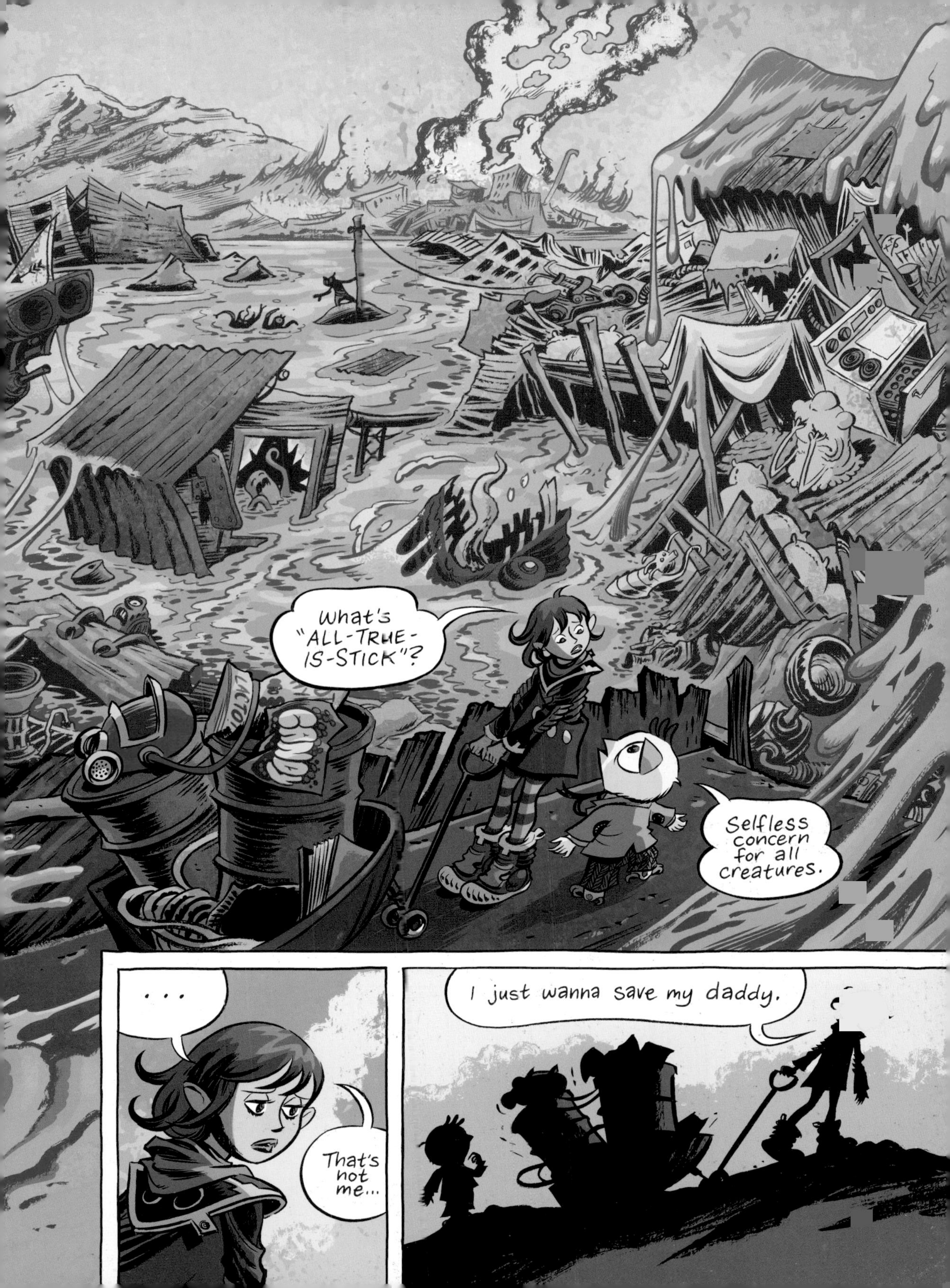
What's "ALL-TRUE-IS-STICK"?
Selfless concern for all creatures.
. . .
That's not me...
I just wanna save my daddy.

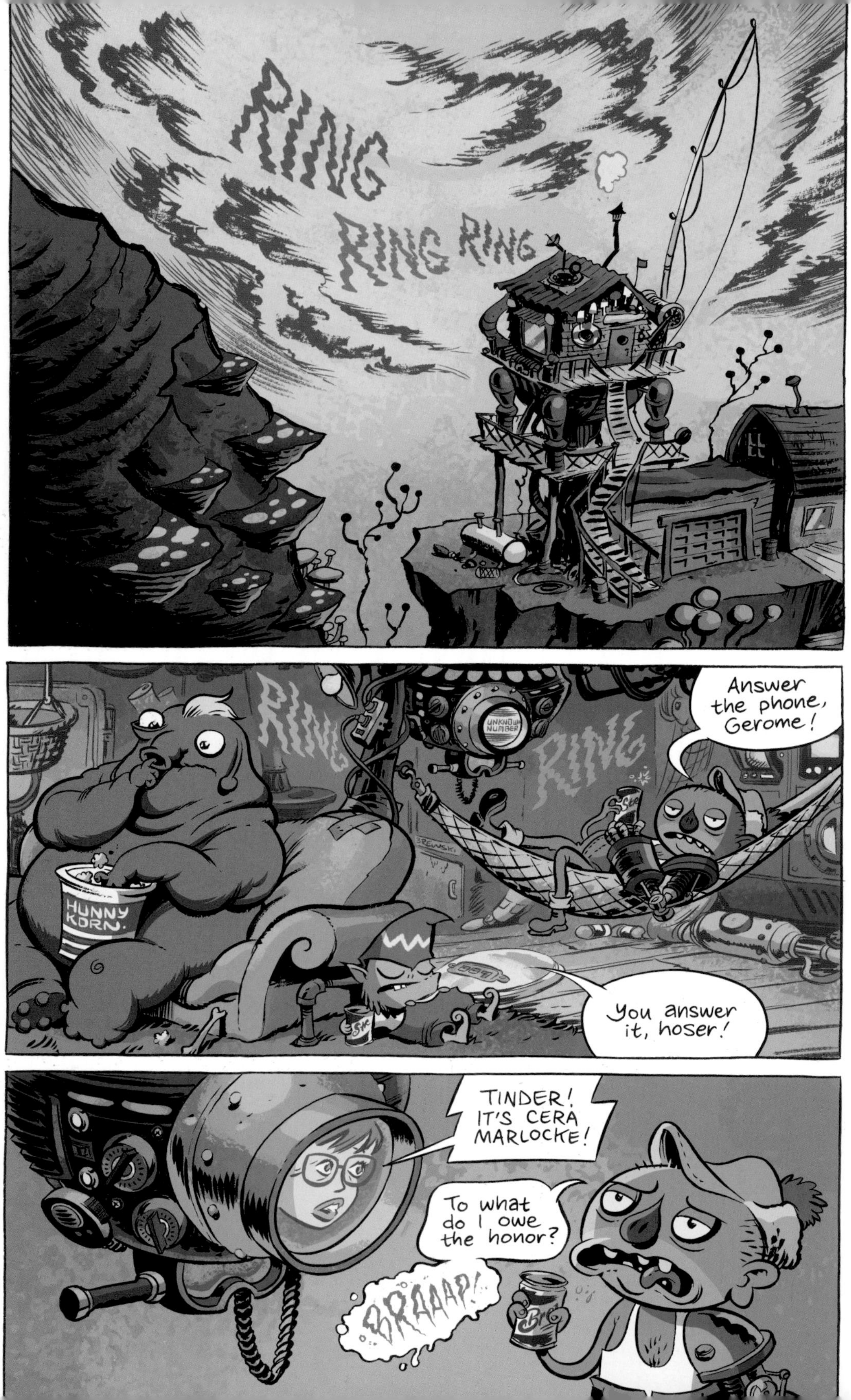
RING
RING RING RING
RING
RING
UNKNOWN NUMBER
Answer the phone, Gerome!
HUNNY KORN.
You answer it, hoser!
TINDER! IT'S CERA MARLOCKE!
To what do I owe the honor?
BRAAAP!

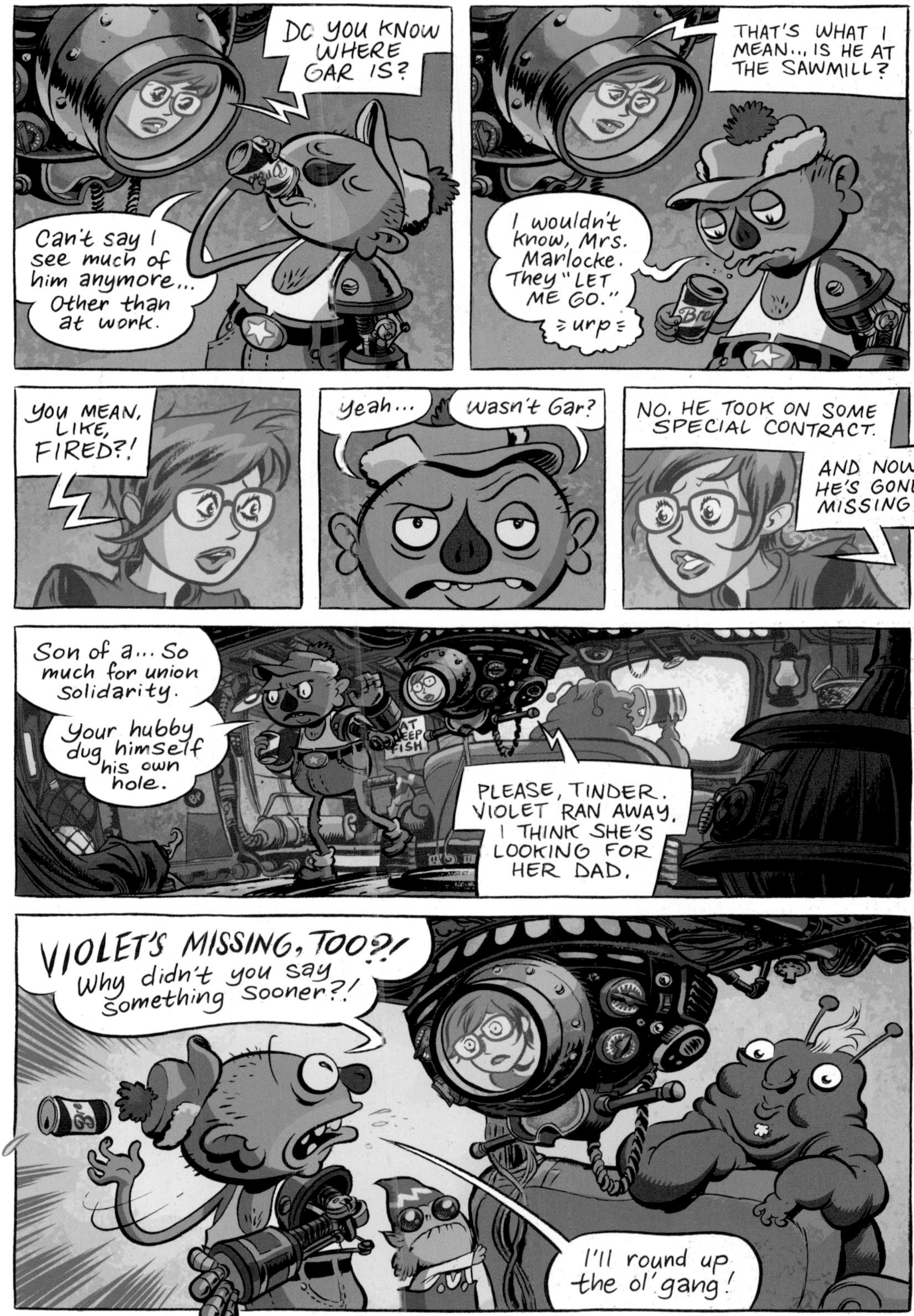
DO YOU KNOW WHERE GAR IS?
Can't say I see much of him anymore... Other than at work.
THAT'S WHAT I MEAN... IS HE AT THE SAWMILL?
I wouldn't know, Mrs. Marlocke. They "LET ME GO."
urp
YOU MEAN, LIKE, FIRED?!
Yeah...
wasn't Gar?
NO. HE TOOK ON SOME SPECIAL CONTRACT.
AND NOW HE'S GONE MISSING!
Son of a... So much for union solidarity.
Your hubby dug himself his own hole.
PLEASE, TINDER. VIOLET RAN AWAY. I THINK SHE'S LOOKING FOR HER DAD.
VIOLET'S MISSING, TOO?! Why didn't you say something sooner?!
I'll round up the ol' gang!

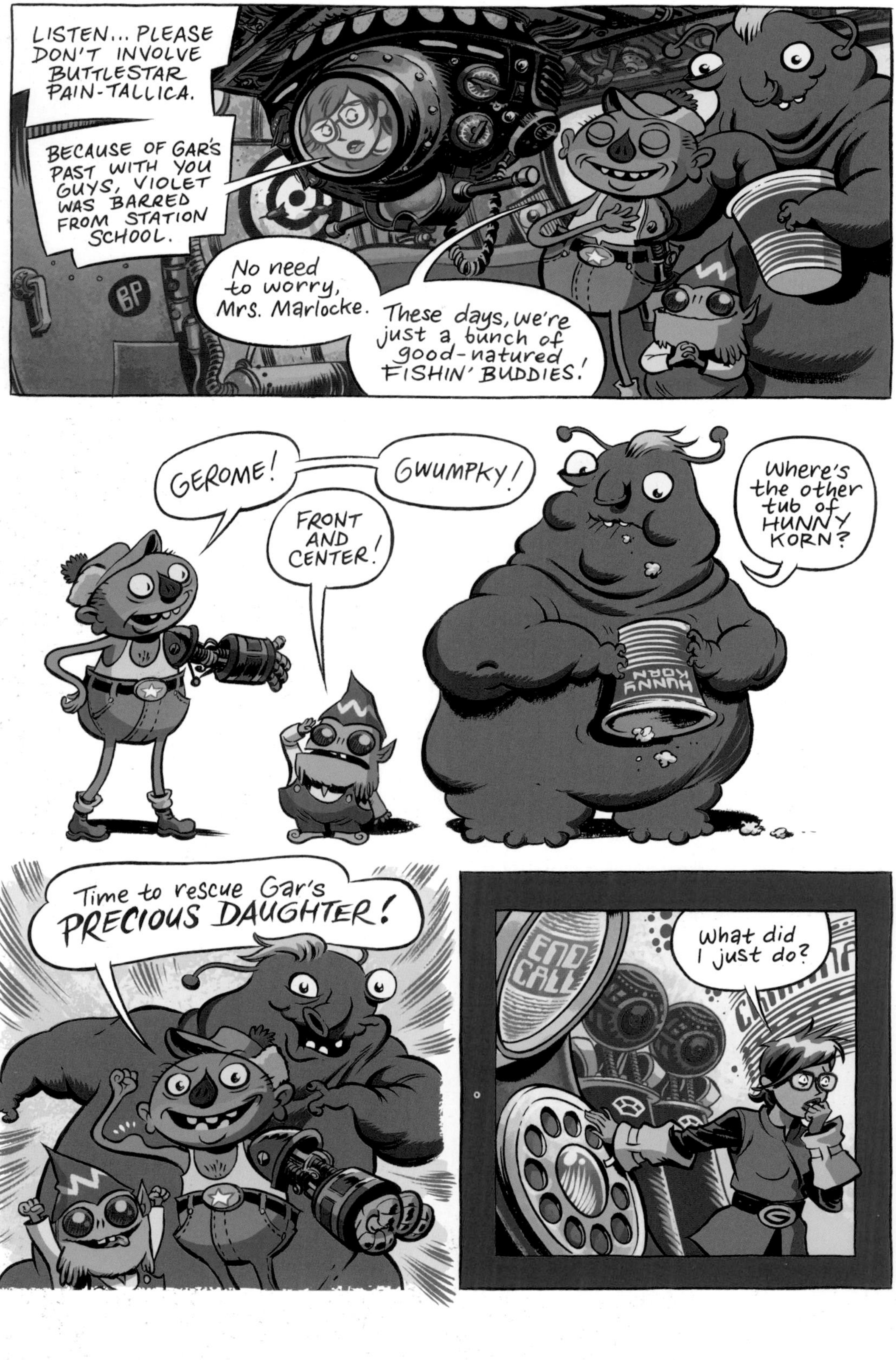
LISTEN... PLEASE DON'T INVOLVE BUTTLESTAR PAIN-TALLICA.
BECAUSE OF GAR'S PAST WITH YOU GUYS, VIOLET WAS BARRED FROM STATION SCHOOL.
No need to worry, Mrs. Marlocke.
These days, we're just a bunch of good-natured FISHIN' BUDDIES!
GEROME!
GWUMPKY!
FRONT AND CENTER!
Where's the other tub of HUNNY KORN?
HUNNY KORN
Time to rescue Gar's PRECIOUS DAUGHTER!
END CALL
What did I just do?

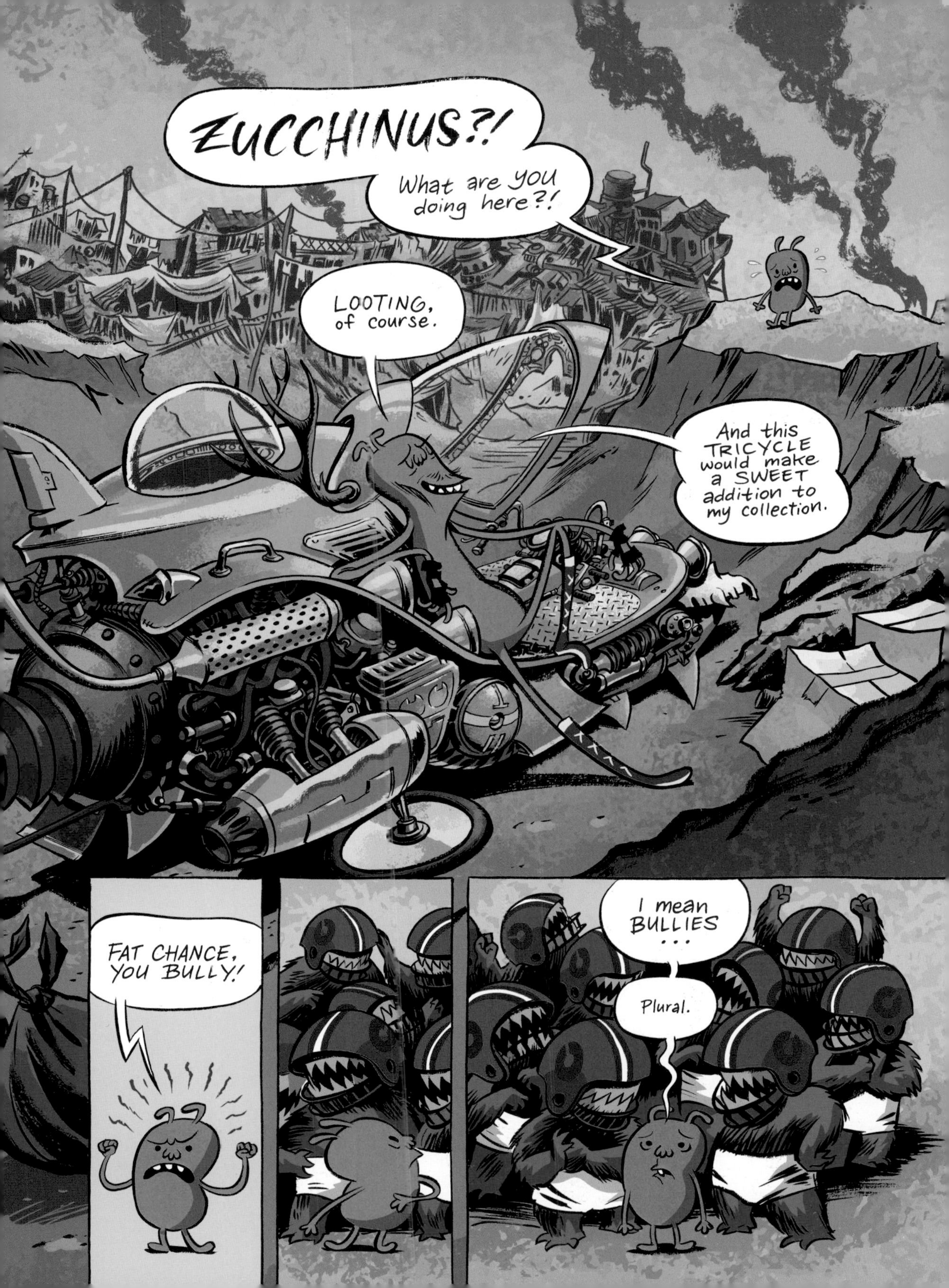
ZUCCHINUS?!
What are YOU doing here?!
LOOTING, of course.
And this TRICYCLE would make a SWEET addition to my collection.
FAT CHANCE, YOU BULLY!
I mean BULLIES . . .
Plural.

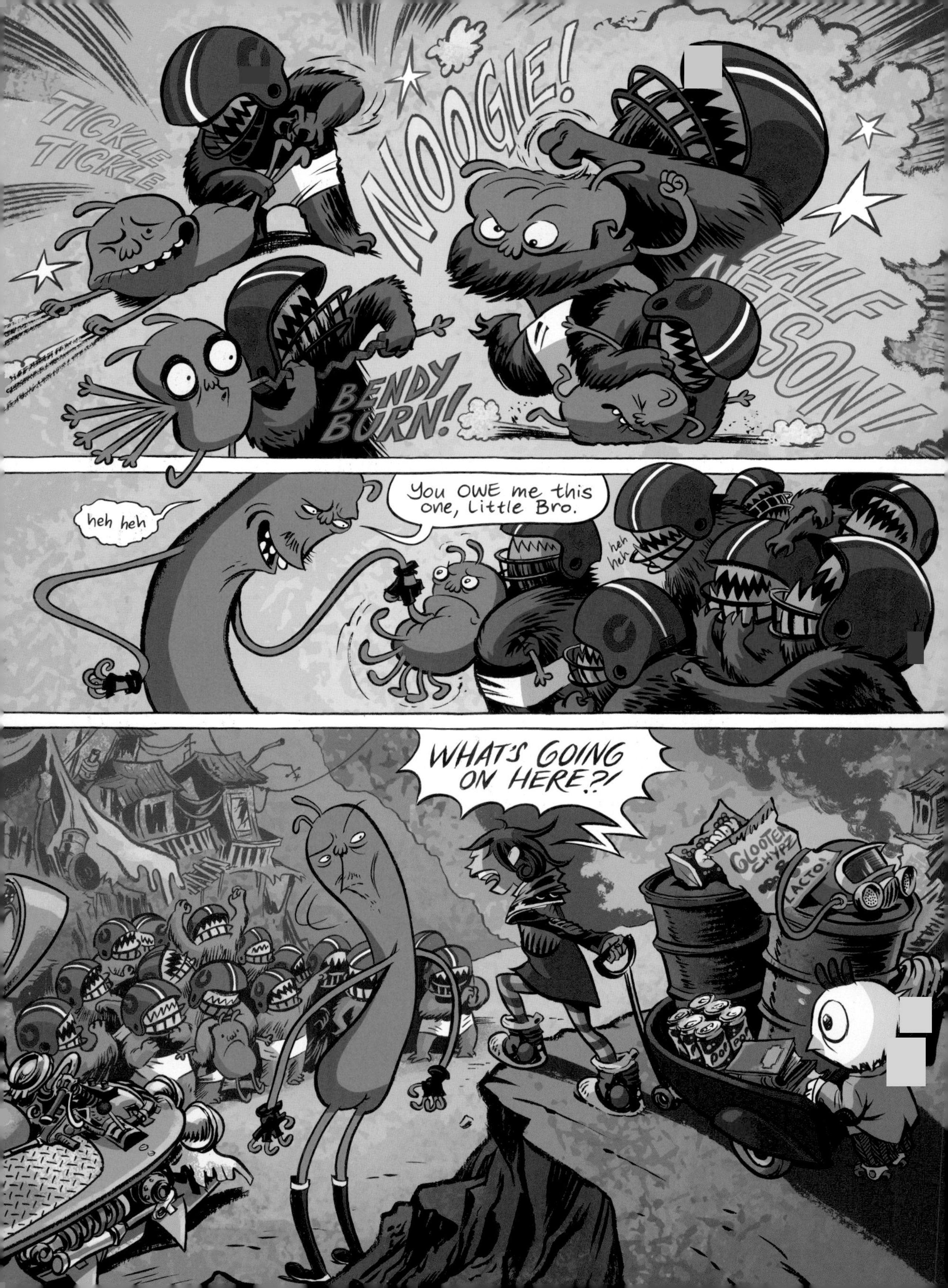
TICKLE TICKLE
NOOGIE!
HALF NELSON!
BENDY BURN!
heh heh
You OWE me this one, Little Bro.
heh heh
WHAT'S GOING ON HERE?!
GLOOTEN CHYPZ
LACTO!

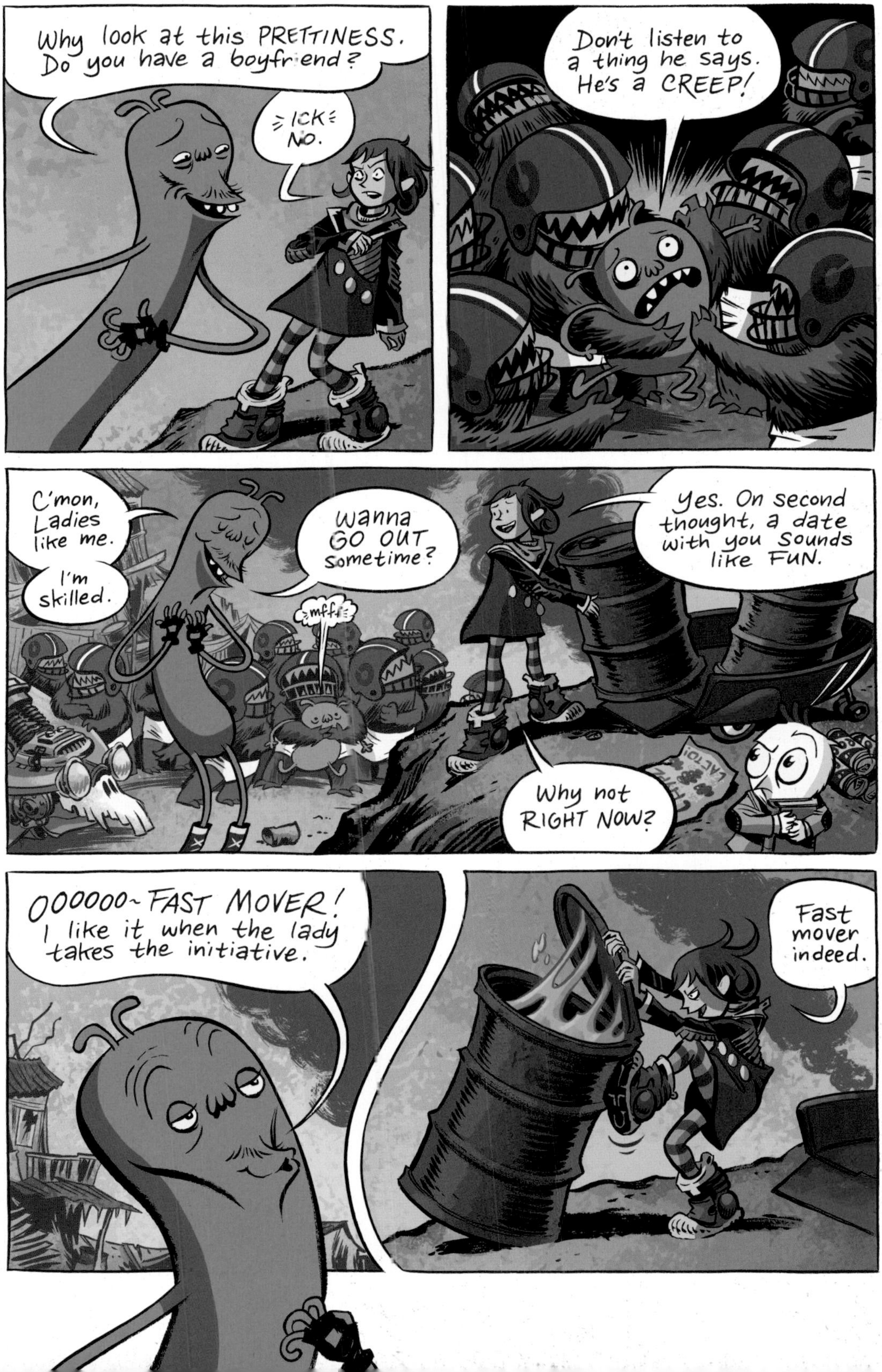
Why look at this PRETTINESS. Do you have a boyfriend?
ICK NO.
Don't listen to a thing he says. He's a CREEP!
C'mon, Ladies like me.
I'm skilled.
Wanna GO OUT sometime?
mfff
Yes. On second thought, a date with you sounds like FUN.
Why not RIGHT NOW?
OOOOOO~ FAST MOVER! I like it when the lady takes the initiative.
Fast mover indeed.

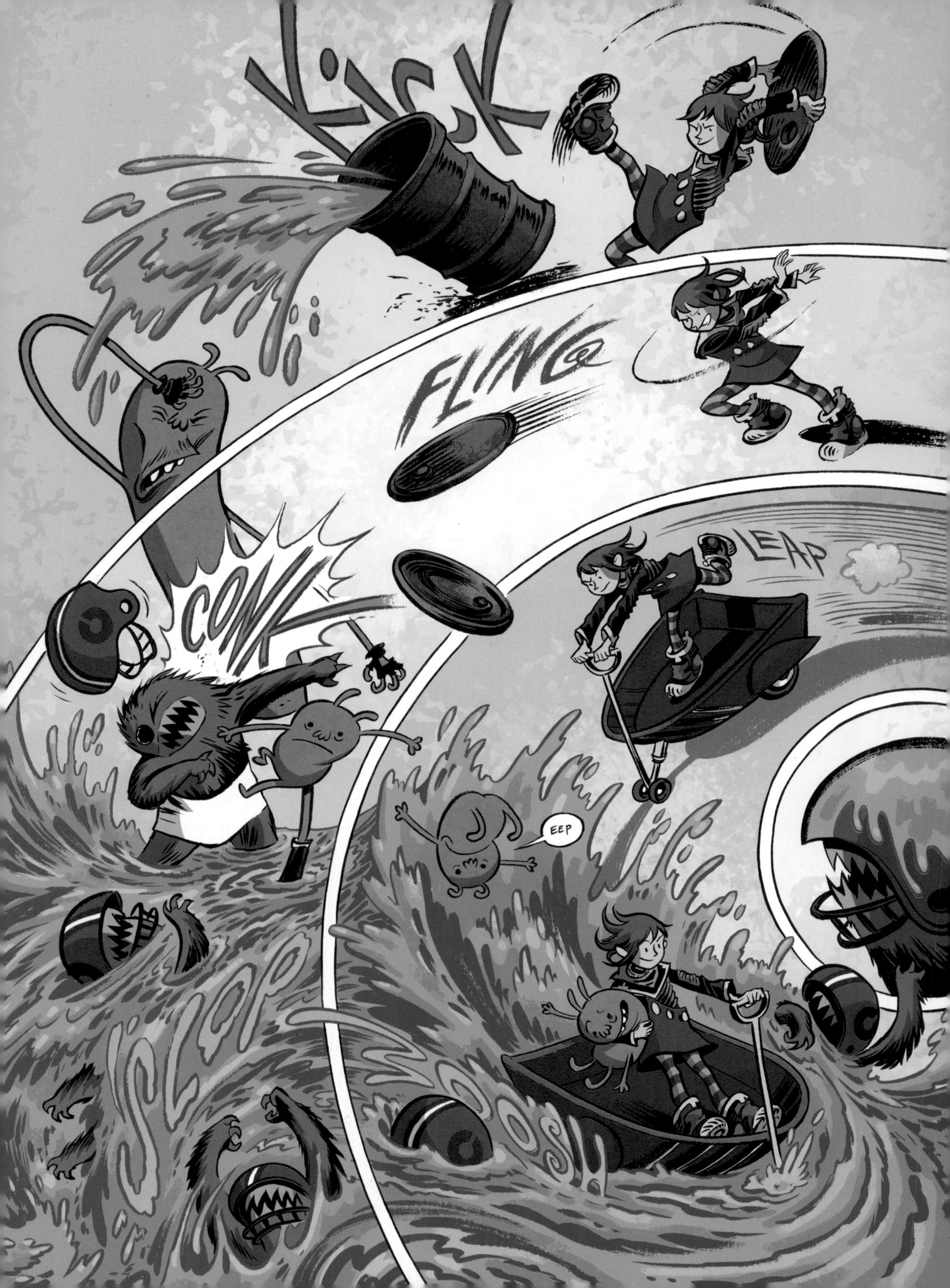
KICK
FLING
CONK
LEAP
EEP

NUNCHUCKS.

NUNCHUCKA NCHUCKA

Dental floss.

WZZZZZZZ

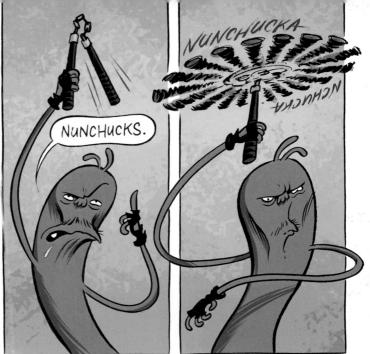

WZZZZZZZ
NUNCHUCKA
NUNHHUCKA
NUNCHUCKA

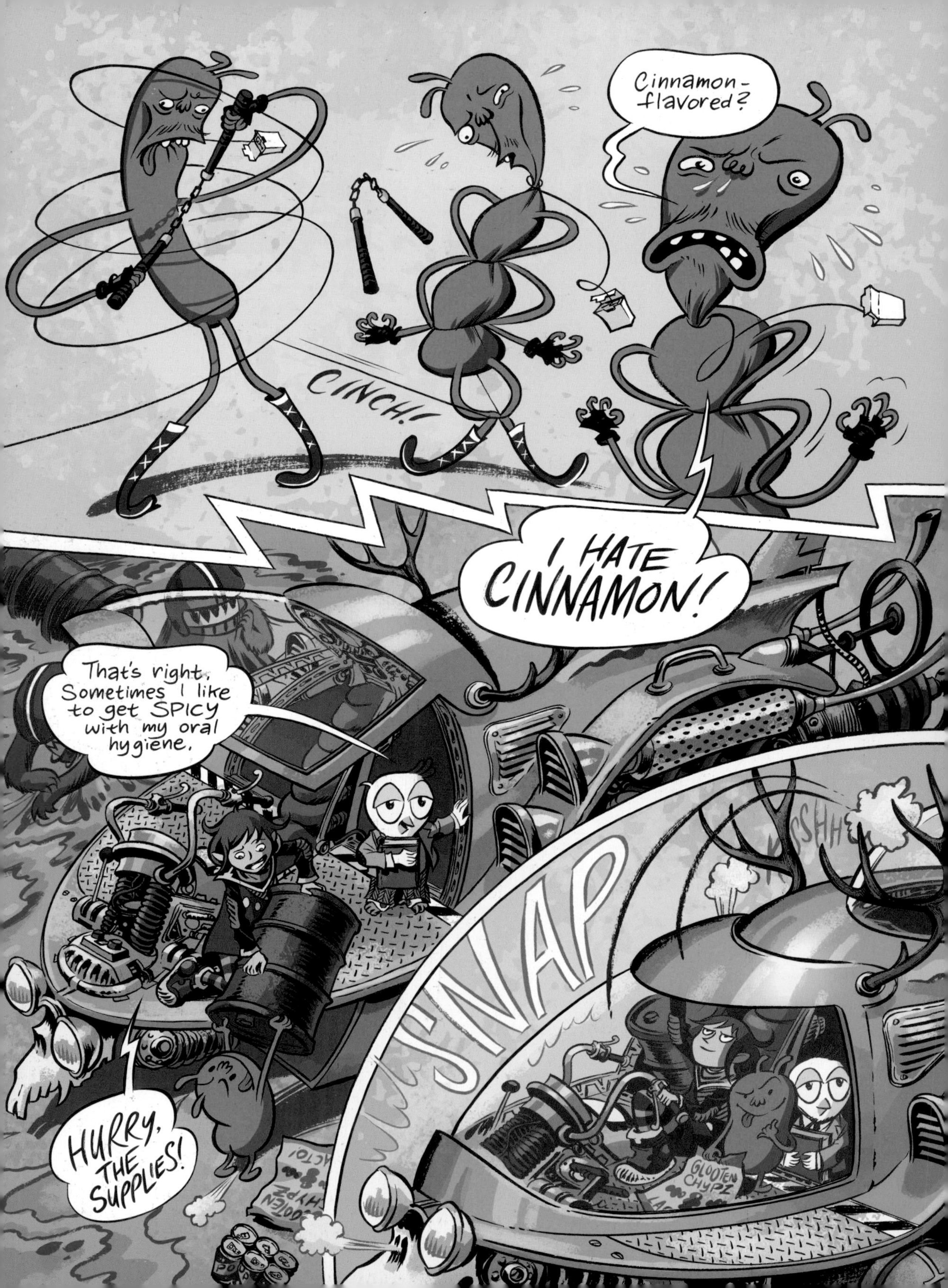
Cinnamon-flavored?
CINCH!
I HATE CINNAMON!
That's right. Sometimes I like to get SPICY with my oral hygiene.
HURRY, THE SUPPLIES!
SNAP
KSSHH
GLOOTEN CHYPZ

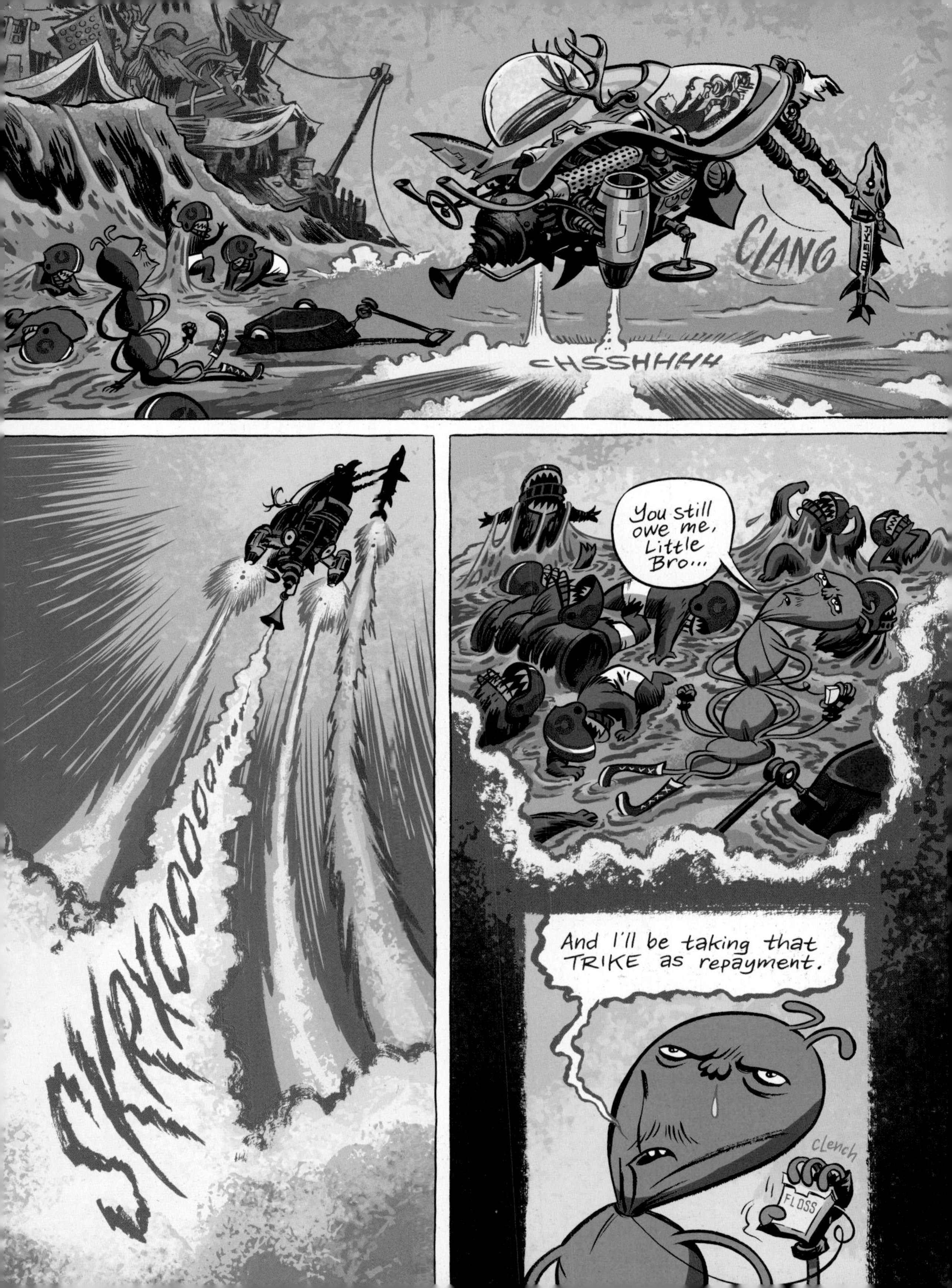
CLANG
MUSKY
CHSSHHHH
SKRYOOOOOO...
You still owe me, Little Bro...
And I'll be taking that TRIKE as repayment.
CLENCH
FLOSS

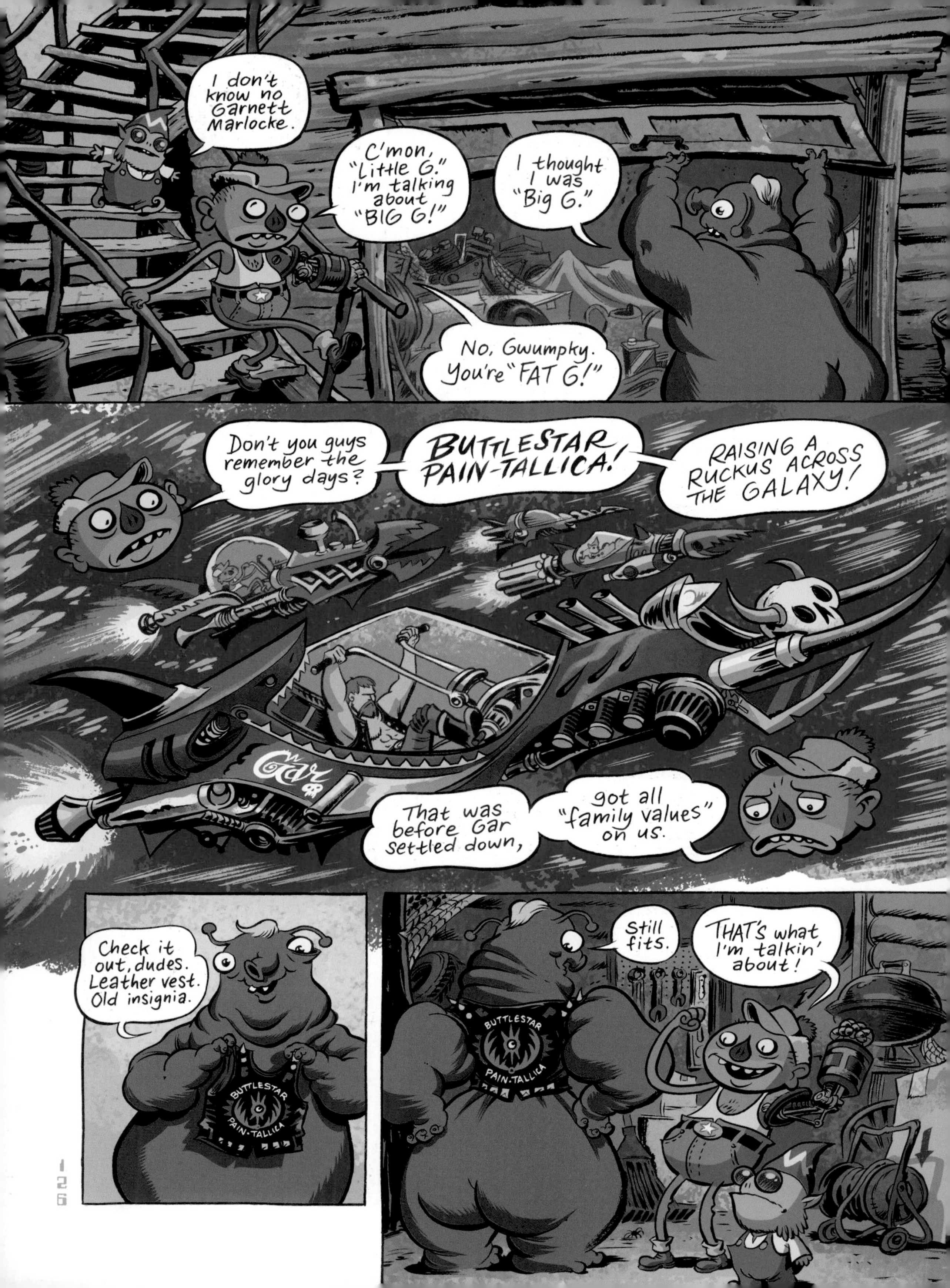
I don't know no Garnett Marlocke.
C'mon, "Little G." I'm talking about "BIG G!"
I thought I was "Big G."
No, Gwumpky. You're "FAT G!"
Don't you guys remember the glory days?
BUTTLESTAR PAIN-TALLICA!
RAISING A RUCKUS ACROSS THE GALAXY!
That was before Gar settled down,
got all "family values" on us.
Check it out, dudes. Leather vest. Old insignia.
BUTTLESTAR PAIN-TALLICA
Still fits.
THAT'S what I'm talkin' about!
BUTTLESTAR PAIN-TALLICA

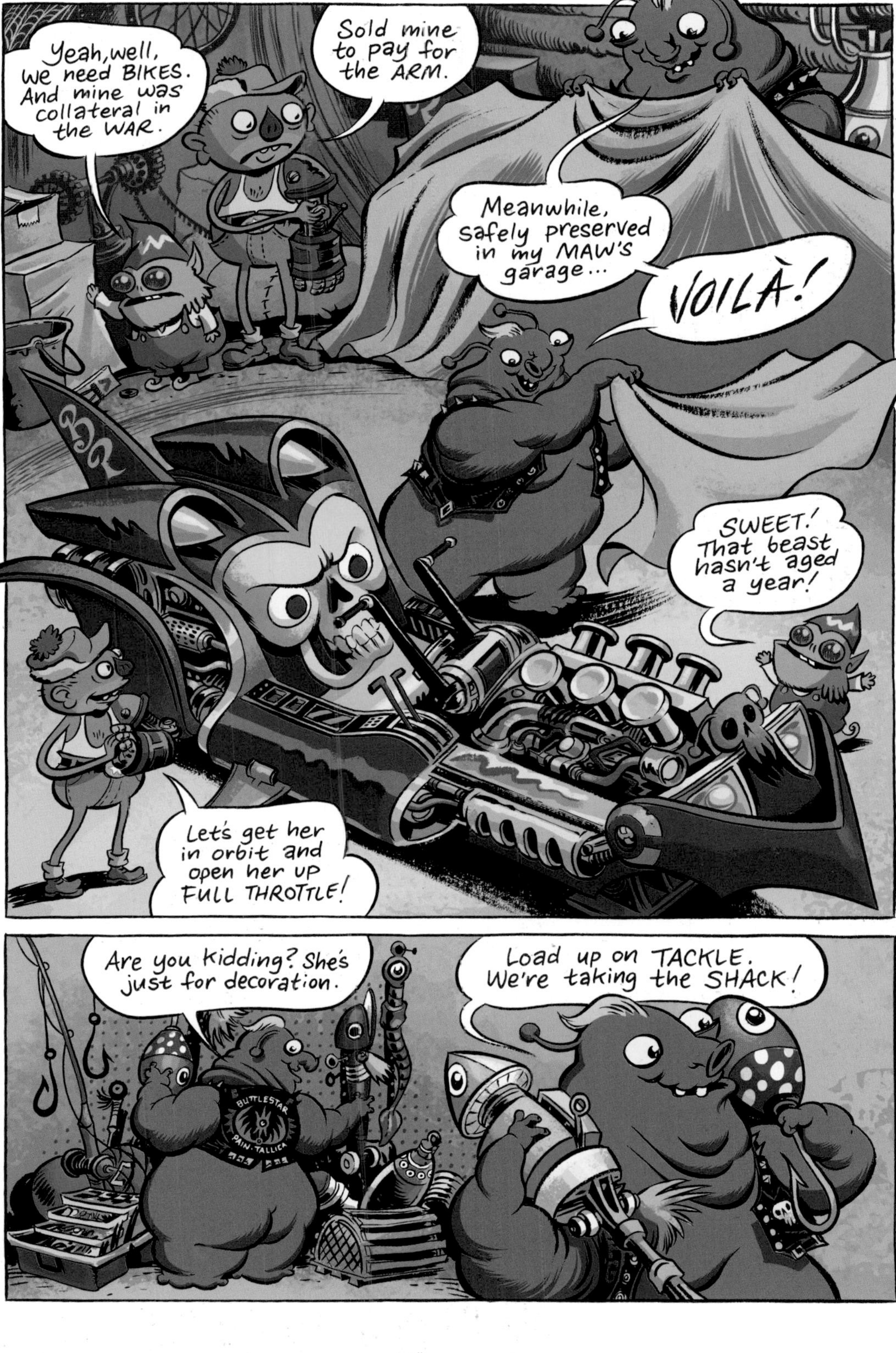
Yeah, well, we need BIKES. And mine was collateral in the WAR.
Sold mine to pay for the ARM.
Meanwhile, safely preserved in my MAW'S garage...
VOILÀ!
SWEET! That beast hasn't aged a year!
Let's get her in orbit and open her up FULL THROTTLE!
Are you kidding? She's just for decoration.
Load up on TACKLE. We're taking the SHACK!
BUTTLESTAR
PAIN-TALLICA

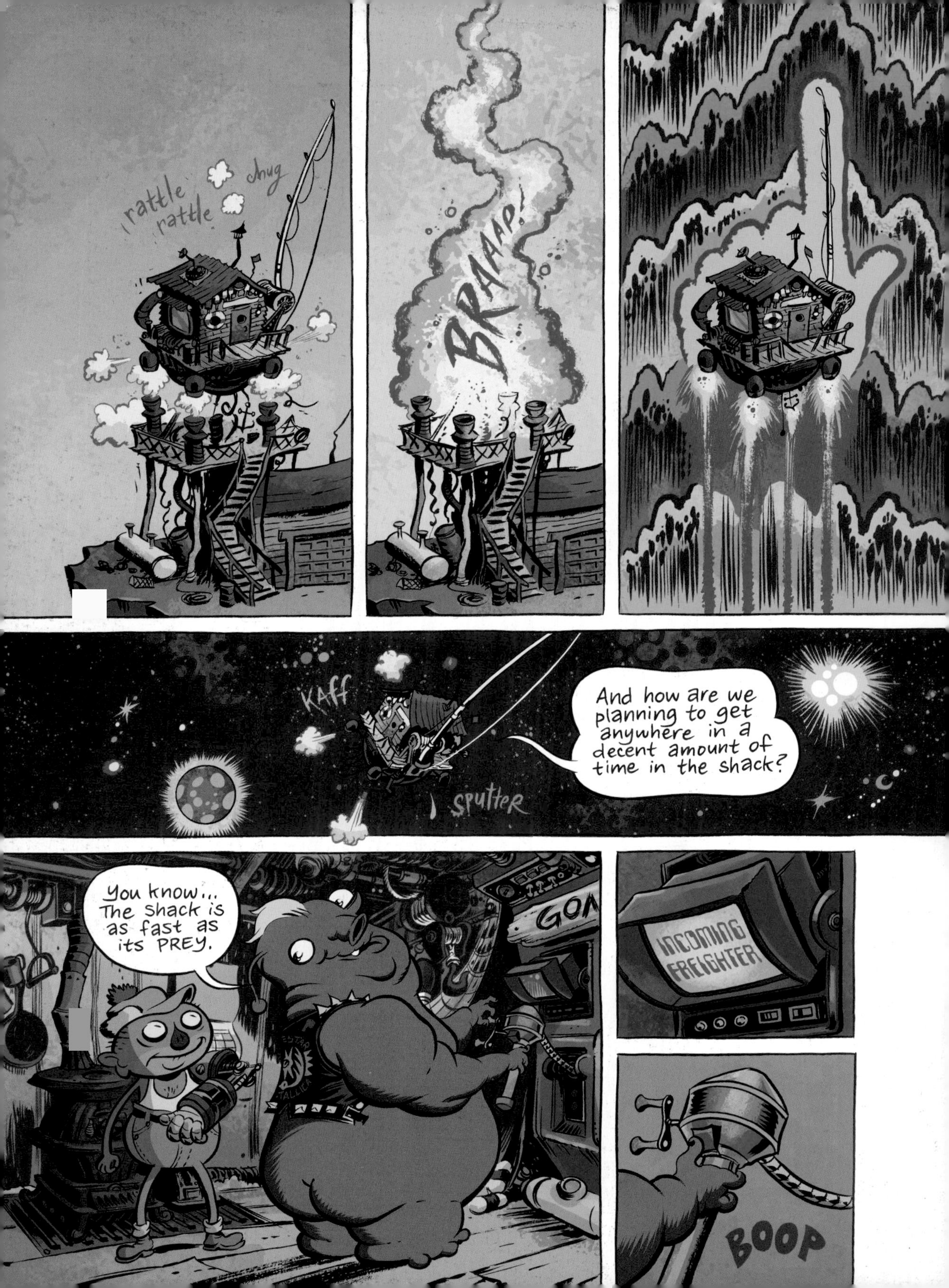
rattle rattle
chug
BRAAAP!
KAFF
And how are we planning to get anywhere in a decent amount of time in the shack?
sputter
You know... The shack is as fast as its PREY.
INCOMING FREIGHTER
BOOP

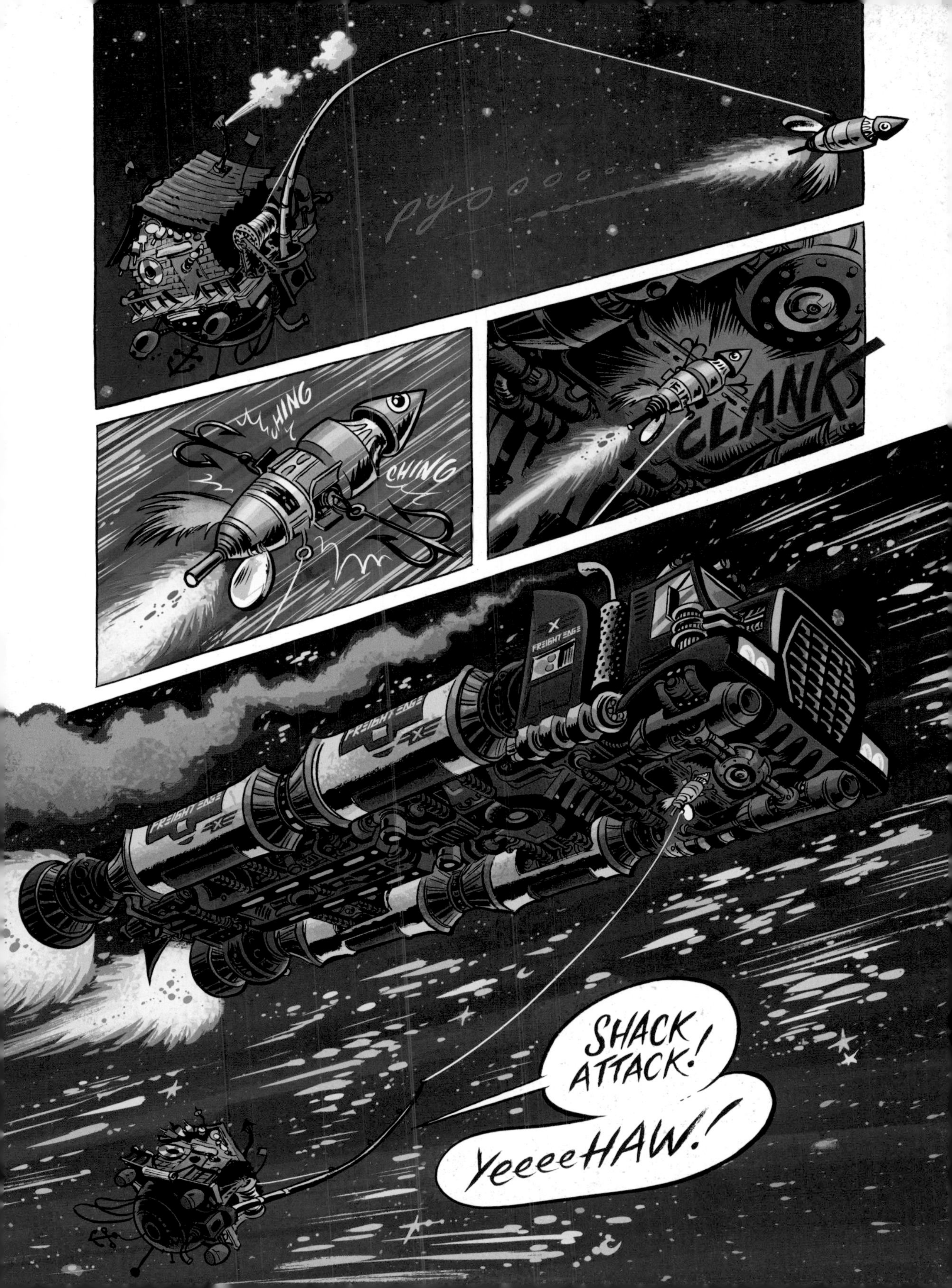
pyoooooo
CHING
CHING
CLANK
FREIGHT EAGLE
SHACK ATTACK!
YeeeeHAW!

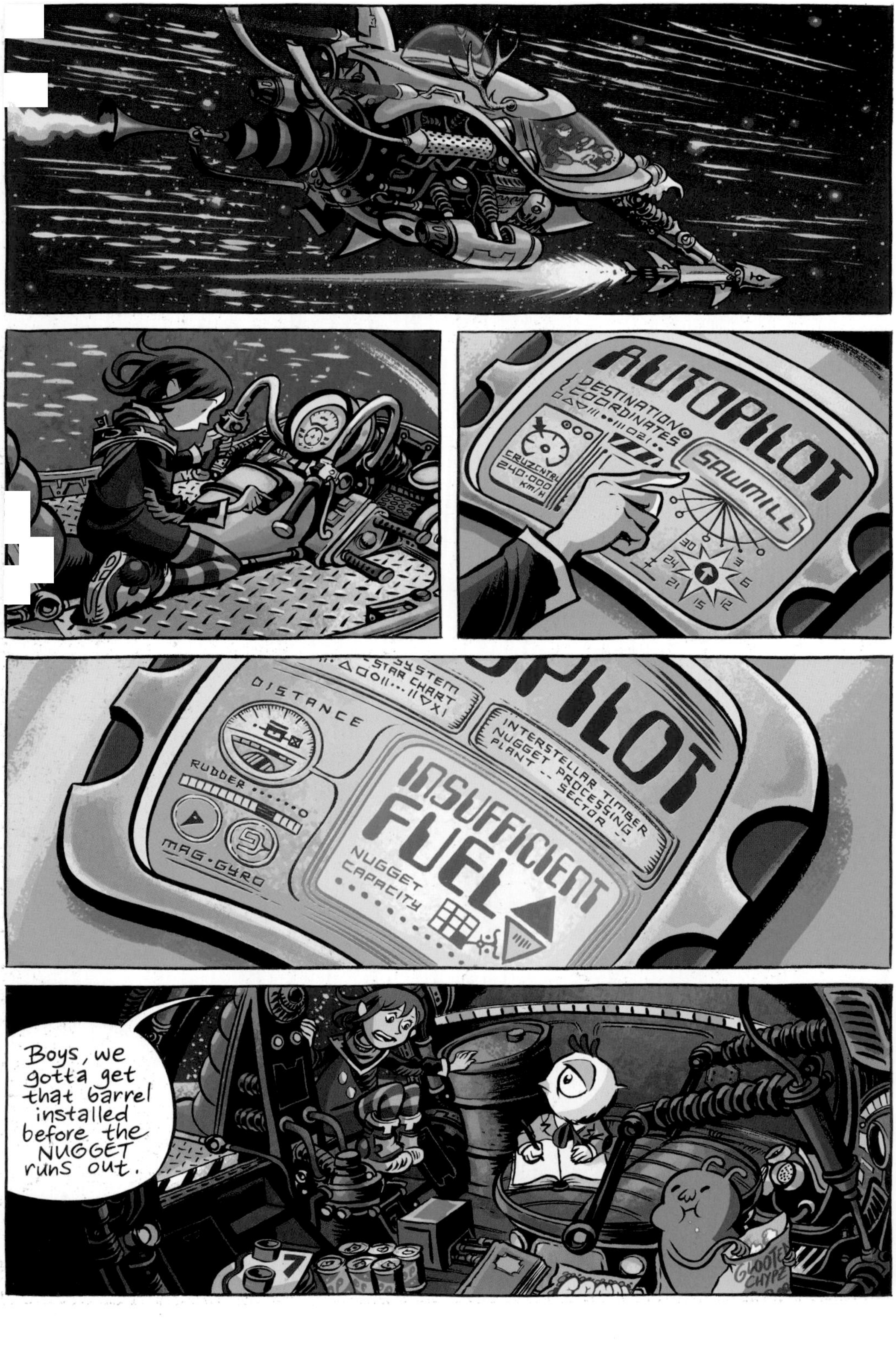
AUTOPILOT
DESTINATION COORDINATES
CRUZCNTRL 240.000 KM/H
SAWMILL
SYSTEM STAR CHART
DISTANCE
RUDDER
MAG-GYRO
OPILOT
INTERSTELLAR TIMBER NUGGET PROCESSING PLANT -- SECTOR --
INSUFFICIENT FUEL
NUGGET CAPACITY
Boys, we gotta get that barrel installed before the NUGGET runs out.
GLOOTEA CHYPZ

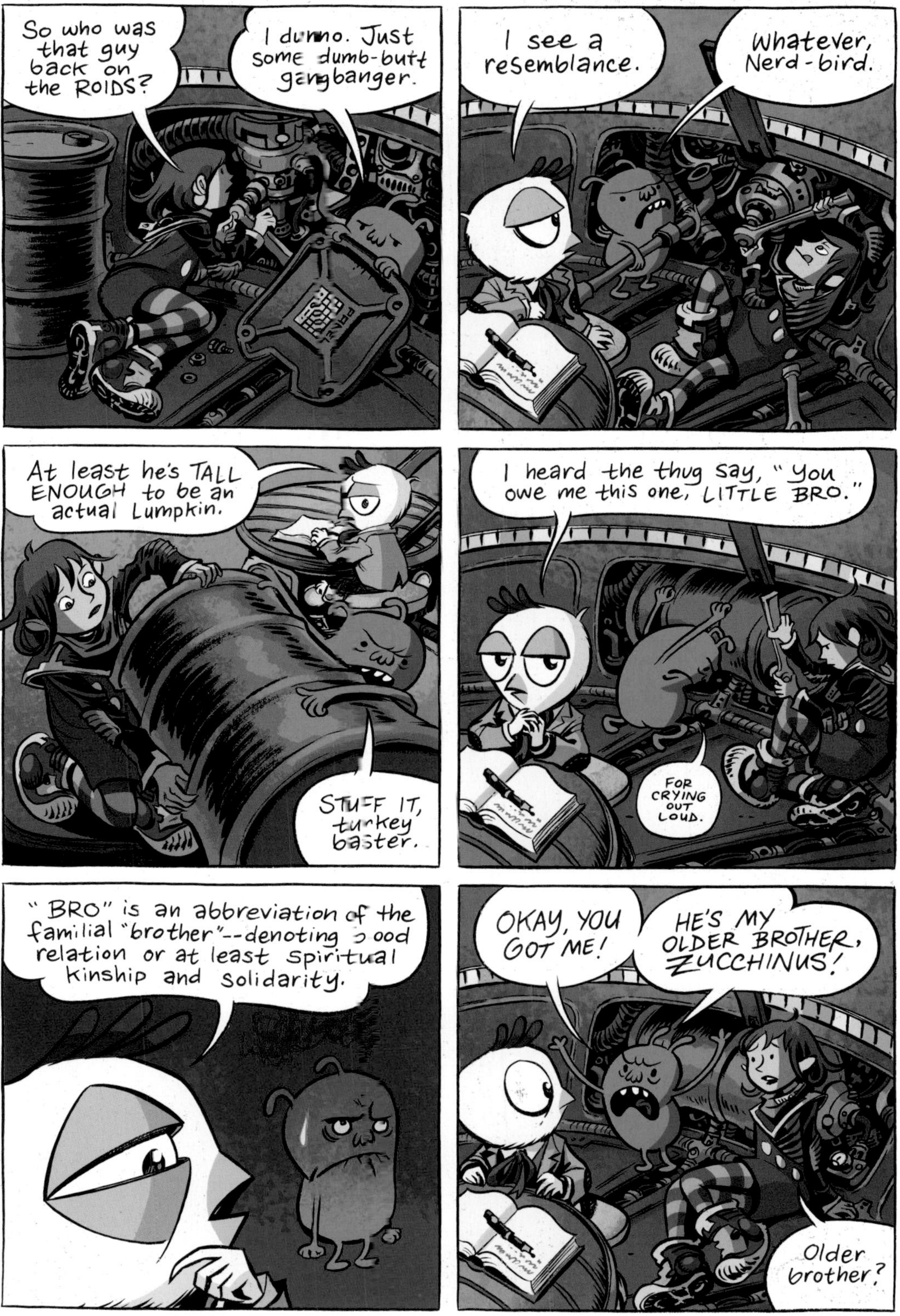
So who was that guy back on the ROIDS?
I dunno. Just some dumb-butt gangbanger.
I see a resemblance.
Whatever, Nerd-bird.
At least he's TALL ENOUGH to be an actual Lumpkin.
STUFF IT, turkey baster.
I heard the thug say, "You owe me this one, LITTLE BRO."
FOR CRYING OUT LOUD.
"BRO" is an abbreviation of the familial "brother"--denoting blood relation or at least spiritual kinship and solidarity.
OKAY, YOU GOT ME!
HE'S MY OLDER BROTHER, ZUCCHINUS!
Older brother?

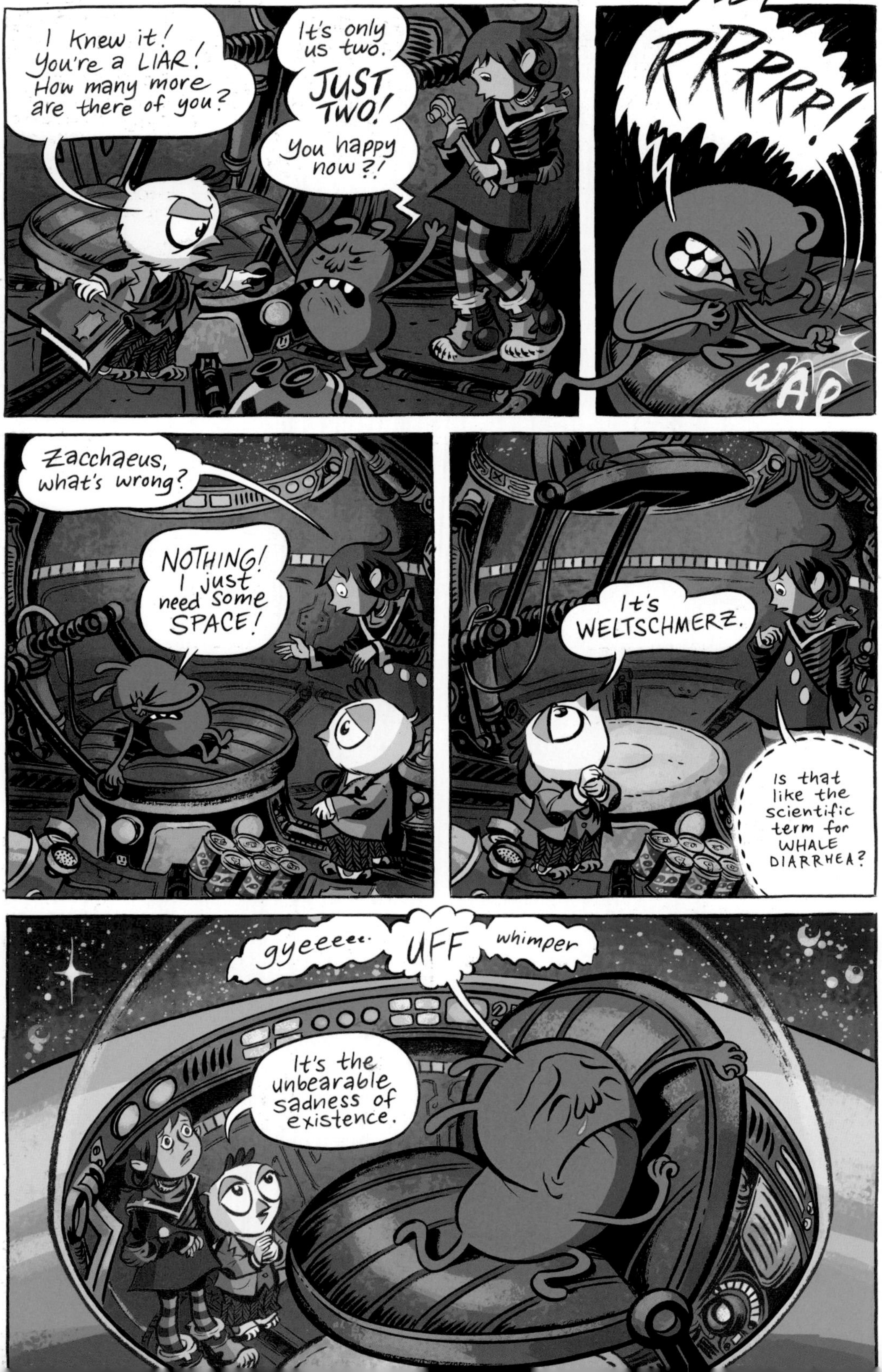

I knew it! You're a LIAR! How many more are there of you?
It's only us two.
JUST TWO!
You happy now?!
RRRRRR!
WAP
Zacchaeus, what's wrong?
NOTHING! I just need some SPACE!
It's WELTSCHMERZ.
Is that like the scientific term for WHALE DIARRHEA?
gyeeeee..
UFF
whimper
It's the unbearable sadness of existence.

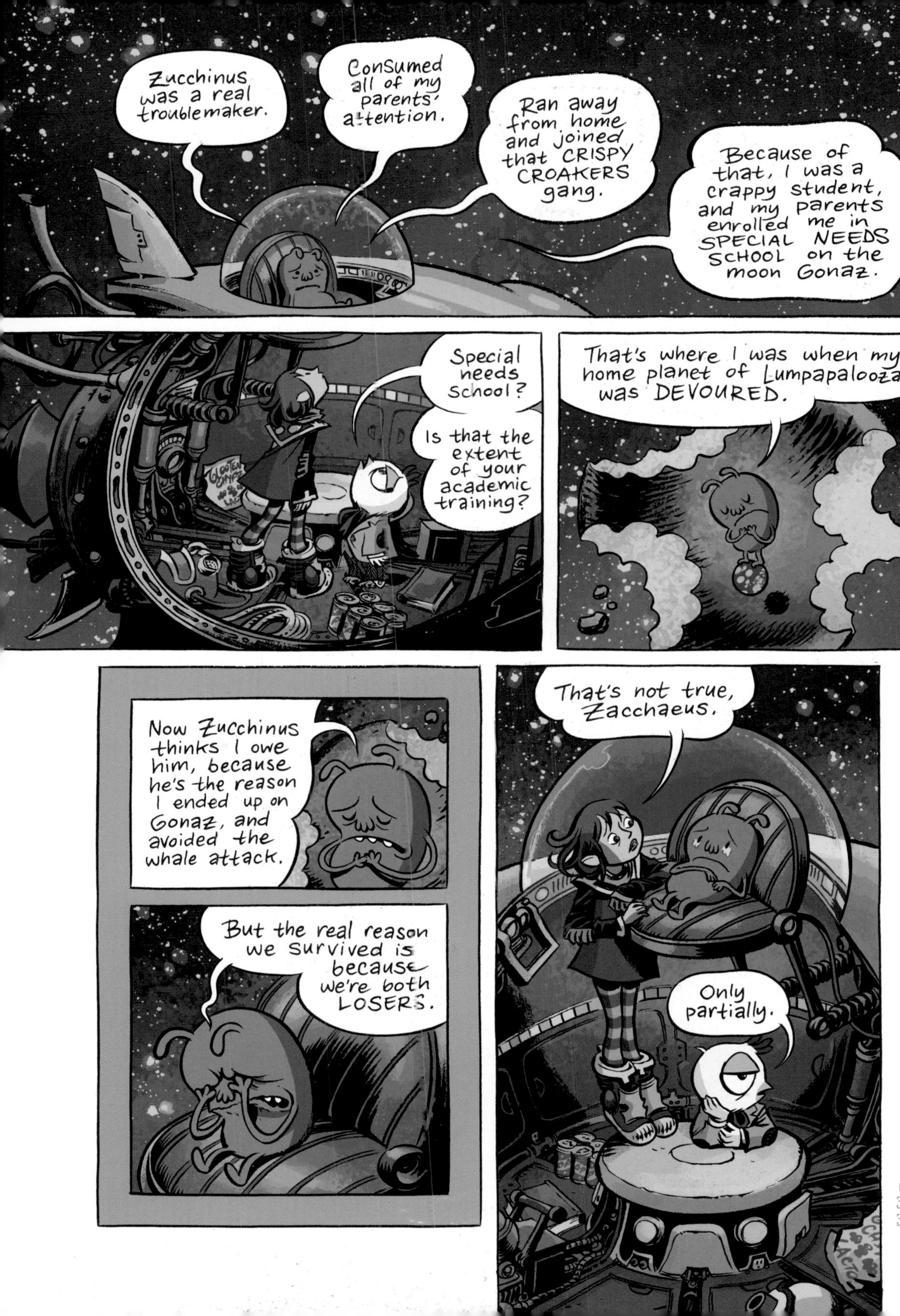
Zucchinus was a real troublemaker.
Consumed all of my parents' attention.
Ran away from home and joined that CRISPY CROAKERS gang.
Because of that, I was a crappy student, and my parents enrolled me in SPECIAL NEEDS SCHOOL on the moon Gonaz.
Special needs school?
Is that the extent of your academic training?
That's where I was when my home planet of Lumpapalooza was DEVOURED.
Now Zucchinus thinks I owe him, because he's the reason I ended up on Gonaz, and avoided the whale attack.
But the real reason we survived is because we're both LOSERS.
That's not true, Zacchaeus.
Only partially.

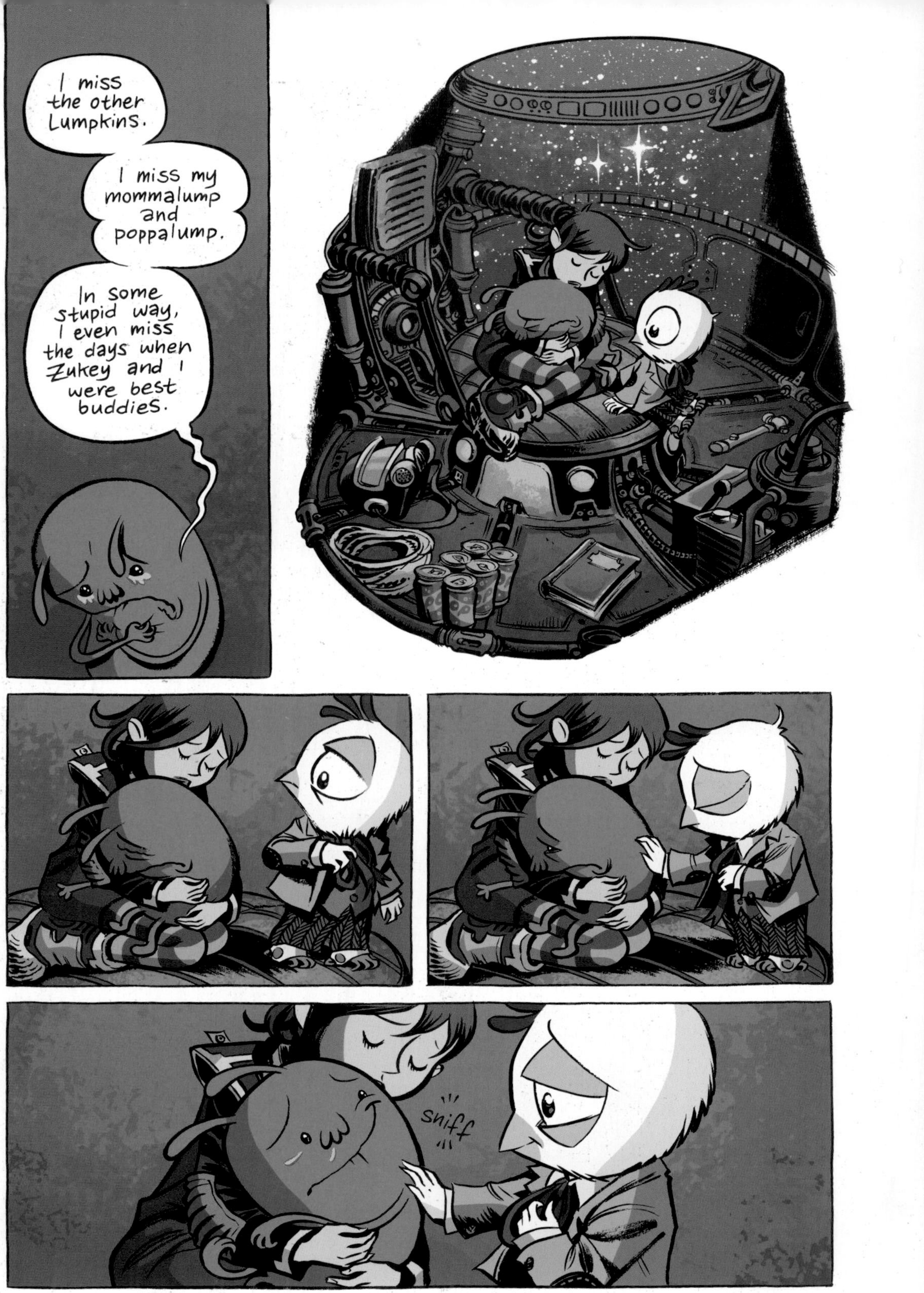
I miss the other Lumpkins.
I miss my mommalump and poppalump.
In some stupid way, I even miss the days when Zukey and I were best buddies.
sniff

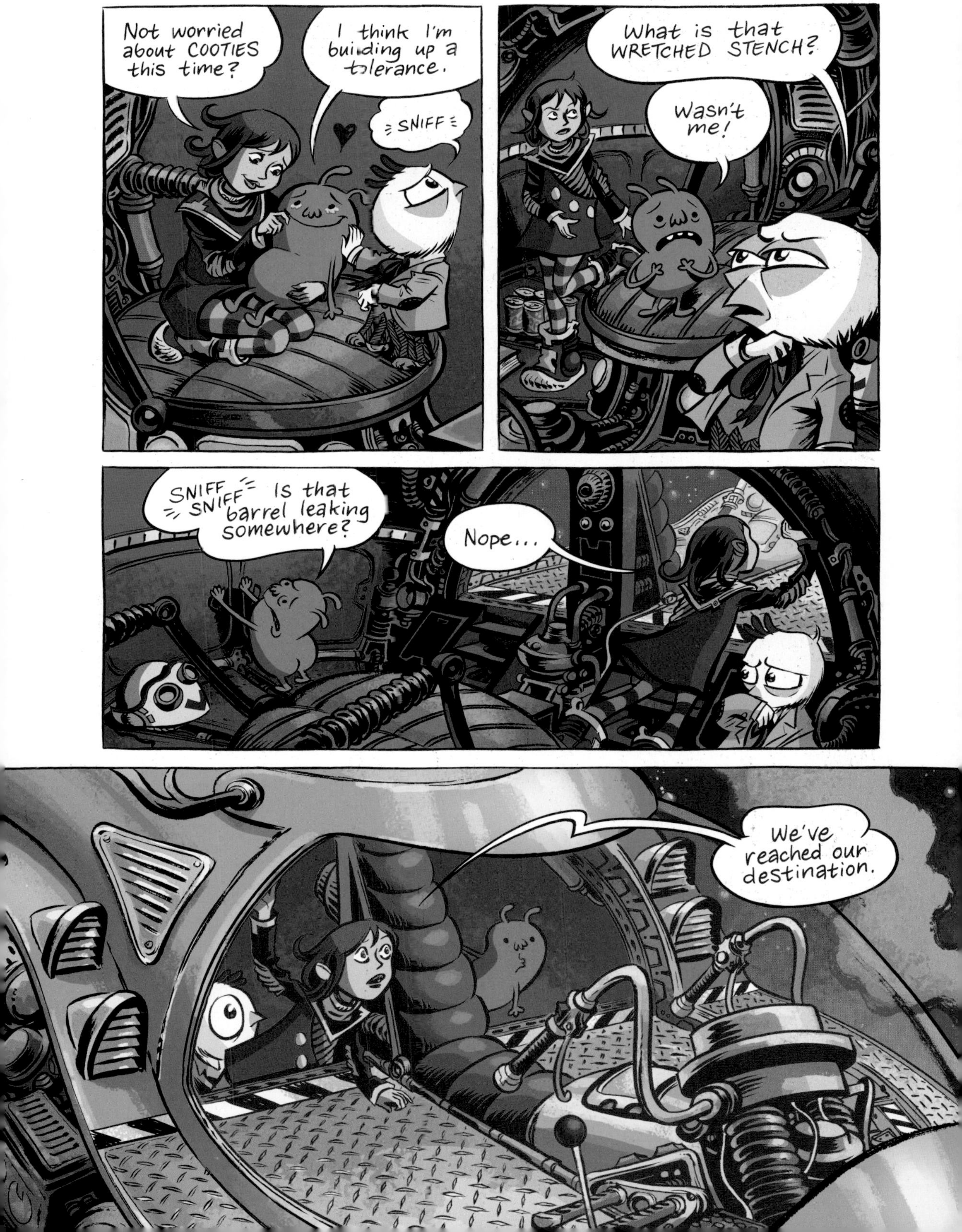
Not worried about COOTIES this time?
I think I'm building up a tolerance.
SNIFF
What is that WRETCHED STENCH?
Wasn't me!
SNIFF SNIFF Is that barrel leaking somewhere?
Nope...
We've reached our destination.

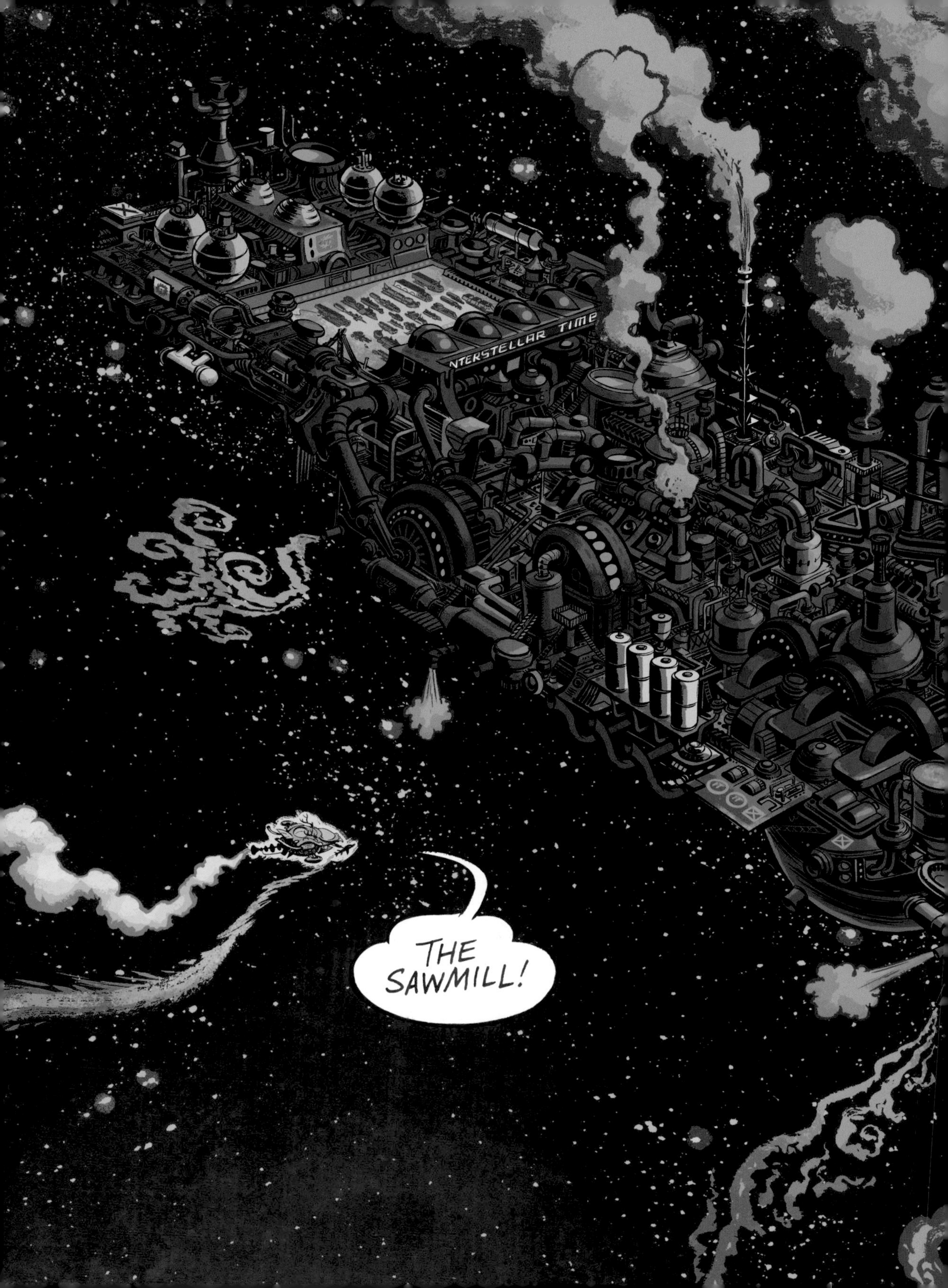
NTERSTELLAR TIME
THE SAWMILL!

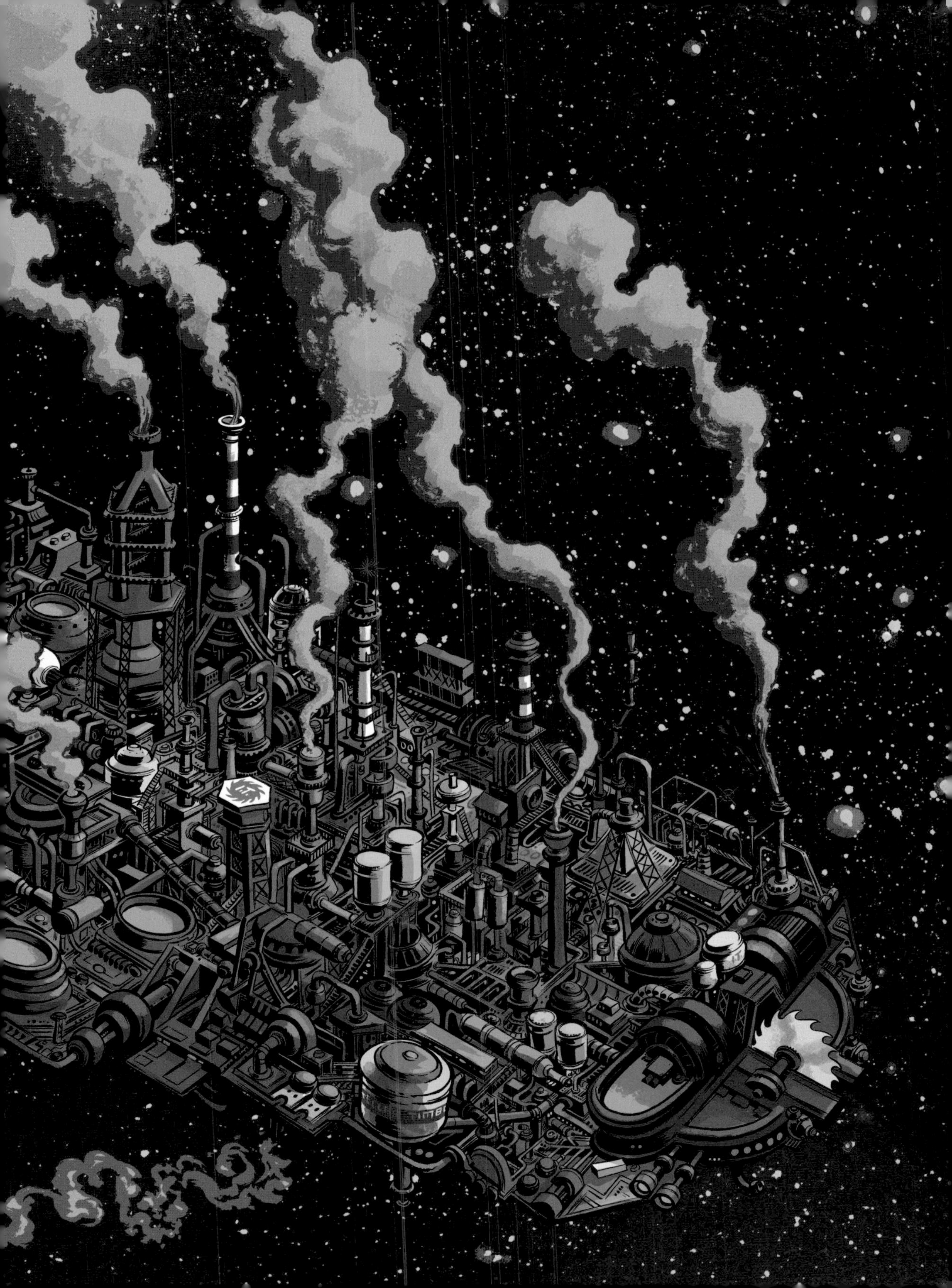

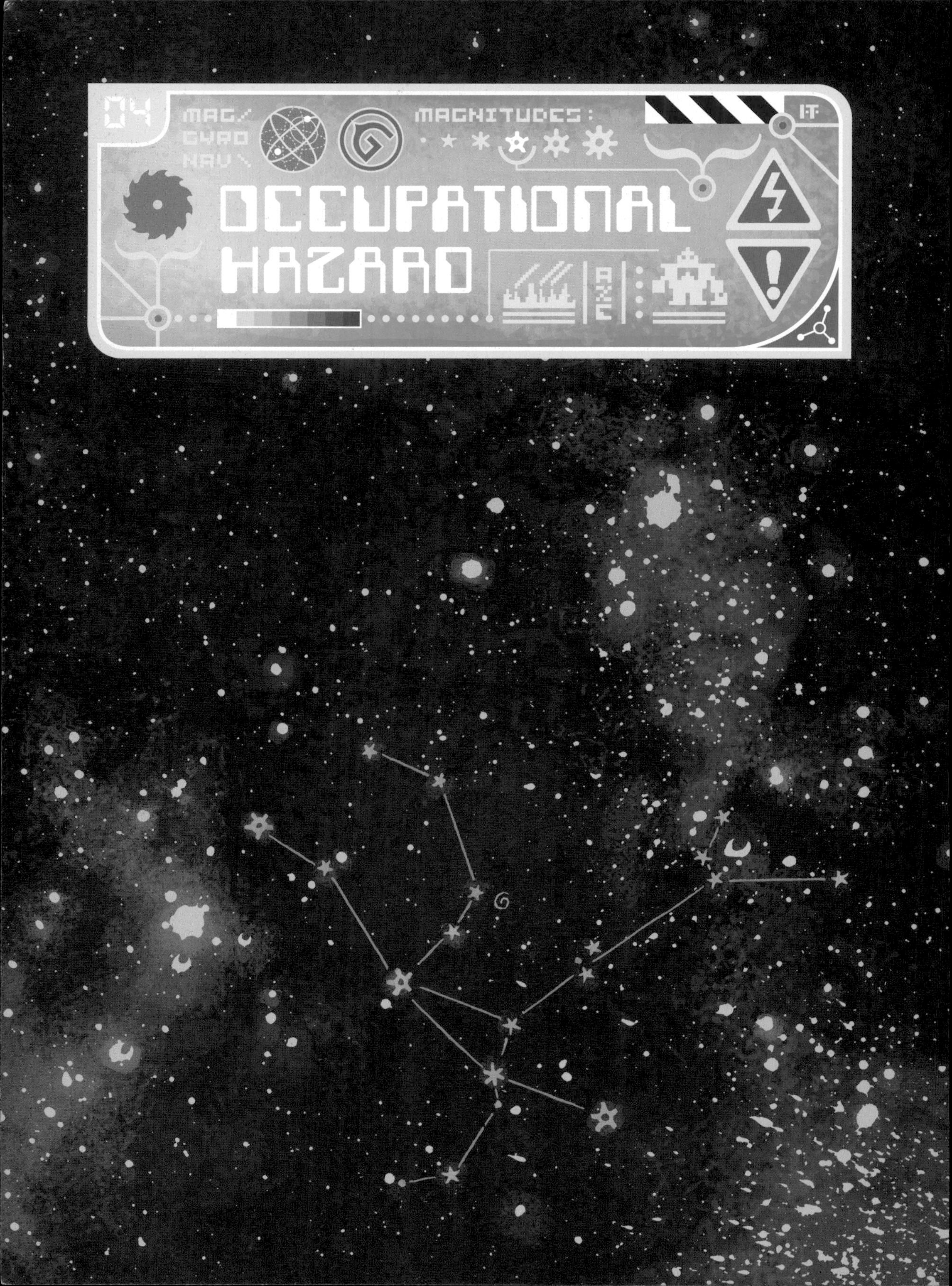
04
MAG/
GYRO
NAV\
MAGNITUDES:
OCCUPATIONAL
HAZARD

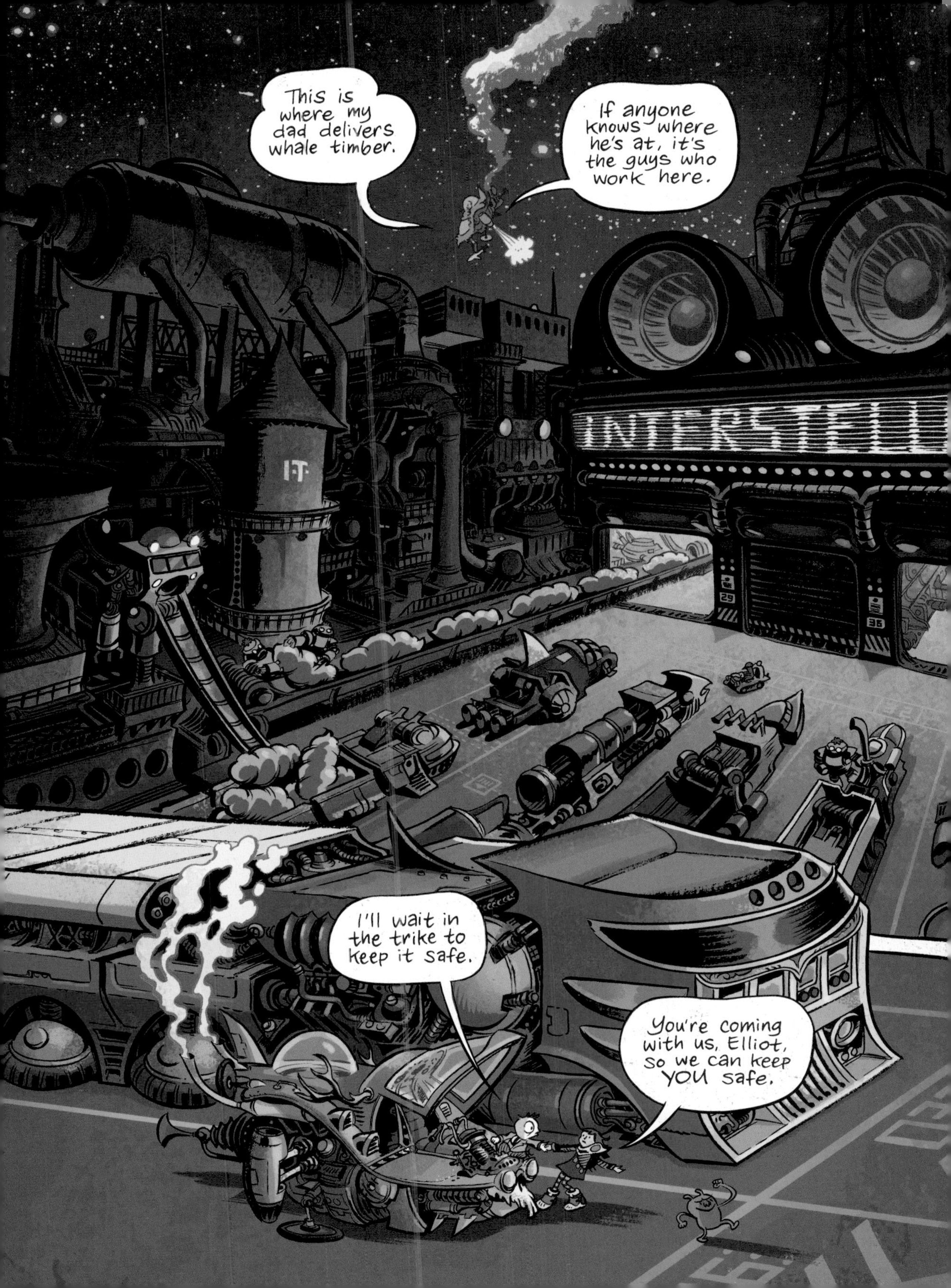
This is where my dad delivers whale timber.
If anyone knows where he's at, it's the guys who work here.
INTERSTELL
I·T·
I'll wait in the trike to keep it safe.
You're coming with us, Elliot, so we can keep YOU safe.

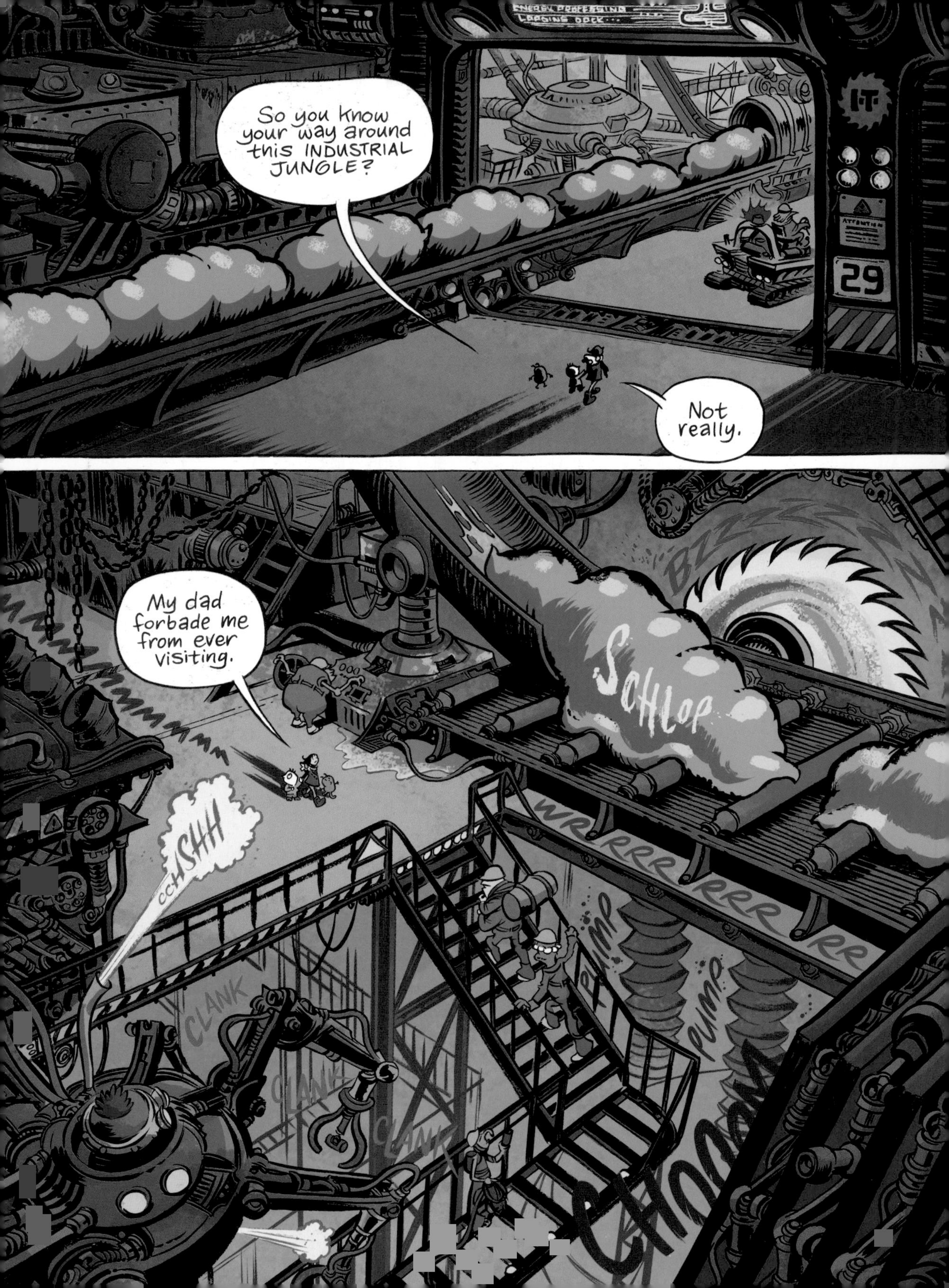

29
So you know your way around this INDUSTRIAL JUNGLE?
Not really.
My dad forbade me from ever visiting.
SCHLOP
CCHSHH
CLANK
CLANK
CLANK
PUMP
PUMP

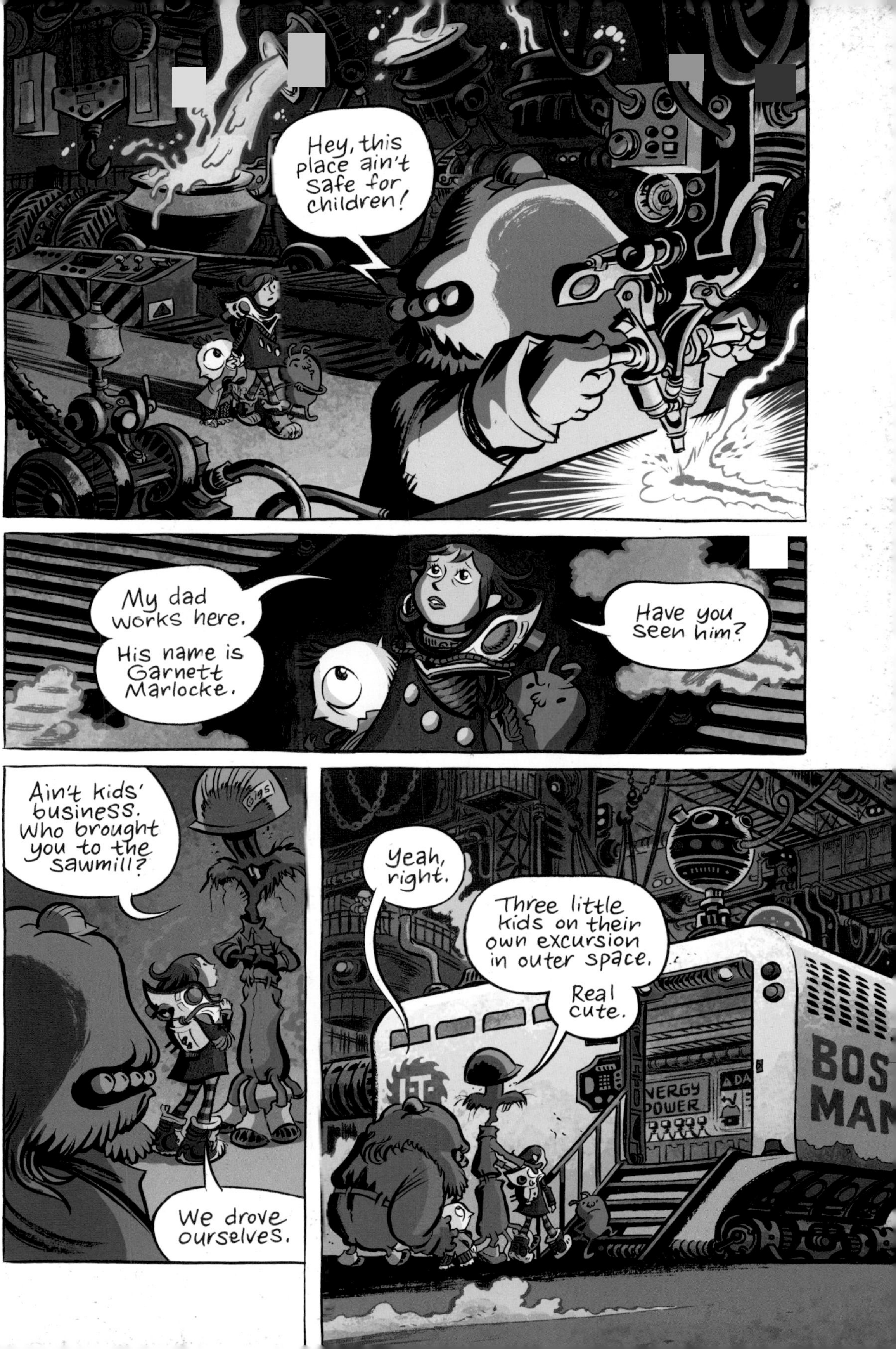
Hey, this place ain't safe for children!
My dad works here.
His name is Garnett Marlocke.
Have you seen him?
Ain't kids' business. Who brought you to the sawmill?
We drove ourselves.
Yeah, right.
Three little kids on their own excursion in outer space.
Real cute.

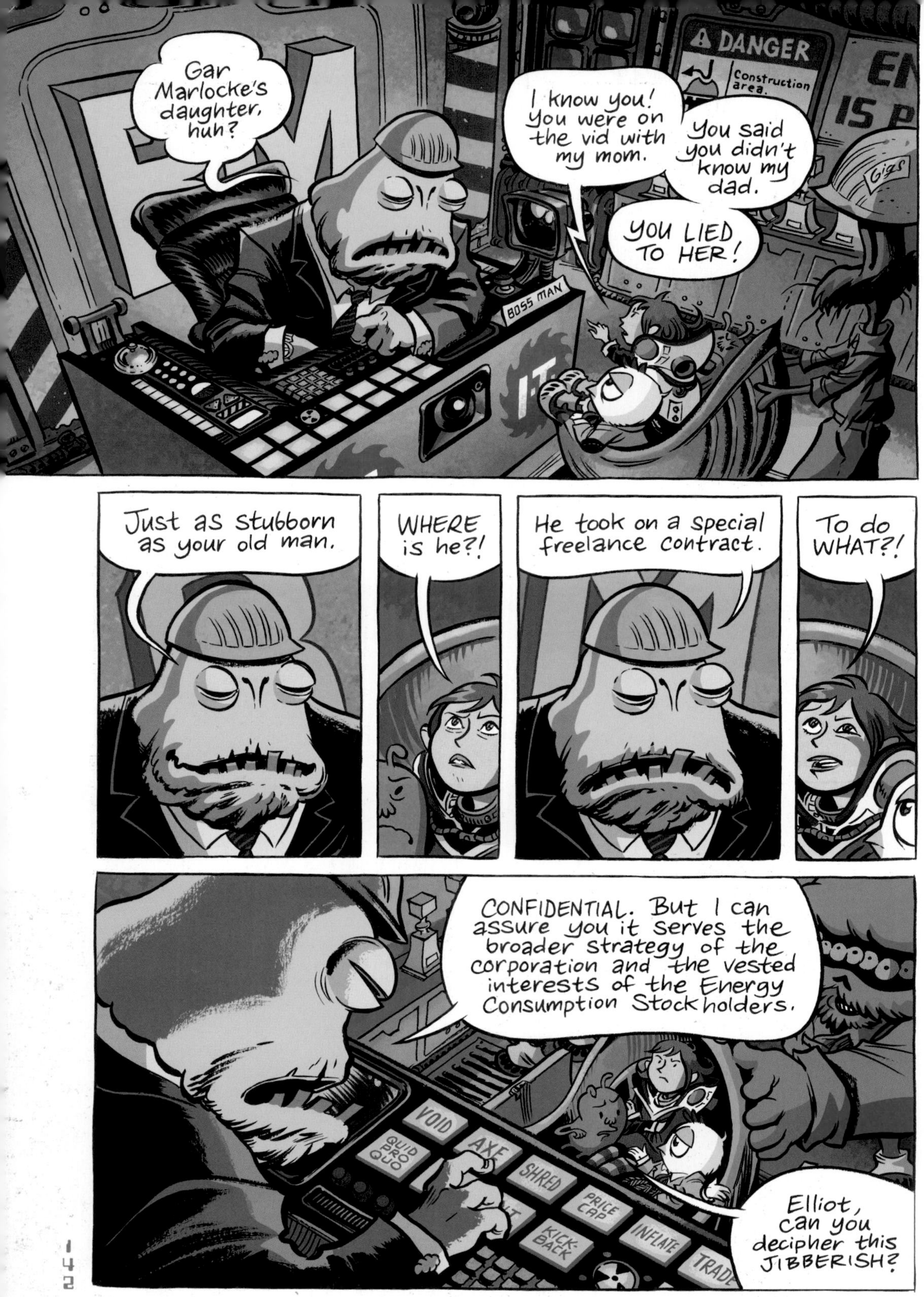
Gar Marlocke's daughter, huh?
I know you! You were on the vid with my mom.
You said you didn't know my dad.
YOU LIED TO HER!
DANGER
Construction area.
BOSS MAN
Just as stubborn as your old man.
WHERE is he?!
He took on a special freelance contract.
To do WHAT?!
CONFIDENTIAL. But I can assure you it serves the broader strategy of the corporation and the vested interests of the Energy Consumption Stockholders.
VOID
QUID PRO QUO
AXE
SHRED
PRICE CAP
KICK-BACK
INFLATE
TRADE
Elliot, can you decipher this JIBBERISH?

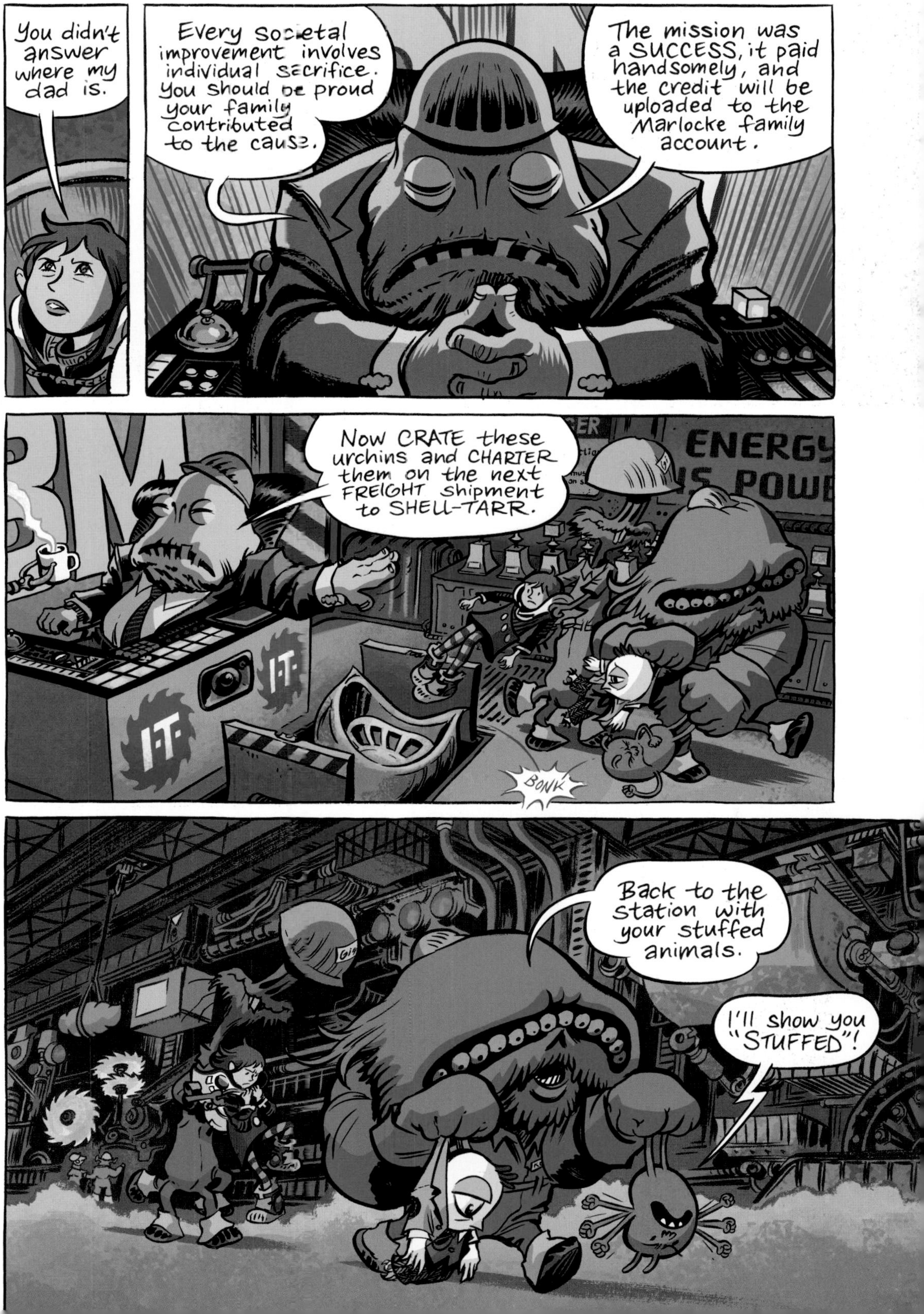
You didn't answer where my dad is.
Every societal improvement involves individual sacrifice. You should be proud your family contributed to the cause.
The mission was a SUCCESS, it paid handsomely, and the credit will be uploaded to the Marlocke family account.
Now CRATE these urchins and CHARTER them on the next FREIGHT shipment to SHELL-TARR.
ENERGY
BONK
Back to the station with your stuffed animals.
I'll show you "STUFFED"!

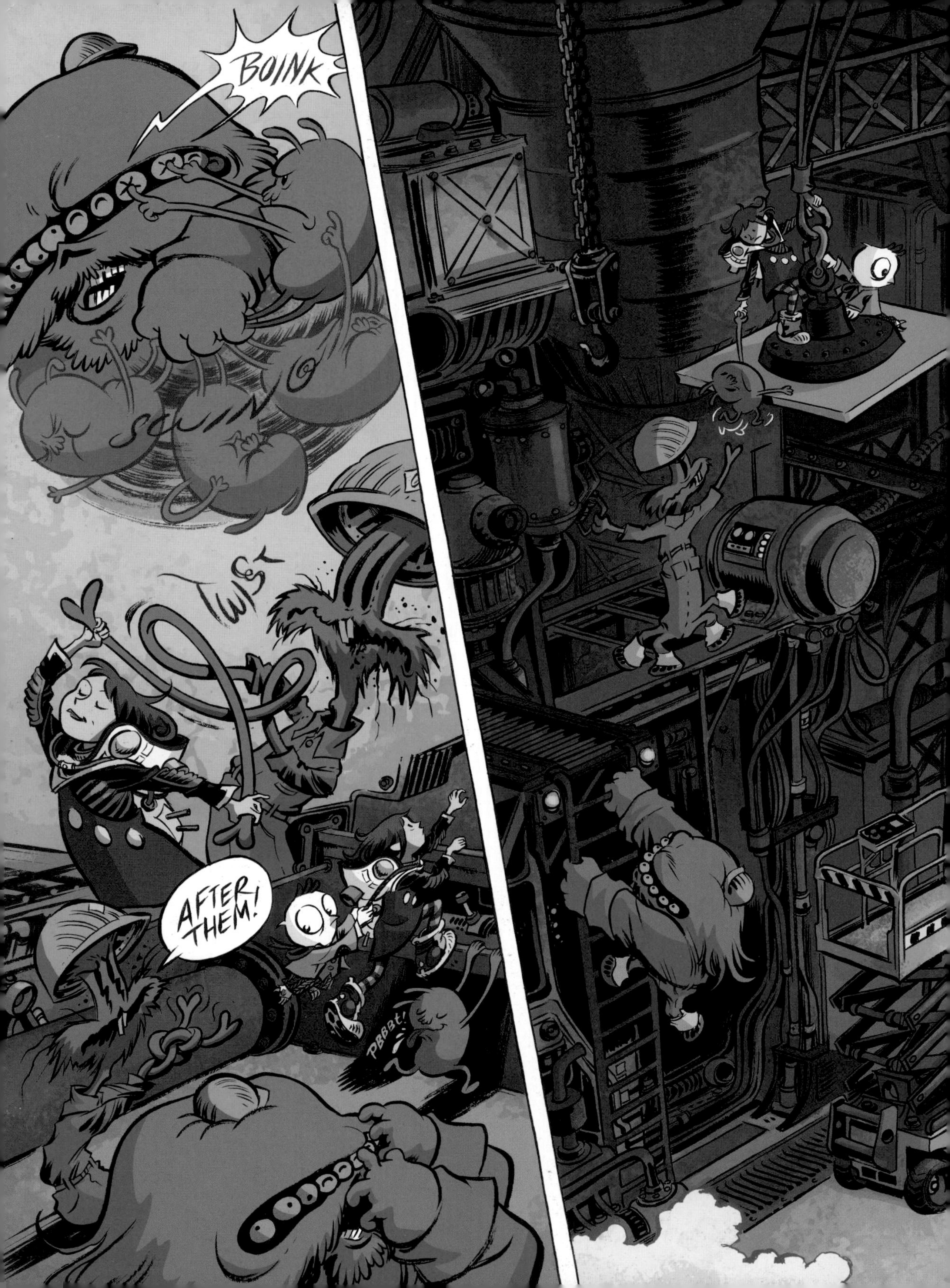
BOINK
SQUINT
TWIST
AFTER THEM!
PBBBt!

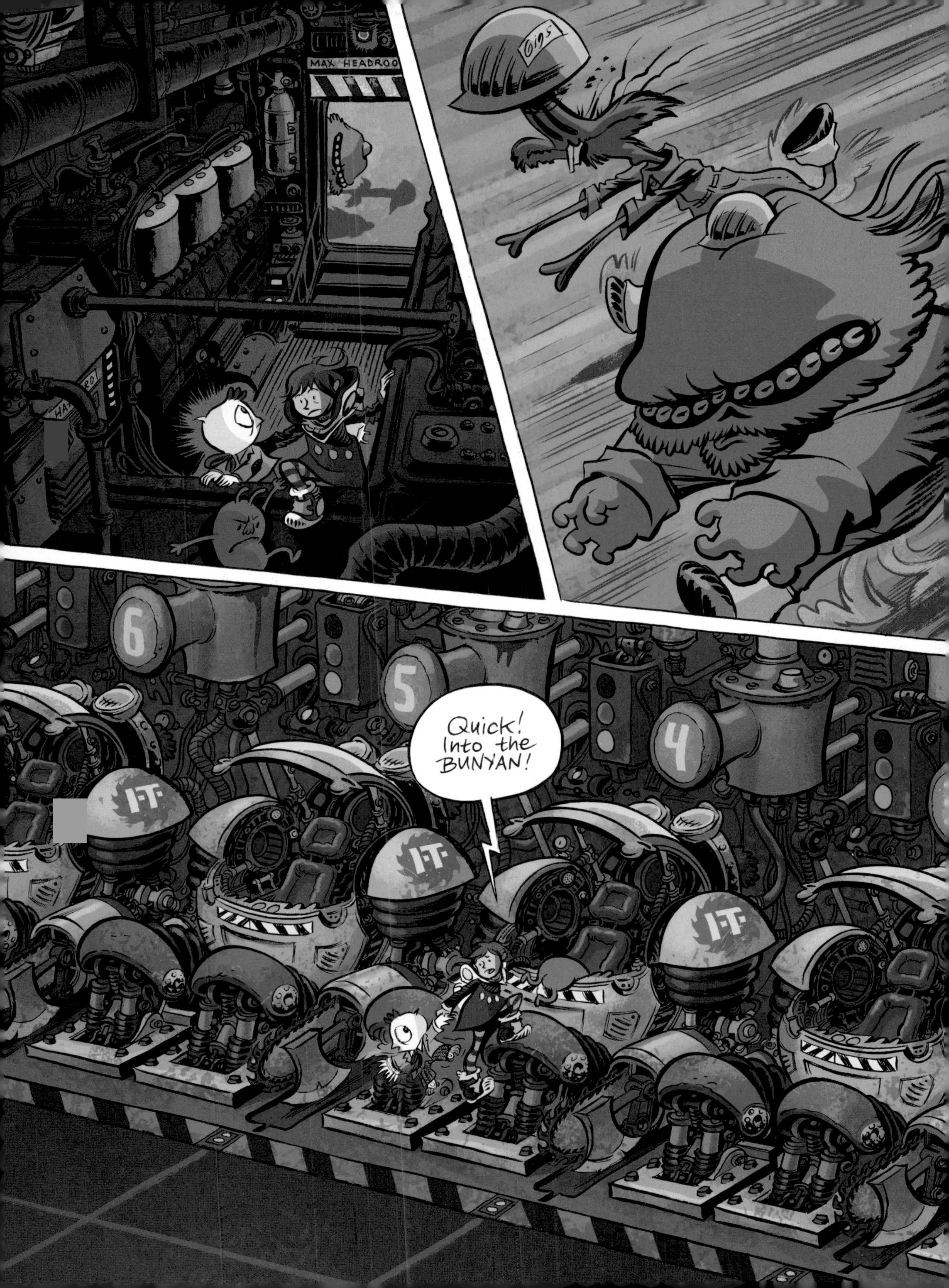
MAX HEADROO
Gigs
6
5
4
Quick! Into the BUNYAN!

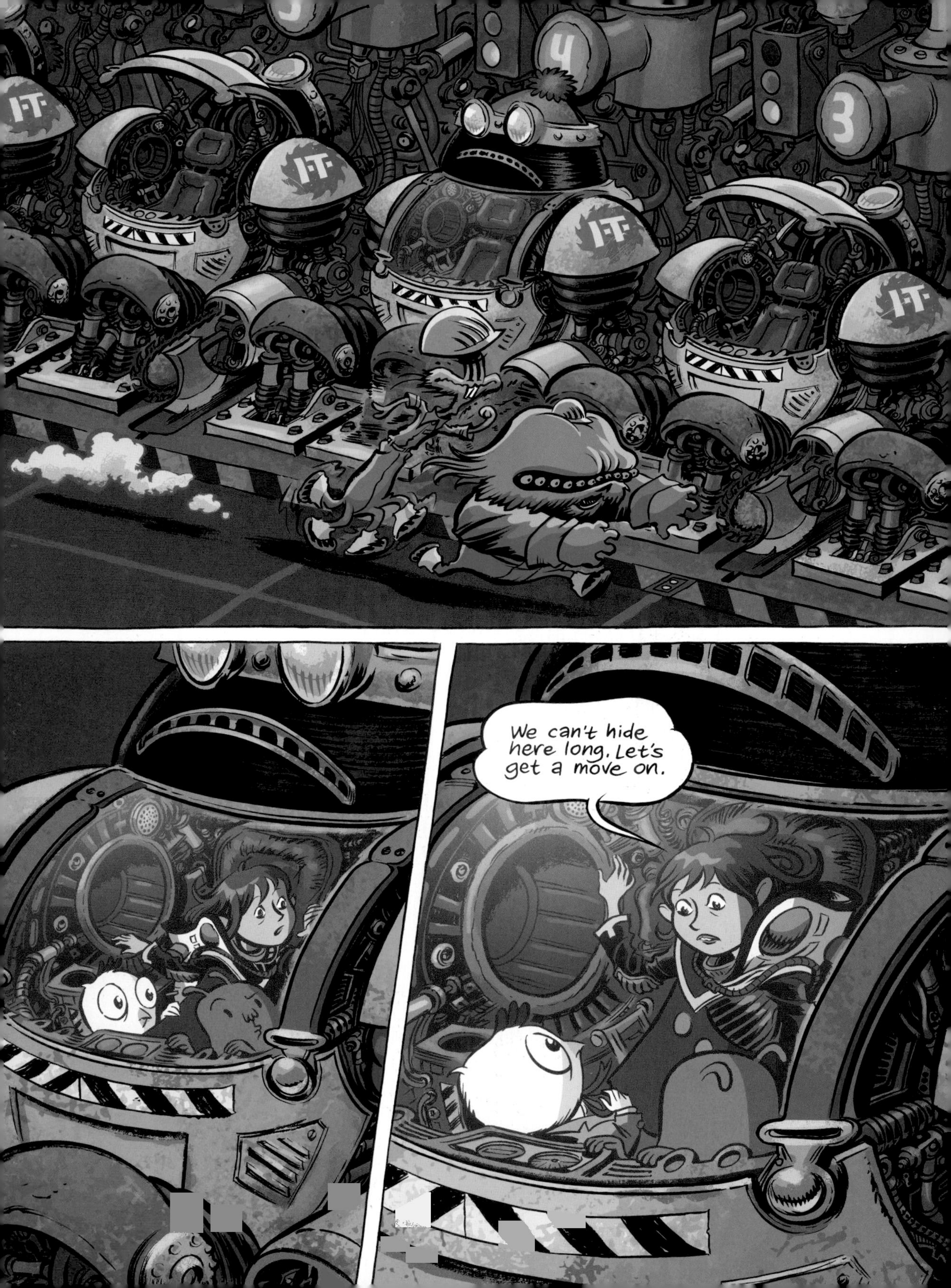
We can't hide here long. Let's get a move on.

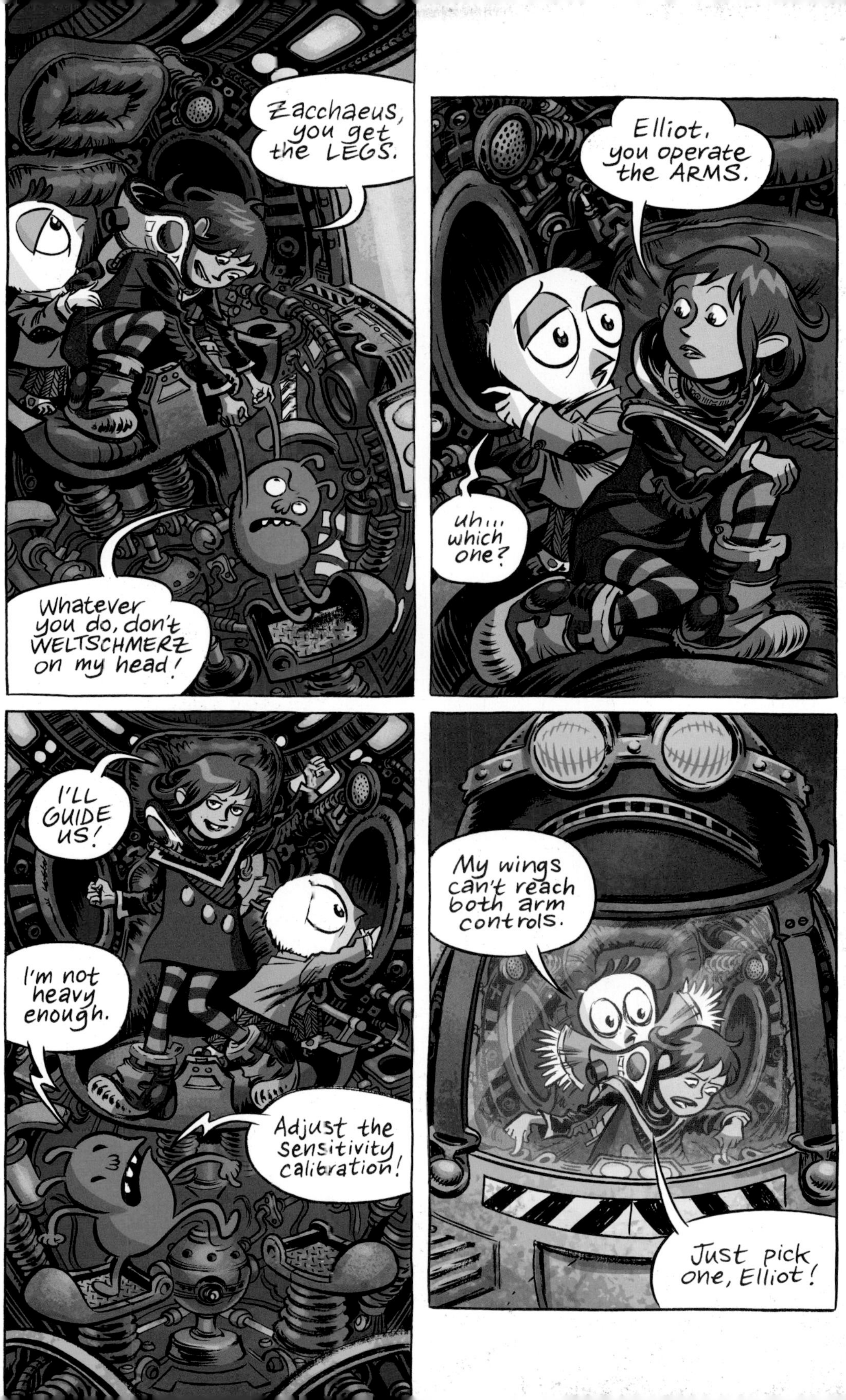
Zacchaeus, you get the LEGS.
Whatever you do, don't WELTSCHMERZ on my head!
Elliot, you operate the ARMS.
uh... which one?
I'LL GUIDE US!
I'm not heavy enough.
Adjust the sensitivity calibration!
My wings can't reach both arm controls.
Just pick one, Elliot!

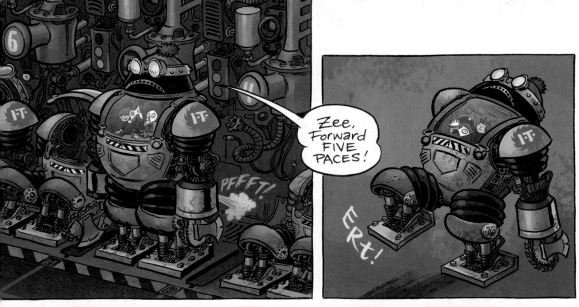

Zee, Forward FIVE PACES!

PFFFT!

ERt!

If I can only operate one arm, it'll be the RIGHT. The LEFT is considered unclean in many cultures.

Can't quite...

CAREFUL!

Watch it!

Okay then, À GAUCHE!

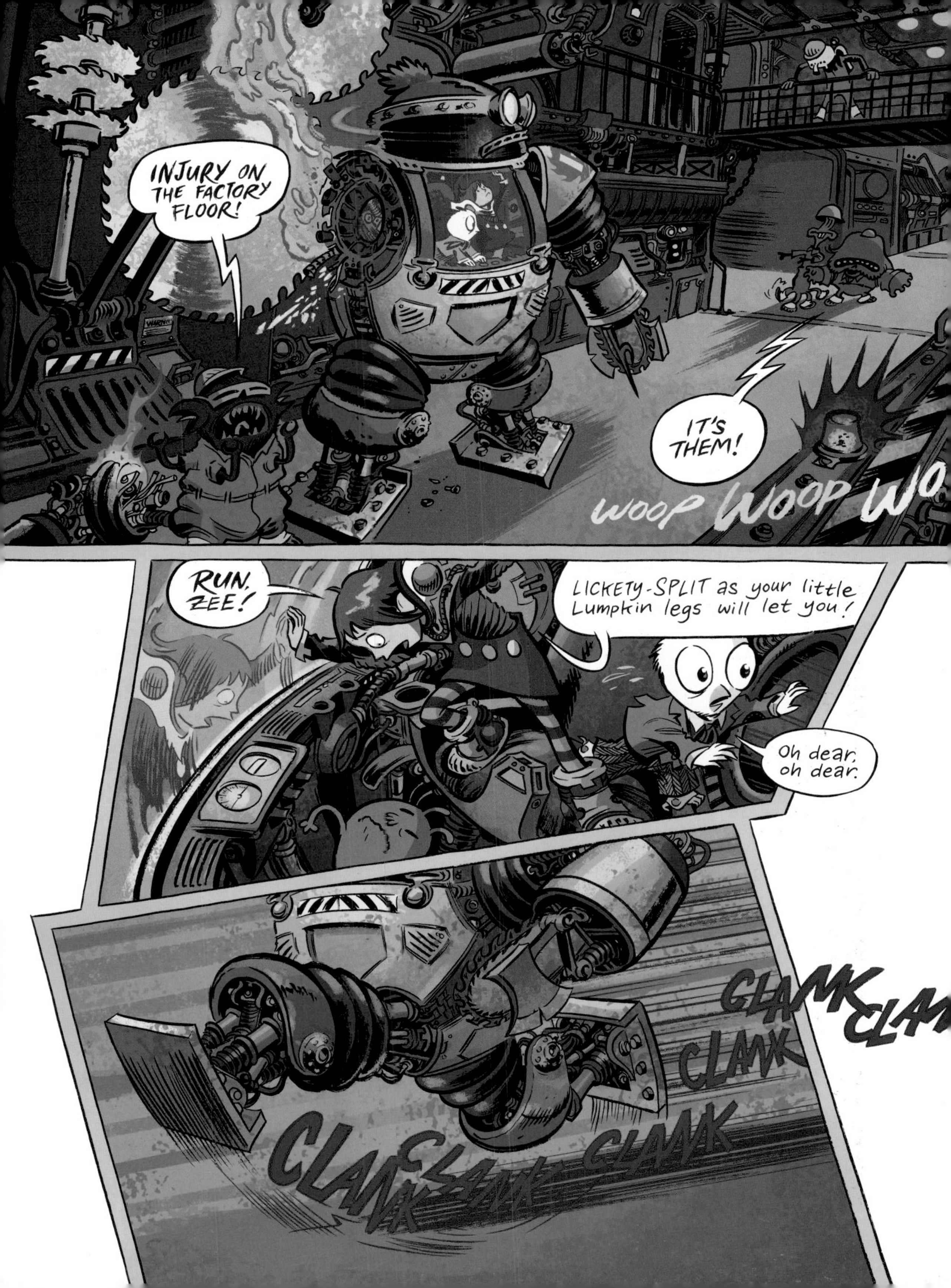
INJURY ON THE FACTORY FLOOR!
IT'S THEM!
WOOP WOOP WO
RUN, ZEE!
LICKETY-SPLIT as your little Lumpkin legs will let you!
Oh dear, oh dear.
CLANK CLANK CLANK
CLANK CLANK CLANK

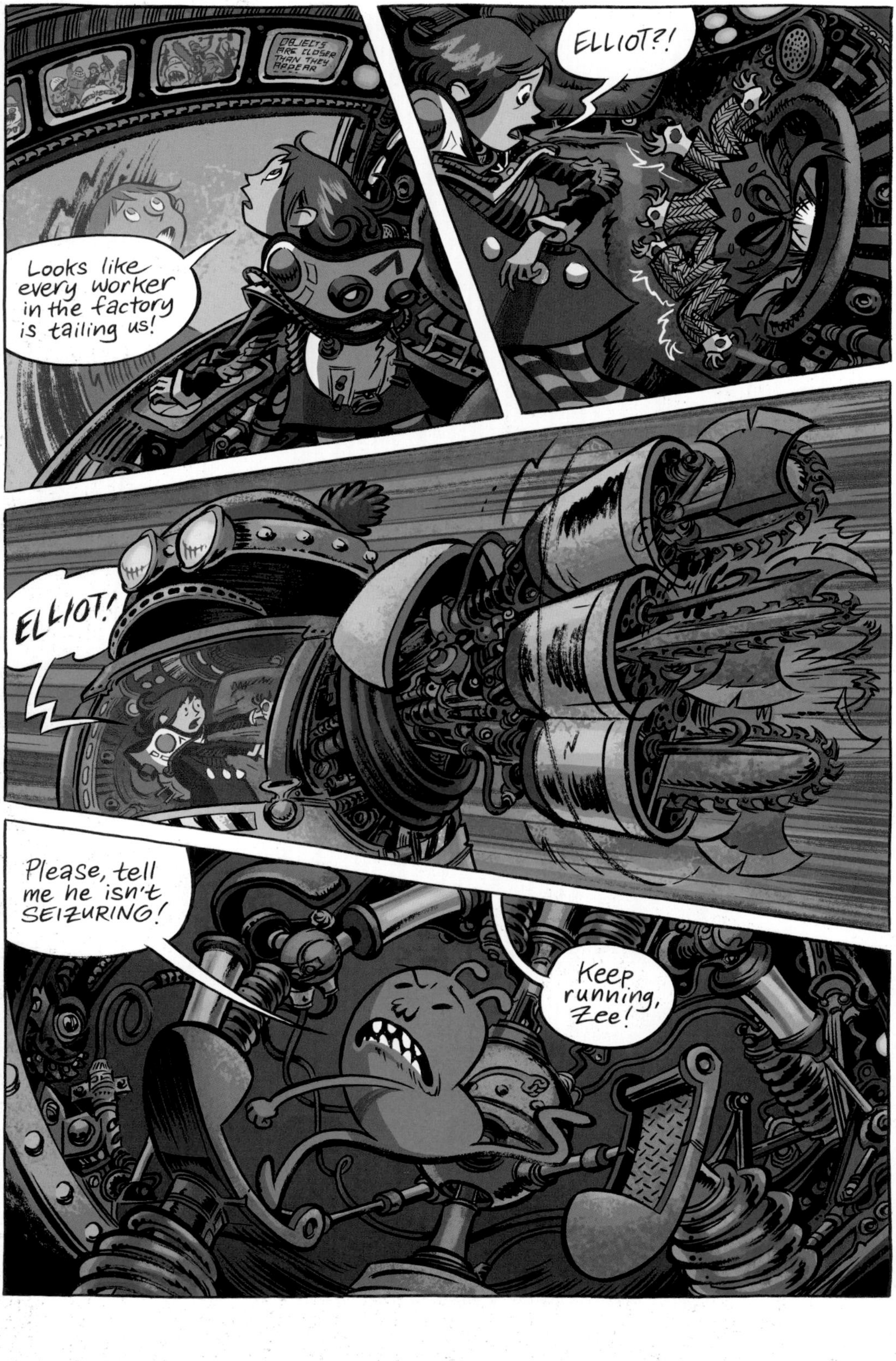
OBJECTS ARE CLOSER THAN THEY APPEAR
Looks like every worker in the factory is tailing us!
ELLIOT?!
ELLIOT!
Please, tell me he isn't SEIZURING!
Keep running, Zee!

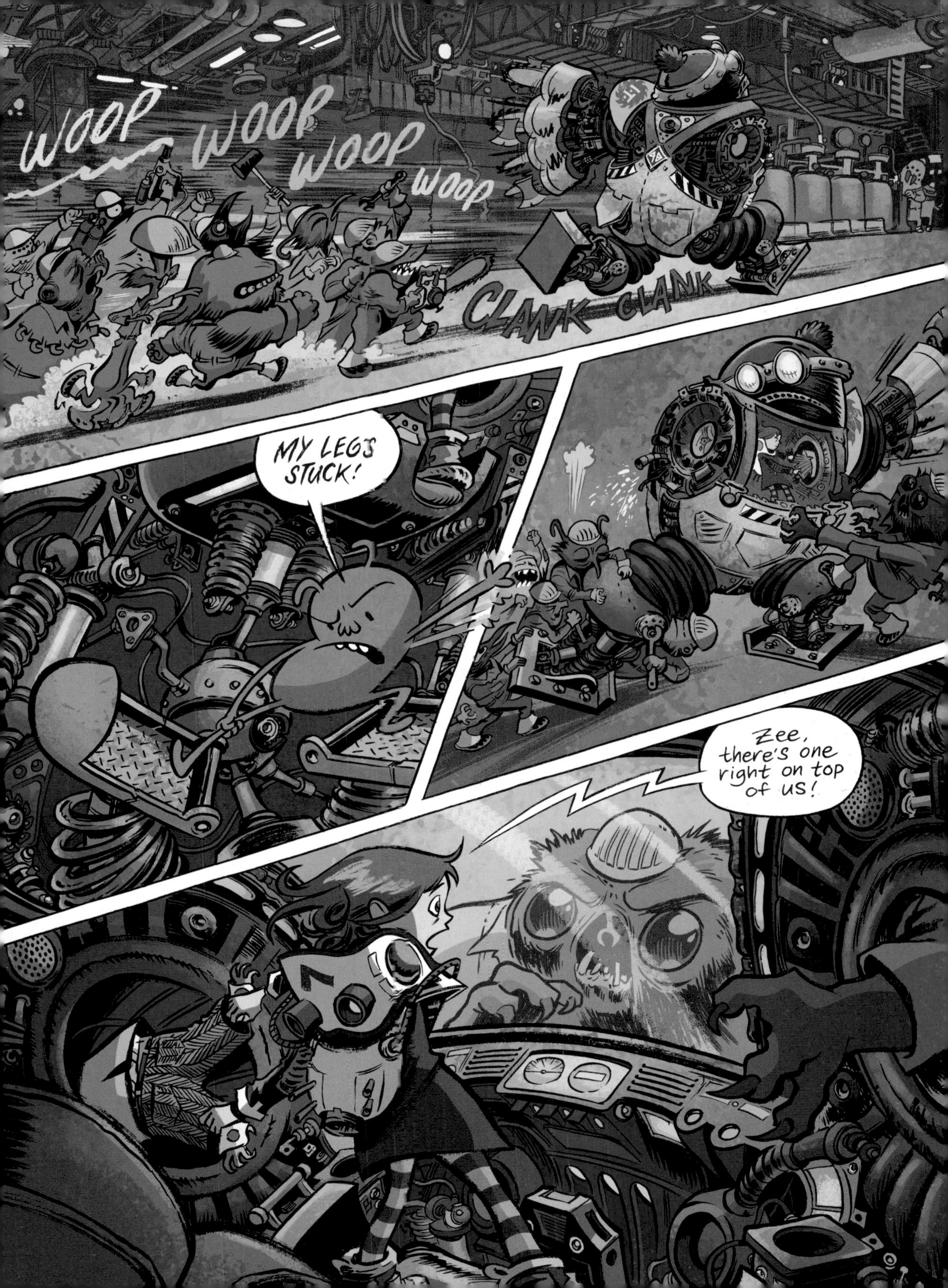
WOOP
WOOP
WOOP
WOOP
CLANK CLANK
MY LEG'S STUCK!
Zee, there's one right on top of us!

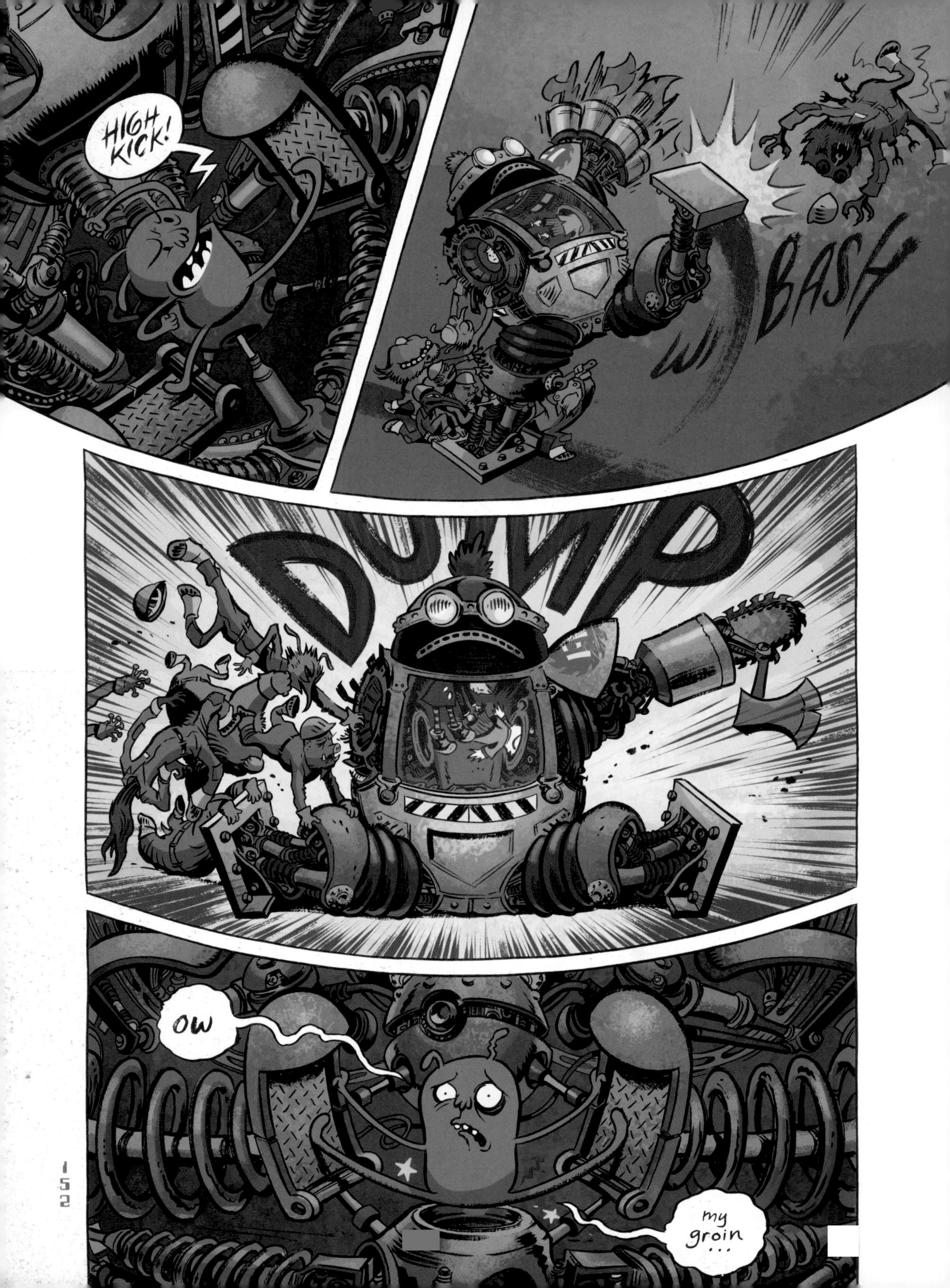
HIGH KICK!
BASH
DUMP
OW
my groin ...

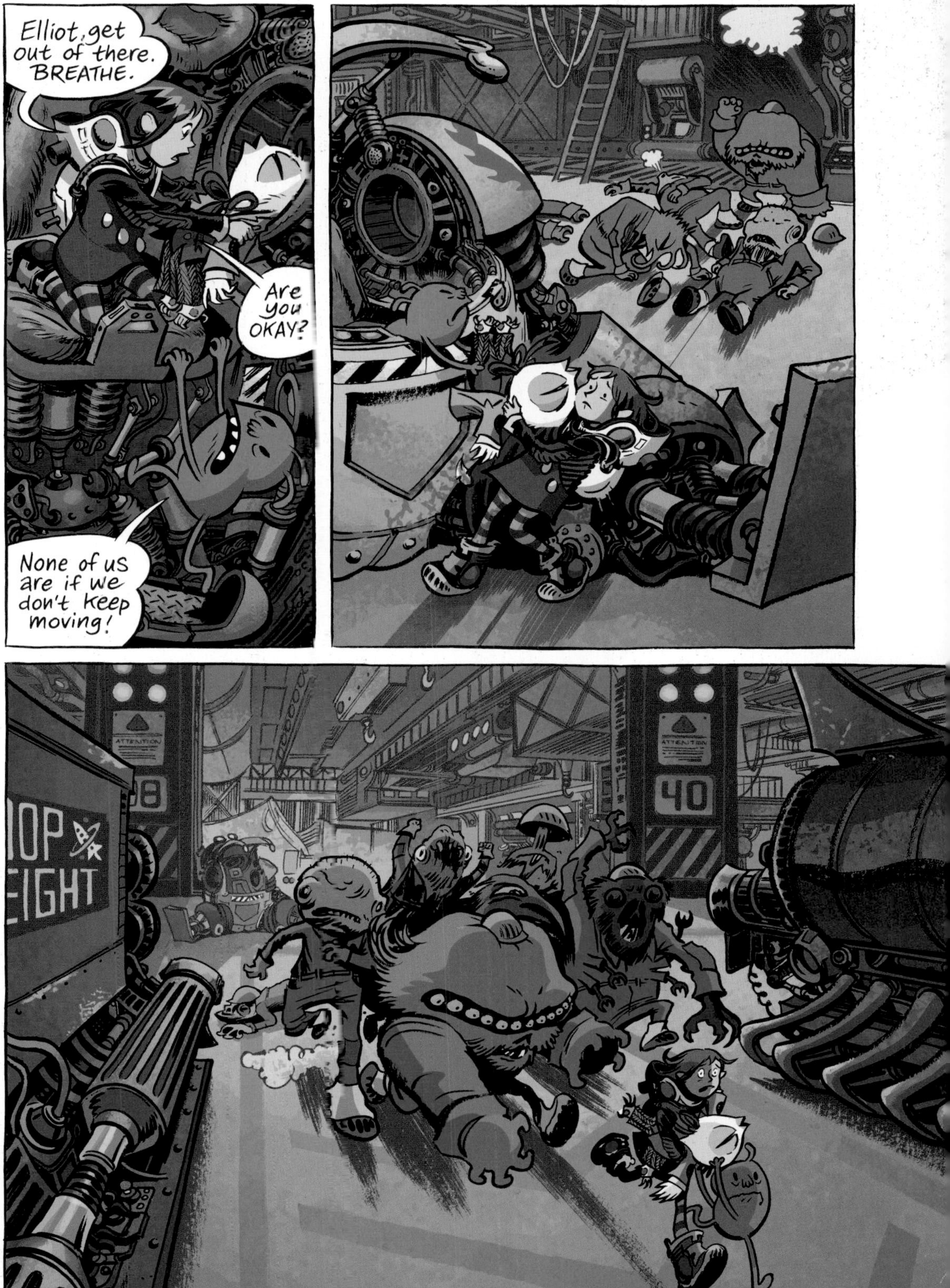
Elliot, get out of there. BREATHE.
Are you OKAY?
None of us are if we don't keep moving!
ATTENTION
ATTENTION
08
40
IOP
EIGHT

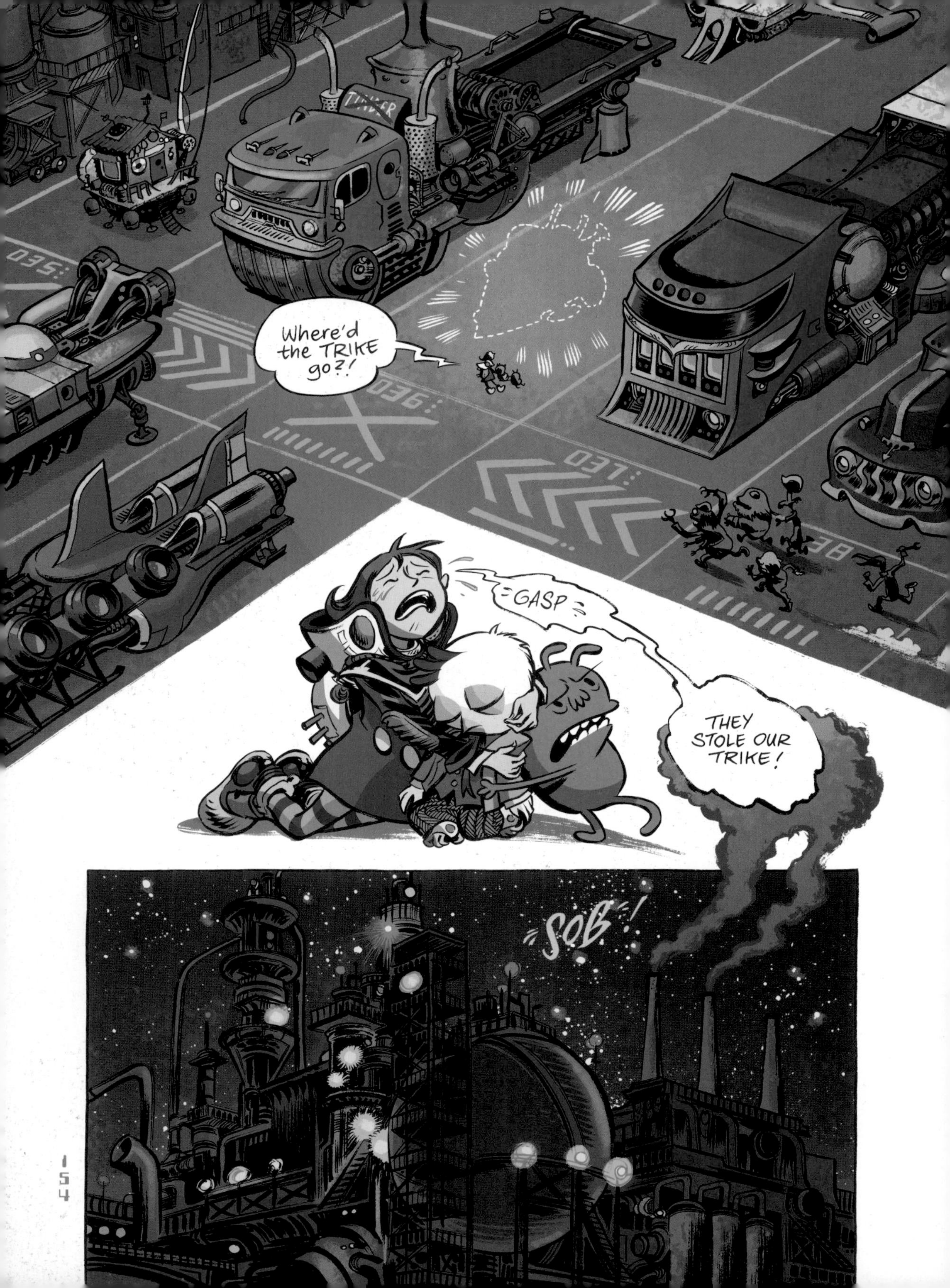
Where'd the TRIKE go?!
GASP
THEY STOLE OUR TRIKE!
SOB!

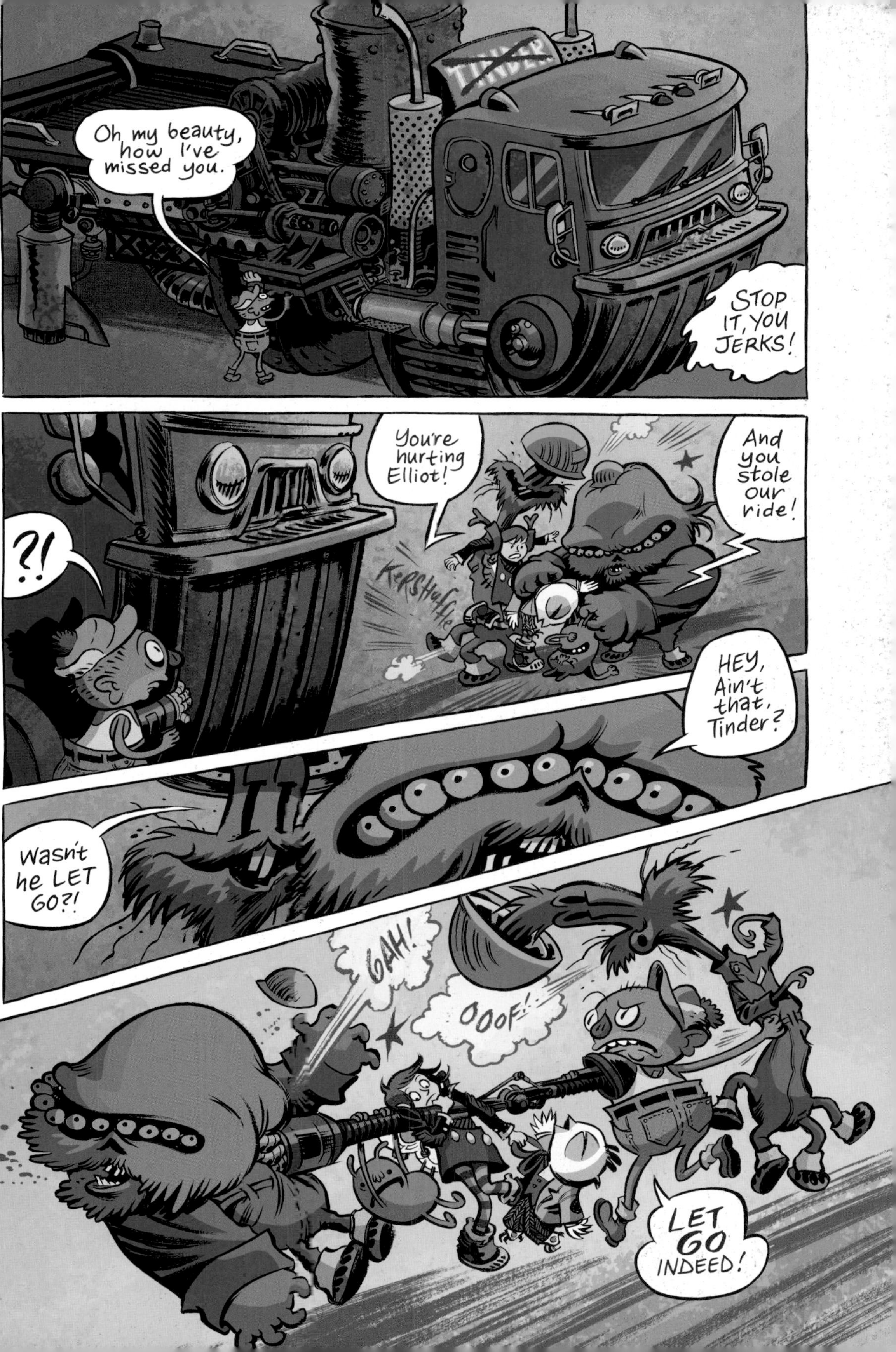

TINDER
Oh my beauty, how I've missed you.
STOP IT, YOU JERKS!
You're hurting Elliot!
And you stole our ride!
?!
KERSHUFFLE
HEY, Ain't that, Tinder?
Wasn't he LET GO?!
GAH!
OOOF!
LET GO INDEED!

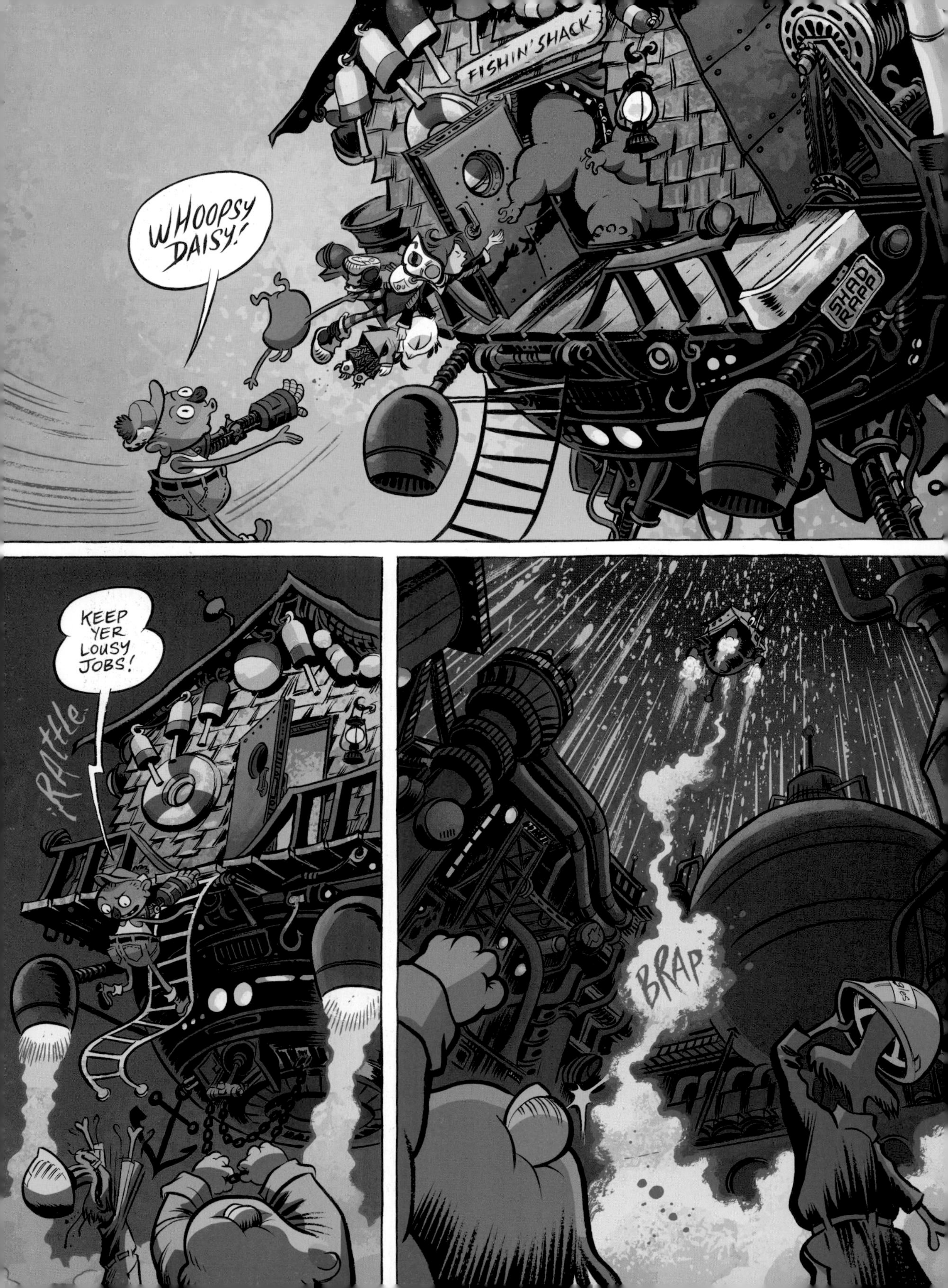
FISHIN' SHACK
WHOOPSY DAISY!
SHAD RAPP
KEEP YER LOUSY JOBS!
RATTLE
BRAP

Elliot needs to sleep off that seizure!

PLOP

SQUISH

I've always wanted my own feathery hug-buddy.

Who are these WEIRDOS?

This is my GODFATHER, Mr. Tinder!

EAT SLEEP FISH

Lieutenant Gerome the Gnome Allen. You can call me Gerry, GG, Little G....

Lieutenant? Were you in the WAR?

DAILY LIFE IS A WAR, LAD.

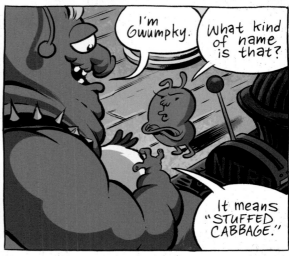

I'm Gwumpky.

What kind of name is that?

It means "STUFFED CABBAGE."

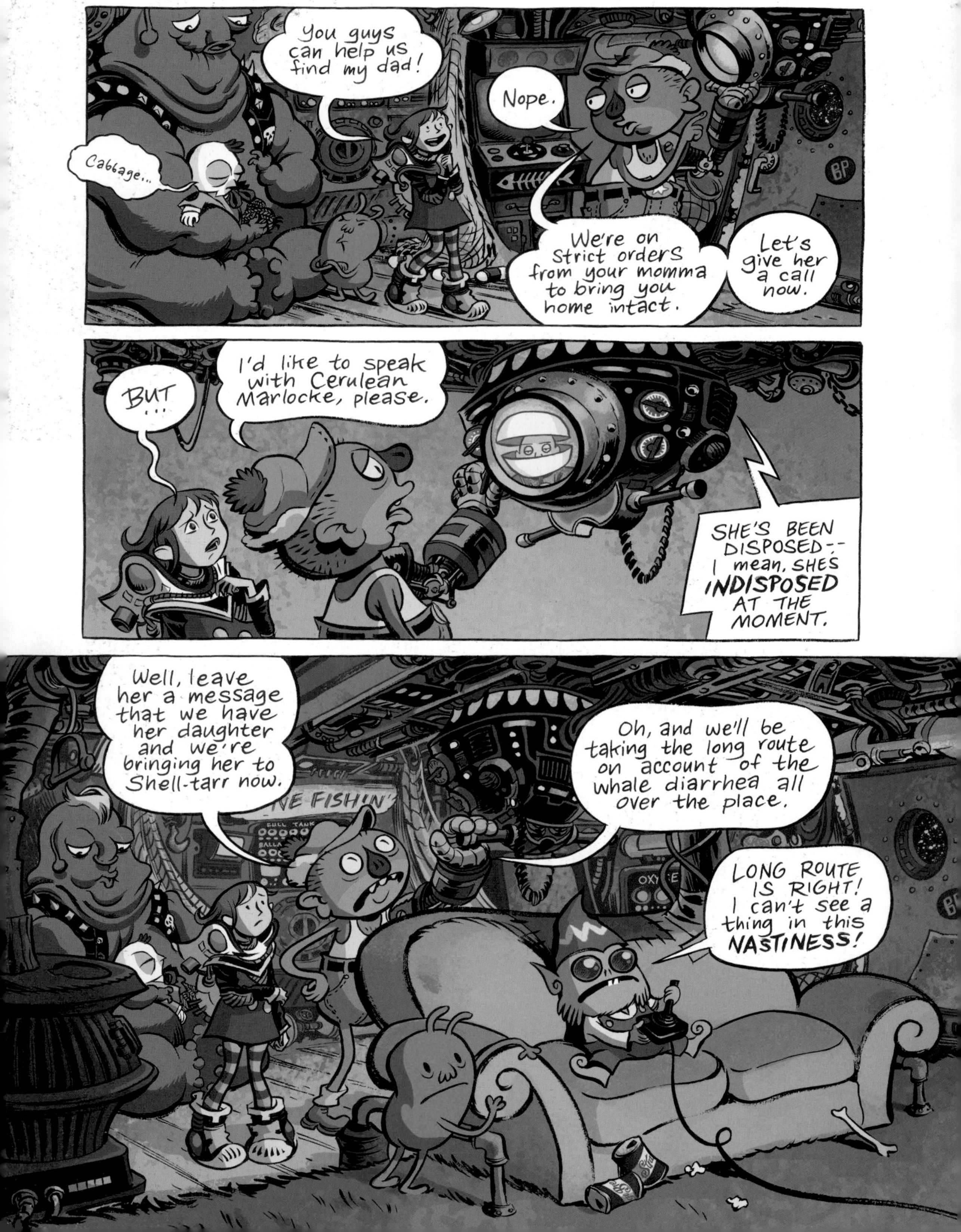
You guys can help us find my dad!
Cabbage...
Nope.
We're on strict orders from your momma to bring you home intact.
Let's give her a call now.
BUT ...
I'd like to speak with Cerulean Marlocke, please.
SHE'S BEEN DISPOSED-- I mean, SHE'S **INDISPOSED** AT THE MOMENT.
Well, leave her a message that we have her daughter and we're bringing her to Shell-tarr now.
Oh, and we'll be taking the long route on account of the whale diarrhea all over the place.
LONG ROUTE IS RIGHT! I can't see a thing in this **NASTINESS**!

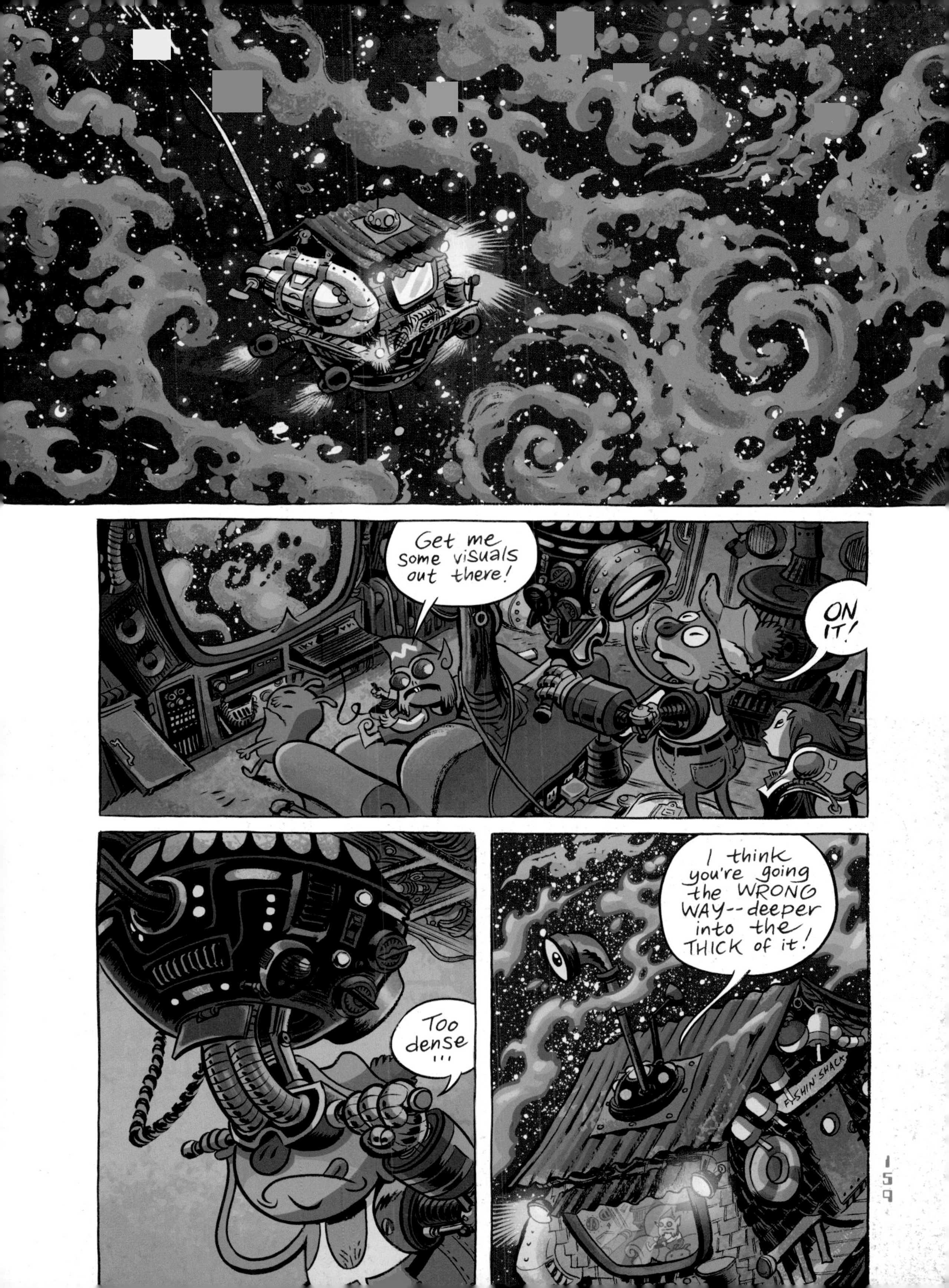
Get me some visuals out there!
ON IT!
Too dense . . .
I think you're going the WRONG WAY--deeper into the THICK of it!
FISHIN' SHACK

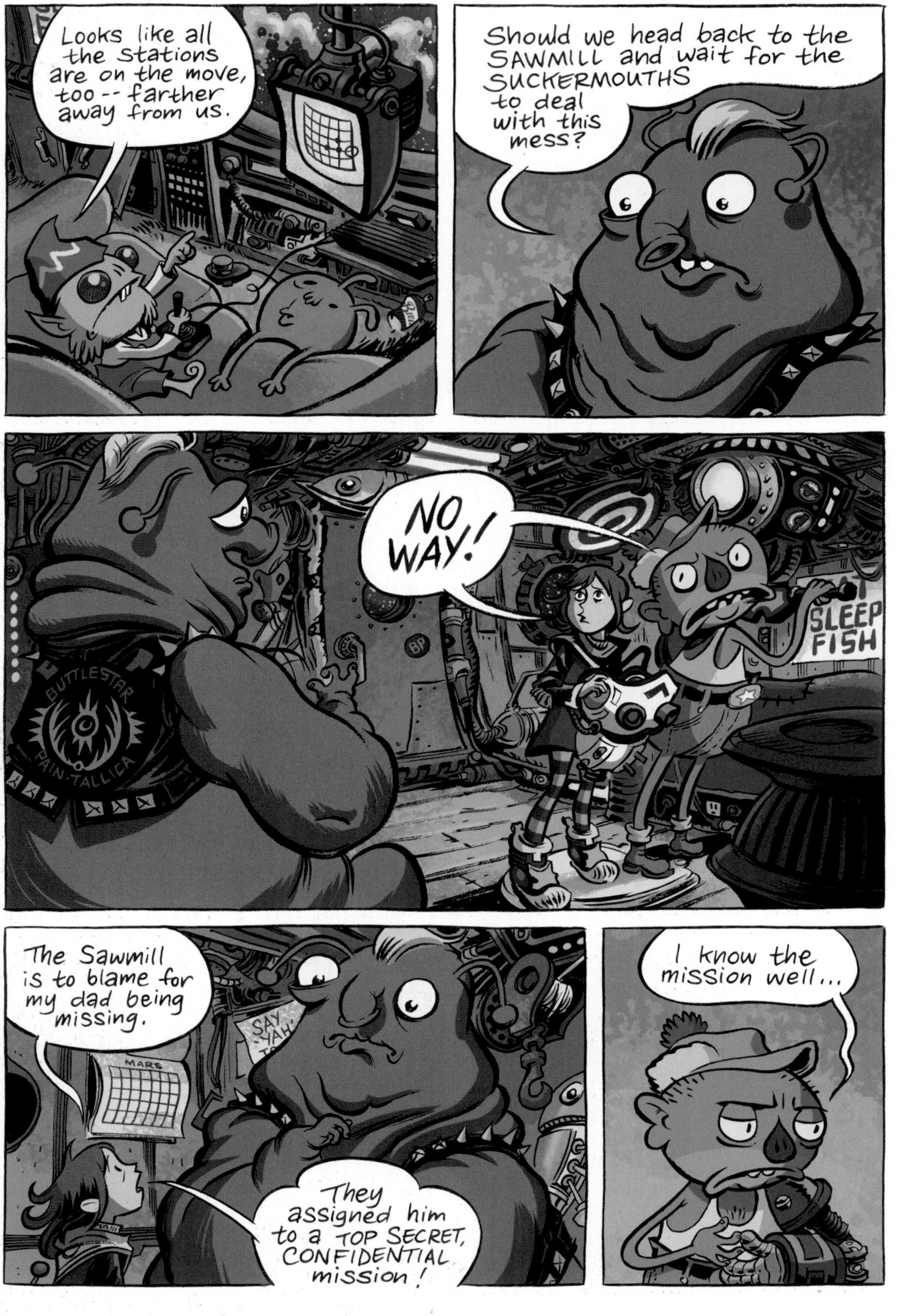
Looks like all the stations are on the move, too -- farther away from us.
Should we head back to the SAWMILL and wait for the SUCKERMOUTHS to deal with this mess?
NO WAY!
EAT SLEEP FISH
BUTTLESTAR PAIN-TALLICA
The Sawmill is to blame for my dad being missing.
MARS
They assigned him to a TOP SECRET, CONFIDENTIAL mission!
I know the mission well...

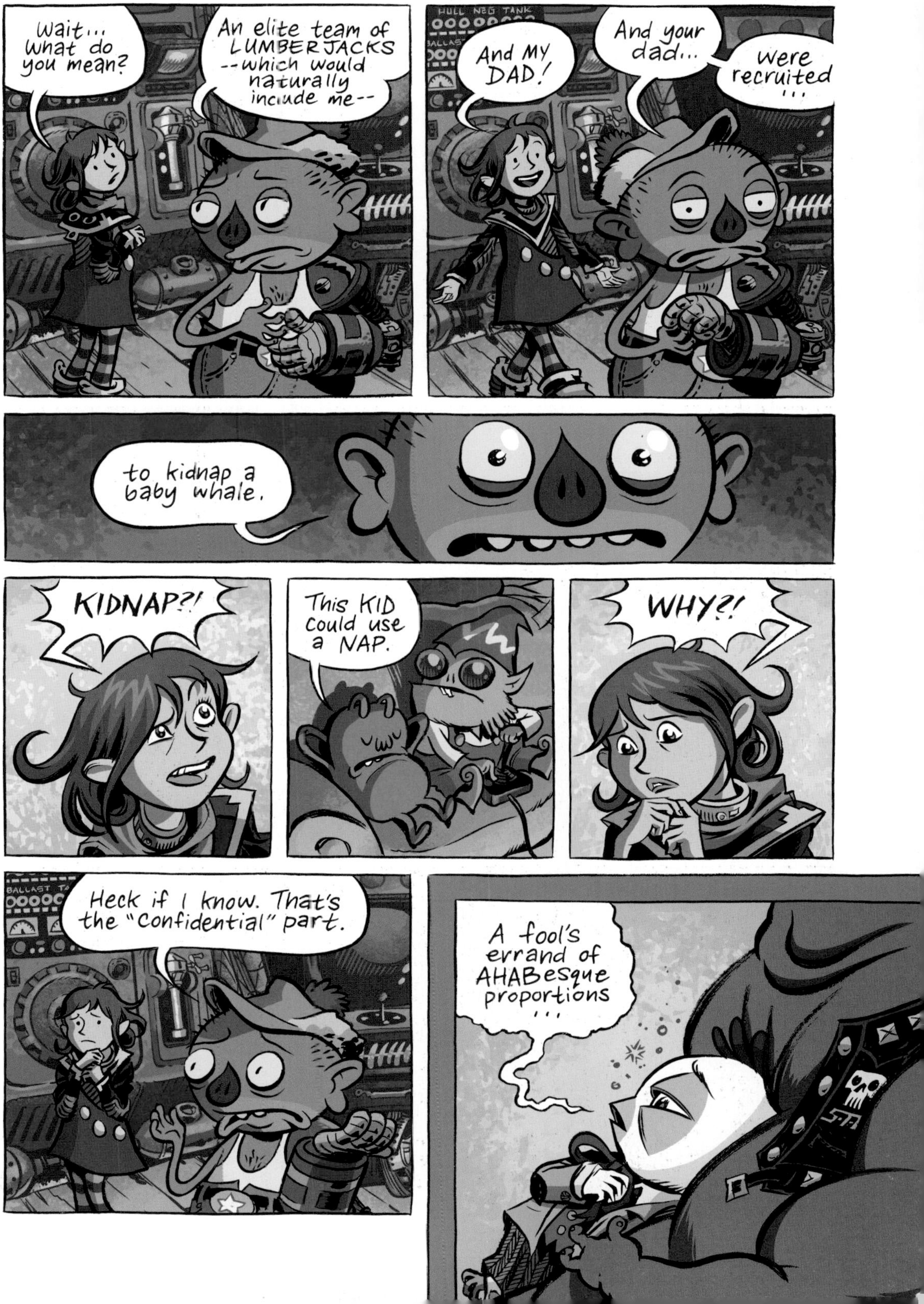
Wait... what do you mean?
An elite team of LUMBERJACKS --which would naturally include me--
And MY DAD!
And your dad...
Were recruited ...
to kidnap a baby whale.
KIDNAP?!
This KID could use a NAP.
WHY?!
Heck if I know. That's the "Confidential" part.
A fool's errand of AHABesque proportions ...

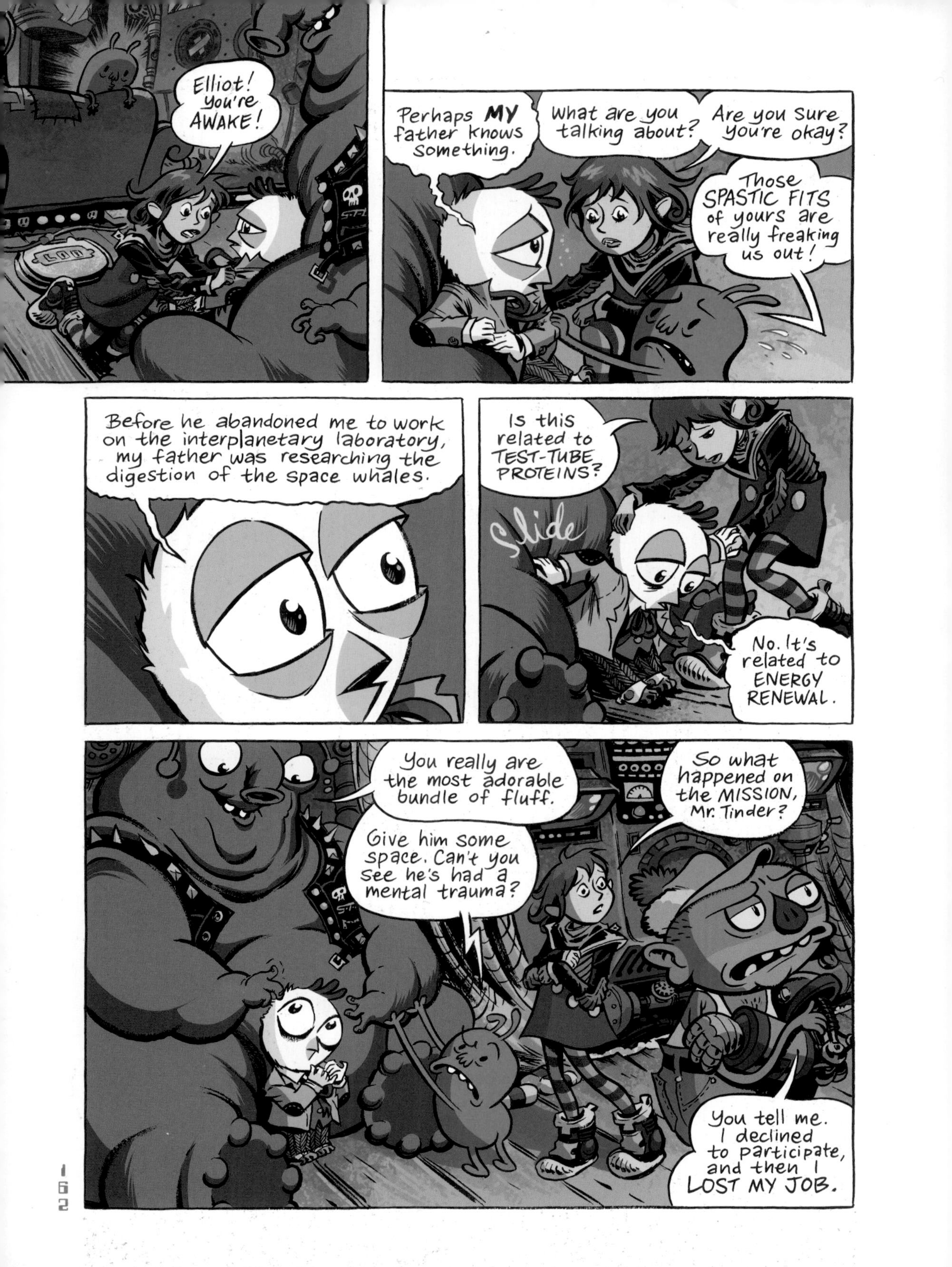
Elliot! You're AWAKE!
Perhaps MY father knows something.
What are you talking about?
Are you sure you're okay?
Those SPASTIC FITS of yours are really freaking us out!
Before he abandoned me to work on the interplanetary laboratory, my father was researching the digestion of the space whales.
Is this related to TEST-TUBE PROTEINS?
Slide
No. It's related to ENERGY RENEWAL.
You really are the most adorable bundle of fluff.
Give him some space. Can't you see he's had a mental trauma?
So what happened on the MISSION, Mr. Tinder?
You tell me. I declined to participate, and then I LOST MY JOB.

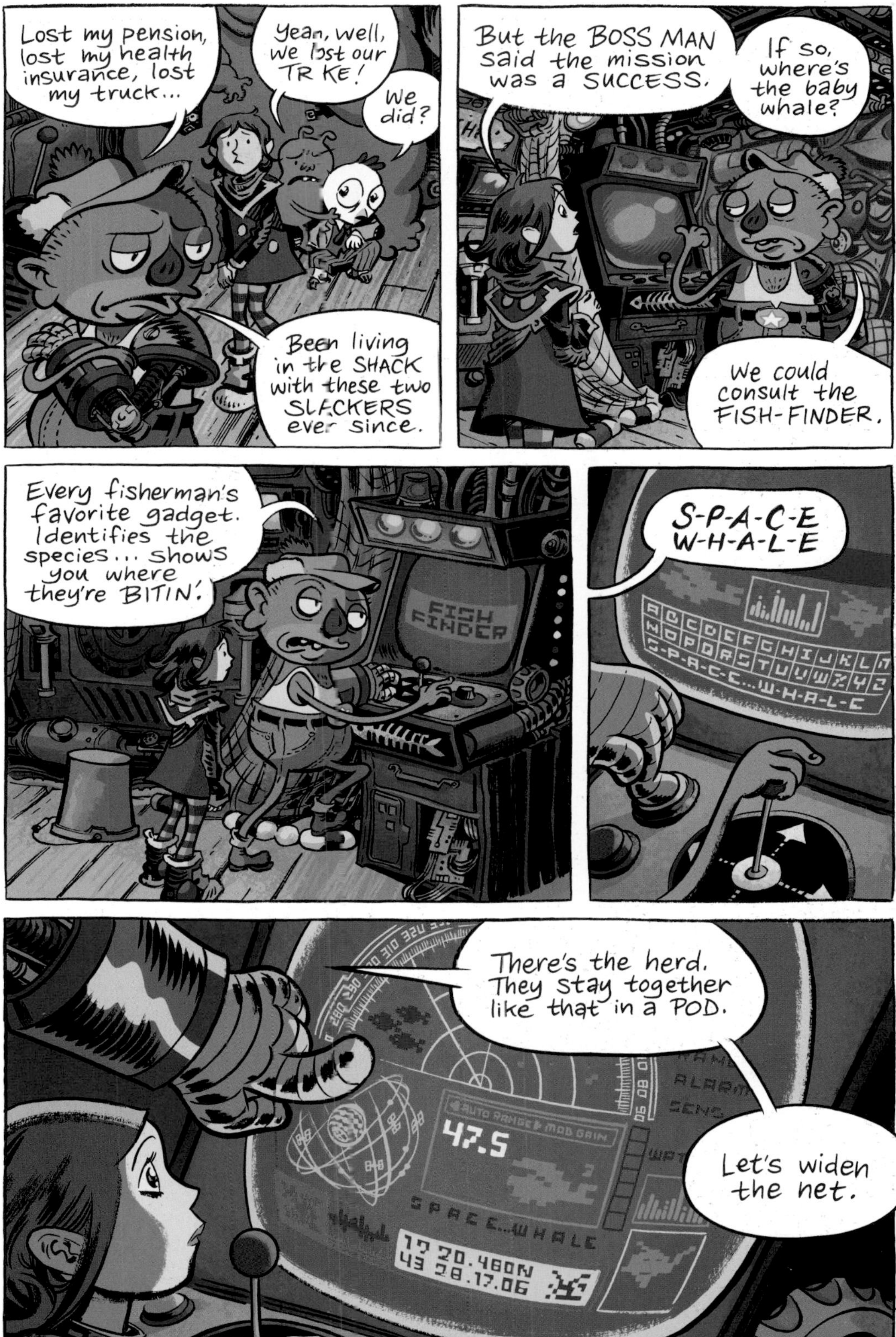
Lost my pension, lost my health insurance, lost my truck...
Yeah, well, we lost our TRIKE!
We did?
Been living in the SHACK with these two SLACKERS ever since.
But the BOSS MAN said the mission was a SUCCESS.
If so, where's the baby whale?
We could consult the FISH-FINDER.
Every fisherman's favorite gadget. Identifies the species... shows you where they're BITIN'.
FISH FINDER
S-P-A-C-E W-H-A-L-E
S-P-A-C-E...W-H-A-L-E
There's the herd. They stay together like that in a POD.
AUTO RANGE
MOD GAIN
47.5
ALARM
SPACE...WHALE
17 20.460N
43 28.17.06
Let's widen the net.

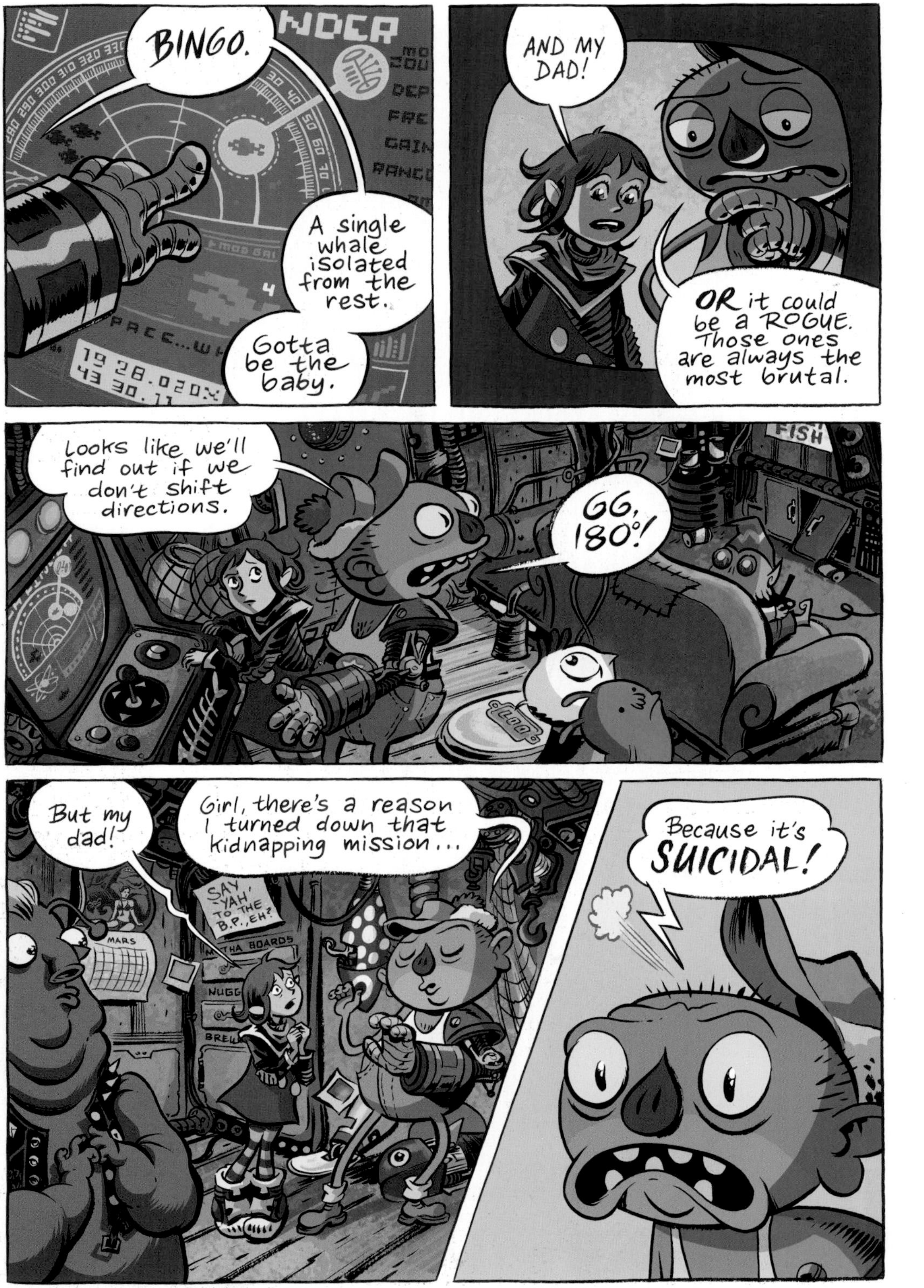
BINGO.
A single whale isolated from the rest.
Gotta be the baby.
AND MY DAD!
OR it could be a ROGUE. Those ones are always the most brutal.
Looks like we'll find out if we don't shift directions.
GG, 180°!
But my dad!
Girl, there's a reason I turned down that kidnapping mission...
Because it's SUICIDAL!
SAY "YAH" TO THE B.P., EH?
FISH
MARS

A lumberjack's duty is to keep a safe distance from those beasts, gleaning the bounty in their wake.

Get too close? Well, space whales eat ships, asteroids... They devour ENTIRE PLANETS, for crying out loud!

AAARGH!

Zach knows.

I know, because the whales ate my school, and then my friends were separated from me.

But I didn't let the whales win.

I made TWO BETTER friends.

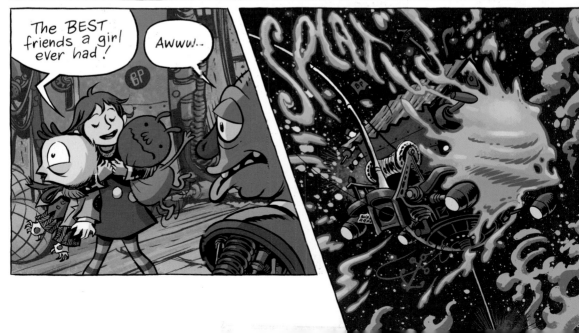

The BEST friends a girl ever had!

Awww...

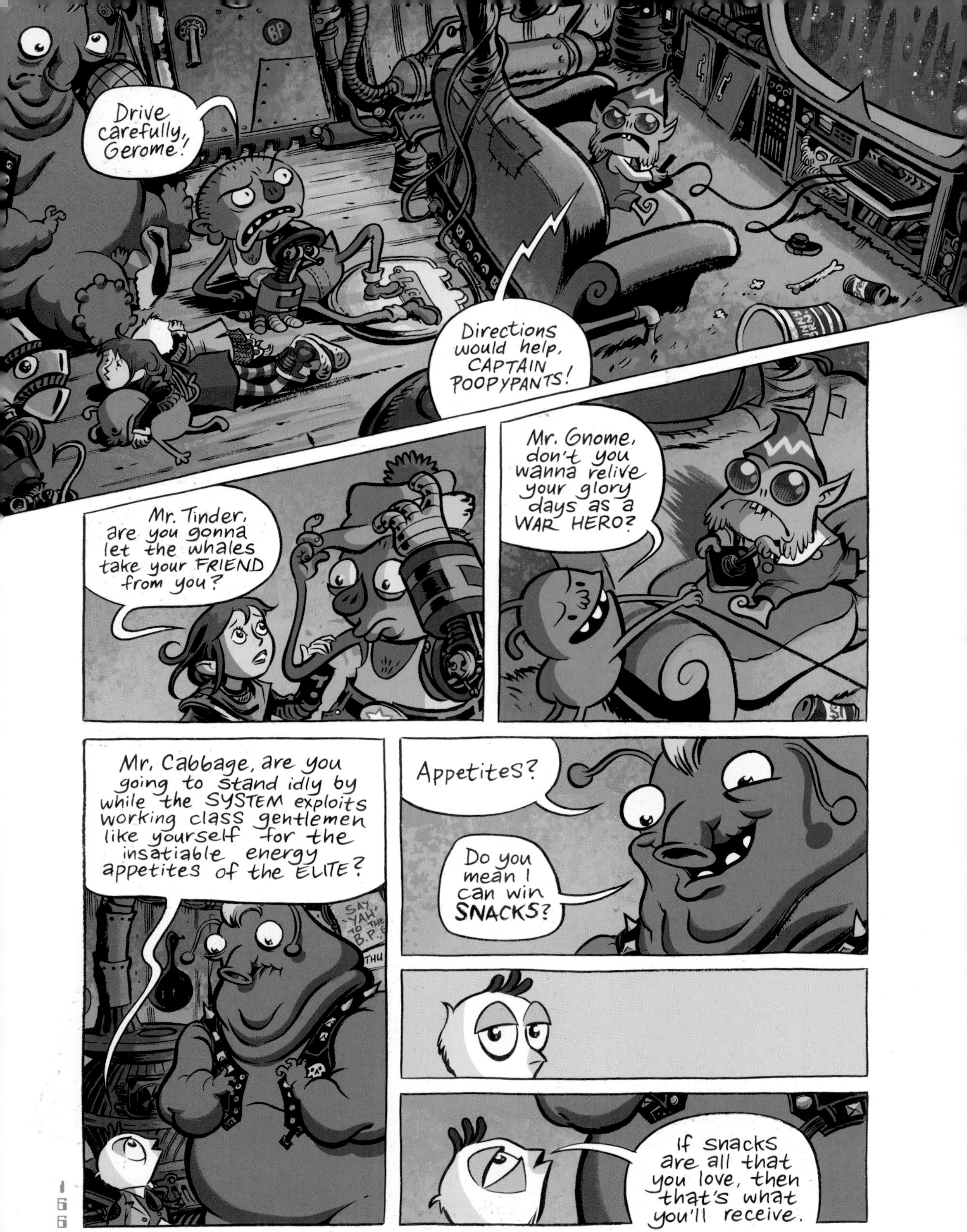
Drive carefully, Gerome!
Directions would help, CAPTAIN POOPYPANTS!
Mr. Tinder, are you gonna let the whales take your FRIEND from you?
Mr. Gnome, don't you wanna relive your glory days as a WAR HERO?
Mr. Cabbage, are you going to stand idly by while the SYSTEM exploits working class gentlemen like yourself for the insatiable energy appetites of the ELITE?
Appetites?
Do you mean I can win SNACKS?
If snacks are all that you love, then that's what you'll receive.

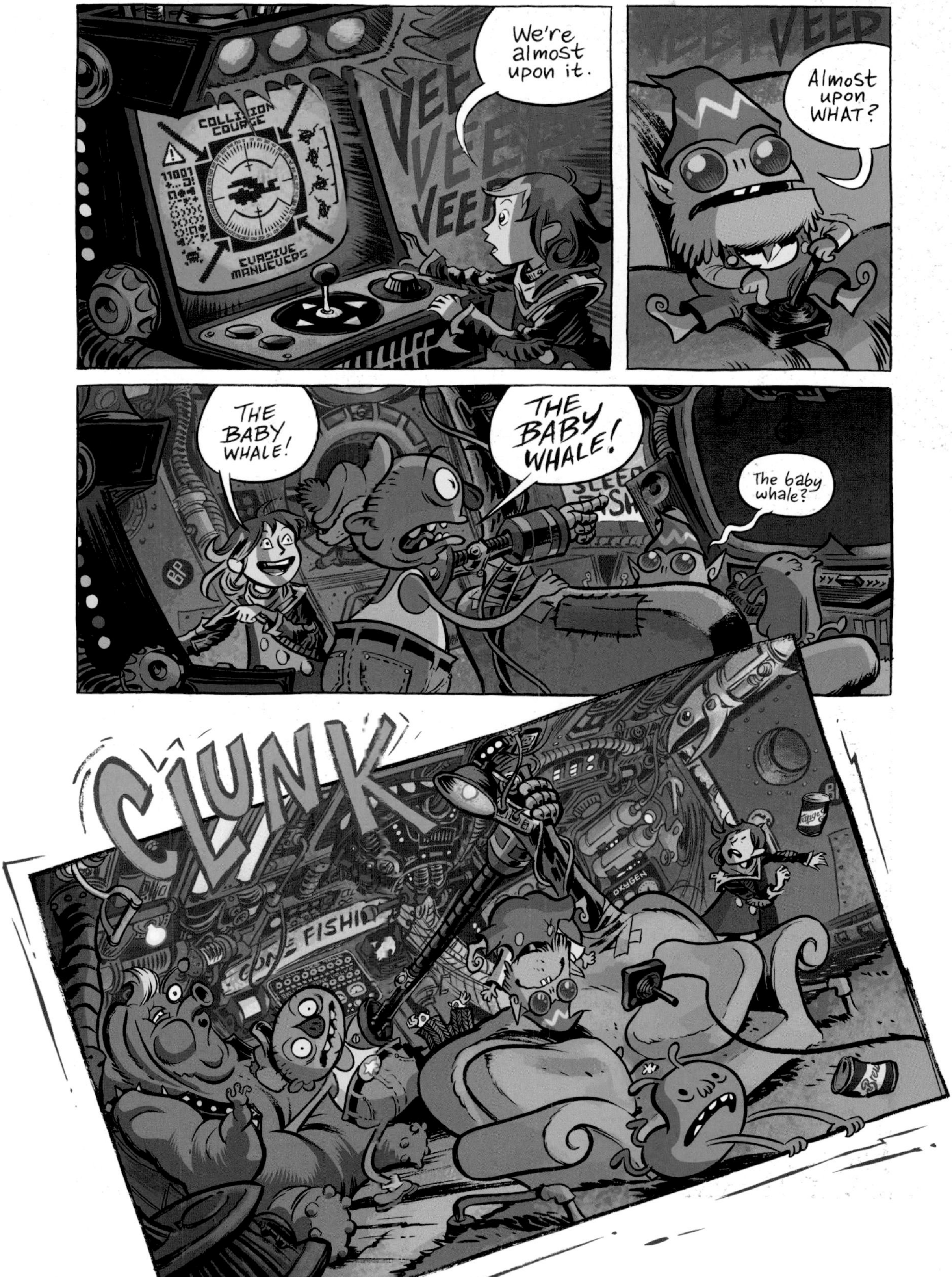
We're almost upon it.
COLLISION COURSE
EVASIVE MANUEVERS
VEEP
Almost upon WHAT?
THE BABY WHALE!
THE BABY WHALE!
The baby whale?
CLUNK
OXYGEN

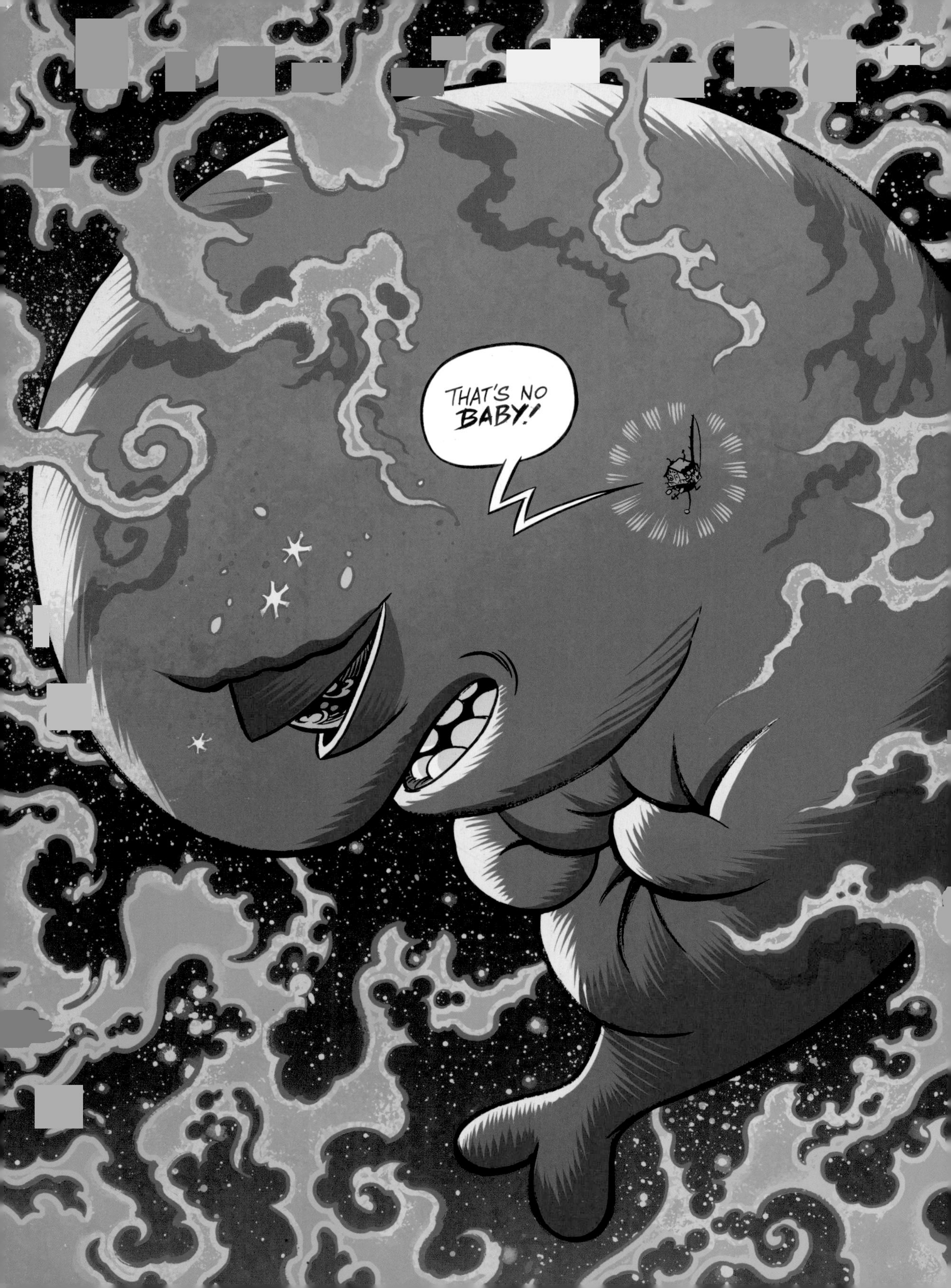
THAT'S NO BABY!

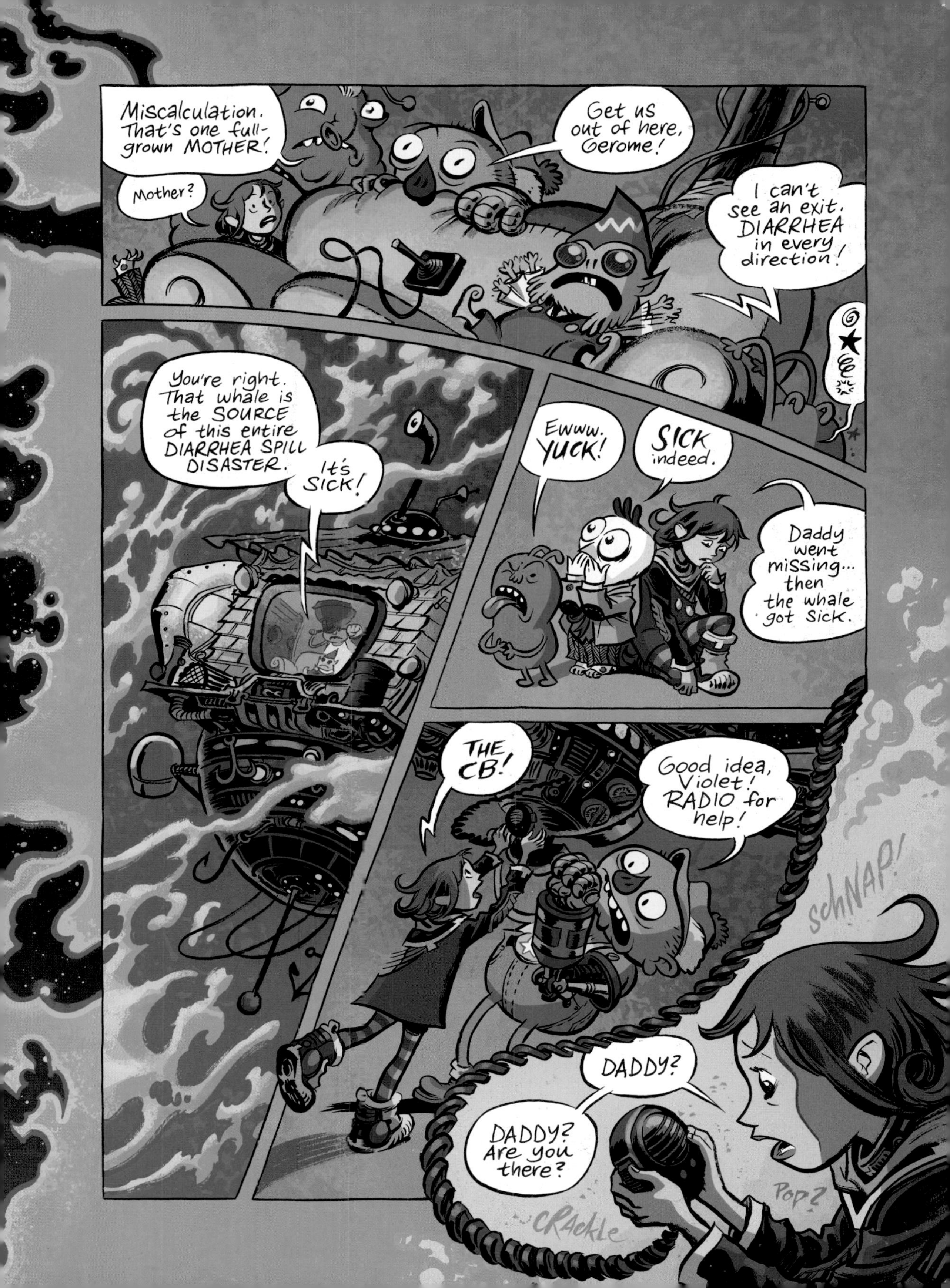
Miscalculation. That's one full-grown MOTHER!
Mother?
Get us out of here, Gerome!
I can't see an exit. DIARRHEA in every direction!
You're right. That whale is the SOURCE of this entire DIARRHEA SPILL DISASTER.
It's SICK!
Ewww. YUCK!
SICK indeed.
Daddy went missing... then the whale got sick.
THE CB!
Good idea, Violet! RADIO for help!
schNAP!
DADDY?
DADDY? Are you there?
Pop?
CRACKLE

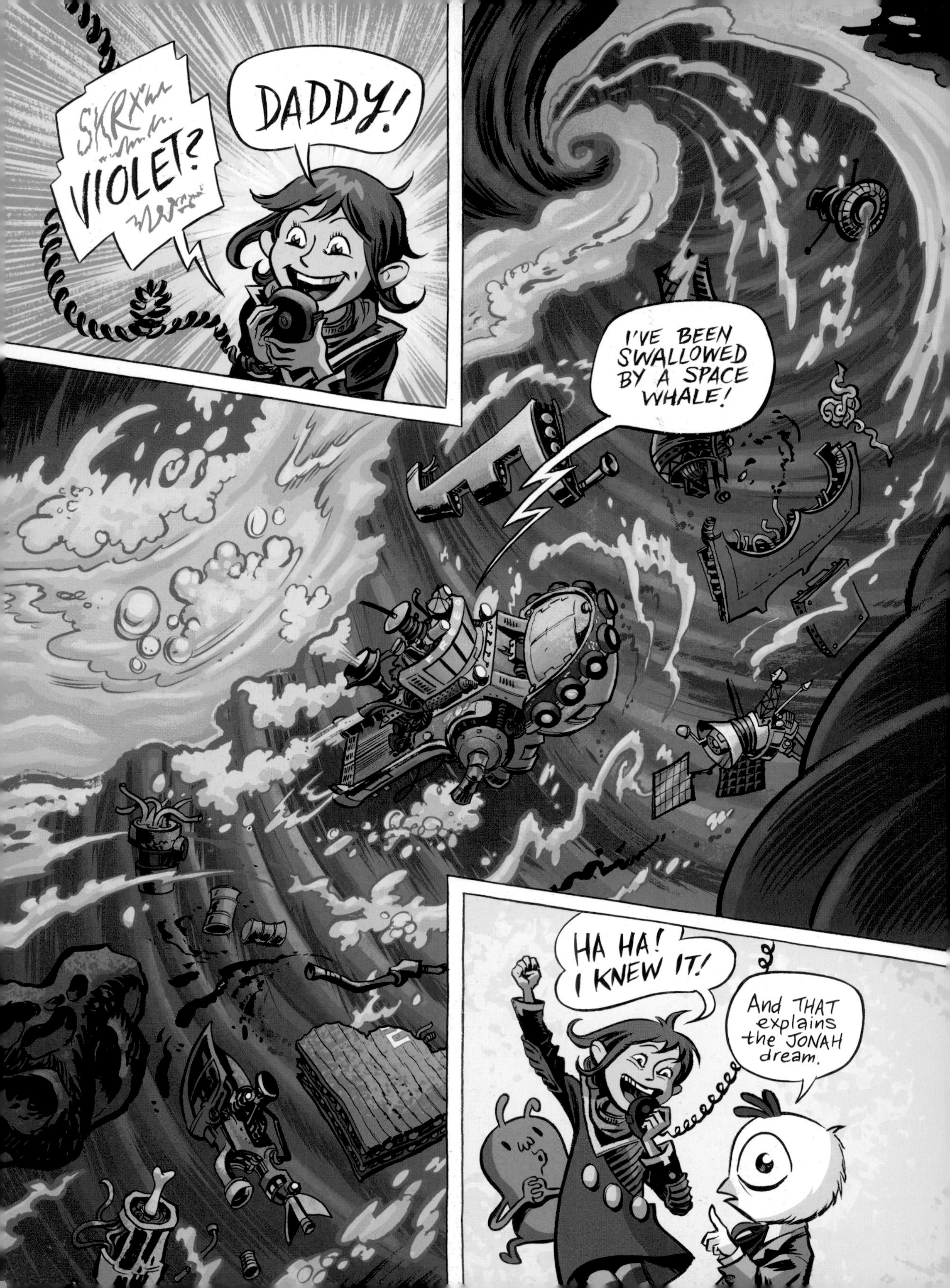
SKRX
VIOLET?
DADDY!
I'VE BEEN SWALLOWED BY A SPACE WHALE!
HA HA! I KNEW IT!
And THAT explains the JONAH dream.

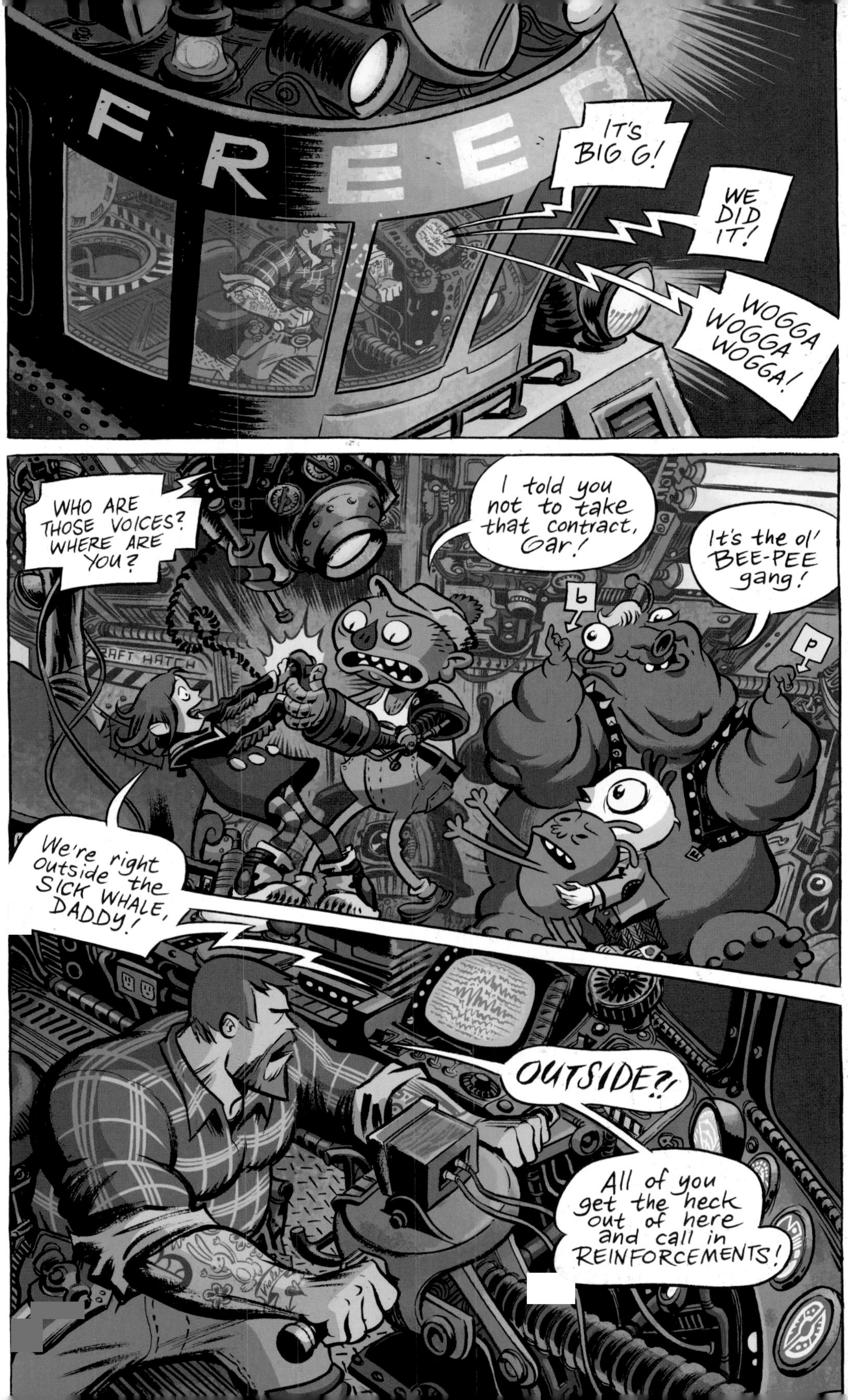
FREED
IT'S BIG G!
WE DID IT!
WOGGA WOGGA WOGGA!
WHO ARE THOSE VOICES? WHERE ARE YOU?
I told you not to take that contract, Gar!
It's the ol' BEE-PEE gang!
b
P
RAFT HATCH
We're right outside the SICK WHALE, DADDY!
OUTSIDE?!
All of you get the heck out of here and call in REINFORCEMENTS!

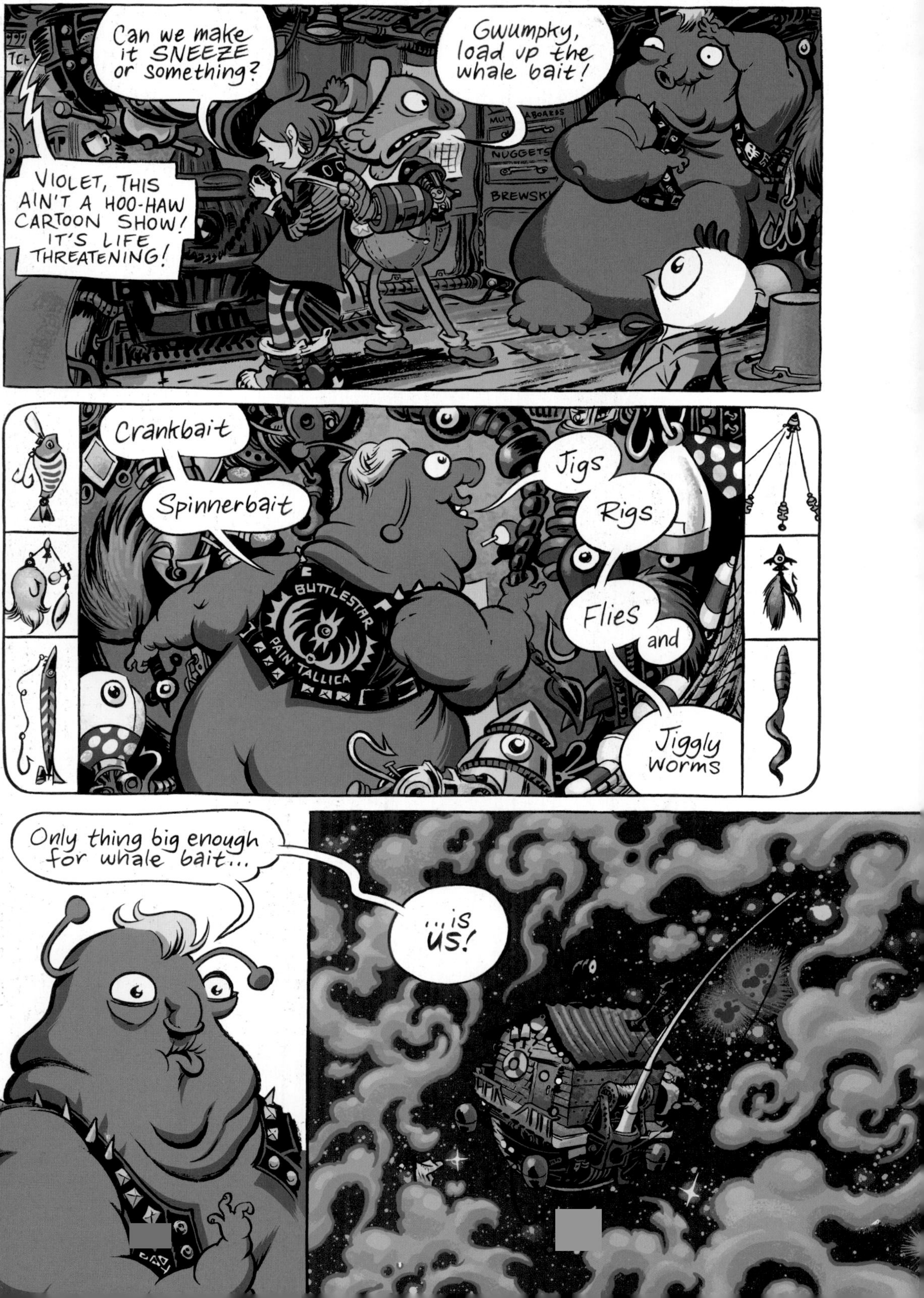

TCH
Can we make it SNEEZE or something?
VIOLET, THIS AIN'T A HOO-HAW CARTOON SHOW! IT'S LIFE THREATENING!
Gwumpky, load up the whale bait!
MUTTABOARDS
NUGGETS
BREWSK
Crankbait
Spinnerbait
Jigs
Rigs
Flies
and
Jiggly Worms
BUTTLESTAR PAIN TALLICA
Only thing big enough for whale bait...
...is us!

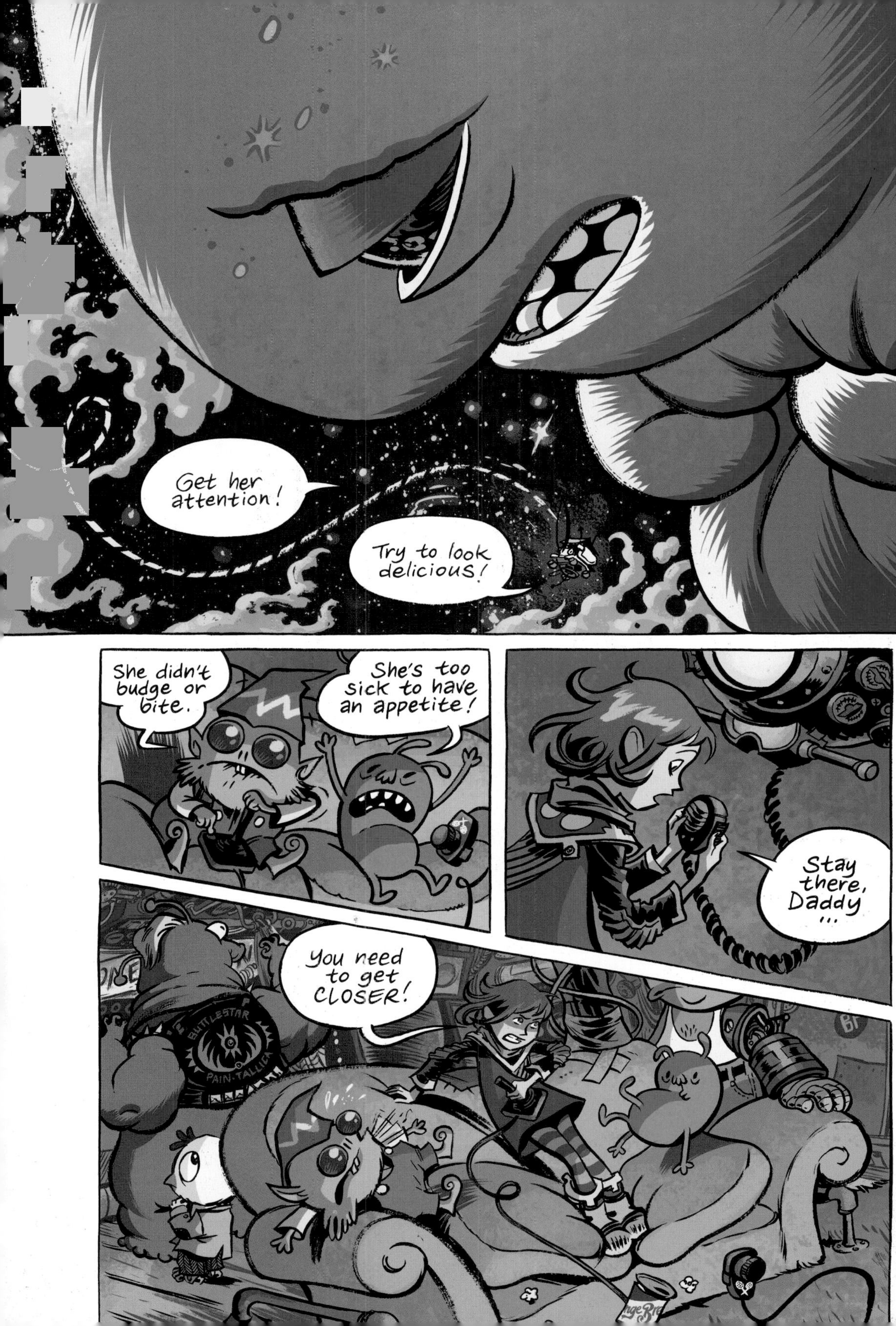
Get her attention!
Try to look delicious!
She didn't budge or bite.
She's too sick to have an appetite!
Stay there, Daddy ...
You need to get CLOSER!

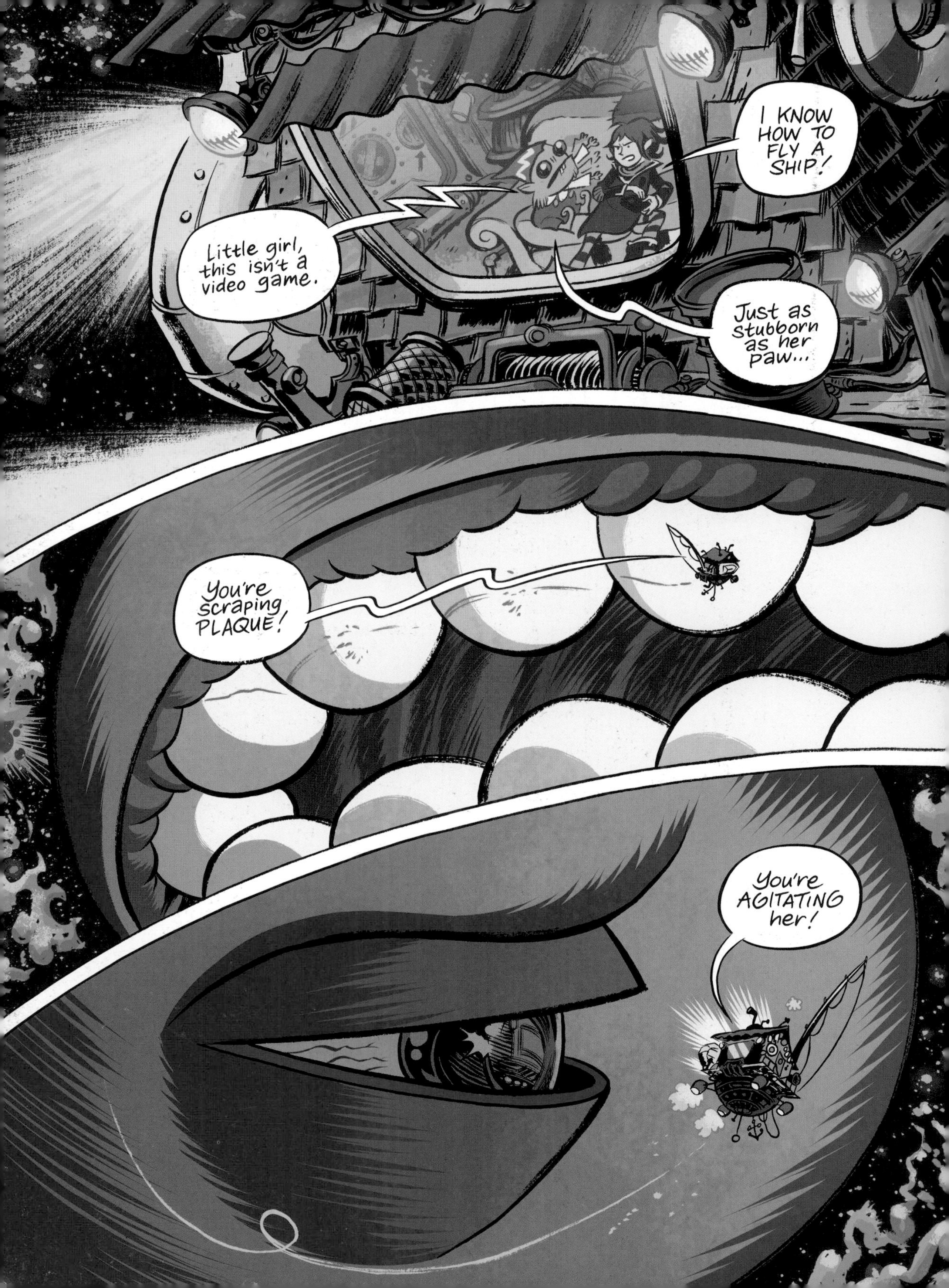
I KNOW HOW TO FLY A SHIP!
Little girl, this isn't a video game.
Just as stubborn as her paw...
You're scraping PLAQUE!
You're AGITATING her!

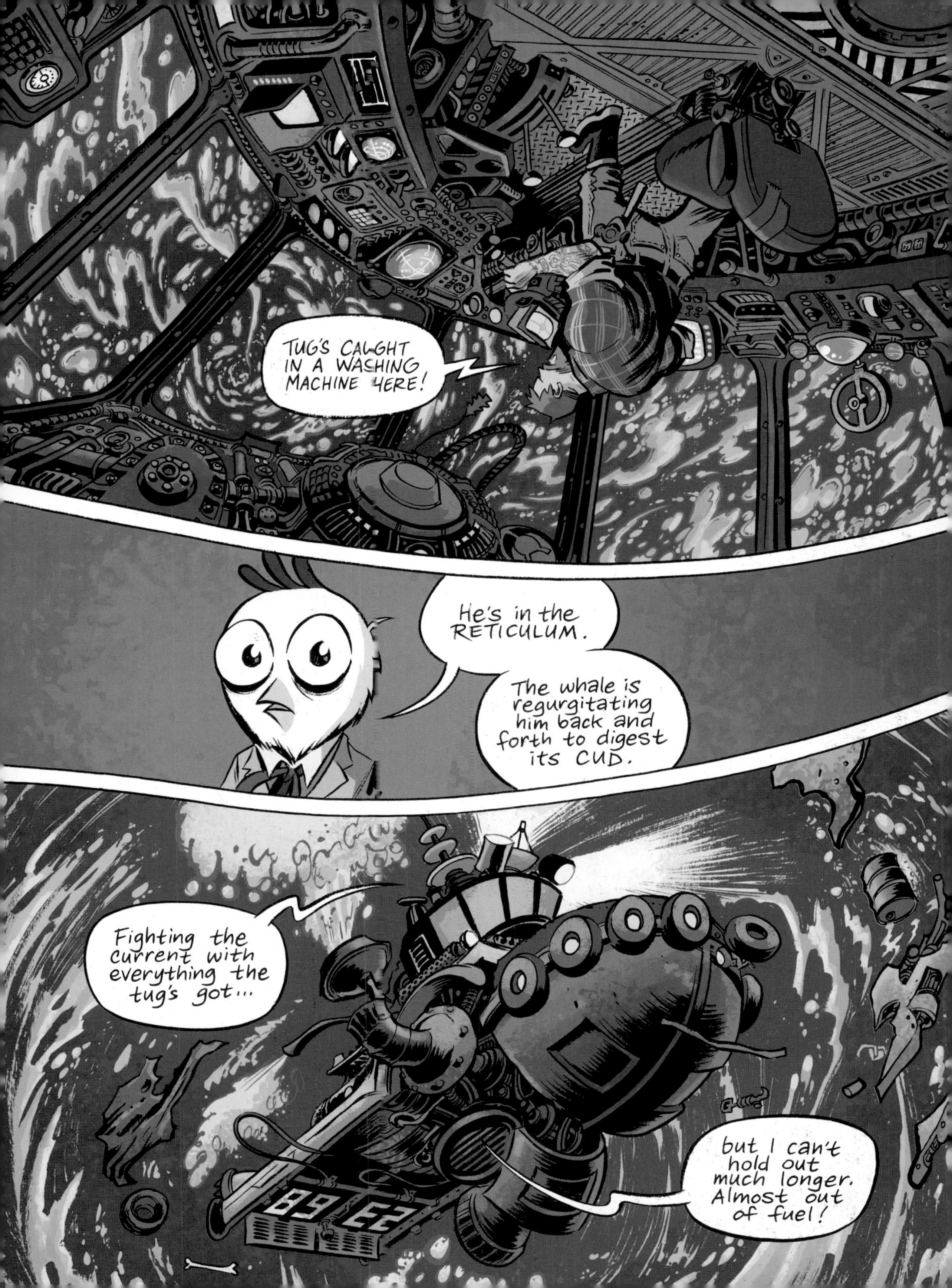
TUG'S CAUGHT IN A WASHING MACHINE HERE!
He's in the RETICULUM.
The whale is regurgitating him back and forth to digest its CUD.
Fighting the current with everything the tug's got...
but I can't hold out much longer. Almost out of fuel!

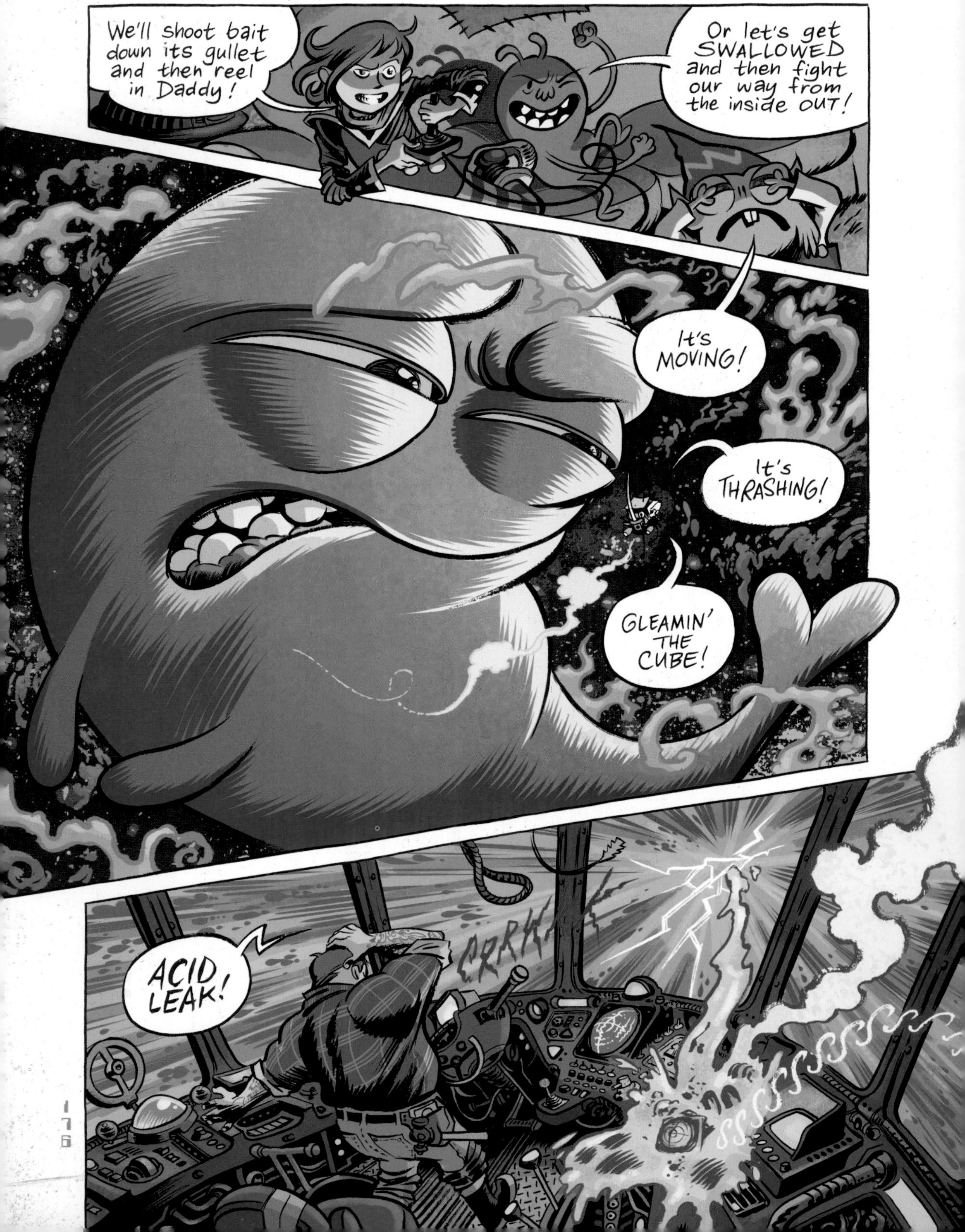
We'll shoot bait down its gullet and then reel in Daddy!
Or let's get SWALLOWED and then fight our way from the inside OUT!
It's MOVING!
It's THRASHING!
GLEAMIN' THE CUBE!
ACID LEAK!

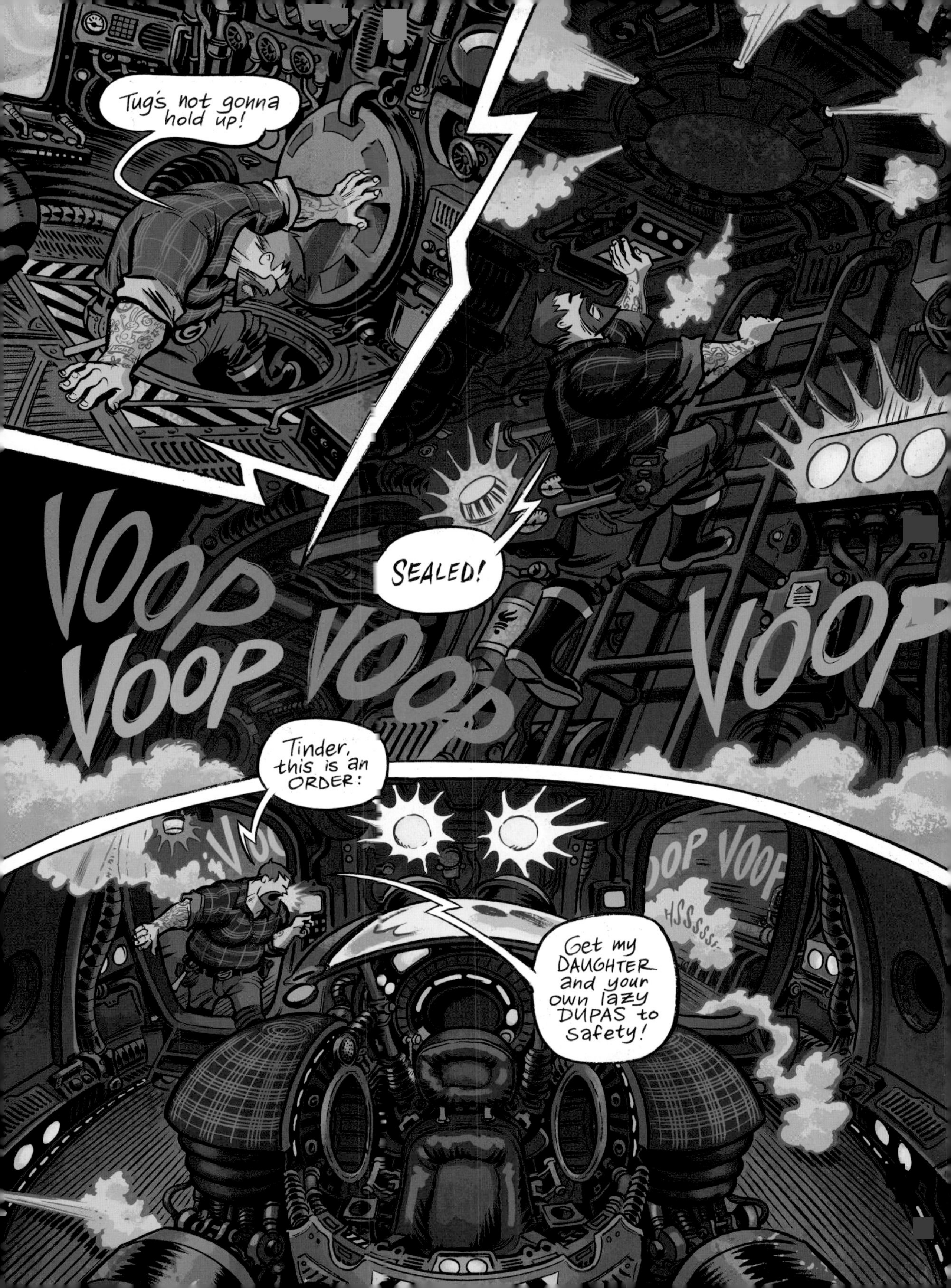
Tug's not gonna hold up!
SEALED!
VOOP VOOP VOOP VOOP
Tinder, this is an ORDER:
Get my DAUGHTER and your own lazy DUPAS to safety!

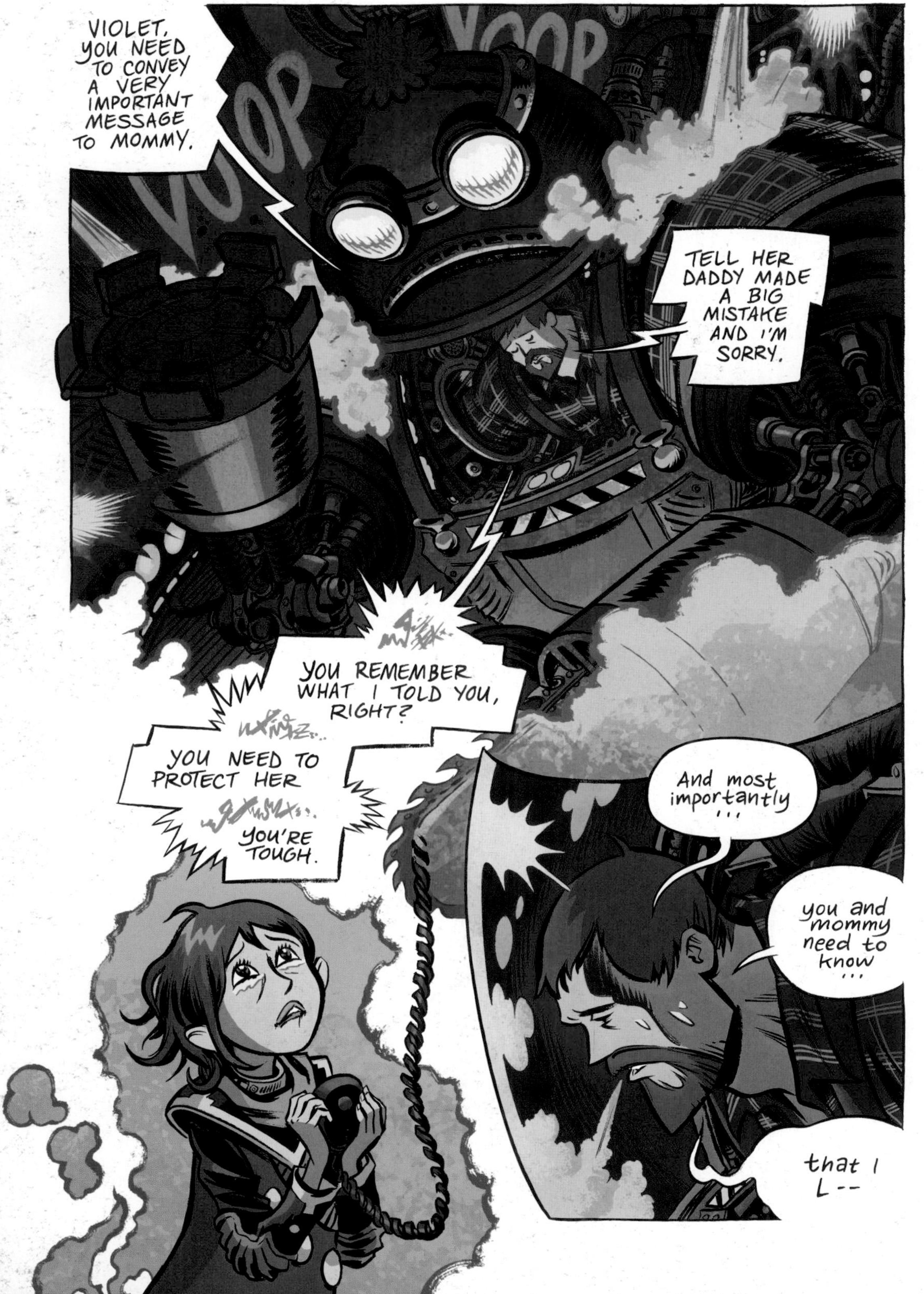
VOOP VOOP
VIOLET, YOU NEED TO CONVEY A VERY IMPORTANT MESSAGE TO MOMMY.
TELL HER DADDY MADE A BIG MISTAKE AND I'M SORRY.
YOU REMEMBER WHAT I TOLD YOU, RIGHT?
YOU NEED TO PROTECT HER
YOU'RE TOUGH.
And most importantly . . .
you and mommy need to know . . .
that I L --

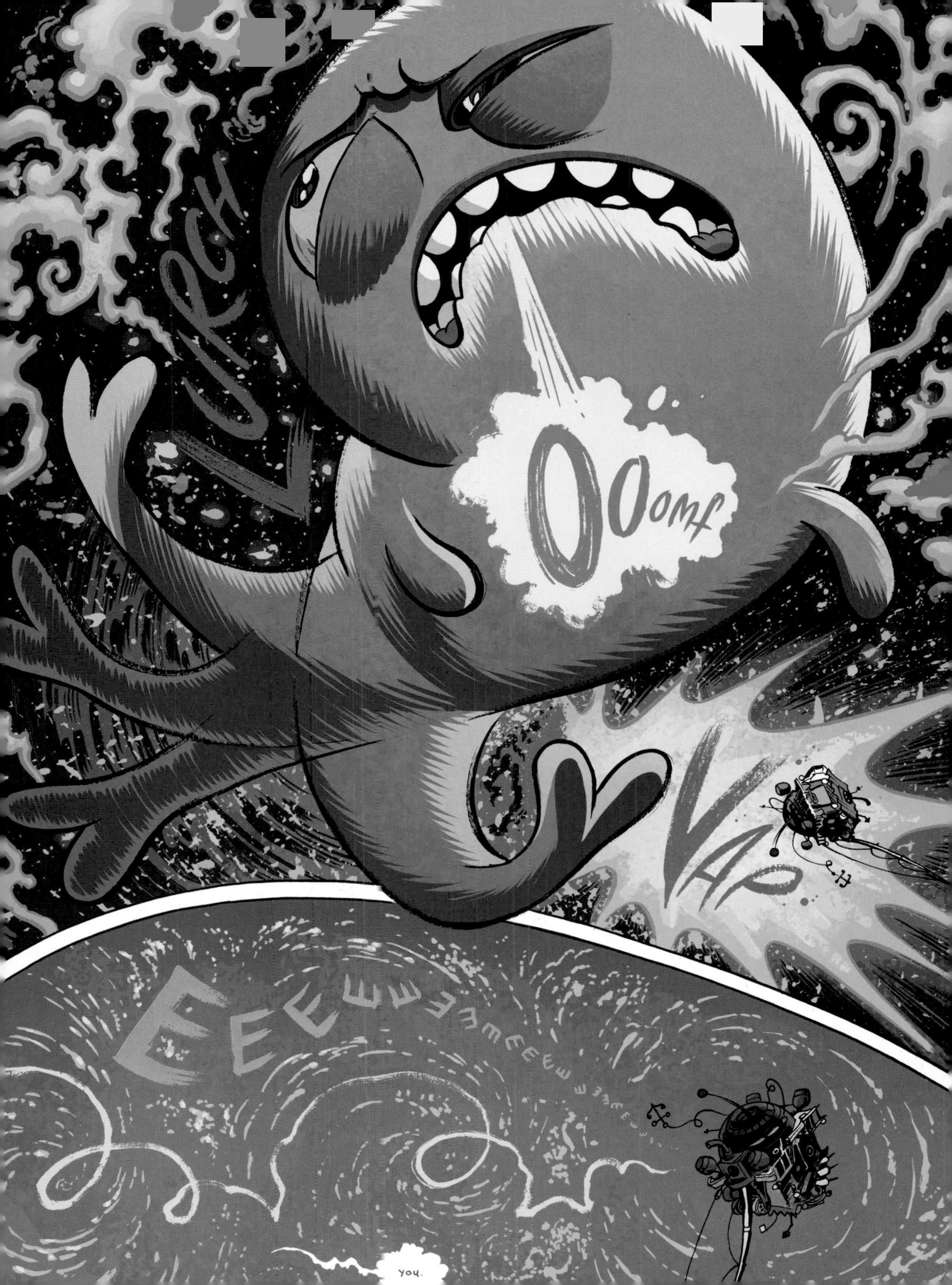

URRCH
OOomf
VAP
EEEEEEEEEEEEEEE
you.

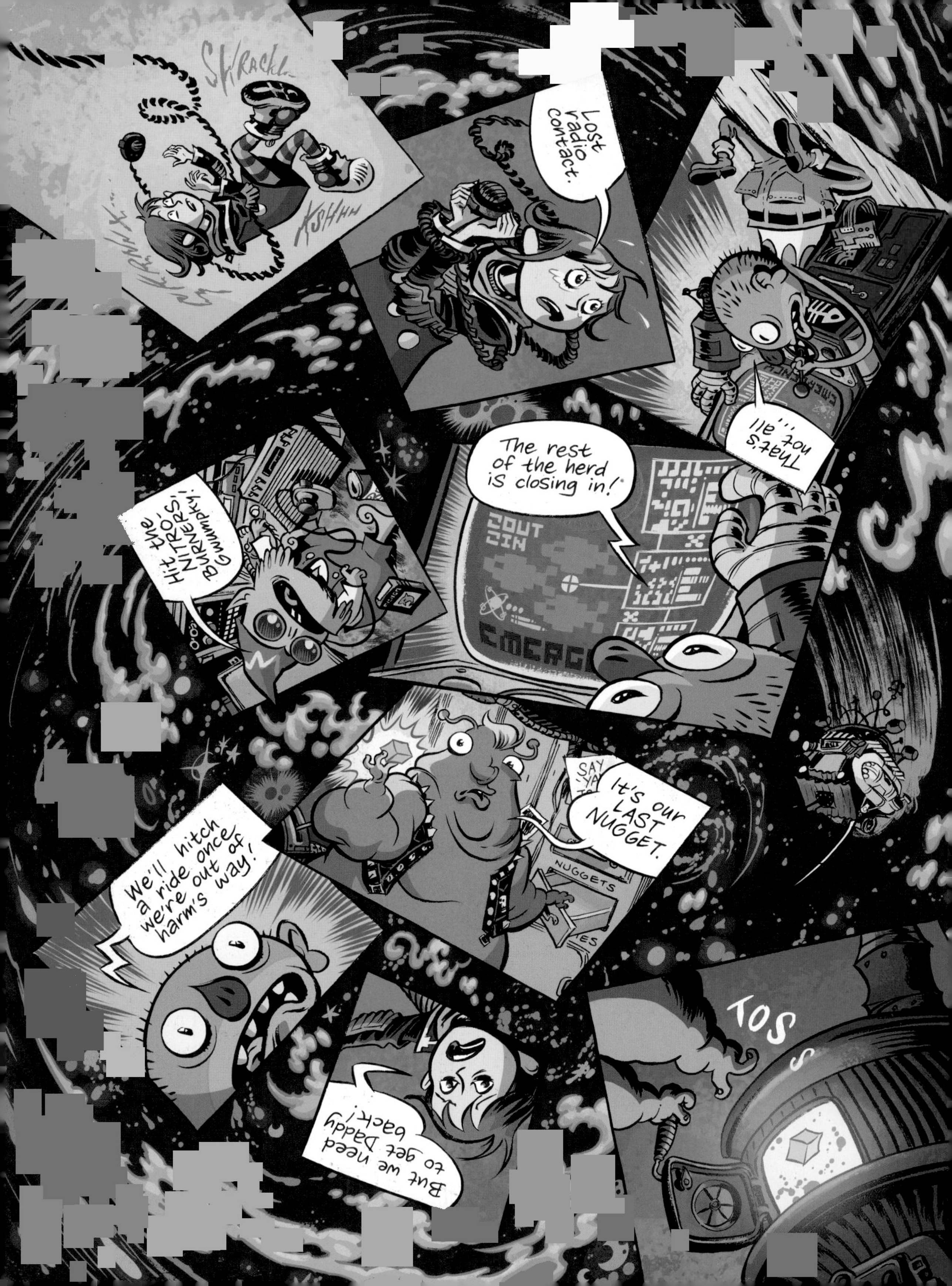
SKRACKL
KSHHH
Lost radio contact.
That's not all...
The rest of the herd is closing in!
Hit the NITRO-BURNERS, Gwumpky!
It's our LAST NUGGET.
NUGGETS
We'll hitch a ride once we're out of harm's way!
But we need to get Daddy back!
TOS

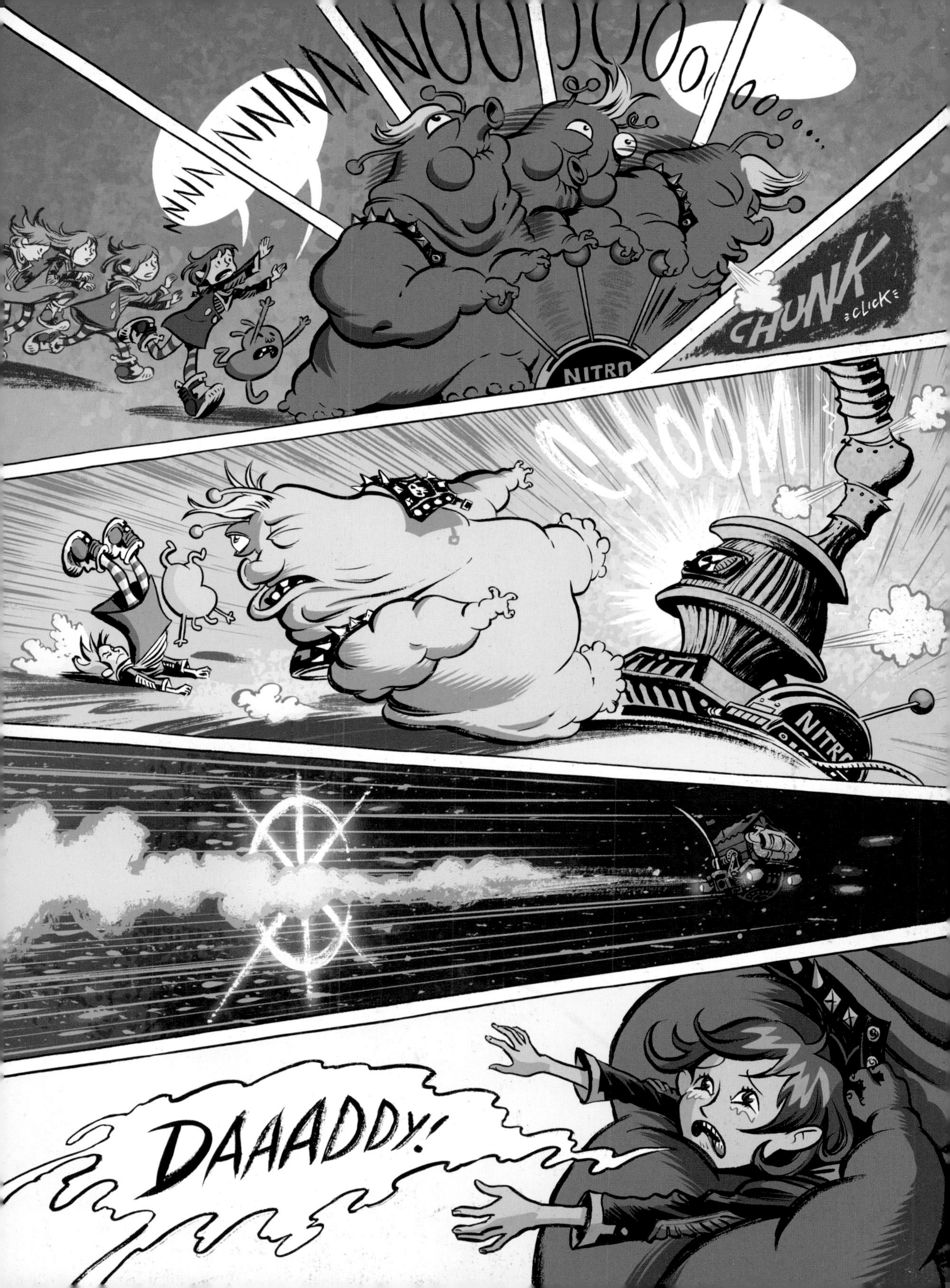
NNNNNNNNNOOOOOOOoooo....
CHUNK
CLICK
NITRO
CHOOM
NITRO
DAAADDY!

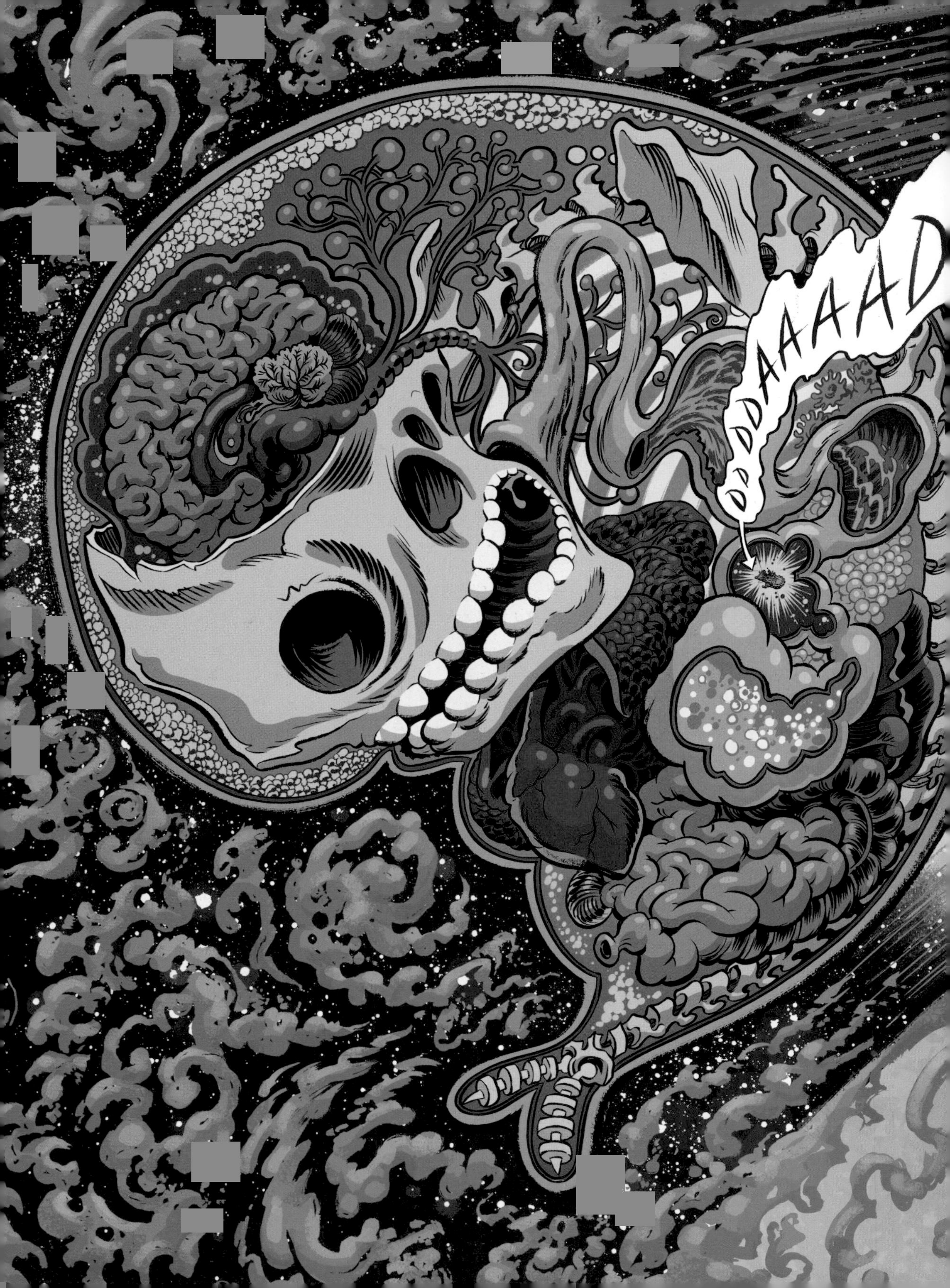
DDDDDAAAAD

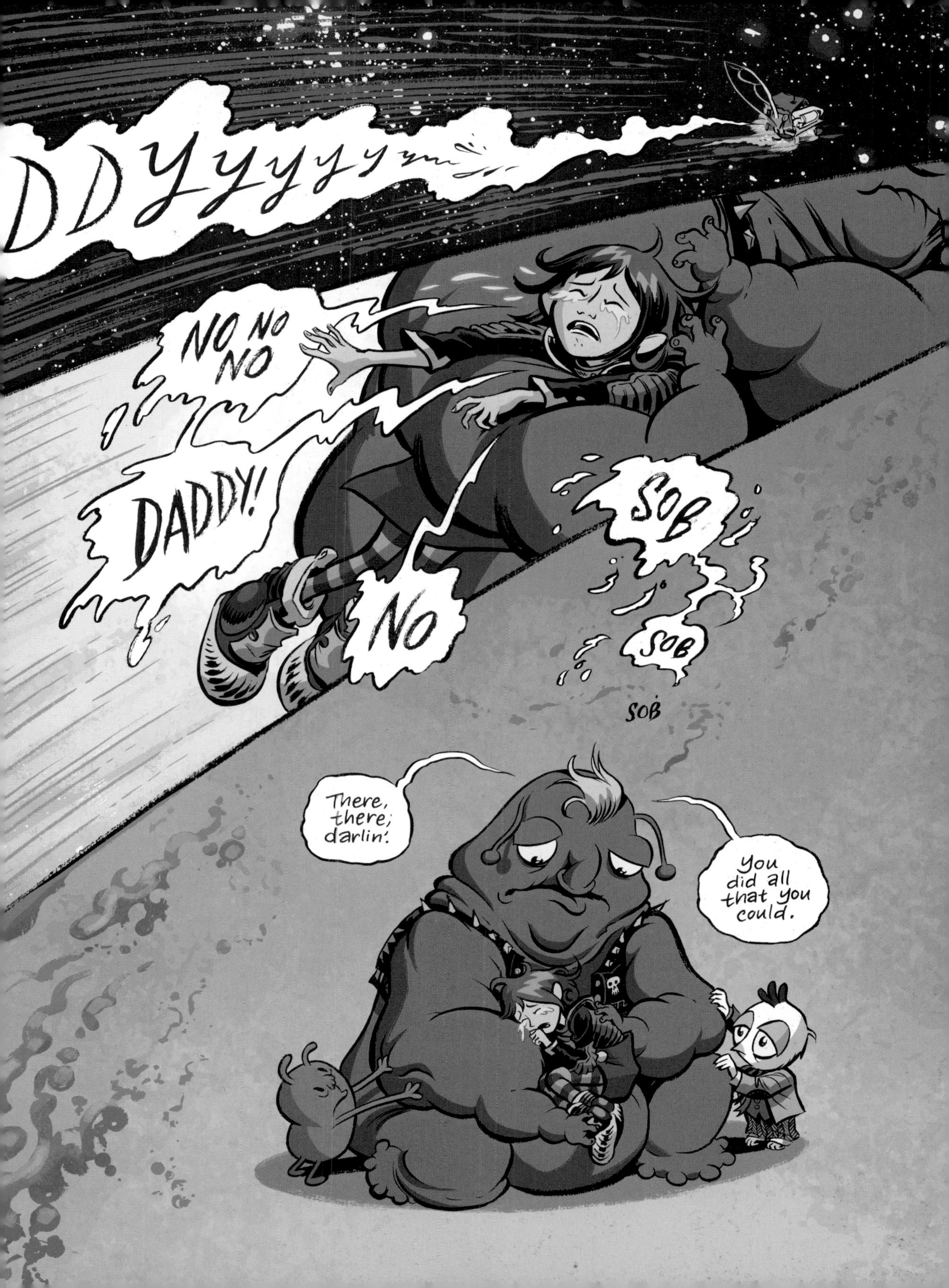
DDYYYYYY
NO NO NO
DADDY!
NO
SOB
SOB
SOB
There, there, darlin'.
You did all that you could.

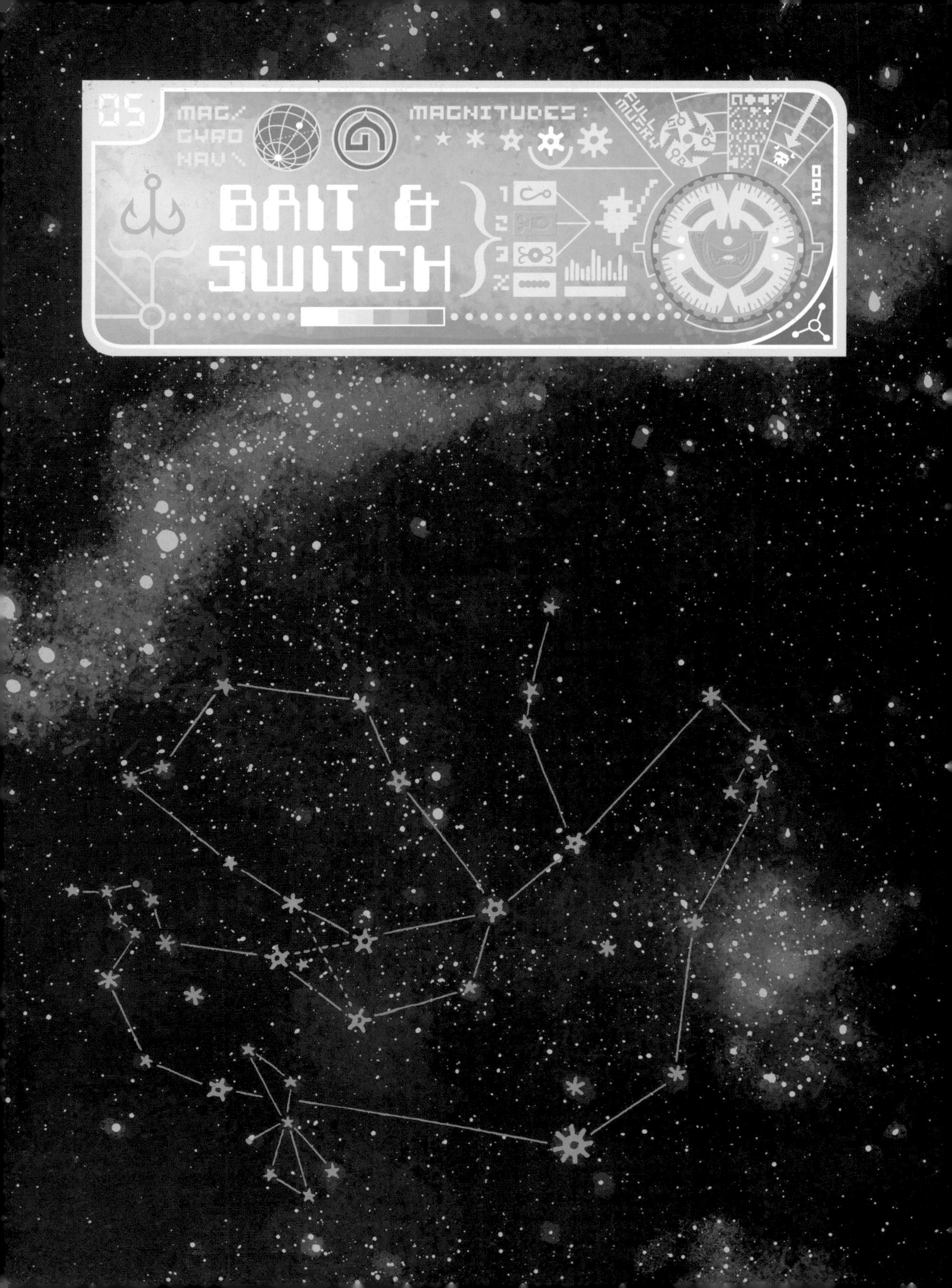
05
MAG/
GYRO
NAV\
MAGNITUDES:
FULL MUSKY
BAIT &
SWITCH

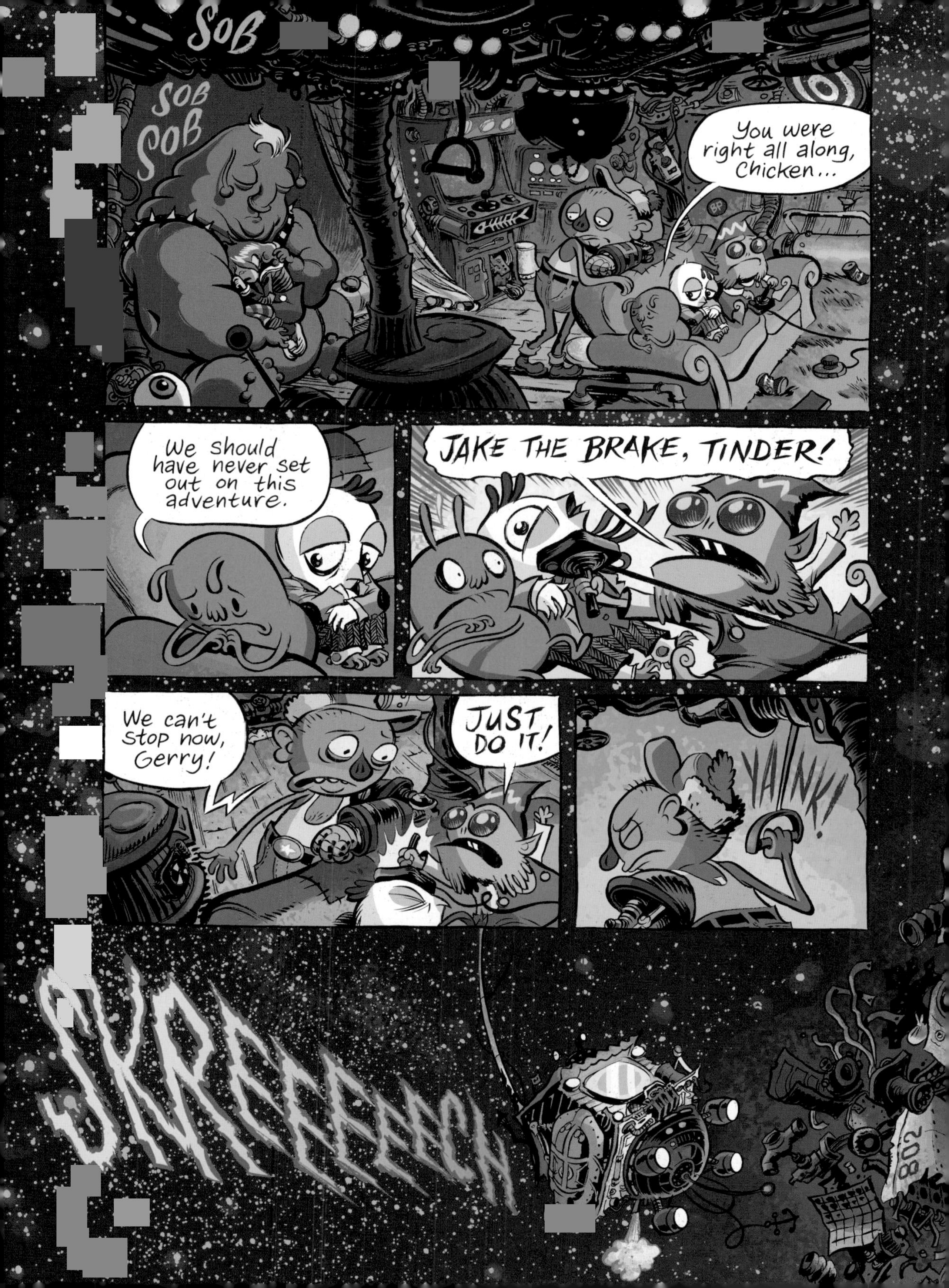
SOB
SOB
SOB
You were right all along, Chicken...
We should have never set out on this adventure.
JAKE THE BRAKE, TINDER!
We can't stop now, Gerry!
JUST DO IT!
YANK!
SKREEEEECH

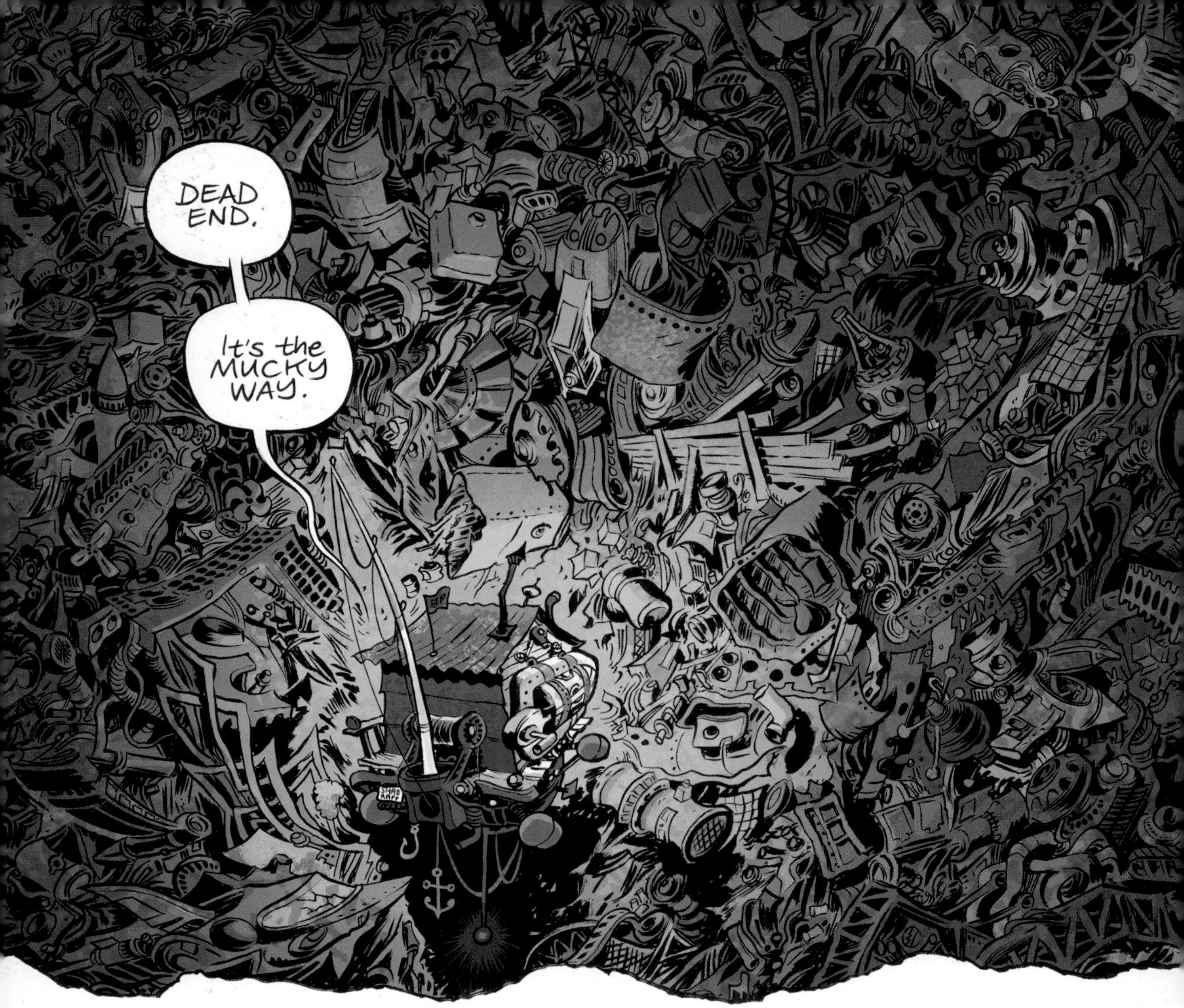
DEAD END.
It's the MUCKY WAY.

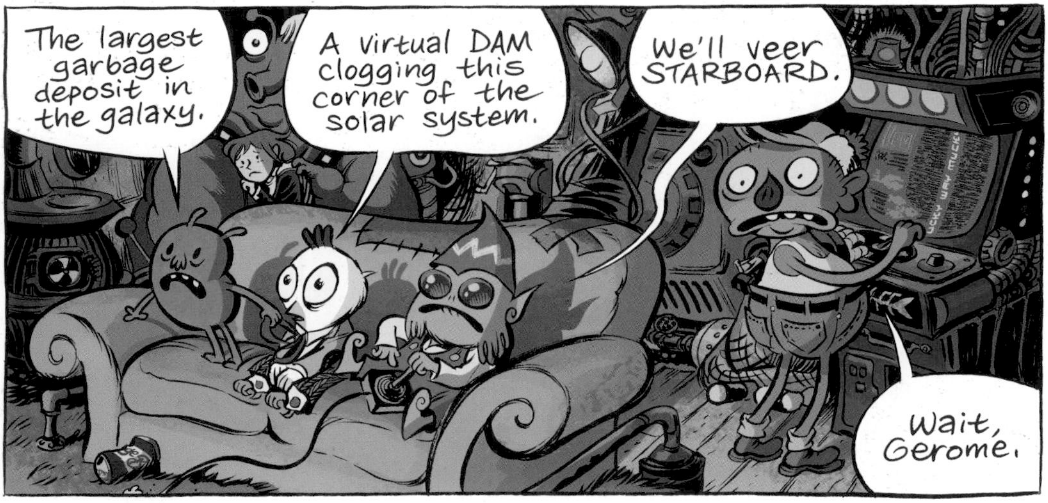
The largest garbage deposit in the galaxy.
A virtual DAM clogging this corner of the solar system.
We'll veer STARBOARD.
Wait, Gerome.

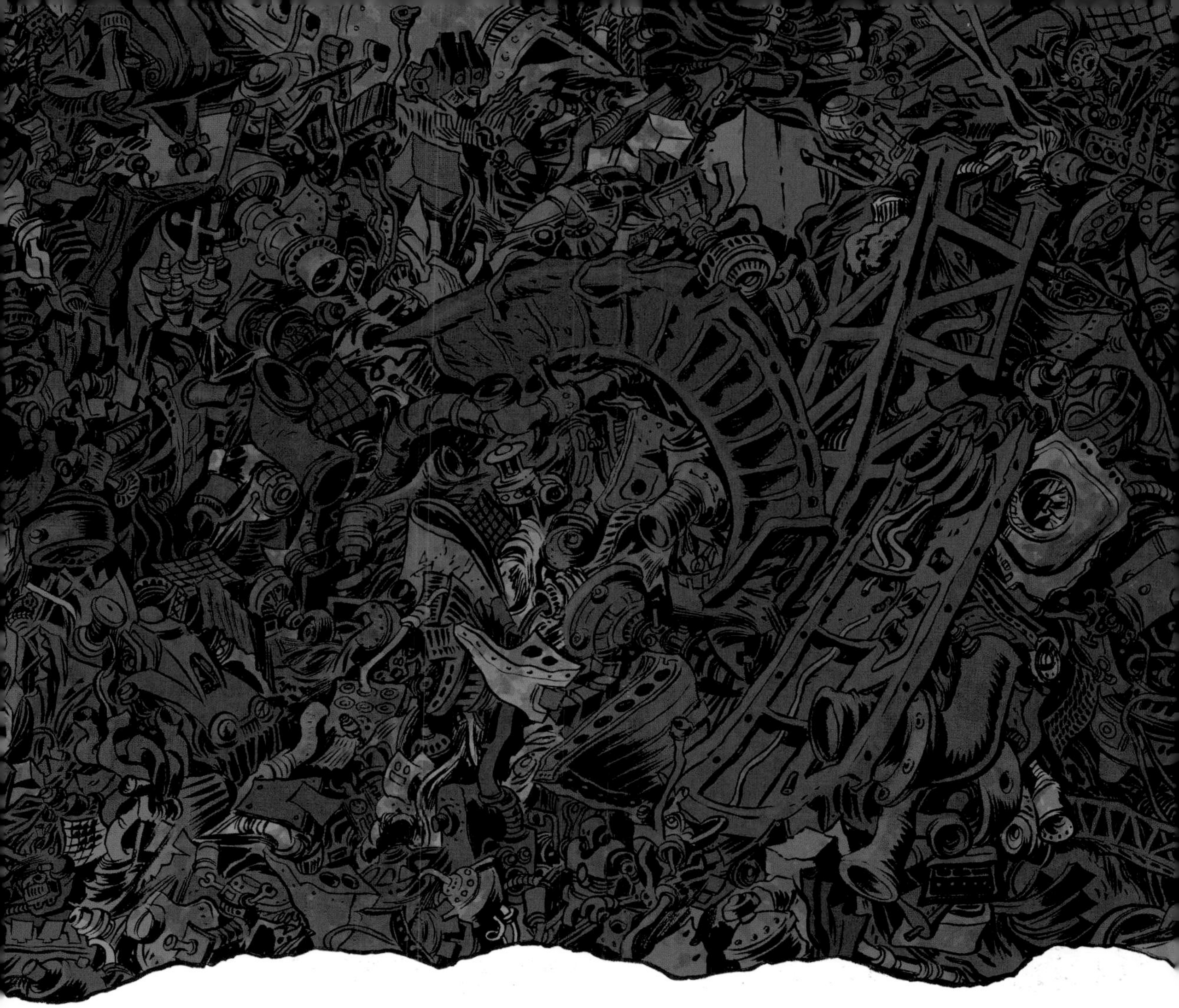

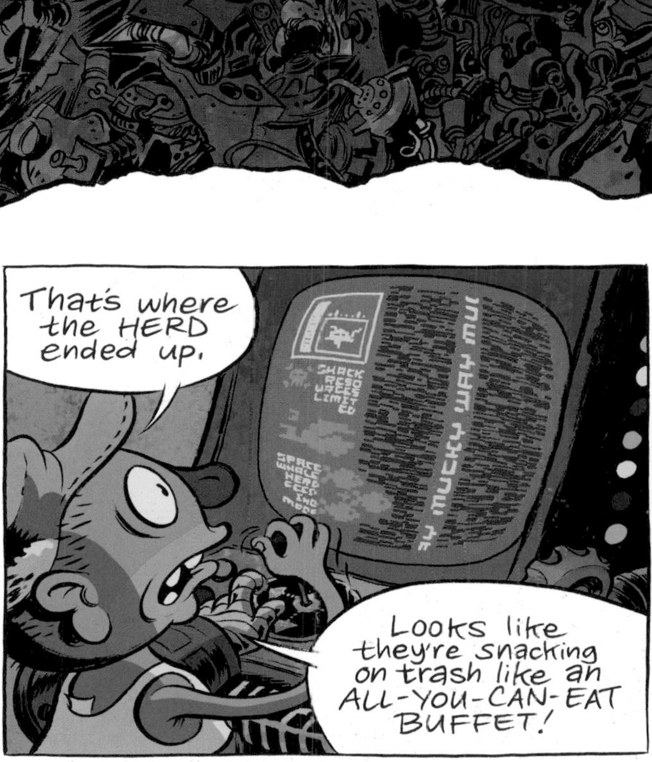
That's where the HERD ended up.
Looks like they're snacking on trash like an ALL-YOU-CAN-EAT BUFFET!

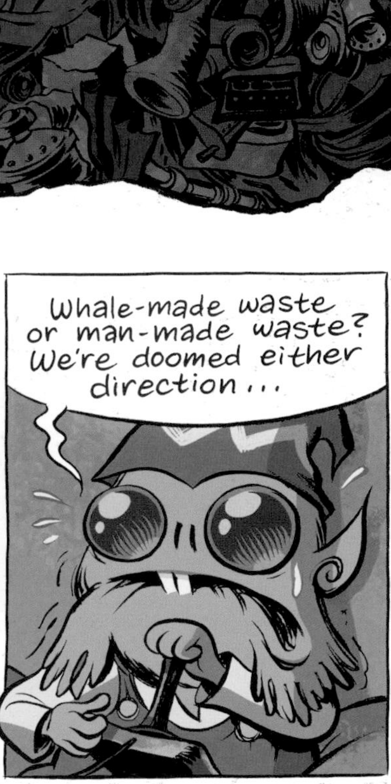
Whale-made waste or man-made waste? We're doomed either direction...

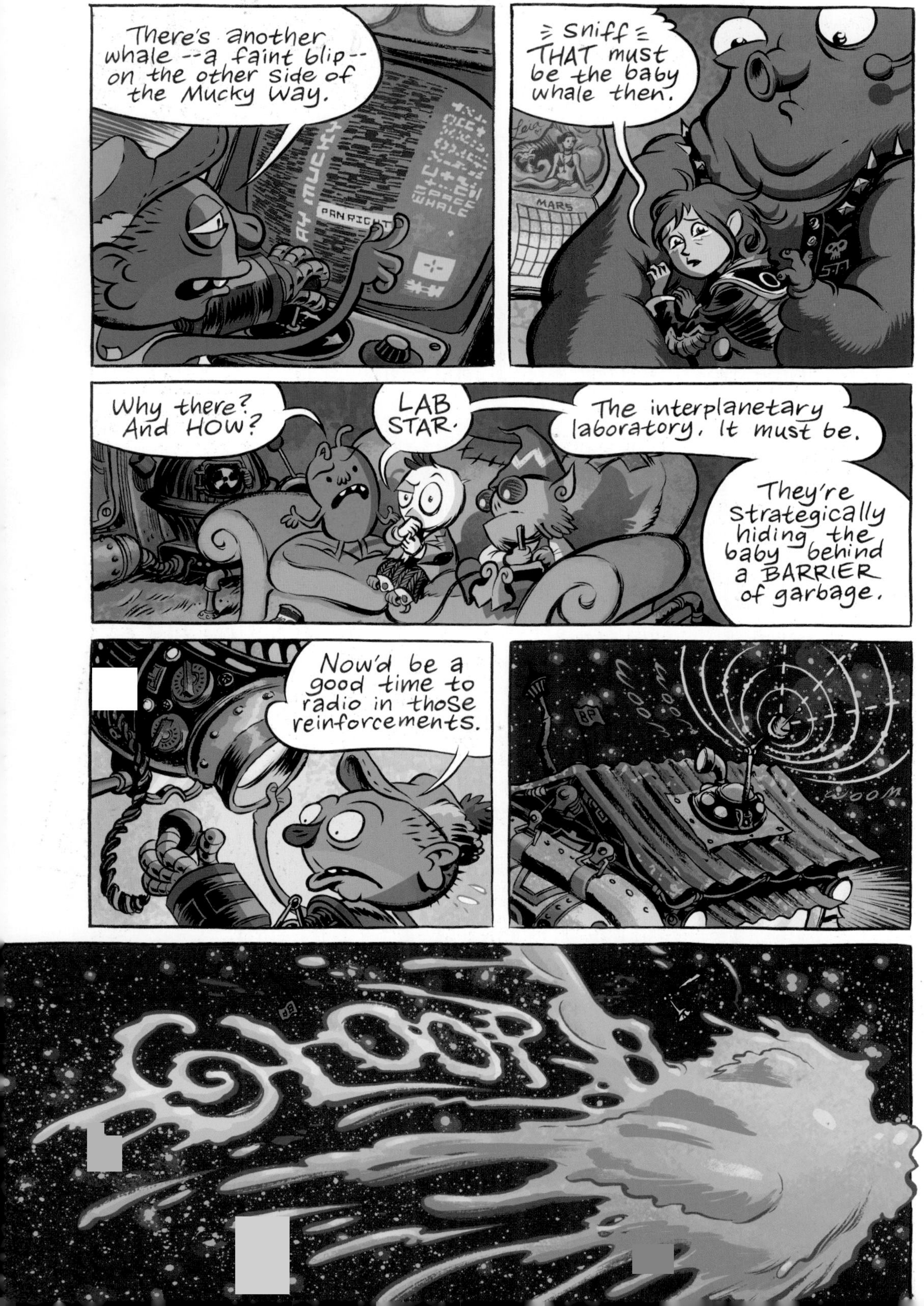
There's another whale --a faint blip-- on the other side of the Mucky Way.
PAN RIGHT
Sniff
THAT must be the baby whale then.
MARS
Why there? And HOW?
LAB STAR.
The interplanetary laboratory. It must be.
They're strategically hiding the baby behind a BARRIER of garbage.
Now'd be a good time to radio in those reinforcements.
WOOM
WOOM
WOOM

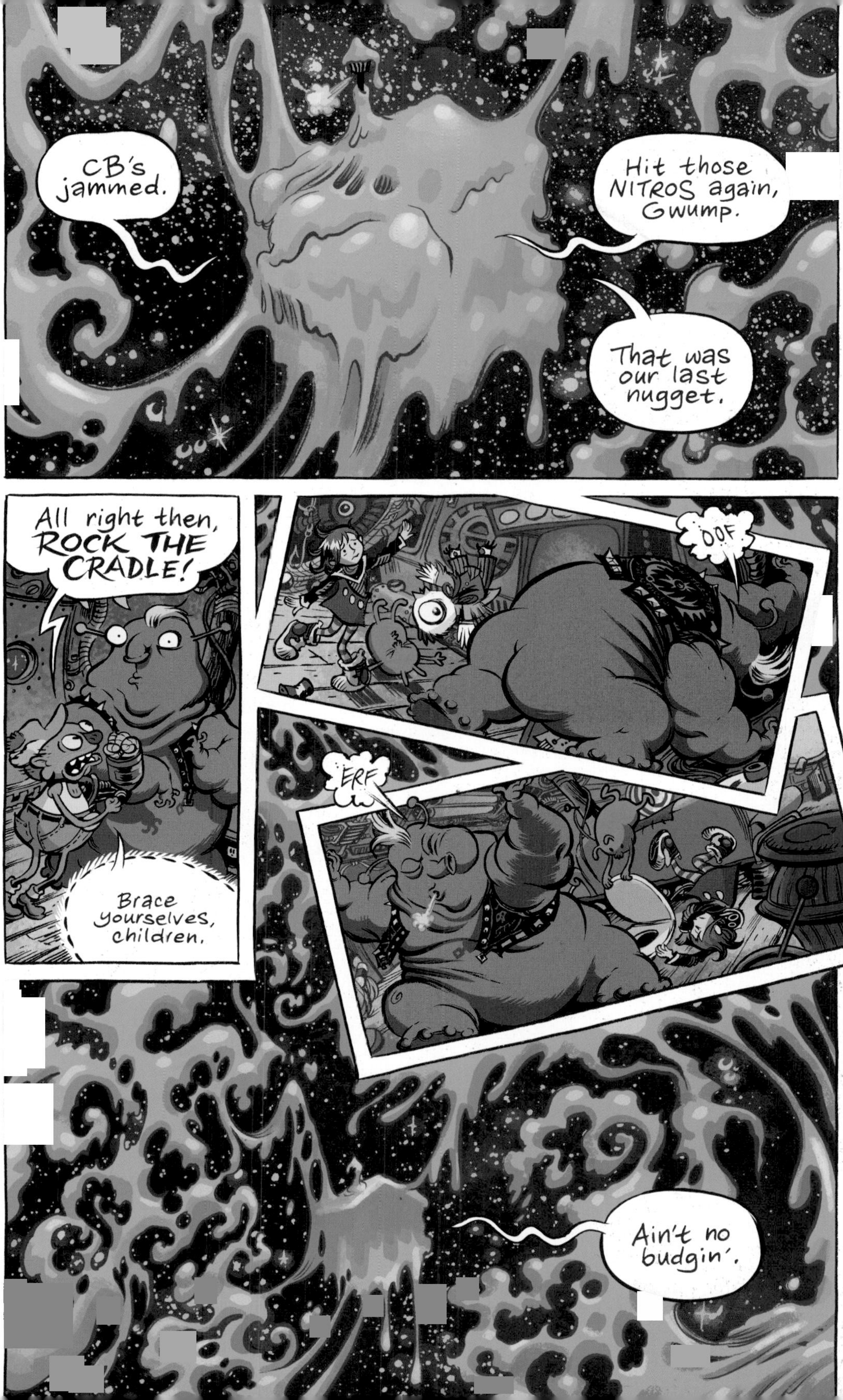
CB's jammed.
Hit those NITROS again, Gwump.
That was our last nugget.
All right then, ROCK THE CRADLE!
OOF
ERF
Brace yourselves, children.
Ain't no budgin'.

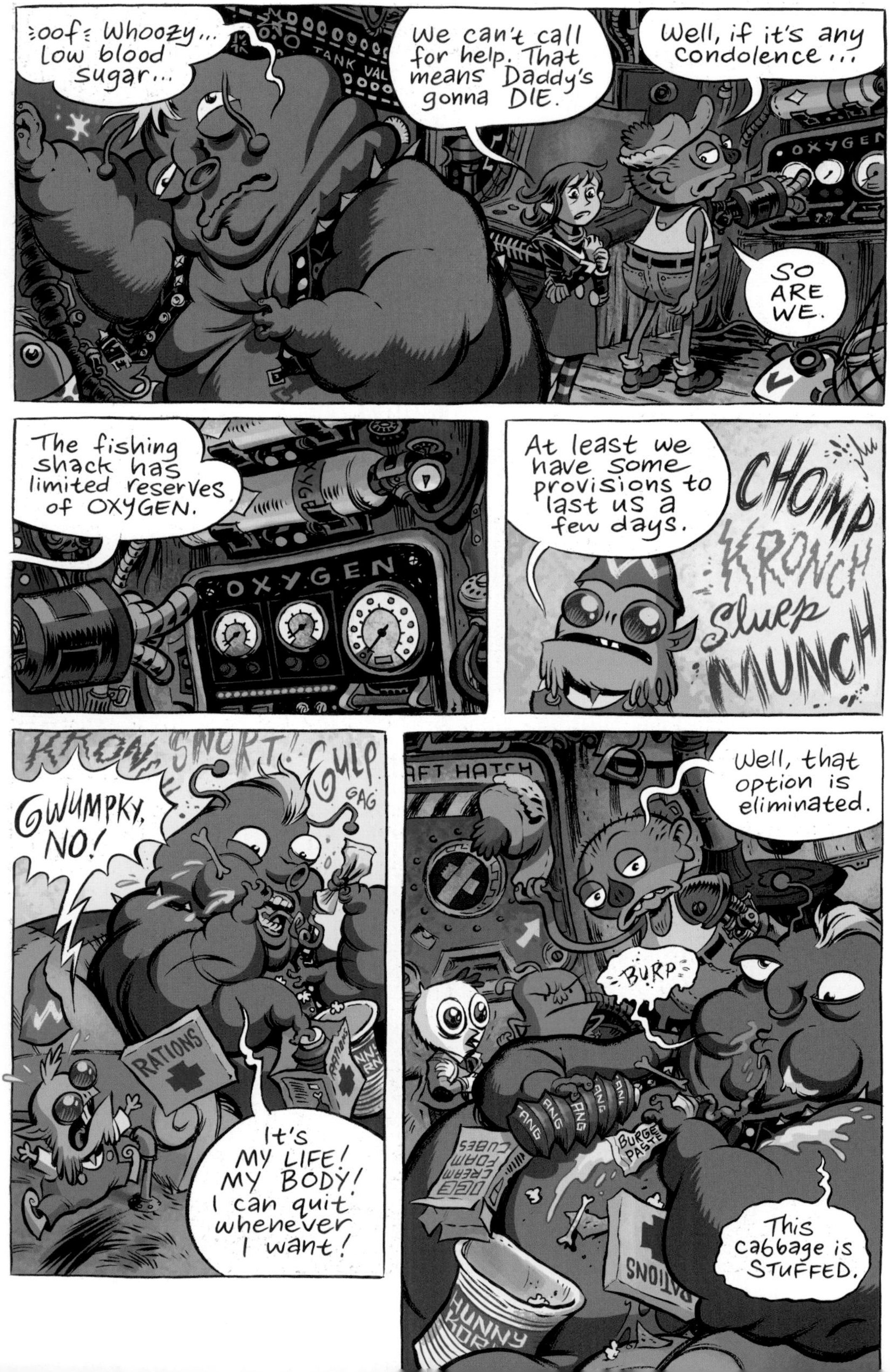

:oof: Whoozy... low blood sugar...
We can't call for help. That means Daddy's gonna DIE.
Well, if it's any condolence...
SO ARE WE.
OXYGEN
The fishing shack has limited reserves of OXYGEN.
OXYGEN
At least we have some provisions to last us a few days.
CHOMP
KRONCH
Slurp
MUNCH
KRON
SNORT!
GULP
GAG
GWUMPKY, NO!
RATIONS
It's MY LIFE! MY BODY! I can quit whenever I want!
AFT HATCH
Well, that option is eliminated.
BURP
This cabbage is STUFFED.
RATIONS

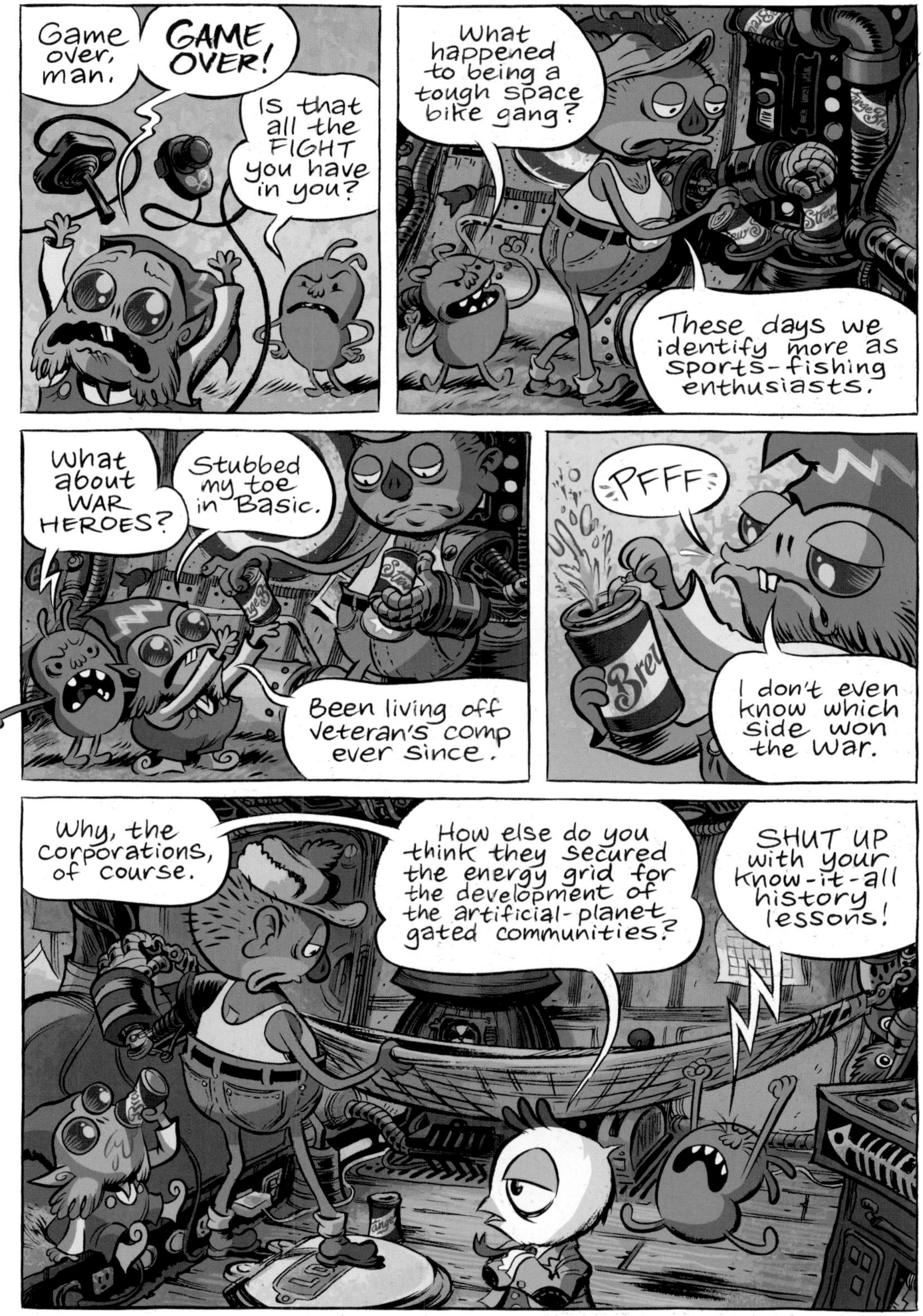
Game over, man.
GAME OVER!
Is that all the FIGHT you have in you?
What happened to being a tough space bike gang?
These days we identify more as sports-fishing enthusiasts.
What about WAR HEROES?
Stubbed my toe in Basic.
Been living off Veteran's comp ever since.
PFFF
I don't even know which side won the War.
Why, the corporations, of course.
How else do you think they secured the energy grid for the development of the artificial-planet gated communities?
SHUT UP with your know-it-all history lessons!

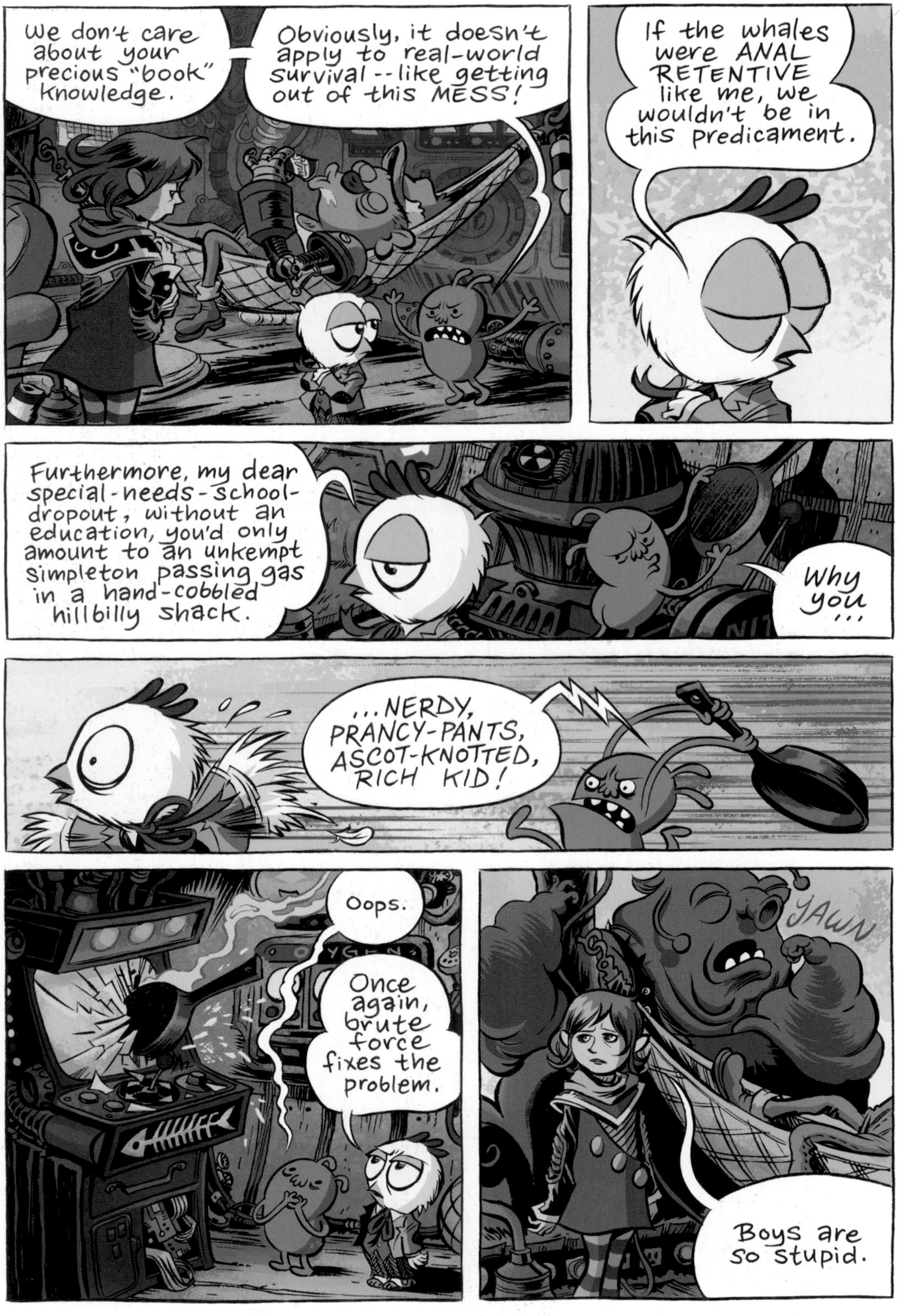
We don't care about your precious "book" knowledge.
Obviously, it doesn't apply to real-world survival --like getting out of this MESS!
If the whales were ANAL RETENTIVE like me, we wouldn't be in this predicament.
Furthermore, my dear special-needs-school-dropout, without an education, you'd only amount to an unkempt simpleton passing gas in a hand-cobbled hillbilly shack.
Why you...
...NERDY, PRANCY-PANTS, ASCOT-KNOTTED, RICH KID!
Oops.
Once again, brute force fixes the problem.
YAWN
Boys are so stupid.

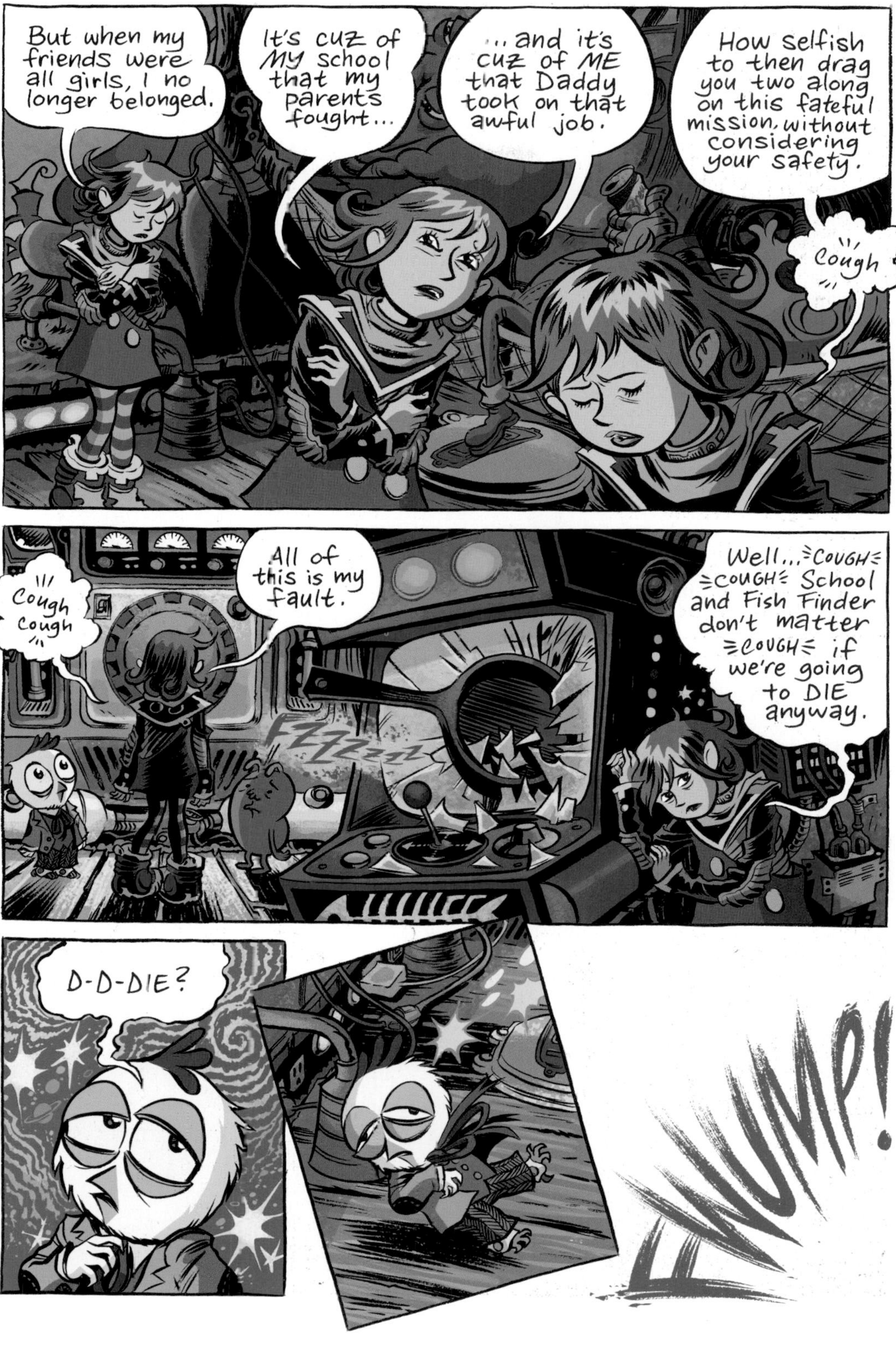

But when my friends were all girls, I no longer belonged.
It's cuz of MY school that my parents fought...
...and it's cuz of ME that Daddy took on that awful job.
How selfish to then drag you two along on this fateful mission, without considering your safety.
Cough
Cough cough
All of this is my fault.
Well... COUGH COUGH School and Fish Finder don't matter COUGH if we're going to DIE anyway.
FZZZZZZZ
D-D-DIE?
THUMP!

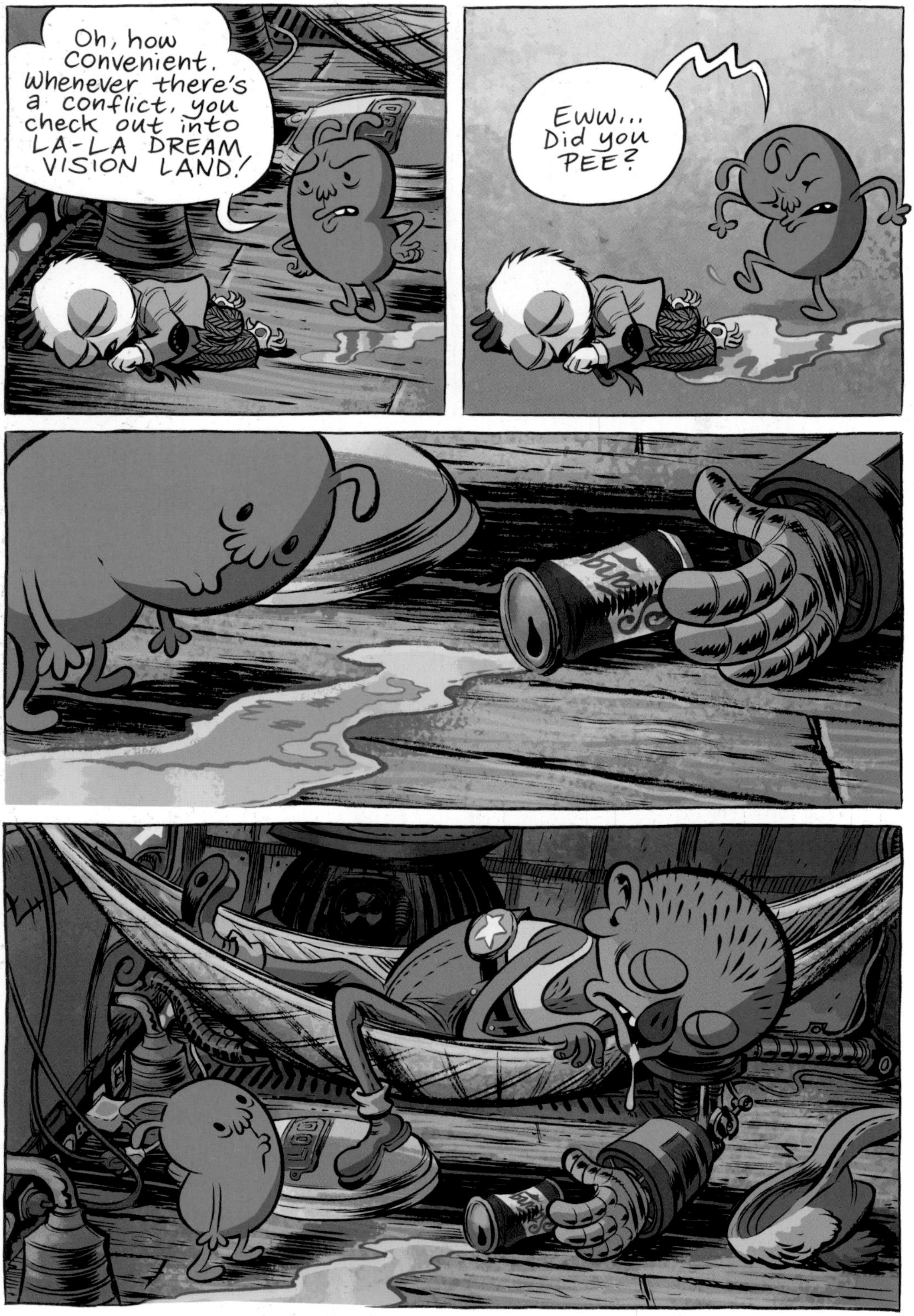
Oh, how convenient. Whenever there's a conflict, you check out into LA-LA DREAM VISION LAND!
Eww... Did you PEE?

RATIONS
NITRO
OXYGEN
GASP
gasp
Khhhhhh
Khhhhhhh

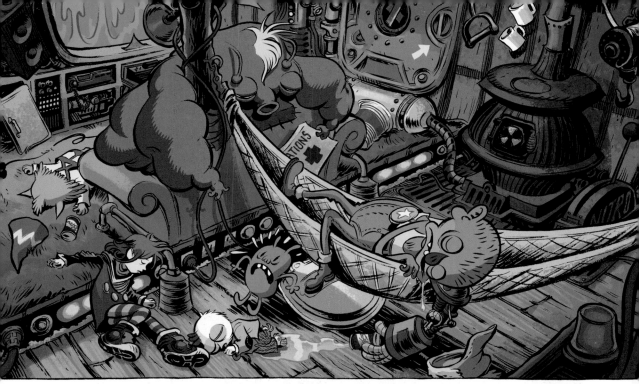

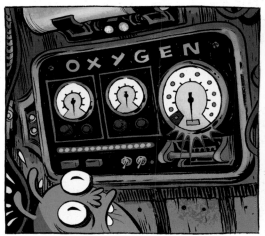

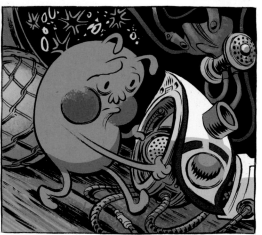

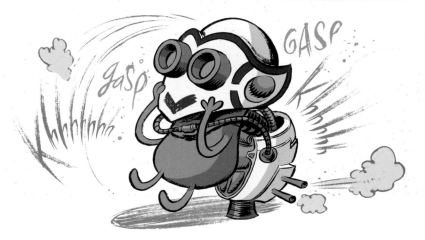

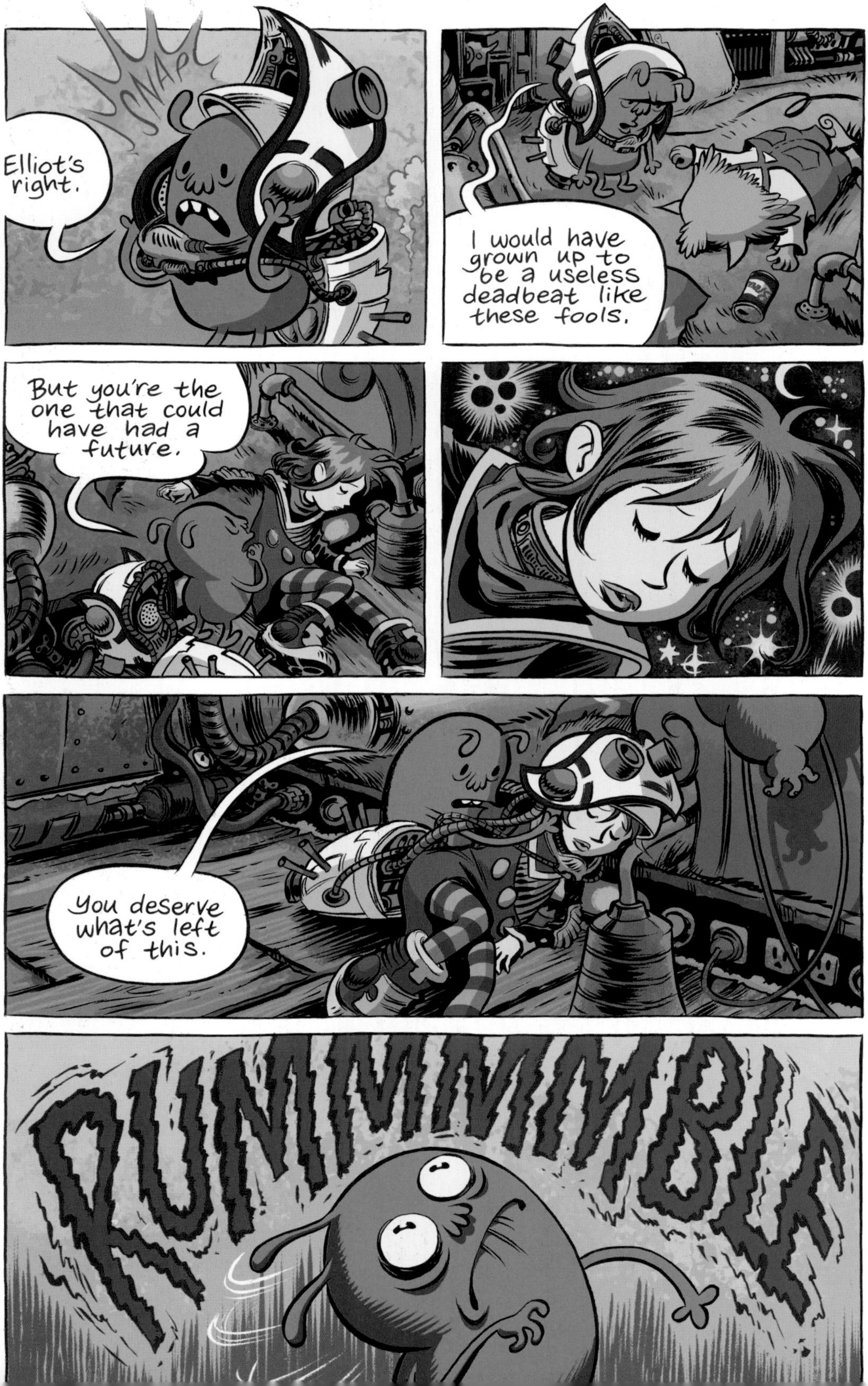
SNAP
Elliot's right.
I would have grown up to be a useless deadbeat like these fools.
But you're the one that could have had a future.
You deserve what's left of this.
RUMMMMBLE

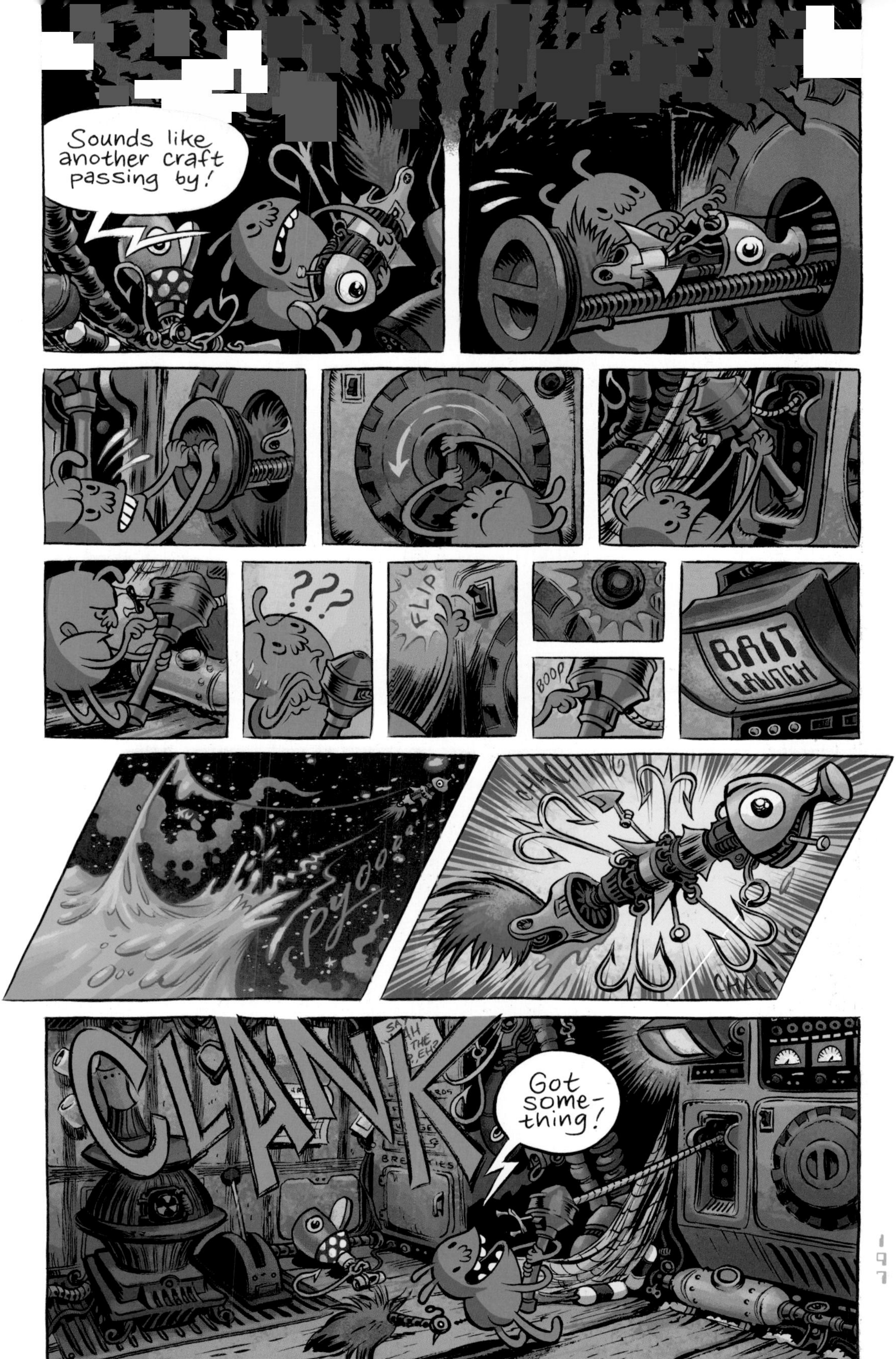
[redacted]
Sounds like another craft passing by!
???
FLIP
BOOP
BAIT LAUNCH
PYOOR
CHACHING
CHACHING
CLANK
Got some-thing!

Feels BIG...
Reeling it in...
SNAP

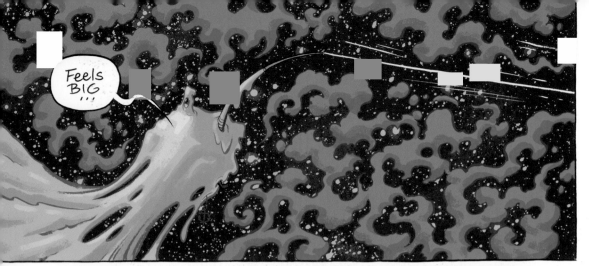

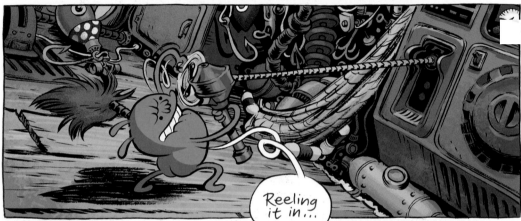

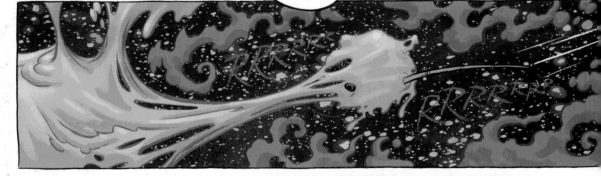

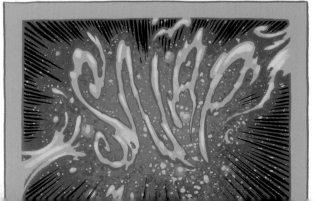

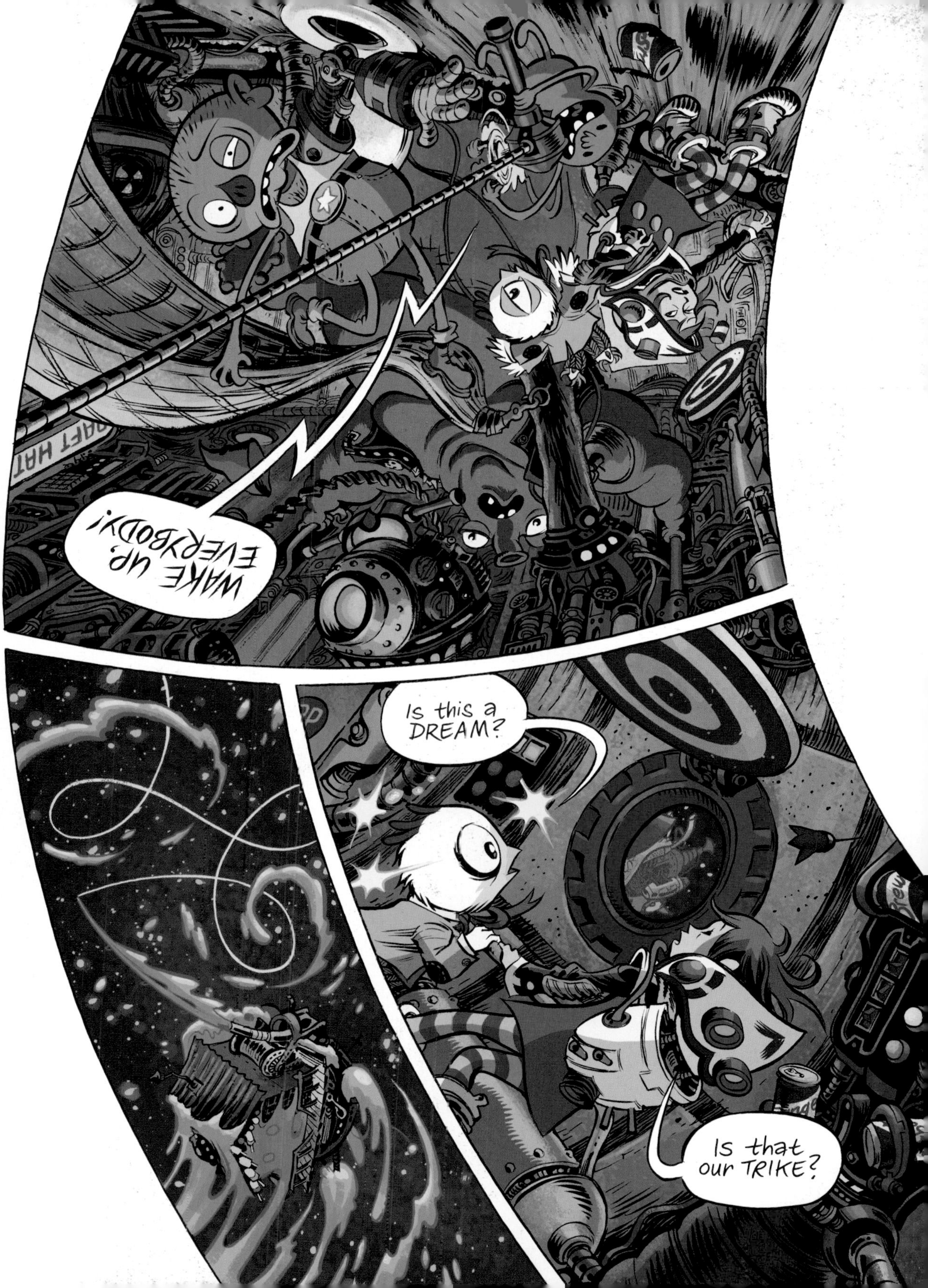
WAKE UP, EVERYBODY!
Is this a DREAM?
Is that our TRIKE?

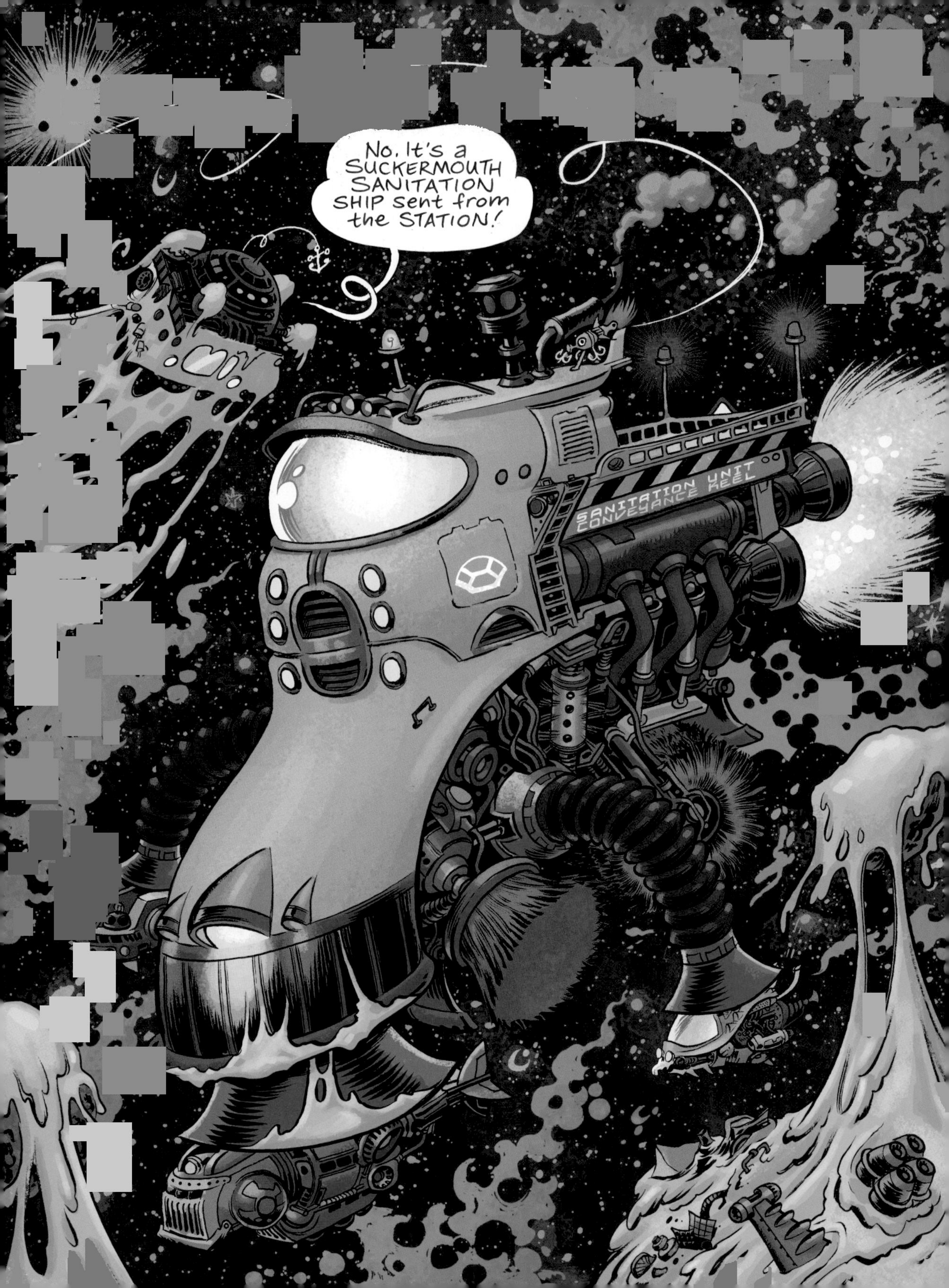
No. It's a SUCKERMOUTH SANITATION SHIP sent from the STATION!
SANITATION UNIT
CONVEYANCE KEEL

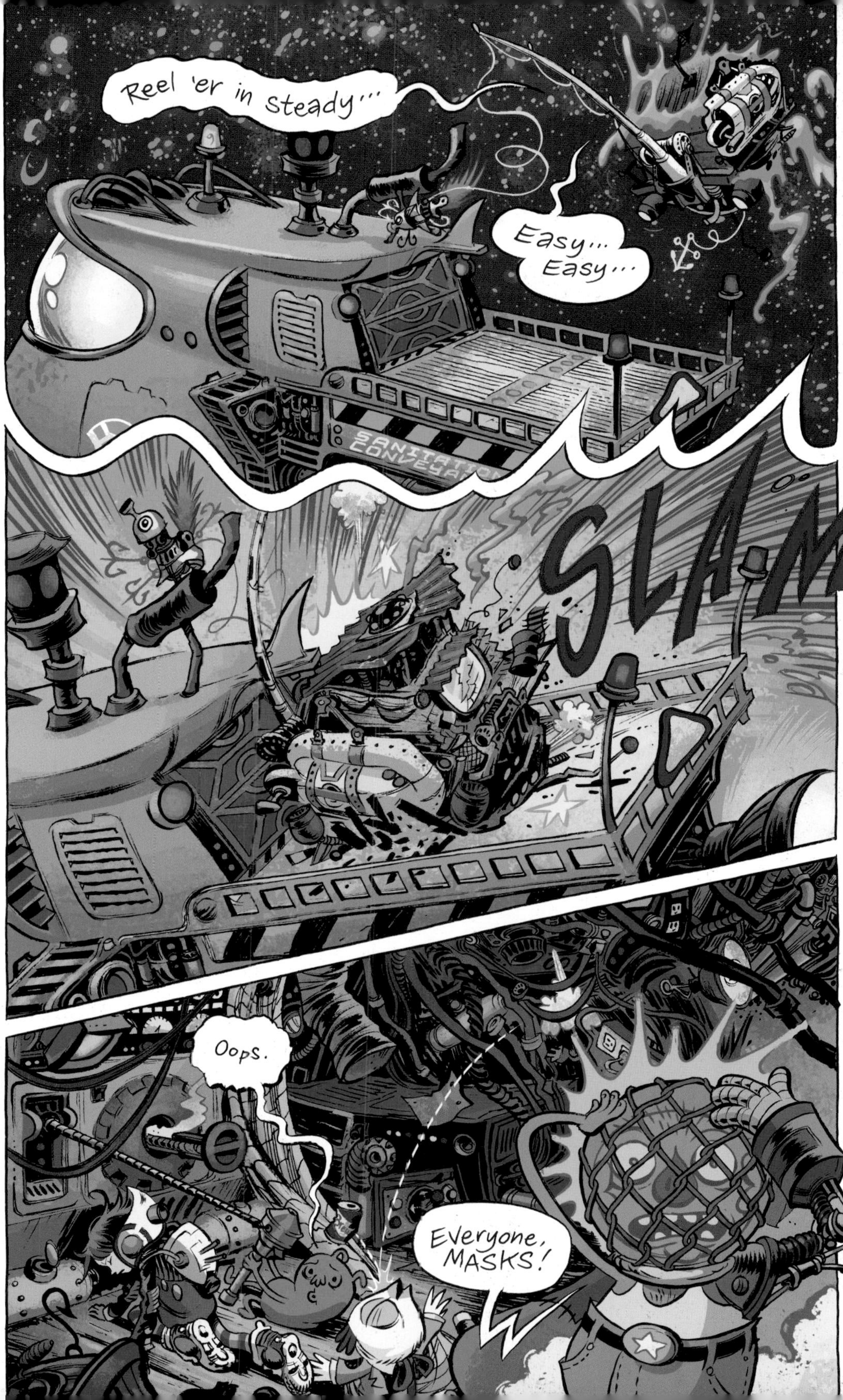
Reel 'er in steady...
Easy... Easy...
SANITATION CONVEYA
SLAM
Oops.
Everyone, MASKS!

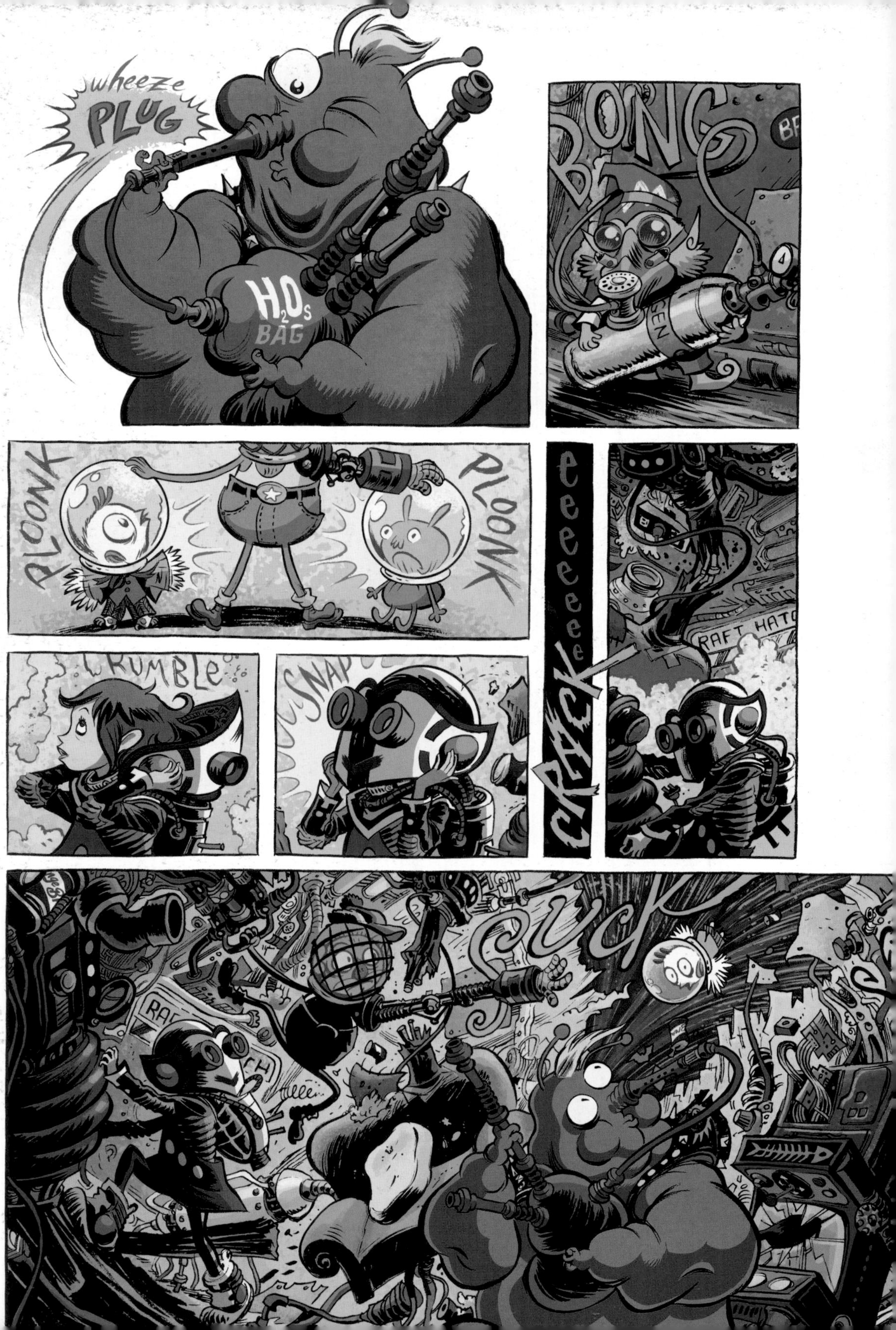
wheeze
PLUG
H2Os BAG
BONG
PLOONK
PLOONK
eeeeeee
CRACK
RUMBLE
SNAP
RAFT HATC

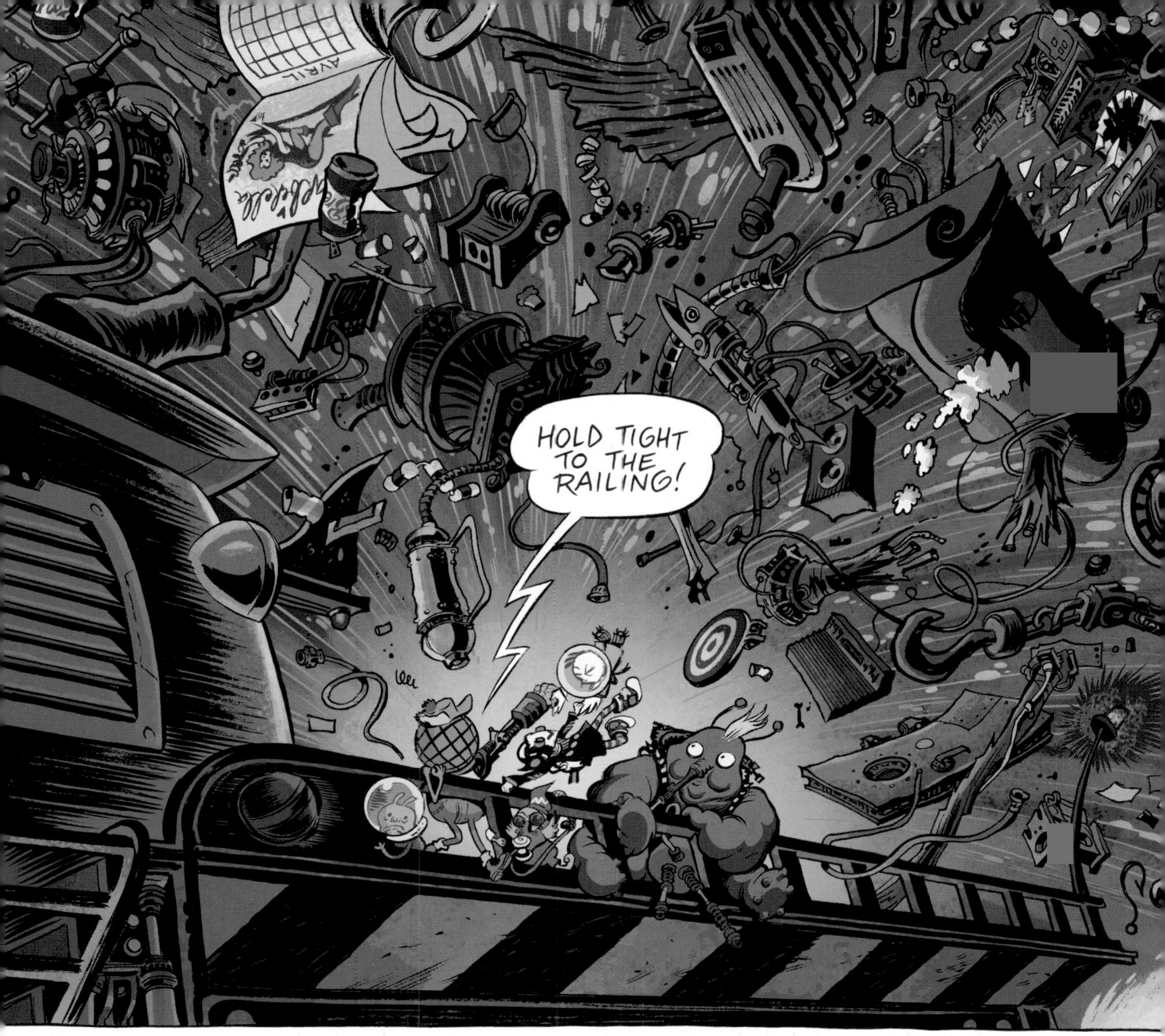
HOLD TIGHT TO THE RAILING!

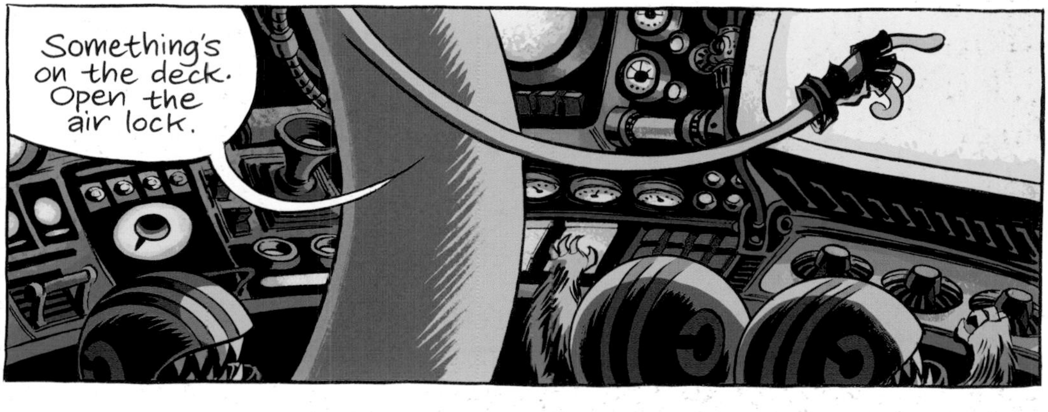
Something's on the deck. Open the air lock.

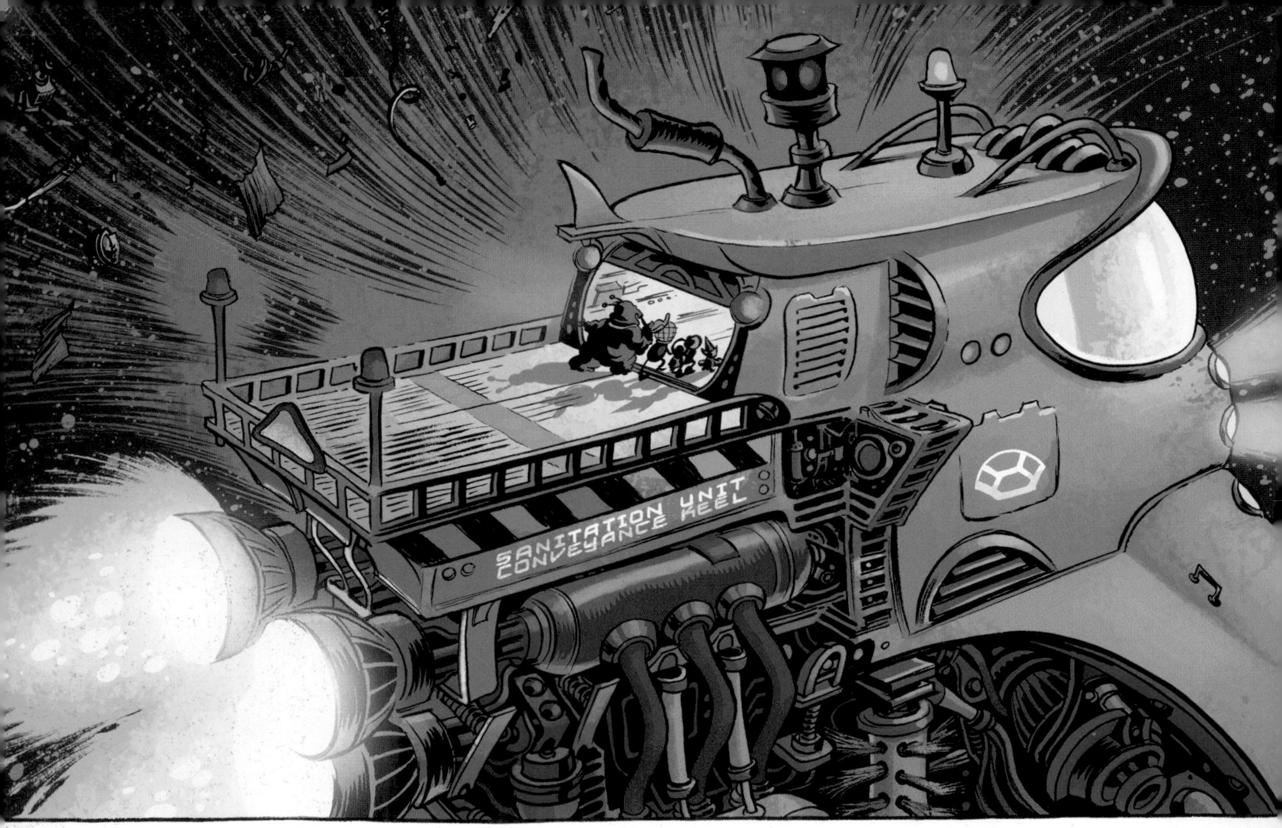
SANITATION UNIT
CONVEYANCE KEEL

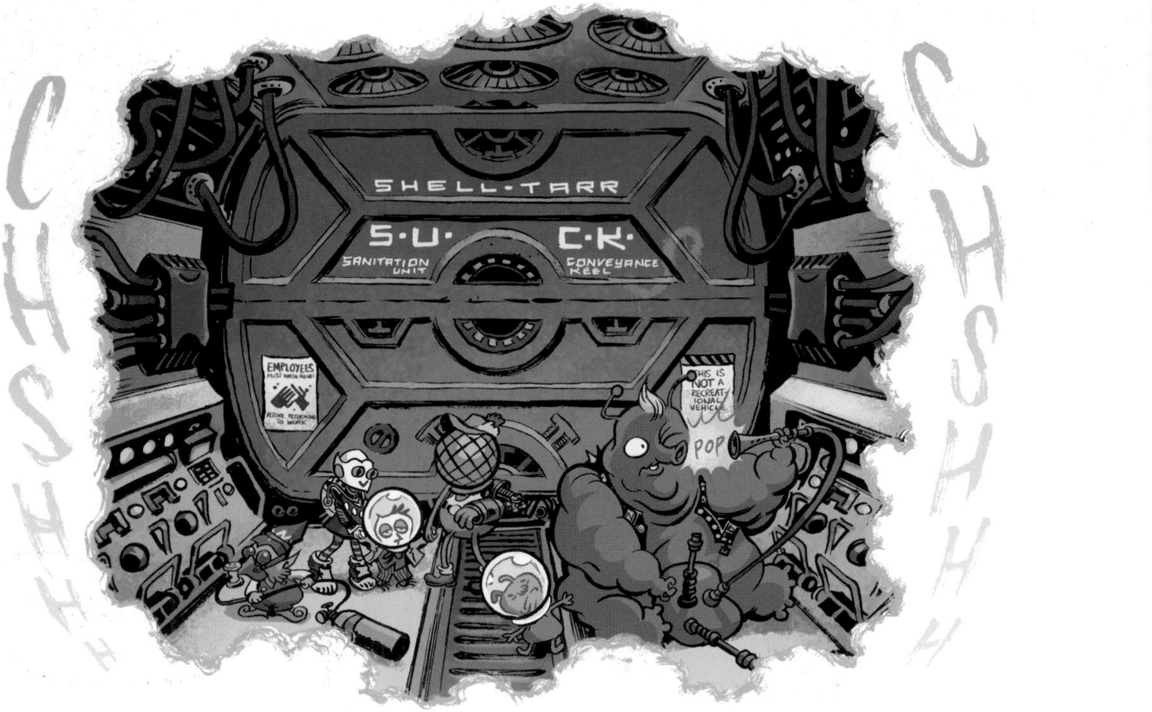
CHSHHH
SHELL-TARR
S·U· C·K·
SANITATION UNIT
CONVEYANCE KEEL
EMPLOYEES
BEFORE RETURNING TO WORK
THIS IS NOT A RECREATIONAL VEHICLE
POP
CHSHHH

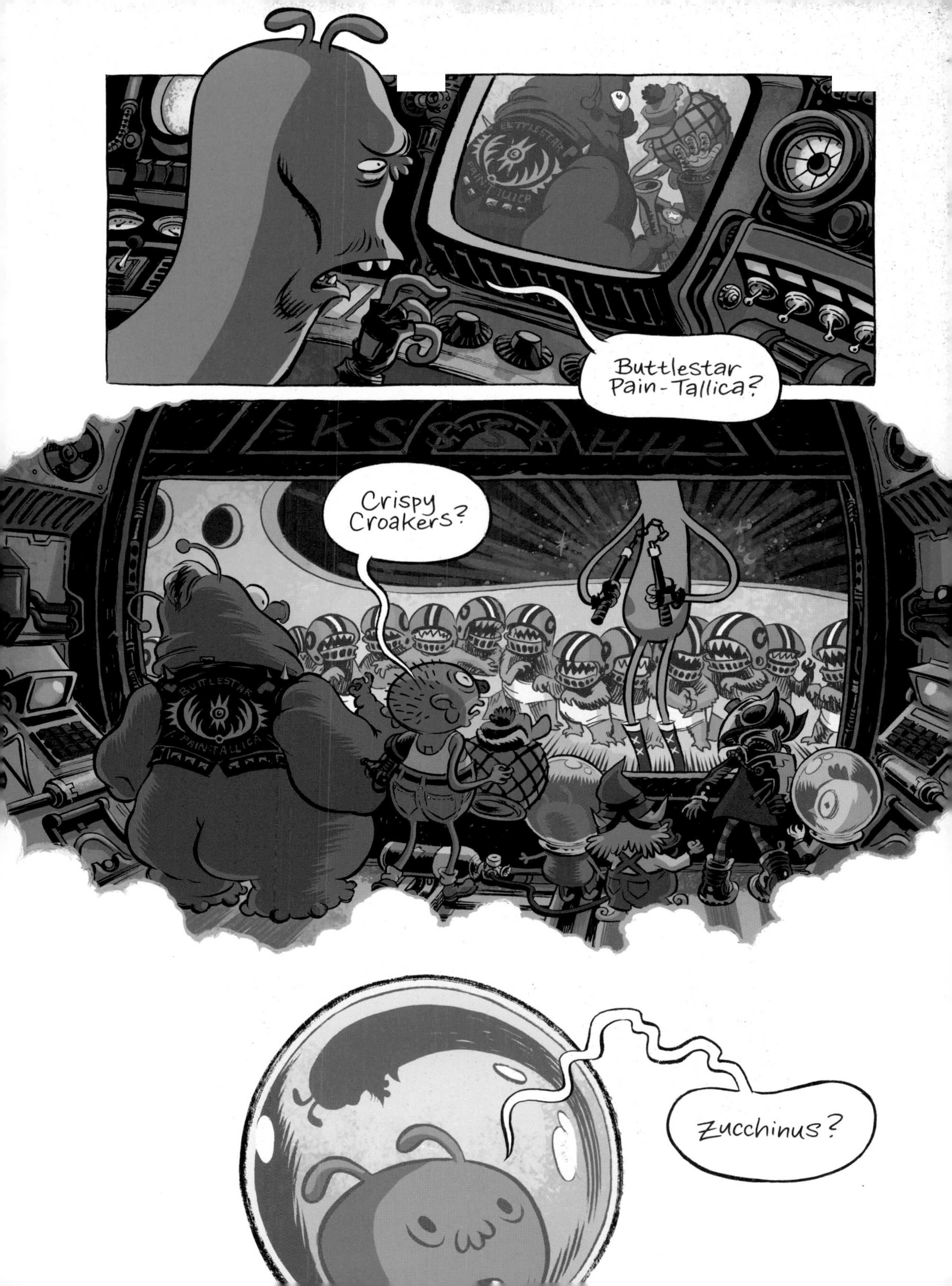
Buttlestar Pain-Tallica?
KSSSHHH
Crispy Croakers?
BUTTLESTAR PAIN-TALLICA
Zucchinus?

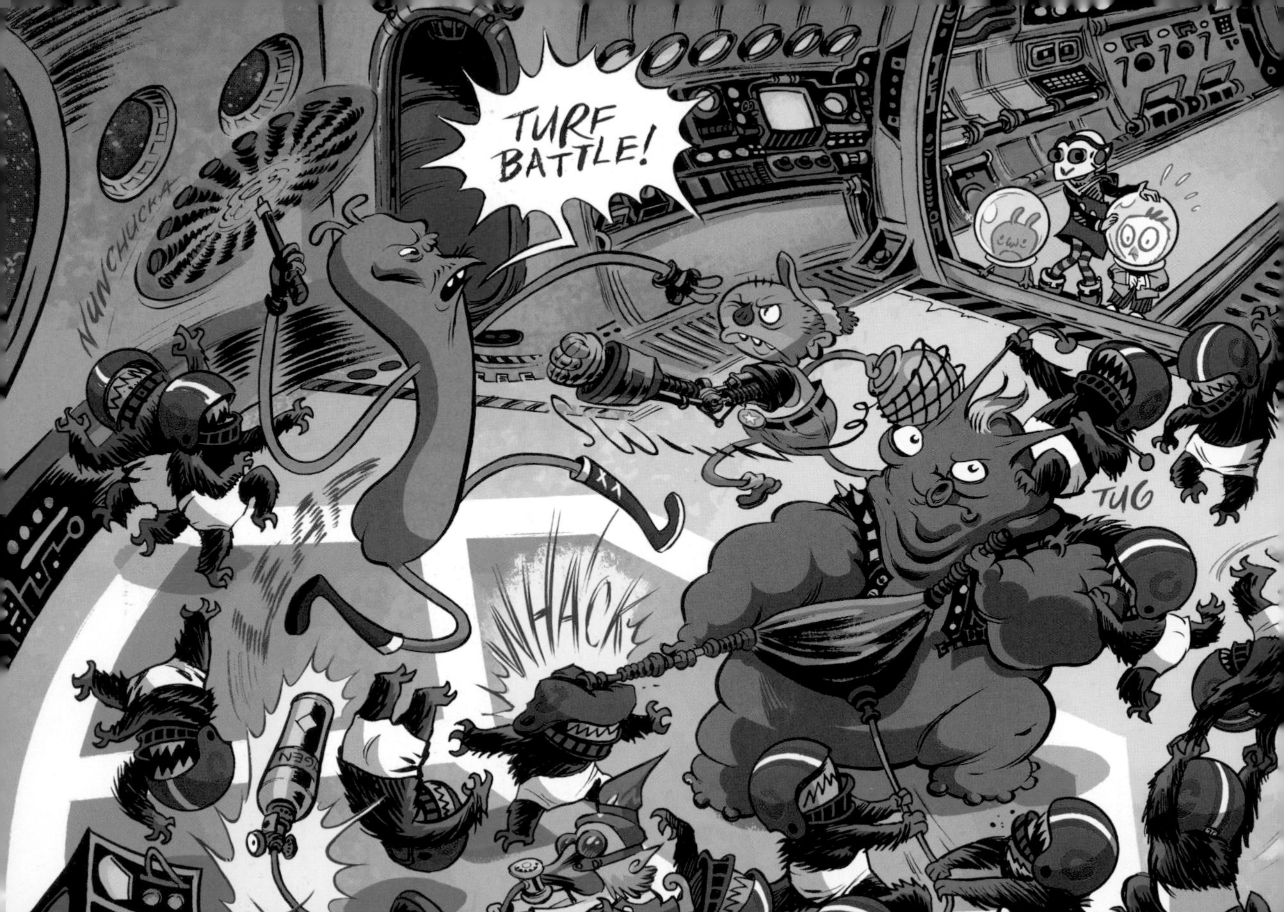

TURF BATTLE!
NUNCHUCKA
TUG
WHACK

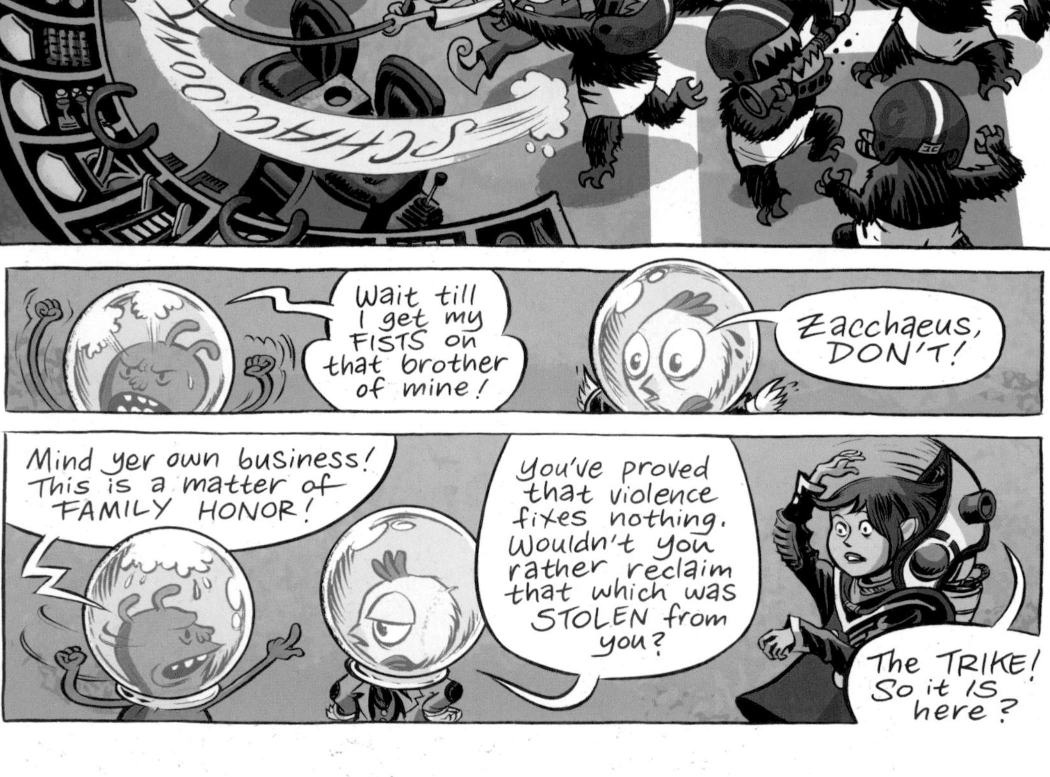

Wait till I get my FISTS on that brother of mine!
Zacchaeus, DON'T!
Mind yer own business! This is a matter of FAMILY HONOR!
You've proved that violence fixes nothing. Wouldn't you rather reclaim that which was STOLEN from you?
The TRIKE! So it IS here?

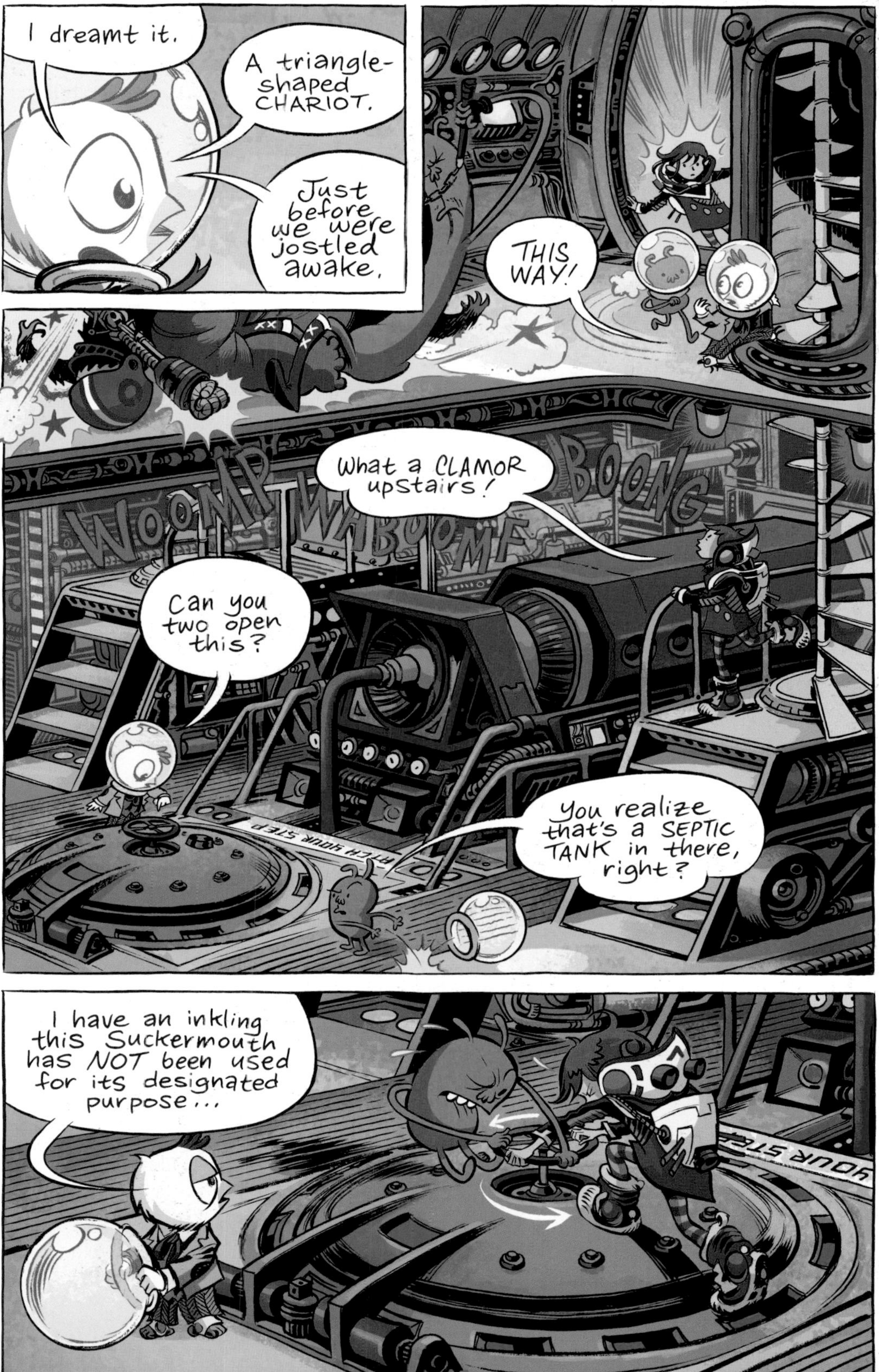
I dreamt it.
A triangle-shaped CHARIOT.
Just before we were jostled awake.
THIS WAY!
WOOMP
WABOOMF
BOONG
What a CLAMOR upstairs!
Can you two open this?
You realize that's a SEPTIC TANK in there, right?
I have an inkling this Suckermouth has NOT been used for its designated purpose...

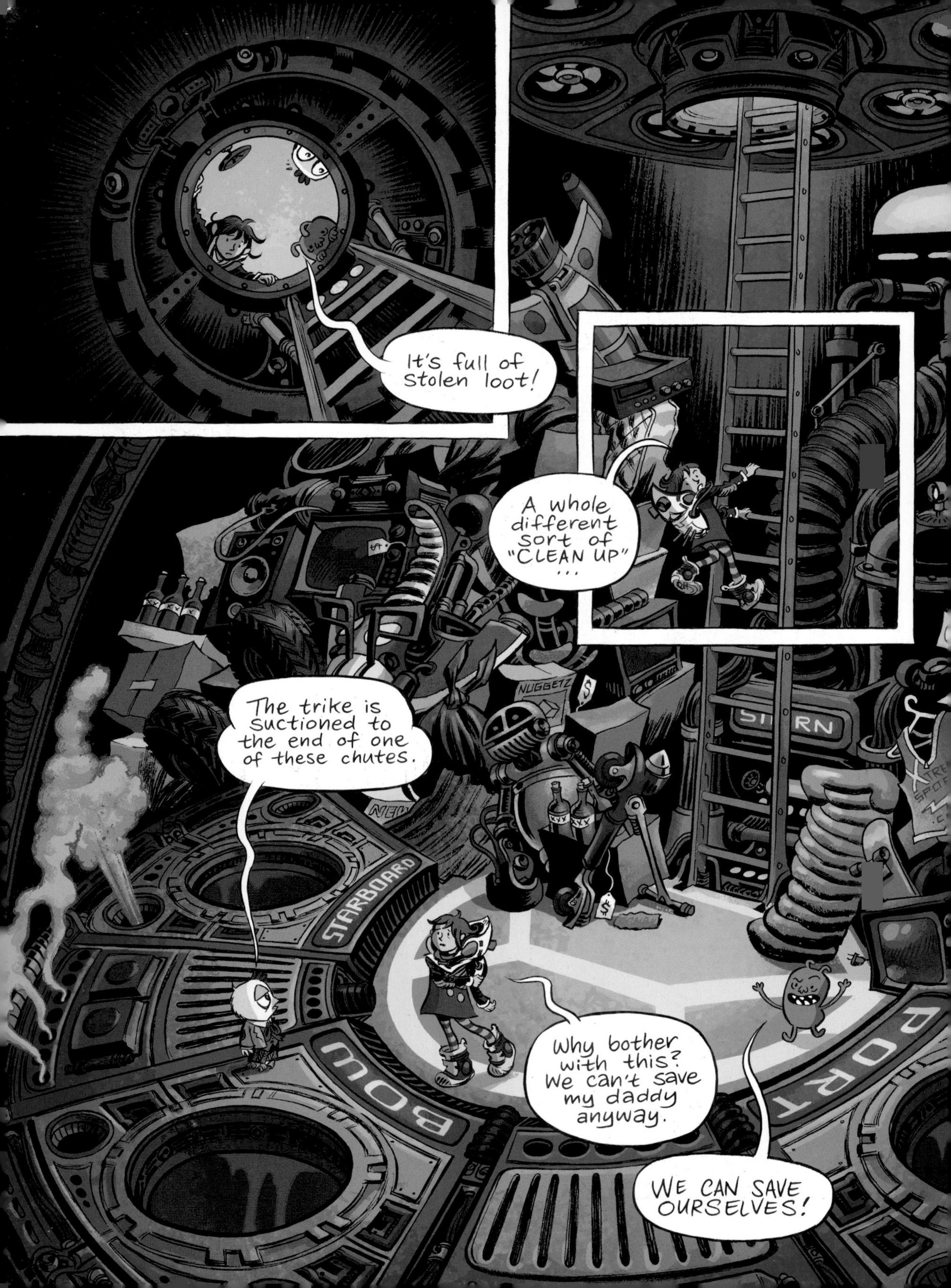
It's full of stolen loot!
A whole different sort of "CLEAN UP" ...
NUGGETZ
STERN
The trike is suctioned to the end of one of these chutes.
STARBOARD
BOW
PORT
Why bother with this? We can't save my daddy anyway.
WE CAN SAVE OURSELVES!

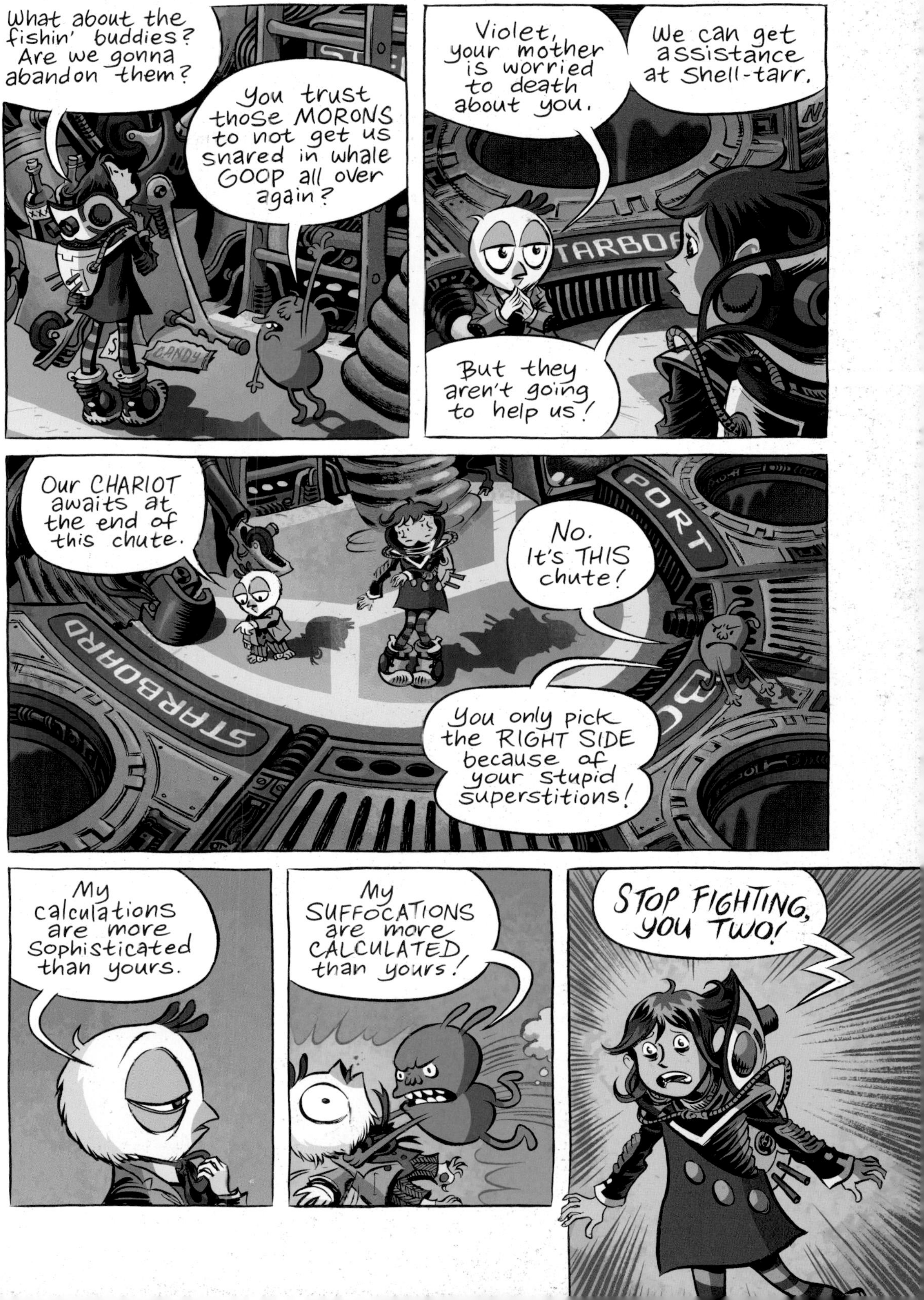
What about the fishin' buddies? Are we gonna abandon them?
You trust those MORONS to not get us snared in whale GOOP all over again?
CANDY
Violet, your mother is worried to death about you.
We can get assistance at Shell-tarr.
STARBOA
But they aren't going to help us!
Our CHARIOT awaits at the end of this chute.
PORT
No. It's THIS chute!
STARBOARD
You only pick the RIGHT SIDE because of your stupid superstitions!
My calculations are more sophisticated than yours.
My SUFFOCATIONS are more CALCULATED than yours!
STOP FIGHTING, YOU TWO!

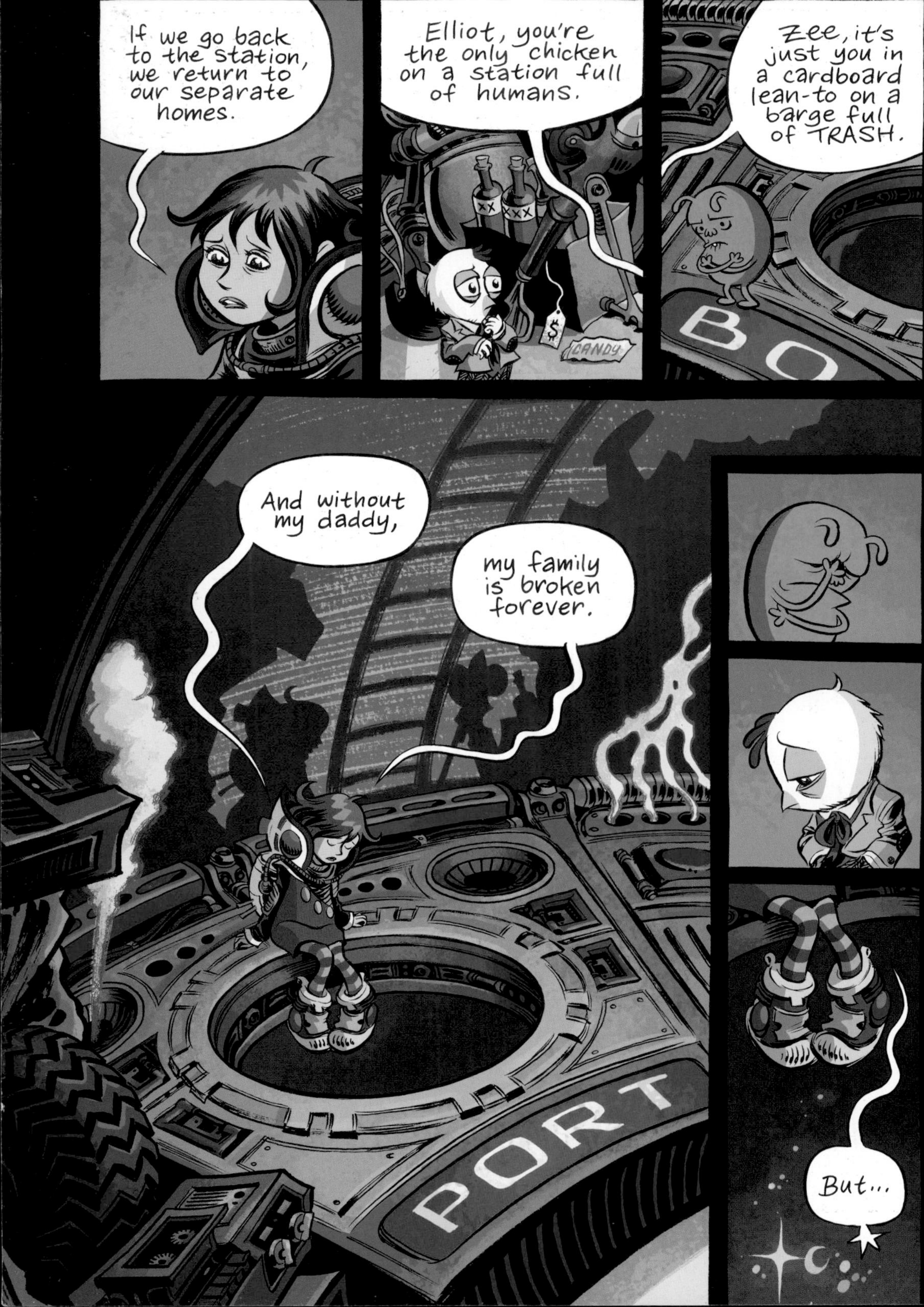
If we go back to the station, we return to our separate homes.
Elliot, you're the only chicken on a station full of humans.
Zee, it's just you in a cardboard lean-to on a barge full of TRASH.
CANDY
BO
And without my daddy,
my family is broken forever.
PORT
But...

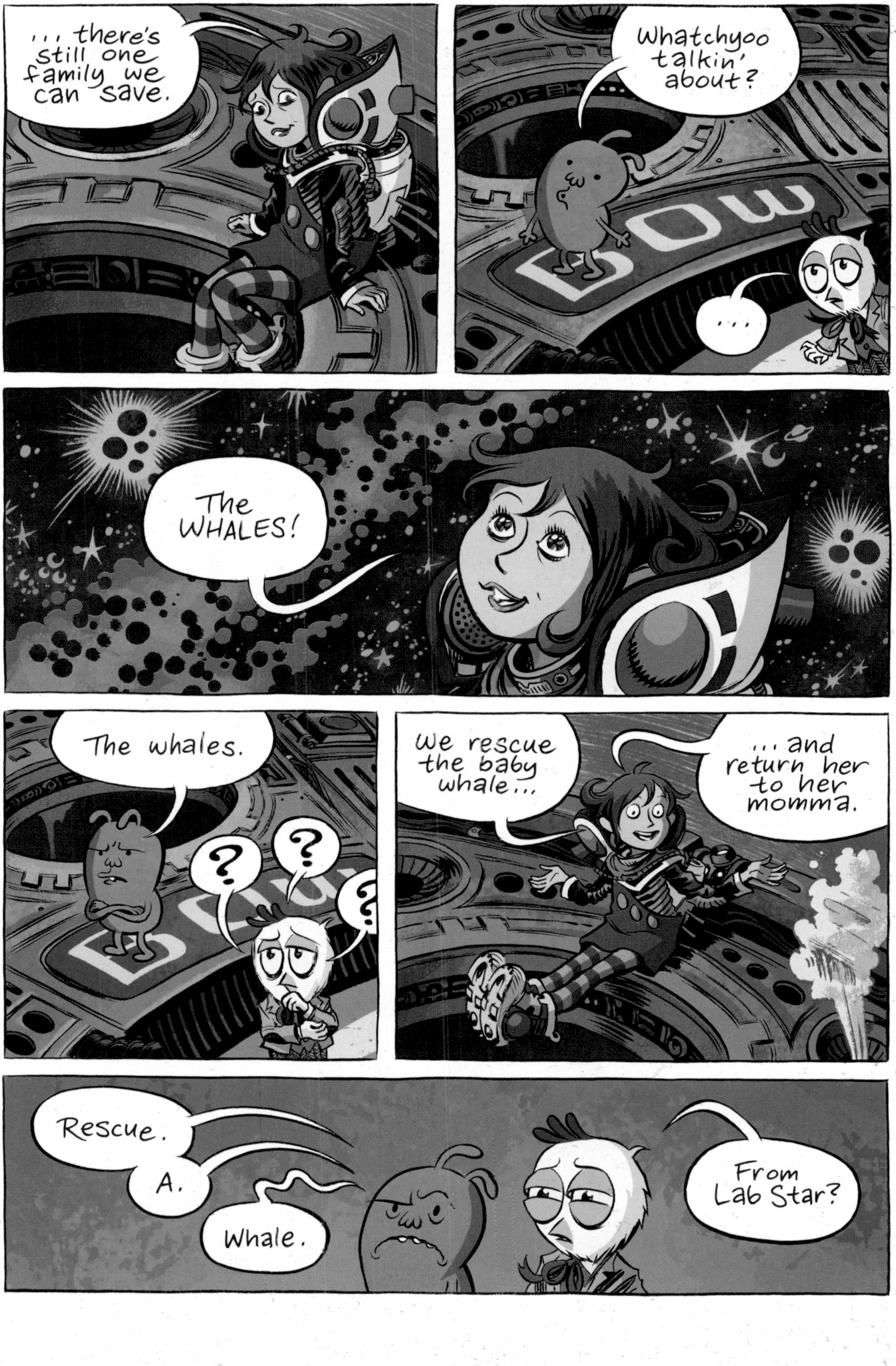

...there's still one family we can save.
Whatchyoo talkin' about?
...
The WHALES!
The whales.
?
?
?
We rescue the baby whale...
...and return her to her momma.
Rescue.
A.
Whale.
From Lab Star?

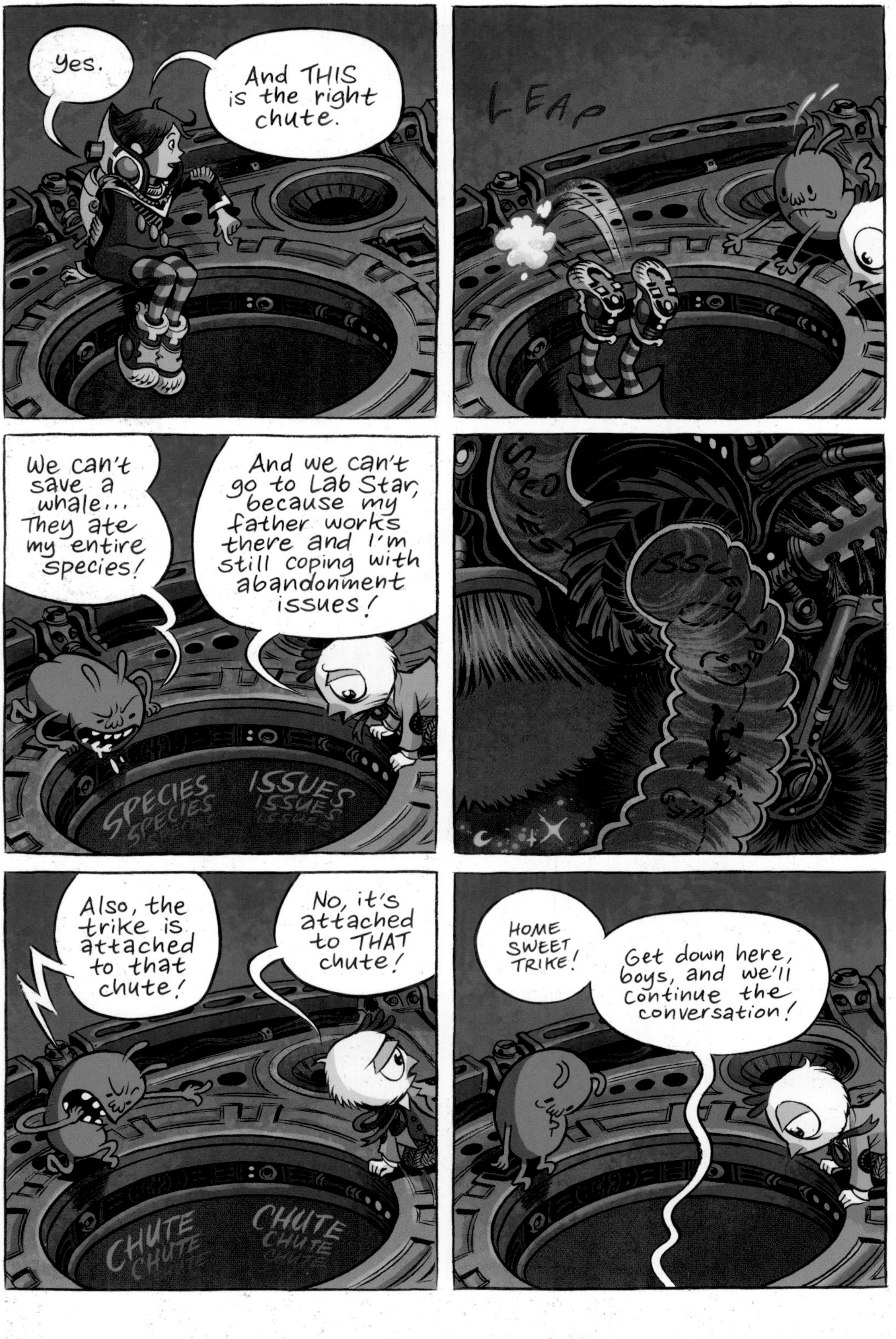
Yes.
And THIS is the right chute.
LEAP
We can't save a whale... They ate my entire species!
And we can't go to Lab Star, because my father works there and I'm still coping with abandonment issues!
SPECIES SPECIES
ISSUES ISSUES
Also, the trike is attached to that chute!
No, it's attached to THAT chute!
CHUTE CHUTE
CHUTE CHUTE
HOME SWEET TRIKE!
Get down here, boys, and we'll continue the conversation!

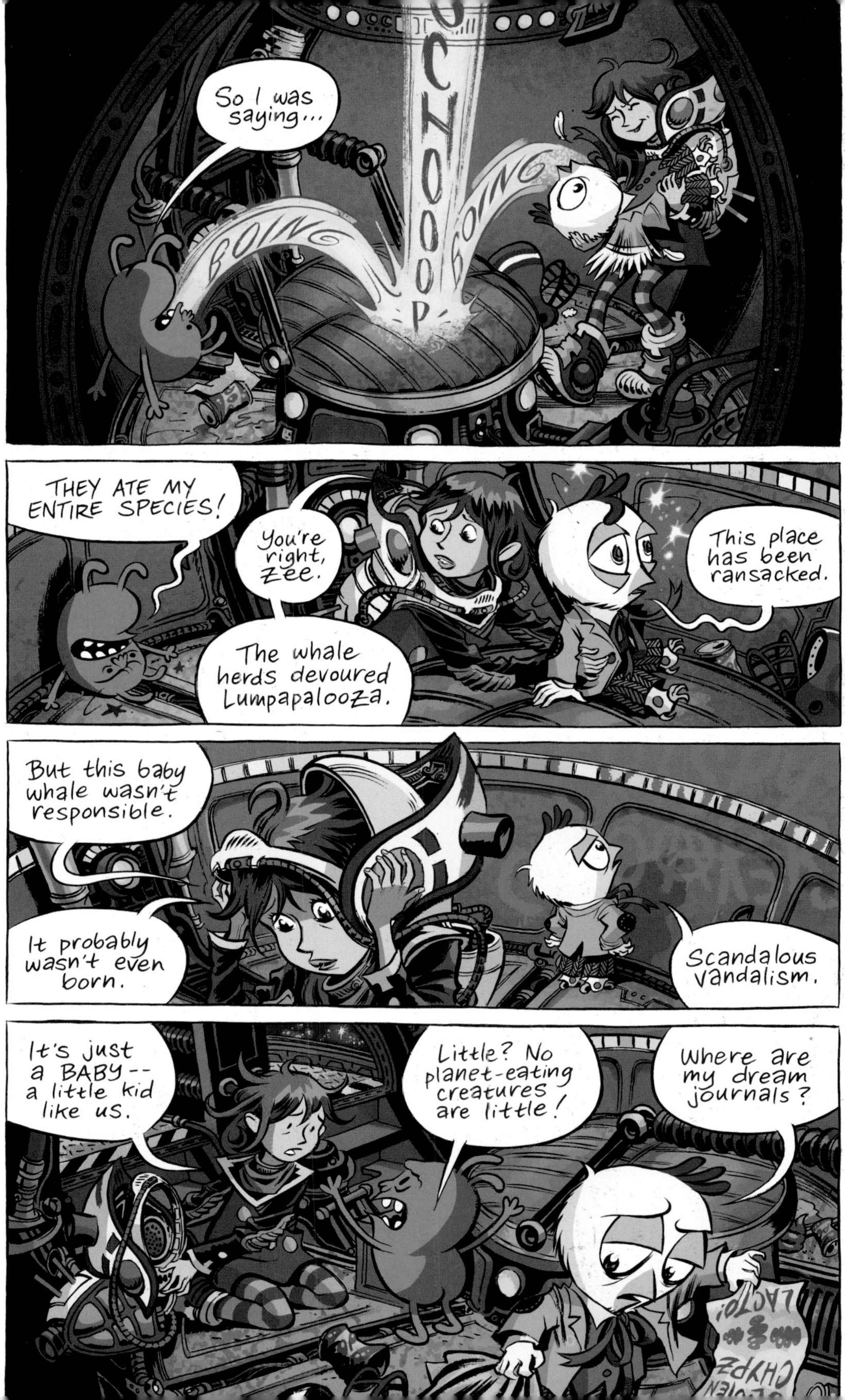
So I was saying...
CHOOOOP
BOING
BOING
THEY ATE MY ENTIRE SPECIES!
You're right, Zee.
The whale herds devoured Lumpapalooza.
This place has been ransacked.
But this baby whale wasn't responsible.
It probably wasn't even born.
Scandalous vandalism.
It's just a BABY-- a little kid like us.
Little? No planet-eating creatures are little!
Where are my dream journals?

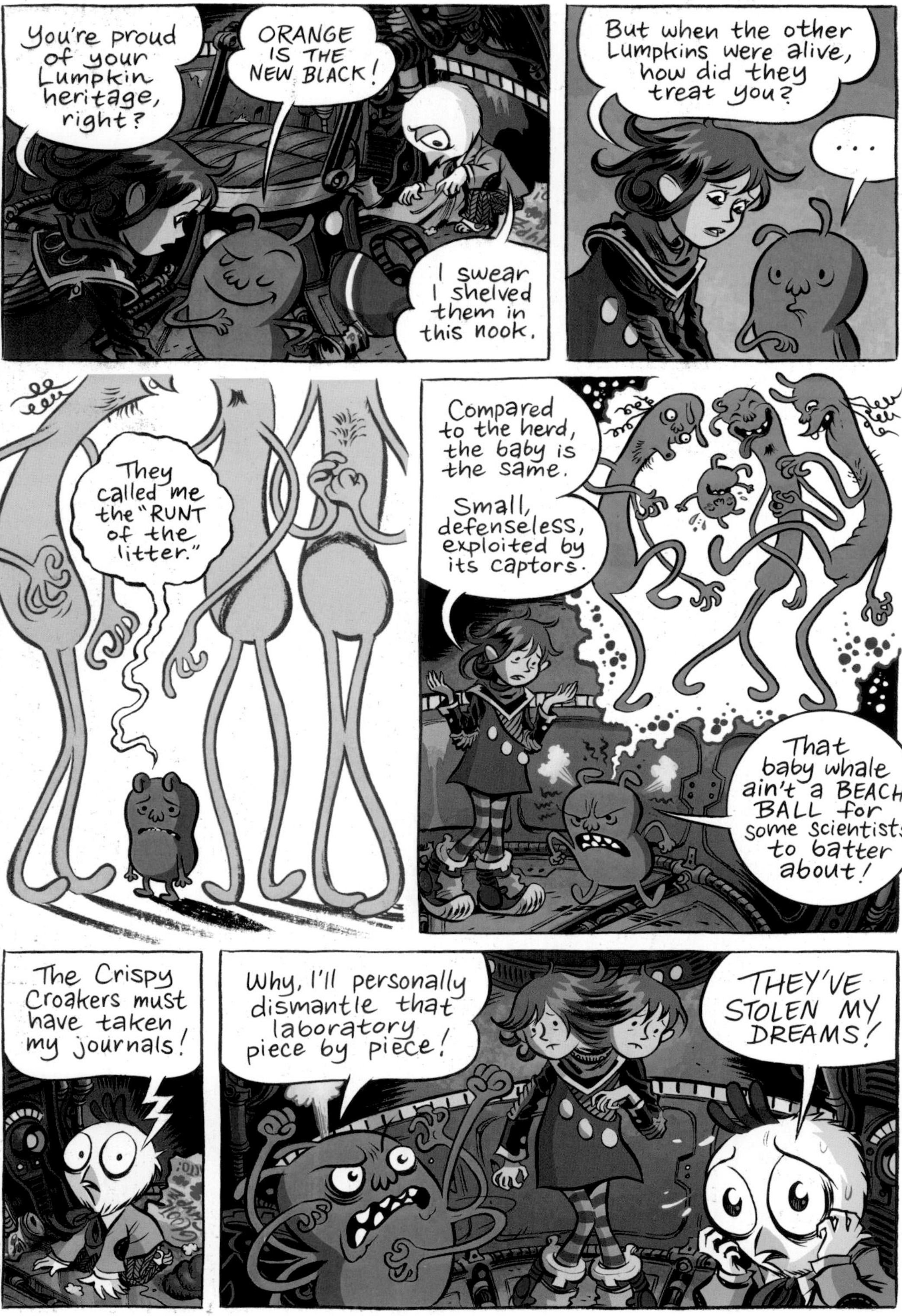
You're proud of your Lumpkin heritage, right?
ORANGE IS THE NEW BLACK!
I swear I shelved them in this nook.
But when the other Lumpkins were alive, how did they treat you?
...
They called me the "RUNT of the litter."
Compared to the herd, the baby is the same.
Small, defenseless, exploited by its captors.
That baby whale ain't a BEACH BALL for some scientists to batter about!
The Crispy Croakers must have taken my journals!
Why, I'll personally dismantle that laboratory piece by piece!
THEY'VE STOLEN MY DREAMS!

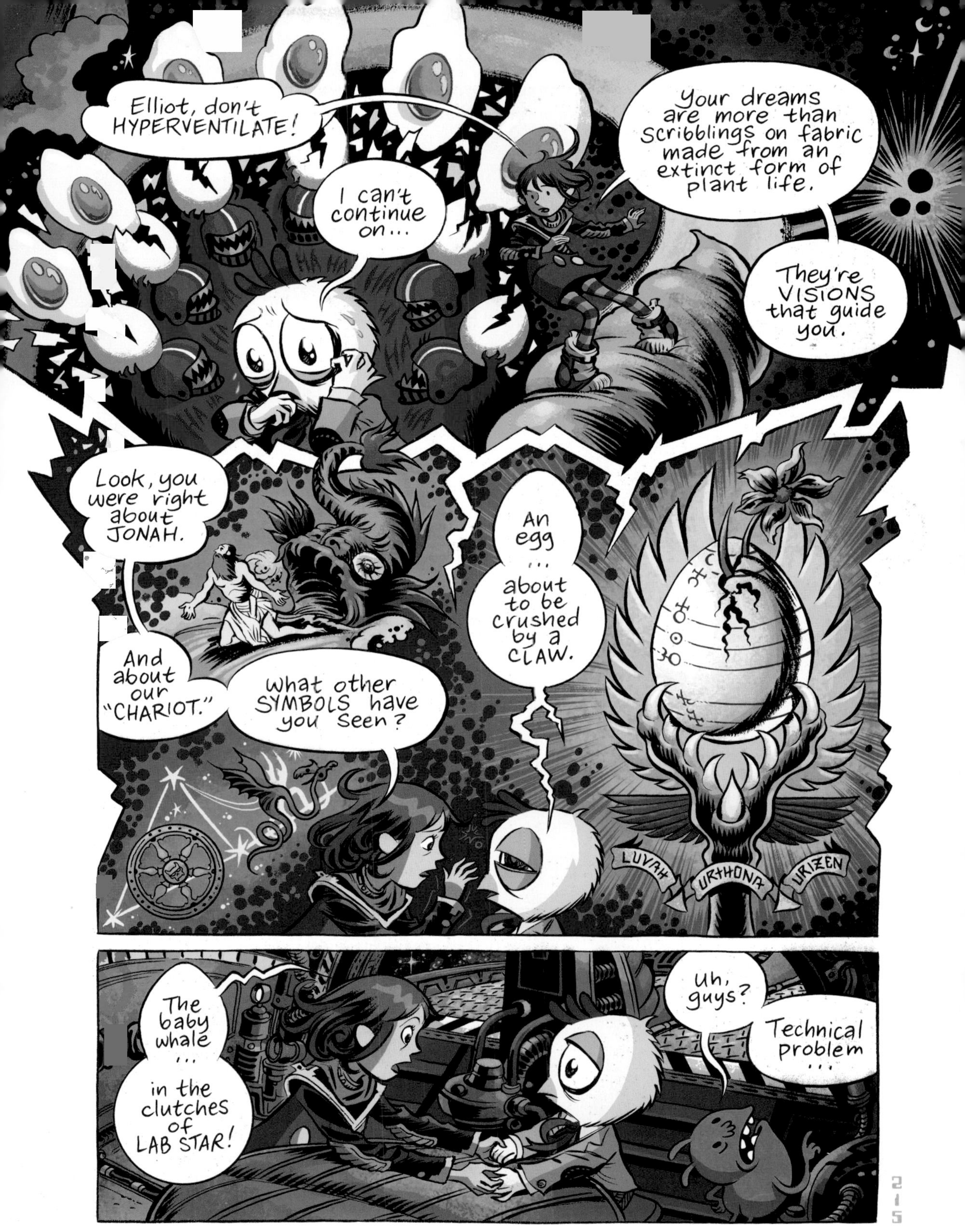
Elliot, don't HYPERVENTILATE!
I can't continue on...
Your dreams are more than scribblings on fabric made from an extinct form of plant life.
They're VISIONS that guide you.
Look, you were right about JONAH.
And about our "CHARIOT."
What other SYMBOLS have you seen?
An egg ... about to be crushed by a CLAW.
LUVAH
URTHONA
URIZEN
The baby whale ...
in the clutches of LAB STAR!
Uh, guys?
Technical problem ...

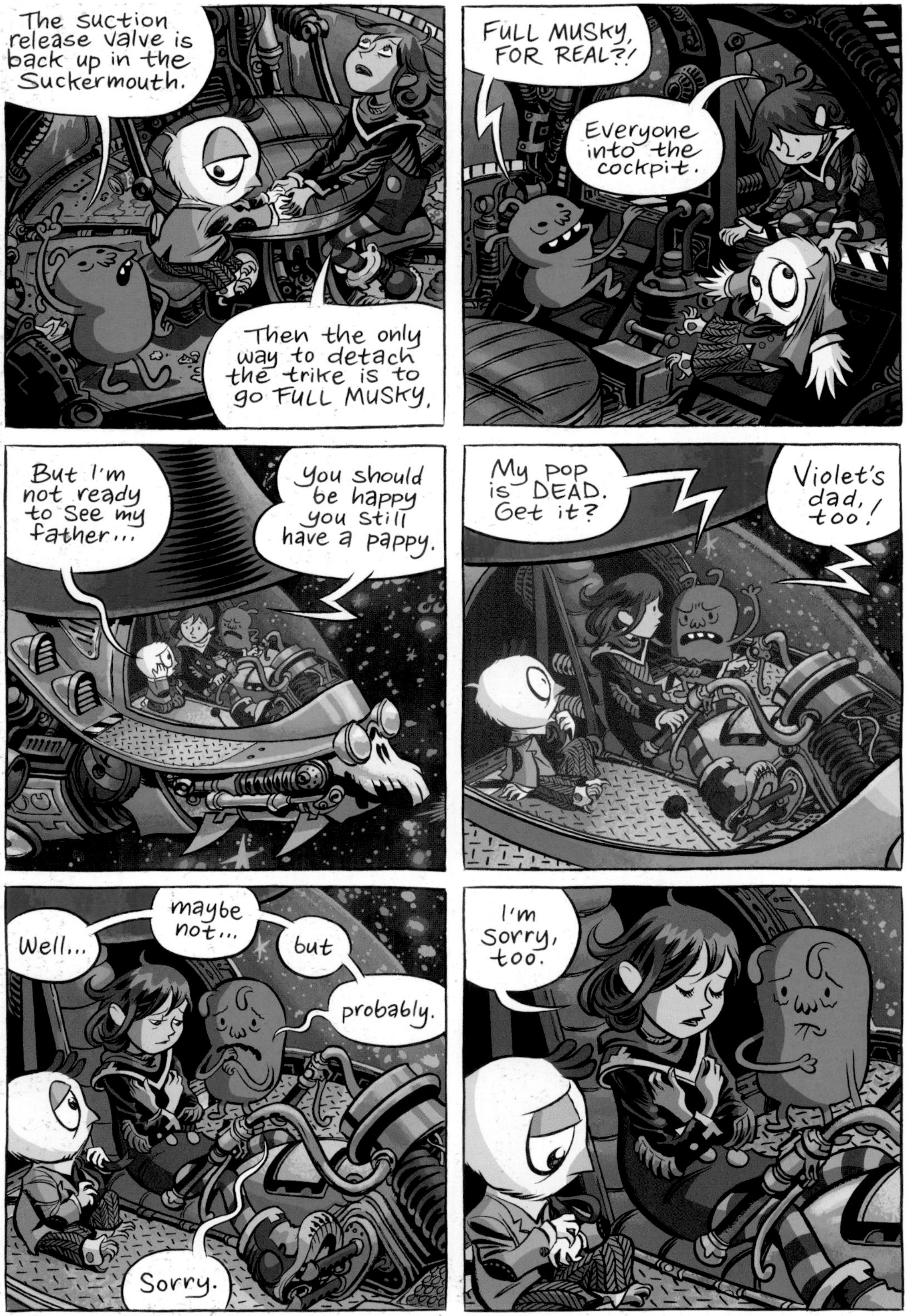

The suction release valve is back up in the Suckermouth.
Then the only way to detach the trike is to go FULL MUSKY.
FULL MUSKY, FOR REAL?!
Everyone into the cockpit.
But I'm not ready to see my father...
You should be happy you still have a pappy.
My pop is DEAD. Get it?
Violet's dad, too!
Well...
maybe not...
but
probably.
Sorry.
I'm sorry, too.

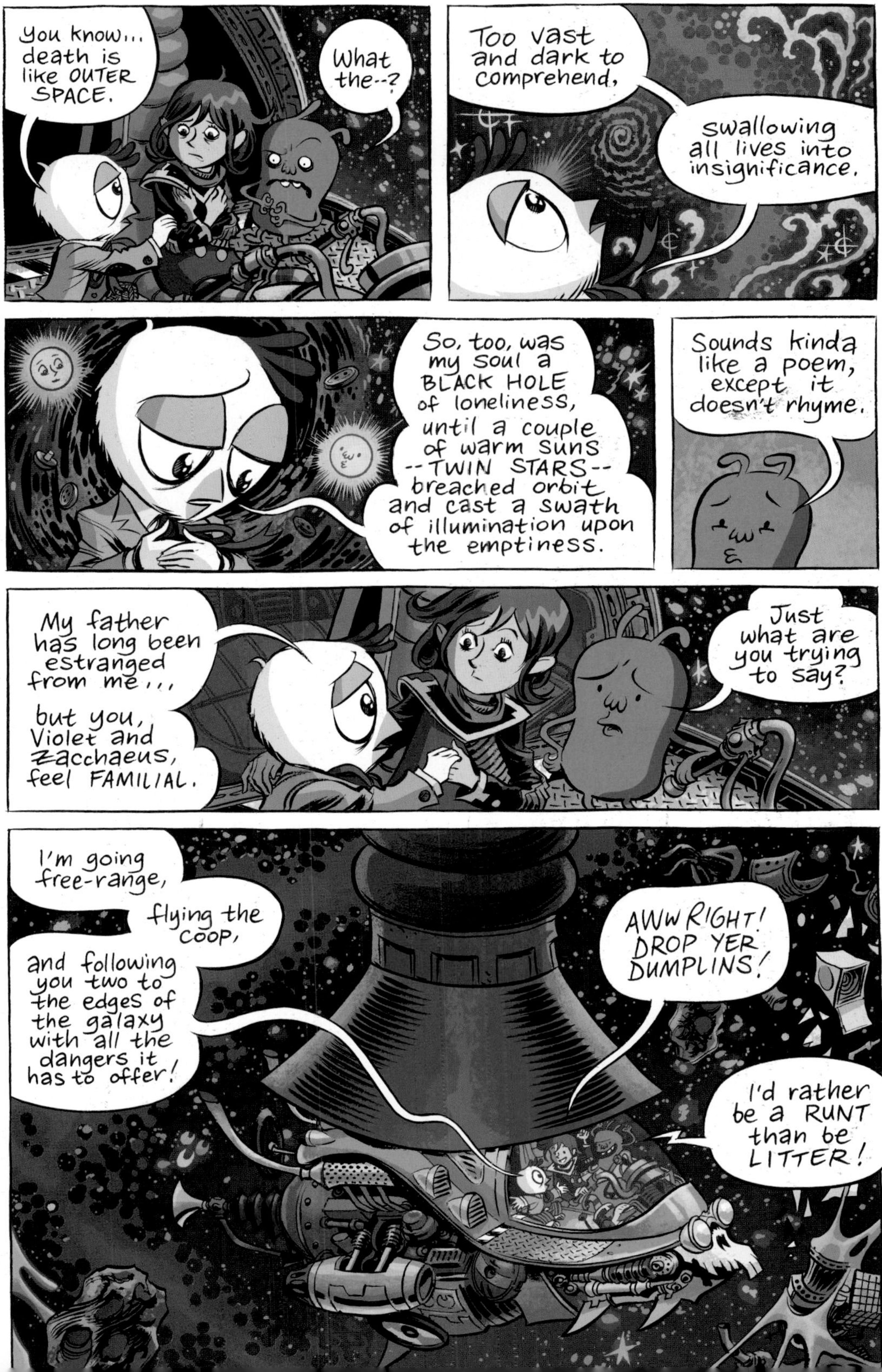
You know... death is like OUTER SPACE.
What the--?
Too vast and dark to comprehend,
swallowing all lives into insignificance.
So, too, was my soul a BLACK HOLE of loneliness, until a couple of warm suns --TWIN STARS-- breached orbit and cast a swath of illumination upon the emptiness.
Sounds kinda like a poem, except it doesn't rhyme.
My father has long been estranged from me...
but you, Violet and Zacchaeus, feel FAMILIAL.
Just what are you trying to say?
I'm going free-range,
flying the coop,
and following you two to the edges of the galaxy with all the dangers it has to offer!
AWW RIGHT! DROP YER DUMPLINS!
I'd rather be a RUNT than be LITTER!

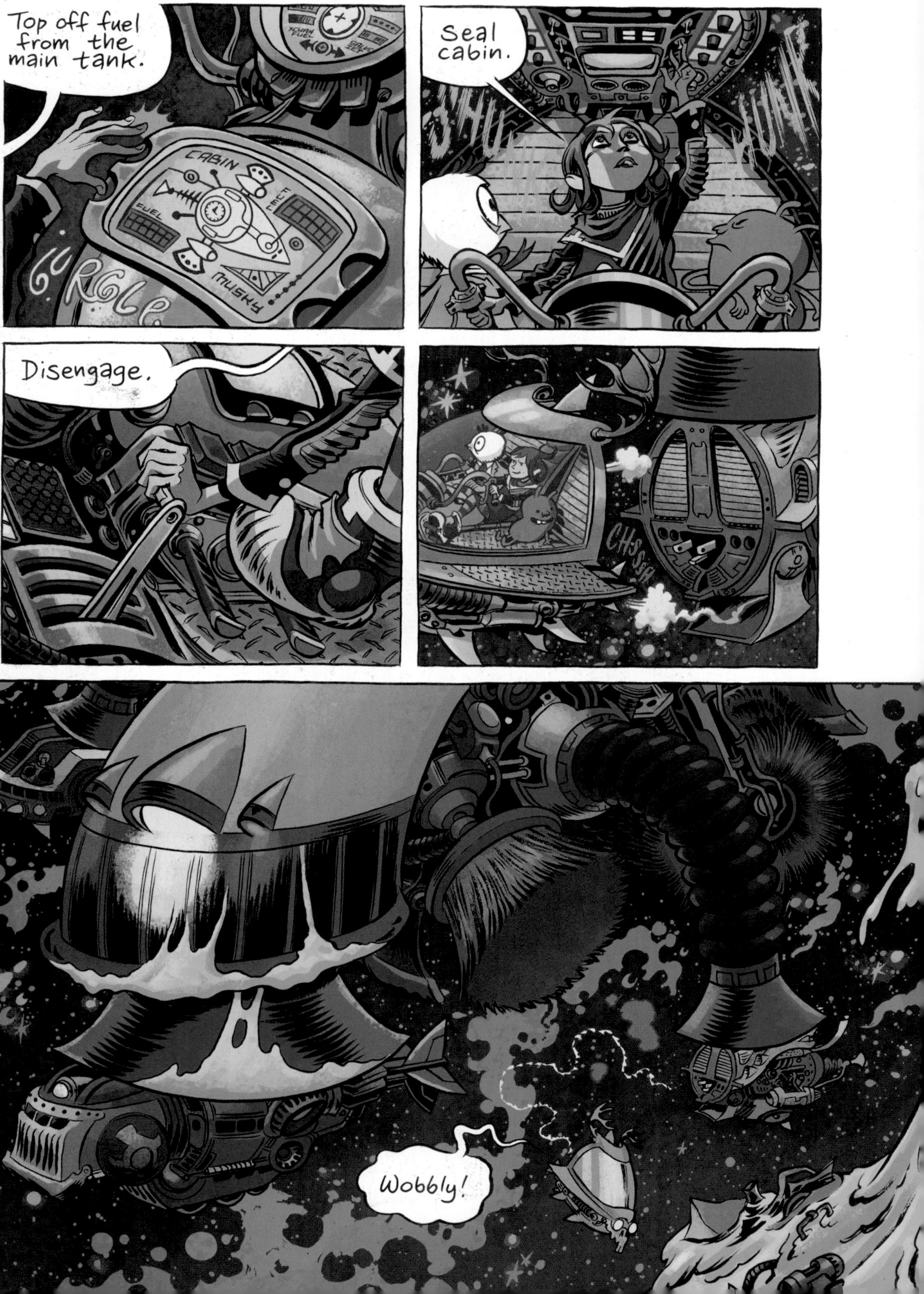
Top off fuel from the main tank.
CABIN
FUEL
GURGLE
Seal cabin.
Disengage.
Wobbly!

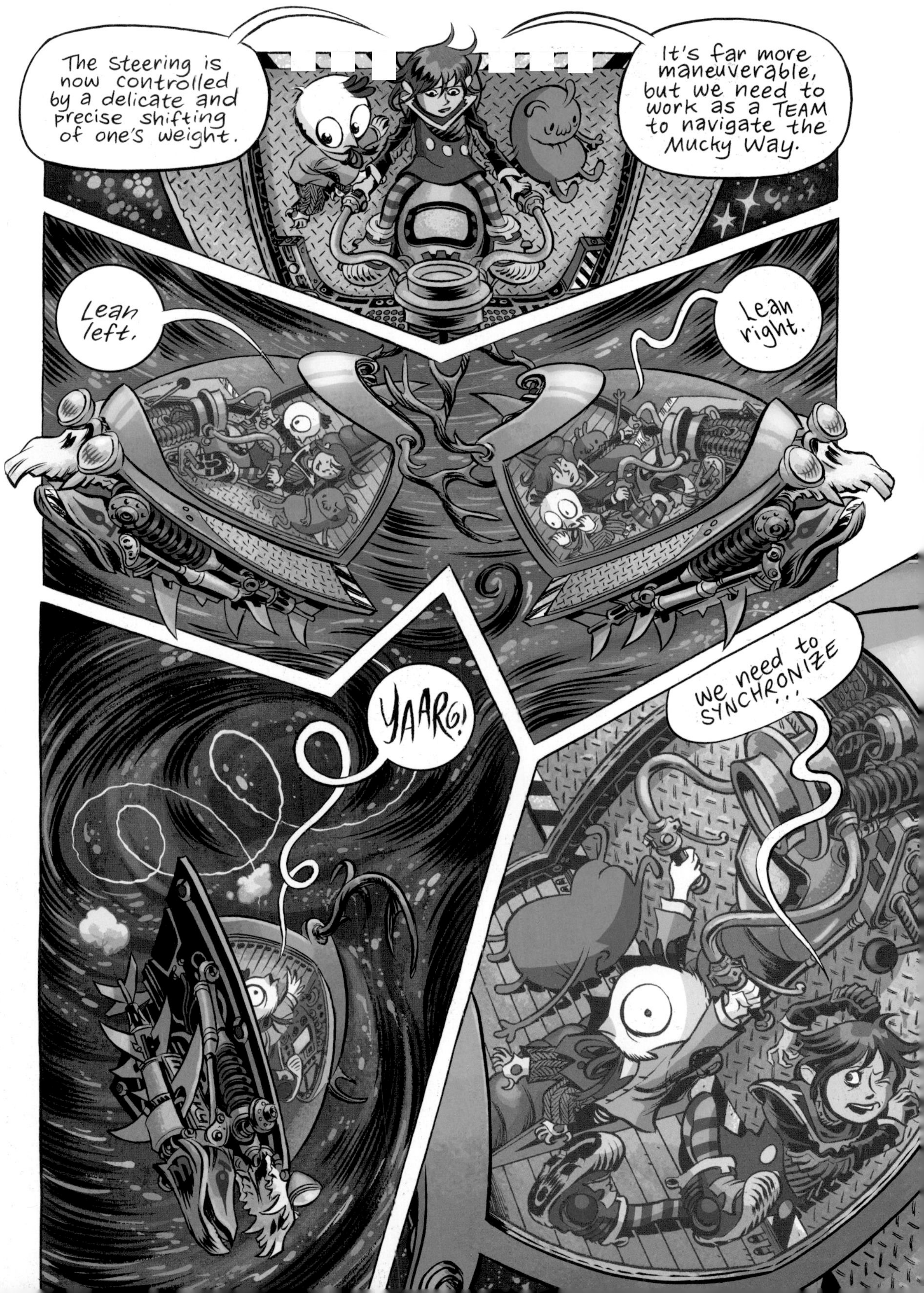
The steering is now controlled by a delicate and precise shifting of one's weight.
It's far more maneuverable, but we need to work as a TEAM to navigate the Mucky Way.
Lean left.
Lean right.
YAARG!
We need to SYNCHRONIZE...

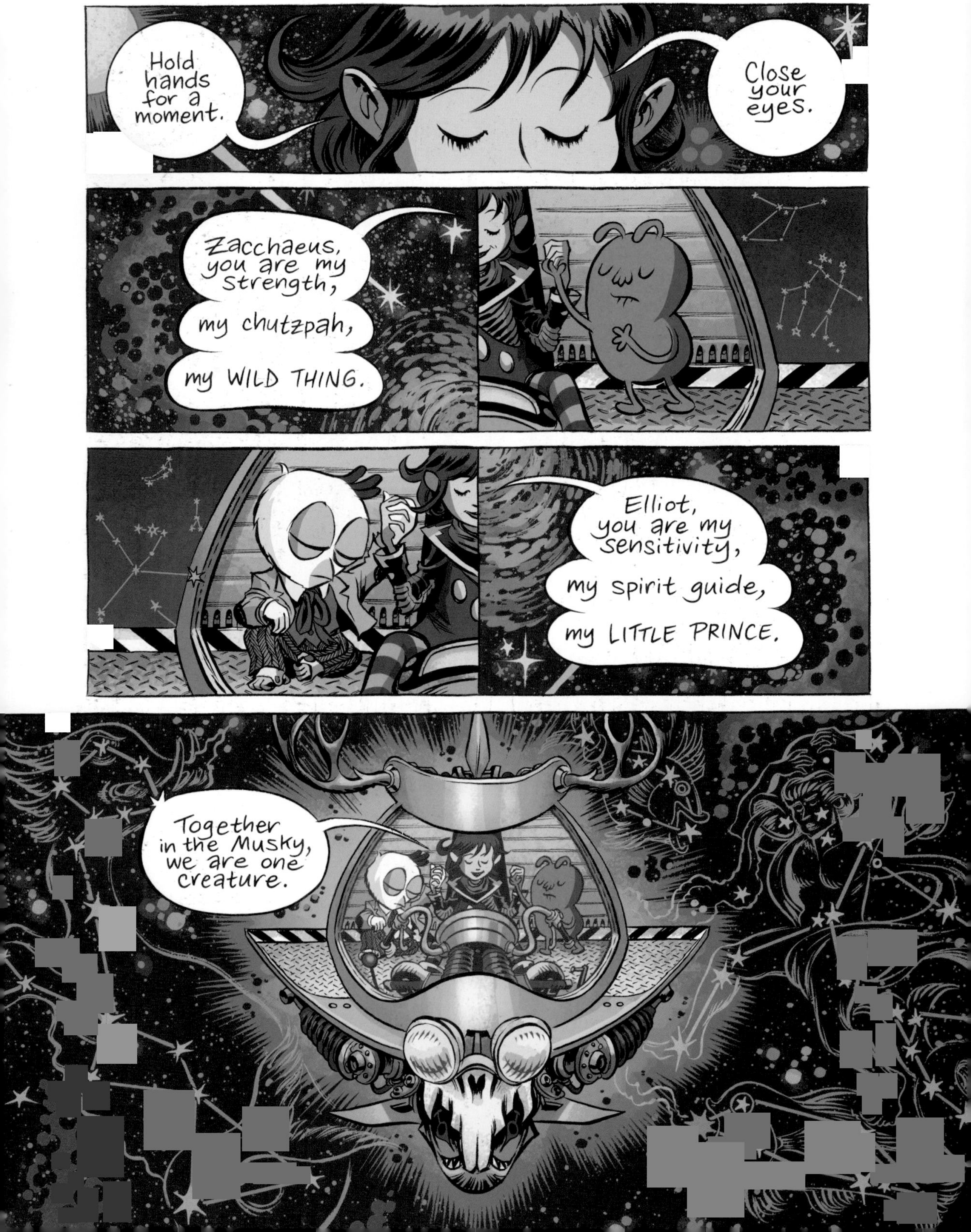

Hold hands for a moment.
Close your eyes.
Zacchaeus, you are my strength,
my chutzpah,
my WILD THING.
Elliot, you are my sensitivity,
my spirit guide,
my LITTLE PRINCE.
Together in the Musky, we are one creature.

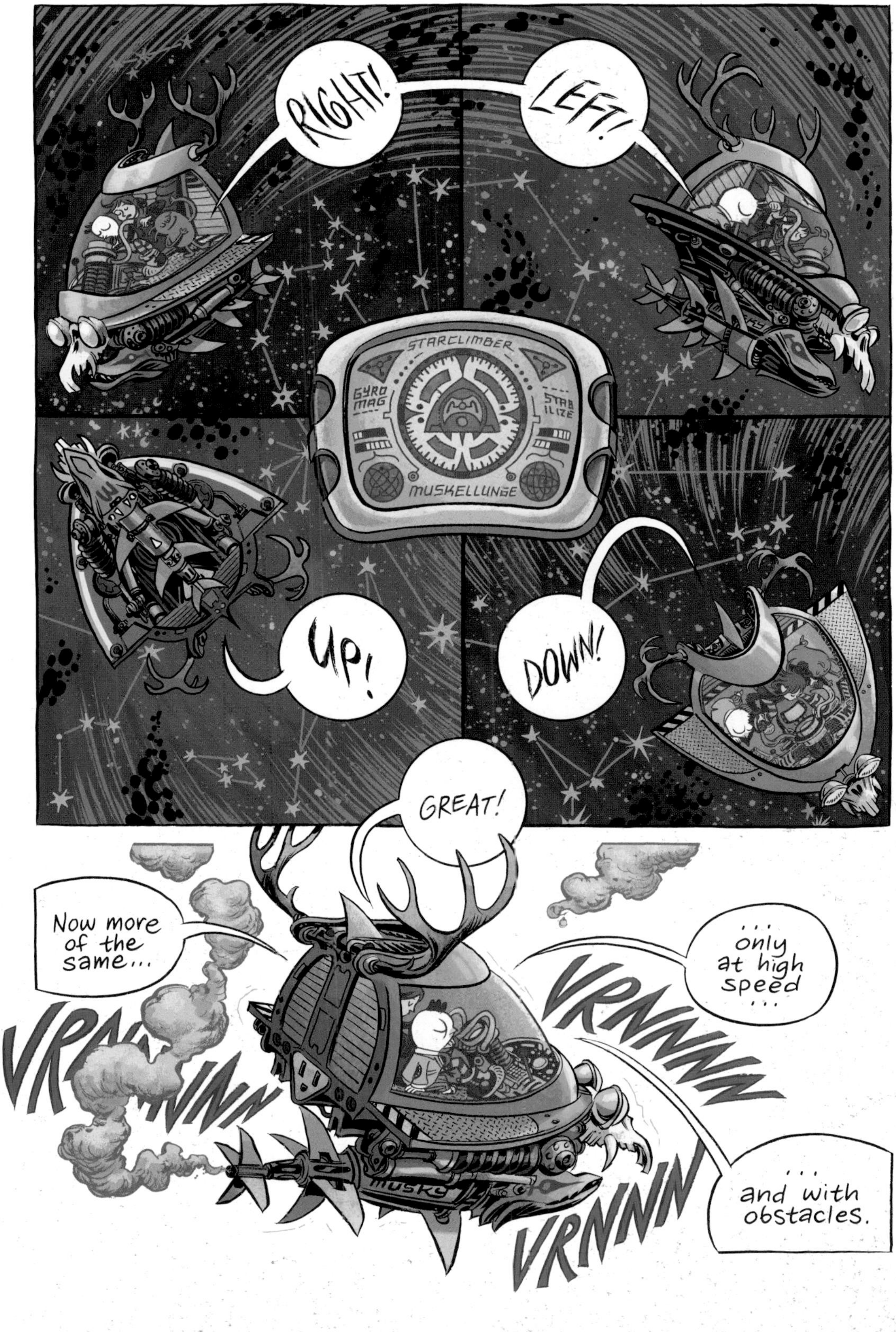
RIGHT!
LEFT!
STARCLIMBER
GYRO MAG
STAB ILIZE
MUSKELLUNGE
UP!
DOWN!
GREAT!
Now more of the same...
...only at high speed...
VRNNNNN
VRNNNNN
...and with obstacles.
VRNNNN
MUSKY

06

MAG/GYRO NAV

MAGNITUDES:

L.I.S.

RED SHELL, BLUE BLOOD

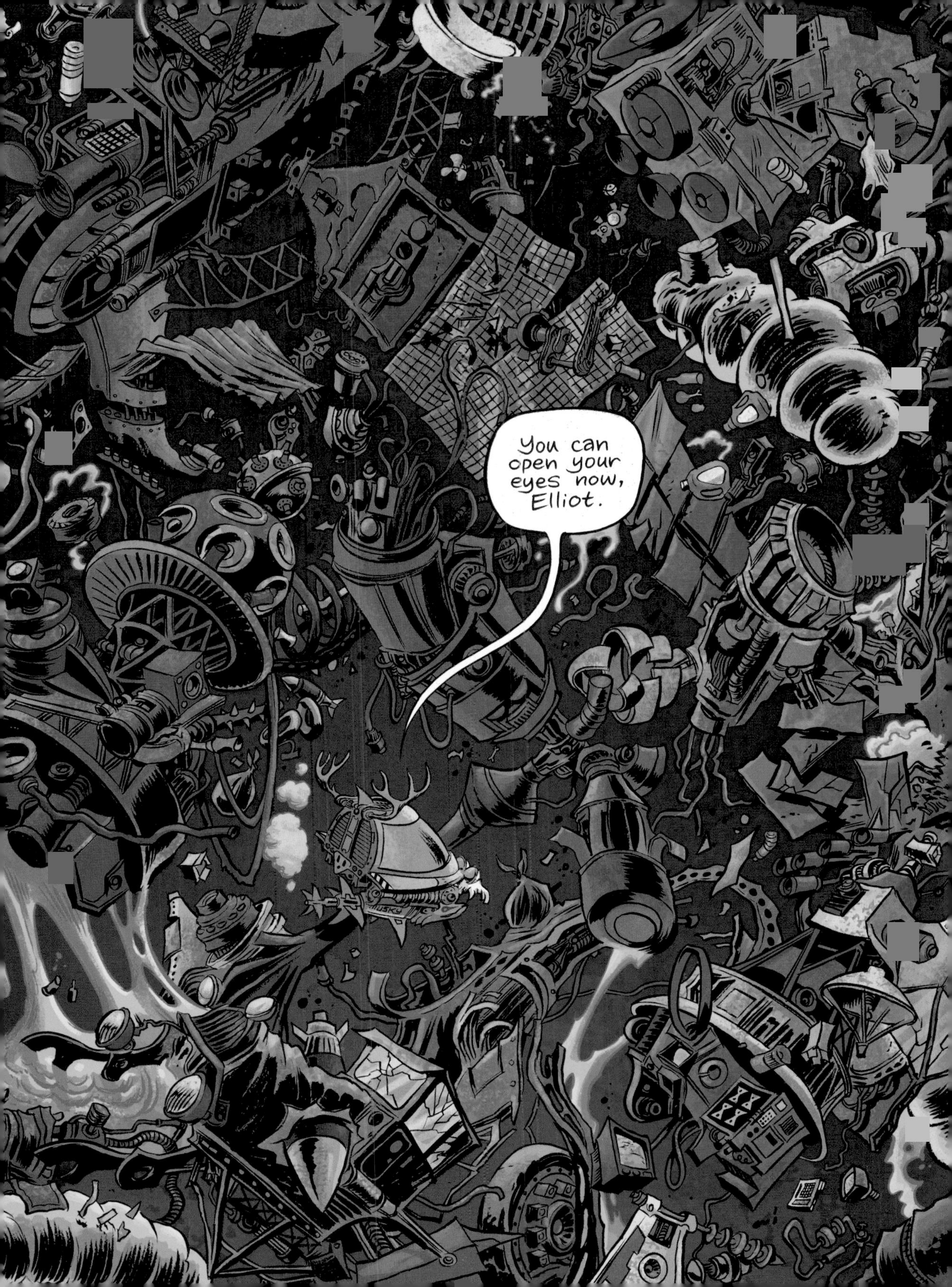
You can open your eyes now, Elliot.

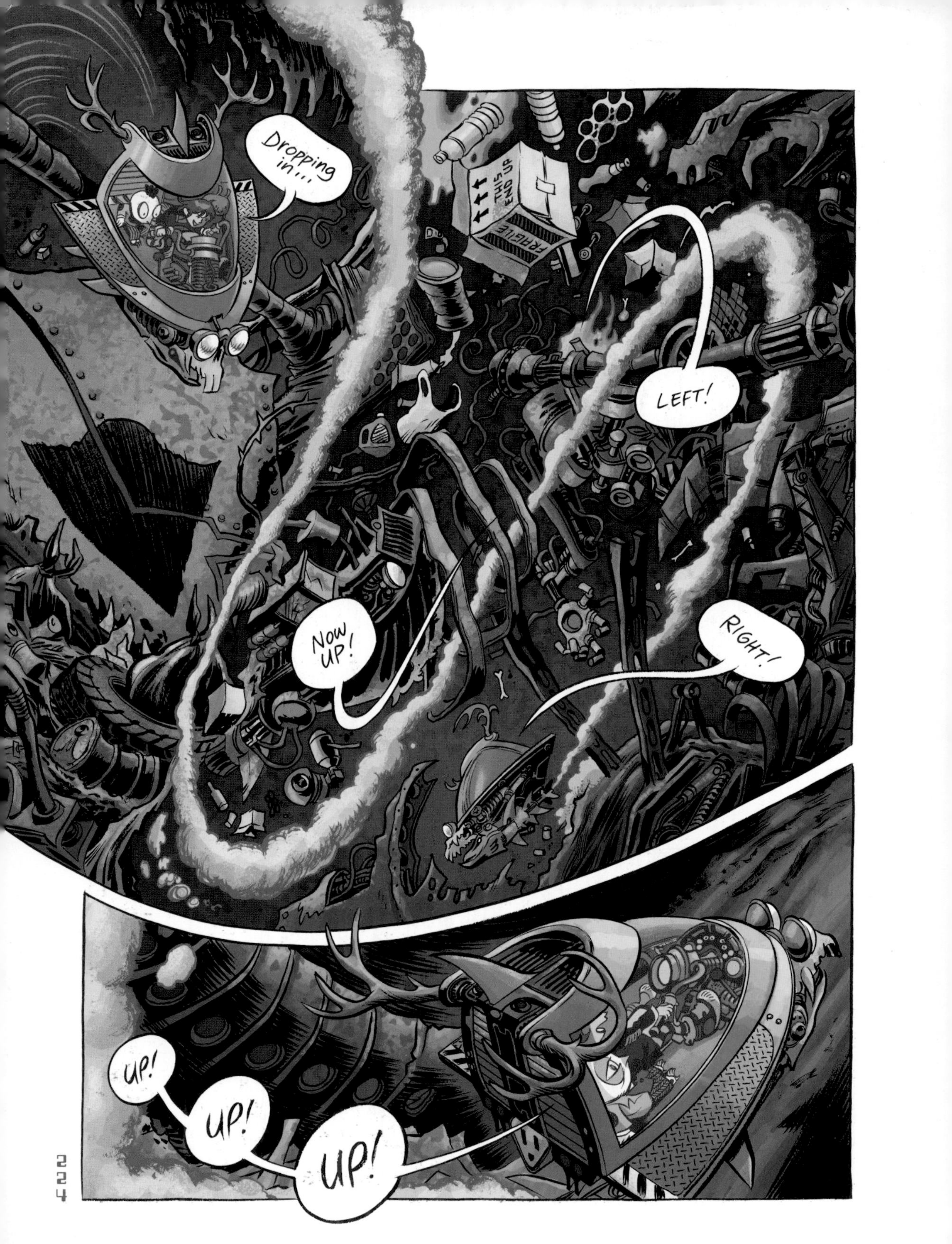

Dropping in...
THIS END UP
FRAGILE
LEFT!
Now UP!
RIGHT!
UP!
UP!
UP!

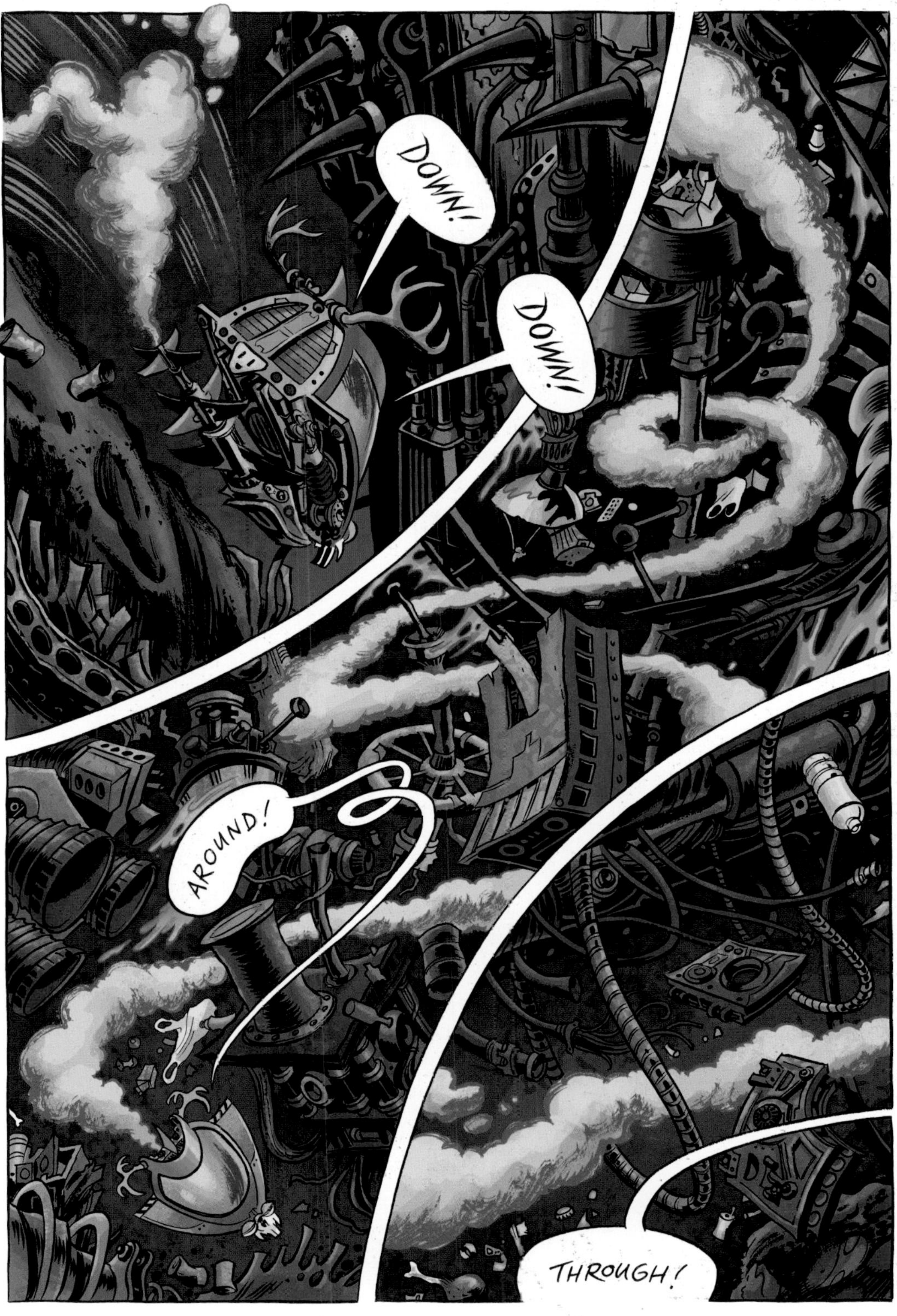
DOWN!
DOWN!
AROUND!
THROUGH!

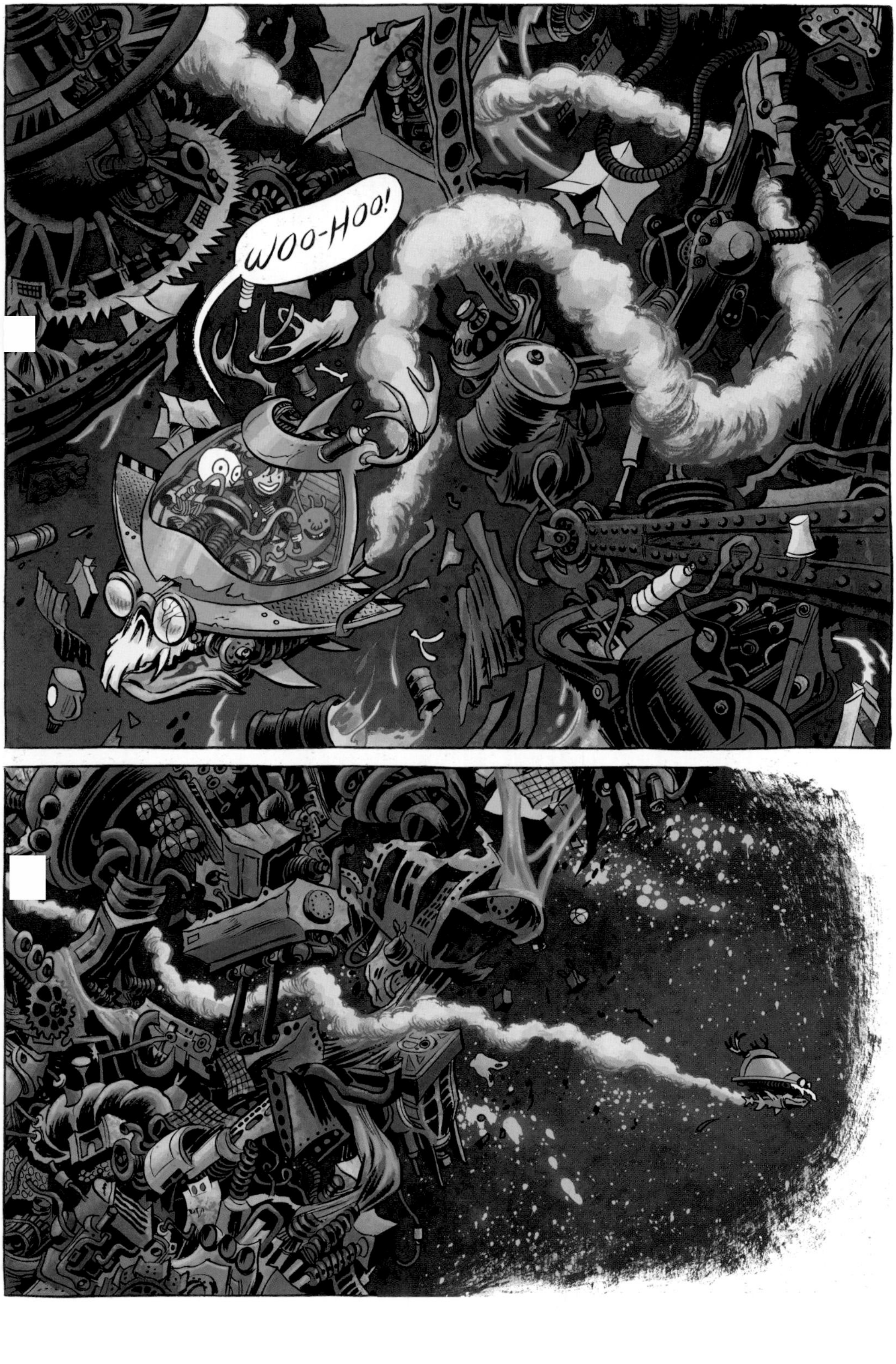
WOO-HOO!

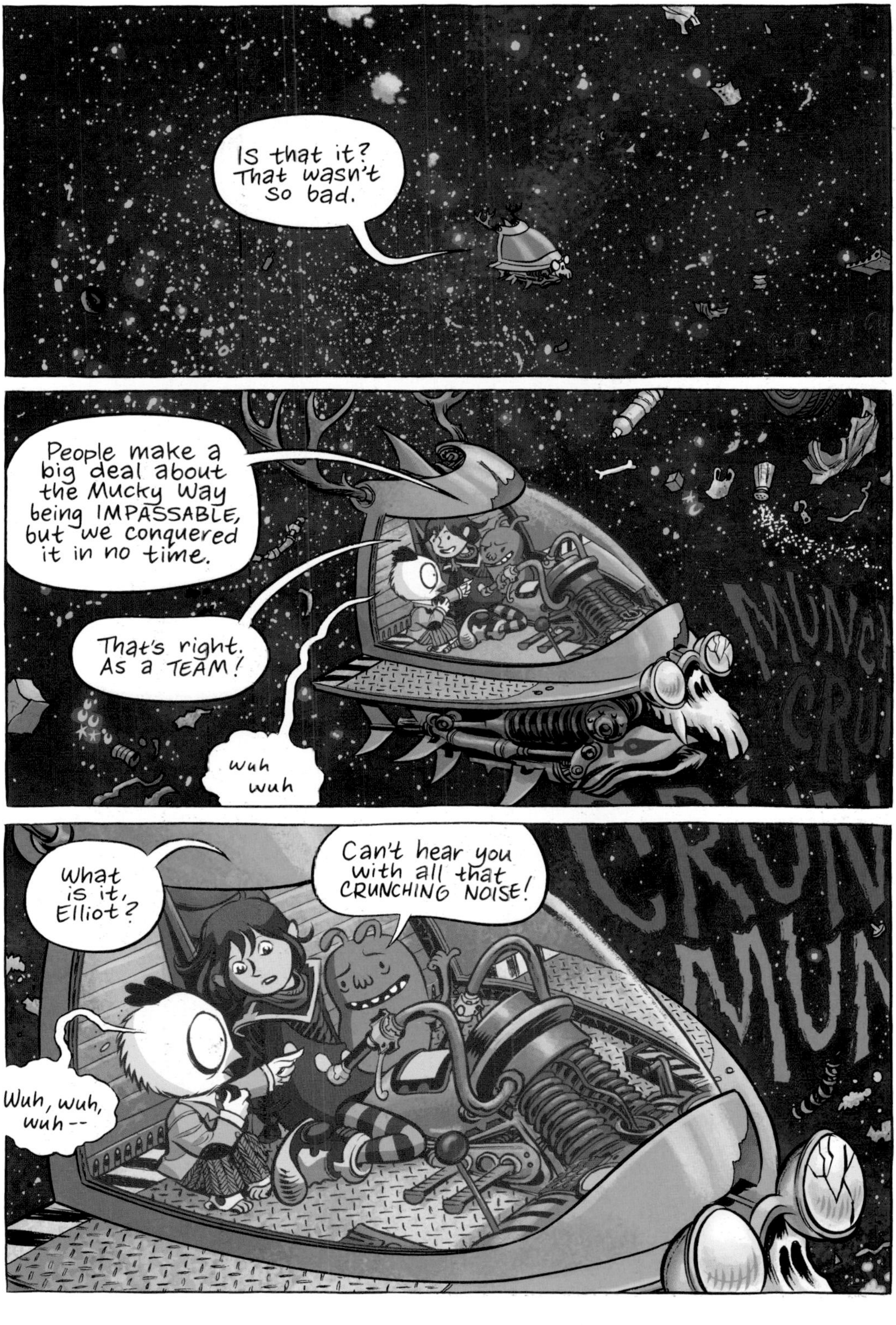
Is that it? That wasn't so bad.
People make a big deal about the Mucky Way being IMPASSABLE, but we conquered it in no time.
That's right. As a TEAM!
wuh wuh
MUNCH
CRU
CRUN
What is it, Elliot?
Can't hear you with all that CRUNCHING NOISE!
MUN
Wuh, wuh, wuh --

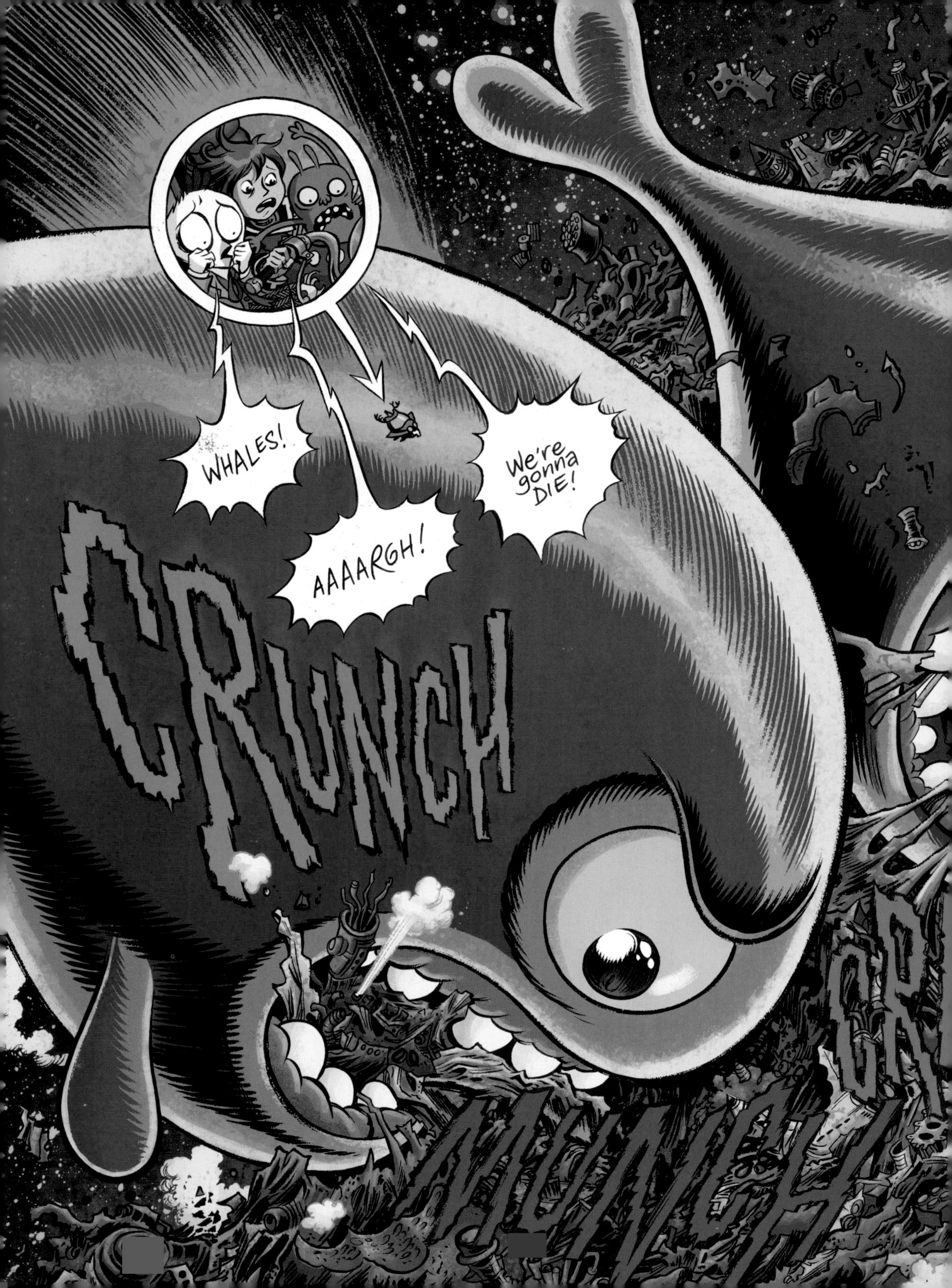
WHALES!
AAAARGH!
We're gonna DIE!
CRUNCH
MUNCH

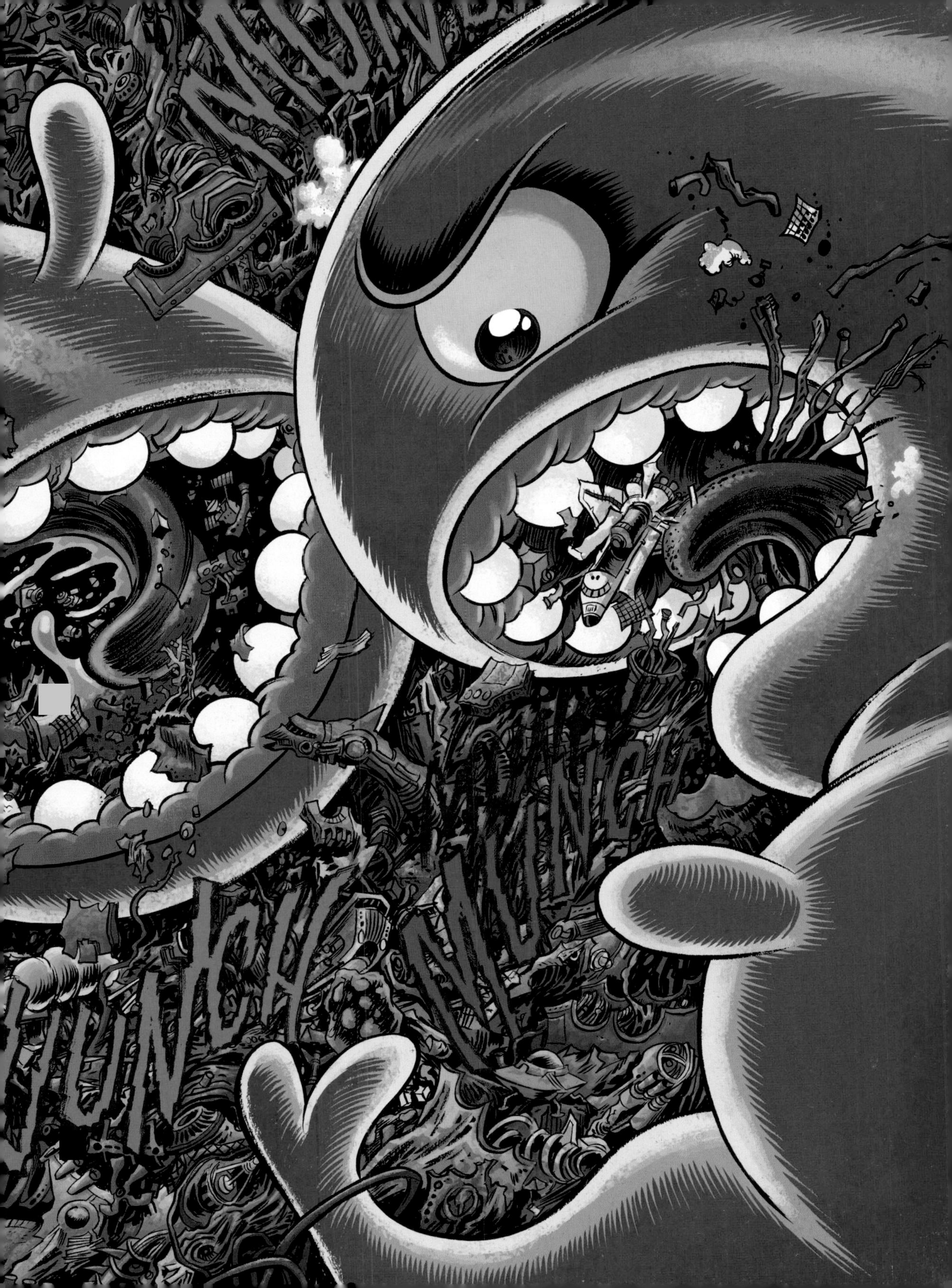
MUNCH
UNCH

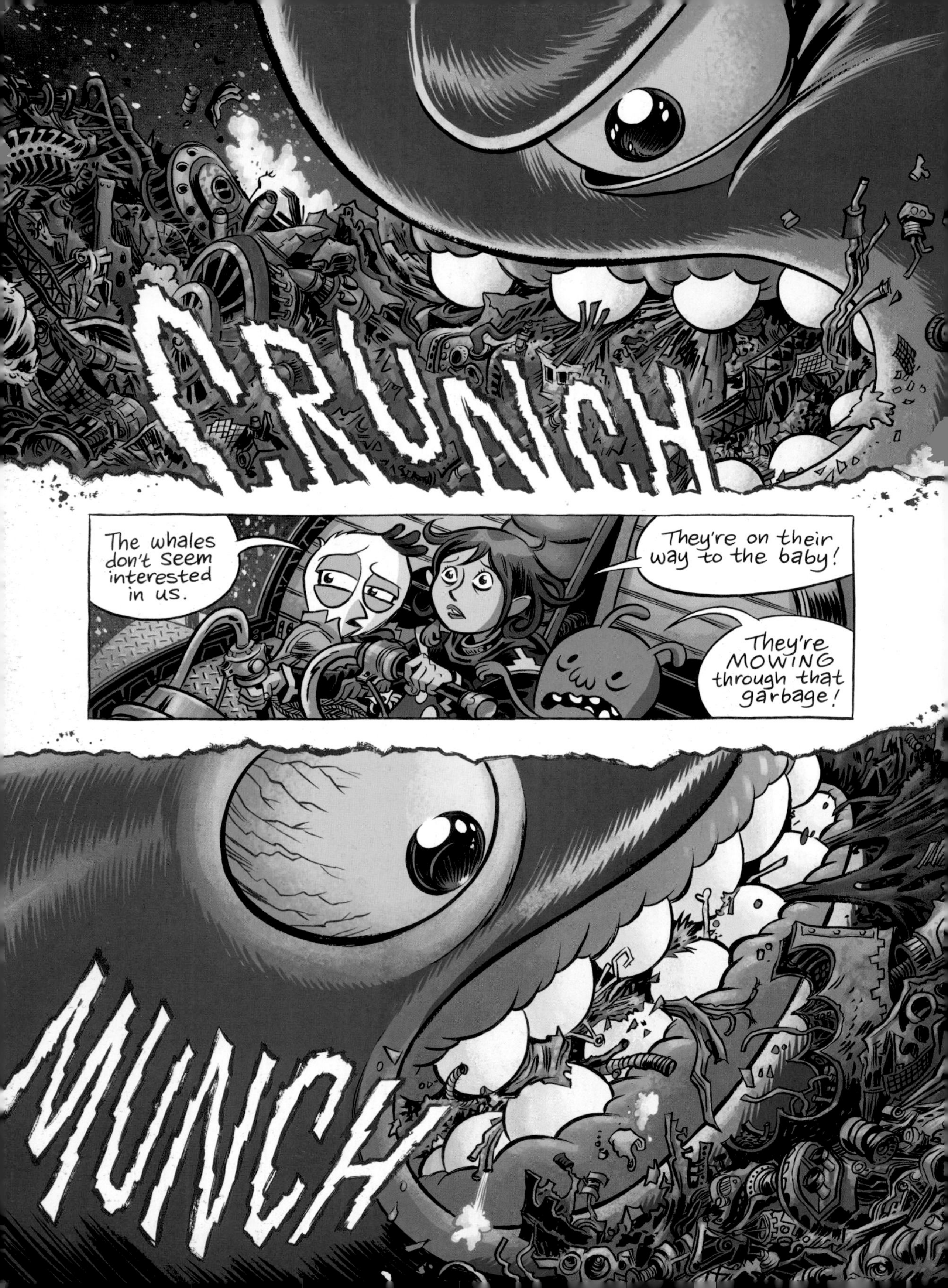
CRUNCH
The whales don't seem interested in us.
They're on their way to the baby!
They're MOWING through that garbage!
MUNCH

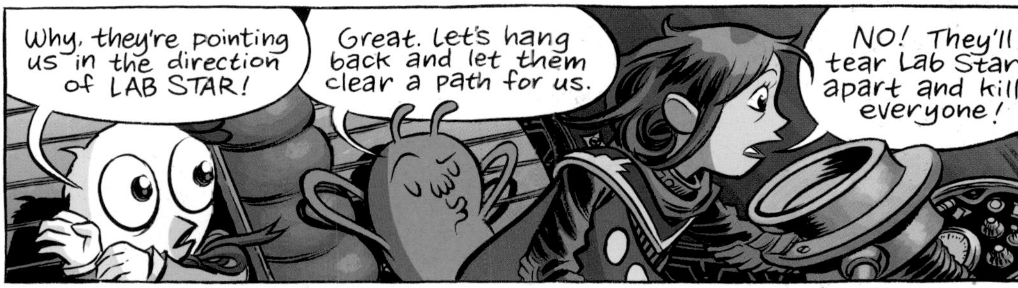
Why, they're pointing us in the direction of LAB STAR!
Great. Let's hang back and let them clear a path for us.
NO! They'll tear Lab Star apart and kill everyone!

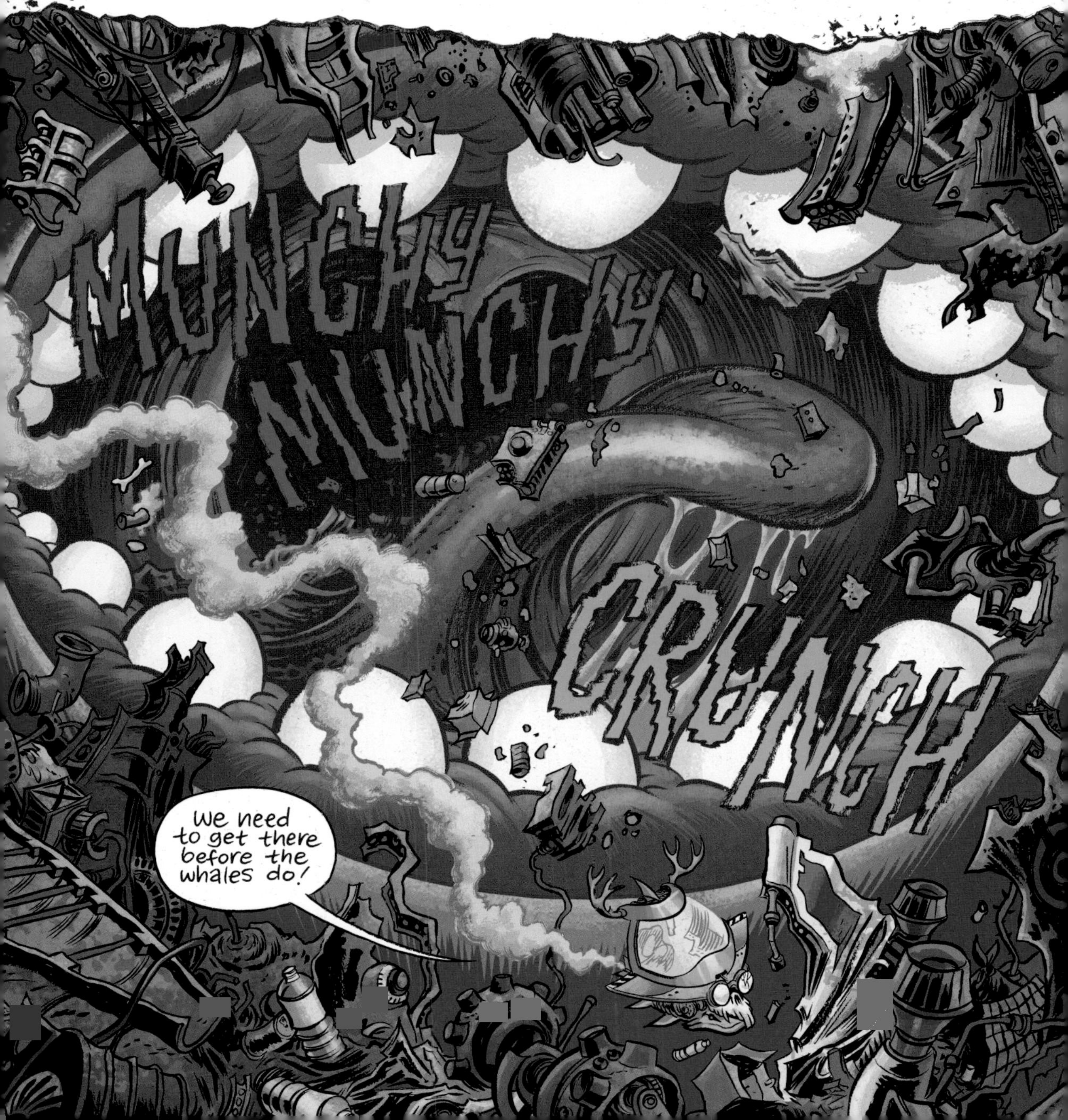
MUNCHY
MUNCHY
CRUNCH
We need to get there before the whales do!

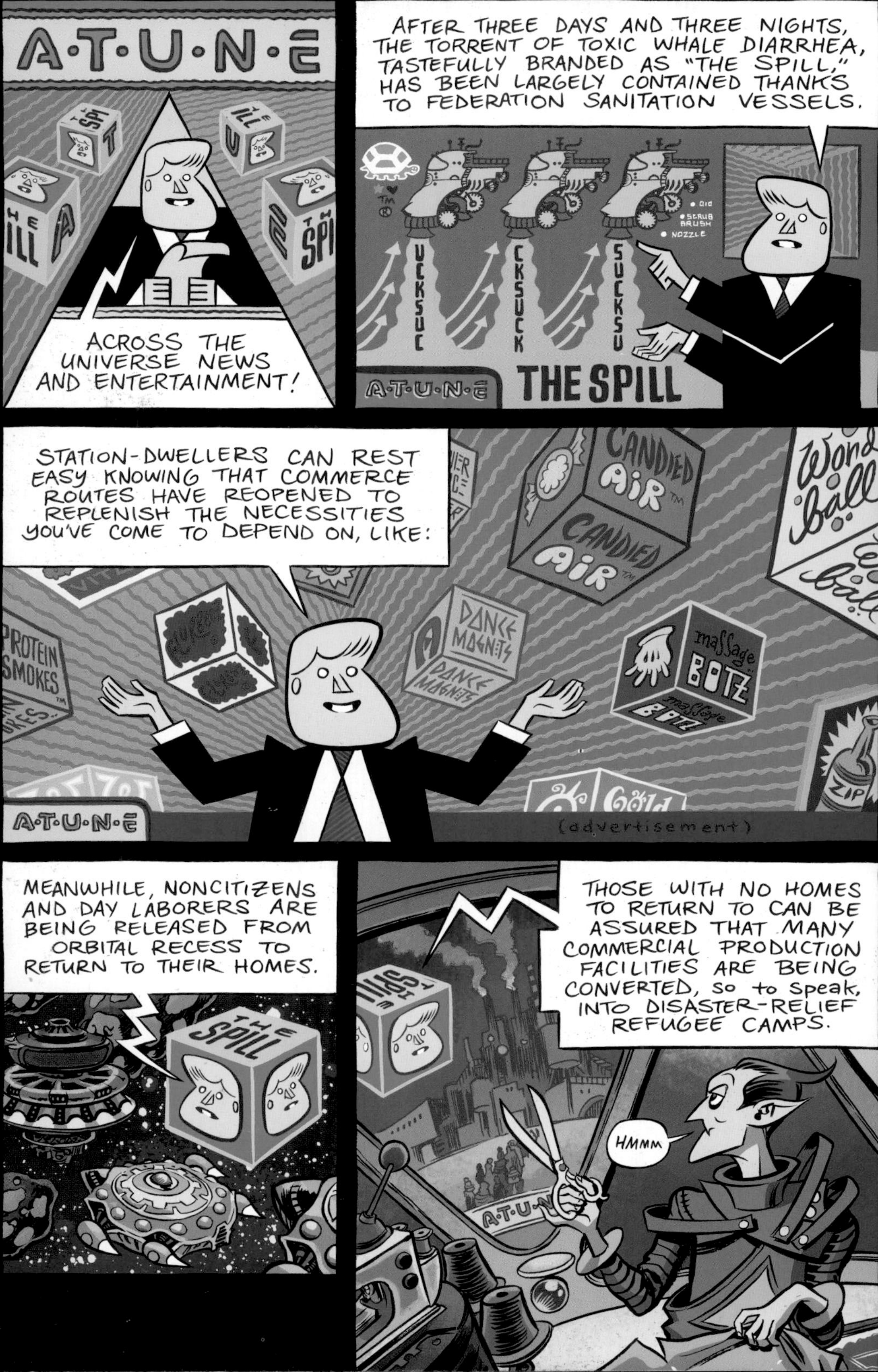
A·T·U·N·E
ACROSS THE UNIVERSE NEWS AND ENTERTAINMENT!
AFTER THREE DAYS AND THREE NIGHTS, THE TORRENT OF TOXIC WHALE DIARRHEA, TASTEFULLY BRANDED AS "THE SPILL," HAS BEEN LARGELY CONTAINED THANKS TO FEDERATION SANITATION VESSELS.
SUCKSU
THE SPILL
A·T·U·N·E
STATION-DWELLERS CAN REST EASY KNOWING THAT COMMERCE ROUTES HAVE REOPENED TO REPLENISH THE NECESSITIES YOU'VE COME TO DEPEND ON, LIKE:
CANDIED AIR
DANCE MAGNETS
massage BOTZ
PROTEIN SMOKES
A·T·U·N·E
(advertisement)
MEANWHILE, NONCITIZENS AND DAY LABORERS ARE BEING RELEASED FROM ORBITAL RECESS TO RETURN TO THEIR HOMES.
THE SPILL
THOSE WITH NO HOMES TO RETURN TO CAN BE ASSURED THAT MANY COMMERCIAL PRODUCTION FACILITIES ARE BEING CONVERTED, so to speak, INTO DISASTER-RELIEF REFUGEE CAMPS.
HMMM

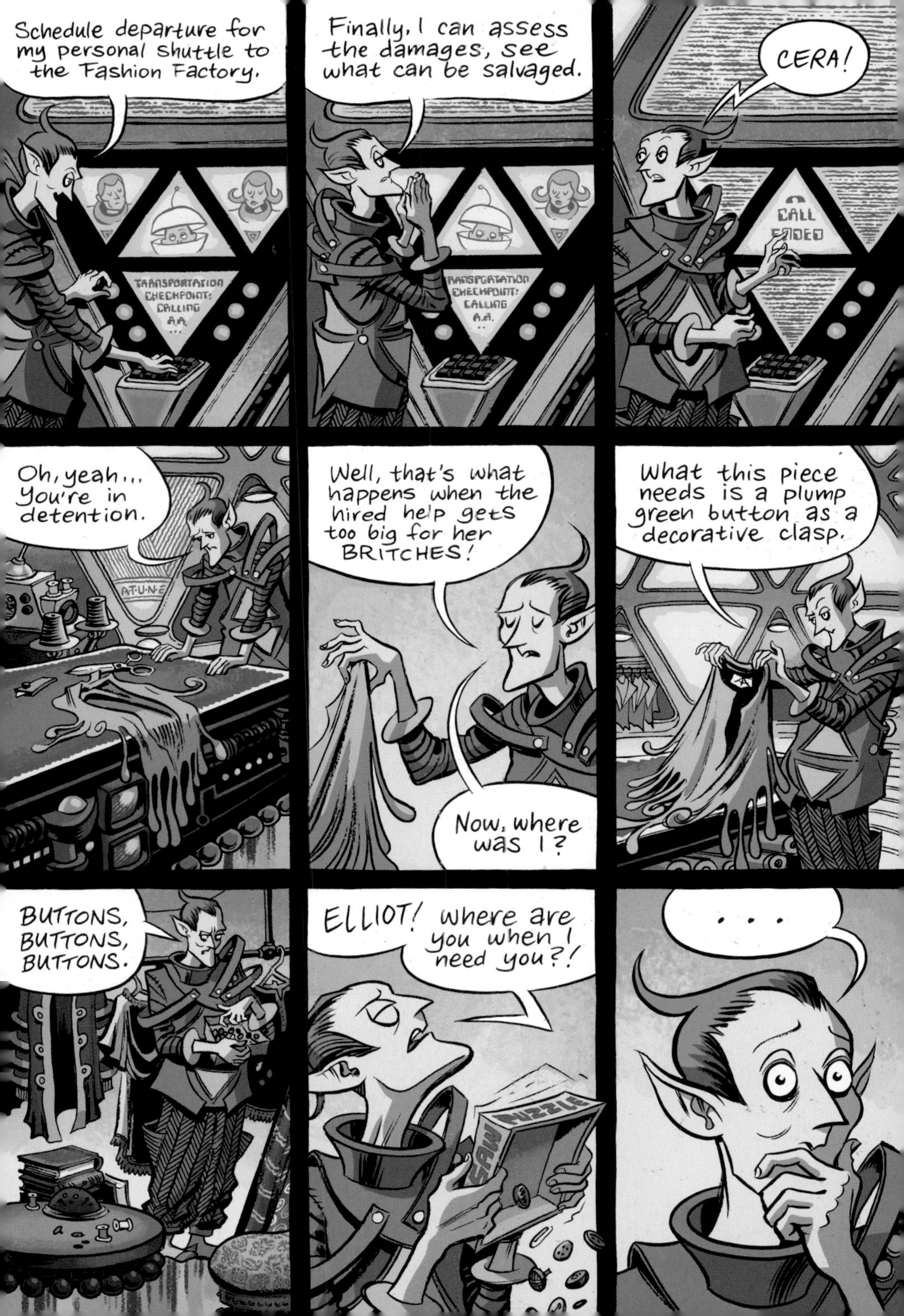
Schedule departure for my personal shuttle to the Fashion Factory.
TRANSPORTATION CHECKPOINT: CALLING A.A. ...
Finally, I can assess the damages, see what can be salvaged.
TRANSPORTATION CHECKPOINT: CALLING A.A. ..
CERA!
CALL ENDED
Oh, yeah... You're in detention.
A.T.U.N.E
Well, that's what happens when the hired help gets too big for her BRITCHES!
Now, where was I?
What this piece needs is a plump green button as a decorative clasp.
BUTTONS, BUTTONS, BUTTONS.
ELLIOT! Where are you when I need you?!
SAW PUZZLE
. . .

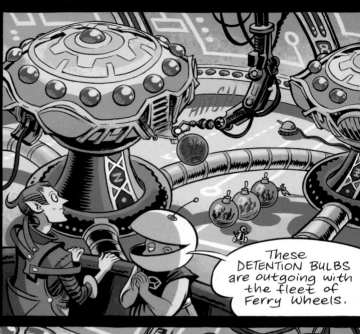

These DETENTION BULBS are outgoing with the fleet of Ferry Wheels.

WAIT!

Where are you taking her?

Back to where she belongs.

This one belongs with ME.

234

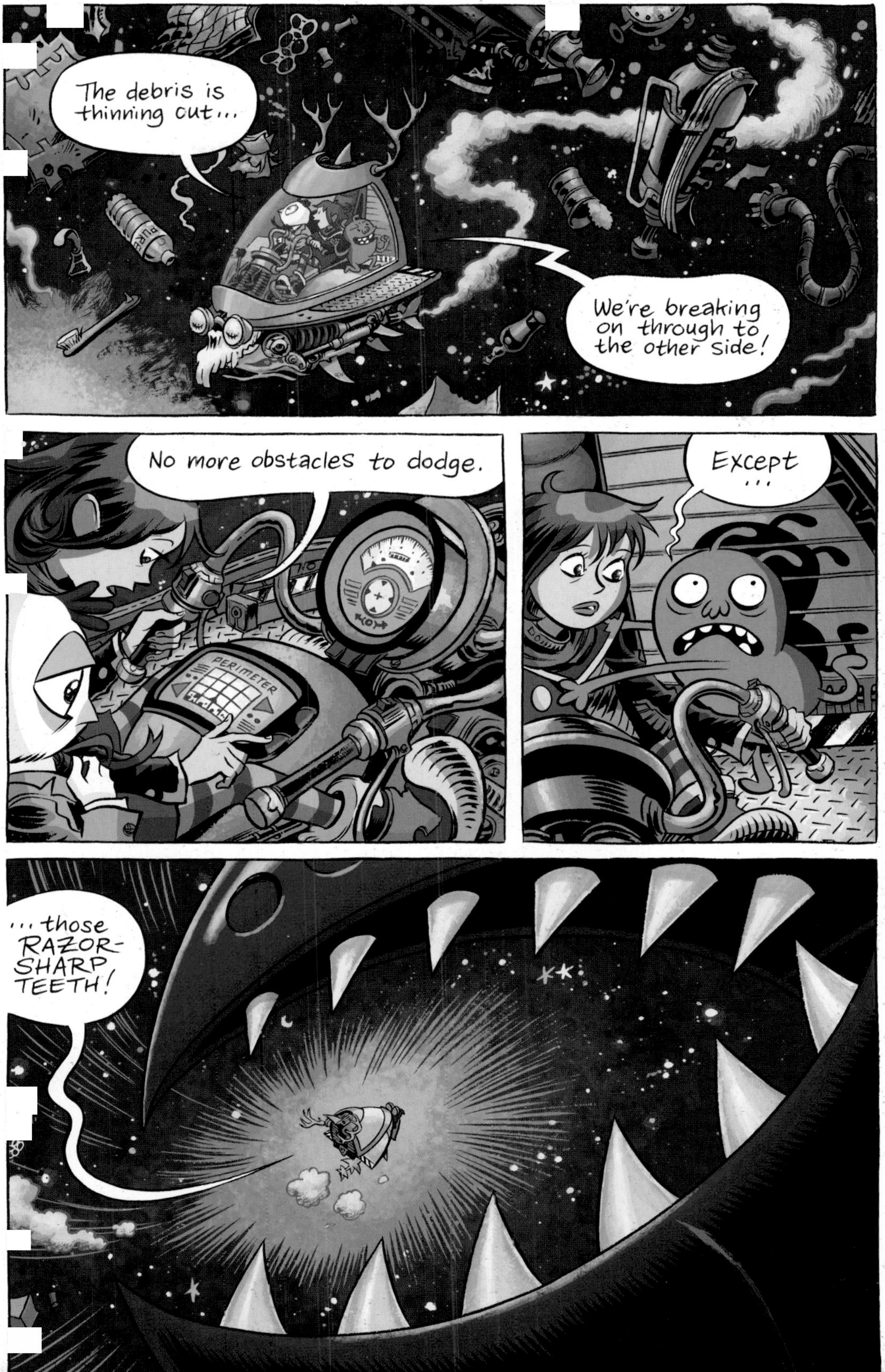
The debris is thinning out...
PURE
We're breaking on through to the other side!
No more obstacles to dodge.
PERIMETER
Except ...
...those RAZOR-SHARP TEETH!

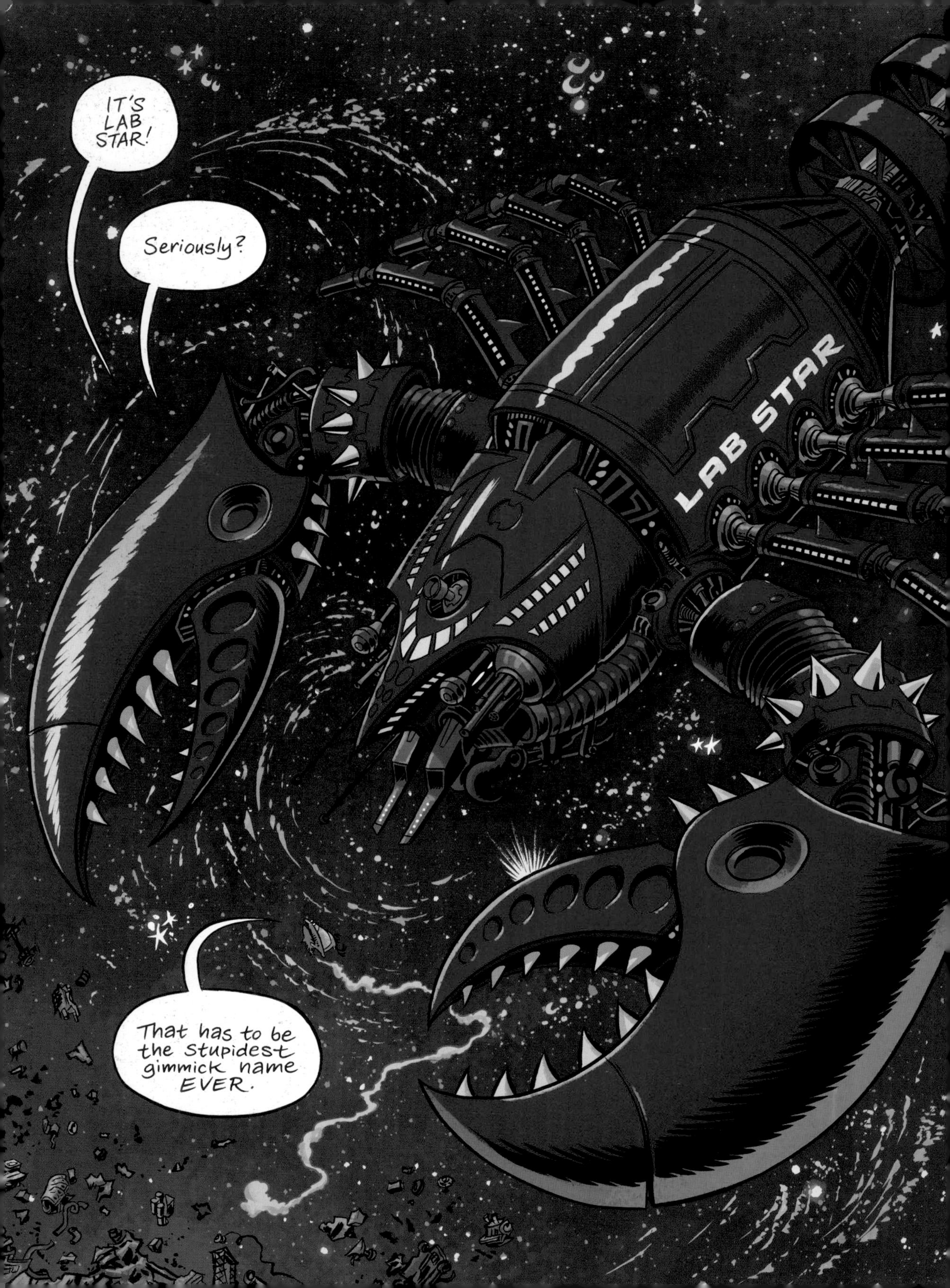
IT'S LAB STAR!
Seriously?
LAB STAR
That has to be the stupidest gimmick name EVER.

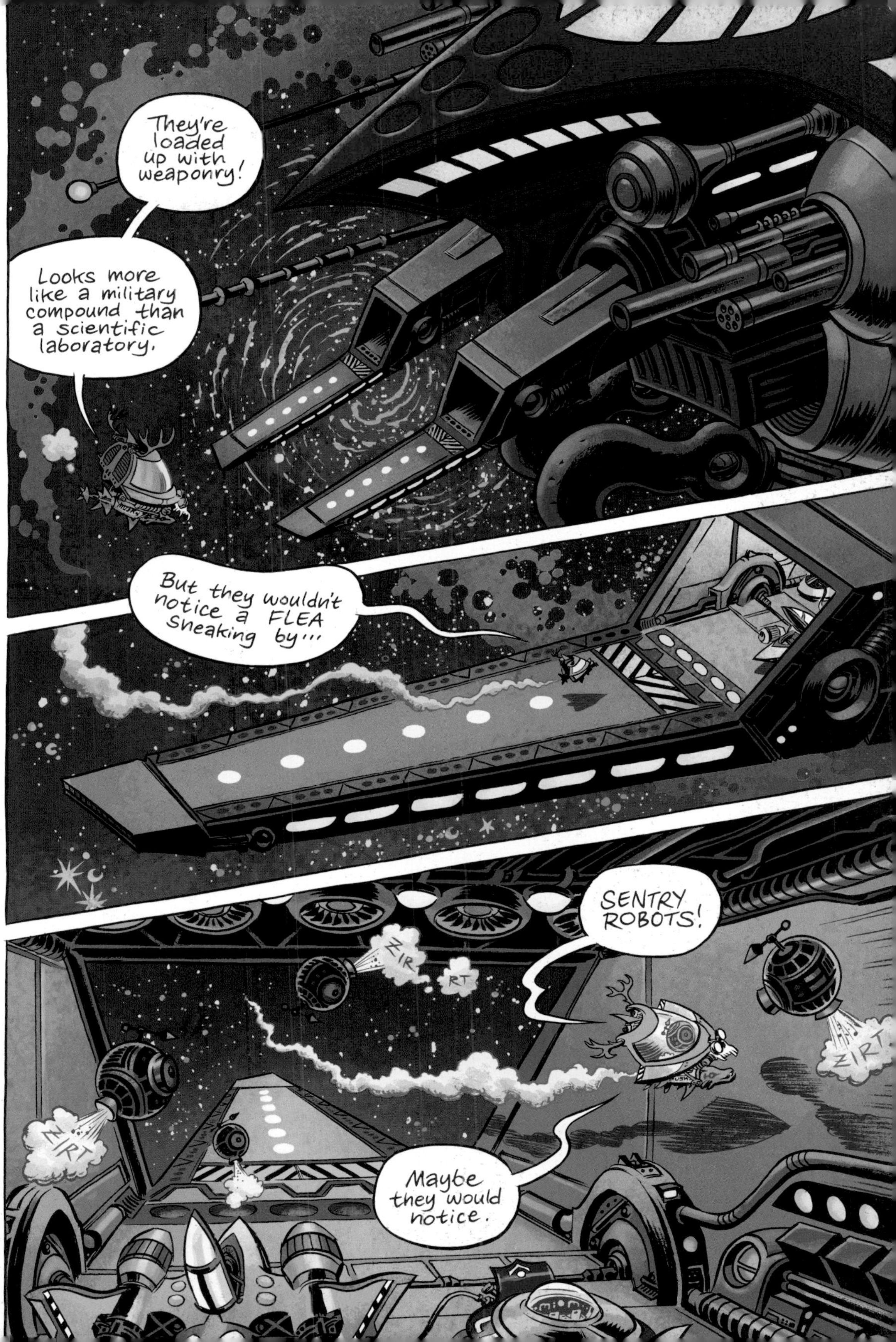
They're loaded up with weaponry!
Looks more like a military compound than a scientific laboratory.
But they wouldn't notice a FLEA sneaking by...
SENTRY ROBOTS!
ZIRT
ZIRT
ZIRT
Maybe they would notice.

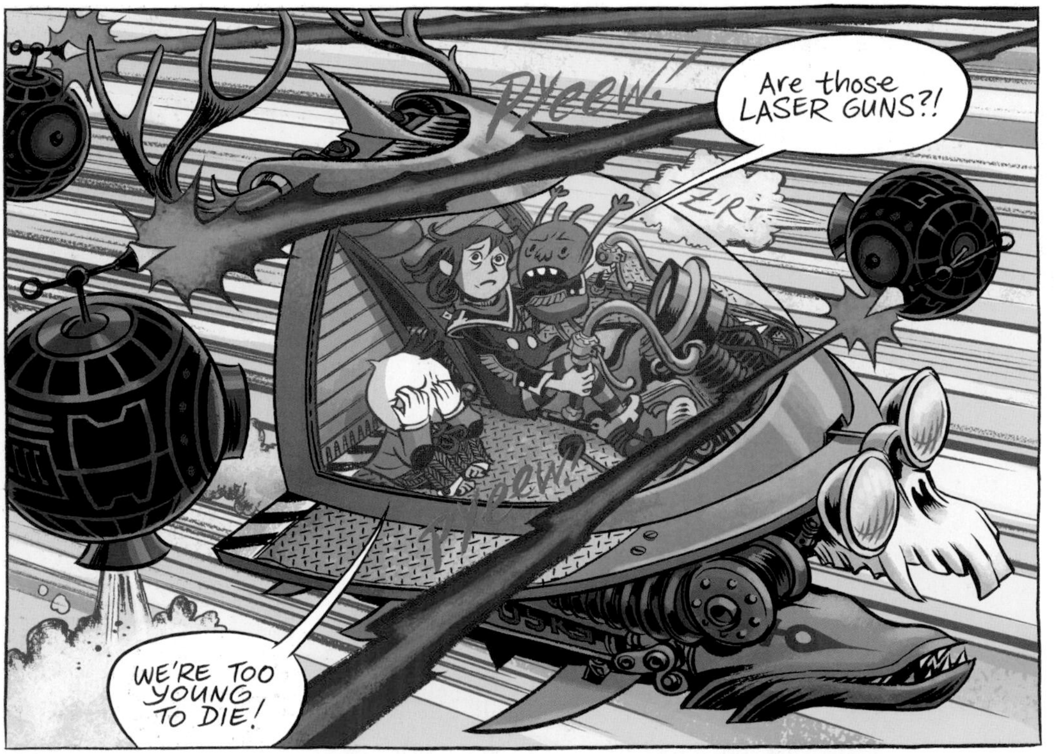
DYEEW!
Are those LASER GUNS?!
ZIRT
DYEEW!
WE'RE TOO YOUNG TO DIE!

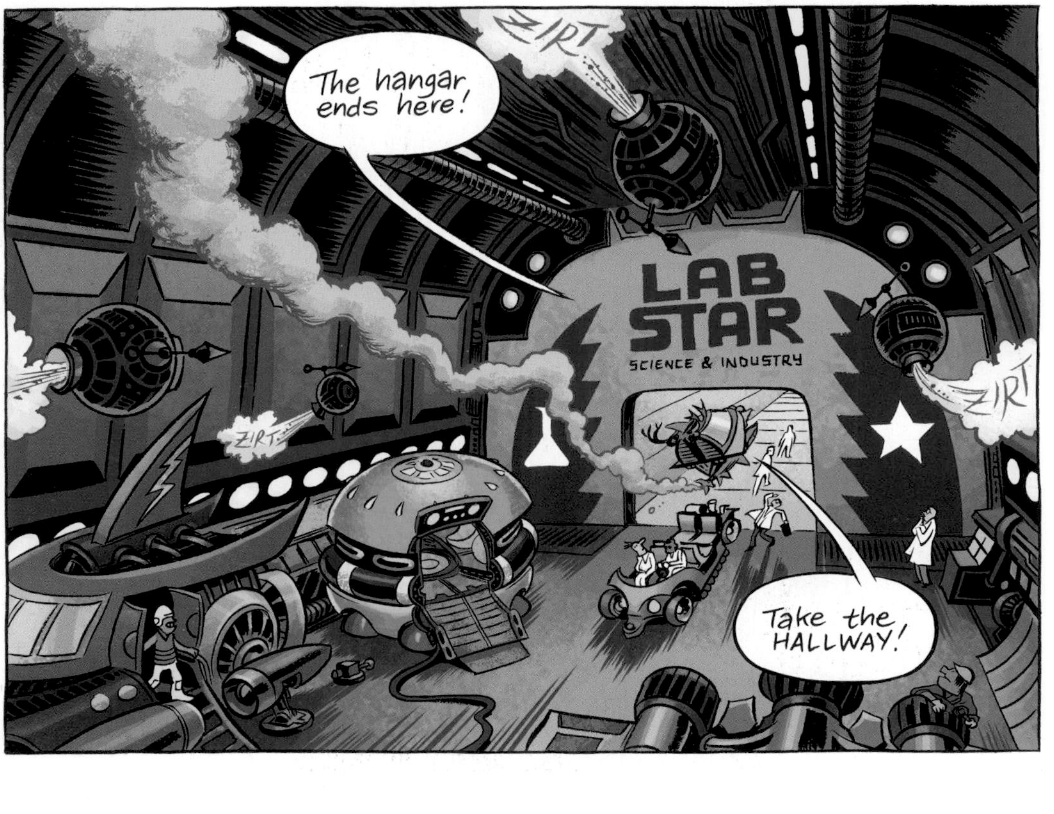
ZIRT
The hangar ends here!
LAB STAR
SCIENCE & INDUSTRY
ZIRT
ZIRT
Take the HALLWAY!

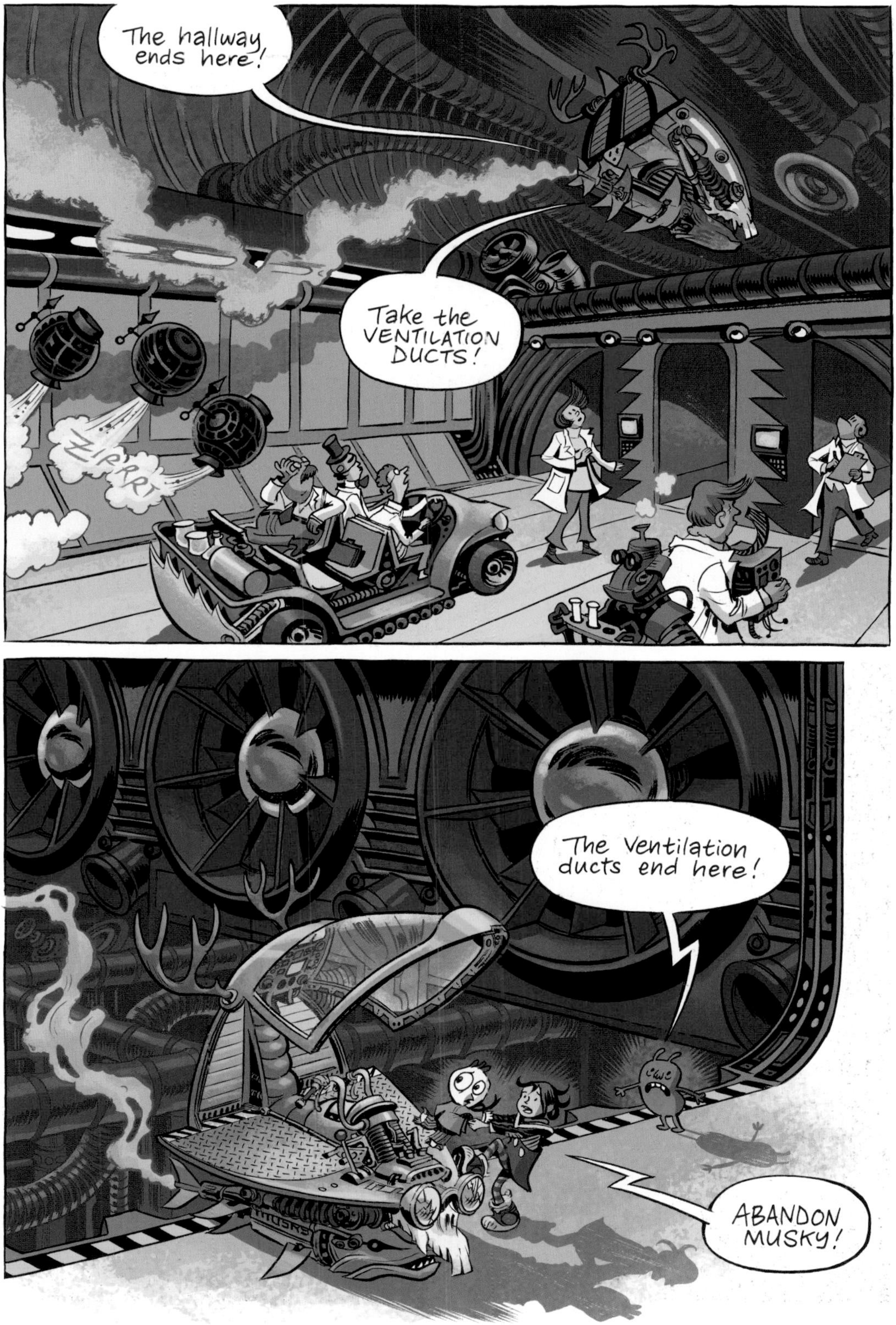
The hallway ends here!
Take the VENTILATION DUCTS!
ZIPRRT
The Ventilation ducts end here!
ABANDON MUSKY!

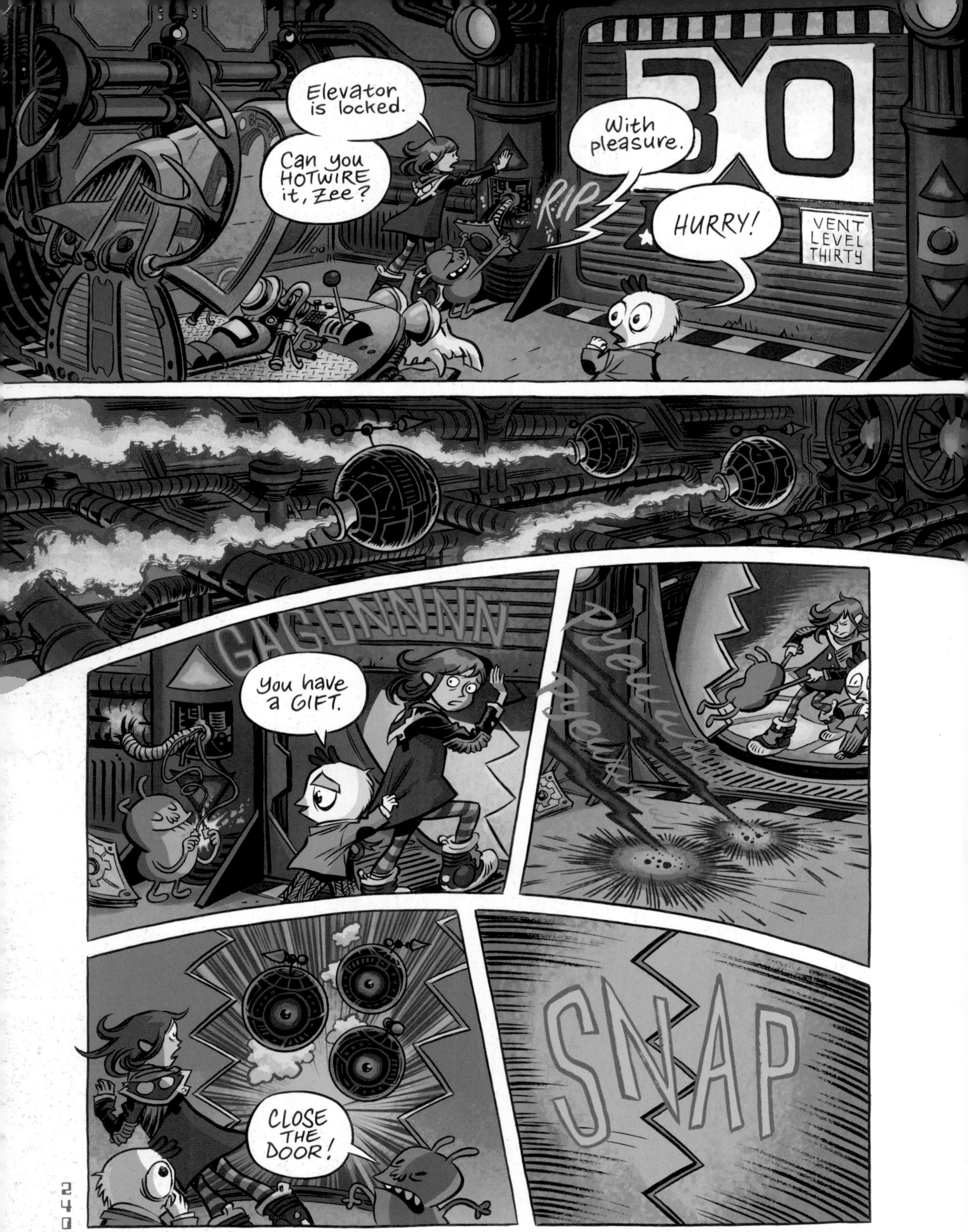

Elevator is locked.
Can you HOTWIRE it, Zee?
RIP
With pleasure.
HURRY!
30
VENT LEVEL THIRTY
GAGUNNNNN
You have a GIFT.
CLOSE THE DOOR!
SNAP

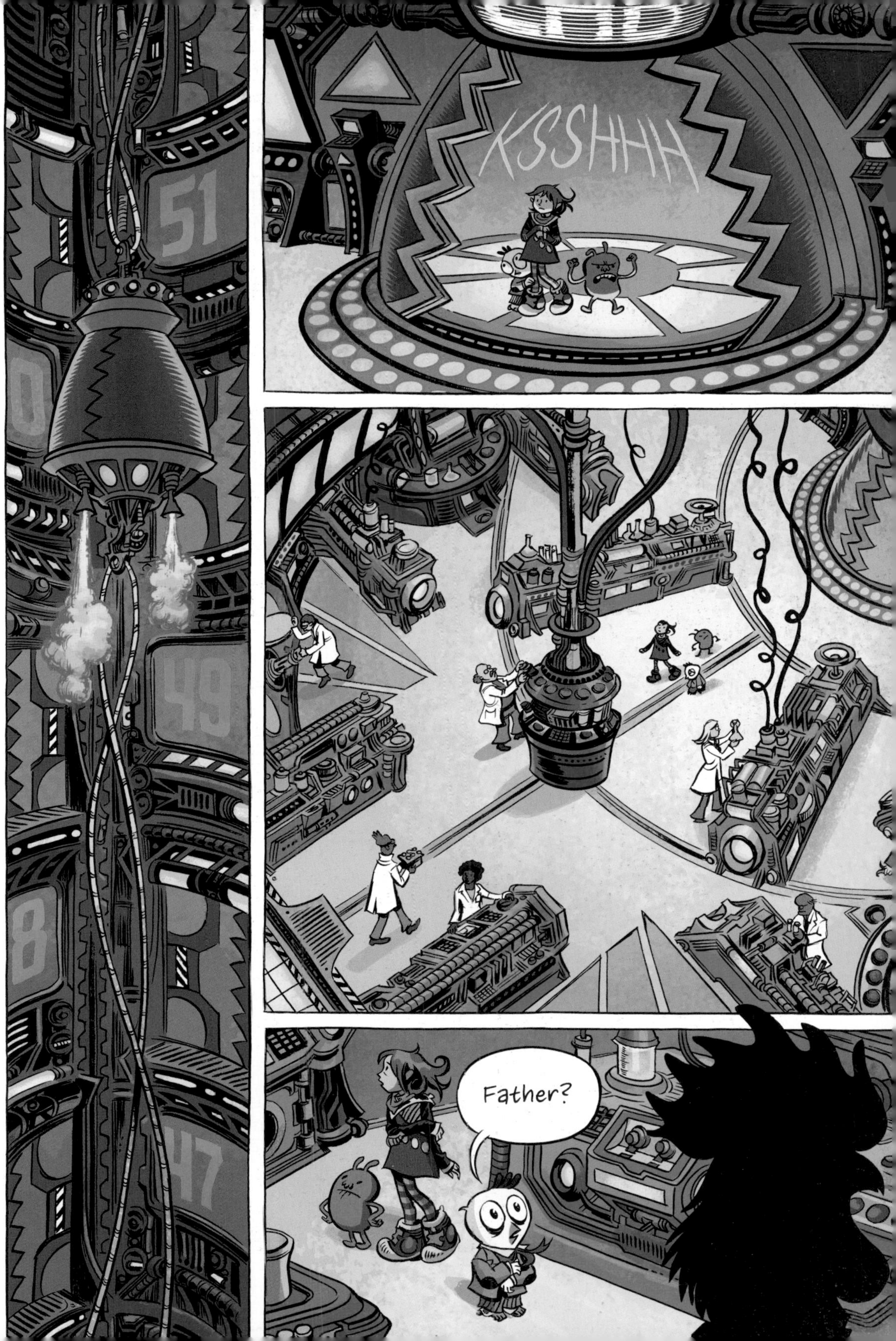
51
49
47
KSSHHH
Father?

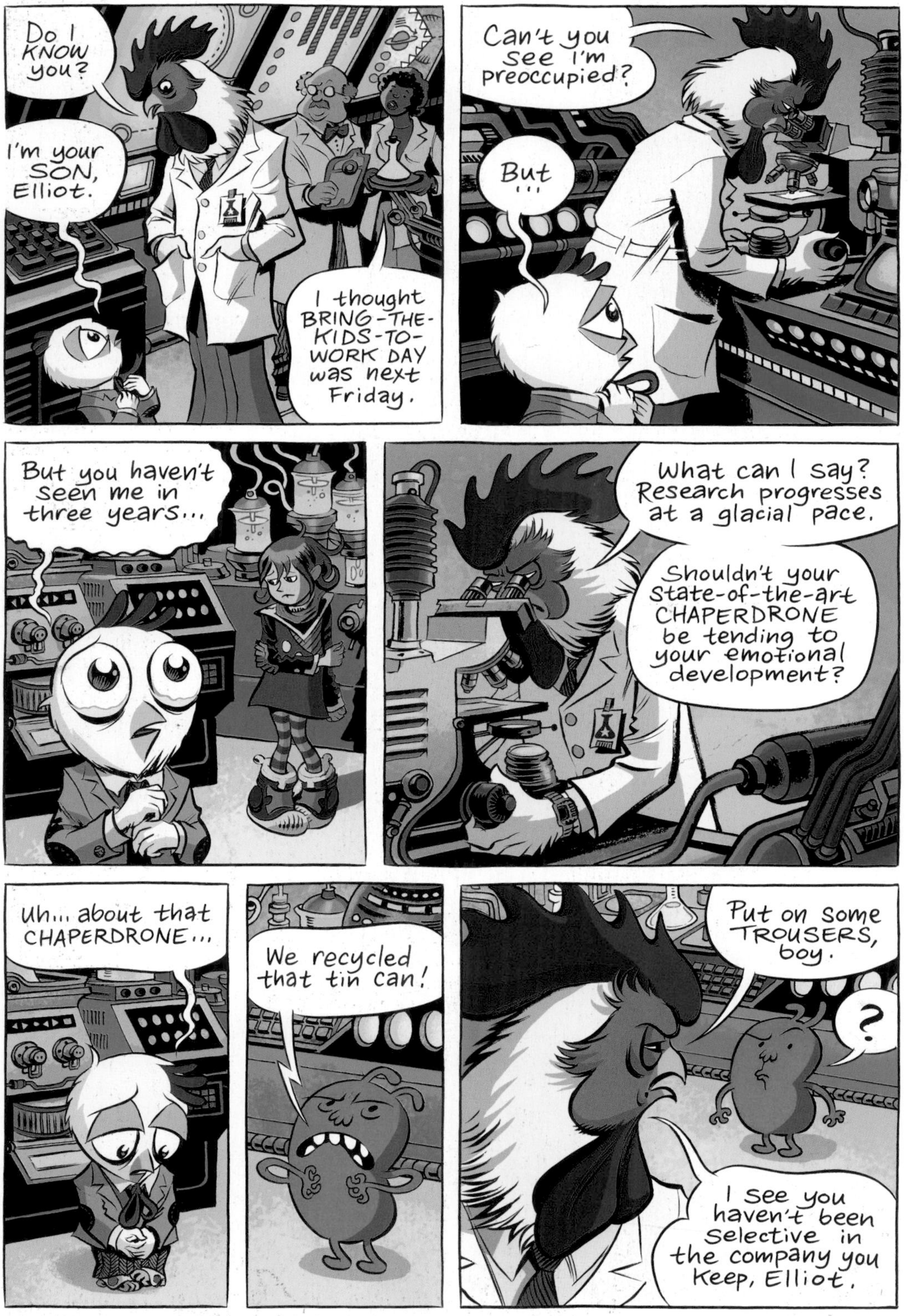

Do I KNOW you?
I'm your SON, Elliot.
I thought BRING-THE-KIDS-TO-WORK DAY was next Friday.
Can't you see I'm preoccupied?
But ...
But you haven't seen me in three years...
What can I say? Research progresses at a glacial pace.
Shouldn't your state-of-the-art CHAPERDRONE be tending to your emotional development?
Uh... about that CHAPERDRONE...
We recycled that tin can!
Put on some TROUSERS, boy.
?
I see you haven't been selective in the company you keep, Elliot.

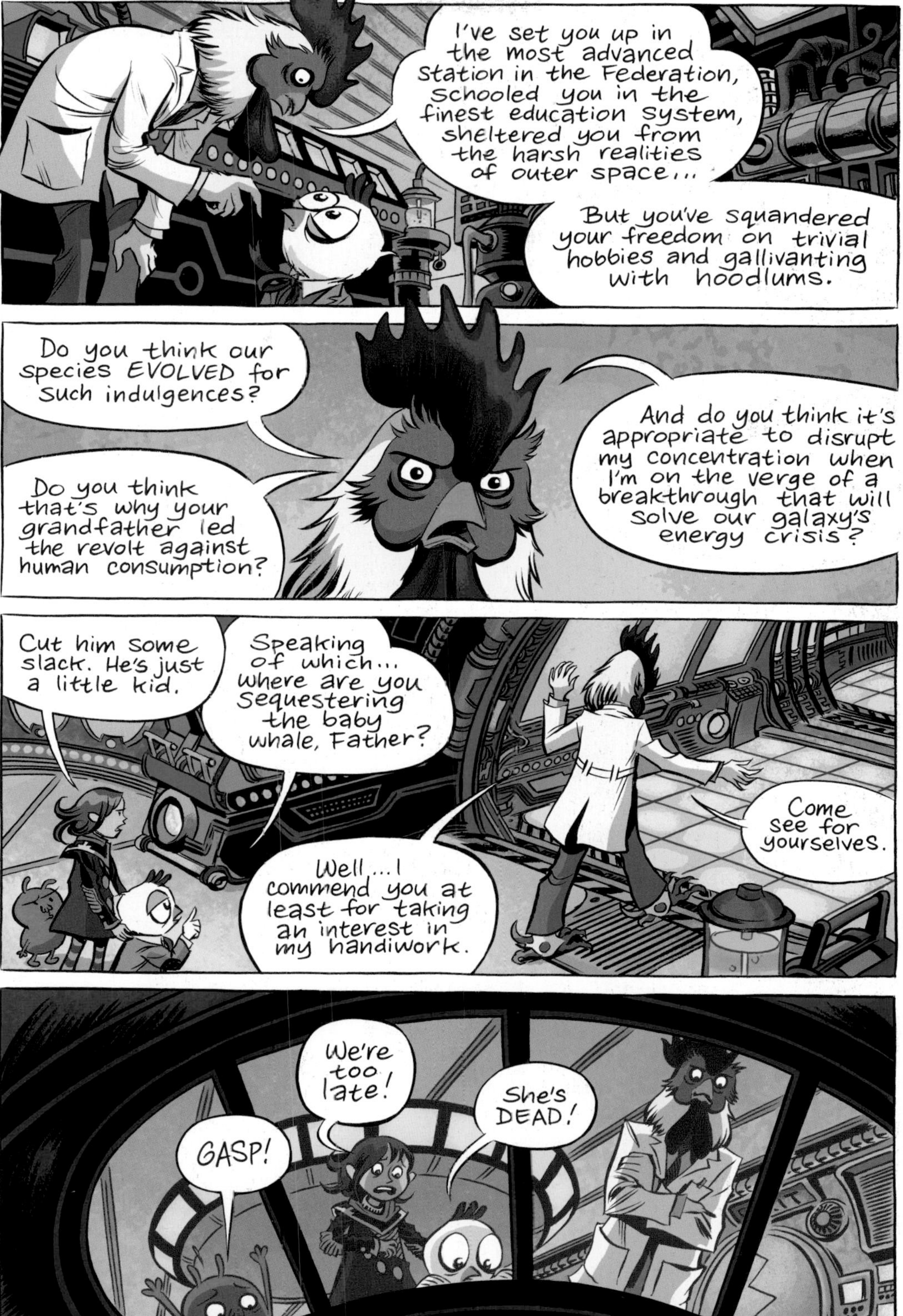
I've set you up in the most advanced station in the Federation, schooled you in the finest education system, sheltered you from the harsh realities of outer space...
But you've squandered your freedom on trivial hobbies and gallivanting with hoodlums.
Do you think our species EVOLVED for such indulgences?
Do you think that's why your grandfather led the revolt against human consumption?
And do you think it's appropriate to disrupt my concentration when I'm on the verge of a breakthrough that will solve our galaxy's energy crisis?
Cut him some slack. He's just a little kid.
Speaking of which... where are you sequestering the baby whale, Father?
Well... I commend you at least for taking an interest in my handiwork.
Come see for yourselves.
GASP!
We're too late!
She's DEAD!

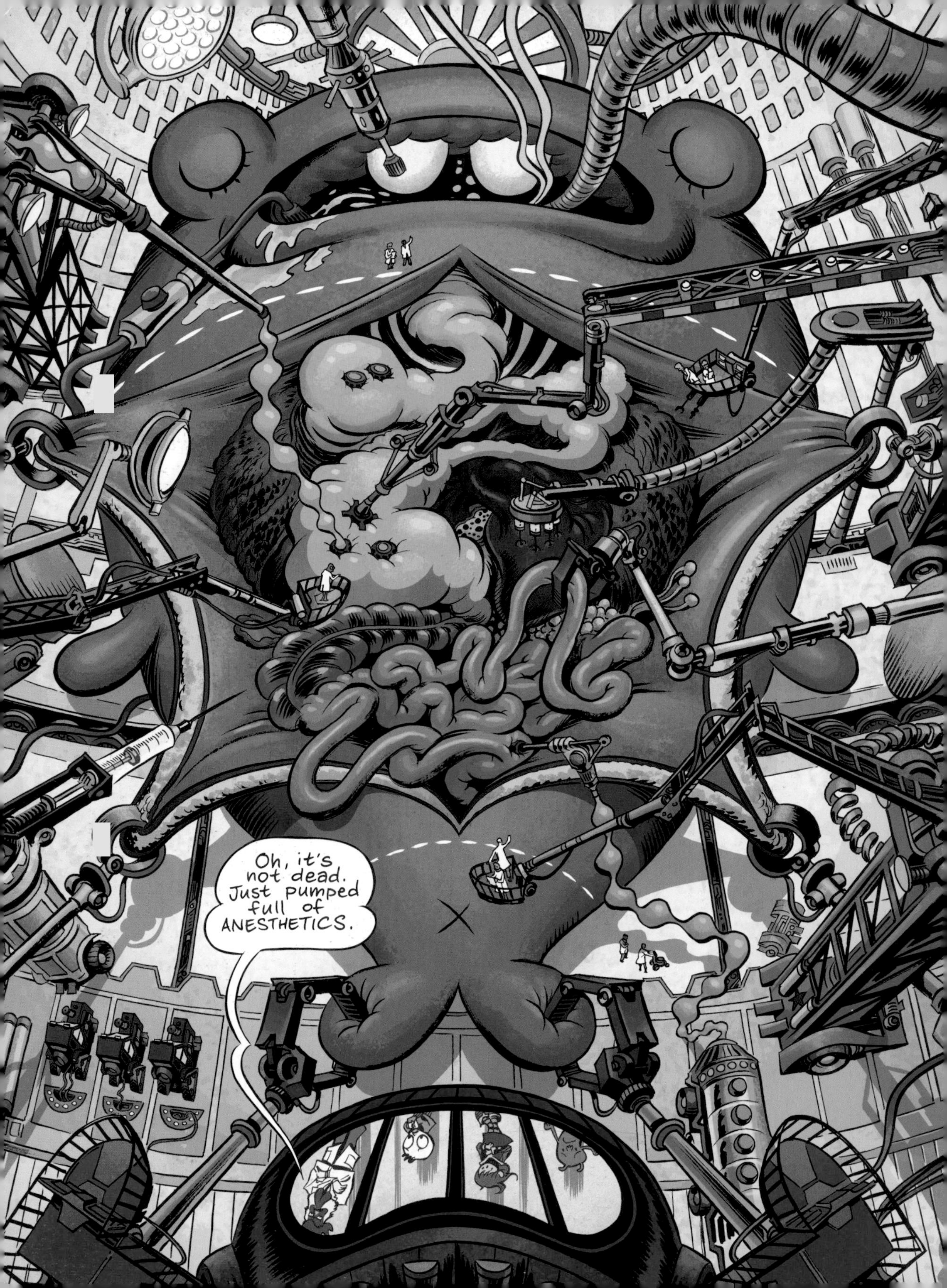
Oh, it's not dead. Just pumped full of ANESTHETICS.

What are you doing to her?!

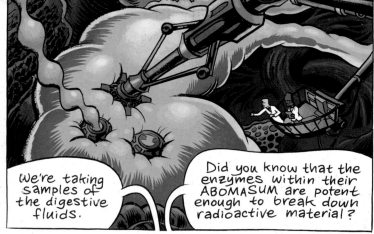

We're taking samples of the digestive fluids.

Did you know that the enzymes within their ABOMASUM are potent enough to break down radioactive material?

This is INSANE! You need to sew her up before the whale herd gets here!

The herd?

The POD has made steady progress through the refuse barrier.

Alert the defense unit!

And restrain these distractions!

CLAMP
CLAMP

CLAMP

You'd be better off an ORPHAN.

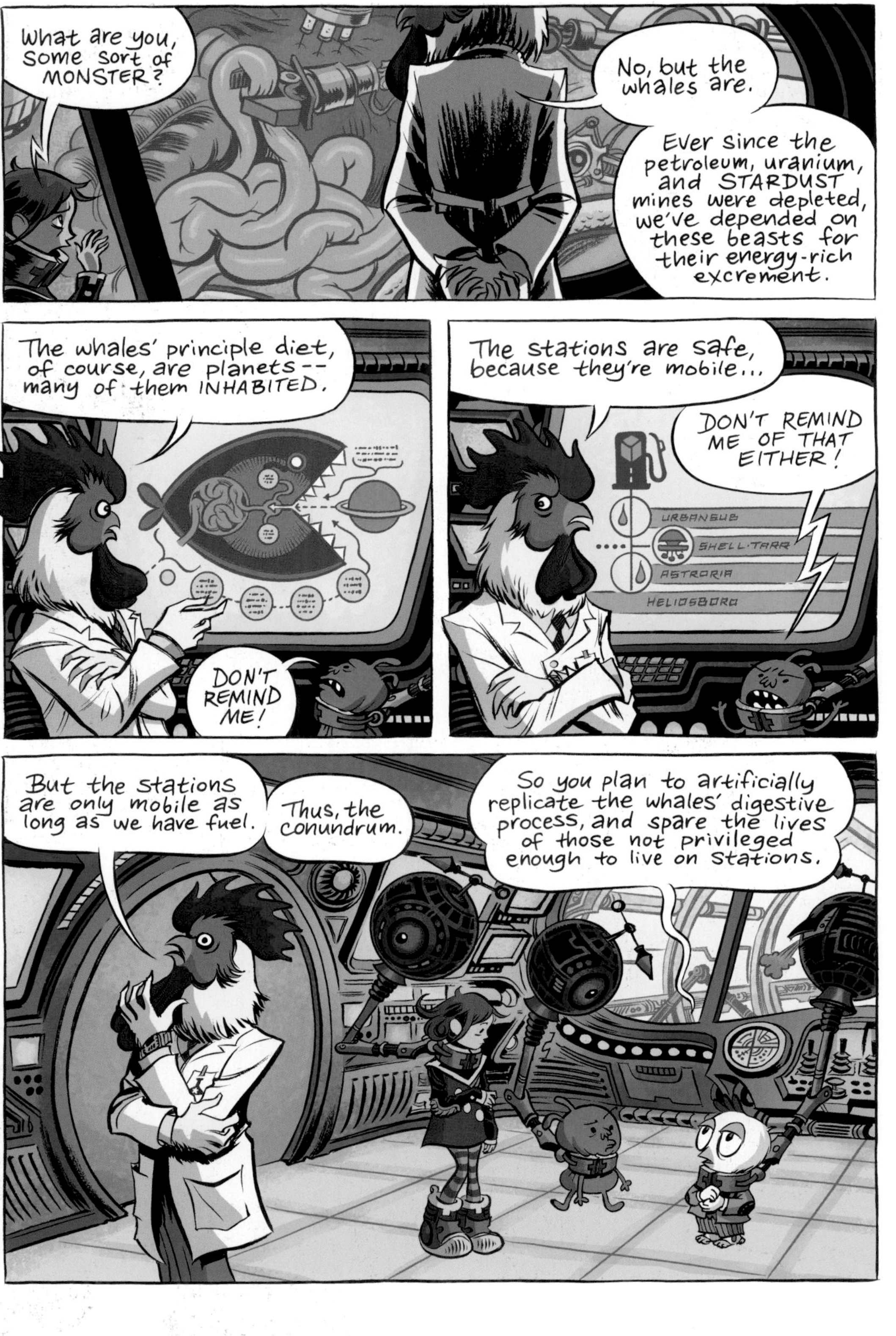
What are you, some sort of MONSTER?
No, but the whales are.
Ever since the petroleum, uranium, and STARDUST mines were depleted, we've depended on these beasts for their energy-rich excrement.
The whales' principle diet, of course, are planets-- many of them INHABITED.
DON'T REMIND ME!
The stations are safe, because they're mobile...
DON'T REMIND ME OF THAT EITHER!
URBANSUB
SHELL-TARR
ASTRORIA
HELIOSBORO
But the stations are only mobile as long as we have fuel.
Thus, the conundrum.
So you plan to artificially replicate the whales' digestive process, and spare the lives of those not privileged enough to live on stations.

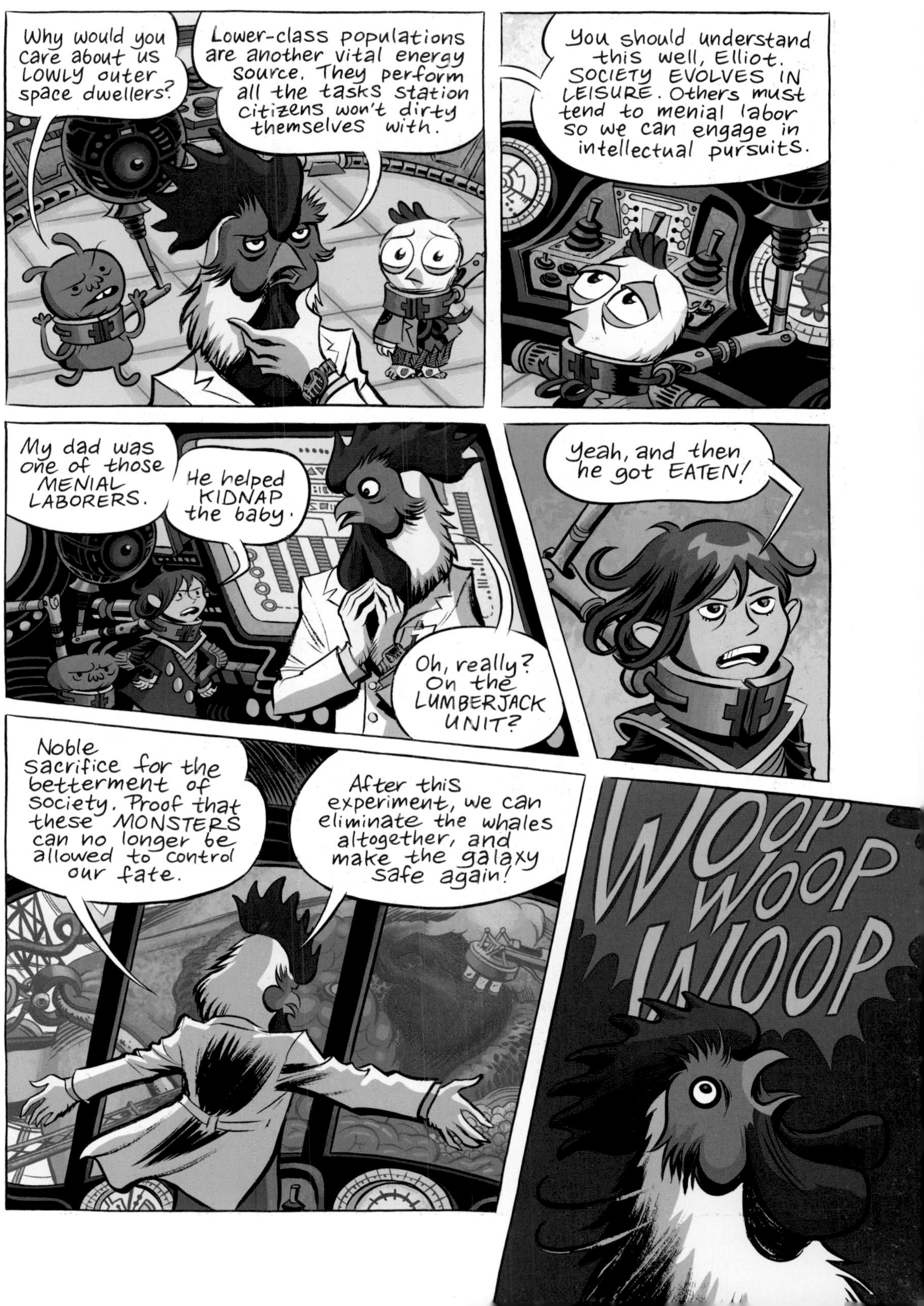

Why would you care about us LOWLY outer space dwellers?
Lower-class populations are another vital energy source. They perform all the tasks station citizens won't dirty themselves with.
You should understand this well, Elliot. SOCIETY EVOLVES IN LEISURE. Others must tend to menial labor so we can engage in intellectual pursuits.
My dad was one of those MENIAL LABORERS.
He helped KIDNAP the baby.
Oh, really? On the LUMBERJACK UNIT?
Yeah, and then he got EATEN!
Noble sacrifice for the betterment of society. Proof that these MONSTERS can no longer be allowed to control our fate.
After this experiment, we can eliminate the whales altogether, and make the galaxy safe again!
WOOP WOOP WOOP

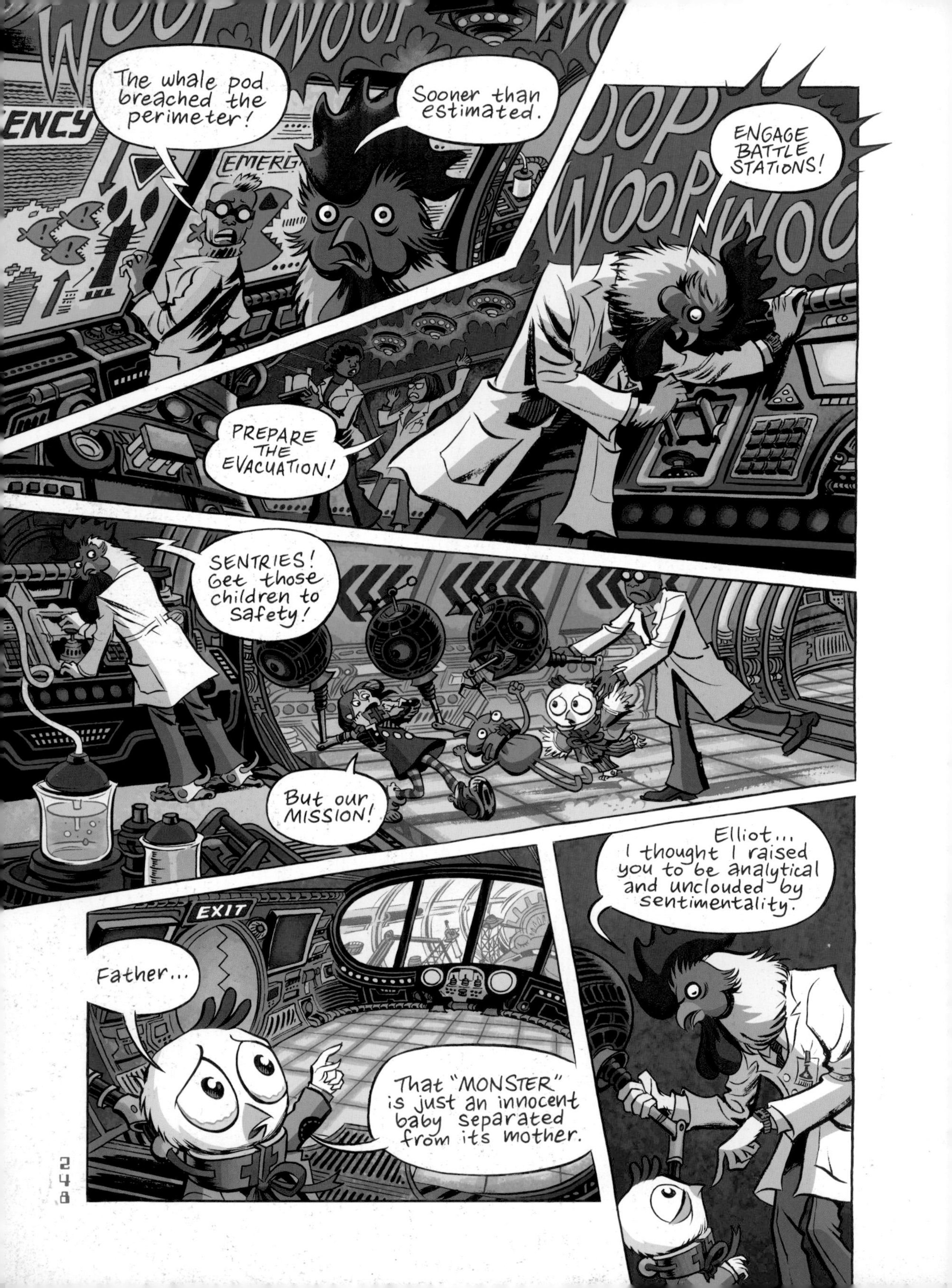
WOOP WOOP
The whale pod breached the perimeter!
Sooner than estimated.
WOOP WOOP WOO
ENGAGE BATTLE STATIONS!
PREPARE THE EVACUATION!
SENTRIES! Get those children to safety!
But our MISSION!
EXIT
Father...
That "MONSTER" is just an innocent baby separated from its mother.
Elliot... I thought I raised you to be analytical and unclouded by sentimentality.

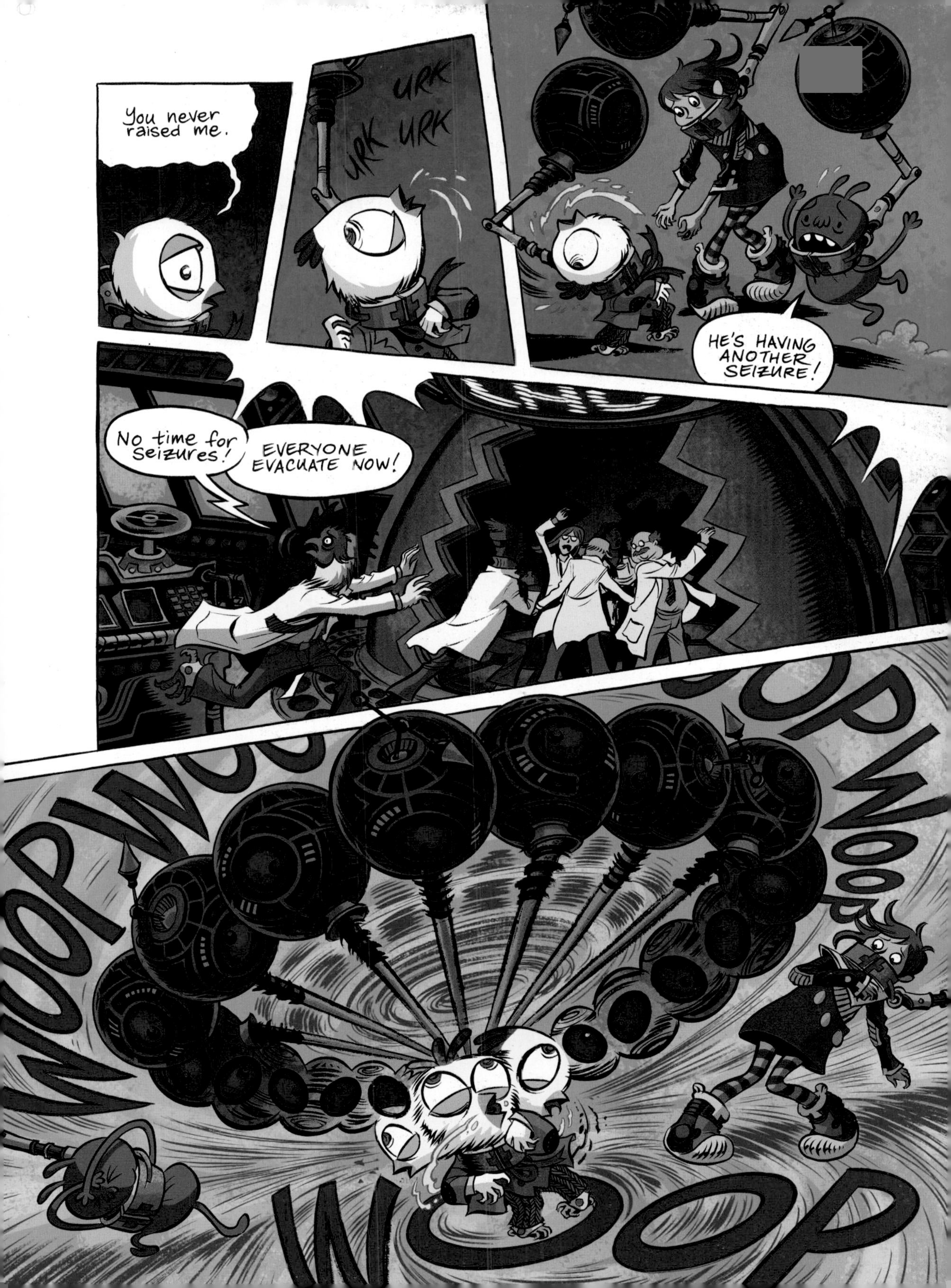
You never raised me.
URK URK URK
HE'S HAVING ANOTHER SEIZURE!
No time for seizures!
EVERYONE EVACUATE NOW!
WOOP
WOOP
WOOP

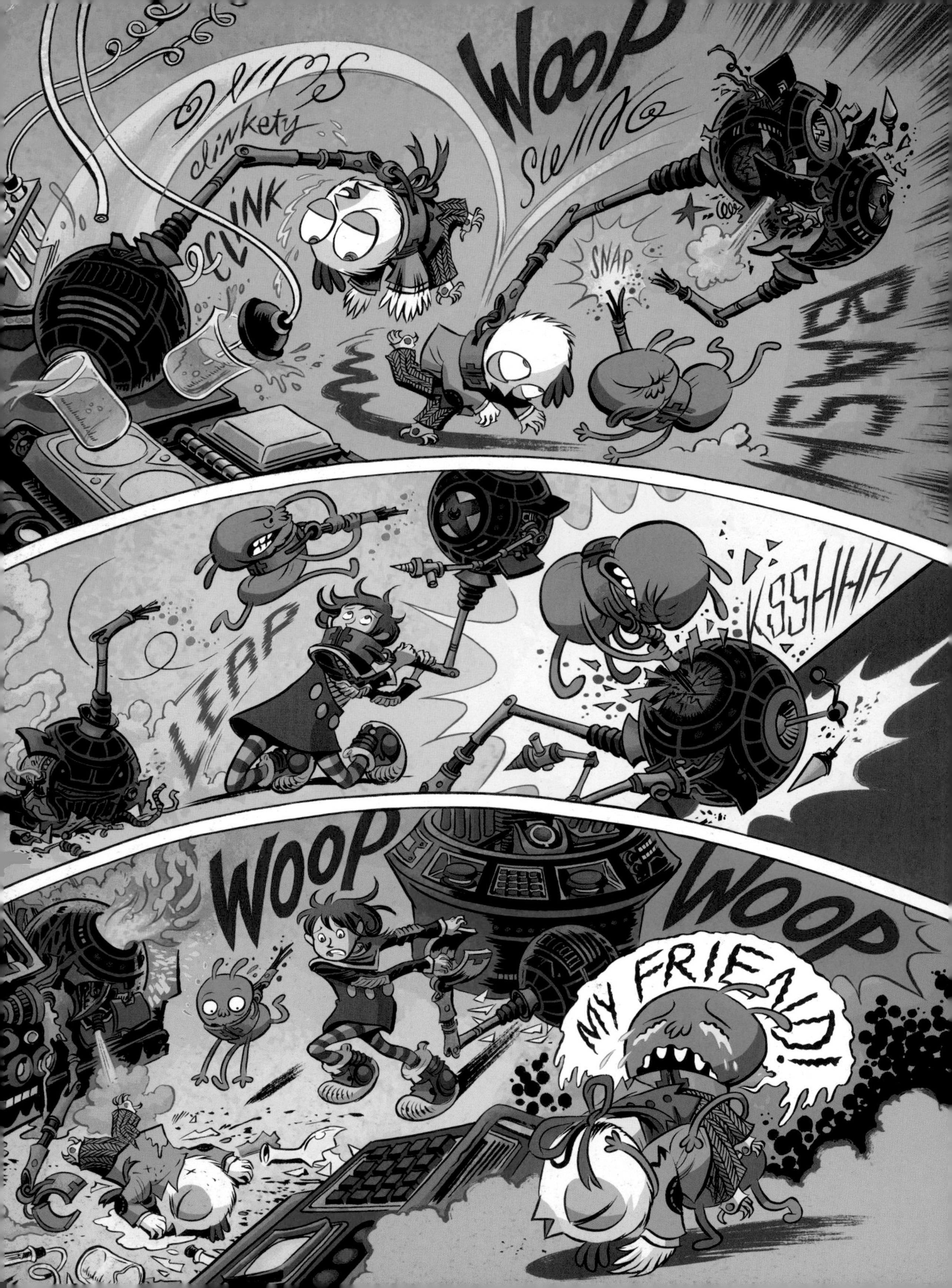

dinkety
CLINK
WOOP
SNAP
BASH
LEAP
KSSHHH
WOOP
WOOP
MY FRIEND!

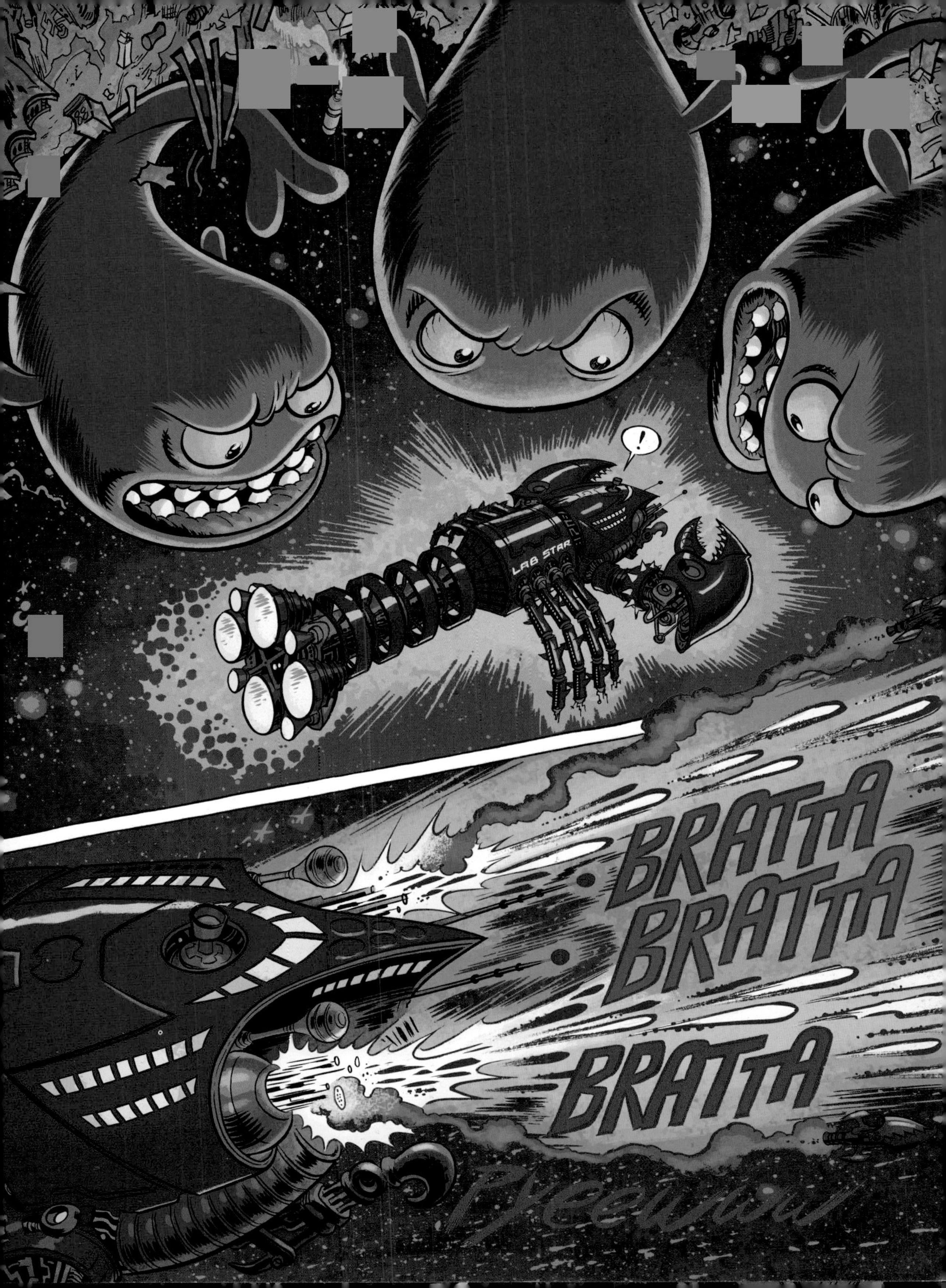
!
LAB STAR
BRATTA
BRATTA
BRATTA

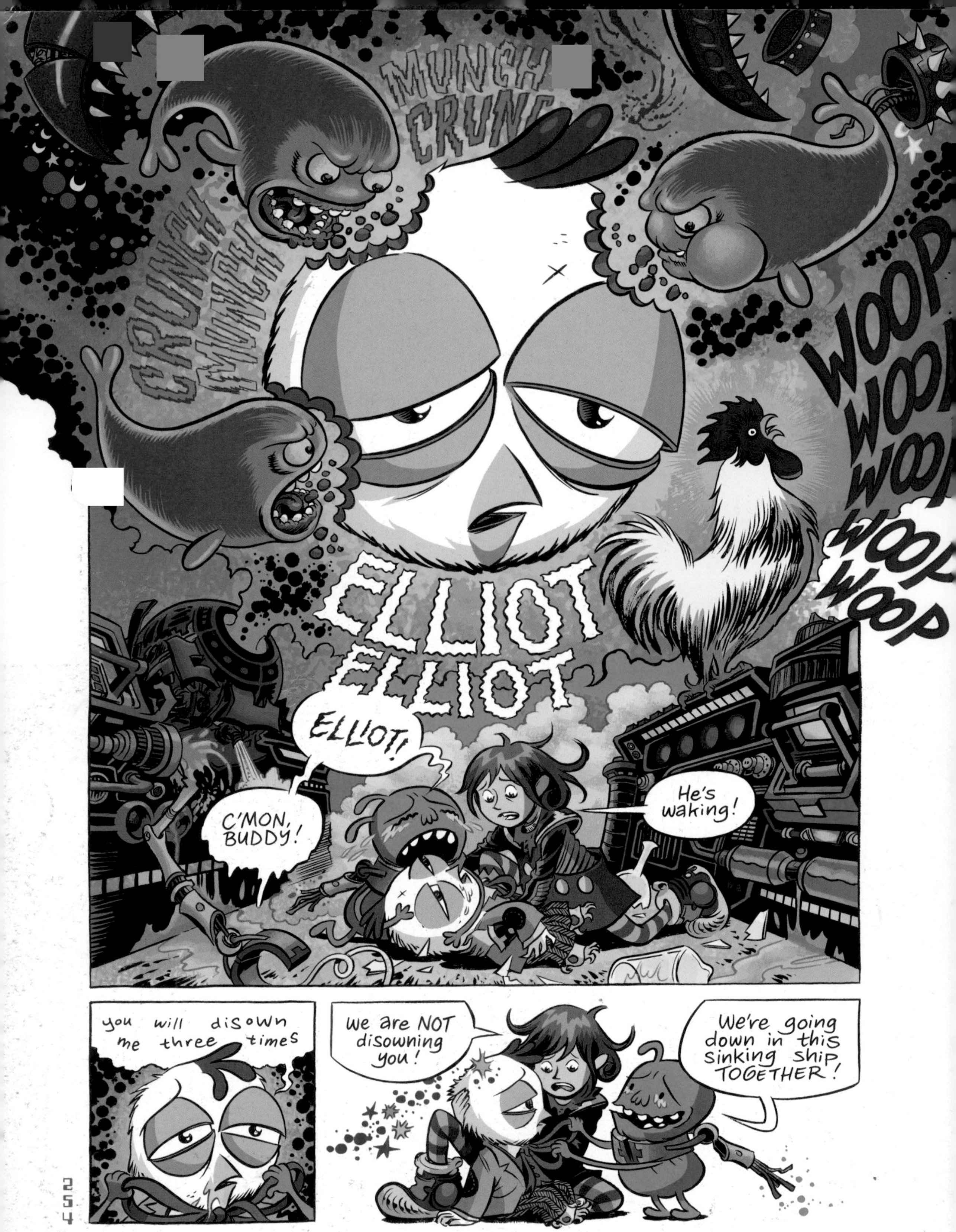
MUNCH
CRUNCH
CRUNCH
MUNCH
WOOP
WOOP
WOOP
WOOP
WOOP
ELLIOT
ELLIOT
ELLIOT!
C'MON, BUDDY!
He's waking!
you will disown me three times
We are NOT disowning you!
We're going down in this sinking ship TOGETHER!

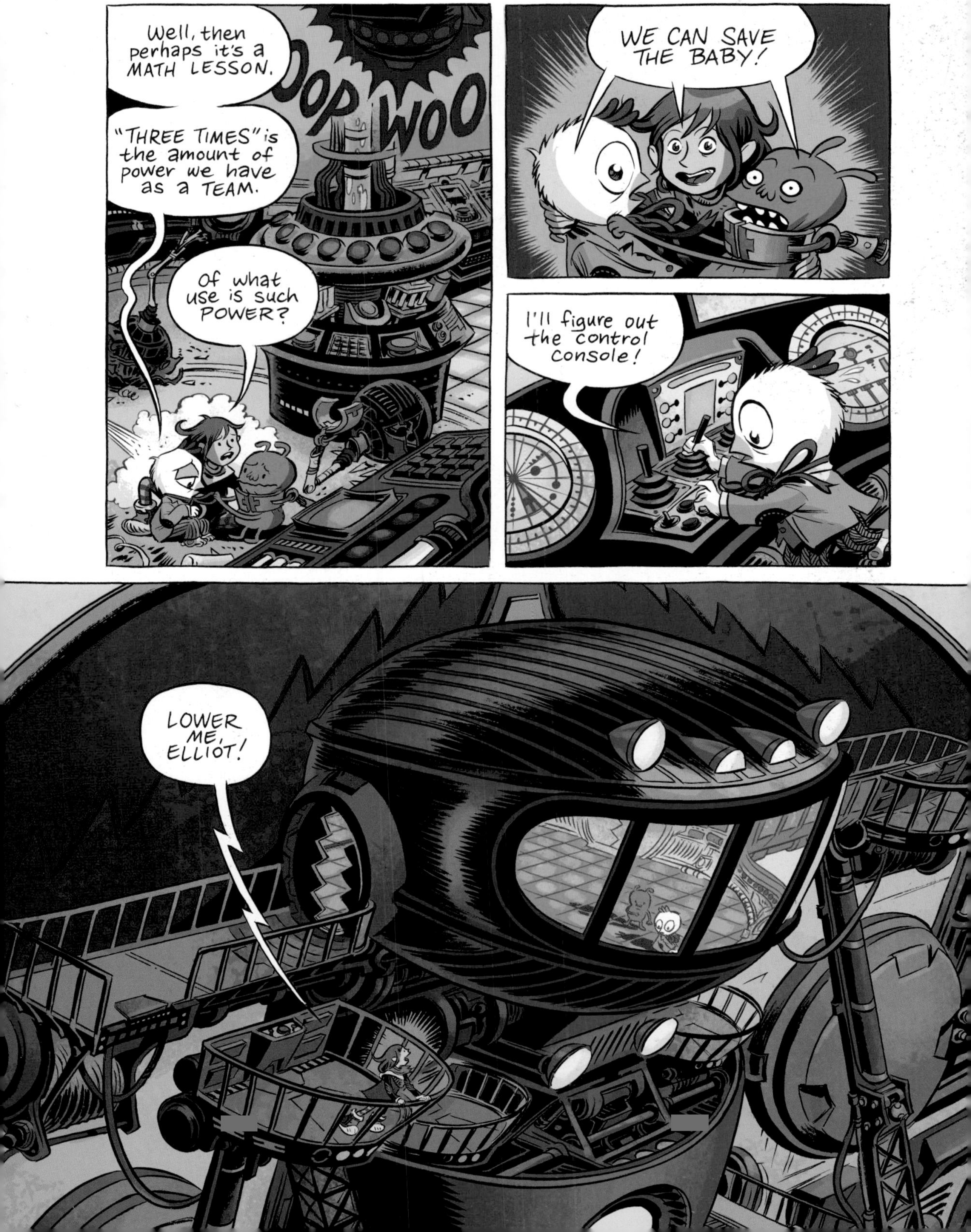
Well, then perhaps it's a MATH LESSON.
WOOP WOO
"THREE TIMES" is the amount of power we have as a TEAM.
Of what use is such POWER?
WE CAN SAVE THE BABY!
I'll figure out the control console!
LOWER ME, ELLIOT!

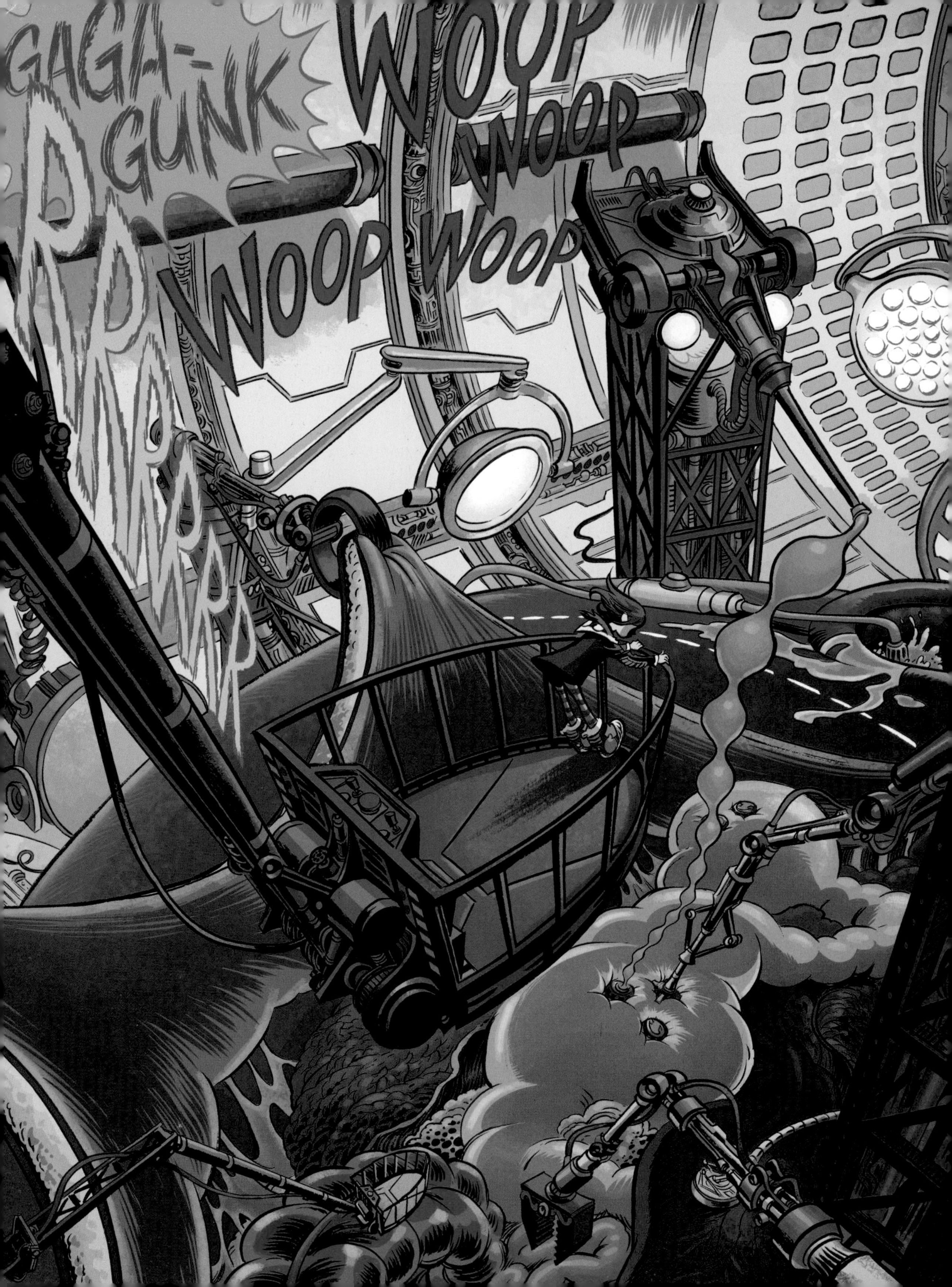
GAGA-GUNK
WOOP
WOOP
WOOP
WOOP

While you two are doing that...

I'll fetch our "ESCAPE POD"!

grunt

REACH REACH grunt

SHOVE

push

...

POUND POUND POUND POUND

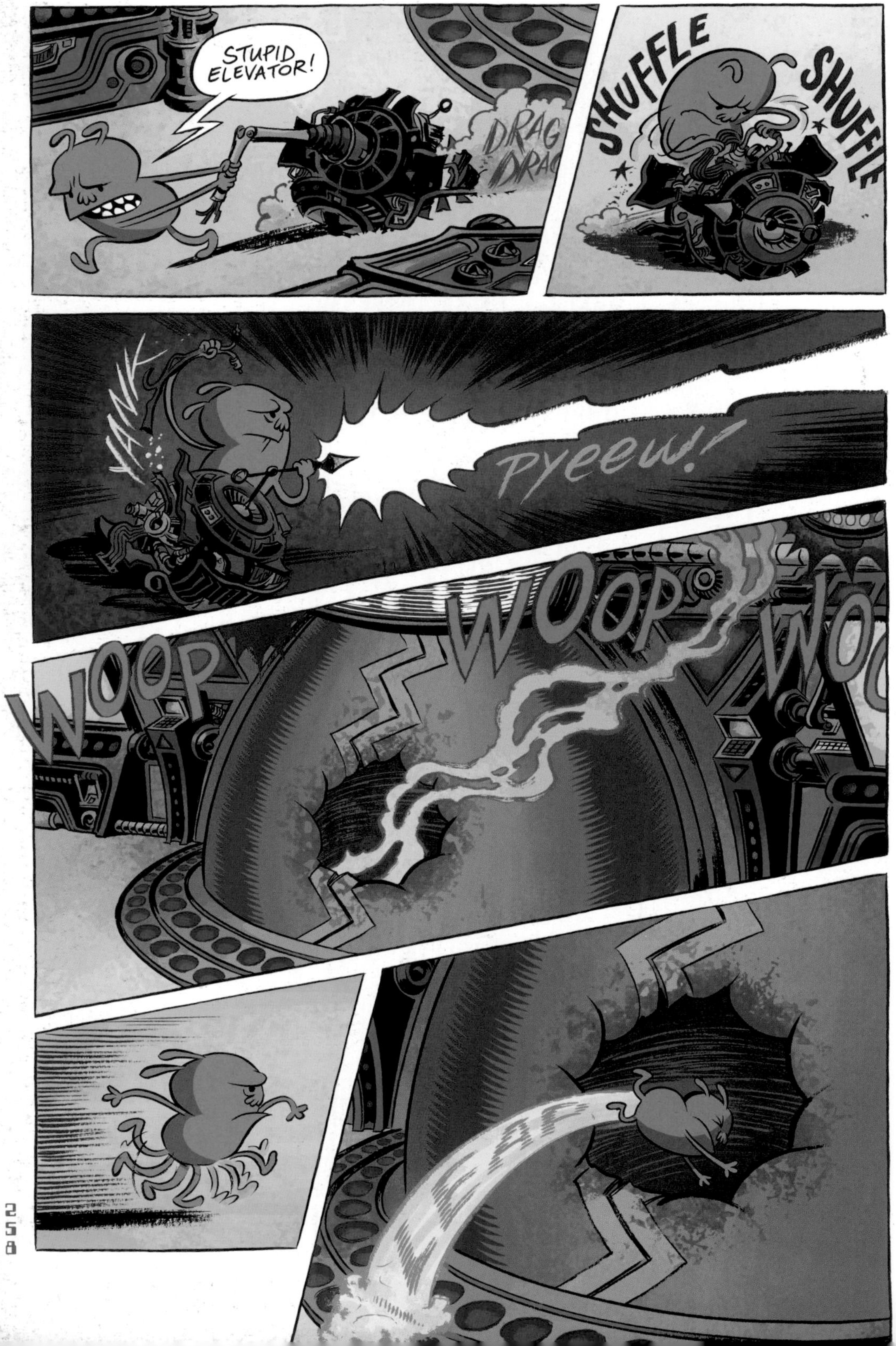
STUPID ELEVATOR!
DRAG DRAG
SHUFFLE SHUFFLE
YANK
Pyeew!
WOOP WOOP WOO
LEAP

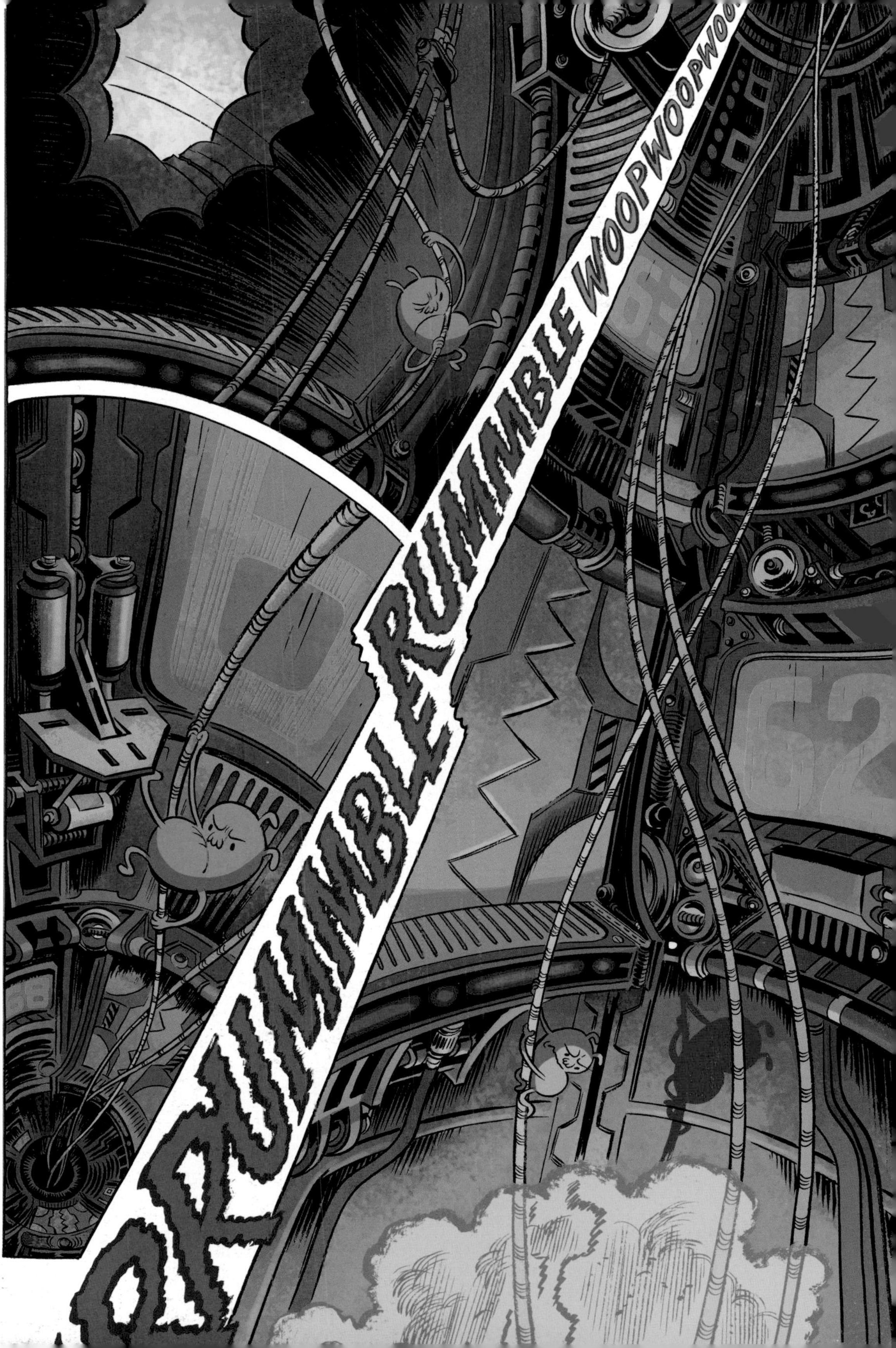
RRUMMBLERUMMBLE
WOOPWOOPWOO

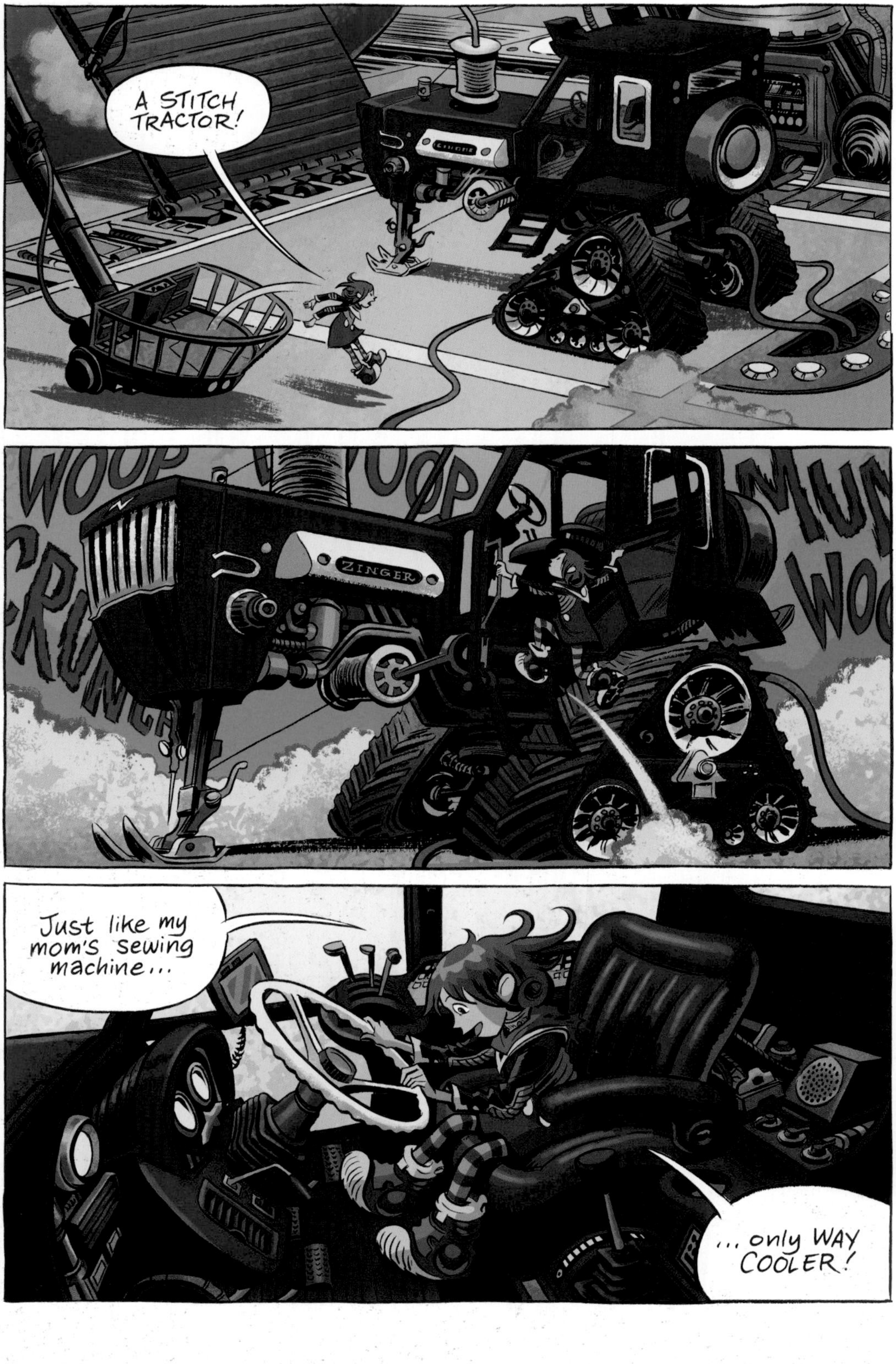
A STITCH TRACTOR!
ZINGER
Just like my mom's sewing machine...
...only WAY COOLER!

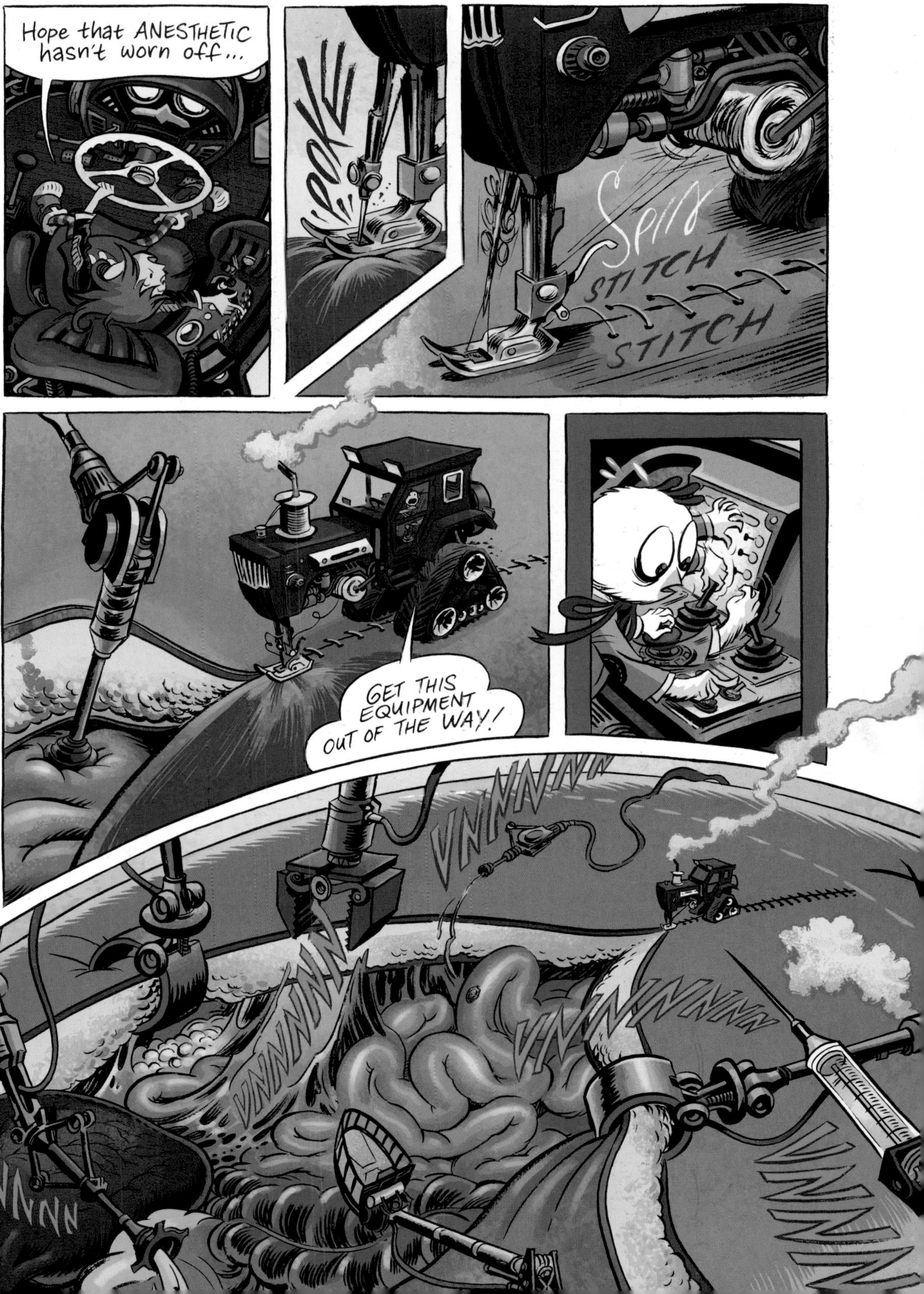
Hope that ANESTHETIC hasn't worn off...
POKE
SPIN
STITCH
STITCH
GET THIS EQUIPMENT OUT OF THE WAY!
VNNNNNN
VNNNNNN
VNNNNNNN
VNNNNNNNN
VNNNNNNN
VNNNNNNN
VNNNNNN

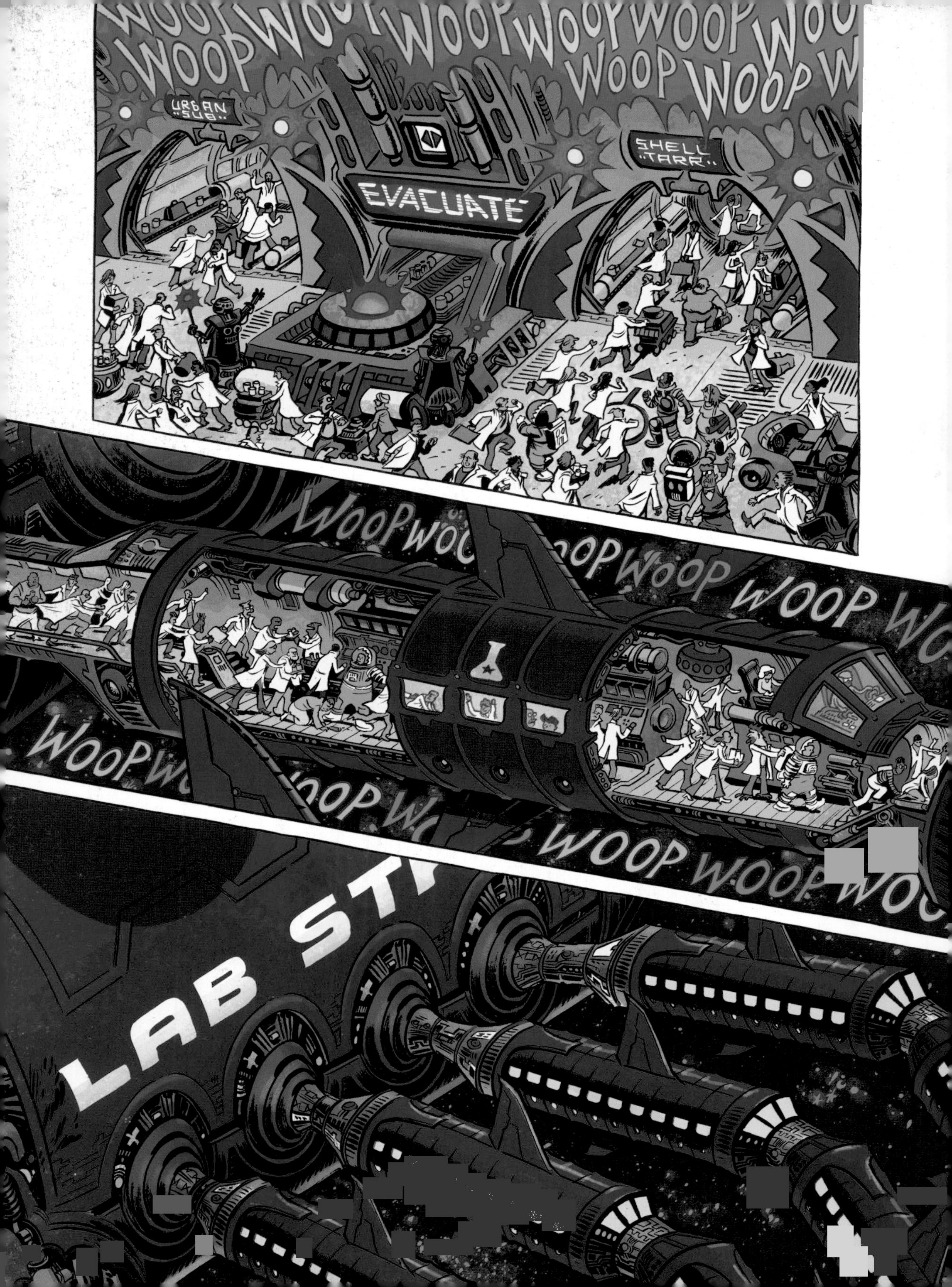
WOOP
URBAN SUB
SHELL TARR
EVACUATE
WOOP
WOOP
WOOP
WOOP
LAB

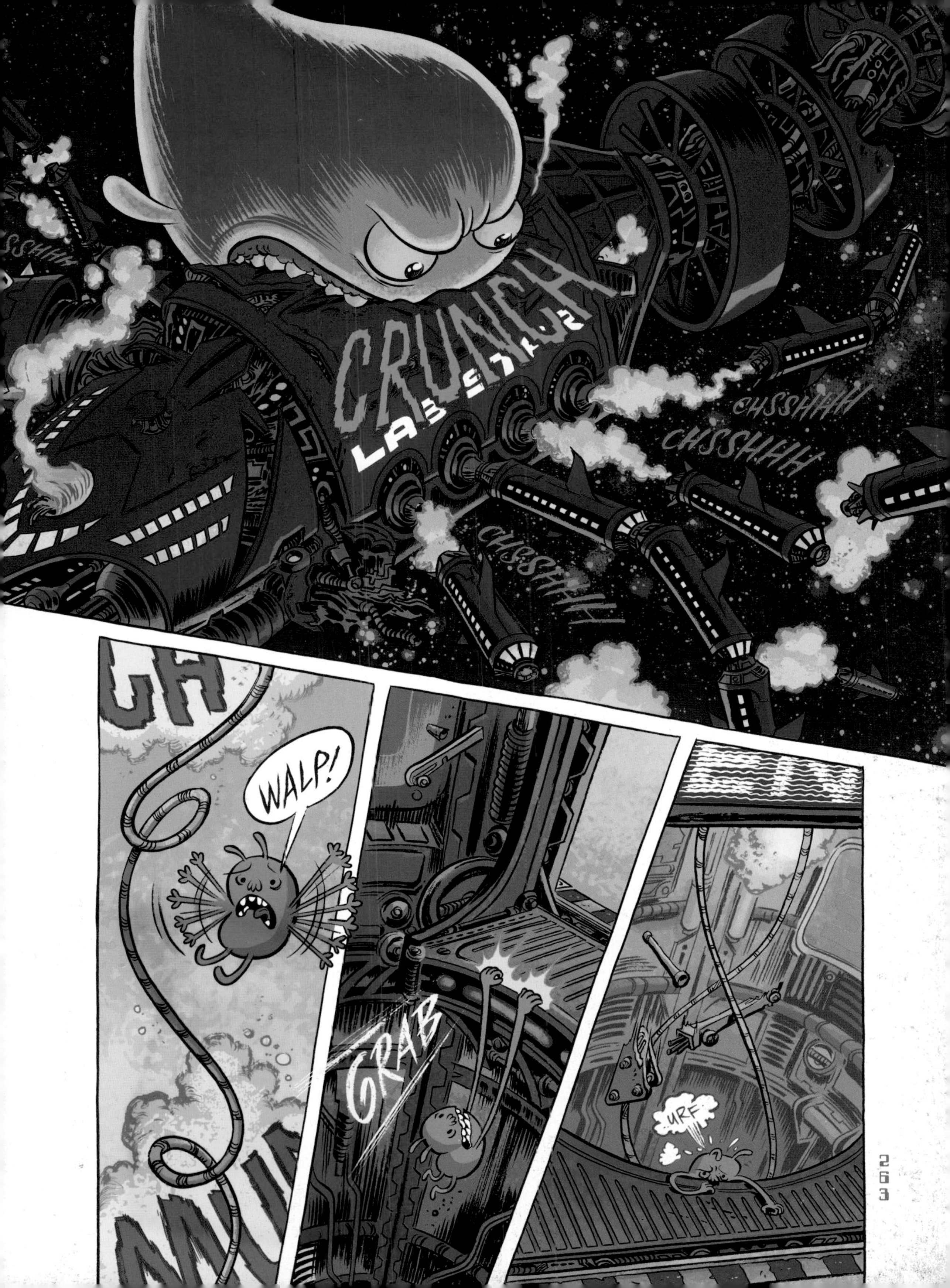
CRUNCH
CHSSHHH
CHSSHHH
CHSSHHH
WALP!
GRAB
URF

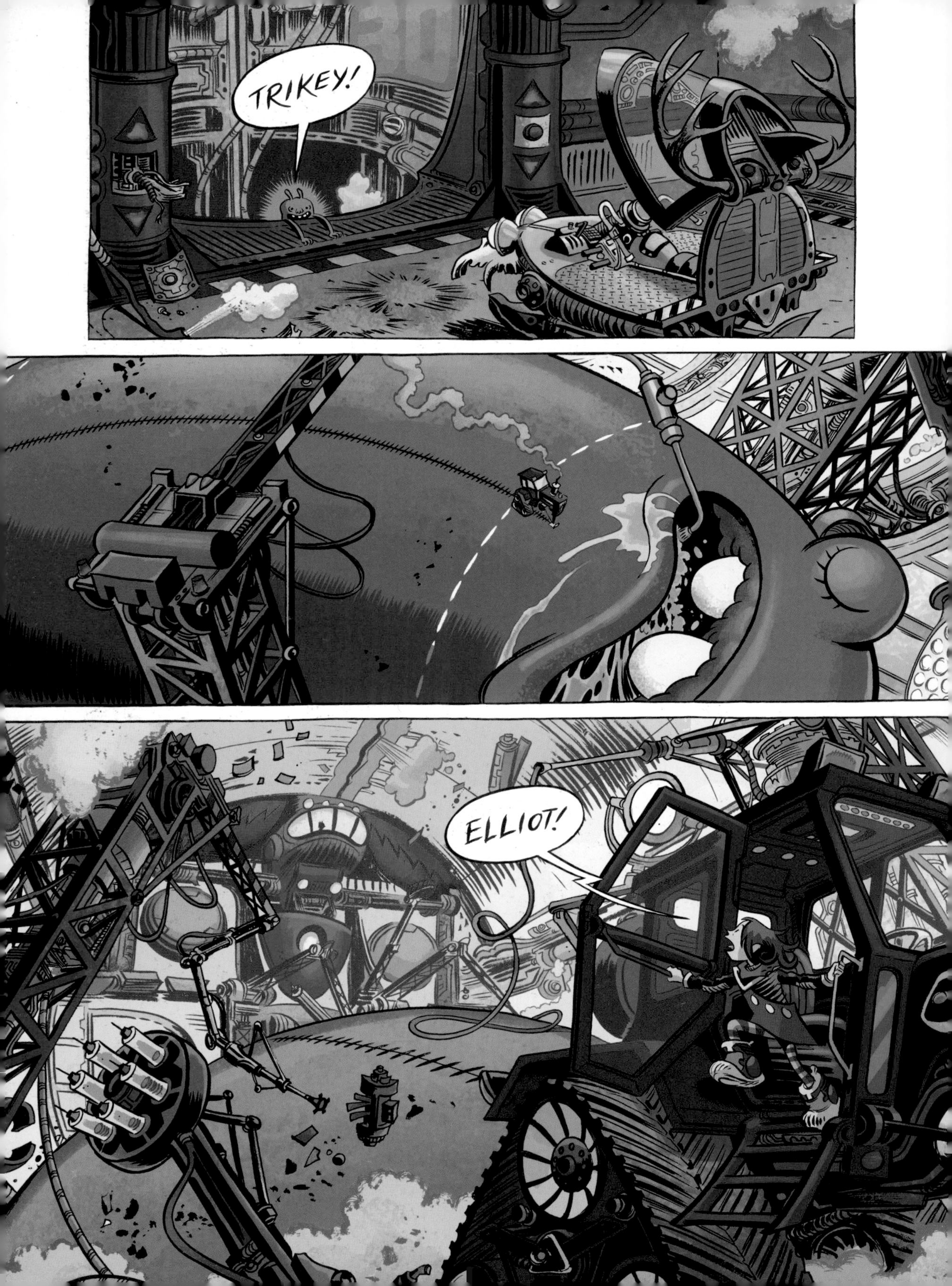
TRIKEY!
ELLIOT!

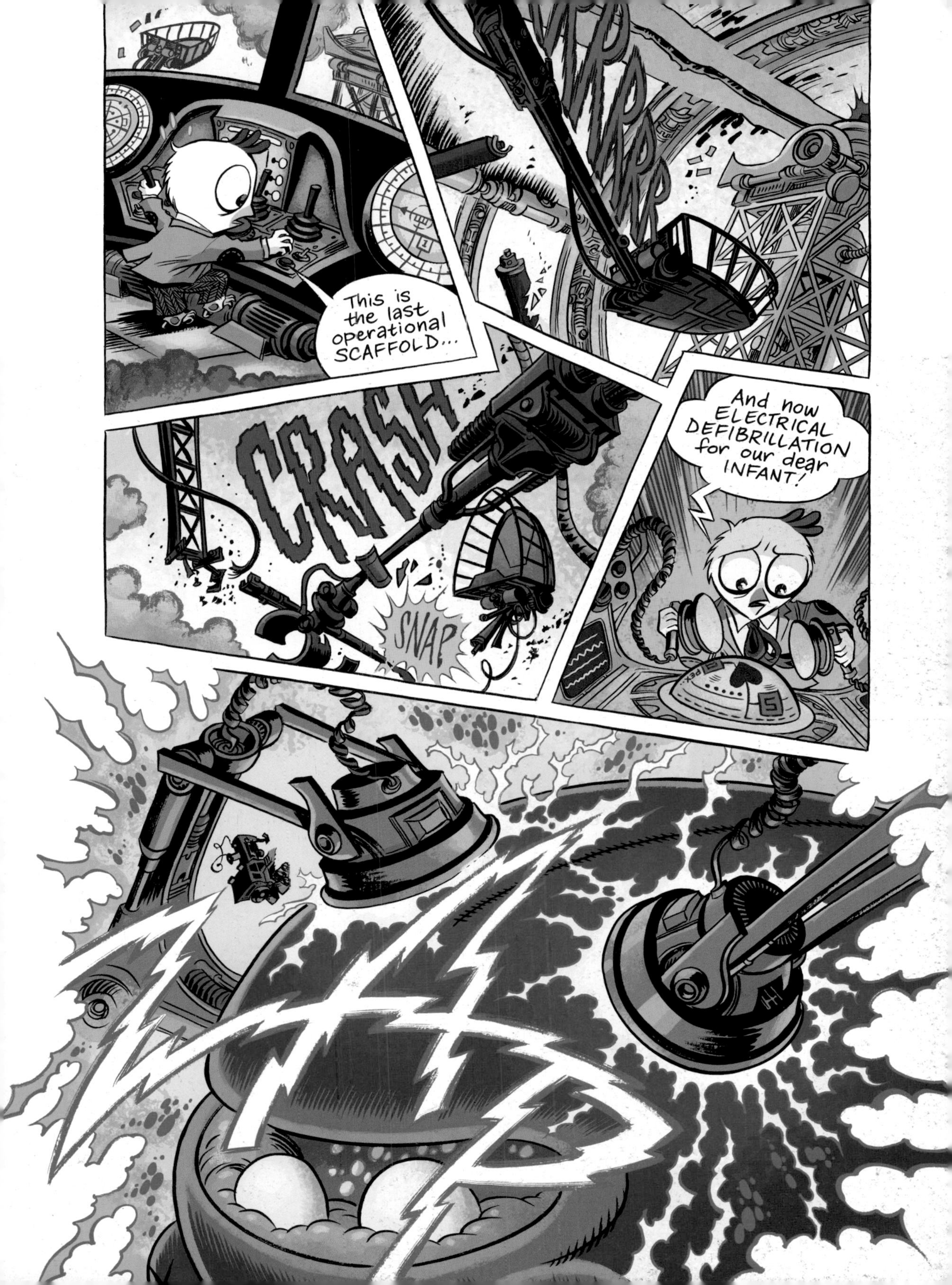

This is the last operational SCAFFOLD...
WRRRRR
CRASH
SNAP!
And now ELECTRICAL DEFIBRILLATION for our dear INFANT!

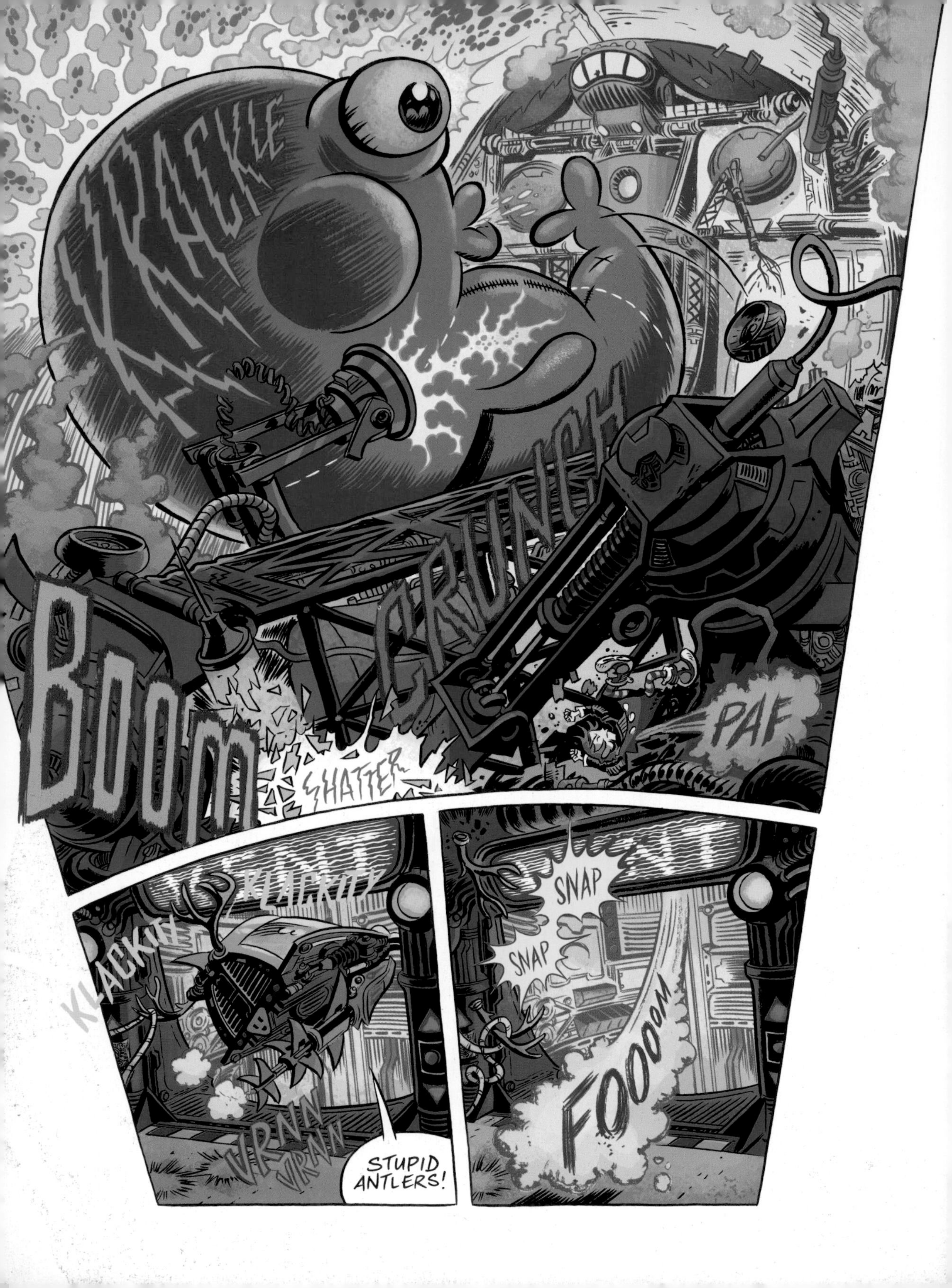

KRACKLE
CRUNCH
BOOM
SHATTER
PAF
KLACKITY
KLACKITY
VRNN VRNN
STUPID ANTLERS!
SNAP
SNAP
FOOOOM

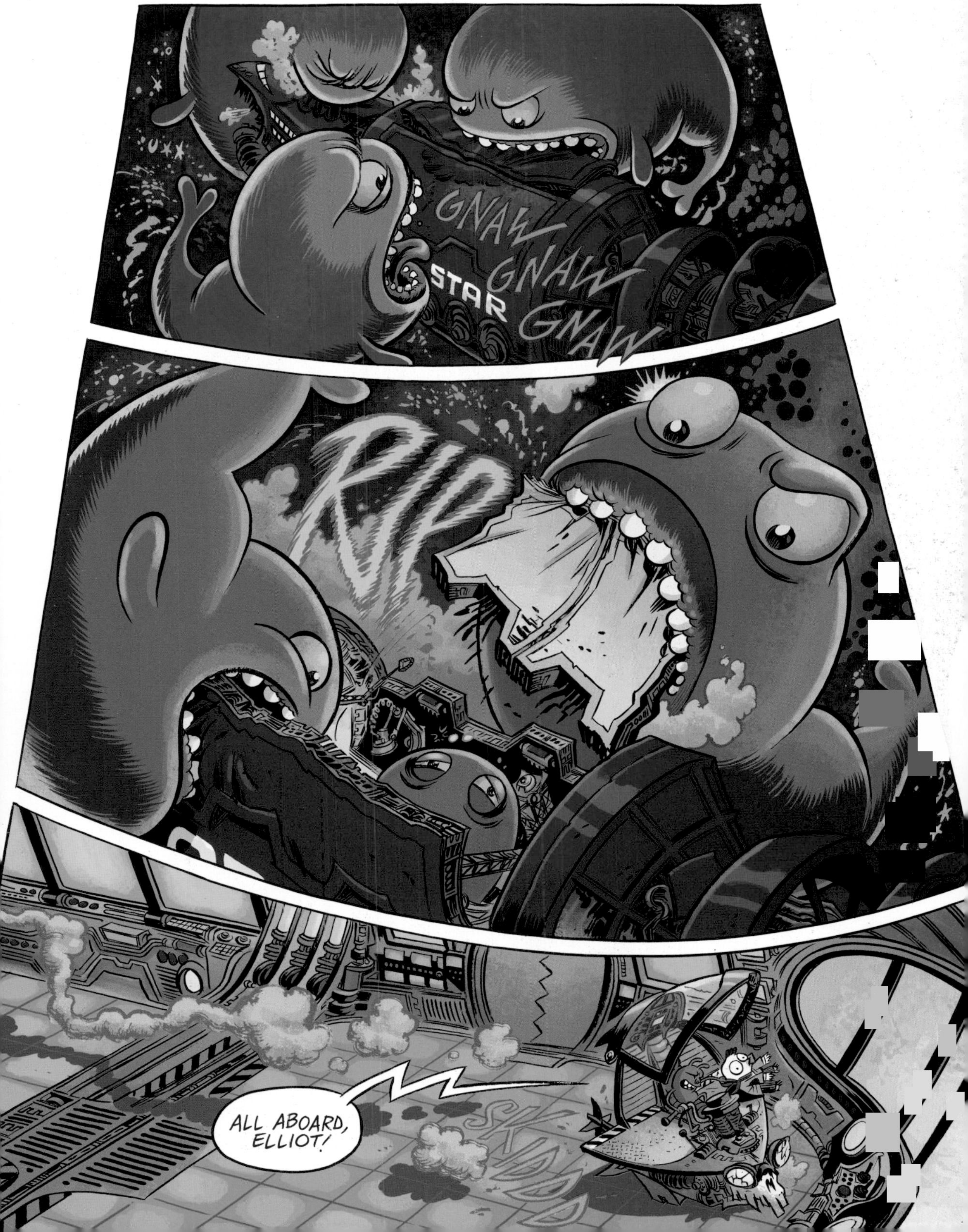
GNAW
GNAW
GNAW
STAR
RIP
ALL ABOARD, ELLIOT!

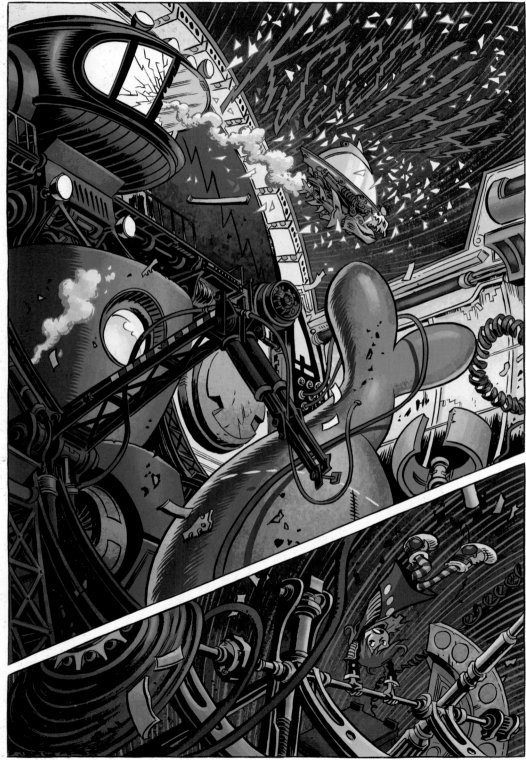

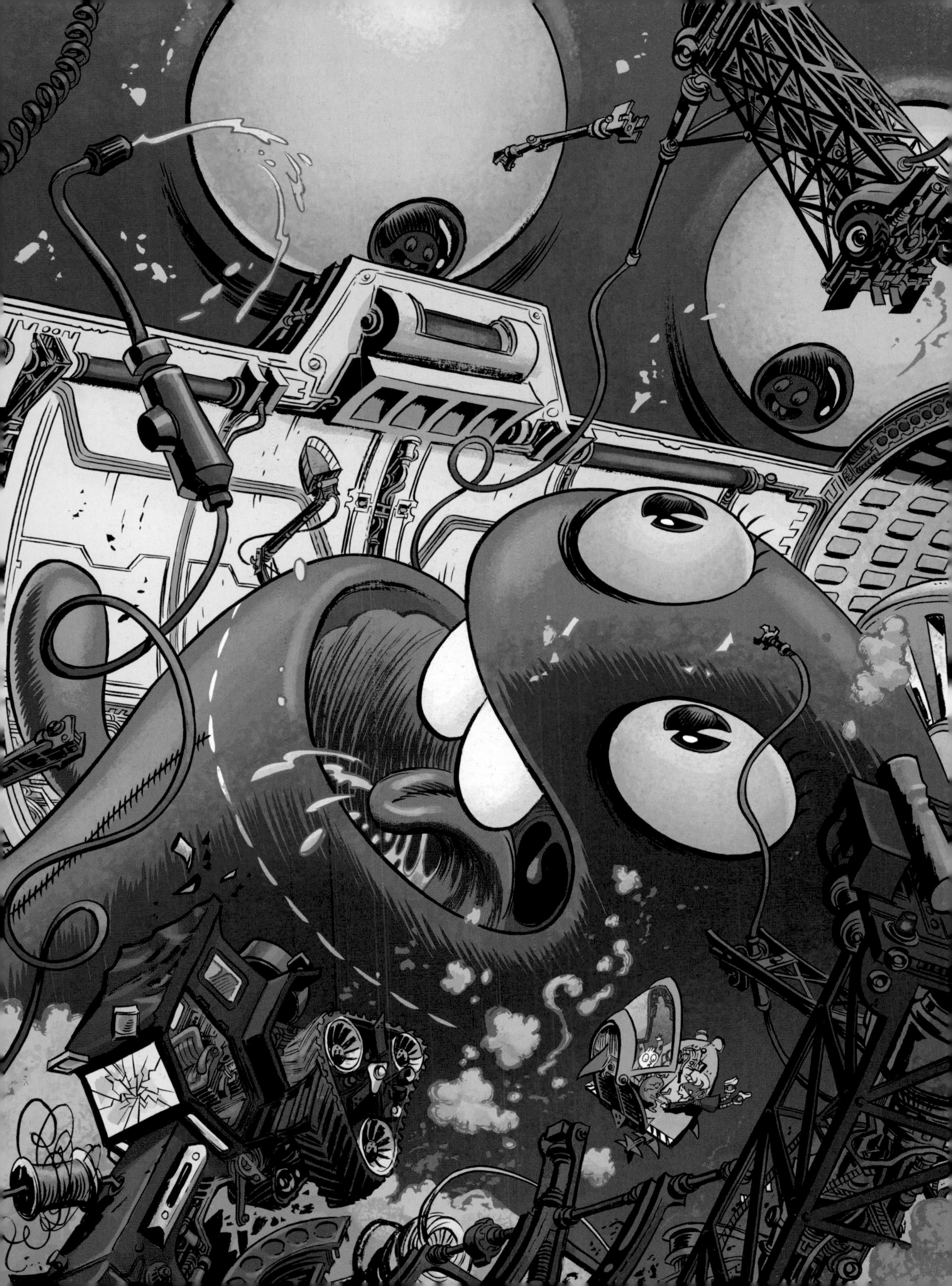

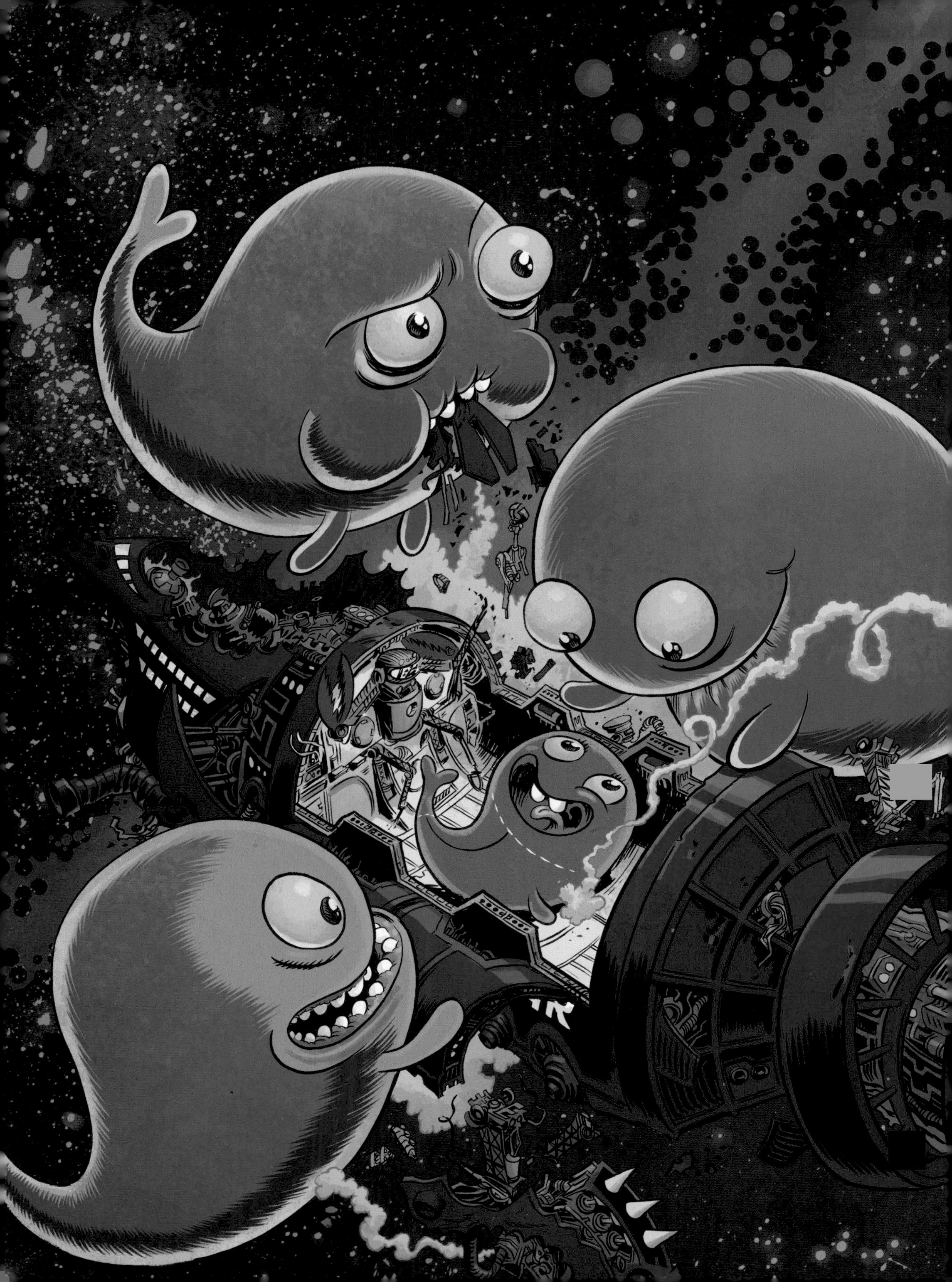

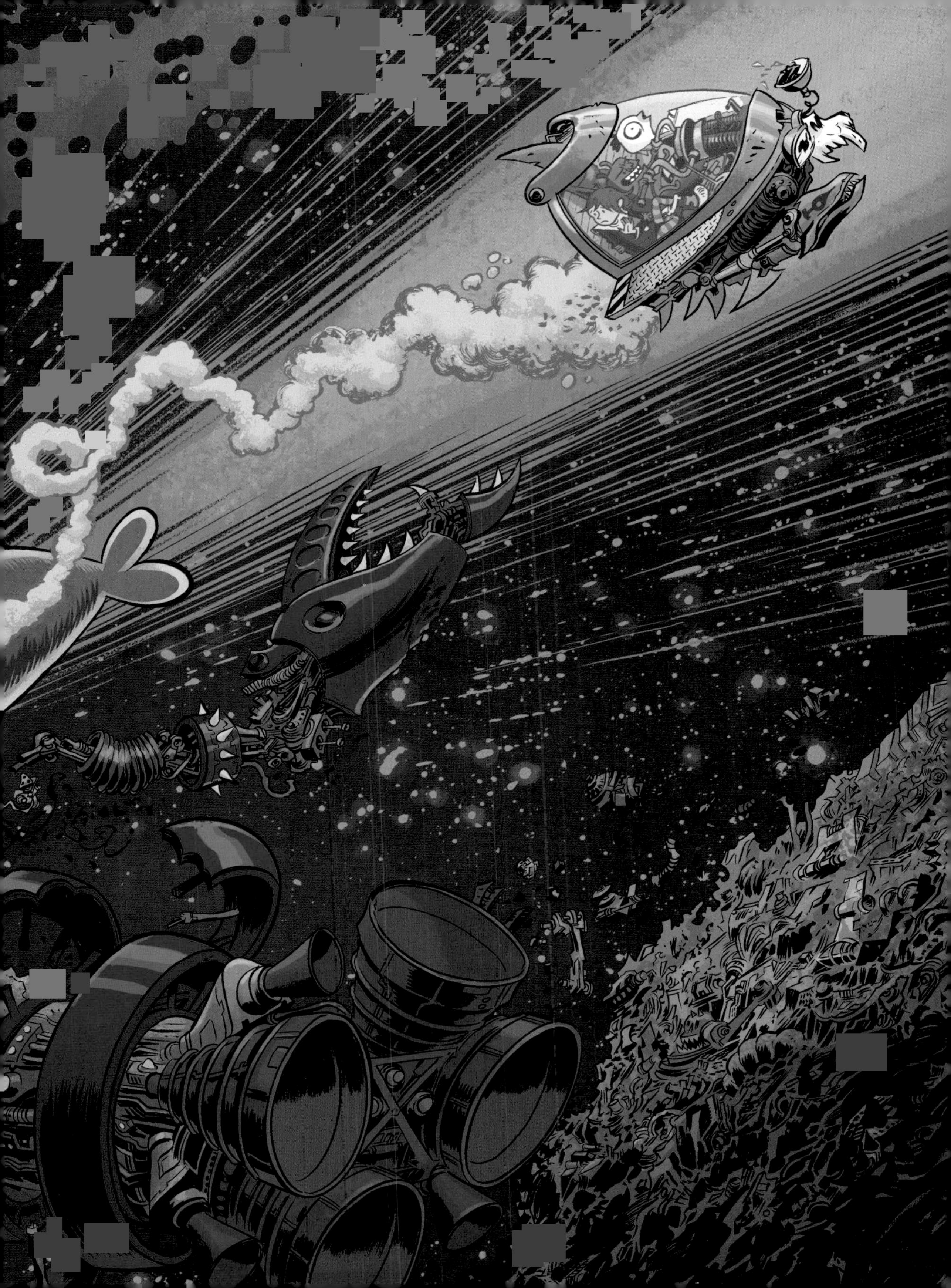

MAG/
GYRO
NAV

MAGNITUDES:

RUDDER

007

FIN OR FLUKE?

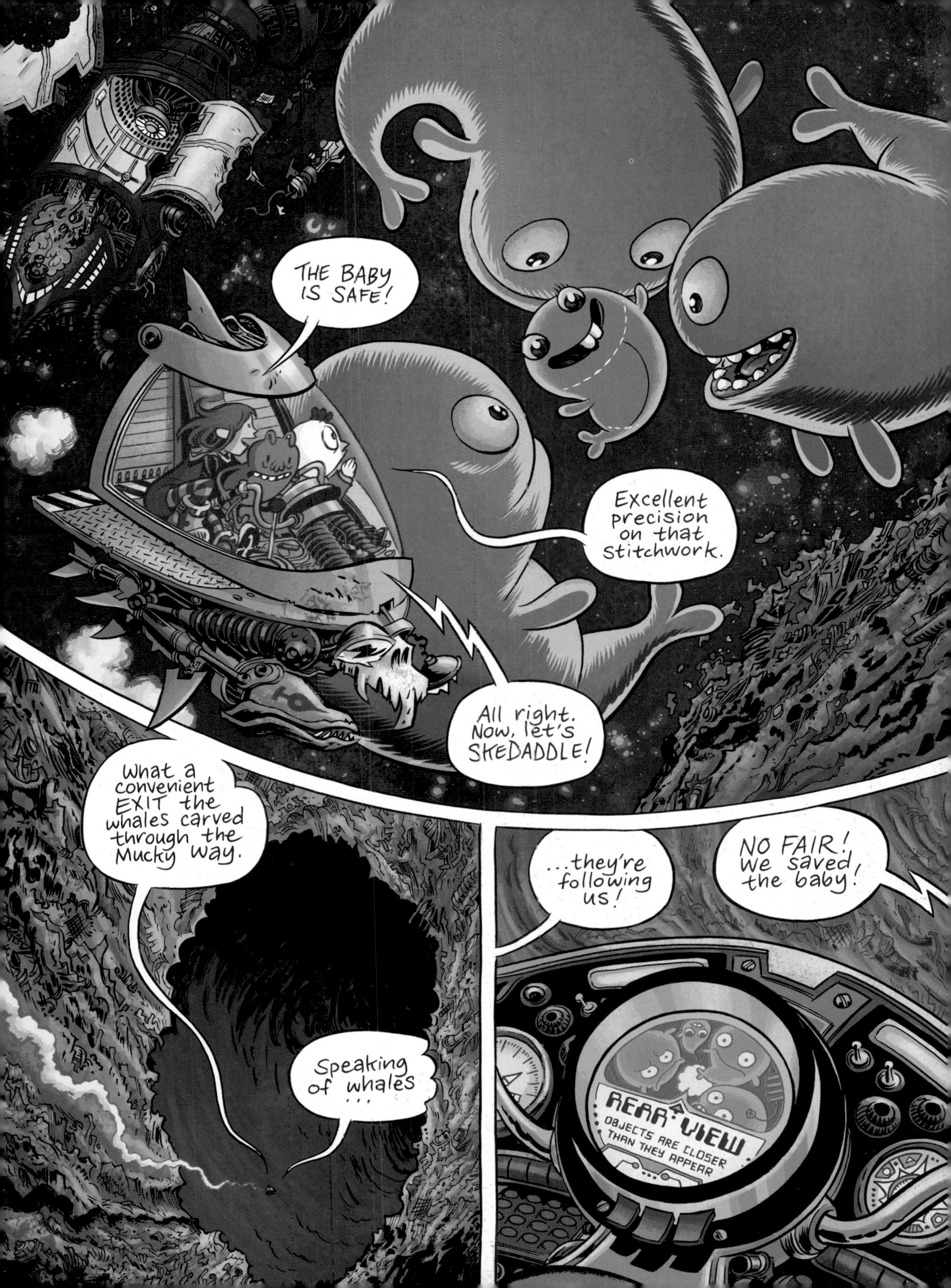
THE BABY IS SAFE!
Excellent precision on that stitchwork.
All right. Now, let's SKEDADDLE!
What a convenient EXIT the whales carved through the Mucky Way.
Speaking of whales . . .
. . . they're following us!
NO FAIR! We saved the baby!
REAR VIEW
OBJECTS ARE CLOSER THAN THEY APPEAR

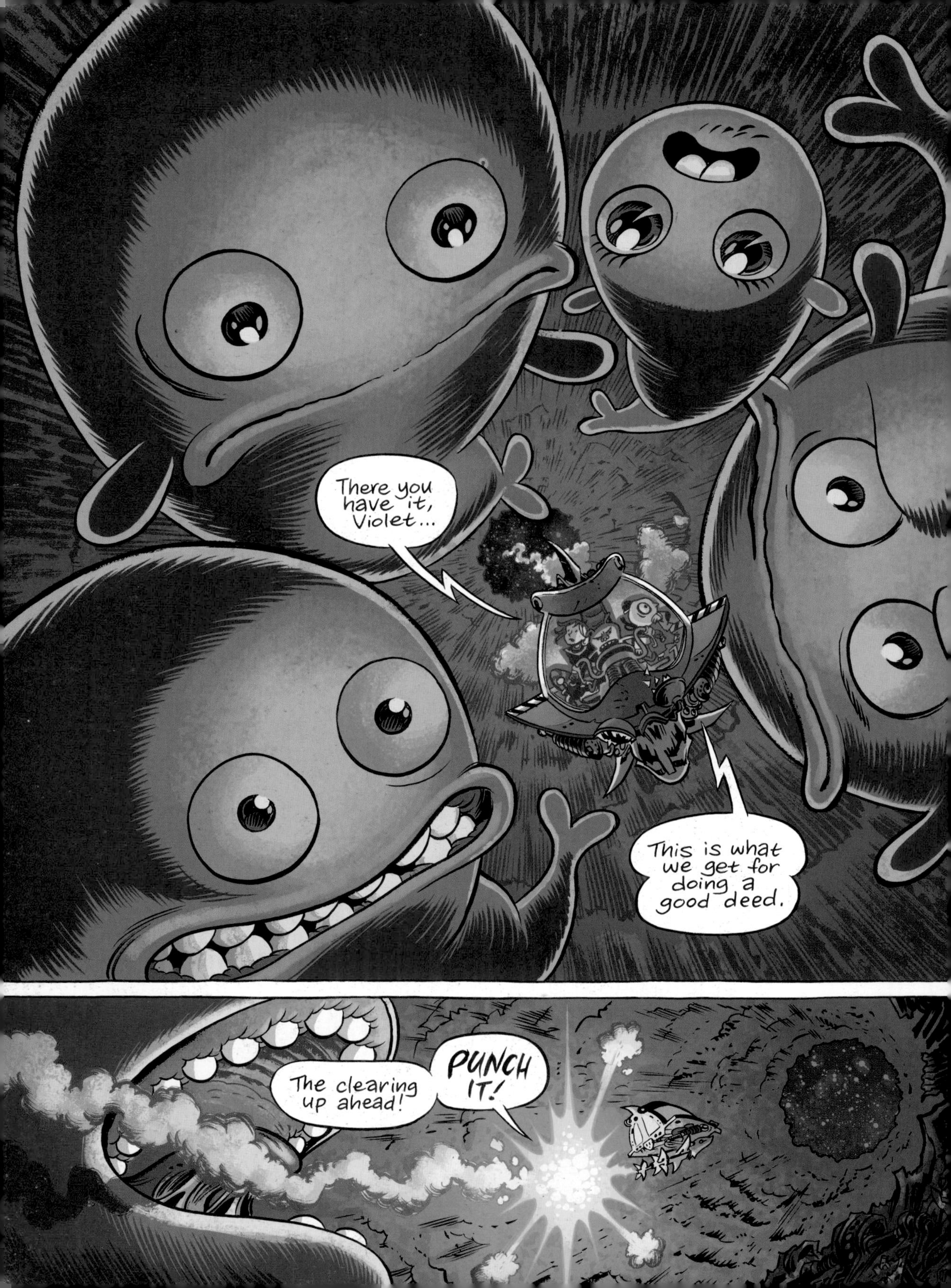
There you have it, Violet...
This is what we get for doing a good deed.
The clearing up ahead!
PUNCH IT!

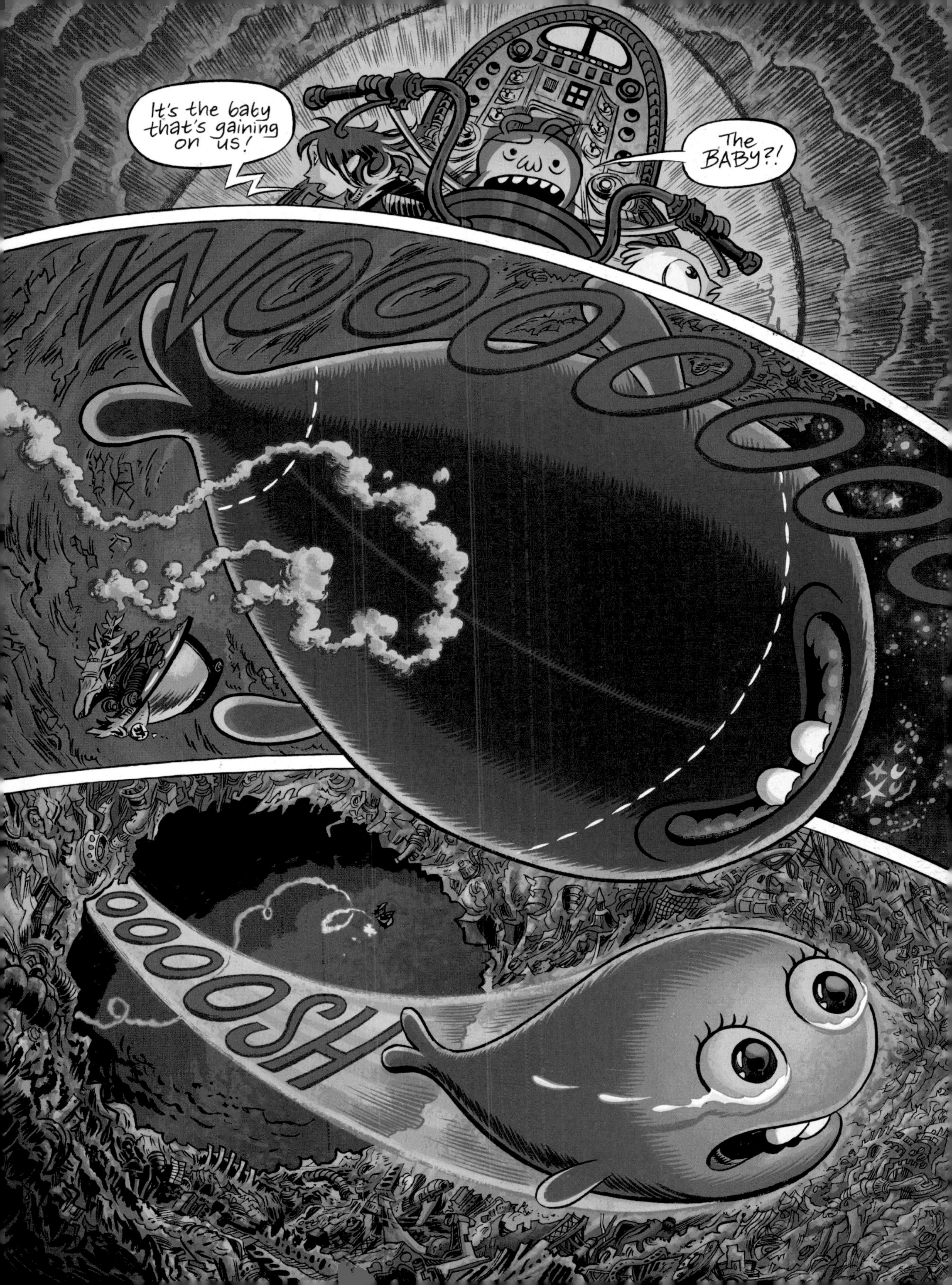
It's the baby that's gaining on us!
The BABY?!
WOOOOOOOOOOOOOOSH

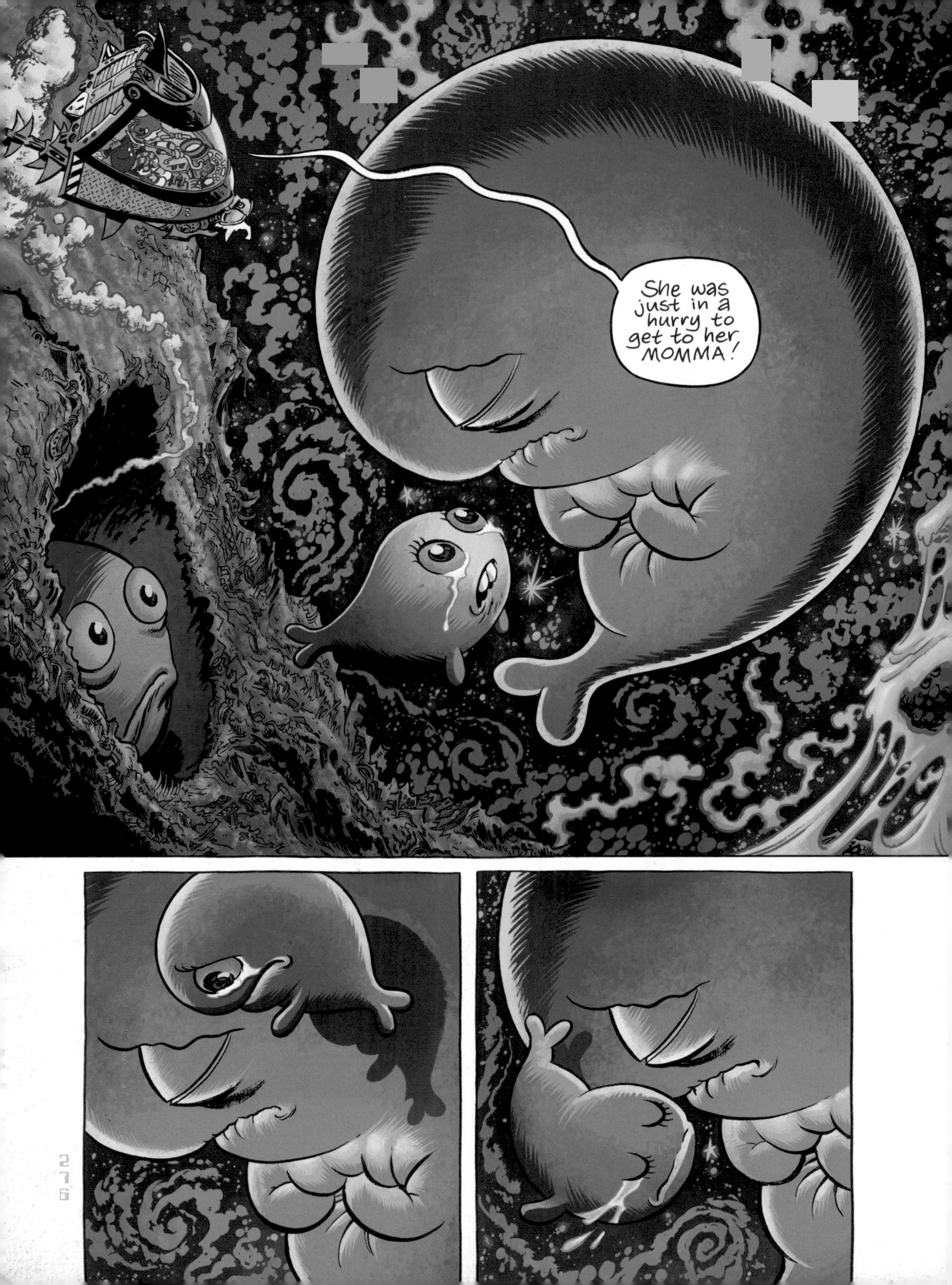
She was just in a hurry to get to her, MOMMA!

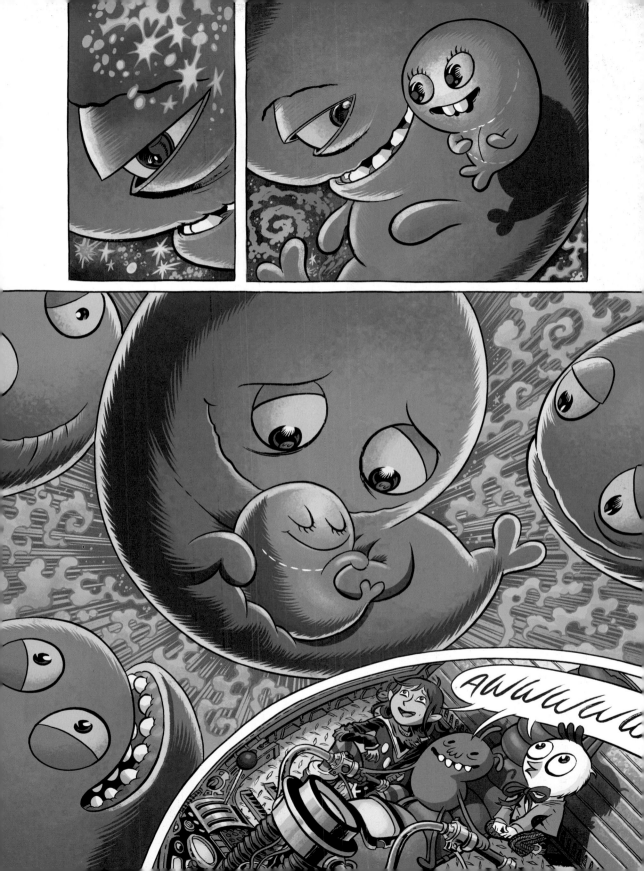

AWWWWW

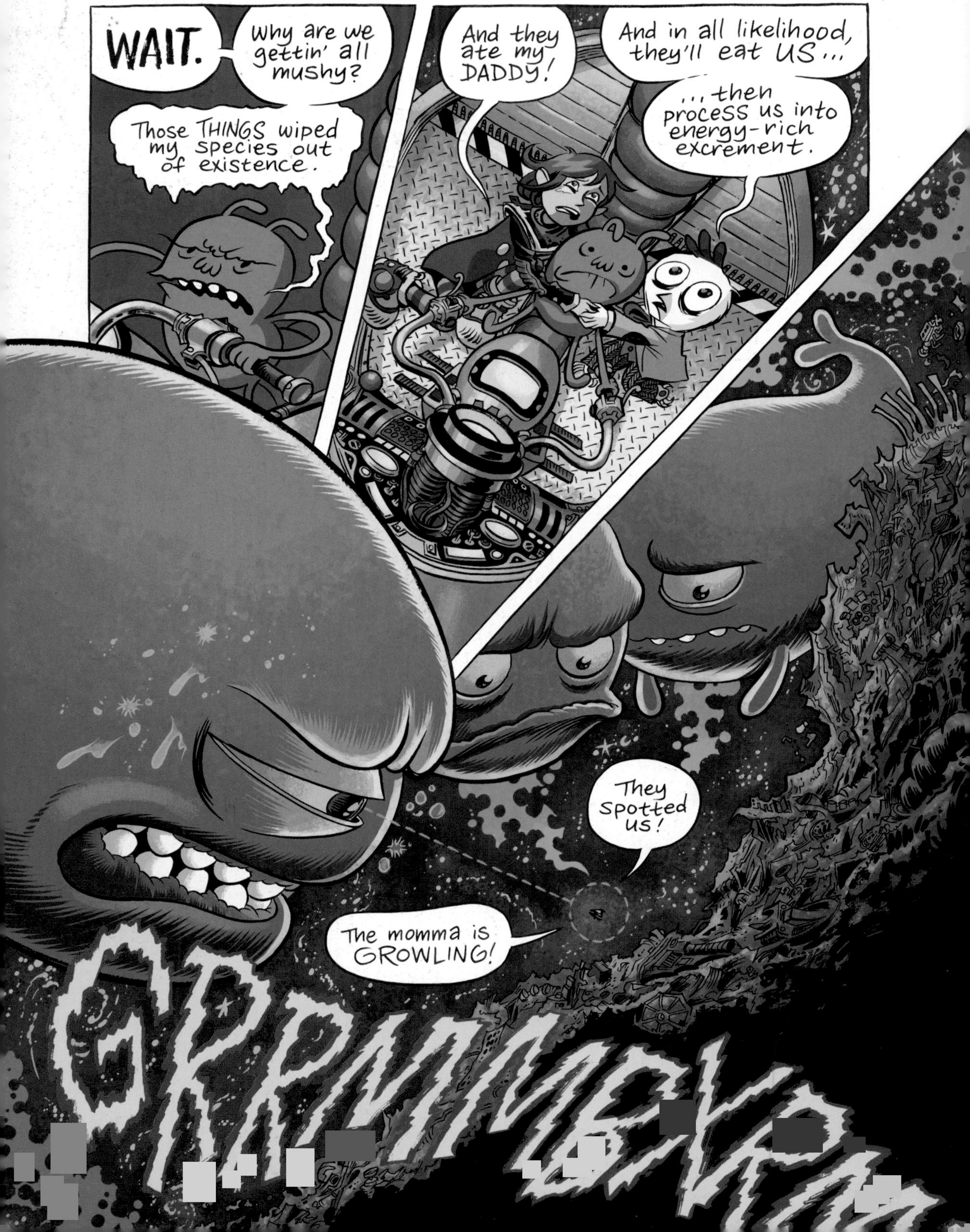
WAIT.
Why are we gettin' all mushy?
Those THINGS wiped my species out of existence.
And they ate my DADDY!
And in all likelihood, they'll eat US...
...then process us into energy-rich excrement.
They spotted us!
The momma is GROWLING!

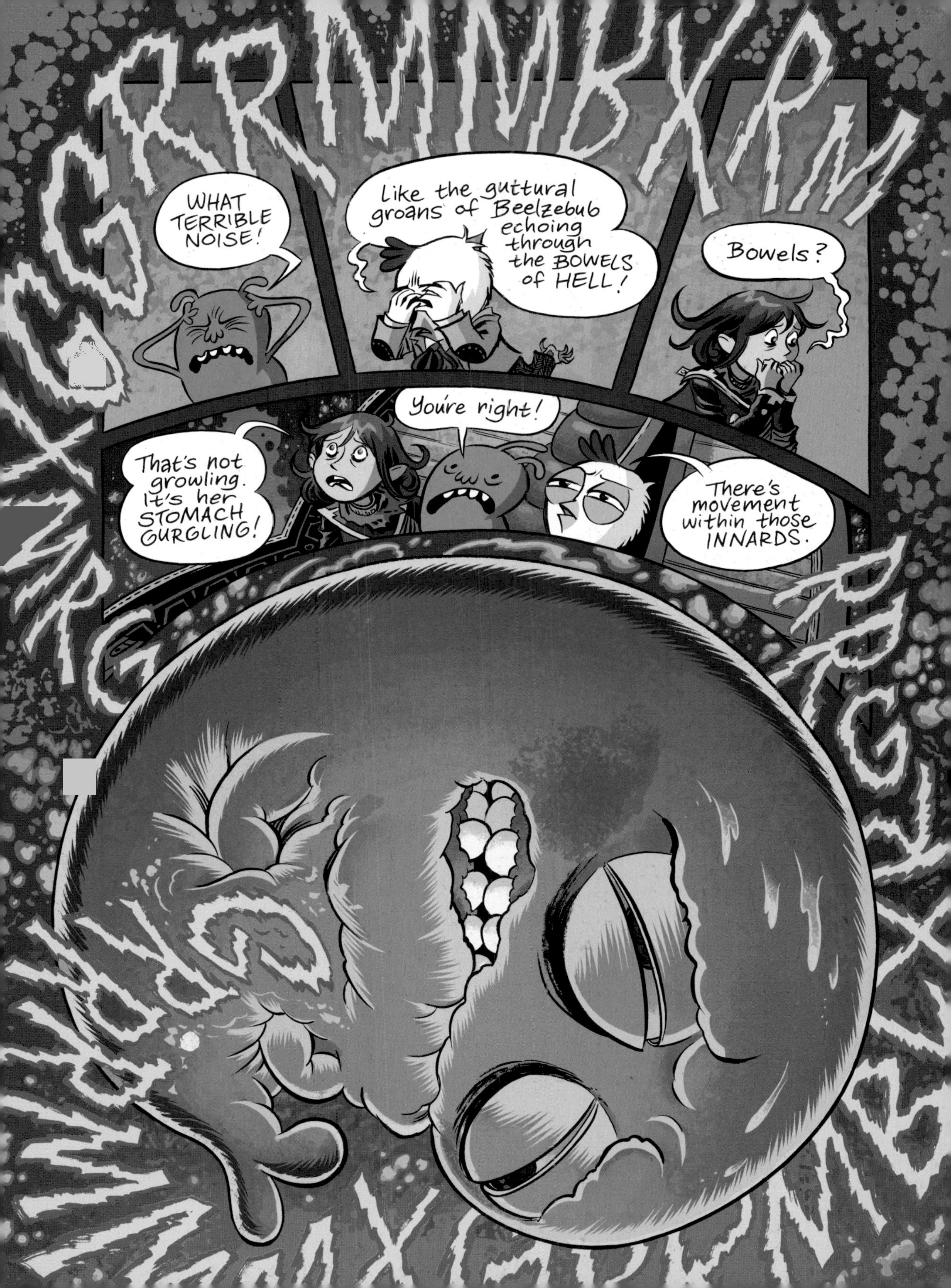
GRRMMBXRM
WHAT TERRIBLE NOISE!
Like the guttural groans of Beelzebub echoing through the BOWELS of HELL!
Bowels?
That's not growling. It's her STOMACH GURGLING!
You're right!
There's movement within those INNARDS.

BURP

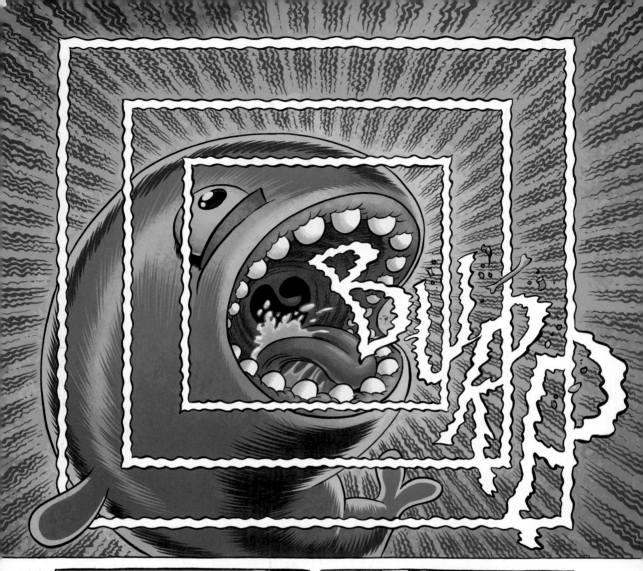

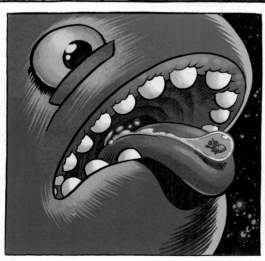

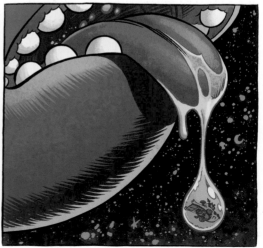

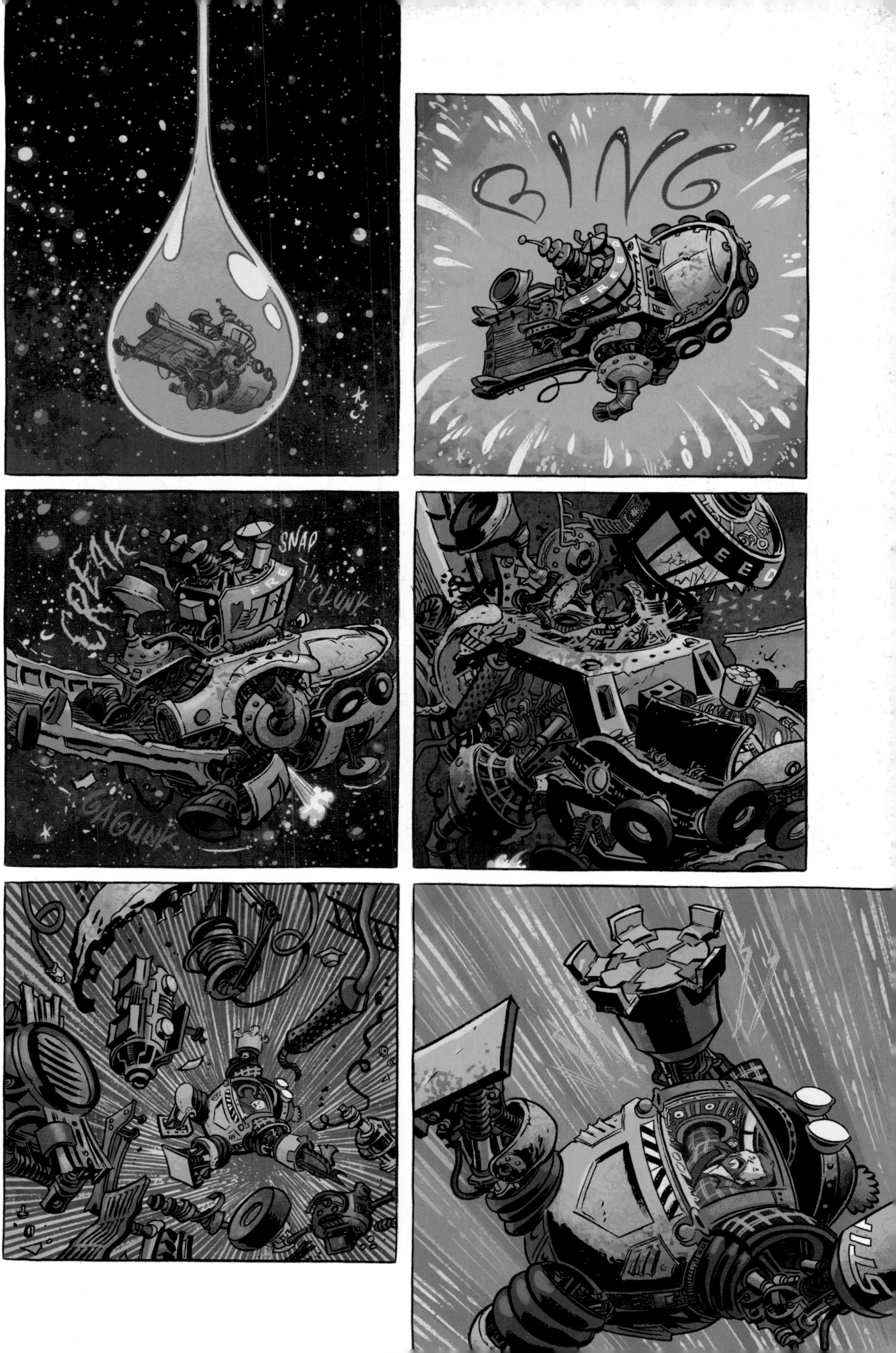
BING
FREED
CREAK
SNAP
CLUNK
GAGUNK
FREED

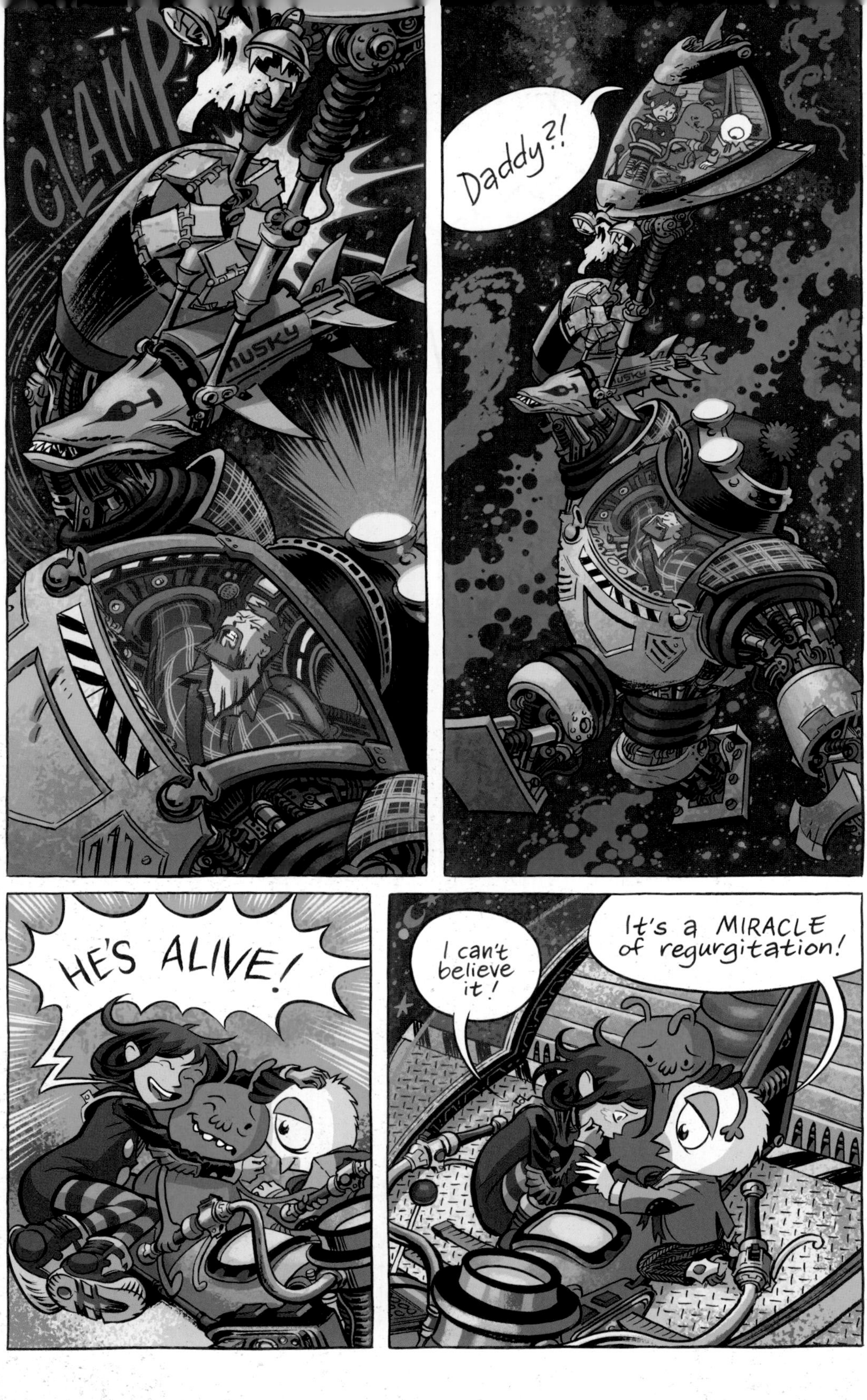
CLAMP!
MUSKY
Daddy?!
HE'S ALIVE!
I can't believe it!
It's a MIRACLE of regurgitation!

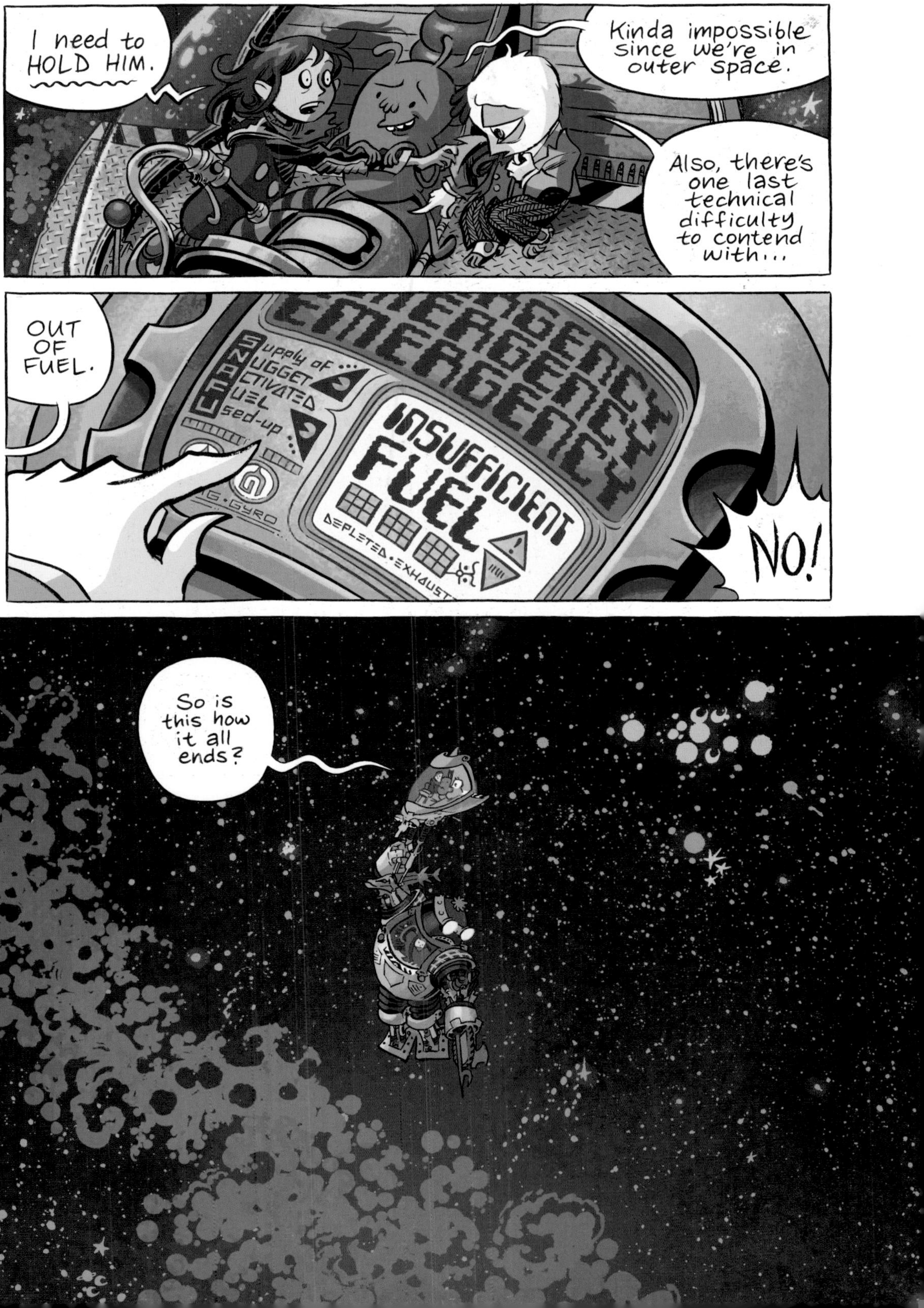
I need to HOLD HIM.
Kinda impossible since we're in outer space.
Also, there's one last technical difficulty to contend with...
OUT OF FUEL.
EMERGENCY
EMERGENCY
Supply of
Nugget
Activated
Fuel
Used-up
G.GYRO
INSUFFICIENT FUEL
DEPLETED • EXHAUST
NO!
So is this how it all ends?

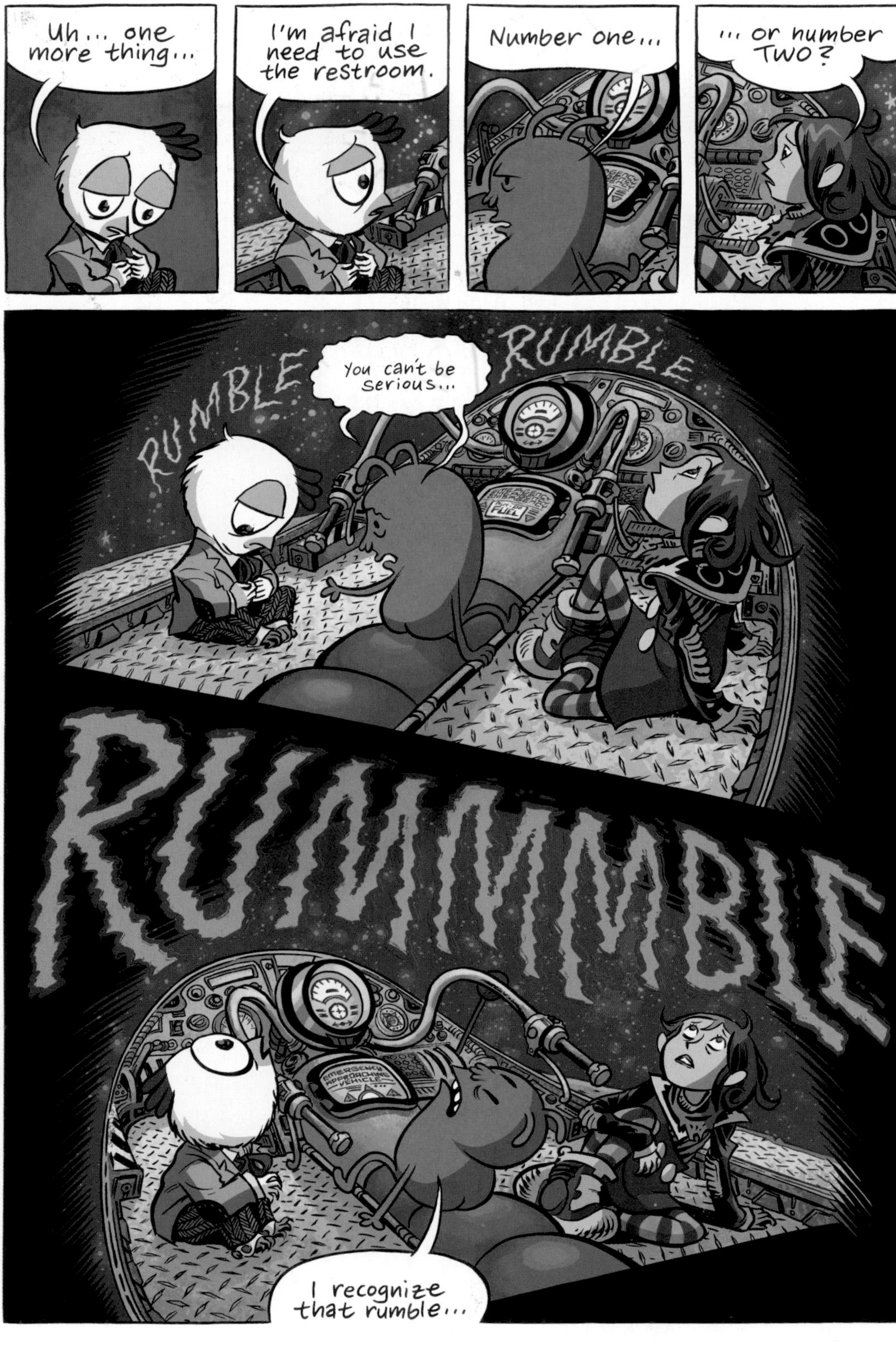
Uh... one more thing...
I'm afraid I need to use the restroom.
Number one...
... or number TWO?
RUMBLE
You can't be serious...
RUMBLE
RUMMMBLE
EMERGENCY APPROACHING VEHICLE
I recognize that rumble...

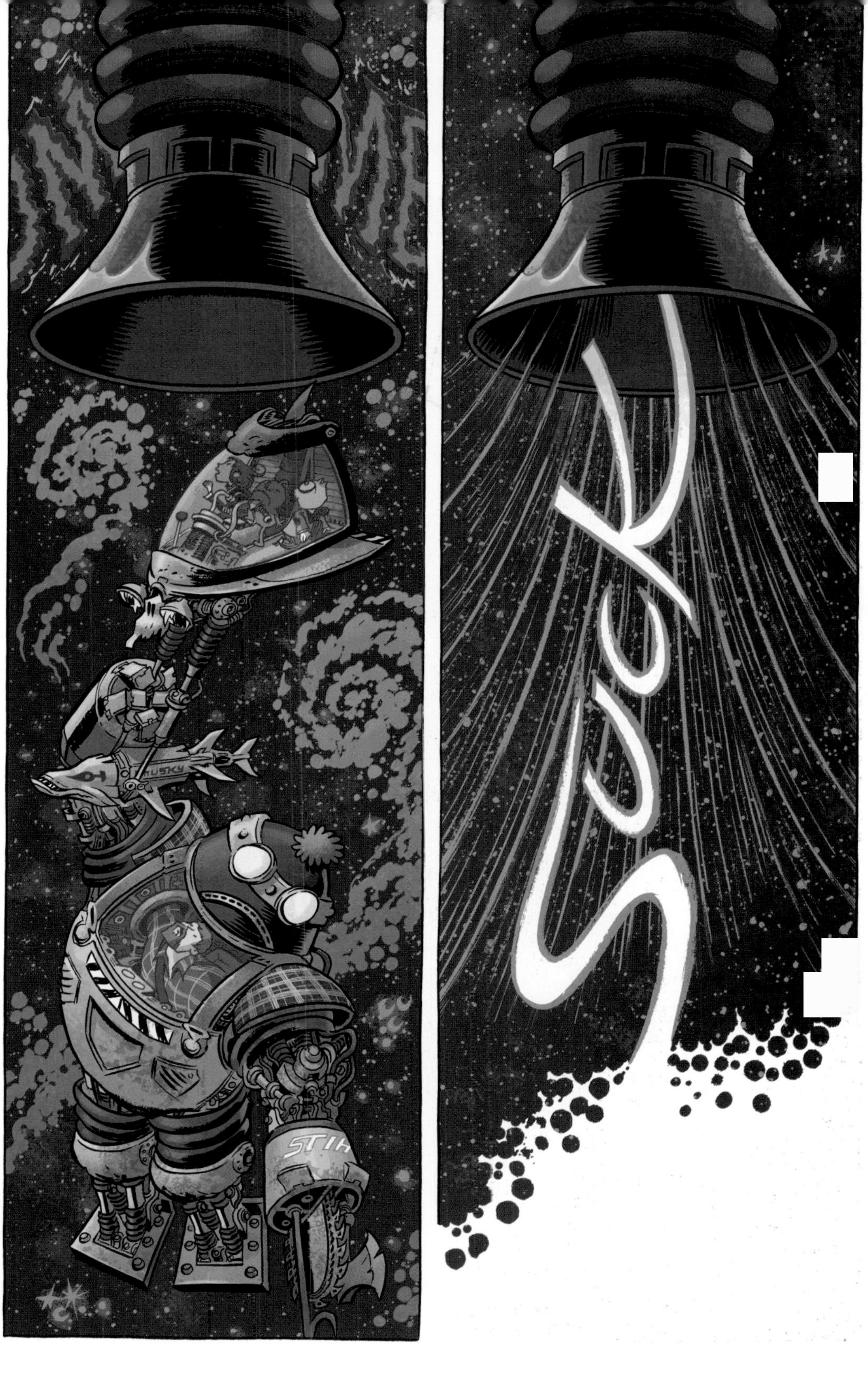
Suck
HUSKY

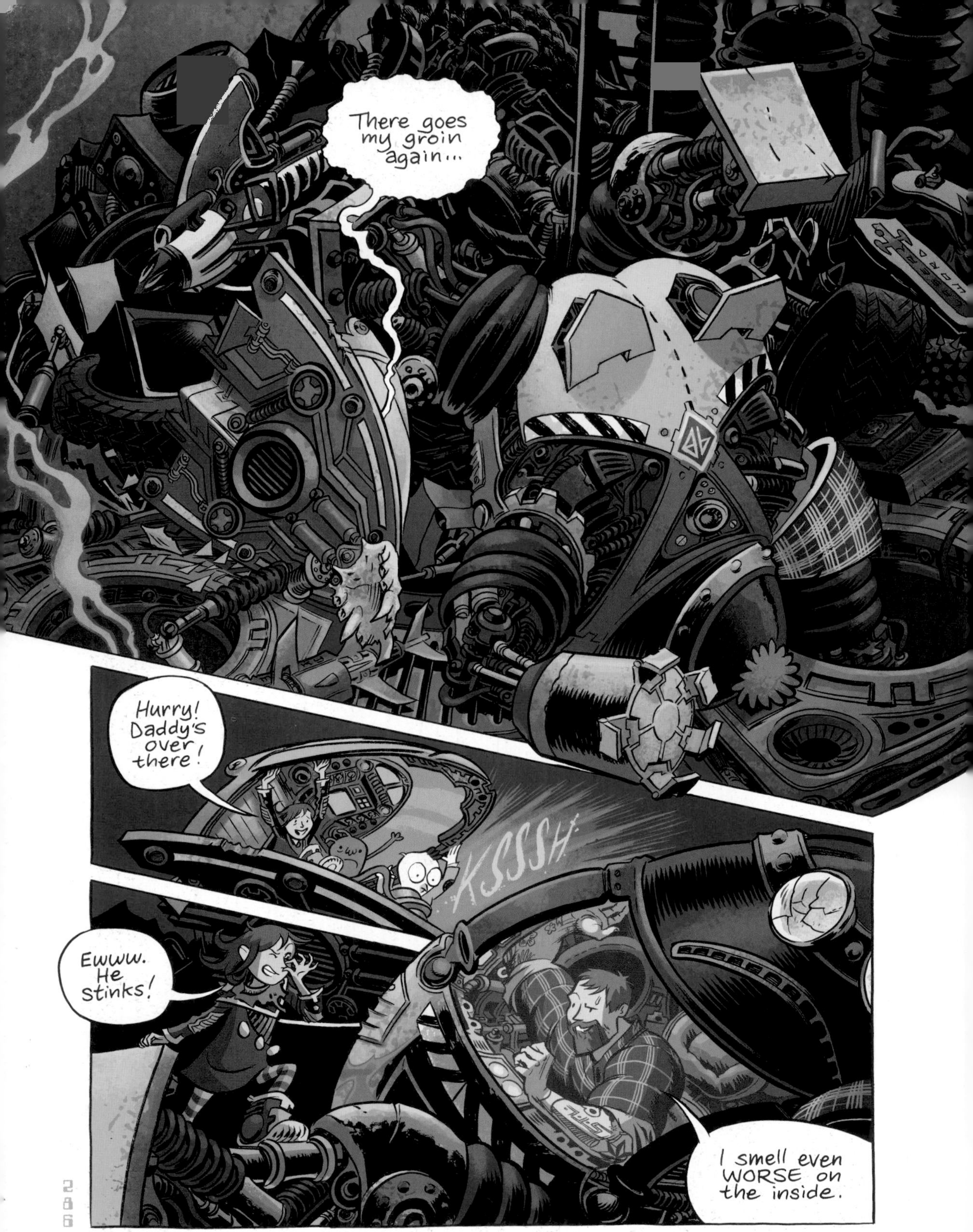
There goes my groin again...
Hurry! Daddy's over there!
KSSSH
Ewww. He stinks!
I smell even WORSE on the inside.

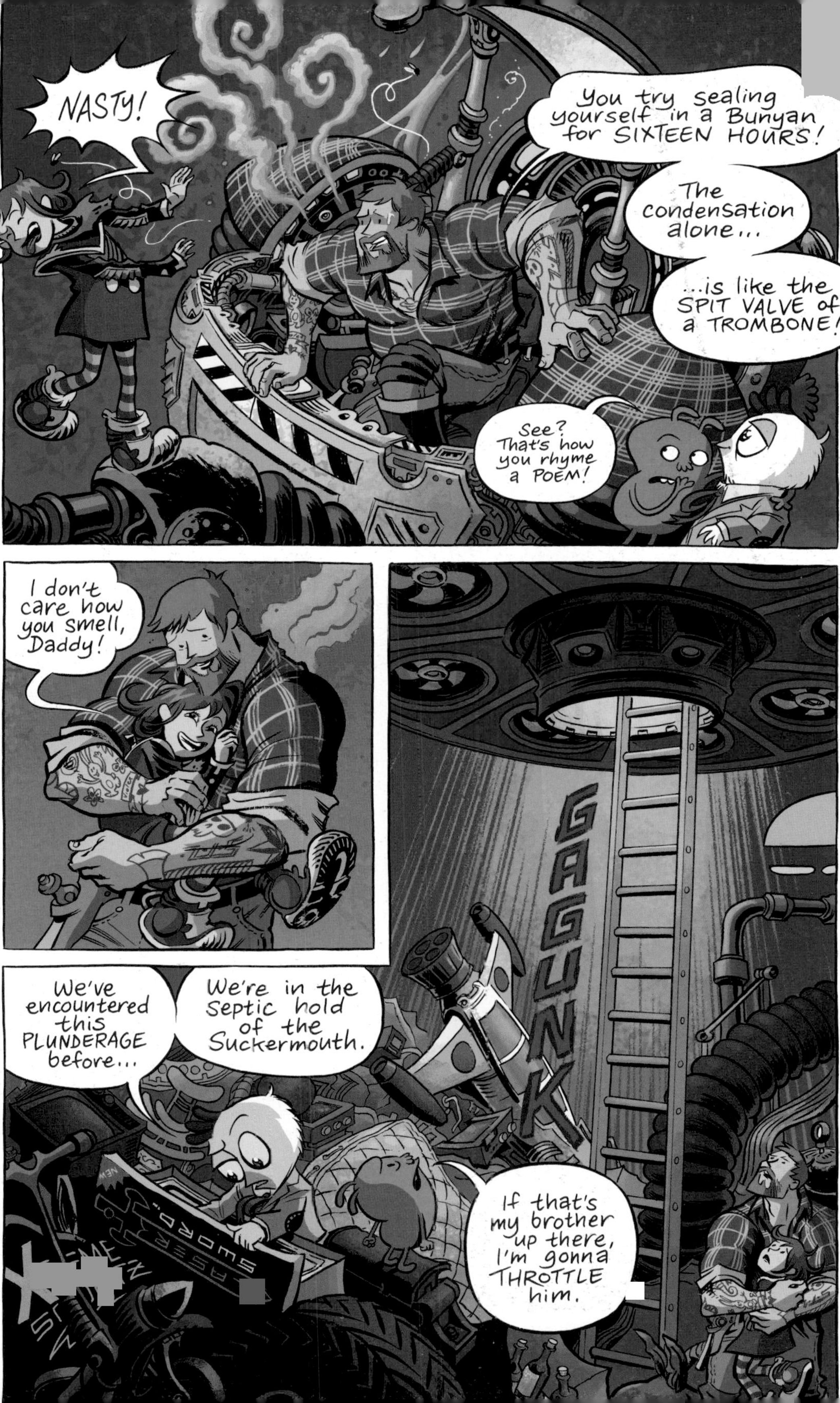
NASTY!
You try sealing yourself in a Bunyan for SIXTEEN HOURS!
The condensation alone...
...is like the SPIT VALVE of a TROMBONE!
See? That's how you rhyme a POEM!
I don't care how you smell, Daddy!
We've encountered this PLUNDERAGE before...
We're in the Septic hold of the Suckermouth.
GAGUNK
If that's my brother up there, I'm gonna THROTTLE him.

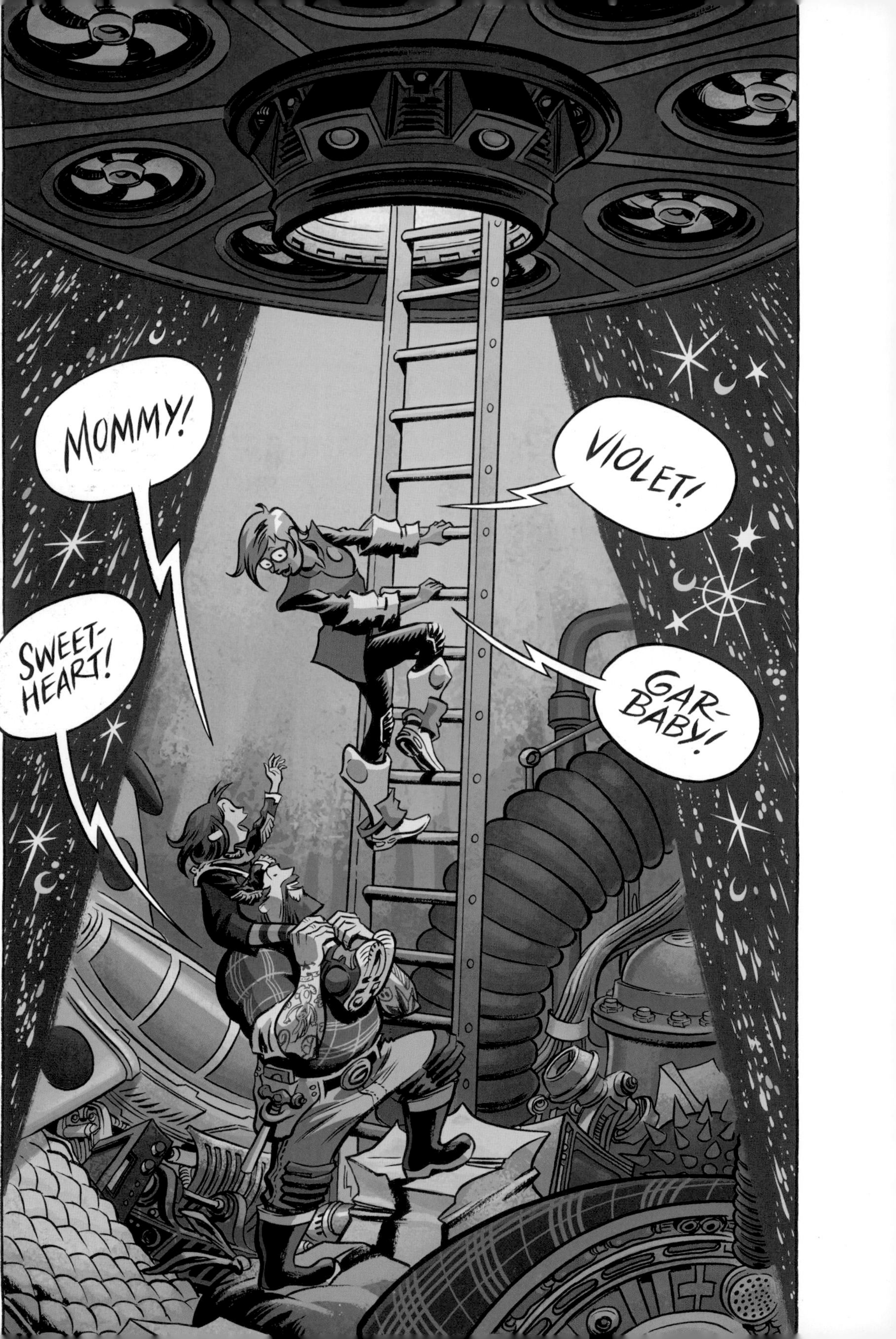
MOMMY!
VIOLET!
SWEET-HEART!
GAR-BABY!

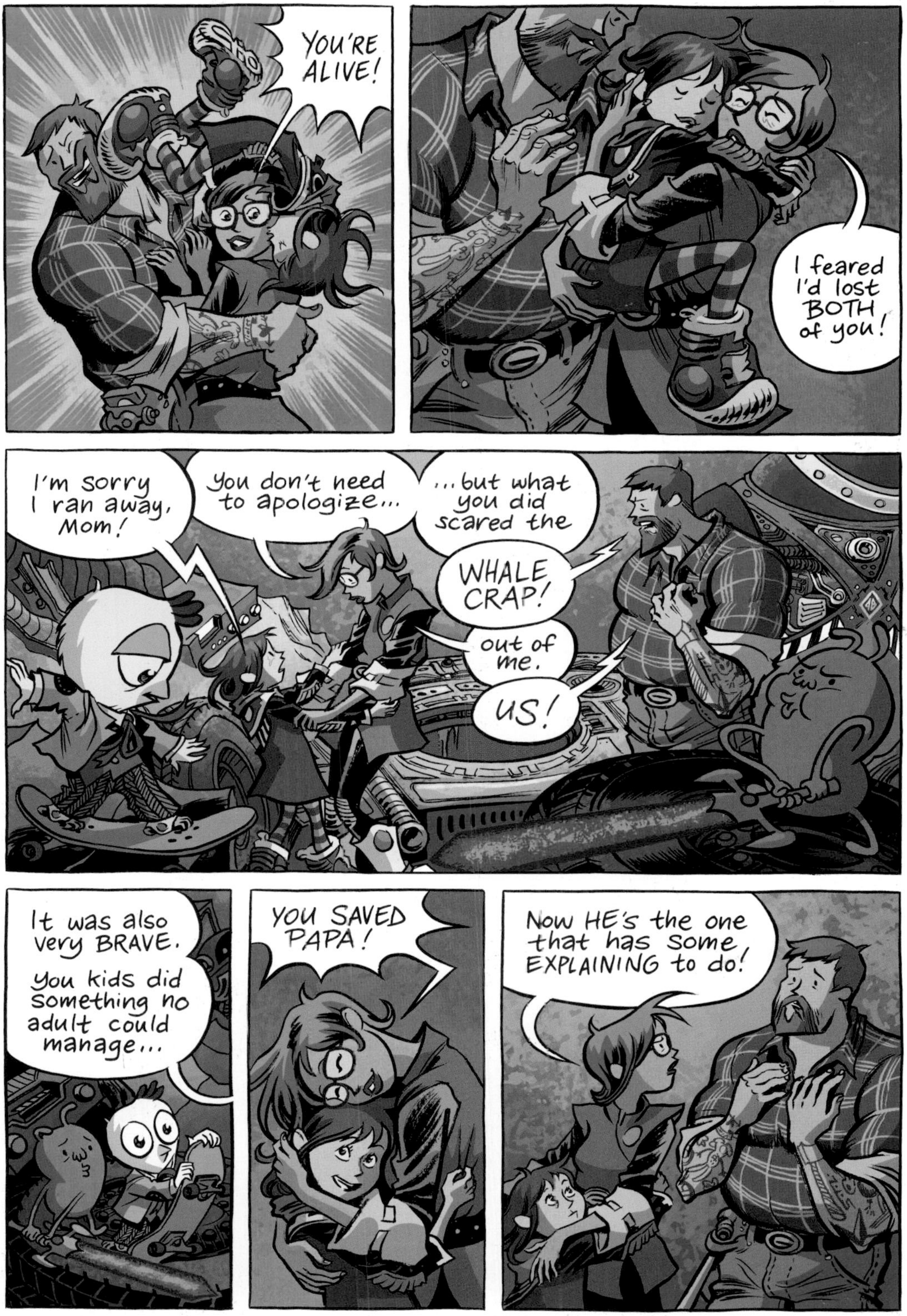

YOU'RE ALIVE!
I feared I'd lost BOTH of you!
I'm sorry I ran away, Mom!
You don't need to apologize...
...but what you did scared the
WHALE CRAP!
out of me.
US!
It was also very BRAVE.
You kids did something no adult could manage...
YOU SAVED PAPA!
Now HE's the one that has some EXPLAINING to do!

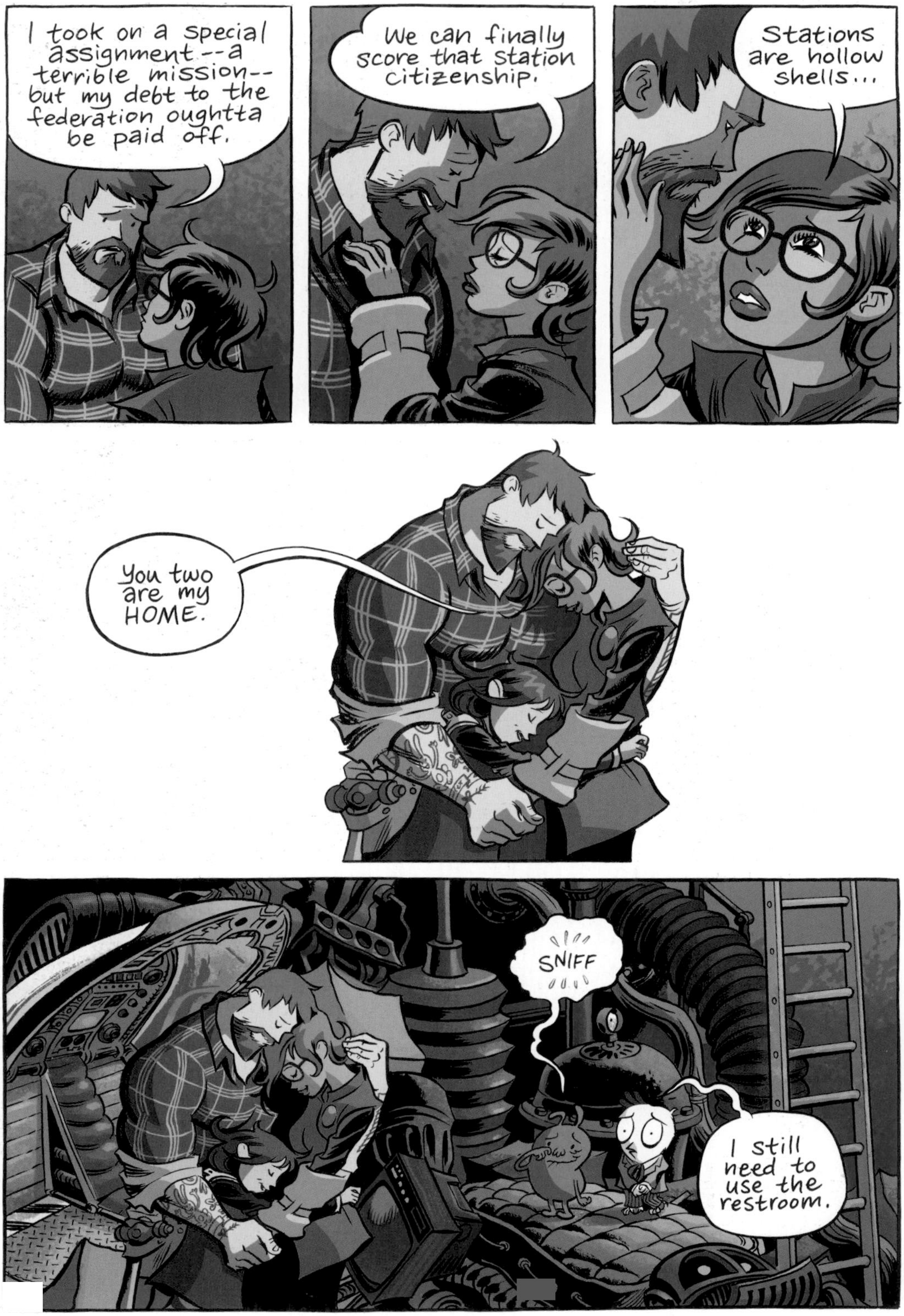
I took on a special assignment --a terrible mission-- but my debt to the federation oughtta be paid off.
We can finally score that station citizenship.
Stations are hollow shells...
You two are my HOME.
SNIFF
I still need to use the restroom.

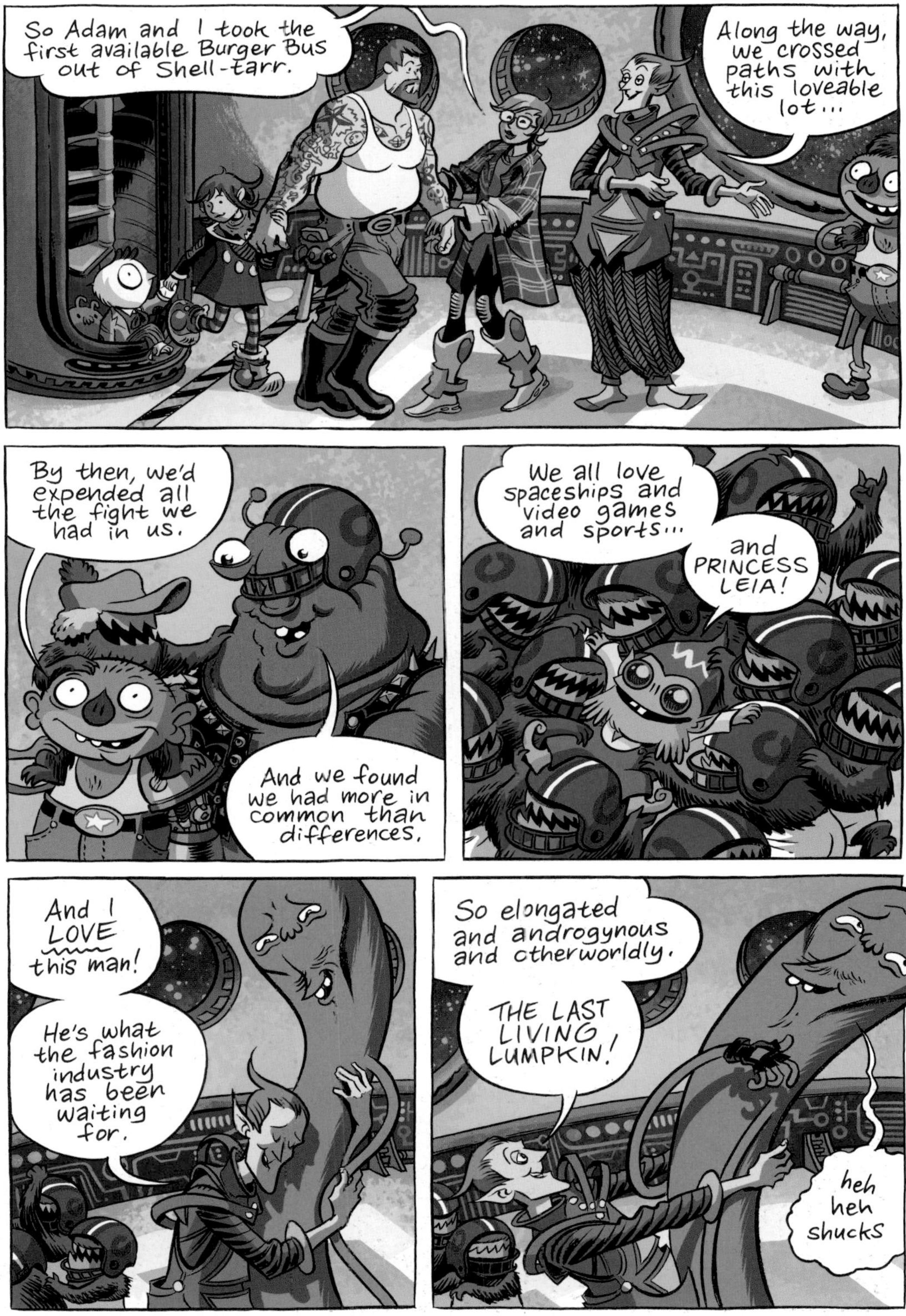

So Adam and I took the first available Burger Bus out of Shell-tarr.
Along the way, we crossed paths with this loveable lot...
By then, we'd expended all the fight we had in us.
And we found we had more in common than differences.
We all love spaceships and video games and sports...
and PRINCESS LEIA!
And I LOVE this man!
He's what the fashion industry has been waiting for.
So elongated and androgynous and otherworldly.
THE LAST LIVING LUMPKIN!
heh heh shucks

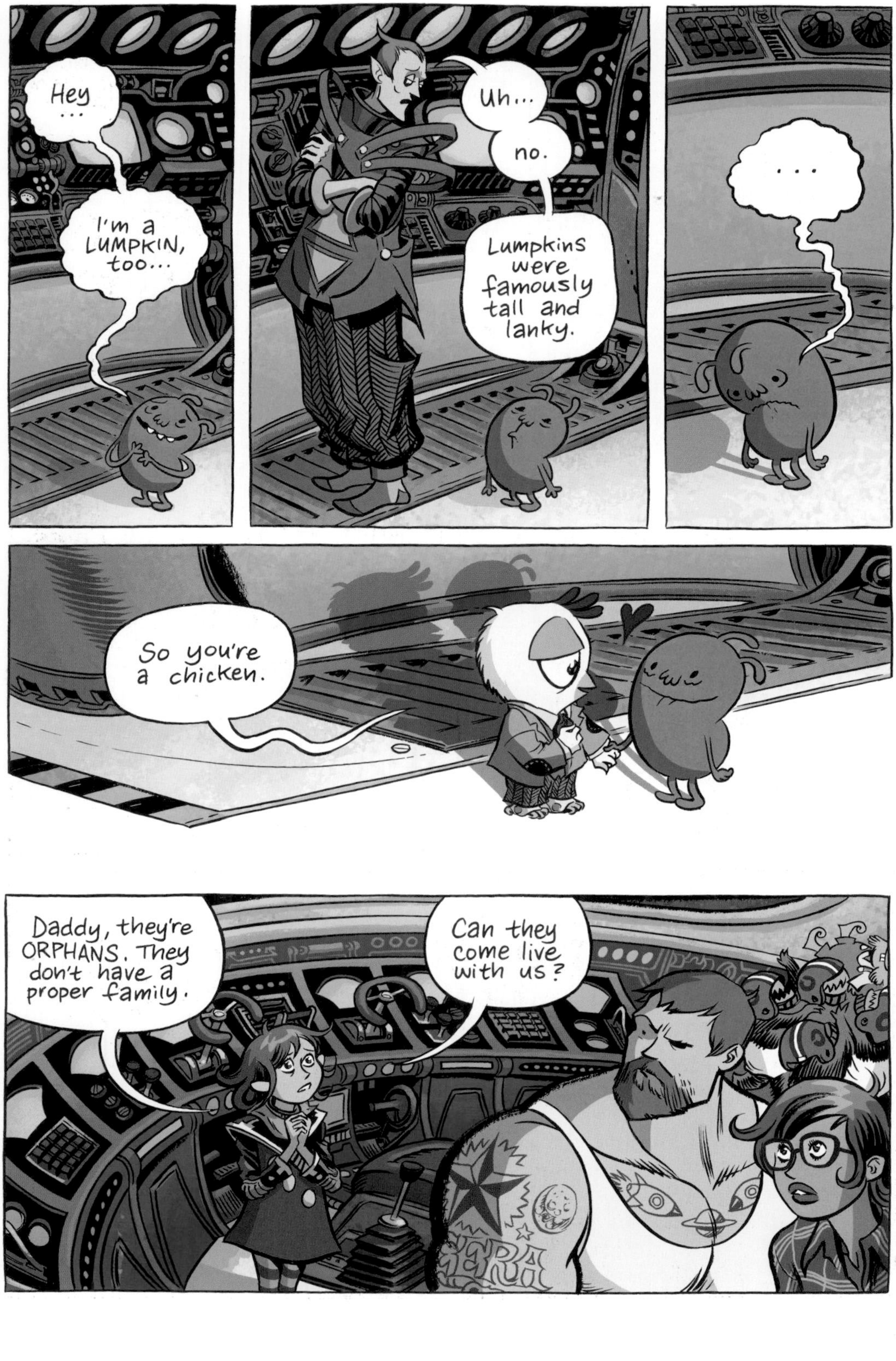
Hey ...
I'm a LUMPKIN, too...
Uh...
no.
Lumpkins were famously tall and lanky.
. . .
So you're a chicken.
Daddy, they're ORPHANS. They don't have a proper family.
Can they come live with us?

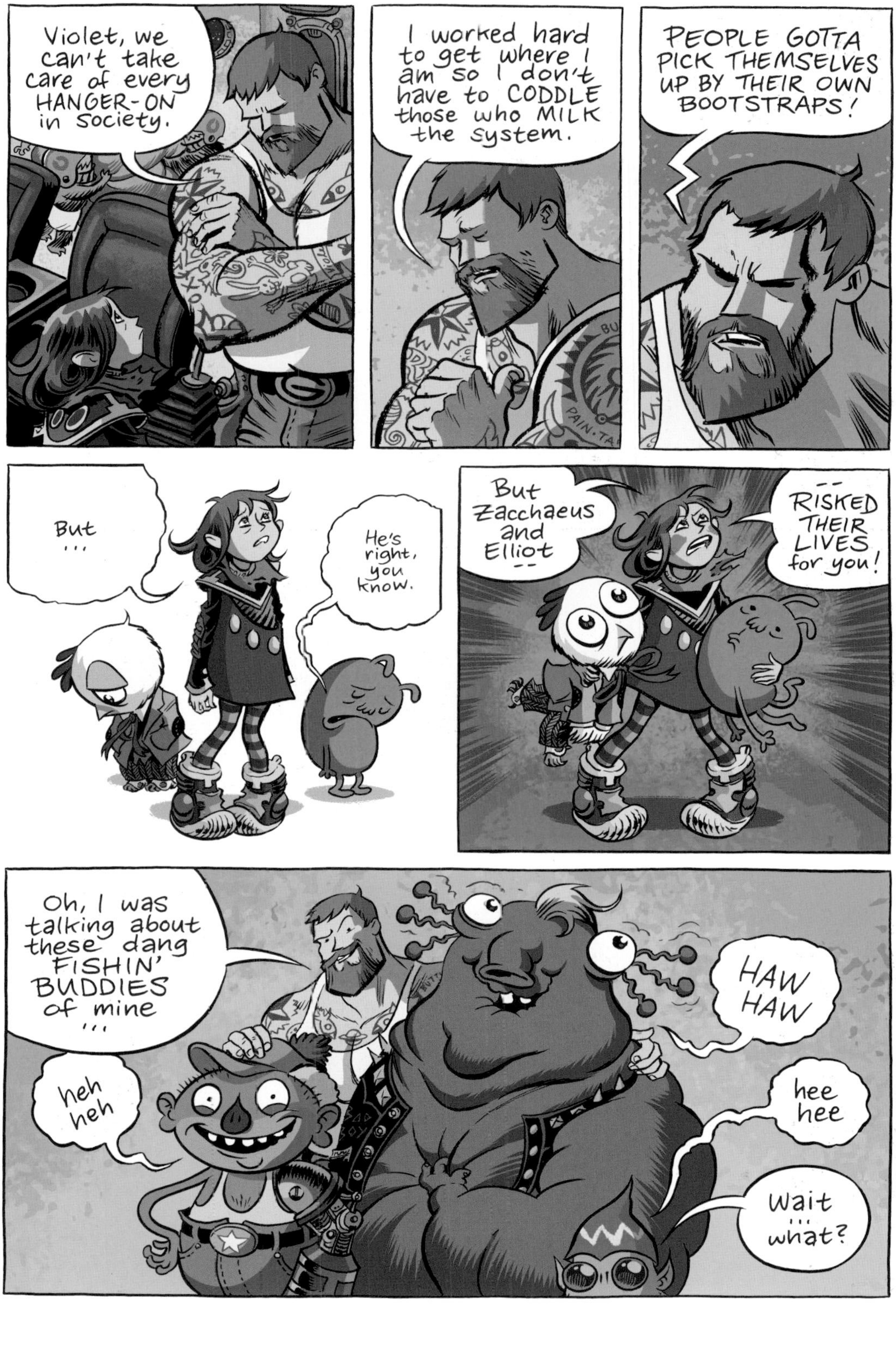
Violet, we can't take care of every HANGER-ON in society.
I worked hard to get where I am so I don't have to CODDLE those who MILK the system.
PEOPLE GOTTA PICK THEMSELVES UP BY THEIR OWN BOOTSTRAPS!
But ...
He's right, you know.
But Zacchaeus and Elliot --
-- RISKED THEIR LIVES for you!
Oh, I was talking about these dang FISHIN' BUDDIES of mine ...
HAW HAW
heh heh
hee hee
Wait ... what?

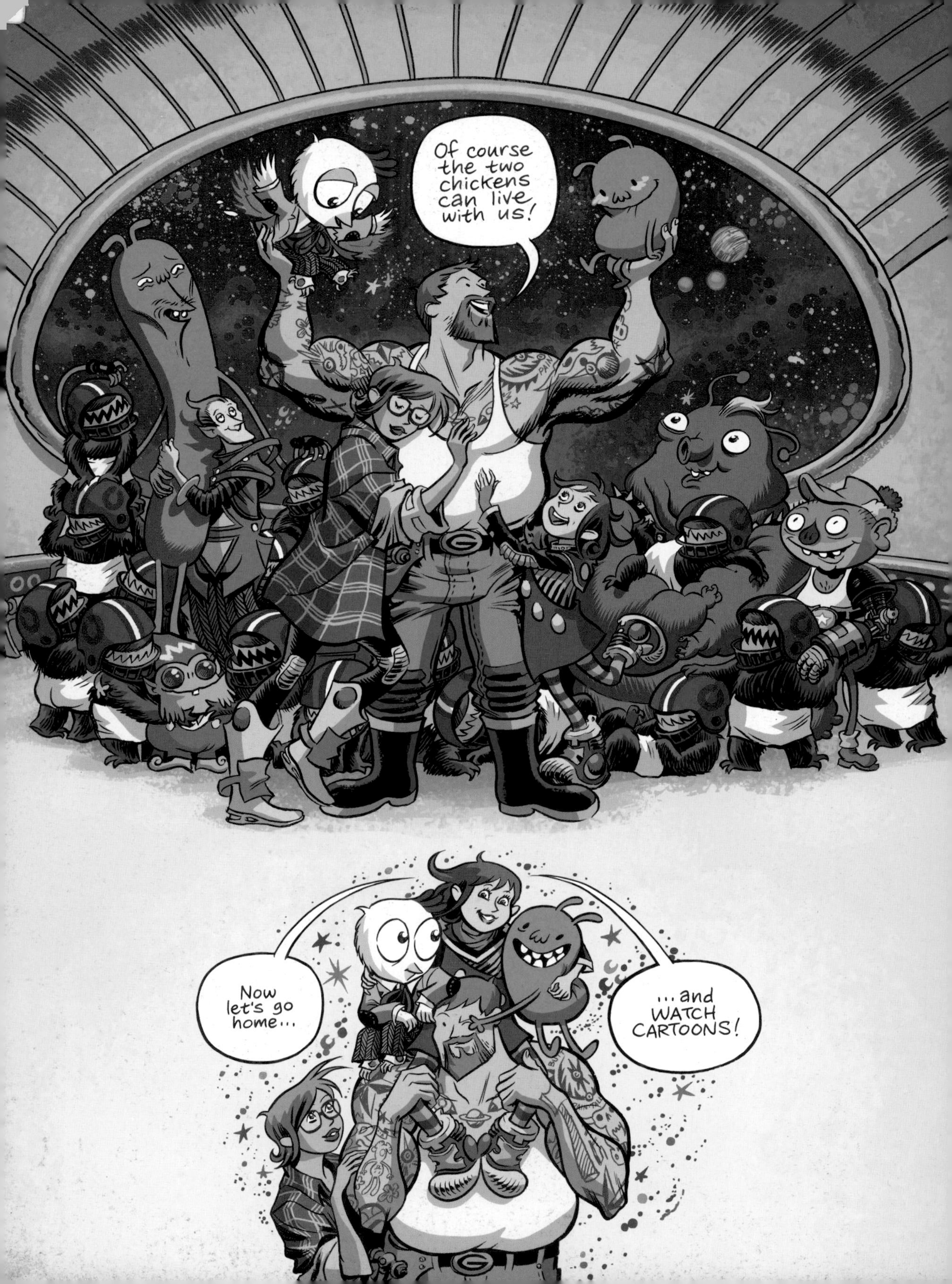
Of course the two chickens can live with us!
Now let's go home...
...and WATCH CARTOONS!

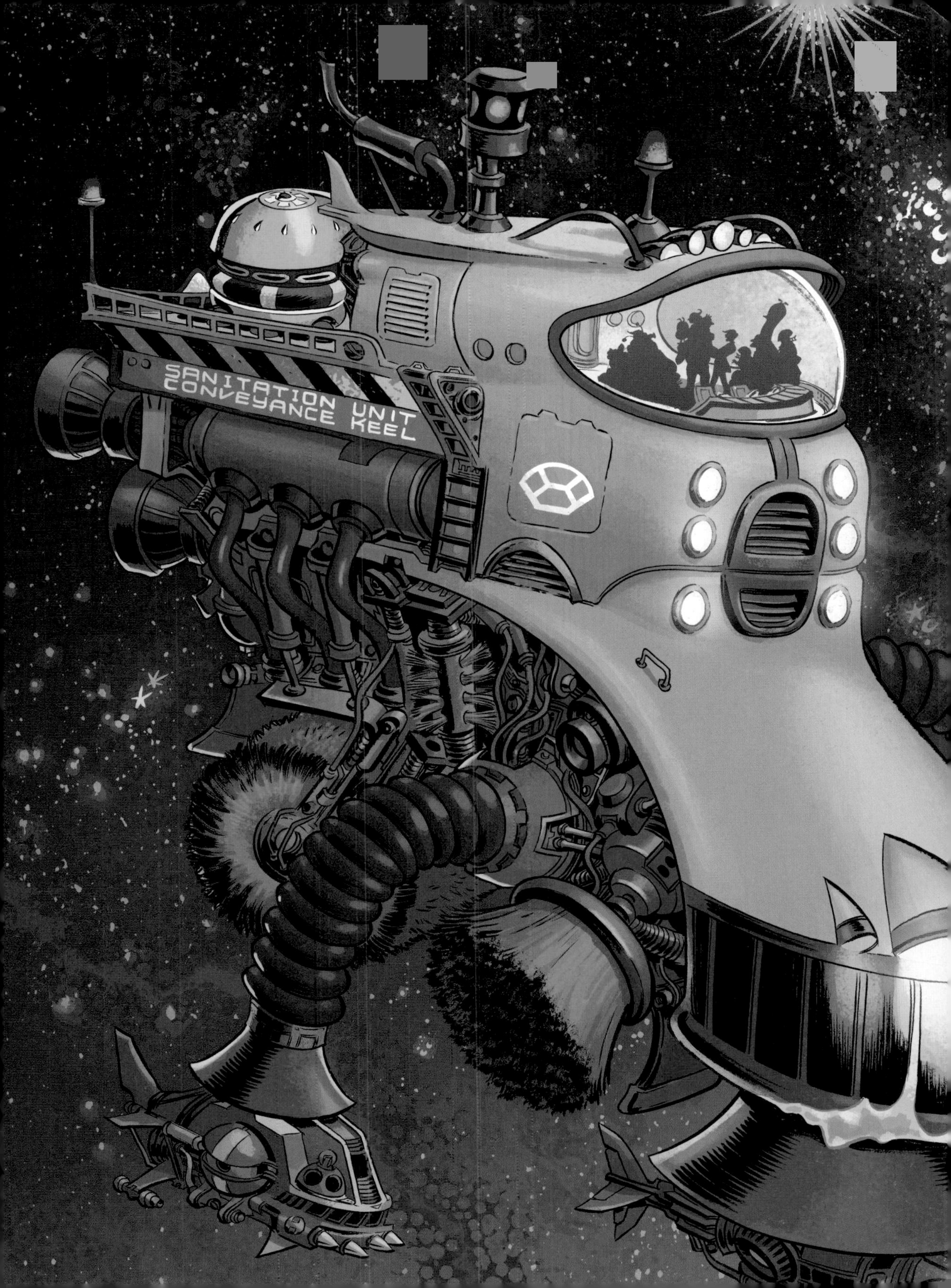
SANITATION UNIT
CONVEYANCE KEEL

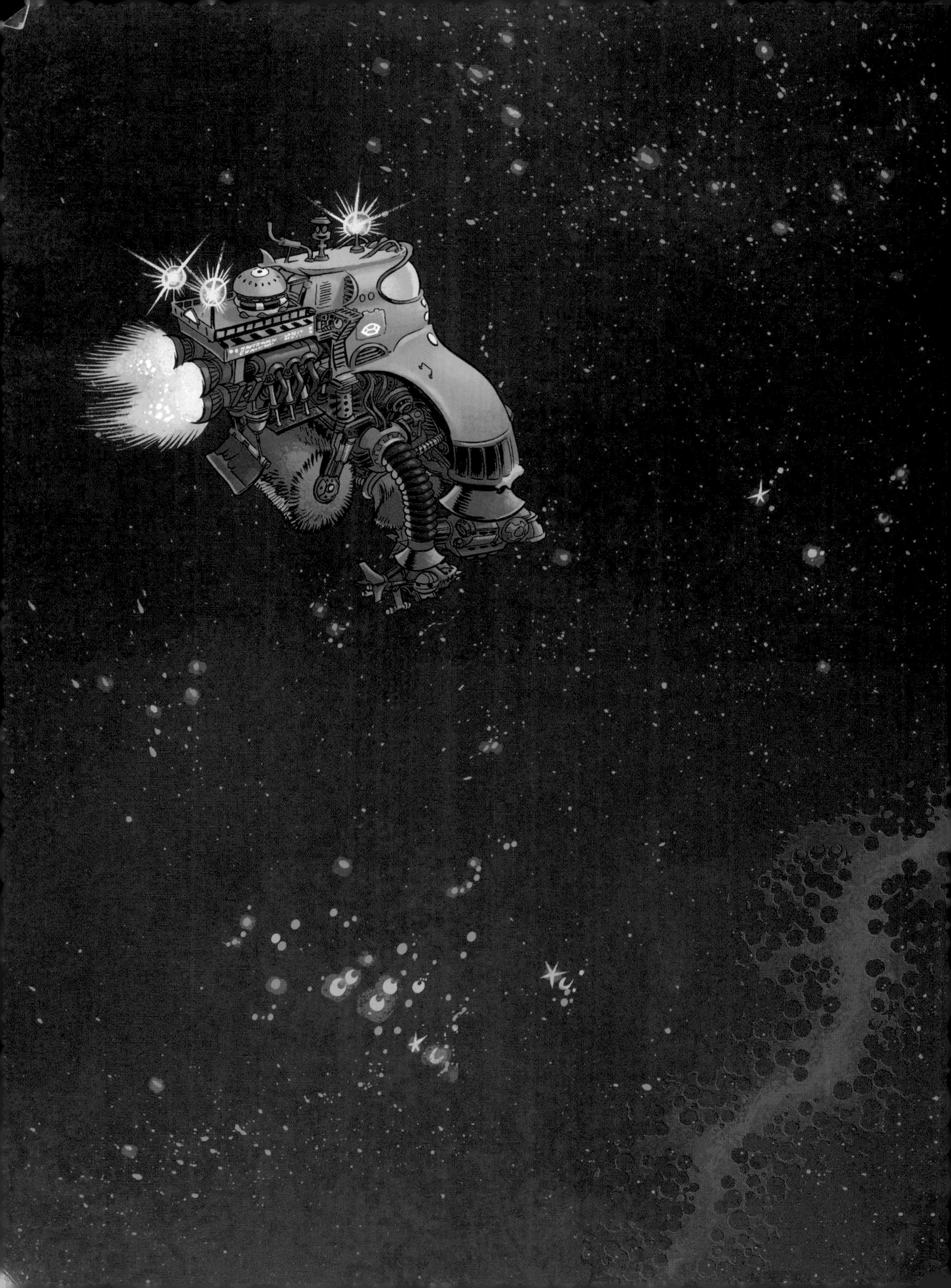

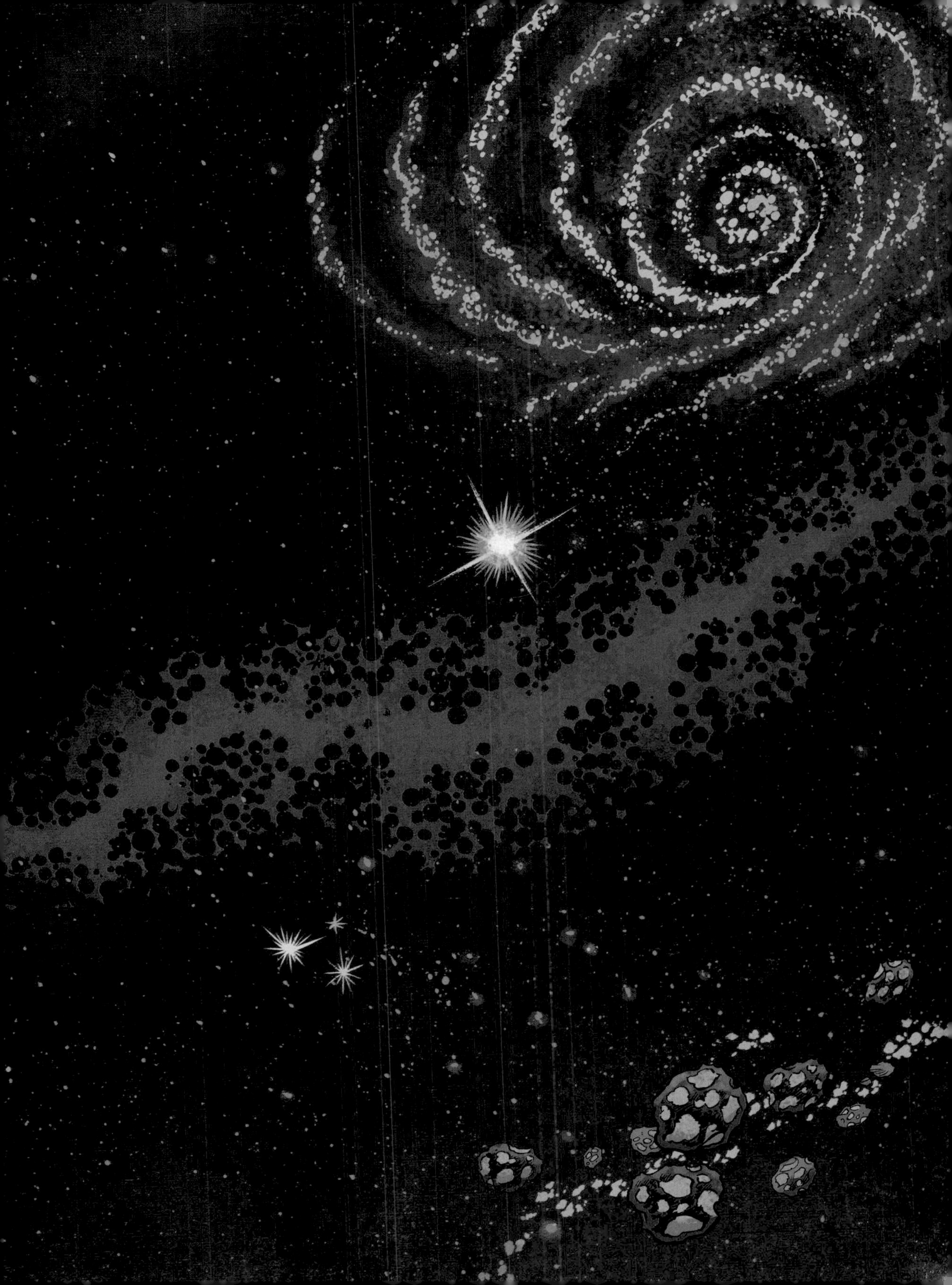

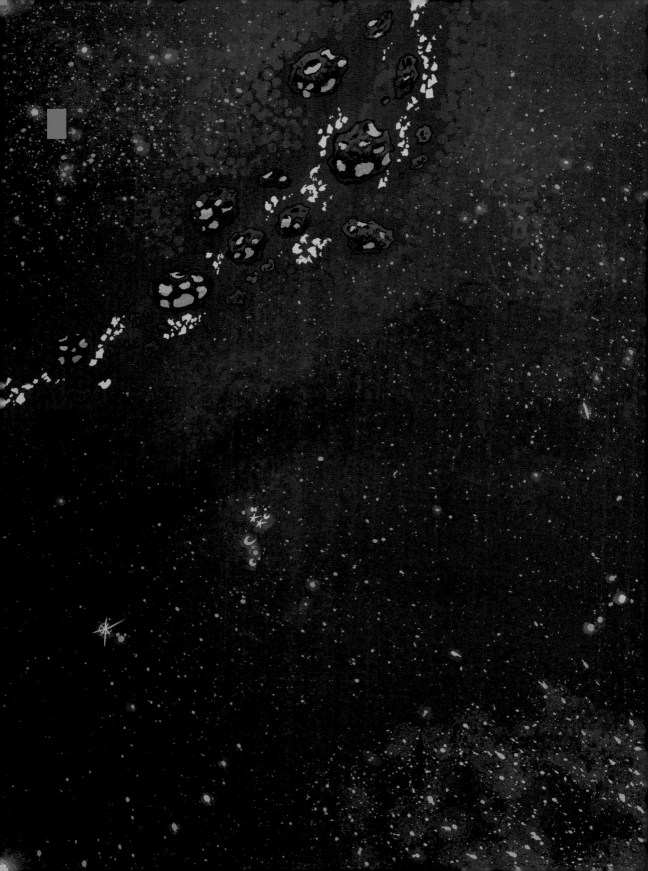

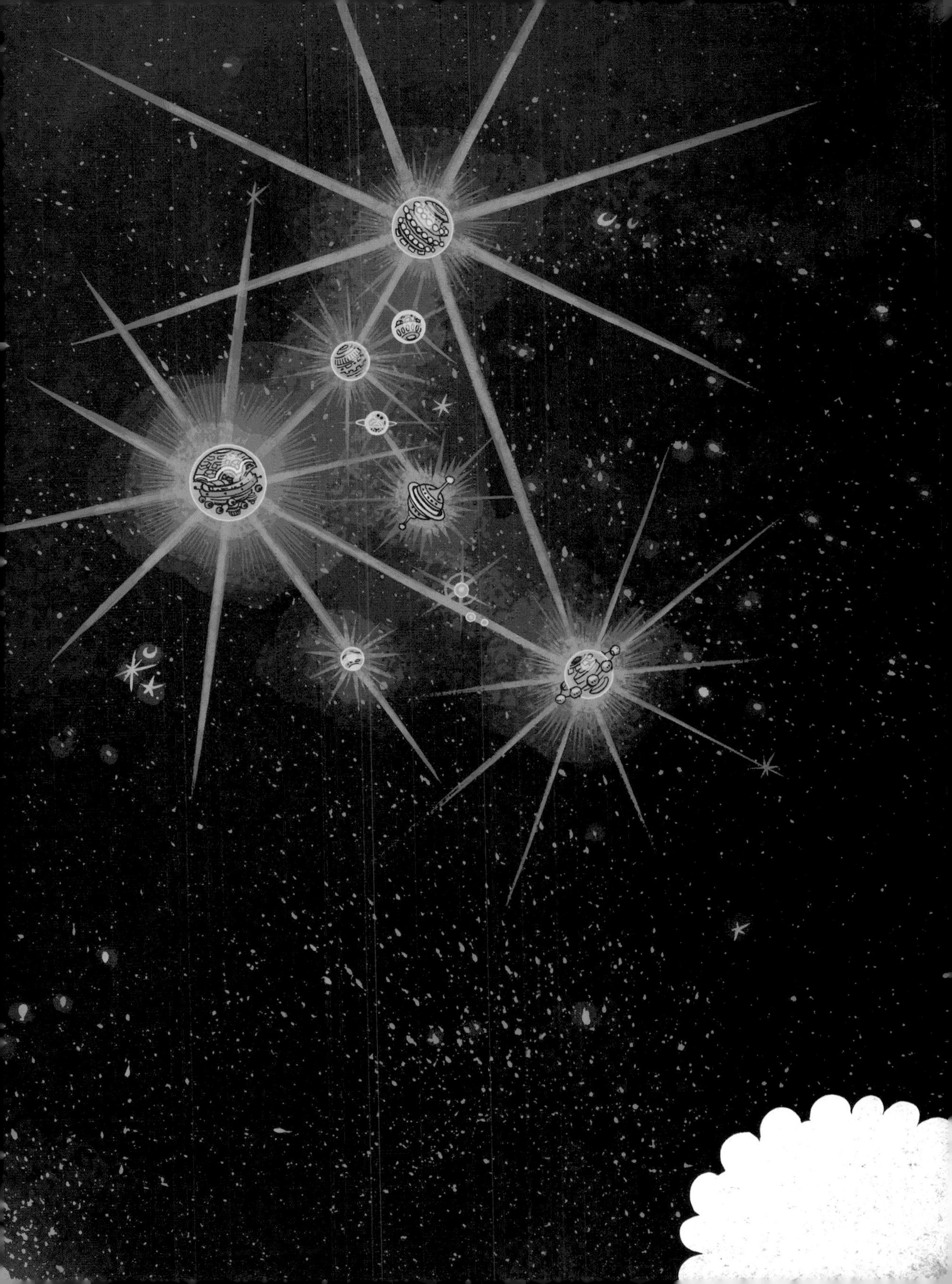

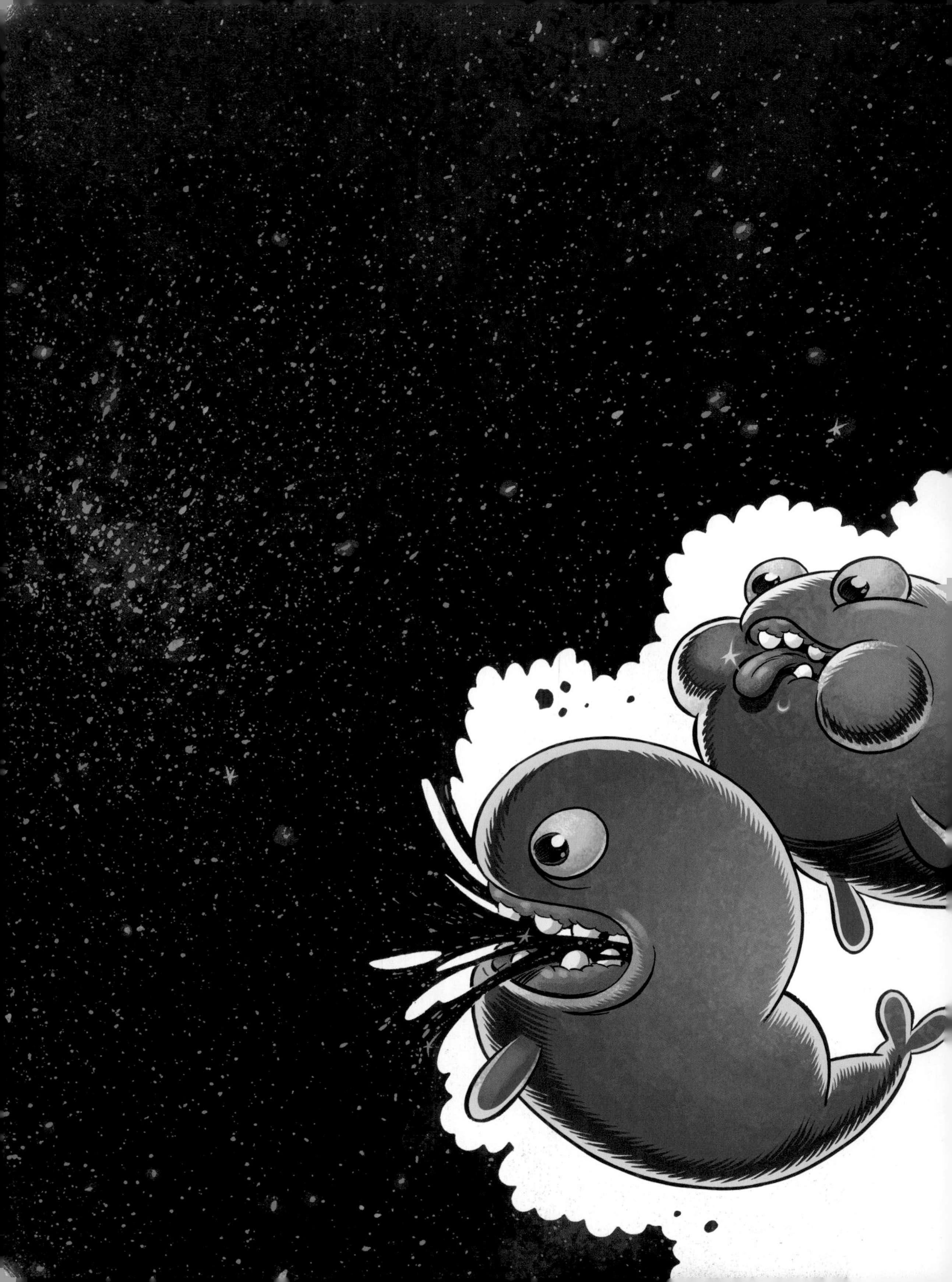

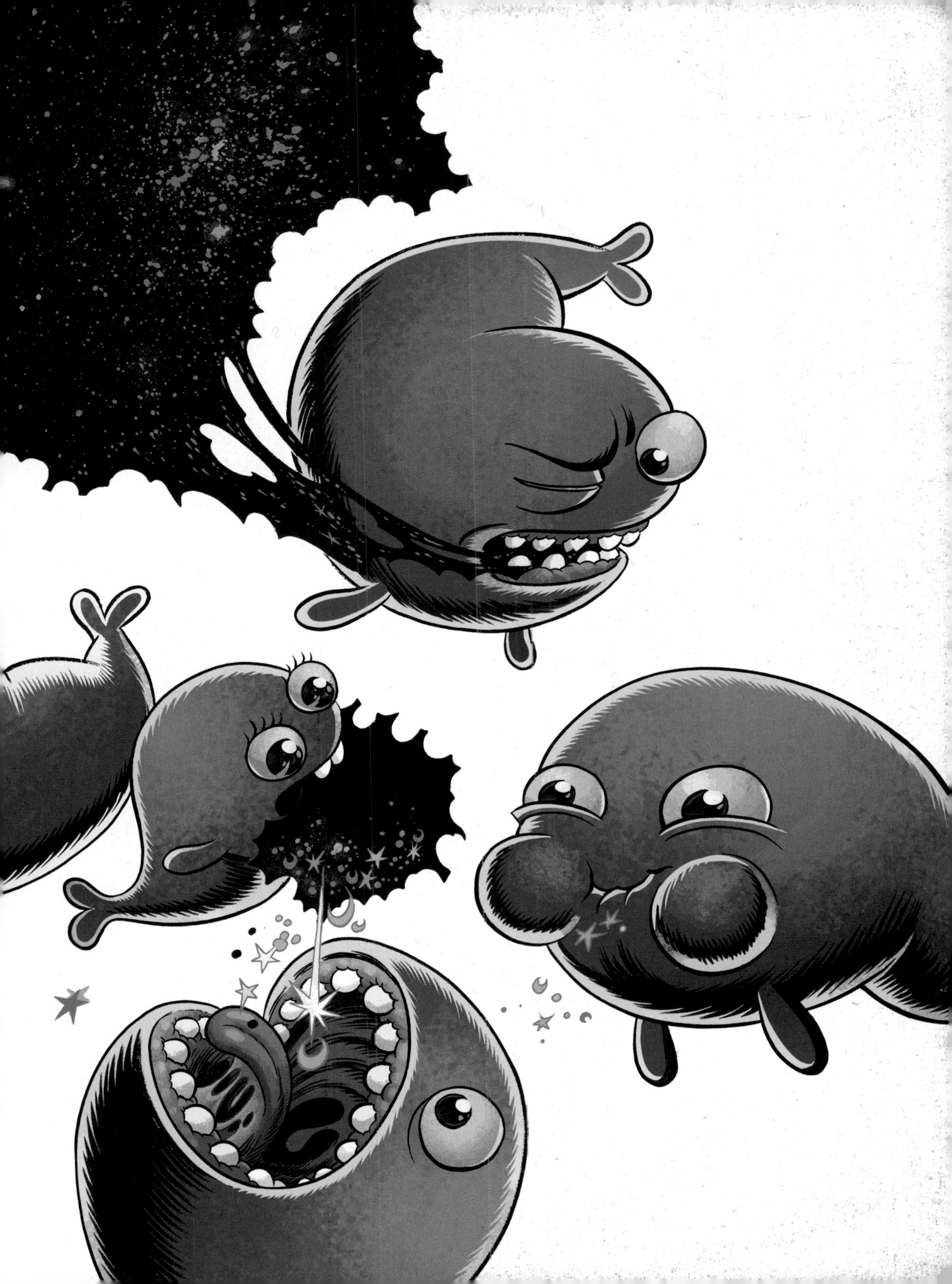

fin.

epilOGue

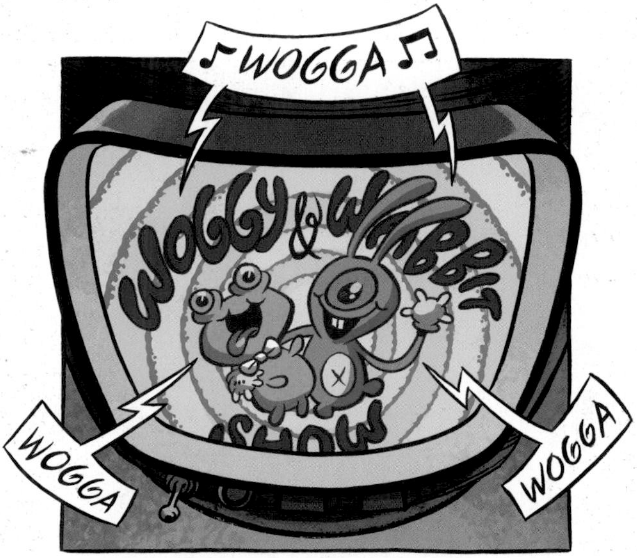
WOGGA
WOGGY & WABBIT SHOW
WOGGA
WOGGA

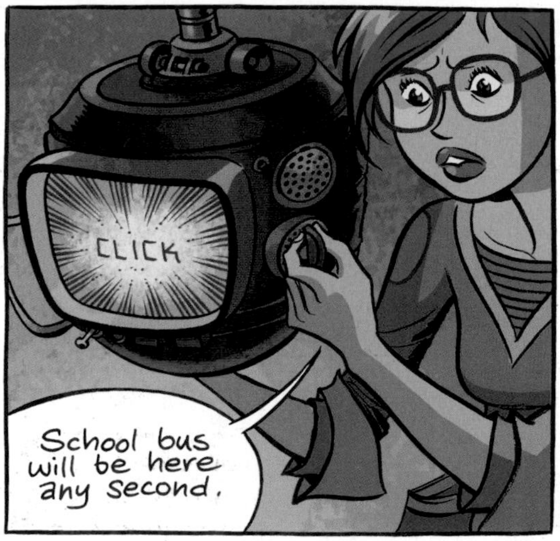
CLICK
School bus will be here any second.

Violet, finish your breakfast!
MY MAWMOFF MUN
Elliot, get your homework in your backpack!
This happens to be PERSONAL work.
Where's Zacchaeus?
"Am I my brother's keeper?"
YANK
Z
: snork whuzzit? :
Get on your UNIFORM, young man.
Then I'll look LAME like Elliot...
Who's HOGGING the bath-room?
That's MY LUNCHBOX!
Why can't I use the PINK one?
WA-WOOPS!
School bus won't stop HONKING.
Test-tube proteins AGAIN?
BURGER PASTE

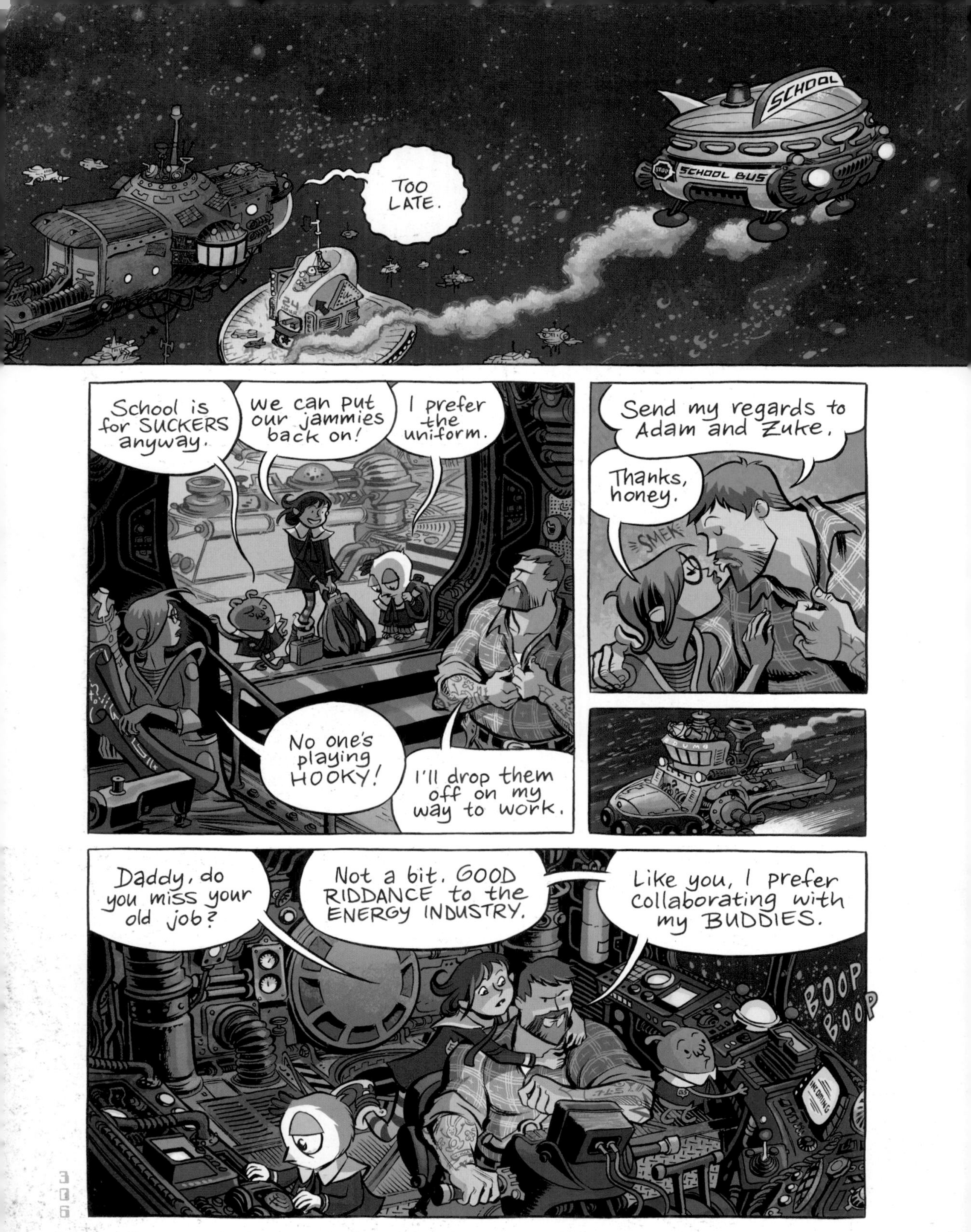
SCHOOL
STOP
SCHOOL BUS
TOO LATE.
School is for SUCKERS anyway.
We can put our jammies back on!
I prefer the uniform.
No one's playing HOOKY!
I'll drop them off on my way to work.
Send my regards to Adam and Zuke.
Thanks, honey.
SMEK
Daddy, do you miss your old job?
Not a bit. GOOD RIDDANCE to the ENERGY INDUSTRY.
Like you, I prefer collaborating with my BUDDIES.
BOOP BOOP
INCOMING

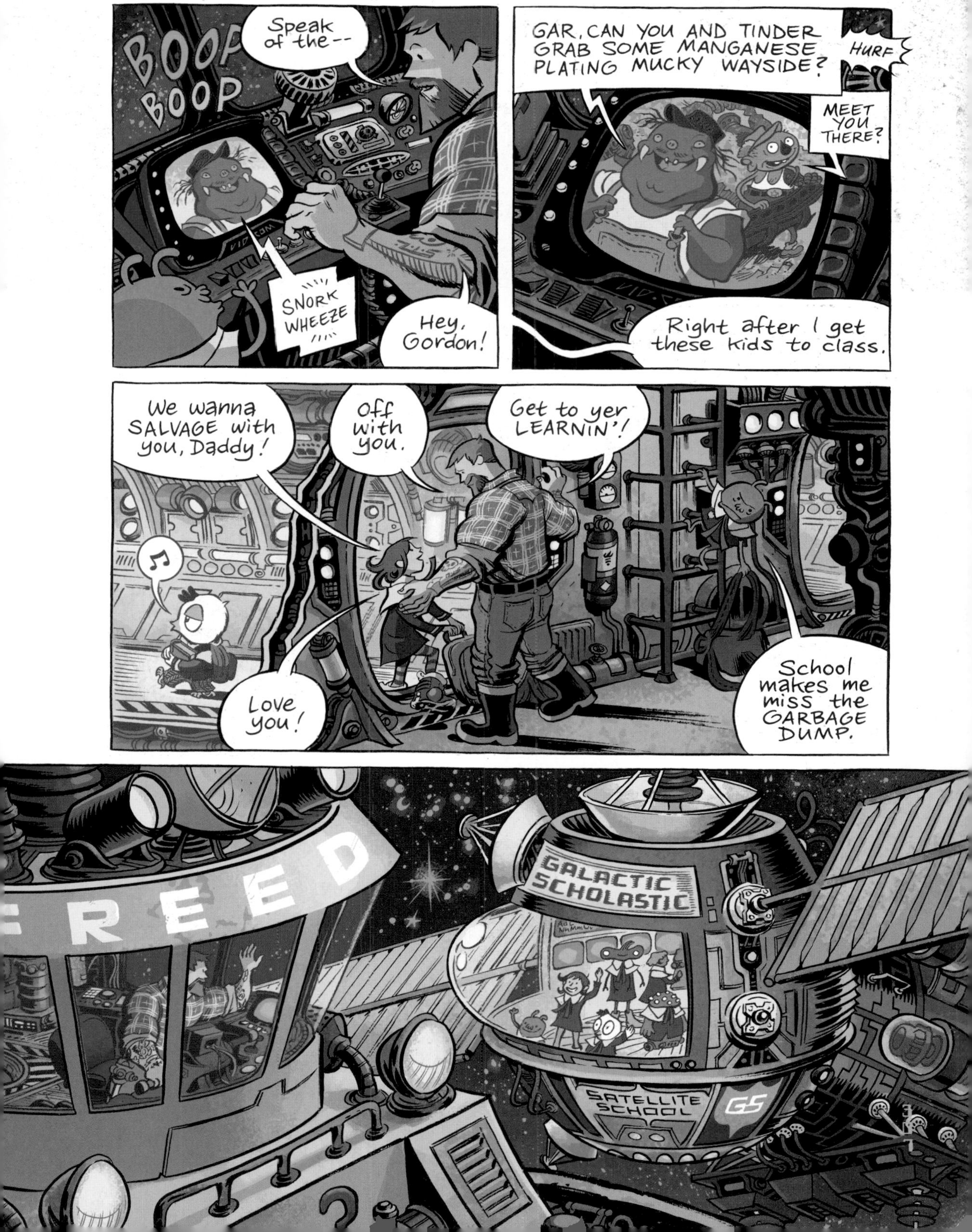

BOOP BOOP
Speak of the--
SNORK WHEEZE
Hey, Gordon!
GAR, CAN YOU AND TINDER GRAB SOME MANGANESE PLATING MUCKY WAYSIDE?
HURF
MEET YOU THERE?
Right after I get these kids to class.
We wanna SALVAGE with you, Daddy!
Off with you.
Get to yer LEARNIN'!
Love you!
School makes me miss the GARBAGE DUMP.
GALACTIC SCHOLASTIC
SATELLITE SCHOOL
GS

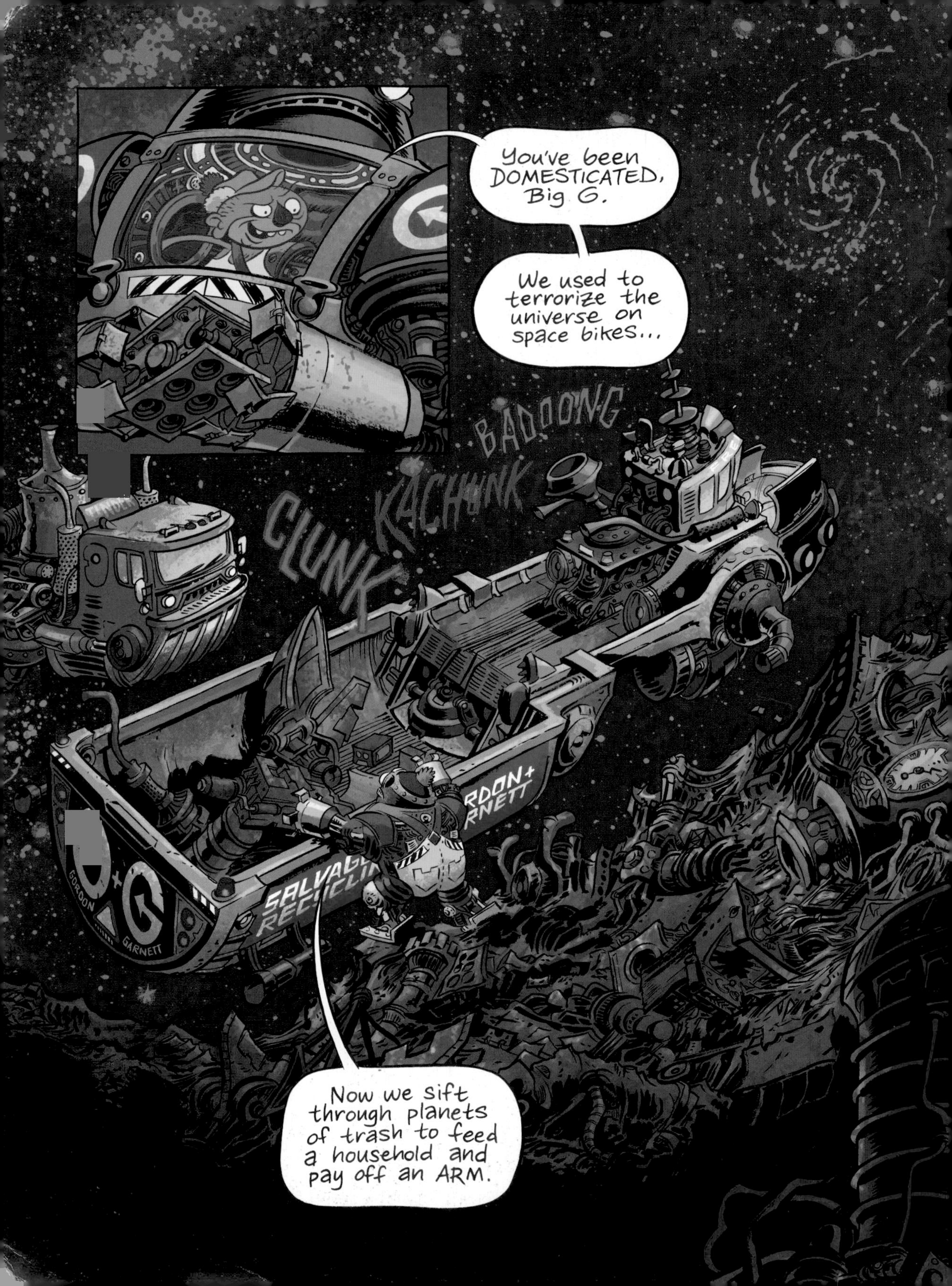
You've been DOMESTICATED, Big G.
We used to terrorize the universe on space bikes...
BADOOONG
KACHUNK
CLUNK
Now we sift through planets of trash to feed a household and pay off an ARM.

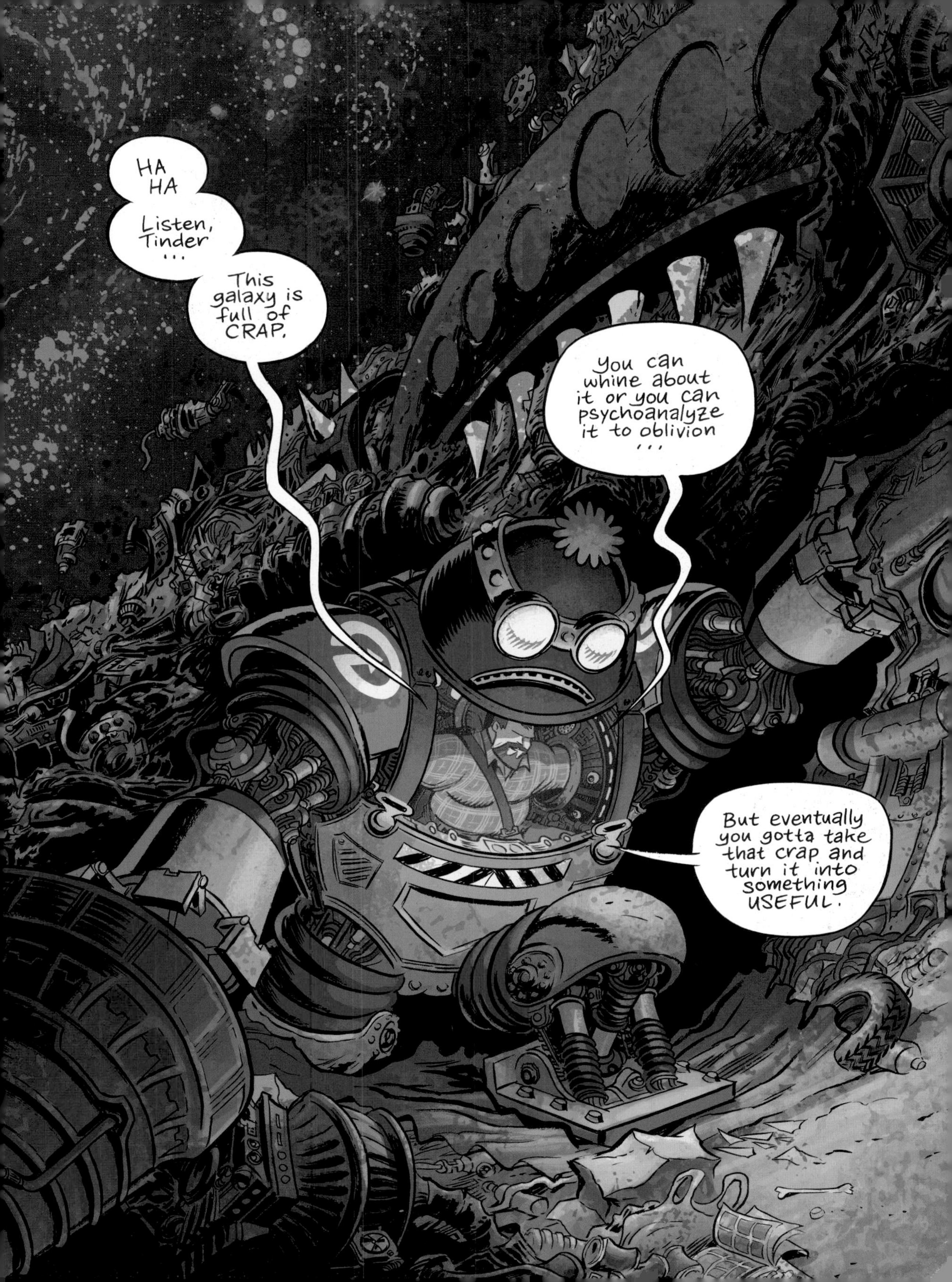
HA HA
Listen, Tinder ...
This galaxy is full of CRAP.
You can whine about it or you can psychoanalyze it to oblivion ...
But eventually you gotta take that crap and turn it into something USEFUL.

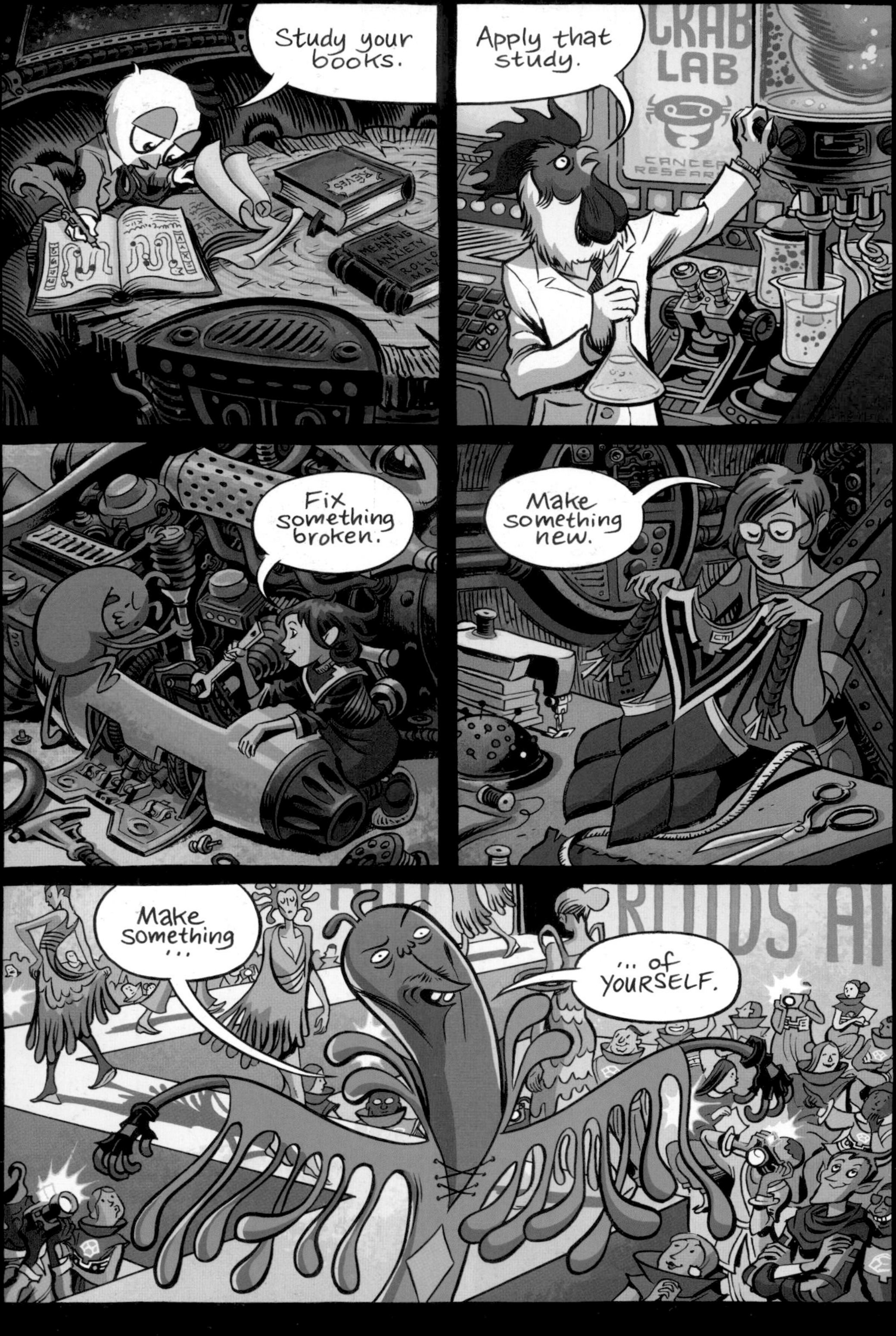

Study your books.
Apply that study.
CRAB LAB
CANCER RESEAR
Fix something broken.
Make something new.
Make something . . .
. . . of YOURSELF.

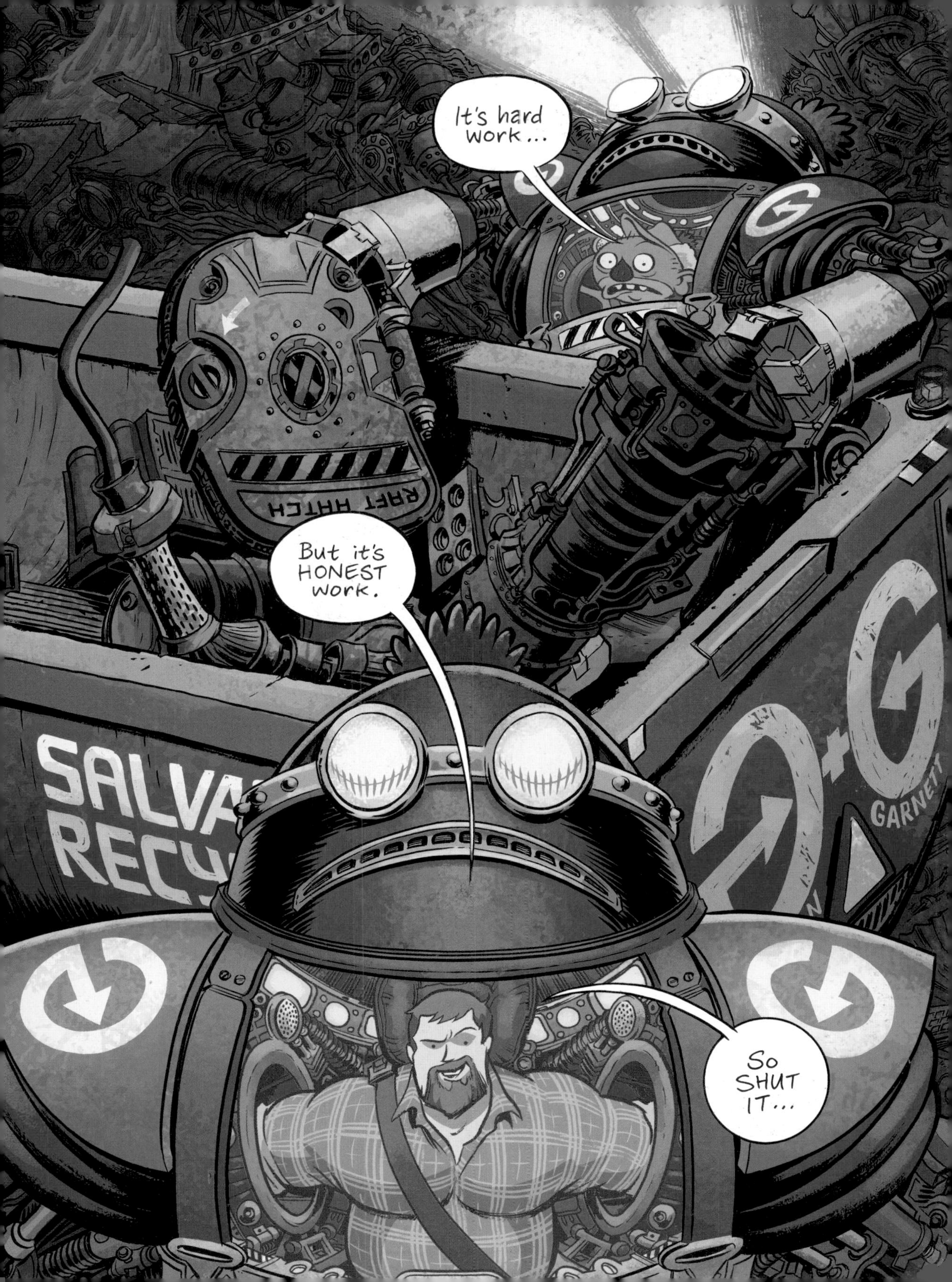
It's hard work...
RAFT HATCH
But it's HONEST work.
GARNETT
So SHUT IT...

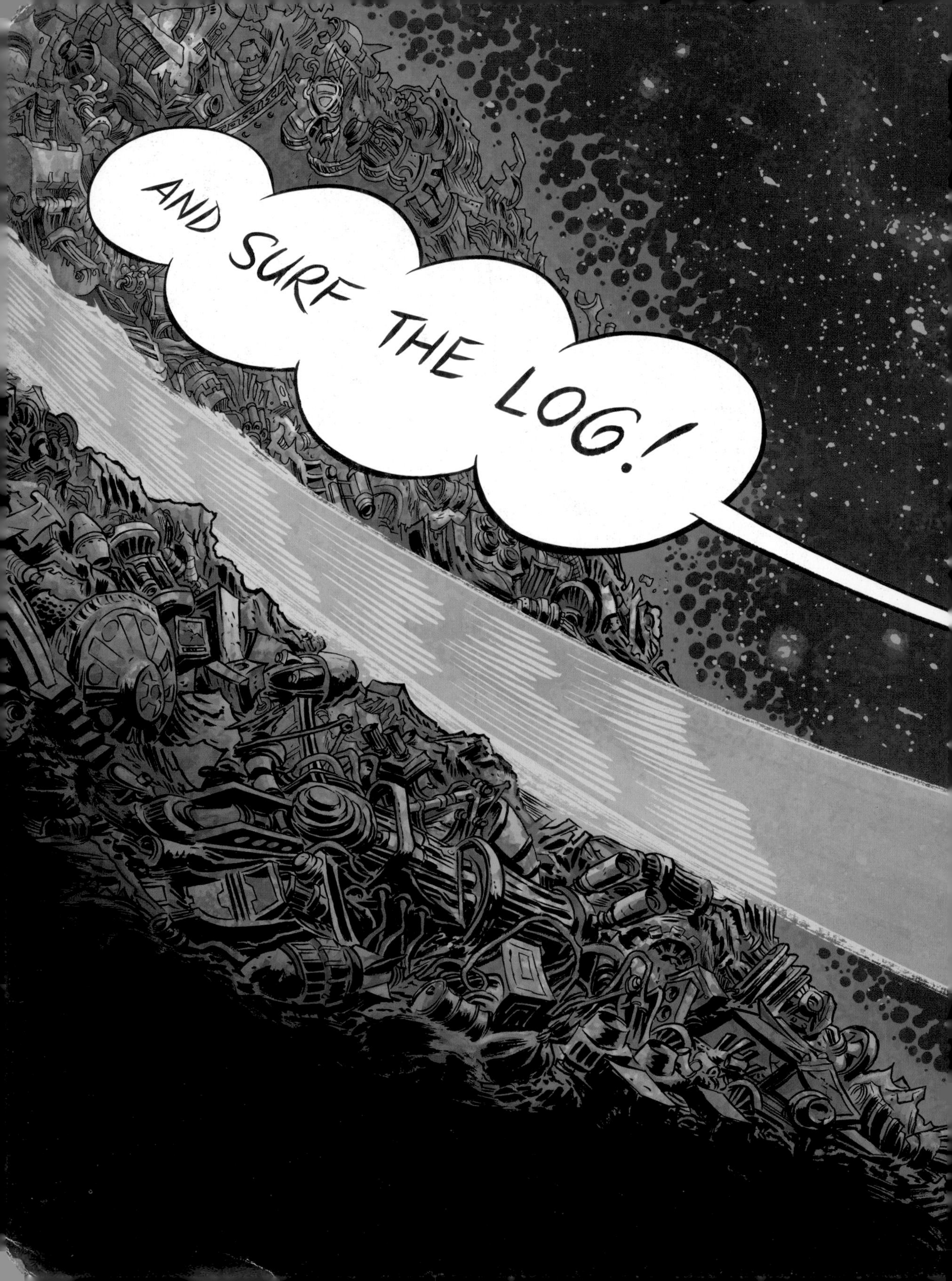
AND SURF THE LOG!

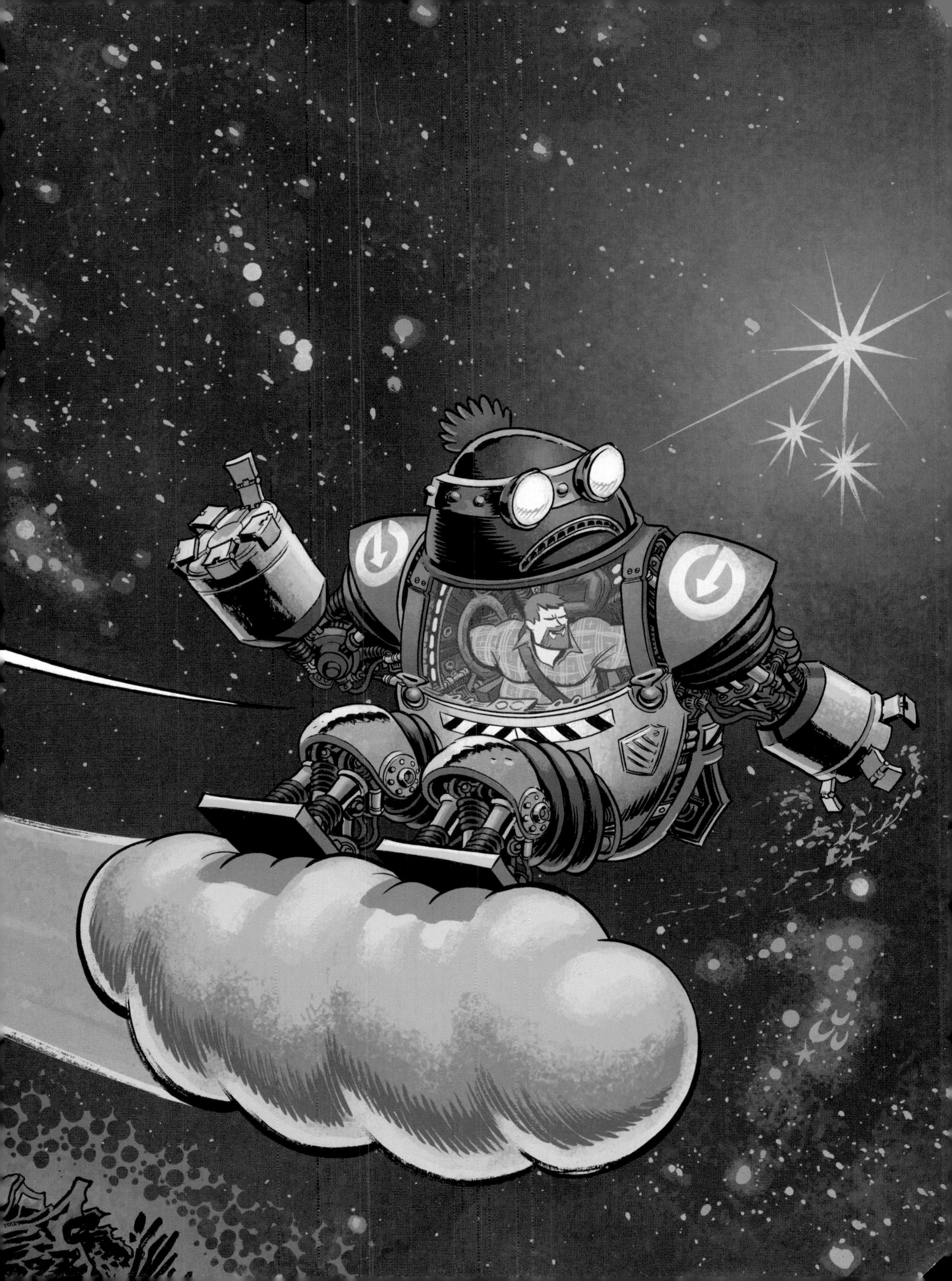

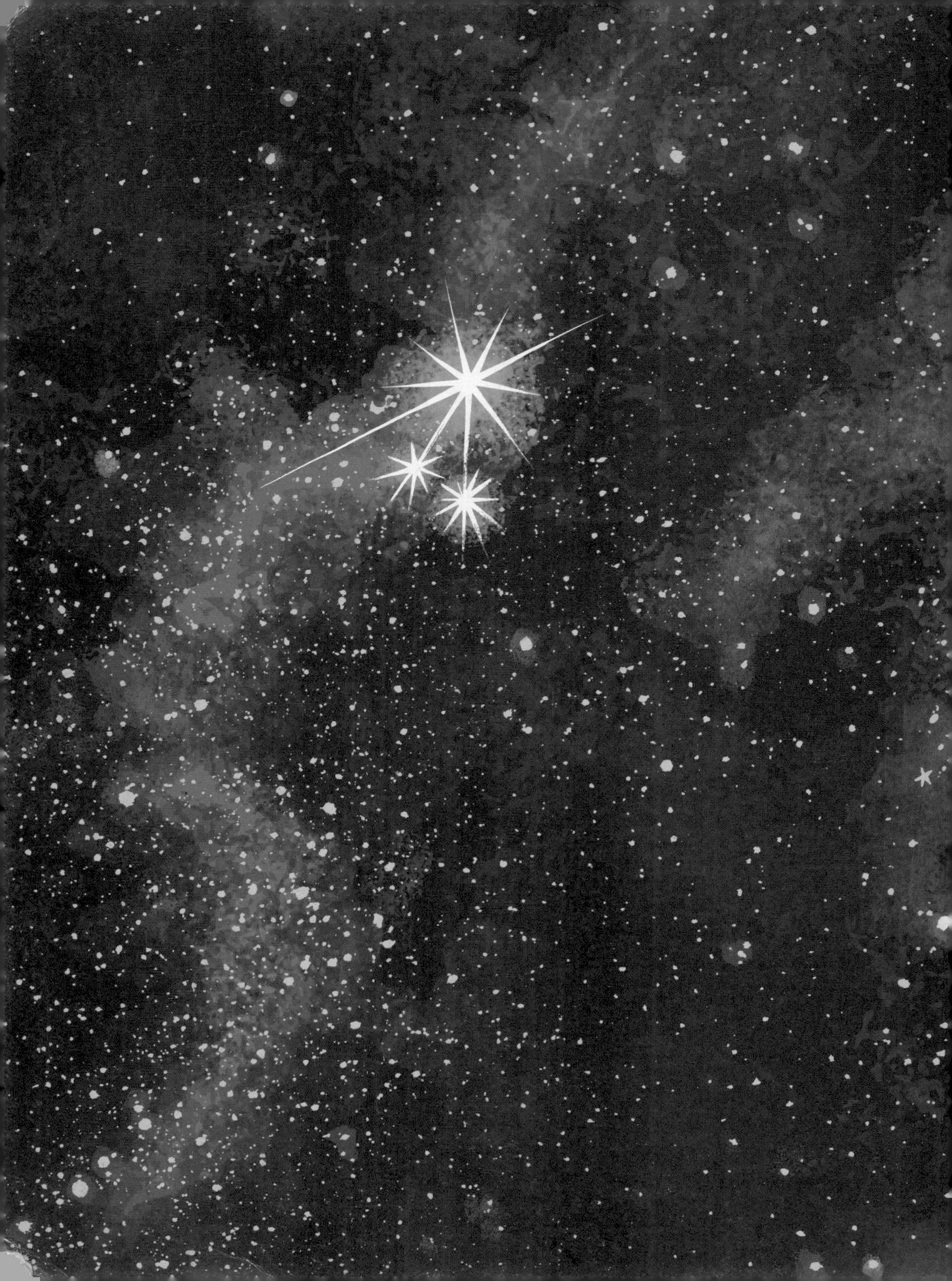

THANKS TO...

Violet, Azure, and Dan, for being the inspiration.

Lily Mason, Stella Sablan, and Joy Wurz, for their girl-hero expertise.

Adam Arnold, for his namesake, and Jeremy Tinder, for his likeness.

Jeffrey Alden, Lucie Bonvalet, Pegi Christensen, Chris Duffy, Alessandro Ferrari, Justin Harris, Georgia Hussey, Rebecca & Brian Hahn, David Naimon, and Ami & Jon Thompson, for being first readers.

Joshin Yamada, for the photos; Timothy Arp, for the spaceship model; Jon Thompson and Bolster, for the video.

Dave Stewart, for brilliant coloring and plenty of patience.

Phil Falco, Adam Rau, David Saylor, and the entire Scholastic team, for believing in the project.

PJ Mark, for being an amazing agent, along with Cecile Barendsma and Marya Spence.

My dear friends and family, for their constant encouragement.

You readers, who stick along for the ride.

And finally Sierra Hahn, for looking after my neurotic Elliot side and my impulsive Zacchaeus side. Also, for being the love of my life.

CRAIG THOMPSON is an award-winning graphic novelist best known for his books *Good-bye, Chunky Rice*; *Blankets*; *Carnet de Voyage*; and *Habibi*. He has received three Eisner Awards, four Harvey Awards, and two Ignatz Awards. Craig lives in Los Angeles, California.

DAVE STEWART is an eight-time Eisner Award–winning colorist best known for his work at Dark Horse Comics, DC Comics, and Marvel Comics.

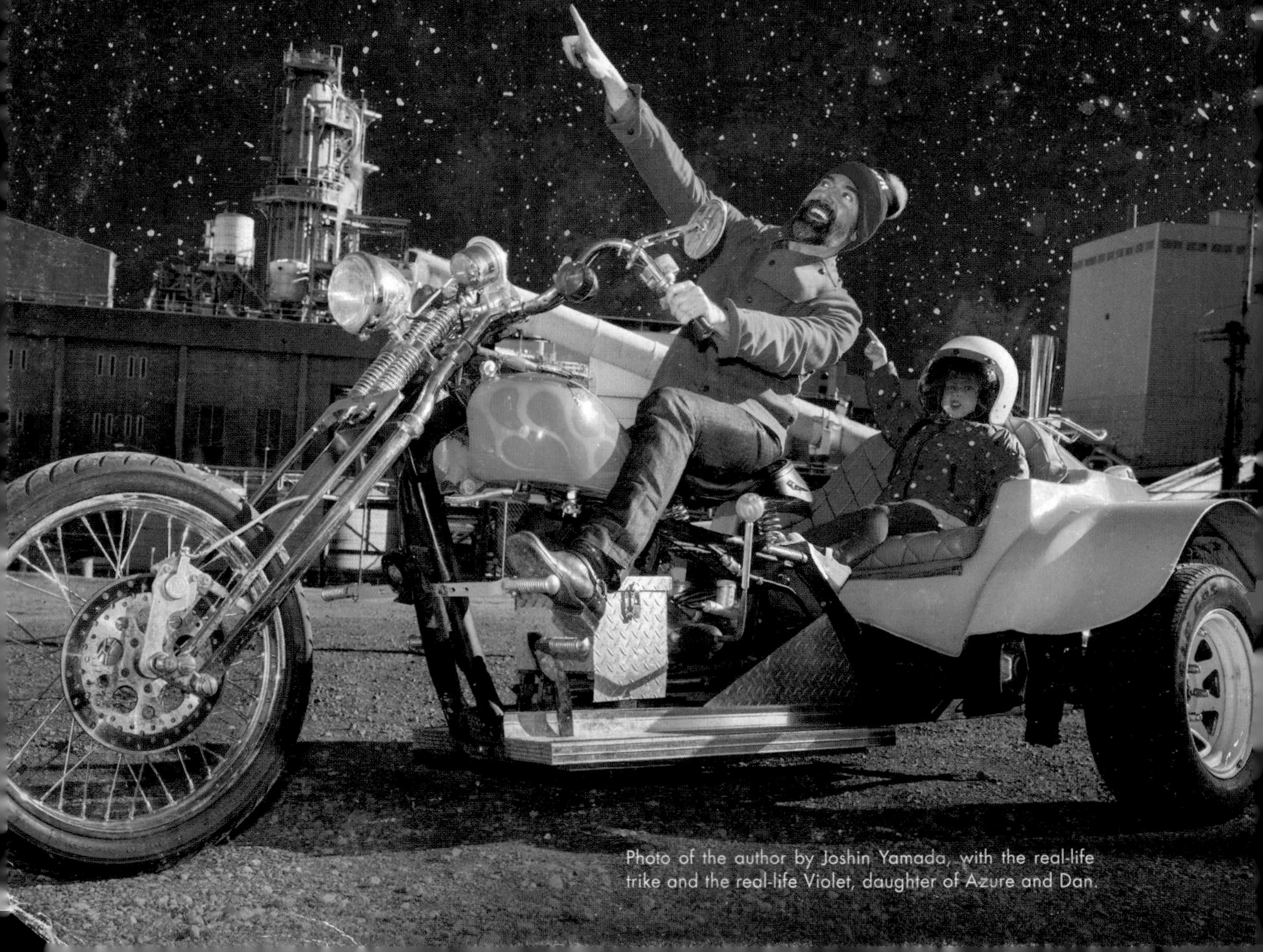

Photo of the author by Joshin Yamada, with the real-life trike and the real-life Violet, daughter of Azure and Dan.